# *Brie Embraces the Heart of Submission: After Graduation*

By

Red Phoenix

Brie Embraces the Heart of Submission



Print Edition



RedPhoenix69@live.com

Edited by Amy Parker

Book cover design by Viola Estrella; Photo by Christina McKenzie Gwin; Phoenix symbol by Nicole Delfs.

Big thanks to Marla Thalassinou, Jennifer Roberts-Hall and Gentle Man

*This book is dedicated to my loveable fans and the remarkable man who inspires all my work*

# Contents

# *Brie Pleases her New Master*

# Her First Lesson

The large commons broke out in applause as the elevator doors closed. Brie couldn't stop the tears from falling, knowing that Sir had given up his position at the Submissive Training Center to claim her.

Her heart melted when he looked down and winked. "No need to cry, babygirl. This is just the beginning."

She smiled through the tears and slipped her hand into his. "Yes, Sir."

"No more tears," he commanded gently.

Brie dutifully wiped them away and took a deep breath. When the doors opened at the first floor, Sir put down his box of office mementoes and took off his jacket. "I can't have you walking out into the cool night like this." He wrapped his jacket, still warm from his body heat, around her naked shoulders. He buttoned it up, picked up his box again and guided her out of the elevator, saying, "Come with me, Brie."

She held her breath, loving those four simple words. Her Master was taking her *home*… She had to pinch herself to believe it.

Sir led her to the farthest corner of the parking lot, to a glossy red car that looked like it belonged in a car show, not at a community college. It was *Batman* hot.

He held out his hand and helped her into the low-lying car. She tried to enter it gracefully but fell into the bucket seat with a plop.

Sir chuckled lightly. "Such style." He slid the door closed and proceeded to the other side, then buckled himself in before starting the roaring engine.

"What kind of car is this?" she asked.

"It's not a *car*, Brie. This is a modified Lotus Evora S."

She hid her smile. Obviously, she knew nothing about his 'baby' and would need to google it later.

He drove like he played with a sub—skillfully, but pushing the limits of the vehicle. Brie flushed in excitement, knowing that Sir was taking her home to play with *her*, alone.

Brie's jaw dropped when he pulled up to the front of a towering high-rise and a debonair valet immediately ran up to greet him. Sir opened her car door, and supported Brie as she made a second attempt at being graceful upon exiting the low vehicle. She smiled and glanced up, mesmerized by the possessive look in Sir's eyes. Her heart skipped a beat when he bent down and kissed her lightly on the lips before handing over his key to the attendant.

Brie took the arm he offered her and they walked through the doors, which were held open by a doorman.

"Good evening, Mr. Davis."

Sir nodded courteously, but said nothing as he guided Brie to the elevator. The foyer of the apartment building was opulent. She couldn't imagine what his apartment must be like. She licked her lips apprehensively, feeling out of place.

"Nothing to be nervous about, babygirl," Sir said.

She whispered, "I've never been here. I feel…"

"At home," he answered for her. Her body tingled at his words.

The bell chimed and the elevator doors opened for them. Sir placed his hand on the small of her back, the electricity of his touch making her whole body quiver. The interior of the elevator was mirrored, so Brie was able to sneak glances at Sir as they traveled up to his apartment. He stared straight ahead with a slight smirk on his face, as if he was already considering what he would do with her.

*Will my heart survive tonight?* she wondered.

At the fifteenth floor, the door opened to a marbled hallway. Sir escorted her out and led Brie to the last door on the right. The door was made of dark wood, engraved with a symbol that looked suspiciously like a BDSM triskele, the emblem for the lifestyle. Was Sir that forthright about it? Did the whole high-rise know what he did for a living…what he *used* to do? A momentary jolt of guilt clouded her joy.

Sir opened the heavy door to a long, narrow hallway with walls covered in various forms of modern art, from sculptures mounted on the walls to alluring paintings. Brie's heels made an attractive clicking sound on the dark marble floor as he escorted her inside. The apartment smelled of Sir.

He walked her to a large, open area with windows from floor to ceiling, with a breathtaking view overlooking the city. "Impressive," she said quietly.

"I quite agree," he answered, unbuttoning the jacket he'd put around her and slipping it off her shoulders. Her nipples were already erect, begging for her Master's attention. "I prefer you like this," he murmured. His lips grazed her neck teasingly, and then he gestured towards the seating area. "Sit while I make us a drink. I would like to talk about our new arrangement."

Brie's heart fluttered as she watched him walk away. She glanced around the large room, noting that it was decorated in a minimalistic style, but the furniture was artfully placed and sensual in appearance. Sir had pointed to a black sofa, but she was drawn to an attractive red chair on the other side of the room. It was curvaceous and thin, made only for one person. She walked up to it, noting its unique shape. It was more like a chaise longue, made for a single person to lie in rather than sit. It had a high, attractively curved back and an equally aesthetic, rounded foot area. She lay down, fitting comfortably in the concave middle of the chair, and looked out over the city from her comfortable vantage point, listening to Sir moving about in the kitchen.

Brie tried to calm her nerves as she came to grips with her new reality. She was in Sir's apartment—*he* was her Master. *Be still my beating heart!*

Sir walked back out of the kitchen holding two martini glasses. When he saw her, he stopped and chuckled. "Of course you would choose that chair."

Brie didn't understand and started to get up.

"No, stay where you are. It's actually perfect." He walked over and handed her a glass. Then he looked out over the cityscape and smiled as he took a drink. Brie regained her composure, and tasted it. The martini Sir had made was slightly dirty, with just the right amount of olive brine mixed with the smooth, high-end vodka.

"Lie back, Brie. I want to enjoy the beauty you bring to my place."

She happily obliged, lying against the back of the sexy chaise, being careful not to spill. Brie lifted one arm over her head casually, knowing it would display her breasts in a pleasing manner for her Master.

"Lovely." He took another sip of his drink with a playful smirk on his lips. Brie wondered what he was thinking but she quietly followed suit, unable to stop the tremor in her hands as she brought the glass to her lips.

"We have much to discuss, you and I. However, I wish to leave the majority of it for another day. I will be putting my consultant work on hold for a few days off so we can grow accustomed to our new relationship, but in truth…I plan to play with you hard and often. Expect little rest."

Brie loved the idea of that, but her practical side took over. "Sir, I am scheduled to work tomorrow night."

He laughed out loud. "I am confident my uncle does not expect to see you so soon after your collaring."

*His uncle.* It sounded adorable to hear Sir call Mr. Reynolds 'uncle'. "May I call and tell him I won't be there, Sir?"

"No, that won't be necessary. I will talk to him myself about the matter. But you will be handing in your two weeks' notice when you return to work on Monday."

Brie couldn't hide her surprise. She'd naturally assumed she would continue working with his uncle at the tobacco shop. "Yes, Master. May I ask what I will be doing instead?"

"You will begin editing your documentary. When you present it to Holloway, the film needs to be perfect. That will take time, and you won't have the time if you are stocking cigarettes on shelves."

Everything in her life had changed in one night. It was thrilling, but also a little disconcerting. "I'm grateful I can say goodbye to Mr. Reynolds and help train my replacement."

"No doubt Unc is going to have trouble replacing you."

She wanted to giggle when he called Mr. Reynolds 'Unc'. It was a casual side of Sir she'd never suspected existed, which made her more impatient to discover Sir's many secrets.

He continued on without interruption. "However, it is not my concern—or yours," he added for emphasis.

*Pleasing Sir and making the documentary is my new reality? Pinch me now!* "I understand, Sir… Master…" She blushed. "What should I call you?" Brie felt foolish for not knowing the protocol with him now that he was no longer her trainer.

He laughed. "It's simple, Miss Bennett. When we have a conversation or are out in public, I expect to be called Sir. However, when we are in a scene I am your Master."

She looked up at him shyly, the word 'Master' having a distinct effect on her. "Thank you for the clarification, Sir." She took another sip of the martini to hide her nervousness.

"I shall also call you by a different name."

That was unexpected news. Brie rested the drink on her lap as she gave Sir her undivided attention. "What name is that, Sir?"

"Téa."

Brie tilted her head, uncertain of its meaning. She dutifully answered, "Thank you, Sir."

He graced her with a heart-melting smile before taking a drink.

*Tay-ah*... She'd never heard a sub called that at the Center. Names were significant—they helped define the role of the submissive—so she waited patiently for Sir to explain.

He set his glass on an end table and approached her with a tender look in his eye. He grazed her cheek with the back of his hand. "My father was half Italian; 'téa' means 'goddess'."

His answer left her speechless. In one fell swoop, he had graced her with a huge compliment and revealed the fact that his father was of Italian descent, but no longer living. Brie was unsure how to respond and whispered, "I am honored, Sir."

"Know that I will think of you as a goddess even as I fuck you like a slut."

His words were powerful and unsettling. Brie quivered in the red lounger and closed her eyes, trying to calm her pounding heartbeat. Was she woman enough for such a man?

"Téa, the only item you are allowed to wear is the collar around your neck."

The tingling fire began in her loins as Brie opened her eyes and nodded. She carefully set down her drink and complied with his instructions. Once she was naked, she bowed low at his feet.

"Walk to the window."

Brie rocked off her heels and stood up, floating on clouds as she made her way to the expansive window. She felt the weight of Sir's stare on her and trembled at the intensity of it. There was an acute sense of vulnerability in being naked in front of the huge window, especially with a similar high-rise just to the right of the building.

In a deep voice he commanded, "Spread your legs shoulder-width apart, put your hands on the window and lean forward so that your nipples touch the glass."

She opened her legs and put her palms on the cold window, leaning slowly forward until her nipples made contact with the chilly glass. Brie gasped softly and waited for his next instruction, but he gave none. She watched Sir's reflection in the window as he stood and admired her while sipping his martini.

The wait, the anticipation, combined with his lustful scrutiny, made Brie exceedingly wet. She closed her eyes, chagrined when she felt a trickle of her excitement run down her leg. Brie was desperate for him, her nipples aching with need, stimulated by the pressure and temperature of the glass.

Her heart skipped a beat when she heard Sir walk out of the room and the distinct sound of the martini glasses being placed on a granite counter. *It begins…*

"Don't move or speak, but you are allowed to come," he murmured as he drew close.

Brie bit her lip when Sir lightly traced her shoulder with his fingertips, her whole body concentrating solely on his touch. She continued to sneak peeks at his reflection, enjoying the erotic contrast of her being completely nude while he remained in his tux, minus the jacket.

Sir's hand trailed down her back and over the swell of her ass. Brie had to consciously stifle her cry when his demanding fingers pressed into her sex and he felt the extent of her need.

His grunt was low and passionate. "Your body betrays you. You stand quiet and demure, but inside you are a raging firestorm of desire."

She struggled to keep quiet when he began playing with her pussy, already oversensitive from need of him. With his expert fingers, he quickly brought her to a swift orgasm.

"So soon?" Sir chuckled lightly in her ear. Then he knelt down on the floor.

Brie about died when she felt his tongue on her still throbbing clit. She made a muffled squeak and closed her eyes tightly, trying to remain upright as he spread her outer lips with his fingers and took a long, drawn-out lick.

"I love the taste of Brie."

*He's making a joke?* She almost burst out in giggles but bit down on her lip hard enough to bring tears to her eyes.

Brie's legs trembled as Sir swirled his tongue over her clit, between her dripping inner lips, until he reached that sensitive area between her opening and her sphincter. Her inner muscles contracted powerfully. To have Sir concentrate his oral attention so close to her ass felt enticingly forbidden. Unfortunately, the area was so sensitive that her knees buckled.

Sir seemed to have anticipated it, because his hands cradled her buttocks as he gave Brie the support she needed to regain her stance. "No moving," he admonished as she returned to the same spot. Brie gasped when he pressed his fingers onto her clit and rubbed in circles slowly, causing a delicious burn.

She was completely held under his spell, his willing and wanton plaything.

"Come," he whispered hoarsely from between her legs.

Her body tensed, initially resisting the command. Soon, however, a cold chill settled on Brie, traveling through her body just before she exploded in a second release, far more powerful than the first. He licked her clit as it pulsed against his tongue.

With a will of iron, she stayed in place and only made small, whimpering gasps. As the last contraction reverberated through her small frame, Sir growled lustfully, "Your ass calls to me."

A cry caught in her throat as he coated his thumb with her juices and slipped it into her tight hole. He played with her ass while he continued to sensually torture her with his tongue. Sir began sucking on her clit in a rhythmic manner, causing her pussy to burn with unbearable heat. When he started thrusting his thumb to match that rhythm, her pussy exploded in violent pleasure.

Brie's legs shook uncontrollably as the third orgasm rolled over her. She was going to fall—there was no way to prevent it. "Sir…" she whimpered just before her legs gave out.

He chuckled as he caught her. "Can't handle your new Master?"

She looked up at him in amazement. *The power of the man…*

"Tsk, tsk," he joked as he helped her up. But then he ordered, "Resume the position, téa."

She had to look down at her feet to make sure they were spread properly, because her entire body had become weak and uncooperative. Brie put her hands on the cold glass and pressed her nipples against it. *Can a woman faint from coming?* she wondered. She knew she was in for a hard fall the instant she heard him unzip his pants.

*Slow breaths, Brie…* She watched Sir's reflection clandestinely as he positioned himself behind her. His hard cock pressed against her wet, overly excited pussy just before he thrust his full length into her, causing her nipples to rub against the cold glass.

*Oh, dear God!*

He grabbed her buttocks and thrust, each stroke pronounced and effective. Brie had to brace her hands against the glass to meet his fervent strokes. He made sure her nipples took the onslaught, and they rubbed up and down the chilly glass with each motion. Electrical jolts from the friction coursed straight to her groin.

She looked at Sir in the reflection, watching the concentration on his face as he delivered exactly what he wanted her to receive. Then he leaned into her, putting his hands on top of hers. She stared at their intertwined fingers, overcome by the sensuality of it.

Sir pressed her body against the glass, growling in her ear, "I've wanted to fuck you like this since the first day I saw you."

Brie closed her eyes and whimpered when his lips came down on her neck and he bit her as if he were a lion subduing its mate. She gave in entirely when her body embraced the chilly wave of her fourth orgasm, no longer needing to concern herself with standing. Sir held her in place with the pressure of his body against hers, his teeth still positioned on her neck. She shuddered afterwards, slowly becoming aware that her cheeks were wet with tears.

"Mine," he stated as he pulled away from her, denying himself his own release.

Brie gasped breathlessly as she realigned herself to Sir's specifications. Legs apart, hands on the glass, nipples touching it… She quivered all over, a bundle of spent energy. He knew how to dominate her mind, body and spirit. Even her orgasms, which she'd considered hers alone to control. It was a profound lesson indeed.

# Lesson Two: The Heart

Sir directed Brie to the bathroom down the hall. "Come back to me when you are refreshed, téa."

She smiled at him, loving the name he had given her. Brie made her way to the bathroom on noodle legs, shutting the door and leaning against the counter for support. The beautiful collar around her neck caught her eye when she looked into the mirror. Brie brushed it lightly with her fingers. She then looked down at the word he had written across her chest: 'Mine'.

*I'm Sir's.*

The thought of that sent a warm shiver through her. Brie quickly cleaned herself off, then ran her fingers through her hair and pinched her cheeks to pinken them before returning to Master.

Sir was sitting on the couch, waiting for her. He made a sweeping gesture and asked, "Where would you feel comfortable sitting?"

He was giving her a choice, but Brie knew exactly where she wanted to be. She knelt beside him on the floor, the same way she had the first night they'd spent time alone together at the Training Center. Thankfully, there was a throw beside the couch, which made the kneeling comfortable. She suspected Sir had placed it there intentionally.

Sir smiled down at her and petted her long, brown curls. "I approve of your choice," he murmured.

"I have longed to sit beside you like this again, Master."

She closed her eyes and reveled in the delightful sensations evoked by Sir's hand. Each time he brushed through her hair, a burst of electrical tingles traveled down her spine. The two sat in silence, absorbing the shock of this new dynamic together—and this new life.

Brie eventually braved the question that had been burning in the back of her mind since he'd mentioned it. "Sir, may I ask you a personal question?"

"Yes, téa."

"When you mentioned your father, you used the word 'was'."

"I did. However, it is not something I care to discuss tonight."

She looked down at the floor, regretting that she'd mentioned it.

Sir commanded, "Look at me."

Brie peeked up at Sir hesitantly.

"You are allowed to ask questions. I encourage it. But tonight I have other plans."

Her gaze traveled to his crotch and she noticed the hardness of his shaft outlined beneath the black material. When she looked into her Master's eyes, she saw lust reflected back.

Sir slowly unzipped his pants, releasing his rigid cock. He opened his legs wider and Brie obediently moved in between, taking his princely manhood in both hands. With slow, luscious licks and light nibbles, she loved his shaft before taking its fullness into her mouth.

The tang of her own juices still covered his cock, mixing with his pre-come. Brie moaned, savoring the taste of their blend. He pulled his pants down farther before he lightly fisted her hair and guided her. She purred, sucking harder as she moved her lips up and down his handsome shaft.

Making love to Sir with her mouth was intimate and powerfully bonding. She flicked her tongue against his frenulum and around the sensitive ridge of the head. He groaned and lay back farther on the couch, spreading his legs more. She relaxed her throat, preparing to take him more deeply, just as his cell phone rang.

Sir opened his eyes and sighed. "I have to take this, but do not stop." He fished the cellphone from the pocket of his open pants.

Brie did not want to distract him from the call by deep-throating him, so she concentrated on his balls and the sensitive spot just below them. She could hear Mr. Gallant's voice in her head: "*The perineum is the area between the testicles and the anus. Do not forget this area.*"

As she pleasured him, she couldn't help listening to Sir's side of the conversation. "No, I won't be able to make it tonight."

There was a deep rumble on the other end.

"I assure you that is not the case."

The phone erupted in a low roll of laughter.

*Rytsar.*

The deep rumbling continued on the other end, to which Sir replied, "Yes, I see no reason not to schedule a trip now." She could hear laughter on the other end. Brie attempted to hide her smile unsuccessfully.

"It appears my submissive is agreeable to the idea, as well."

Brie's heart melted at being called *his* submissive. A trip to Russia to visit the infamous Rytsar in his homeland would be an adventure, but truly, nothing could compare to now. She lavished even more attention on Sir's cock, wanting him to feel how profoundly she loved him.

"Fine. I'll work out the details later. I'm sure you'll understand why I am hanging up on you." Sir shut his phone with a snap and stuffed it back in his pocket. Brie took it to mean she could begin deep-throating him, and slid the head of his shaft to the back of her throat, relaxing her muscles so she could take him deeper.

"No, not yet," he stated. She released her hold on his cock and looked up at him from between his muscular thighs.

"Do you know what that is?" he asked, pointing to the stylish red lounger.

"An artful chair, Sir."

He raised an eyebrow suggestively, making her loins quiver. There was no doubt it was more than a simple lounge.

"It's called a Tantra chair, téa. Especially designed for the Kama Sutra. Are you familiar with the Kama Sutra?"

"I've heard of it, Sir. But no, I don't know anything about the Kama Sutra."

He lifted her chin up and leaned over to kiss her. "My naïve submissive, there is still so much you have yet to learn."

She smiled at him with love. "I'm honored to have you as teacher."

He nodded and then replied huskily, "And Master. Sit in the chair for me."

Her whole body trembled as she got up from the floor and lay down in the arc of the red chaise. Brie took a deep breath, trying to calm her racing heart as Sir shed his clothes in front of her, his belt hitting the marble floor with a satisfying clink. She marveled at Sir's masculine body. Dark hair covered his toned chest and powerful thighs, and framed Sir's handsome shaft, thick and physically pleasing. Truly the most beautiful cock she had ever seen—or felt.

Brie was surprised when he left her there, and instead walked down the hall of his apartment. She turned her head towards the window to look at the city lights. She loved the beauty of LA at night. It spoke of hope, magic and dreams coming true…

When she heard Sir, she started to turn her head but he ordered, "No, stay as you were."

Brie settled back onto the chair, biting her lip to stop the questions spurred by his command. She pretended to stare out at the city lights, but she was intently watching his reflection.

Sir looked as magnificent naked as he did dressed, and he carried himself with a confidence that made his being nude seem completely natural—preferred, actually.

She could tell he had something in his hand, but was unable to identify it. Brie watched as he approached her. She held her breath when he stood over Brie and gazed at her body. She saw Sir hold up his hand just before all the lights went out.

"Master?"

"Hush…"

She waited, listening to the sound of his breathing behind her. Sir eventually broke the silence with his low, compelling voice. "The dark allows for a more intense connection, both of us dependent on senses other than sight."

The experience reminded her of the hood that Master Anderson had used on her once. However, this was far more alluring because Sir would be equally challenged. The thought thoroughly aroused her.

Brie felt his hand begin caressing her thigh. He said nothing as he ran his fingers over her skin slowly, sensually. He explored her body, taking in every part as he found his way into every untouched crevice—between toes, behind knees, the sensitive area behind her ears, and even her unbearably ticklish armpits. Nothing escaped his scrutiny.

His warm hands glided over her ass, grasping and releasing, kneading her buttocks lustfully. "I love the flesh of a woman's ass. Pliable…sensuous…irresistible."

Brie purred softly in response.

He traced the letters he had written on her chest after the collaring as if he could see them. The individual letters tingled even after he removed his finger. Sir then placed her hand on his own chest, where she had written her word.

"Master, yes, but for this session you will call me Sir," he commanded.

She was curious what he had in mind, but answered quietly, "My pleasure, Sir."

As if he knew her thoughts, he added, "Everything I do has a purpose, a simple lesson for you to learn. What was the lesson of the window?"

She swallowed hard before replying, "Even my orgasms answer to you."

"Good." Sir found her lips with his fingers, leaned over her and kissed Brie on the lips. "Now I will teach you another."

Brie felt him cup her buttocks in his strong hands. Sir gently pushed her up the angled back of the chair as he climbed between her legs. "Tuck in your legs, téa."

As soon as she did, the smooth head of his shaft rested against her sex.

Still cradling her ass, he pressed his cock into her. Gravity helped the depth of his penetration as he lowered her down onto his shaft. "The beauty of the Tantra chair is that it allows for the perfect angle," he murmured, his cock nestling deep inside her.

"Sir…" she gasped as he began rolling his pelvis, using his hands to support her. Brie slid up and down the back of the chair effortlessly as he thrust his shaft into her, hitting the perfect spot with each stroke.

He sought out her lips again, the kisses tender. When he broke away his warm breath caressed her ear. "I shall make love to you now." His lips returned to her mouth. Both his tongue and his cock expressed his deep passion for her.

Sir's lovemaking was an ethereal experience. Brie soaked in the emotional wave of it even as her body responded to his skill and expertise. She prayed it would never end. "I love you, Sir, with all my heart."

Instead of giving a verbal response, he surprised her by leaning over the side of the chair to pick up something from the floor. "Give me your left wrist."

Brie lifted it to him and felt Sir's hand trail up her arm to her wrist. He joined them together with a soft cord without the aid of light and announced, "We are bound together as one." His warm lips pressed against the binding before he lifted their hands over her head, holding her firm. He kissed her deeply then, thrusting with slow, fluid movements.

Brie was overcome by the profound gesture and opened herself completely to her Master, holding nothing back as he claimed her heart. He made love to her tenderly while he held her captive. It was the best of all worlds and for the first time she felt utterly…complete.

Sir growled in her ear just before his cock swelled and the powerful surges began, filling her body and soul with his masculine essence. She responded with a gentle orgasm of her own. It was like sweet ambrosia.

Sir slipped his free hand under the small of her back and pressed her to him possessively afterwards. They lay there in the dark; the only sound was their labored breathing. She matched hers to his and reveled in the added connection. Alone, bound together, skin against skin… Held in his tight embrace, Brie knew with confidence she would never love another as deeply as Sir—his claiming was complete.

# Misguided Service

Brie woke up before daybreak to the sound of Sir's relaxed breathing beside her. She was tempted to pinch herself. Here she was, sleeping next to Sir, in *his* bed. Brie lay in the dark, drinking in the moment.

When he rolled over, she quietly slipped out of bed and made her way to the kitchen. She was determined to make him the best damn omelet known to man. She shivered as she tiptoed through his dark apartment, the chill of the marble freezing her toes.

When Brie reached the kitchen, she flicked on the light in the hallway and glanced over at the red lounger, a smile playing across her lips. Last night, Sir had taught her that he commanded not only her body, but also her heart. She sighed happily and scanned the panoramic view of the city. Considerably fewer lights than before twinkled below as LA prepared for the beginning of a new day. She caught a glimpse of Sir's white shirt on the floor beside the couch. Brie walked over and picked it up, crushing it to her chest to drink in his smell.

Brie purred, loving the sexy feel of his shirt wrapped around her naked frame as she buttoned it up. The shirt hung down, barely covering her ass. Its thin material provided little protection from the cold, but the knowledge it was Sir's warmed her immensely.

She returned to the stylish kitchen to assemble the ingredients. His kitchen was clean and artfully decorated, like the rest of his house. Black granite countertops, stainless steel appliances and recessed lighting made it look like it belonged in a magazine. It was a bit intimidating, but Brie refused to be deterred.

She was delighted to see there was a whole carton of eggs. Plenty to make a mistake or two… She then searched through the fridge to gather the rest of the ingredients. Brie set them out before her and replayed the recipe in her mind, going over each step. She found an appropriate pan, bowl, and whisk, making only the tiniest of noises, being extra careful not to wake Sir. She sat down at his small, round kitchen table and waited for Master to wake up. Unfortunately, she was feeling too anxious to sit for long.

Brie decided it would be wise to do a quick run-through first. She cracked the eggs and separated them like a pro. She got the pan heating while she whipped up the egg whites. In no time, she had a fluffy, expertly cooked omelet sitting on a plate. *Wouldn't Marquis be proud?*

She felt kinda sad when she tossed it into the trash, but focused her energy on cutting up the veggies and shredding the cheese for the real omelet. As she was dicing up the ham, she heard movement behind her.

"Continue," Sir said as he settled down at the kitchen table to watch. She noticed he wore only boxers. *Oh, my God—he looks hot.* Naked, dressed, or in boxers, it didn't matter—the man was a stunning example of masculinity.

Brie's heart began to race. It was one thing to cook without an audience, but to have Sir watch her… She took a few deep breaths before beginning. She cracked the eggs and groaned silently. *A shell!* She poured them into the sink and started again. This time she succeeded and quietly cheered. She turned on the burner and proceeded to whip and fold the egg mixture, sneaking glances at Sir while she worked. He remained stoic, but Brie swore she saw a slight smirk.

*No matter.* This morning she would prove to him that she could cook—omelets, at least. She poured the eggs onto the bubbling butter in the pan and turned to Sir. "What would you like in your omelet, Sir?"

"Put in whatever you assume I'd like."

She nodded. His odd answer made her feel a bit anxious over her choice, but she went ahead and sprinkled in a little chive, ham and sharp cheddar cheese. She swirled it around, noticing that the cheese was burning on the sides of the pan. *Crap, I'm supposed to wait to add cheese!*

Her nerves hit and she froze. It was ruined. She hesitated before tossing it in the trash so she could start again. Sir said nothing.

Brie began the process again. She almost burnt the butter, but saved it in the nick of time. She added the proper ingredients and mixed it up before putting it down to wait for it to set. Everything looked good; this would be a perfect omelet. She could just see the proud gleam in Sir's eyes when he tasted it.

She went to pick up the pan to swirl it, not noticing that Sir was behind her until he grabbed her wrist and turned her around. He lifted her onto the cold granite counter and began unbuttoning the shirt.

Brie glanced over at the eggs nervously. They would be ruined if she didn't get them off the stove now, but Sir was slow and deliberate as he unfastened the last button and slowly slid his shirt off her shoulders.

He kissed her on the collarbone and then slowly made a trail down between her breasts. The whole time, Brie stared anxiously at the eggs, but she quickly returned her attention to him when he looked up. Sir gave her a mischievous smile and kissed her on the lips.

When he pulled away, she couldn't hold it in any longer. "Sir, the eggs…"

He lifted her chin up and kissed her again, as if he hadn't heard. The unpleasant smell of burnt egg began to swirl around her nostrils. Her perfect omelet was ruined.

Without breaking the kiss, Sir pushed the pan off the burner and turned it off. Then he pulled away from her, wearing a serious expression. He lifted Brie off the counter, removing the shirt completely before asking her to sit.

Brie didn't know what was happening, but it was obvious she had failed somehow.

Sir sat across the table from her and stared at Brie for several moments before speaking. "Do you know what you did wrong, téa?"

She blushed and whispered, "I burnt your eggs, Sir."

"No."

Brie looked up at him, now suddenly far more alarmed. "Sir, did I pick the wrong ingredients?"

He shook his head once. "No. Apparently, you are unaware that you have made three grievous errors this morning."

Her lips trembled. *How?* What could she have done wrong when all she'd wanted to do was impress him?

"Shall I explain?" he asked.

Brie looked down at the glass tabletop to avoid his disappointed stare. "Please, Sir."

"Look at me."

She forced herself to look up and meet his solemn gaze.

"First, you left my bed without permission. A grave error on your part that shall not happen again. Second, you disobeyed a direct order."

She shook her head in disagreement. "No, Sir, I would never—"

He looked at her sternly. "Last night I told you that you were only to wear the collar."

She opened her mouth to protest but then nodded, realizing that he had. "Yes, you did, Sir." She looked down at her feet, completely mortified. "I am sorry, Sir. I deserve to be punished."

"Why did you disobey me?"

"I assumed it was a command only meant for the moment." She bit her lip to stop it from trembling. Once Brie had regained her composure, she added, "I never meant to disobey you, Sir. Please know that."

"I accept your apology. See that it does not happen again."

"Never, Sir."

"Never is a long time, my little sub. Do not be quick to use such words."

She looked at the table again, crushed to be failing so badly on her first morning with him. A glutton for punishment, she asked, "How did I fail you the third way, Sir?"

"You did not ask what I wanted for breakfast, or if I wanted breakfast at all."

Her shoulders slumped in defeat, but she quickly straightened them, not wanting to offend him further. "I was foolish not to ask, Sir."

"There is something you should know."

She looked up at him sheepishly. "What, Sir?"

"I hate eggs."

Her jaw dropped and she squeaked, "You do?" How could it be that her Master hated the only thing she knew how to cook well?

Sir crinkled his nose. "The smell makes me nauseous and now my whole apartment reeks."

She sat in stunned silence, feeling sick to her stomach.

"Do not fret, téa. I only punish willful disobedience. Today I was curious what you would do. In your eagerness to please, you forgot your training."

She closed her eyes. "Yes. You're right, Sir."

"Of course I am," he answered.

She snuck a peek and was relieved to see his expression was relaxed, not angry. When he motioned Brie to his lap, she literally jumped up and ran to him. He gathered her into his arms, and chuckled. "When Marquis told me the only things he was able to teach you to cook were an omelet and spaghetti, I had to laugh."

"Don't tell me you hate spaghetti, too?" she whimpered.

"I am not a fan of tomatoes."

"Oh…" she said dejectedly. Brie rested her chin on his strong shoulder and sighed. "You are going to starve because of my cooking."

His answer was quick. "No. Unlike you, I know how to cook."

She gasped, but noted the glint in his eye. "I'd say that is below the belt, Sir."

"It's the ugly truth."

Brie grabbed her stomach and grunted loudly. "It hurts, it hurts…"

Sir swatted her bottom. "You are fortunate I do not eat breakfast. Thankfully, that is one less meal you can ruin."

She basked in Sir's playful mood and traced his masculine jaw before kissing him. "Thank you, Sir, for hating breakfast. Is there any way I can make up for my lack of culinary talent?"

He furrowed his brow, stating, "No. There is nothing you can do to make up for your atrocious cooking skills."

She pouted prettily, smoothing out the wrinkles from his frown with her fingertips. "Are you sure?"

He snorted. "You will find your feminine charms have little effect on your Master."

Brie gave up and buried her head in his chest, mumbling, "I guess I'm hopeless."

He stroked her long hair and replied in a deceptively soothing voice, "Useless, yes, but not hopeless."

His sense of humor was brutal and she loved it. Brie was about to object, when he gave her a direct command. "Take a quick shower and ready yourself for me."

Those words were music to her ears. "My pleasure, Sir!" she replied, jumping off his lap and heading straight for the shower.

# Lesson Three: A Matter of Ego

In less than a half hour Brie was washed, shaved, and primped. She opened the bathroom door and called out his name. "Sir?"

He answered with a low, sultry, "Come," from the front of the apartment. Brie glided over the smooth marble, wanting to make a favorable impression. Since she wasn't capable of cooking, she damn well would make up for it with her other skills. *Man does not live on bread alone!*

Sir was waiting for her beside the red chaise with a silver chain in his hand. She followed the trail of links down and saw that it was attached to a leg of the chair. "Kneel before me, téa."

*Kneel before me, goddess…*

Sir certainly had a way with words. Brie bowed before him and willingly accepted the cuff he secured around her ankle. "You will not be released until the lesson has been learned."

She looked up at him questioningly. "What lesson, Master?"

He smiled. "That is for you to figure out."

Brie had to hide her frustration. Mr. Gallant's upfront method of teaching was so much easier and involved a much smaller chance of failure.

Sir read her like a book. "You are no longer at the Training Center. Lessons will not be spoon-fed to you. Growth must be earned."

She bowed low, her head touching the floor. "I understand, Master." Then she added softly, "But I don't want to fail you."

Brie squealed when he picked her up. He held her so that she was eye to eye with him. "You cannot fail unless you are unwilling to try."

"Yes, Master."

His intense look communicated confidence in her abilities, and her fears receded. He set her back on the ground and slipped off his boxers.

Sir lay down on the lounger and motioned her to him. The clinking sound of the chain echoed through the room as she moved to straddle him. She couldn't help thinking of her Auction Day when she'd played Captain's pet. It brought a smile to her lips, but she let go of the memory. Brie looked down at her handsome Dom now, her heart bursting with pride that she was his—and his alone.

The red lounger was so narrow that both her feet touched the floor when she straddled him. It was a different position already, heightening the sense of adventure the chain already inspired.

"This first part of the lesson is easy. Make love to your Master."

Her eyes widened as she realized he was giving her free rein over his body. "Anything I want, Master?"

"Unless I tell you to stop."

Brie immediately leaned over to kiss him. All those weeks in class she had watched those lips, fantasized about them, and now they were hers for the taking. She lightly brushed her mouth against them, and was thrilled when he closed his eyes and groaned in response.

It seemed decadent to kiss him like that—like eating fine chocolate. She should show some restraint, some level of sophistication, but she could not. Brie kissed him over and over again. Sir met her enthusiasm by running his hands over her body, further igniting her hunger for him.

"I love you, Master," she declared, finally burying her face in his neck and breathing his manly scent. Sir was a combination of masculine musk with a hint of sweet like a summer's day; no artificial scents covered up his intoxicating smell. Brie took another long sniff, purring softy. However, she could not ignore the hard shaft cradled between her lower lips.

Brie rubbed herself against him, loving the feel of his stiff cock pressed against her sensitive clit. She used it, shifting her pelvis to enjoy different angles without letting the head of his cock slip inside. Sir did not object. He seemed to enjoy watching her pussy coat his manhood with her abundant excitement.

Alas, there was only so much self-teasing she could take. Brie lifted herself up and positioned his handsome cock so that it barely touched her opening. She teased herself for a little longer by not settling down onto his rigid manhood. She leaned over to kiss his lips again, savoring the agony of being so close to satisfaction, but delaying her own pleasure…and his.

Sir put his hands on her hips and squeezed her buttocks, but to her surprise he did not thrust. He continued to let her control the level of torturous penetration. His level of restraint did Brie in, and she ever so slowly, millimeter by millimeter, lowered herself onto his shaft. The unique chair gave her a level of control she hadn't experienced before.

Brie moaned loudly when her pussy hit the base of his cock. All of Sir. Inside her. While they kissed. *Pure, unadulterated heaven.*

"Damn, woman, you feel good," Sir said hoarsely.

Brie kissed him again, reveling in the fact her body was pleasing to Master. She began to move up and down his thick shaft, using the power of her legs. Sir helped guide her with added force so that each stroke was fully realized. No movement was wasted, making it incredibly intense.

She cried out as time after time his cock surged into her, filling her completely. He began thrusting faster as he threw his head back. A low groan rumbled in his chest.

*Oh, God! To watch Sir come…*

He suddenly stopped and held her hard against his rigid manhood. The pulses that had been building inside her could not be halted. She bit her lip, having not been given permission to orgasm. He opened his eyes and grinned as he started the thrusting motion again. It distracted her enough to stave off the climax.

She let out a small gasp, remembering his previous lesson. *Even my orgasms answer to him.* She trembled at his control.

Brie leaned over to give him another kiss, but felt her pussy contract when his tongue parted her lips. She had to pull back. Brie closed her eyes. *Do not come. Do* not *come.*

Sir's hands glided over her skin, caressing her stomach before moving up to her breasts. He flicked the nipples with his thumbs as he squeezed her ample breasts. "You're breathtaking, téa."

She automatically responded to his praises by kissing him again. This time he grasped the back of her neck as he parted her lips, claiming her mouth. She instinctively struggled to get out of his embrace in an effort to prevent what was about to happen.

"Relax," he whispered between kisses.

The instant she let down her defenses, her orgasm crashed over her. It was powerful, having been denied before. Her pussy continued to pulse long after her climax had ended.

Sir released her and grabbed her hips again. She followed his lead, moving slowly up and down his shaft, whimpering softly because of the sensitivity of her freshly-come pussy. He threw his head back again, closing his eyes and groaning loudly. Through gritted teeth he told her, "When I tell you to stop, don't move."

"Yes, Master," she breathed.

Brie watched Sir intently as his whole body stiffened. "Stop," he grunted as he pushed deep into her. She braced her hands against his chest and became still. He clenched his jaw, breathing heavily. Sir opened his eyes just before the spasms began. It was incredibly hot to gaze into Sir's eyes as he came deep inside her.

Afterwards, he turned her around without disengaging (a hidden benefit to the oddly shaped chair) and wrapped his arms around her—one around her waist, while his other hand rested comfortably around her neck in a possessive embrace. Brie closed her eyes and drank in his loving ownership.

They lay like that, in a state of peaceful harmony, for what seemed like hours. There was nothing but the beauty of now and Sir's embrace. He let out a long, satisfied sigh.

Her body flushed in response. Connecting like this with Sir was amazing, and it made her crave even more intimacy with him. Questions pricked her consciousness and she broke the pleasant silence by asking the one foremost in her mind. "Master, may I ask about your father now?"

She felt his whole body tense, but he answered evenly. "Yes."

"How did he die, Sir?"

He paused for a second. "My father committed suicide."

Brie felt her heart crush inward. The mood in the room had completely changed with his revelation. "I shouldn't have brought it up. I'm sorry, Sir."

"No." He sighed quietly. "It's important you know. Continue."

"Thank you, Sir." She paused before asking her next question, not wanting to upset him. "How old were you?"

"Fifteen."

Her sympathy poured out to him as she imagined what it must have been like to lose his father at such a pivotal age in his life. "What about your mother, Sir?"

His voice dropped an octave. "She is dead to me."

Brie shivered and stopped the line of questioning. She squeezed the arm he had wrapped around her middle.

Sir continued of his own volition, "My father was...extremely talented, a world class violinist." He readjusted himself, holding her tighter. He added, almost as an afterthought, "An unusually gifted musician who was idolized by his fans."

Brie imagined an Italian hunk with dark hair and dark, soulful eyes, standing on stage alone, playing for an enraptured audience. She couldn't help wondering how that had affected Sir growing up. Had he been close to his father or had the man been absent from his life? Had the constant traveling caused an estrangement between his mother and father? There were so many questions to ask, but at the moment she felt only empathy for Sir and remained silent.

His voice was distant when he spoke again. "I still find it difficult to believe he's gone. Such a force in the world. How can that disappear as if it never existed?"

Brie suddenly felt inadequate, not knowing what to say but feeling a need to break the deafening silence. "Death is cruel, Sir."

"Have you lost someone?" he asked quietly.

"Yes, my grandfather when he was eighty. Nothing as great as your loss, Sir."

He tightened his hold on her. "Good. I would not wish that on anyone."

She decided her words would be useless, so she rested her head against his chest and surrounded him with loving thoughts instead.

He spoke a few minutes later. "Suicide is brutal."

"I can't think of anything worse," she answered softly.

"No, neither can I... That last image of him is seared in my brain and I will *never* be free of it." He snarled under his breath and abruptly lifted Brie off him. The chain rattled as he placed her feet on the floor. "Let's return to your lesson, my wayward sub."

Sir stood up and formally kissed her on the forehead, as if it were part of a ritual. He then pulled a mat out from under the Tantra chair and laid it down beside her. His voice changed, once again unruffled and commanding. "Kneel. Legs closed, hands behind your head so that your breasts are displayed."

After the command Sir walked away from her, his tight ass flexing as he moved. Despite the seriousness of his mood, she couldn't prevent herself from admiring it. The man was majestic naked.

Brie obediently lowered herself to the mat, wondering if she had been wrong to say anything. She looked out of the window at the clouds drifting in the sky and tried not to second guess herself.

When she heard the shower, she found herself imagining Sir's hands running over his muscular body as he lathered up. How she wished she could join in the fun. Brie sighed, wanting to free Sir from the taint her questions had caused.

He returned to her, fully dressed, and picked up his house key from the counter. "I have a few errands to run, including retrieving your car and purse from the Training Center. Thankfully, Marquis thought to lock your handbag in the safe."

Brie had totally forgotten about those mundane, but exceedingly important, details. "That is kind of you, Sir."

"Kindness has nothing to do with it, téa. I have assigned you a task. Therefore, I will take care of this while you complete it."

"Yes, Sir," she answered meekly.

"Remain in this position until I get back. You are only allowed to release yourself to use the restroom. Be prepared to tell me the lesson I am teaching you with this."

Brie bowed her head in answer.

"And téa?"

She looked up timidly.

"Asking about my father was not an error on your part. If I hadn't wanted you to know, I would not have spoken of it."

She smiled up at him gratefully. "Thank you, Sir."

Sir nodded and left the apartment, shutting the door quietly behind him. Brie sighed as the electricity of his presence left with him, leaving behind an emptiness that weighed upon her.

Brie was unsure why Sir was having her practice kneeling again, but she felt certain it was not meant as a punishment. It concerned her that the purpose of the lesson eluded her, especially since Sir expected an explanation upon his return.

Worrying about it wasn't producing answers, so Brie closed her eyes and thought of her friend, Lea. Brie wondered what the bubbly jokester was doing the day after graduation. *Probably sleeping in…*

If Lea had to guess what Brie was up to, she would never believe Brie was enduring another kneeling lesson. It had been their first kneeling lesson at the Training Center that had marked the beginning of the girls' friendship. That day, Lea had cracked jokes when they'd been ordered to kneel quietly. Brie had chosen to stand up for her, despite Marquis' threat to punish Brie for Lea's transgression. All because Mary had decided to tattle.

*Mary…*

Brie's lips curled into a snarl. She could not believe the bitch had attempted to steal Faelan from her on the night of graduation. It was low, even by Mary's standards. But then, Mary had always gone after any Dom Brie had shown an interest in. Up until last night, Brie had been willing to forgive her, knowing that Mary was a hurting unit who desperately needed a friend. Brie had been foolish enough to believe that over the six-week course she'd been able to break through the barriers Mary had put up and develop a real friendship with the woman.

*Yeah… I'm a freakin' idiot!*

She'd been completely blindsided, never suspecting that Mary would betray her so brazenly. Brie would never forget the shock of seeing Faelan enter Mary's room, or the sounds of the bitch's cries of passion during their 'interview' together.

*Thank God for Marquis…*

Brie opened her eyes and let out the pent-up rage she'd been holding in since last night. "Fuck you to hell, Mary!"

In another apartment, she heard the muffled barking of a tiny dog. Even the dog hated Mary.

It didn't matter that things had worked out for the best. The simple fact was that Mary had deliberately stabbed Brie in the back by picking Faelan. But the bitch hadn't left it at that. No! She'd had to fuck him in the adjacent room, *knowing* Brie could hear them.

Suddenly Faelan's blue eyes loomed before her. He was no better than Mary. Brie understood that school protocol had required him to join Mary for the interview, but anything that had happened during the interview itself had been *his* choice. It sickened Brie to think that she had even considered Faelan as her potential Master. Thankfully, her eyes had been opened before she'd made her decision at the collaring ceremony.

Mary's treachery had inadvertently forced Brie to make the right choice. But as long as she lived, she would never forgive *or* forget Mary's betrayal.

*Fuck the bitch and Faelan both!*

Inside her head, she heard Mr. Gallant's voice reprimanding her for those ugly words. She rolled her eyes and reworded her thoughts, wanting to think and behave like a proper submissive. *I hope Mary and Faelan get exactly what they deserve, Mr. Gallant.*

Brie sighed in satisfaction afterwards. It did feel better not to cuss. "Thank you, Mr. Gallant," she said out loud, smiling at the walls. The only way she could remain a sub worthy of Sir's dominance was to consistently behave like one. It would not do to be submissive only in his presence. Perfect obedience at all times. *A true submissive obeys in mind and body, whether or not Master is present.*

She nodded once, confident in her fresh resolve. Brie ignored her hurting knees and aching back, staring out of the scenic window with a contented sigh. Cars inched along the tiny streets. People were busy navigating their lives while she knelt on the floor alone, anxiously waiting for *him.*

Brie wondered if Sir was thinking about her as he went about his business. Was he secure in the knowledge that his newly acquired sub was obeying his command? That she was kneeling beside his sexy Tantra chair, earnestly awaiting his return?

Brie glanced around the room suddenly, wondering if Sir had cameras, but she quickly dismissed the idea. Why would he? This wasn't the Training Center. Still, it helped to think that he was watching her remotely. It caused her to straighten her back more, keeping her lips supple and her body relaxed. Yes, that was how she would endure the wait—by pretending that even now Sir was secretly watching her, pleased with her level of commitment.

"I love you, Sir," she whispered.

Brie's heart skipped a beat when she finally heard the key turn in the lock hours later. *Master's back!* She was embarrassed to admit to herself that she felt just like a little puppy eager to greet its owner.

Sir entered the apartment and placed her purse on the counter before going to the kitchen with several bags in his hands. He didn't even glance her way as he walked by.

It was reminiscent of her objectification lesson and she actually felt an odd thrill. Brie waited patiently, although her stomach started growling when she heard him cutting up food in the kitchen.

Sir came out briefly and smiled. "Well done, téa." His words of praise thrilled her overly much, forcing her to show great restraint to avoid grinning like a fool. He commanded smoothly, "You may stand and sit on the chair, legs spread for my pleasure."

Brie choked on the groan that erupted from her lips when she tried to get up off the floor. The chain accentuated her lack of grace, making random clinking sounds as she struggled with her stiff limbs. Thankfully, Sir had returned to the kitchen and missed her graceless transfer from floor to chaise.

He returned soon after with a plate in his hand. Sir walked over and sat on the foot of the chair. "Before we eat, I want to hear what you've learned."

Her heart raced as she voiced her answer, terrified she might be wrong. "I learned two lessons, Sir."

"Go on," he said, sounding surprised.

Brie suddenly panicked. Was it okay to learn more than one thing per lesson? *Of course*, she chided herself. "Sir, it is important for me to think like your submissive at all times, even when you are not beside me."

Sir remained silent for a moment and then stated, "I would have assumed you already knew that, after six weeks of training."

She looked at him self-consciously. "Sir, I *knew* it in my head, but I hadn't lived it until now."

He nodded. "Very well. What else did you learn?"

"The only thing I care about is pleasing you, to be worthy of your domination."

"Answer me this. If pleasing me was your motivation this morning, what went wrong?"

Brie thought back on it. Her mistake had been to assume he wanted what she would cook, but it was more than that. She had wanted to show off her meager cooking skills. Why? To prove that she was good enough for him.

"I wanted you to be proud of me."

"And why was that a problem?"

She looked down at the leather cuff around her ankle as she thought about it. "Because…" She stalled, and then suddenly it came to her. "In the end it had to do with stroking my own ego, not pleasing you, Sir."

"Exactly," he replied, holding up a bite-sized piece of green apple. "Open."

Brie parted her lips and took the apple in her mouth, appreciating its sweet tartness.

He spoke while she chewed. "I am confident in my choice of sub, despite the fact the decision was thrust upon me last night. To doubt yourself is to doubt my choice, and *that* I will not tolerate."

Sir had gifted her with a clear understanding. Even though she had chosen Sir at the collaring ceremony, the truth was it had been his choice to accept her as his submissive. In fact, he'd turned her down initially. She shuddered, remembering it, but the pain of that rejection was like a long-lost echo now.

The fact Sir cared enough to address her fear of inadequacy endeared him to her even more. Brie looked up at her Master, declaring with heartfelt conviction and a smidge of humor, "Sir, I will not doubt your fabulous choice of sub."

His eyes softened as a smirk played at the corner of his lips. "I believe you are in need of another lesson." Sir fed her another piece of apple and then took one for himself. "But this lesson is best done on an empty stomach." He got up and placed the dish in the kitchen before coming back to her. He undid the chain around the leg of the chair and started down the hallway.

"Come, téa."

# A Little Restraint

Brie followed behind Sir, quivering in excitement. Having waited for him for hours, her body was revved up and ready for whatever he desired.

Sir led her into his bedroom, which was a stark contrast to the rest of the apartment. Whereas the color scheme of the rest of his place was dark and stylish, his bedroom was a sultry crimson with gothic accents of ironwork. It alluded to unspeakable acts of the sensual kind.

He proceeded to attach the chain to the leg of the bed. He then left her, disappearing into his closet before returning with several items in his hands. The one that grabbed Brie's attention was the spreader bar.

Sir noticed her focusing on it and grinned. "Oh, yes, you will be quite restrained for this session. Feel free to call a safeword at any point, for I will not be asking."

Brie's knees shook. There was no doubt Sir was going to push her limits with him. The thought both excited and terrified her. Such an experienced Dom would be used to compliant, fearless subs.

*He knows you, Brie,* she reminded herself.

Sir knelt down at her feet and caressed her ankle before he attached the first cuff. She felt the fire begin. His touch was like an electrical storm, sending jolts of sensation upward.

"Spread your legs," he said evenly.

Brie stared down at him as she moved to comply with his command. Sir wrapped his strong hand around her ankle to help her get the proper distance. She moaned softly as he buckled her into the cuff. Sir stood up with a satisfied look.

His eyes met hers and she caught her breath. The hunger she found in those eyes was overpowering. Sir laid out a large towel at the end of the bed and then picked her up. He placed her at the foot of the bed, pressing her stomach down onto the mattress. "Wrists."

Brie put her wrists behind her. He quickly and adeptly bound them with cord. Sir then took a silk scarf and tied it over her eyes. Her whole body was trembling by then. He'd effectively subdued her, leaving her defenseless to his ravenous appetite.

"You are mine."

"Yes, Master."

He moved to the side of the bed and she heard the lighting of a match. The scent of sulfur wafted through the air. Then the sound of music filled the room, intense and beautiful. She felt the bed move as Sir leaned over and whispered in her ear, "A favorite composer of mine, Giuseppe Verdi." Brie listened to the music, carried by the impassioned sound of violins. He moved to her other ear. "The opera is called *La Traviata.* A poignant tale of love and sacrifice. We must see it sometime."

Brie was instantly transported back to their last opera, the night he had played the role of Khan. There in the theater he had played out her King fantasy, with another male acting as the priest. God, how she had wanted him that night, but she had been denied the pleasure. Now here she was, bound and blindfolded, about to be fucked by Master. His choice of music added a sense of sophistication and substance to the intense scene.

Sir stood behind her. "The oil will be warm."

Brie instinctively jumped when she felt the first few warm drops fall on her skin, as he poured it over her lower back and down the crack of her ass. The oil was incredibly erotic as it rolled down and slowly trickled off her mound, one drip at a time. Then he began to rub the oil into her skin—first her back, then her buttocks, until Sir was concentrating all his attention on her tight little hole.

"Deny me nothing," he stated, slapping her ass resoundingly. Brie's surprised squeal rivaled the high notes of the woman singing in the background.

He growled hoarsely, "I will hear your passion as I use you for my pleasure, téa." He slapped her hard on the other cheek, causing another cry to escape her lips as she instinctively struggled to avoid the pain. The spreader bar kept her in place, her body helpless and open to his ravenous need.

The skin on her tender ass tingled as he changed tactics and played with her buttocks, lightly slapping and squeezing them—reacquainting her with the sensual power of his touch. She lay there, helpless and completely turned on.

Sir knew her, knew exactly how to make her body crave him.

His play stopped and then he left her again. She heard the sound of running water from the adjoining bathroom before he returned. Suddenly, Sir's hand was between her legs, confirming her state of desire. "My goddess is dripping for her Master."

"Most desperately, Master," she agreed.

Brie soon heard the distinct sound of Sir liberally applying lubricant to his cock. Sir was silent as he coated the outside of her anus with gel and then eased more inside her tight hole. He made sure her ass was thoroughly prepared for the pounding she was about to receive. He separated her buttocks with his slippery hands and she felt the warm head of his shaft slip into the valley of her ass.

Sir's cock rested against the entrance of her taut hole. He grabbed her hips and began pressing his thickness into her. Despite being willing, Brie's body resisted his manly conquest—making the encounter that much more exhilarating.

In the past, Sir's entering had been gentle but demanding. This time was different. He pressed into her with more force, slapping her ass lightly to weaken her resistance. "Give yourself to me," he demanded. She consciously relaxed her inner muscles and cried out as his generous shaft opened her up, body and soul.

Sir used her hips to give him leverage, thrusting deeper into her ass while the music swirled around them. It was surreal, profound. When he was buried deep inside her, Sir grabbed her bound wrists and remained motionless, pressing even harder, forcing her to take all of him.

Brie's body struggled to embrace the fullness of Sir. She gasped and then moaned as he began moving, slowly stroking her tight recesses with his impressive cock. "I remember when you struggled to take me halfway."

Brie remembered their first encounter well. She'd had no idea then how forbidden their coupling had been. It hadn't been until the next day, when she had almost been kicked out of the program and Sir had been asked to resign, that she'd understood the ramifications. It still amazed

Brie that Sir had been willing to risk his career to be the one to take her anal virginity.

Had he suspected what the final outcome would be? Had that been his method of marking his potential mate? The possibility of it excited her.

"I love your cock, Master."

"My cock loves your ass, téa."

She purred, but soon cried out as Sir held her down more securely and fucked her hard. In an instant there was nothing but Sir's cock powering into her ass. Master held nothing back as he dominated her with his formidable shaft.

Brie gasped, her face buried in the bedcovers as she desperately tried to hold on to reality. Her whole body began to tingle as it slowly moved to another level of awareness. When he slowed down and snaked his fingers below, rubbing her clit furiously, she could only gasp for air like a fish out of water.

"You are my instrument. Sing for me," he stated. The violins sounded in the background as Sir pushed deep into her and brought her over the edge with his skillful manipulation. Brie suddenly found her voice and screamed out in ecstasy.

Before the last contraction had ended, he was pounding into her again. Her body was no longer hers, transformed into his instrument of pleasure. She began crying in pure joy, loving his hands clasped around her bound wrists, the restriction of the spreader bar, the opera music swimming in her head and his masterful cock that demanded everything of her.

He suddenly changed angles and she tensed. The head of his shaft began hammering her in a spot that made angels sing. She lost all connection with her surroundings as she felt her spirit floating upwards; exploding in pure rapture the moment Sir released his hot seed.

Brie slowly came back down to a light caress on her cheek. She opened her eyes and gazed straight into Sir's, blinking several times. All her bindings had been removed and the music was now playing softly in the background, more like a whisper than a song. Sir was lying naked beside her.

"My pleasing little sub, how you do fly."

She smiled and closed her eyes again, needing to concentrate on his touch. His soothing voice gently brought her back down to earth.

"I love you, babygirl."

# The Wolf Returns

Brie arrived at the tobacco shop early on Monday, but it seemed weird to her now and she actually blushed when she saw Mr. Reynolds. At her graduation ceremony, she'd found out he was Sir's uncle, and he'd seen her bare-chested.

Thankfully, Mr. Reynolds did not behave differently. He nodded as he priced the tins of tobacco. "Good to see you, Brie."

She walked up to him and smiled sadly, handing over her letter of resignation. "I'm sorry, Mr. Reynolds, but I am going to be moving on."

He took her letter reluctantly. "I can't say I'm surprised."

Jeff came up from the back. "What? Are you quitting, Brie?"

Brie ignored him—she had no respect for the boy. However, Mr. Reynolds responded to his inquiry. "Yes, we are losing Miss Bennett in two weeks."

"Fuck that. I quit." Jeff walked out of the front door without another word.

Mr. Reynolds shrugged. "Well, he just made my job easier."

Brie chuckled. It was true. Jeff had been a lazy employee who'd caused more problems than he was worth. "Will you get in trouble with the owner?" Brie asked, worried for her kind boss.

"I've wanted to fire the punk for a year. I can't be blamed if he quits."

"I'll be happy to train two people for you, sir."

He turned his head at the sound of the title she only meant informally. A smile suddenly spread across his face. "The two of you were certainly the talk of the evening after you left. I was told such a thing has never happened in the history of the Center. Are you still confident of your unorthodox choice?"

She grinned. "Yes, there is no doubt in my mind."

"Good. Thane is a good man," Mr. Reynolds said, sounding pleased. "You have balls of steel, young lady. My heart dropped when he said no."

Brie shuddered. "That was the hardest thing I've ever done, but there was no other choice for me."

Mr. Reynolds' expression changed, and she noted sadness in his eyes. "Thane has had a difficult time opening up to people ever since…"

He stopped, so she finished his sentence. "Since his father's suicide?"

Mr. Reynolds' face became pale. "My brother-in-law's death changed the boy, but walking in on it would change any man."

Brie was shocked by the revelation. Sir hadn't just seen his father's body; he had been present when the man had died. It broke her heart.

She saw the raw grief in Mr. Reynolds' eyes when he spoke. "The boy lost himself when Alonzo died. We took him in, but he was in too much pain and far too independent to accept our help. He petitioned for emancipation at age sixteen, and was granted it. I've tried to be there for him as much as he would allow." Mr. Reynolds' expression changed, as if he regretted what he'd said. "I'm sorry. It isn't my place to talk about this. Forgive me."

"It's obvious everyone was hurt by it," Brie offered. She found it odd that Mr. Reynolds hadn't mentioned his own sister. What part, if any, had she played in what had happened?

His voice caught, the emotion hard for him to contain. "It's a damn shame. An extraordinary talent lost and a young man scarred for life." He turned away and wiped his eyes before he looked at her again. "I can't tell you how grateful I am that you've come into his life."

She shook her head. "Oh, no, I'm the grateful one."

"It's good you feel that way, Brie. Thane is much like his father," he paused and smiled sadly, "in that he is honorable to a fault."

"Sir is an honorable man," Brie agreed, returning his smile. "I'm thrilled he has chosen me to partner with."

Mr. Reynolds wrapped one arm around her. "As much as I hate to lose you, I can't think of a better reason."

"At least I don't have to say goodbye." She gave him a tentative hug. "Now that I'm part of the family, *Unc*."

"You are not allowed to call me that at work. Nepotism and all that."

She nodded and stepped away. "I understand. I'm sorry, Mr. Reynolds. It won't happen again."

He laughed out loud. "I'm just kidding, Brie. We're surrounded by nepotism here. Truly, I have never had an employee who worked as hard, or treated me with the respect you do."

"I hope you are allowed to hire good people this time, Mr. Reynolds."

He shook his head. "I doubt it. I've been told there are several nieces and nephews looking for jobs."

"I'll do my best to train them well, then."

Mr. Reynolds chuckled. "You do that for me."

She spent a pleasant morning at the shop, ringing up customers and stocking the shelves. At noon, her phone binged with a text. She took a quick glance and saw that it was Sir. As texting was not allowed at work, she asked for permission before answering it. "I know it's against policy, Mr. Reynolds, but it's Sir. I really need to take this."

He smiled in understanding. "Yes, Brie. You have my permission to answer his texts only, just as long as customers are not present."

She beamed at him. "Thank you, Mr. Reynolds!"

Brie held her breath as she clicked on the text. The butterflies began when she read it. *Tonight we will play a game.*

It left her in a constant state of excitement for the rest of the day. What did Sir have planned for the evening? The possibilities gave her goosebumps.

When five o'clock finally rolled around, she bade Mr. Reynolds goodbye and headed out, a bundle of sexual tension. *Going home to Master!*

As she was walking to the car, she heard her name being called. "Brie! Brie Bennett."

She turned and saw Faelan loping up to her. "What are you doing here?" she asked, stunned to see him at her place of work.

"I've been waiting to talk with you alone."

"I can't," she exclaimed, taking a few steps back. "I don't think Sir would approve."

"But this is between us—it doesn't involve him."

She did not feel comfortable and turned to leave, not wanting to have a confrontation with Faelan in the middle of the parking lot. He quickly caught up with her and took hold of her arm. "We're just going to talk. What's the harm in that?"

"I don't think we should," she insisted.

"Brie." Blue Eyes cocked his head and smiled sadly. "Don't you think I deserve an explanation?" His eyes drew her in and she became acutely aware of the pain behind them.

"Todd..." She quickly corrected herself, addressing him properly. "Mr. Wallace."

He shrugged off the formality, calling her by her given name. "Brie, we are two of a kind, you and me." When he came nearer, she decided not to bolt. *We have to talk this out sooner or later.* "I knew the minute I met you that you and I were meant to be. Hell, my one thought this whole time has been to become the man, the Dom, you needed."

She shook her head indignantly, remembering how he'd made her feel on graduation night. "It didn't appear that way at my graduation."

"Blossom."

She stiffened when he used his pet name for her. "Don't call me that."

"Fine." He put his hands in the air as if in surrender. "But you need to know that I didn't touch Mary."

Brie turned towards her car, not wanting to hear his version of that night. "I heard her, Fae...Mr. Wallace! Don't even go there."

He advanced cautiously, as if he were afraid she might get spooked and run if he moved too fast. "Mary needed a little pain, so I delivered what she asked for. There was no sex involved."

She glared at him. "If that was the case, you should have explained it to me when I asked, but you didn't! And now it doesn't matter." She took a defiant stance with her hands on her hips and her head held high. "I'm Sir's now. There is no going back."

Pain washed over those ocean blues, but he said with conviction, "We are meant to be together, Brie." He backed her into the side of her car, putting an arm on either side of her. "Headmaster Davis stole you from me." His stare pierced her with its intensity. "Why the hell did he spend all that extra time training me just to steal you away?"

Faelan's close proximity felt as if it were a force, immobilizing her. It needed to stop—it *had* to stop. She gazed into those deep blue eyes and said softly, "I chose him."

He snarled, "It's because of that damn Mary, isn't it? She's the one who screwed it up for us."

"No, but she helped me to realize I can't trust you." He was about to interrupt, so she forged ahead. "When I asked if you wanted Mary, you answered, 'Yes'. I knew then you didn't care about me."

"What? Did you expect me to lie? Any guy who told you he wasn't attracted to the girl would not have been telling you the truth. Come on, Brie…" He lifted her chin, forcing her to look at him. "Just because I find her attractive doesn't mean I want to collar her. I was clear about that."

His answer threw Brie off. She scooted from under his arms and walked to the driver's side of her car.

Todd stated quietly, "I deserve a chance."

She attempted to unlock the door with a trembling hand. "None of this matters. It's too late."

"I need you, blossom." He was beside her again, covering her hand with his. "You are my reason."

She slowly pulled the key back out of the lock and looked at him. "No…"

"Brie, I didn't understand who I was until I met you. You opened my eyes to the truth and freed me from the hell I've suffered. Don't turn your back on me now."

She shook her head. "Please…stop."

"If you knew the truth you would not be so callous towards me now."

"I'm not being callous, Todd. But this," she gestured at the two of them, "doesn't do either of us any good. We can't change what happened. I—"

Faelan lifted his hand to caress her cheek. She turned her head to avoid his touch just as Mr. Reynolds opened the door of the shop and called out to her. "Brie, is this man harassing you? Do you want me to call the police?"

Brie shook her head. "No, everything is fine, Mr. Reynolds. We're done here. I was just leaving." She unlocked her car door and looked back at Faelan. "Don't talk to me again. You'll only get yourself in trouble." She jumped into her car, grateful for her boss' interruption.

On the drive home, she debated whether or not she should tell Sir. She decided against it. Faelan had been hurt enough, and Brie didn't want to add to his pain by making Sir furious at him.

But how disconcerting to find out that Blue Eyes hadn't fooled around with Mary. It didn't change her heart, because she knew without a doubt she was with the right man. However, it made her sad.

She hoped Faelan would be able to move on. It would be a shame if Blue Eyes walked away from the lifestyle because of her. Sir had mentioned seeing Faelan's natural talent and she'd had the pleasure of experiencing it herself. There was no doubt he would make some submissive very, very happy.

Sir was not home when she arrived. The first thing she did was undress so that she was naked except for the beautiful collar around her neck.

While she waited for him, she decided to cut up a salad. She might not be able to cook, but she was capable of cutting vegetables. As she searched through the refrigerator she noticed a lone tomato. It melted her heart. Sir hated the little red fruit, which could only mean one thing: he'd bought it specifically for her. She picked it up and kissed it before placing it back in the fridge to admire.

Once the salad was prepared she went to the door, choosing to greet Sir in the kneeling position he had assigned her at the Center. Her stomach was full of butterflies every time she heard the elevator open. A whole day away from Sir had her anxious to please her handsome Dom.

While she waited, she reflected on Mr. Reynolds' revelation of the deep pain Sir carried. It made her love him all the more. If love could heal wounds, she would love Sir to wholeness.

Her heart sped up when she finally heard the key in the lock. She bowed her head when the door opened. She heard it shut and then felt Sir's hand on her head, along with the familiar jolt of warm passion his touch inspired.

"Stand and serve your Master, téa."

His words warmed her loins. She gracefully stood up and felt his finger under her chin. She lifted her head up and he kissed her. Brie's soul sighed in contentment. "Welcome home, Master."

"How was your day?" he asked as he placed his key on the counter and unbuttoned his jacket. She took it from him and hung it on the hook in the hallway.

"It was good, Sir. Jeff quit, which made the day so much nicer."

Sir chuckled. "I can imagine Unc was pleased by that."

"Yes, he was, Sir. Now I can train both replacements for him. I hope to do Mr. Reynolds justice by training hard workers."

He smiled down at her. "No reason not to try, my optimistic little sub." Sir handed her his briefcase. "Set it by the couch and wait for me there."

While she followed his orders, he disappeared down the hallway. She stared out of the large window, thrilled by this new life of hers. Sir was an exceptional person, and not just an experienced Dom. He was caring and conscientious in everything he did. Truly, she was the luckiest sub in the world.

He returned wearing only black sweatpants. His toned chest begged to be caressed and kissed. Sir sat on the couch and motioned for her to lay her head on his knee. He began petting her hair as he had each night since her arrival. It was something she adored; the ritual made her feel especially cherished.

After more than a half hour in silence, he spoke. "Today was quite successful. I have procured another client. A large client, in fact. Now that I am free of the Training Center, I plan to expand my accounts overseas. Mark my words, your Master will become a prominent force in the business world, téa."

She looked up at him, beaming with pride. "I am not surprised, Sir. You are exceptionally talented. I'm positive you would succeed in anything you tried your hand at."

He caressed her cheek. "Such blind confidence, but I appreciate your certainty." His finger traced the outline of her lips. "I must admit, it seems odd not to be at the Center tonight. Normally, I would be sifting through the paperwork of the new recruits." His hand trailed down to her chest. "However, I find this far more pleasurable…"

Brie closed her eyes and purred inside as he fondled her breasts. Sir made her feel fiercely feminine and desirable. Her body responded to her Master, her loins longing for his cock, her nipples aching for his mouth's attention.

"Are you ready to play my game, téa?"

Her heart beat rapidly when she answered. "Yes, Master."

Sir's cell phone rang on the counter. Its unusual ring made Sir stir on the couch. "Lie on the Tantra chair and play with yourself while I take this."

Brie kissed his hand reverently before she got up and walked to the red chair. She lay down and closed her eyes as she ran her fingers over her ever-wettening pussy. Just knowing Sir was going to play with her had her close to coming.

Sir's smooth voice filtered through her naughty thoughts. "This is an unexpected surprise." She opened her eyes and was startled to see a serious look on his face. "I understand. No, I am grateful for the information."

He hung up and glanced over at her. "Change of plans. I'll be leaving for a bit. Have dinner waiting for me when I return. I don't care what you make."

Brie stopped rubbing her clit and sat up. "Master?"

"An unexpected complication has come up. I need time to sort it out," Sir stated as he exited through the front door.

She was worried for Sir. He had been so elated about his new client and now he was facing a serious setback. The fact Master had asked for dinner, knowing her cooking skills, meant that he was so distraught he didn't care what he ingested.

Brie went to the kitchen and began her best attempt at baked chicken to go along with the salad she'd made. She googled how to cook breast meat so that it would not be so dry, a common problem whenever she cooked meat. While it baked, she set the table, smiling as she imagined them sitting together, eating her simple but lovingly made meal. She hoped that Sir still planned to introduce her to his game. It had been frustrating to have it end just as it was about to begin.

An hour later, Sir returned and joined her at the table. He still seemed lost in thought, but smiled when she placed the chicken in front of him. Sir asked her about her day again, as if he'd forgotten that they'd talked about it earlier.

Brie decided to entertain him with a conversation she'd had with an older customer who loved dogs—all kinds of dogs. She shared how the elderly gentleman had gotten out his wallet and shown her at least twenty different canines he'd had the privilege to own. She laughed. "It was as if he was showing me his grandchildren. It was sweet, Sir."

Brie felt a pang of guilt at not mentioning her encounter with Todd. However, she'd noticed that he hardly touched his meal and didn't want to add to his stress. Besides, there was no point in getting Faelan in trouble over nothing.

When Sir announced he was done, he ordered her to join him over at the couch once she was finished with the dishes. She glanced at him several times as she made quick work of the kitchen. Sir was entrenched in paperwork, poring over a presentation he was going to give the next day. He hardly noticed when she knelt at his feet.

Brie didn't mind. It was an honor to watch him work and she felt doubly blessed when he shared his presentation with her before bed. Sir was an inspiring speaker, leaving her in no doubt why he was highly esteemed in the business community.

When he finished, she smiled. "If they follow your suggestions, Sir, there is no reason they shouldn't see an immediate increase in production."

"That is the key," he replied. "It is one thing to be presented with what needs to be done and another thing entirely to follow through with those changes. My job is to motivate that change."

She blushed. "I guess you do the same with businesses that you do with submissives."

He did not reply as he gathered his papers and turned off his laptop. She expected to be ordered to pleasure him orally; in fact, she had been counting on it. Instead, he stated, "You have failed me tonight." With that, he got up, turned off the lights and walked to his bedroom.

Brie's heart jumped into her throat. He *knew* about Todd's visit at the tobacco shop! He'd been waiting all night for her to say something about it.

She closed her eyes, realizing that it must have been Mr. Reynolds on the phone earlier that evening. It was natural that he would want to inform his nephew about Faelan's visit. She didn't blame him. No, this was her own fault. In trying to spare everyone from unnecessary distress, she had managed to make things so much worse.

It disturbed her that Sir wasn't even asking to hear her side of the story. Brie remained on the floor, feeling like an idiot. "Sir…" she called out.

He answered by shutting the door.

Tears rolled down her cheeks. It had been a terrible mistake not to say anything. She understood that now. All she wanted was to make things right with Sir. Whatever he demanded as punishment would be fine, as long as he could forgive her for the mistake.

Brie laid her head on the couch, feeling utterly bereft. She spent the night kneeling beside the couch in the dark, watching Sir's bedroom door. She noted when the light finally went out and stared at the door all night long, praying the light would turn back on and he would come for her.

Sir did not.

# Repentance

Brie was on alert when she heard him stir in the morning. She heard the shower and a short time later his bedroom door opened. She waited with bated breath as he walked down the hallway to her. Sir was fully dressed in a business suit, his hair still slightly damp.

He did not waste time, coming directly to her and commanding, "Stand."

With great difficulty, Brie urged her stiff limbs to support her wobbly legs. She dared not look him in the eye.

"Not speaking of the encounter with Wallace is the same as lying."

"I'm sorry, Sir. I did not mean to lie to you."

"What possible reason would make you keep it from your Master? Do you respect me so little?"

She braved a look at him, wanting Sir to know her heart. "No, Master! I didn't think it was important enough."

"Anytime another Dom touches my sub, it is very much my business."

She bowed her head. "I didn't think of it that way, Master."

"Do you have feelings for the boy? Is that why you covered it up?"

"No, Sir. I love you. I want no one else."

His voice became deadly serious. "Know this, Brie." For the first time, her name sounded distasteful on his lips. "I consider you talking to another Dom without my permission an act of betrayal on your part."

The air left her lungs.

"I will not abide disloyalty."

She could barely get the words out. "I understand, Master. I deeply regret my actions."

"Any interaction with a Dom is worthy of my attention. A lie of omission is still a lie."

She bowed on the ground before him. "I understand, Master. I will not lie to you again."

"No, you will not. Look at me." Brie looked up at his imposing stature, afraid and in awe of him. "I must know the real motivation behind your deception."

She swallowed once, to force her throat to relax enough that she could speak. "I did not want Mr. Wallace to get in trouble, Master. I felt guilty that I caused him pain by choosing you, and I didn't want to add to it by making you angry with him."

"Foolish," he growled. "Wallace is a grown man. He knows the protocol. If he chooses to ignore it, he *must* suffer the consequences."

Her heart sank for Faelan. Instead of sparing Todd, she was certain she had made things much worse for him. "I understand, Master. I was wrong and deserve to be punished."

"Yes, your willful disobedience must be addressed."

As much as she hated being disciplined by Sir, she craved it, because it would put her right with him. Harmony with Master was all she wanted, and she would do anything to get it back.

"Get ready for work. You will spend the day out of contact with me. When you return home, I want you to remain fully dressed while you wait. I will dole out your correction tonight."

Sir grabbed his key and left the apartment. Brie slowly pulled herself up off the floor and headed to the bathroom. Her sense of failure was so great, she could taste it in her mouth.

The day was a trial. Mr. Reynolds knew there was something wrong, but wisely chose not to get involved. Instead, he interviewed the owner's family members applying for the job. Since there were four of them, it gave her boss some control over who would be working with him. Brie took care of the front, and spent the rest of the time taking inventory to keep her mind off her troubles.

It made for a long and terrible day. She dreaded going home to Sir, but longed to be in his good graces again. This would be her first punishment by her Master. Would he be like Ms. Clark, and use an instrument to bring pain? The thought frightened her, but she would willingly submit to his authority and endure it.

When she arrived home, she had to wait in the oppressive silence of the apartment. It was actually humiliating not to undress, because it only highlighted the fact she was not pleasing to Sir. She knelt by the door and listened to the lonely ticking of the clock in the kitchen. Each tick accentuated the dread building in her heart.

He came home just as the sun disappeared behind the horizon. The apartment was dark when Sir opened the door. He flicked on the light and walked past Brie, setting his key on the counter. She heard his retreating footsteps as he walked to his room.

Several minutes later, Sir returned and addressed her. His voice was detached and unemotional. "I will not touch you until your punishment is complete."

Not to have his reassuring touch made this horrible moment that much harder, and a tear fell down her cheek.

"Why are you being corrected?"

"I failed to tell you of my interaction with Mr. Wallace, Master."

"Why is that unacceptable?"

"No Dom is allowed to interact with me without your consent. My silence is the same as lying, Master."

"Are you repentant?"

"Yes, Master." A sob escaped her lips. "I am deeply sorry."

"Then I shall correct your repentant heart," he replied. Sir proceeded to place a ball gag in her mouth and secured it tightly around her head, being careful not to touch her with his hands. "The gag represents your willful silence."

Her jaw stretched uncomfortably to accommodate the gag, and then the saliva began to build. She understood it was an appropriate instrument of punishment for her transgression.

"You acted like a disobedient child, therefore I shall treat you like one. Go to the kitchen and get the bag of rice."

She quickly retrieved the rice and handed it over to him with her head bowed. She couldn't imagine what he had in mind.

Sir took a handful of rice and spread it in a line on the floor. Then he took a second handful and covered the line with another layer. He handed the bag back to her. "Put it away and return to me."

She did so with trepidation. What did the rice represent?

"Because you are unworthy to be naked before me, pull your pants up so that your knees are exposed." She did so, watching with mortification as a long strand of saliva escaped her mouth and dribbled slowly to the floor when she bent over to roll up her jeans.

"I do not enjoy punishing you."

She actually felt bad that her actions were forcing Sir to do this, and bowed her head lower in shame.

"Kneel on the rice with your weight resting on your knees."

Brie knelt down slowly, positioning both knees on the hard little pellets. It didn't become painful until she did as he commanded and put her full weight on her knees. She moaned in distress, the ball gag muffling her cry of discomfort.

"You will remain this way for twenty minutes."

He went to the couch and began his work. She watched from the floor, trying to ignore the agony each tiny grain caused as it dug mercilessly into her knees. It seemed unreal that something so miniscule could cause such considerable pain.

As the clock ticked away the minutes, she tried to blink away the tears. Although it hurt, it was knowing she'd disappointed Sir that made the punishment truly unbearable. Thinking on it, she realized that not mentioning her encounter with Faelan was the same as putting the boy before Sir. It was glaringly clear to her now.

Being completely open and honest with Master was the only thing that mattered. How it affected others was not her concern. Brie accepted the pain as her obligation as a disobedient submissive. She would learn from it and would not let it happen again.

When the twenty minutes were up, Sir spoke to her again. "Get the broom and dustpan. Clean up your mess and then come stand before me."

Brie could not immediately stand because of the debilitating pain, and was forced to roll to one side. She brushed off the rice still clinging to her skin and pulled her knees to her chest, wrapping her arms around them, rocking gently to comfort herself. Once the torturous ache had subsided enough for her to stand, she picked herself up and did his bidding before presenting herself before Master.

Sir put his work down and stood up, holding a small towel in his hand. He undid the ball gag, and cleaned up the copious amounts of spittle that came with it. Once she was presentable again, he spoke.

"Have you learned your lesson?"

"Yes, Master. I will not keep anything from you in the future."

"Fine. You may undress, then."

With stiff movements, she took off her clothes and laid them in a neat pile beside her.

Sir held out his hands to her. "It's okay, téa. I forgive you."

Brie broke out in a sob and fell into his arms. He picked her up and carried her to his bedroom, then laid her down on the bed. After he'd shed his clothes Sir joined her, gathering her into his protective embrace. She could not stop the tears as she cried against his chest. Sir allowed her to weep, holding her tight. Eventually he whispered, "Hush now, Brie. You are my good girl."

There was no hot sex afterwards, no sexual games, just a Master holding his repentant submissive in the dark.

"I love you, Sir." Being reconnected with him was like being given a new lease of life. She felt she would burst with joy.

Sir nuzzled her neck and then bit down hard. She instantly became putty. "Tomorrow we are going to visit the Training Center."

"Why, Sir?" She gasped as he began sucking on the delicate skin of her throat.

"There is something I want to show you." Brie whimpered in pleasure, a host of images filling her mind. "Oh yes, my little sub. It's about to get rough for you…"

# *Brie Submits to her Master*

# Visiting the Center

Brie stared at Sir as the first of the sun's rays flooded through the window. His face took on an almost boyish quality while he slept. It was sexy and so incredibly sweet. She was tempted to gently caress his cheek, but Sir must have sensed her inclination because he opened his eyes.

Brie gasped softly, her whole body quivering.

"Morning, téa."

She broke out in a shy smile. "Good morning, Master."

"Waking up to your beautiful face has moved me." He threw back the covers so she could admire his hard awakening. "Service me."

Her smile grew wider as she crawled between Sir's legs and took him into her mouth. Brie lavished her love with an eager tongue, swirling around his smooth head before sucking lightly to bring added pleasure. She moaned when he fisted her long hair and began guiding her with his hand. Did Sir know it melted her insides when he did that?

"I love starting the morning with your pink lips wrapped around my cock."

She looked up at Sir as she continued to suck his handsome manhood. He pushed her down deeper on his shaft and she gladly took its fullness, letting the head of his cock slip down her throat.

"Oh, yes," he growled.

Her muffled moan expressed the pleasure she felt at being his. Sir was not rough, but always demanding. He had a way of using her for his own gratification, but making her feel completely cherished in the process.

Brie's pussy pulsed of its own accord in response to his pleasure. When he released deep in her throat there was a significant exchange of power: his male dominance over her, and her total submission to him—balance. It was the perfect way to start the day.

Afterwards, Brie laid her head on his thigh and looked up at him lovingly. Sir stroked her hair with a contented look on his face. "Tonight we shall visit the Center. I hope you are ready for what I have planned."

Her loins contracted with a mixture of excitement and trepidation.

Brie spent the day at the tobacco shop showing the two newest employees the ropes. It looked like Mr. Reynolds had at least *one* good worker. The niece was a whiny little thing, complaining constantly and texting her friends instead of listening. Brie knew Laurel would be nothing but a pain for her soon-to-be ex-boss—a perfect replacement for Jeff. However, the nephew was acceptable. Mike was a quick study and showed respect towards Mr. Reynolds. Brie was tempted to tell Mr. Reynolds to fire the girl and only keep the boy, but her boss had no real control over the hiring at the shop.

When she arrived home, she was surprised to find that her entire apartment had been moved into the spare bedroom. The large room was now completely stacked with boxes and cheap furniture. Upon entering Sir's bedroom, she noticed her old uniform laid out on the bed. It was exactly the same: the dark brown miniskirt and leather corset, as well as the six-inch heels. However, the crotchless pantyhose had been replaced with lace garters and silk thigh-highs. The thong was noticeably missing.

She picked up the card that was lying on the bed and read his note:

*Had your belongings moved. We will discuss placement later.*
*Dress in your uniform and wait for me at the door.*

Brie dutifully dressed, feeling nostalgic as she tightened the laces of the corset and slipped on the fuck-me heels. She took a quick peek at herself in the mirror before leaving the bedroom, looking herself over critically.

Would people confuse her for a trainee at the Center because of the outfit? She turned her head from side to side and twirled slowly, staring at her reflection. The garters and new hose were a sexy touch, giving her a more refined look. The collar certainly helped to state her position, but she still felt very much like a trainee in the outfit. Was that Sir's point?

She settled down before the door and waited for her Master to come home. Exactly at six, she heard the key in the lock. He walked in and graced her with a pleased smile. "Ah, my little student. Are you ready for class to begin?" He placed a hand on her head and commanded, "Stand and serve your Master."

She stood before him as he held out his arm. She was mortified when her stomach growled as she was wrapping her arm around his. He looked down at her and smiled knowingly.

Brie felt heat rise to her face. How unsexy to greet Sir with a growling stomach.

He made no mention of it, but when Sir got to the car he reached behind his seat and pulled an apple out of his briefcase. "I believe in the adage, 'An apple a day…'"

Brie took the fruit and murmured, "Thank you, Sir." She smiled to herself as she bit into the tart green apple, grateful she had such a thoughtful Master.

He remained silent on the drive, leaving Brie free to conjure up all kinds of different scenarios Sir might try on her. He had specifically mentioned the night before that things were going to get rough. What did that mean? Was he going to test her pain tolerance? The thought of that was definitely *not* sexy, but she trusted him to bring her through it if that was his intent.

Perhaps he was going to punish her further for her deceit involving Faelan? Brie quickly dismissed that idea. She knew in her heart that Sir was a fair man. She had endured the punishment for her indiscretion and had received his complete forgiveness.

Brie licked the sweetness from her lips as they pulled into the Training Center parking lot. It was strange to be back, knowing she was no longer a student.

Although classes for the Submissive Training Center were on hiatus, the business college was still in full swing and the parking lot was full. Unlike before, Sir did not park in the spot reserved for the headmaster of the Center. It remained empty, announcing the fact that a new one had not been appointed yet. It gave her a pang of guilt to know Sir had stepped down from his position to become her Master. She wondered if he was feeling similar pains of regret.

"I will open the door for you, téa," he stated. The use of her sub name let her know the protocol. She was to treat him as Master at the Center. No eye contact with other Dominants and no speaking unless spoken to by her Master.

As he helped her out of the car, he ran his hand down the length of her curves. Goosebumps followed. Such simple contact, but it instantly set her focus on him and reminded her of the power of his caress.

They walked into the school, arm in arm. The receptionist greeted him. "Good evening, Headm—I mean, Sir Davis. It is good to see you again."

"Likewise, Miss Lewis."

He continued to the elevator, putting his arm around Brie when a group of students walked past. Brie kept her eyes lowered, basking in his manly protection.

Sir took her down to a wing of the school she had never been before. As she passed through the doorway, she read the words 'Faculty Lounge' on the gold plate. The scent of rich tobacco filled the air, along with the sounds of many familiar voices.

"Couldn't stay away, I see," Master Anderson said. He came over to Sir and slapped him on the back with the same casual familiarity the two had shared the first time she'd been introduced to him.

"I have no problem staying away, but damn if you people didn't insist I come back."

Master Coen's voice rang out from the other side of the room. "I apologize, but we didn't anticipate assigning a new headmaster just before a new session. There are many loose ends to be addressed."

"So you say," Sir answered jokingly. "I accept it as the price I must pay to have free rein of the place after we are done here today."

Brie's insides quivered at the thought of Sir unleashed.

A woman's soft voice floated through the air. "How are you, Sir Davis? Are you happy with your new submissive?" Brie kept her eyes glued to the floor. Her mind raced to place the feminine voice, quickly identifying her as the Asian Domme who owned Boa. Boa, the sub with a python for a cock.

Brie held her breath, waiting for Sir's answer. Would he expose her mistake with Faelan in front of the other trainers?

"I'm finding the experience challenging and *quite* stimulating."

Master Anderson laughed. "I bet you are, Thane. You picked a fine one to partner with. She won't let you rest, I'll wager." He hit Sir so hard on the shoulder that he momentarily lost his balance. "I have to admit, though, I was a little put out when you stepped down. It was enjoyable working with you; reminded me of our college days."

Sir's low chuckle was like music to Brie's ears. "College was—"

Master Coen interrupted their reverie. "Enough of the reminiscing. We have work to do. Where's Clark?"

The door opened as if on cue, and Ms. Clark's voice rang out loud and clear. "Back already, Davis? Wait… Miss Bennett, what are you doing here?" The woman stopped abruptly in her tracks and said sarcastically, "You do realize this is a *faculty* lounge."

Sir's reply was controlled, but with a slight edge to it. "Address me, Samantha. Not my submissive."

Oh, what fun having Sir correct Ms. Clark on her behalf! Brie wished she could peek just to see the look on the female trainer's face.

"Forgive me, Sir Davis. I am still wrapping my head around the fact you broke all protocol and collared a student. My apologies."

"It is precisely due to protocol that I resigned, Samantha," he said dryly.

Brie heard the disdain in his voice when he used Ms. Clark's given name. But *why* was he calling her by her first name? Did they have a history together?

"It was foolish," Ms. Clark snorted. "We've lost a perfectly good headmaster and the Center's reputation has been compromised because of your impulsive actions."

Mr. Gallant's warm voice filled the room, making Brie's soul sigh with happiness. "That is not true. Although people are certainly talking about the collaring ceremony, I have not heard any ridicule towards the school, nor towards Sir Davis himself. Do not exaggerate, Ms. Clark."

There was one voice that was suspiciously silent. *Marquis Gray.*

"Regardless of your opinion, Samantha, I am asking that you treat Miss Bennett and I as you would any D/s couple. You are not allowed to speak to her directly without my permission."

"Fine," she snapped. "But I demand your submissive leave the faculty lounge."

"Fair enough," Sir responded. Before commanding Brie to leave, he addressed Master Coen. "I did have a question for you."

"Certainly," Master Coen replied, moving across the room to join him.

"Would you be able to fashion an iron brand for me?"

"Not a problem. What is it you want?"

"The letter 'T', exactly an inch in height and half an inch wide."

Brie gasped. *A brand?*

"That should be easy enough. How soon do you need it?"

Sir's voice was pleasant when he answered. "There's no rush."

"Good, then I'll start work on it after we get the new recruits settled in."

"That should be fine." Sir turned to Brie and said, "Téa, Ms. Clark is correct. Submissives normally stay in another room, at the end of the hall to your left. I will collect you after our work here is concluded."

She stole a glance at him when she answered, hoping to gain some insight into the exchange he'd just had with Master Coen. "Yes, Master."

The mischievous twinkle in his eyes let her know he had plans for that brand—and they most definitely included her. A chill coursed down her spine. Did he mean it as a warning or an honor?

Brie bowed to Sir before quietly leaving the room. She let out a huge sigh once the door was closed. She was concerned about Marquis' absence, but it was the brand that had all of her attention. She had not forgotten the day Master Coen had convinced her he was going to brand her with the school logo. She shuddered, feeling quite certain that Sir was not into 'mind-fucks' the way Master Coen was.

No, Sir had already warned her that everything he did had purpose. She didn't believe for one second it had been meant as a joke. There was a lesson there she was expected to learn. She shook off her trepidation as she pushed open the door to the new room.

To her surprise, Boa was sitting on a couch. He nodded at her. "Ah, it's Brie. The sub who captured the headmaster. You have quite the reputation around the Center these days."

"Good or bad?" she asked, sitting down on a lounge chair opposite him. The smell of food caused her to sneak a quick glance at the table laden with gourmet fare. It reminded her of her training nights. She was curious why so much food had been laid out when there were only two of them.

"It all depends on who you ask. Subs who were hoping to snag the headmaster themselves are quite pissed at you, but the rest of us are rather impressed. You've done the impossible." He clapped his hands lightly in mock appreciation.

"You should know that I'd never been so terrified in my life."

"Ah, but for good reason. You dared to offer yourself in the face of certain failure."

Brie didn't care to relive that moment, and was relieved when her stomach growled loudly. "Do you mind if I get myself something to eat?"

"Not at all."

She got up and tried to be ladylike as she filled her plate with smaller portions than her hunger demanded. It was weird to be in the same room with Boa. They'd done a scene together—a very hot scene—and here they were, just talking like casual acquaintances.

Brie dropped her napkin and bent down to pick it up, completely forgetting her lack of panties.

"Damn…" Boa growled.

She quickly stood up and grabbed another napkin. Brie walked back to the seat, feeling the heat of her blush when she noticed his large cock straining against the tight confines of his jeans.

"My Mistress will not be pleased if I have a hard-on when she comes to retrieve me."

"Sorry," she mumbled, taking a huge forkful of salad and looking towards the door.

"You can bet my Mistress is chuckling to herself right now, fully expecting to catch me with a stiffy so she can punish her randy sub. But I won't let that happen." He readjusted himself, pushing down on his massive cock as if it were a mischievous animal. "Tell me about your childhood," he blurted. "Make it something sad."

"Oh, um… Sad, you say?" Brie's childhood had been fairly easy: good parents, stable family life, and excellent care because she was an only child. Although her parents had never had extra money, all of her needs had been met. There was nothing notable about her childhood other than that horrible experience at school. "Well, I suppose I could tell you something I've shared with my trainers at the Center. When I was twelve, my family moved to a predominantly black neighborhood. I didn't have any siblings, so I pretty much had to fend for myself."

Boa chuckled harshly. "That can be true, even if you have siblings."

She shrugged. "I suppose that's true. Most of the families in our neighborhood were struggling to make ends meet, just like we were.

Looking back on it, I guess I became the token punching bag to release their frustrations on. The ringleader was Darius. I don't know why he had it in for me, but just seeing my face upset him. He'd have his friends wait until I was off school grounds before they pounced. I told my teachers, but they just shrugged it off, saying it wasn't their problem because it wasn't on school property."

Brie growled under her breath. "He never played fair. There were always three or more. He'd hold me down while the girls kicked me in the gut." She closed her eyes, lost in the feelings of helplessness the memory conjured up. "I didn't tell my parents. My dad finally had a job and there was no way I was going to ruin it for him." Brie opened her eyes, smiling sadly. "Darius was smart. He made sure the attacks happened off school grounds and they never hit me in the face. It allowed me to hide the bruises."

Boa looked down at his crotch. "It's helping. Please continue."

Brie rolled her eyes, amused that her life story was being used as an erection detractor. "Everything changed the day he used the needle…" Her breath came faster as she relived that moment. "He had me on the ground, pushing my face into the dirt and telling me to eat it. I refused. He spat in my face and ordered the others to hold me down. He looked around wildly until he spied a used needle lying by the chain-link fence. When I saw him going for it, I started to kick and scream violently. I was terrified of needles. He picked it up and ordered them to turn me over onto my stomach. I was screaming bloody murder by the time he got next to me, so Darius ripped off my shoe and stuffed one of my socks in my mouth. 'If you won't eat the dirt then you must pay the price,' he declared before he started stabbing me in the ass repeatedly with the needle."

Brie felt sick and closed her eyes, forcing herself to calm down before she continued. "The others suddenly got quiet and let me go—like they knew a line had been crossed. I guess I must have totally freaked out because I remember screaming hysterically and then the next thing I remember, I was standing in the principal's office."

She snorted in disgust. "You know what's funny? At first, I wasn't taken seriously. I was forced to pull down my panties in front of both the principal and vice principal to show them my wounds before they believed my story. My parents were called and I was rushed to the emergency room for tests."

Boa was now leaning forward, engrossed in her tale.

"I was too young to be worried about HIV or all the other countless things the needle could have carried. No, you know what I was terrified of?"

He shook his head.

"My parents." She smiled sadly. "It went down just as I'd feared. My dad quit his job. Mom and I lived in a shelter for over half a year while my dad searched for another one. He eventually found work in Nebraska and that's where I stayed until I moved out here."

Boa's cock was completely flaccid by the time she finished—her work was complete.

He tilted his head charmingly and surprised her by saying, "Everyone carries scars, Brie. I never forget that, especially when someone is being an ass towards me."

Brie nodded, both Ms. Clark and Mary instantly coming to mind. "I think it's only fair that you share your story, Boa."

He looked down at her untouched plate. "I think you should eat first."

While Brie was finishing up, Boa's Mistress walked in. Her eyes went straight to his groin and a sly smile formed on her lips. "Good boy."

He stood up and bowed to her. "What is your pleasure, Mistress?"

"We're leaving." When he walked up to her, the Domme caressed his flaccid cock, making it flaccid no more. "Come, pet. I think playtime is in order."

They left the room without acknowledging Brie. She smiled to herself, taking a bite of a ripe peach. Brie wiped away the juice that rolled down her chin. It made her think of Boa pleasing his Mistress. There was no doubt he was in for a treat, having passed his Mistress' test.

# Lea and the Subs

Brie sat alone in the room for a long time. She wondered what Sir was discussing with the trainers. Were they picking the new headmaster? She sighed, a fear nagging her; would there come a time when he resented the path his life had taken the day she had knelt at his feet?

She was grateful for the distraction when she heard a group of girls chattering in the hallway. They stopped at the door just before it swung wide open. All the chattering stopped the moment they saw Brie.

She smiled self-consciously, feeling embarrassed, until a familiar voice rang out. "Oh, my gosh! What are *you* doing here?"

Lea broke through the small crowd and rushed at her. She grabbed onto Brie and they jumped around in circles like schoolgirls. Brie couldn't stop smiling. It seemed like ages since she'd seen Lea, although it had only been a few days.

"You're supposed to be pleasing your Master, girl. You have no business being here!"

"Sir was called in and he asked me to join him."

One of the other girls huffed and the group moved as one to the table laden with food. Lea remained with Brie, bursting with numerous questions. "I wonder if Sir has special plans for you afterwards." She poked Brie in the ribs.

Brie swatted her away. "As a matter of fact, he does."

"Oh, God, how is it, Brie? Having a Master… Sir, no less. I can't even imagine!"

Suddenly the entire room became silent. Apparently, everybody wanted to know. "Sir is…" But she didn't want to share her experiences with everyone else, so she finished by simply saying, "I'm seriously in love with him, Lea."

Her best friend squealed and hugged her again. "Every sub here wishes they were you, you know. Having the headmaster all to yourself… Heck, I feel honored just to know you." Lea got on her knees and went to kiss Brie's feet.

Brie backed away, laughing. "Stop!"

An older-looking sub interrupted their silliness. "I'll be surprised if it lasts. Sir Davis was simply flattered by your youthful rashness."

Lea picked herself up from the floor and chided the woman. "Don't be like that, Ruby. Brie is one of the finest people I know, period. She and Sir are perfect for each other." Lea turned to Brie and smiled. "I knew it on that first day when he touched you. I felt the electricity between you, even then."

Brie quickly changed the subject, not wanting her love life open for discussion. "So, girl, what the heck are *you* doing here? I imagined you would take some time off before the new session started."

"Heck, no! They are running us subbies through their paces. The Center has to make sure the Dominant training is top-notch. I've already had practice sessions with Baron and Tono."

Brie caught her breath when Lea mentioned Tono's name. She wanted to ask Lea how he'd seemed, but did not feel comfortable asking in front of the other subs. "Did they put you through the wringer?" she joked lightly.

"Oh, yeah. Baron teased me mercilessly with the swing. Had to beat me with a flogger to get my pussy to obey." Lea grinned and whispered, "I kinda cheated."

Brie laughed, imagining it in her head. "Did he complain about what a difficult student you were?"

"No. But Master Night, the head trainer for the Dominant class, took me aside afterwards. He was less than amused."

One of the other subs broke in. "Lea is always pushing the boundaries."

Brie nodded, wrapping her arm around her high-spirited friend. "It's one of the things I love most about her."

Lea knew Brie well enough to know the question she could not ask. "As far as Tono…" she began. Brie tried to hide her interest by picking up and chewing on a stray piece of carrot. "He showed me his style of Kinbaku yesterday. I must say, he is a gentle teacher."

Brie looked into her eyes. "Yes, that is true."

"I found him a bit preoccupied," Lea continued, "but overall the experience was quite enjoyable."

A curly-haired blonde sub spoke up. "God, when he tells you to breathe with him I just want to die!"

Brie quickly changed the subject, not wanting to hear about their experiences with Tono. "So Lea, got any plans this weekend?"

Her face brightened. "Why? Do you think we can get together? I would love that!"

"Yeah, I can show you my new crib. Maybe you can help me unpack my stuff."

Lea smiled wickedly. "You want me to invite Mary?"

Brie swatted her on the butt. "I can't believe you just went there, Lea! I retract my previous invite."

Lea pouted. "No…I'm sorry. I want to see your new place. Let me make it up to you. Why did the submissive cross the road?"

Brie shook her head.

"To get some hits."

"That was pathetic, Lea. You get no brownie points for that one."

"Okay, okay. If you are hankering for a spirited spanking, when your Dom tells you to look him in the eye, look at him cross-eyed."

Brie couldn't help it—she giggled at the stupid joke.

"There! See, I made you laugh. Now you have to let me come and help you unpack."

Several of the other subs chuckled in the background. Brie looked at them for sympathy. "Was that *really* worth a re-invite?"

Most smiled and voiced their support of Lea, but the oldest sub—the one who had expressed her doubts about Sir's choice—glared at her.

Lea jumped in. "There you go. They said yes, so now you have to let me come."

Brie was about to answer when the door opened. Sir appeared in the doorway, filling the small space with his commanding presence. Brie instantly jumped to attention, bowing her head.

His aura filled the room. The silence expanded until Sir asked, "How is the additional training going, Ms. Taylor?"

"Great, Sir."

"No issues?"

She hesitated for only a second before answering truthfully, "I do have my areas of weakness, Sir."

"As do we all," he replied generously before asking the group, "How are the rest of you faring?"

All of the girls answered at once, making it impossible to understand them. He chuckled lightly. "I see… I expect that each of you is putting forth your best effort."

Sir addressed Brie last. "Come, téa. I have something special for you."

She loved that he'd called her by pet name in front of the others. It emphasized her new status. Brie shivered in pleasure when he placed his hand on the small of her back. "Good evening, ladies," he stated as he led Brie out of the room. She felt the jealous glares as she left, but she didn't mind—not one bit.

"Did you enjoy your time with the other subs, téa?"

She looked up at him and smiled. "It was good to see Lea, Master. I've missed her."

He chuckled. "You two are unusually close. It was pleasant to watch as you were training. I appreciated it when you brought Mary into the fold."

Brie snorted in disgust.

"Do not be so quick to dismiss her," Sir stated as they walked down the hallway.

Brie attempted to hide her resentment. "I will try not to, Master."

"Téa, *try* is not what I am asking of you."

She realized what he was demanding of her and reformed her answer. "I will do my best, Master."

He smiled down at her. "See that you do."

Brie pressed her cheek against his muscular arm, grateful that he challenged her to think beyond herself. "Master?"

"Yes?"

"Would it be agreeable if Lea helped me unpack this weekend?"

He chuckled at the request. "I suspect the apartment will be filled with laughter. Yes, I find that agreeable."

"Thank you, Master." Brie squeezed his arm.

"Unfortunately, I have some unpleasant news, téa. Tonight I learned that Celestia, Marquis' sub, suffered a burst appendix while visiting her parents in Seattle. Marquis Gray has traveled to attend to her."

"Is she okay?" Brie hated to think of anything bad happening to the kind-hearted woman. Celestia had been with her the night of graduation, and had proven to be quite a comfort during Mary's betrayal.

"She underwent emergency surgery and, from what I was told, she is recovering well. We will visit and provide a meal on their return."

She noticed that he was leading her towards the kitchen area and her heart sank. The last thing she wanted was another cooking lesson.

Brie glanced up and saw a playful smirk on his lips. She dutifully slowed down as they approached the dreaded room forty-two, but Sir walked past it. So cooking was not on the schedule for the night!

"Normally, non-trainers are not allowed back here. However, while the classes are on hiatus, and in honor of my service, the staff has graciously offered me free run of the lower level."

There were still rooms Brie had yet to explore. Her heart raced faster the farther down the hall they went. What was waiting for her behind those closed doors? Which one would it be?

Sir finally stopped at the end of the hall. They couldn't have been any farther from the others—no one would hear her screams.

"Tonight's training begins."

As he opened the door, the butterflies began. What did Sir have planned for her this time?

The opposite side of the room was covered in mirrors. In the center was a small table and an apparatus that looked like a padded balance beam with a vertical wooden pole attached to the head of it.

"My own invention. It allows the sub control over the scene even when gagged. It also requires complete focus. Excellent for building a sub's endurance."

Brie stared at it, her eyes growing wider with each passing second.

Sir laughed warmly. "I am not planning to torture you. Where's the trust, my little sub?"

She glanced up at Sir apologetically. "Momentary lapse of reason, Master. I trust you completely."

He turned from her and muttered, "Maybe you shouldn't."

Her mouth fell open. Was he teasing her?

As Sir walked towards a cabinet in the far corner, he instructed, "Undress completely and lie on your back. I want you to hold onto the pole with both hands."

Brie's whole body was trembling as she undid her corset and slipped out of her garter and hose. Sir already had her tense with anticipation. With his limitless experience, anything was possible tonight.

She gingerly lay down on the beam, which looked to be about eight inches wide. Sir was right—she had to concentrate to balance her body on it. Brie bent her knees and placed her feet together to keep her balance. She then lifted her hands over her head too fast and nearly fell off the beam. She stopped to regain her composure before gripping the pole tightly with both hands.

Sir returned to her with a metal box in one hand and several items in the other. He looked down at her and smiled. "You must maintain your balance the entire time, téa. No matter what I do to you."

She nodded, looking up at him apprehensively, but unable to hide the excitement he inspired.

He put down the items on the table and proceeded to run his fingers over the length of her. Brie bit her lip, her skin tingling with the intensity of his touch, her nipples already painfully erect with need. He slipped his fingers between her legs. "As I expected. You enjoy the prospect of the unknown."

Sir picked up a piece of cloth. "Let's add to the experience. Lift your head and open your mouth." He quickly placed the cloth in her mouth and tied it. There was an added sense of vulnerability in not being able to speak.

"If I do anything you cannot handle, let go of the pole. The instant you do, I will stop. Do you understand?"

She nodded with lustful eyes, watching his every move.

"Instead of a blindfold, I have something more romantic." He opened the white box and pulled out a huge red rose. He lifted it to his nose and smelled it, smiling at her. Then he put it under her nose and she breathed in its sweetness. He rubbed the soft petals against each nipple, then crushed the flower in his hand. "Close your eyes."

Brie did as he asked and felt the cold, velvet petals fall on her eyelids.

"A slight turn of your head and they will fall away. You are in complete control of this session, even though you are figuratively blind and bound."

Brie's chest was rising and falling rapidly. He hadn't even started yet and she was a delicious mess.

She heard him unsnap the lock on the metal box. He began rifling through, chuckling softly to himself. She heard him lay several items on the table, then shut the case.

"The human brain is a hotbed of imagination, capable of taking a simple stimulus and magnifying it many times greater than it is. I am going to leave you here, téa. Let your mind run wild."

She whimpered when she heard him walk away.

"This is my gift to you," he said before shutting the door.

Brie lay there on the thin length of wood, smiling to herself. Sir certainly knew how to play her. Would he watch her from a camera, or had he rejoined the others while she contemplated what he would do?

Brie felt the tension of her stomach muscles as she remained stagnant on the balance beam. Luckily for her, the temperature of this room was pleasant and did not distract her.

She imagined what he had placed on the table beside her. Was one of the items a Wartenberg wheel? Her skin instantly developed goosebumps at the mere thought. Could it be a variety of colored waxes? Brie's nipples ached at the thought of the hot wax rolling down them. Maybe he was planning something more intense. Were there clothespins or possibly nipple clamps on that table?

Would he do something she'd experienced before? *Probably not…*

When she heard him standing outside the door she held her breath, not wanting to lose her balance as her yearning for him increased.

# His Electric Touch

Sir entered the room quietly. She heard his footsteps as he walked to the far corner of the room. She silently questioned what he was doing until he volunteered the answer. "I do not care to have our private affairs recorded." So he was blinding the camera. It made the encounter seem much more personal, but also a little dangerous.

The distinct sound of his dress shoes as he approached made the butterflies in her stomach swarm. "Are you ready to begin, téa?"

Brie nodded slightly, so she did not displace the petals.

She heard him pick up something from the table, and then buzzing filled the room.

*A violet wand…*

Brie wobbled on the beam as he drew near. "We begin on the lowest setting." She felt the contact of the smooth glass as the sound of static filled the air and tiny electrical bursts tickled her stomach.

She giggled into her gag, loving the feel of it. Sir moved it over her body, letting every area of her skin feel the stimulating effects of the device, from her shoulders to her toes.

*No wonder Lea likes it so much!*

He disengaged for a moment and she heard the frequency of the wand increase. She whimpered, inadvertently jumping when it sparked against her skin. She had to quickly right herself or risk falling off as Sir glided it under the swell of her breasts before lightly touching the tips of her nipples. The current was still light enough to be tingling and she moaned into her gag, a gush of wetness flowing between her legs.

Sir slowly lifted her right leg and brushed the sole of her foot. Her pussy contracted in pleasure. With careful precision he lifted her other leg, holding her so that she did not fall as he caressed the sole of her left foot with the wand. She squealed into the gag when he slowly moved up her leg towards her mound. He brushed it lightly, and a feeling of fizzy bubbles lingered after the pass.

Then he gently put her legs back down and let her regain her balance before he let go and turned off the wand. A few seconds later it was on again, the frequency of the wand much louder.

"Now, this is where your concentration will come into play. The intention is not an exercise of endurance; it is about embracing a new stimulation. When it becomes unpleasant, I want you to let go of the pole."

Brie swallowed hard. So far, it had been refreshingly ticklish. Nothing like the electric shocks she had been expecting. Now she was about to feel the bite of the device. The buzz itself was intimidating, but knowing that Sir had turned up the intensity had her quaking on the beam even before contact.

He had attached a different apparatus; it was not a smooth surface, but felt more like a pointed tip. It concentrated the electricity considerably. He ran it down the length of her torso. Brie really did jump this time, and had to tighten her grip on the pole to steady herself. It made the hairs on her skin stand up, but the sensation reminded her more of a nail being dragged across her skin than the intense stinging she'd expected.

"Would you like to try another pass?" he asked with a lustful growl.

There was something incredibly sexy in the exchange of pleasure and pain with her Master. She nodded and the stinging burn traveled down the other side of her torso. Sir's fingers found their way between her legs and he groaned. "Your pussy speaks clearly." He played with her slippery clit, rubbing it sensuously.

Sir slipped his finger inside Brie and stroked her G-spot several times, teasing her before pulling out and slowly dragging the wand over her pelvis. She whimpered in pleasure. "Open your legs," he commanded.

With trepidation she placed the soles of her feet together and pulled her legs up carefully so that she did not lose her balance. Sir turned off the wand and replaced the attachment with yet another apparatus, turning up the intensity even higher. She yelped as the multiple tails of a metal flogger caressed her skin with little bites of electricity. Sir dragged it up her right thigh. The closer he got to her sex, the more her body contracted in fear and pleasure. He lifted the toy before he made contact with her mound and started on her left thigh. It took everything in Brie not to wiggle and twist. The idea of that metal flogger touching her clit had her squirming inside, but she lay still, taking deep breaths as it inched towards her pussy.

Just before it electrified her clit, he pulled it away, leaving her gasping into her gag. The violet wand went silent. She wondered what he planned next and was surprised when he said softly, "Lift your head an inch, but do not dislodge the petals."

She carefully lifted her head and he untied the gag. Brie put her head back down and lay there, trying to keep her breath calm as her pussy pulsated of its own accord.

The crackling noise of the violet wand started up again at a lower frequency. Sir leaned over her and she felt his warm breath on her lips. "I am electrified, my dear." She gasped in surprise as his mouth brushed against hers, making her lips tingle with electricity. His kiss was quick but he returned again, locking his lips with hers and causing her mouth to burn with current. She whimpered when he pulled away. Sir leaned in for a third time. His energized tongue darted into her mouth and she cried out in surprised pleasure.

He broke the kiss and she felt his tingling caress as his hands moved over her chest. Sir pinched her sensitive nipples, the electricity giving an extra bite.

"Oh, Master…" she purred. She squirmed under his touch and nearly fell off the beam because she refused to let go of the pole. Luckily Sir righted her, his laughter warm and deep.

His tingling fingers spread her thighs and then lightly caressed her mound. She cried out, overcome by the sensation of his electrified touch. Then he did the unthinkable—she felt his hot breath just before he licked her clit.

Brie froze.

Sir licked the length of her pussy the second time, his tongue burning with the current. She shook her head violently, the rose petals falling to the floor, but she refused to let go. She looked down and whimpered, swearing she could see sparks jump from his tongue. "Oh God, Sir…oh, my God!"

He lifted his mouth from her pussy. "Your Master commands your orgasm."

Brie closed her eyes and willingly gave into the sensations his electrified tongue created. He pressed his tingling hands against her, holding her still as the fire built up inside her, his fluttering tongue shooting current with every pass. Brie screamed wildly when the orgasm finally crested and she came against his sparking tongue.

She was grateful for his support, still trembling even after the orgasm had ended. Sir wiped his mouth with a smirk. "Electricity feels odd on the tongue, but is certainly worth the effect." He turned off the device and placed it on the table before undressing. His rigid cock left no doubt that the encounter had been equally arousing for him.

Sir picked up Brie in his arms and carried her over to the mirror, lifting her up. She instinctively wrapped her legs around his torso as he impaled her with his manhood. Her passionate screams continued when Sir powered his shaft into her. Brie slid up and down the glass as he fucked her against the mirrored wall, his labored breathing totally turning her on.

"I love being fucked by you, Master!"

He growled, clutching her thighs as he plowed in deeper. Sir let her have the full effect of his uninhibited passion. His fingers dug into her flesh as he bruised her with his powerful thrusts. All of it was welcomed, all of it wanted.

Master roared when he came. It was deliciously violent, taking her breath away in its ferocity. Sir buried his head in her neck afterwards, panting as he regained his composure. He slowly disengaged and lowered her to the floor. Sir kissed her on the lips. "My slut; my goddess."

He walked her over to a lounge chair in the corner and sat down. Brie crawled into his lap and curled up in his arms. They sat there for a long time in silence.

She smiled to herself, overcome by a feeling of intense love. "My Master, my Sir."

He chuckled. "I remember when you had the arrogance to call me that the second night of class."

She looked up and stated with conviction, "I think my spirit knew you, even before I understood."

He looked at her solemnly. "Yes, téa. I would agree."

She nestled up against him, loving the warmth of his embrace. "Thank you for finding me, Sir."

"Do you believe in fate?" he asked.

"No. I've always believed I make my own life what it is, Sir."

"I am undecided, myself," he answered, crushing her against his chest before letting her go. "Dress and clean the mirror with the spray you'll find in the cabinet."

She walked over to her clothes and dressed quickly, watching Sir meticulously clean the instruments as well as the beam.

They left the Center only after the room had been returned to its original state. Several people greeted Sir as the two walked out, obviously pleased to see the ex-headmaster. It hurt Brie's heart. *He belongs here.*

On the way home, Sir asked, "What was the lesson for tonight?"

"I'm undecided, Sir. I learned tonight that pain can act as an aphrodisiac when applied by you. At the same time, being forced to balance on the beam helped me to control my reactions. Being in control like that improved my ability to govern my mental response."

He reached over and stroked her cheek tenderly. "Those are fine answers, téa."

# The Haven

Brie received a text from Sir at noon the next day while working. *Tonight you shall be on display. To prepare yourself, every other hour you will remove a piece of clothing. You must send a photo of each piece. Begin now. Tell no one.*

Brie shut her phone and sighed nervously. He hadn't specified which pieces which meant the decision was up to her. She would have to be smart so that she wasn't left exposing herself by the end of her shift.

"Mr. Reynolds, can you watch the front for a moment? I need to use the bathroom."

Her boss looked at her strangely because she had just come off a break. "Sure, but make it quick."

"Yes, Mr. Reynolds." She hurried to the small bathroom, cursing because she had worn heels without stockings. Two items eliminated from her selection. With little time to think she went for the quickest, peeling off her panties. She took a picture with her phone and sent it to Sir. He immediately texted back. *Surprised by your first choice. It will be a long day of not bending over, my dear.* Brie had no place to put her panties, so she ran to the back of the store and stuffed them in her purse before returning to the front.

"Are you feeling okay?" Mr. Reynolds asked with genuine concern.

She blushed, quite aware of her lack of underwear as they conversed. "Yes, I feel much better. Thank you."

It was disconcerting to work without her panties. She was conscious of it every time she moved, making sure to bend her knees so that she never exposed herself to the two trainees as she unpacked the cigarettes and helped to stock them.

When two o'clock rolled around, she asked Mr. Reynolds for another quick break.

"Again? What did you eat for lunch?"

"Sorry," she stammered, running to the bathroom. With ample time to think beforehand, she'd already decided on the next piece. Brie unbuckled the stylish little belt around her waist, taking a quick picture before rolling it up. After she hit send, Sir responded: *I do not consider that clothing, téa. No fashion accessories.*

Even though her time was short, she didn't want to disappoint Sir and quickly texted back. *Should I take off something else, Sir?*

*Yes.*

She unbuttoned her blouse and removed her lacy camisole. She dutifully took a pic and sent it to Sir. He did not return a text back. She worried for a second, but decided he must have been distracted by a business call or a visit from a client. Just as she was exiting the bathroom, Mr. Reynolds met her at the door. "Is everything all right, Brie? Do you need to go home?"

She held the camisole behind her back and stuttered, "No…no, sir. I'm just… It's…" She couldn't lie to her boss, but she didn't want to break Sir's explicit command either. The tension made her queasy, so she answered truthfully, "My stomach is a little upset."

He broke out in a huge, paternal grin. "I'm not going to be a great-uncle, am I?"

She stared at him in shock. "No! Oh, no, Mr. Reynolds."

He chuckled good-naturedly. "I'm just kidding, Brie. Have to admit, though, the look on your face was priceless."

She wasn't able to go to her purse, so she stuffed her camisole underneath the register. Brie definitely felt more exposed, knowing her white bra could now be seen through the thin material of her blouse, yet Sir's unique challenge also made her feel more alive than she'd ever felt at the tobacco shop.

At four, Brie was able to avoid asking Mr. Reynolds, who happened to be at the back door signing for newly arrived shipments. She went directly to Mike, instead. "Can you man the register until I get back?"

"I haven't learned how to work it yet," he protested.

"That's okay. If a customer comes, just tell them to wait. I won't be long."

"You need some Pepto-Bismol or something? I'm sure the old man must have some stashed somewhere."

Brie unintentionally snorted in laughter. "Ah, no…"

She closed the bathroom door and started giggling quietly to herself. In no time flat, she had her shirt off and her bra undone. She took a picture of the frilly thing and sent it to Sir.

His response was, *Now you will truly be on display.*

Brie balled up her bra and stuffed it behind the trashcan. With Mr. Reynolds in the back, she had no way to deposit it into her purse. Did Sir know how difficult this assignment was? *Probably…* He must have counted on the fact she was being challenged by the task.

She took a quick glance downward as she walked back up to the front. Sure enough, her pert nipples were poking through the thin blouse. She picked up a box and covered her chest with it when she addressed both trainees. "You guys should put out these tins. They go over on the end display by the door."

Laurel grinned, although Brie wasn't sure what she found so amusing. "Sure thing, princess."

Mike took the box from her and headed straight for the display. Brie took heart that Mr. Reynolds would have a fine replacement. It made leaving him much easier.

One of their regulars came in and asked for his normal carton of Salems. His gaze went straight for her chest as he handed her the money. Brie held her head a little higher to fight the urge to bolt.

She handed over his change, counting it out quickly. "And thank you for coming today, Mr. Abrams."

"Have a lovely day, Miss Bennett," he replied, tipping his hat.

She struggled with her feelings of embarrassment and feminine pride.

At ten before six, Mr. Reynolds came up to her. "You must be anxious to get home. Go ahead and cut out a little early. Hopefully whatever ails you will have passed through your system by tomorrow." To his credit, his attention never traveled from her face.

"It's really not necessary," Brie told him, feeling a little guilty.

"No, Brie. I insist."

She went to the back to gather her purse. Laurel met her there and, holding up Brie's bra, demanded, "What kind of game are you playing?"

She snatched it from the girl. Since she made a lousy liar she didn't even try. Instead Brie answered with a simple, "It's none of your business."

"Hey, I'm just telling you there's no need to try so hard. Mike is an easy catch. He'll bed any girl who gives him the time of day."

"I'm not interested in Mike."

"Oh! So it's the old man you're gunning for."

Brie shook her head. "No, it is not like that. You have no idea what you're talking about."

Laurel laughed, obviously not believing her. "Hey, don't worry, chick-ie. Your secret's safe with me." She leaned in and whispered, "Personally, I think you should set your sights a little higher. That old man is married and doesn't make all that much."

Brie looked at her in disbelief. "Thanks for the advice, Laurel. I've got some, too. If you aren't going to work hard for Mr. Reynolds, quit now and save everyone the trouble. He deserves only the best."

As Brie walked away, Laurel sang out childishly, "Brie's got a crush on Mr. Reynolds…"

No doubt everyone in the tiny shop had heard it, so Brie did the only thing she could. She held her head high, stuck out her chest with pride and walked out of the door with a smile on her lips. *People can think what they want.*

Sir was already home when she got there. He had her twirl in front of him so he could see the effects of his little game.

"You do look good without a bra, babygirl," he complimented.

He slipped his hand under her skirt and caressed her ass cheek before teasing her clit with his middle finger. "Bet they all wanted to do that," he growled before kissing her hard on the lips.

Brie closed her eyes, enjoying the magnetic pull of his dominance.

He withdrew abruptly to explain, "We will eat a light dinner before we head out. There are several people I have to meet with tonight at The Haven. But, rest assured, I also plan to scene with you while we are there."

Brie let out an excited squeak. Scening in public with Sir would be a dream come true!

"While I talk with them, feel free to walk around and observe the other performances. Let me know if there are any that stimulate you."

"Sounds thrilling, Sir!"

His voice took on a serious tone. "I have also invited someone to join us there to talk with you."

She wondered whom it was, but noticed he wasn't providing a name. Sir did like to keep her guessing. He enjoyed trifling with her intense curiosity, knowing it was a characteristic she needed to gain control over.

After their simple meal, which Brie struggled to eat because of her elation, Sir directed her to dress. She skipped down the hallway to the bedroom and saw that he had laid out a black leather halter top, shiny vinyl skirt, and crotchless panties with cutouts in the back to nicely frame her heart-shaped ass. Instead of his preferred garters and hose, he had picked out thigh-high boots to go with the ensemble. It gave her a much edgier look, making her wonder what he had planned for their scene. Sir was capable of anything.

He nodded his approval when he saw her. He had changed into black slacks and a solid black, button-up shirt. He still looked formal, but with an edgier feel that matched hers. "The exact look I was going for. You look absolutely edible, téa."

She basked in his lustful gaze. "Thank you, Master."

Brie was not surprised to see The Haven's parking lot full when they drove up. It was the 'hot place' to be for those in the local BDSM community. She was feeling a little nervous, though. With Sir being such a prominent member, all eyes would be on them tonight. It was a lot of pressure, especially knowing there were many out there who found Brie unworthy of Sir's collar.

*He chose you*, she reminded herself as he opened the door and helped her out of the car. He pulled a black duffle bag out of the trunk and slung it over his shoulder before he escorted her to the club.

The sights and sounds of The Haven assaulted her senses. The place was packed and every alcove was already in use, with various BDSM scenes being played out. Brie soon found herself surrounded as people crowded Sir, eager to talk to him. Brie kept her eyes on the floor, sensing that many of them were Doms. There was no way she was going to break protocol here.

After several minutes Sir insisted on moving along, guiding her with a hand on her back through the crowd. He walked her around the large central room, letting her glance at the scenes available for her viewing pleasure in each alcove.

She had to hide her shock when she saw Tono performing Kinbaku. A huge crowd had gathered to watch his artful performance. She had never admitted to anyone that Tono had been her choice during the collaring ceremony—up until the point she had met the eyes of his disapproving father as she had approached Tono with her collar. Brie had to force herself to remain calm, totally unprepared for seeing him in this environment.

Sir moved her on to the next scene. "You may enjoy watching Cat O' Nines. She is well known for her intense play."

Brie concentrated on the new scene, putting all her focus into it. The Domme's dramatic show fascinated Brie. The performance was enhanced by the powerful music she had chosen to accompany her work, a haunting melody with intense instrumentals.

Cat O' Nines' submissive was strapped to a St. Andrew's cross and already had red lash marks on his thighs and back.

She had just put down a cane and picked up a flogger with evil little knots on the end of each tail. She swung it in the air several times, showing the crowd her wicked-looking nine-tail before striking her submissive. His cry filled The Haven. Brie shifted uncomfortably, imagining that flogger making contact with her own skin.

The Domme played with her sub, striking several times and then cupping his ass or running her long nails between his legs. She continued like that, his cries of pleasure-pain building in intensity. Brie was horrified that she found it sexually arousing as welts appeared on his back.

There was a break in the action as Cat O' Nines unbound him and turned him around to face the crowd. His strong erection made it obvious that he thoroughly enjoyed his Mistress' attention. The Domme bound him again and began on his thighs, moving ever closer to his rigid cock. Brie was riveted.

"I must leave you, téa," Sir said quietly. "Feel free to walk around and observe. Once I am done with this meeting, you and I will enjoy our own scene."

Brie's heart raced as he walked away. *I hope it's a short meeting.* Just then, the masochistic sub roared out in pain, but Brie couldn't bear to look and headed back to Tono's scene instead.

The Asian Dom spent several minutes securing the girl's legs and then moved to her arms. He was very precise, needing her body to be perfectly supported by the rope because he was preparing to lift her in the air. Long ropes, attached to her body, had already been slipped through the large metal ring hanging from the ceiling. However, it was easy to see the girl was nervous. Tono stopped what he was doing and wrapped his arms around her, whispering something in her ear.

The girl's face began to relax when she closed her eyes. Brie knew the sub was matching his breath and she found herself subconsciously doing the same. The instant she felt the harmony, Tono looked up and stared directly into her soul.

Brie stumbled backwards, then turned and ran to an alcove on the other side of the room. She pretended to watch a paddling session as she tried to regain her bearings. Brie hadn't expected her connection with Tono to remain as strong. She knew in her heart she must eliminate the emotional ties that bound her to the gentle Dom, but she had no idea how.

# Toasted Brie

Brie had no idea how long she'd been standing there, staring blankly at the scene, but she was brought back to life the moment she felt the warm breath of her Master on her neck. He growled in her ear, "Are you ready, téa?"

"Yes, my Sir."

He chuckled softly, kissing her on the top of her head. "What we are about to do will not hurt. I've been told by those I've scened with in the past that it is actually quite relaxing, but it will require your trust." He began guiding her through the multitudes, adding, "It is certain to draw a crowd."

"What are you going to do, Sir?"

He just smiled and said, "Trust me."

Brie sighed in nervous excitement. She loved the thrill of the unknown and Sir knew that—knew how it added a heightened sense of exhilaration. She practically skipped beside him as he took her to an empty alcove. This one was dark, with midnight-blue walls and low lights. There was a table set at a slight incline in the center, and the faint scent of cinnamon filled the small space.

"Take off all your clothes except your panties and lie face down on the table."

As Brie complied with his command, Sir began taking items from the duffle bag. She glanced over to get a better idea of what he had planned for her, but the only item she recognized was a bottle labeled '70% Isopropyl Alcohol'.

*Oh, boy…*

Brie lay down on the table and turned her head towards Sir, ignoring the crowd that was already gathering. It appeared that everyone wanted to see Sir play with his newly collared sub. She forced herself to take long, slow breaths to combat her nervousness. The last thing Sir took out from the duffle bag was a CD player. He turned on music that featured a female with a lilting Celtic voice.

"We will begin by warming you up first," Sir said soothingly. He ran his fingers over her back and down her legs. As always, Sir's touch thrilled her. His hands traveled back up her legs and gave her framed little ass a light smack. Brie giggled, not expecting it.

She glanced at Sir and saw his smile as he began to caress with more pressure, causing her whole body to relax. Brie held her breath when he began tapping her skin, much the same way that Marquis Gray had when he'd flogged her. Brie quickly peeked at the items again, but noted there was no flogger.

"Curious, are we?" he murmured, as his hands danced over her back and down her thighs. This time Sir slapped her buttocks twice, with a much greater force, so that the sound of it echoed in the small alcove.

Brie yelped. "A spanking session, Master?"

"No, I just love playing with your ass, téa." He winked at her as he smacked her again.

She heard several whispers and turned her head to see that the crowd had grown significantly in that short time. Sir moved away from her and came back with a brush. He began brushing her hair, binding it in a high ponytail so that it lay away from her shoulders. "We cannot have any hair in the way," he stated.

Sir went back to the duffle bag and pulled out a small fire extinguisher. Brie shuddered involuntarily.

"Do you wish to continue, téa?" Sir asked.

She hesitated for just a second before answering, "Yes, Master."

"There is nothing to be frightened of."

"If she doesn't want to, I volunteer!" an uncouth submissive shouted from the crowd.

Sir ignored the unwelcomed offer, keeping his eyes solely on Brie. "In my opinion, fire is far more elegant than the violet wand. Truly a beautiful display." He peeled off her panties and asked her to keep her legs closed.

"Cross your arms and lay your head down in a comfortable position. You must stay still at all times."

He lightly brushed her back with his fingers before walking over to the table. He poured the alcohol into a small container and put what looked like a large cotton swab into it. "The process is simple, téa. I will apply the alcohol and then light it. I will snuff out any lingering flames with my hand. You will not be burned. I have done this many times and am experienced in the art." He traced her backbone with his fingers before dragging the swab over her spine. "It feels cool initially as it evaporates," Sir lit a slow-burning match, "but that is about to change."

He leaned over and kissed her cheek, careful to keep the flame away from her. "Are you ready?"

"Yes, Master."

Sir tapped the flame on her skin and intense heat raced up her back. Sir's hand swept the area in a fluid motion and the heat was gone. The crowd murmured their appreciation. It must have looked impressive.

"How was it?"

"Interesting. I would like to feel it again, Master."

"But of course…" Sir dragged the wet swab over her spine and tapped the flame against it. Again, the fire raced up her back. It was too fast to cause pain, although the heat was brief and concentrated. Sir swept the flames away before they could burn her skin.

"I believe your ass is craving a little attention, téa."

Brie bit her lip as he caressed both cheeks with his free hand. Where his fingers touched, the alcohol soon followed.

"I always said you had a hot ass." The crowd chuckled as he tapped her right cheek with the match and spanked it out with his hand. Then he moved to the left cheek, slapping that one several times just for fun after the flames went out.

Brie closed her eyes as Sir explored her body with the flames. Always, his caress came before the cool liquid and the burning heat. He had been right; it was relaxing and it was made all that more pleasant because of the abundant touching it required.

"Now we will ramp it up a notch," he announced to the crowd. Brie turned in time to see Sir take a swig from another cup on the table just before a fireball shot from his lips up into the air.

People broke out in enthusiastic applause. Brie glanced over and saw that the crowd was huge now. Sir rinsed his mouth out with water before leaning down and giving Brie a kiss on the lips. "Turn over, téa."

She turned herself onto her back so that she was facing Sir. The reflection of the fire in his hand danced in his eyes, giving him an almost sinister look. "Now you can witness the beauty of the flames."

Sir blew out the match and put it back on the table. Like he had done for her back, he caressed her skin, warming it up before the fire play ensued, but this time he interspersed the touches with gentle kisses all over her body. Brie purred silently. Could there be anything better than this?

He turned up the volume, letting the lilting Celtic melody set the scene. Then he traced a line on her thigh before following it with the alcohol. Sir lit the match and said with a grin, "Toasted Brie," just before he tapped the flame on her thigh and the fire raced up her leg.

Brie gasped in surprise. It was exhilarating to actually see the flame as she felt its heat. "Oh, Sir…"

"Do you like, téa?"

She looked into his flaming eyes. "Very much, Master."

"My fiery goddess," he growled as he caressed her other thigh. Brie held her breath as she watched him set fire to her skin. The flames danced upon her body before he swept them away. It was extremely sensual on a level she had not experienced before. She could feel the excitement of the crowd as they watched Sir skillfully control the fire to the graceful rhythm of the music.

He leaned forward and whispered in her ear, "This may feel a little hotter, my dear. Nipples are sensitive bits."

She looked at him in fear. "Master…"

He smiled down at her, his eyes blazing orange. "Do you trust me?"

She did not hesitate this time. "Completely, Master."

"As it should be."

Brie noticed that Sir picked up a towel and soaked it with water before announcing to the crowd, "You know you have a superior sub when she will let you do this."

He swirled the cotton tip over her right nipple, leaving only a trace of the fuel. He put it down and returned to her. With a sinuous movement, he tapped the flame on the tip of her erect nipple and Brie cried out as the fire consumed it. In an instant, Sir had swept the flame away with the damp towel and his warm mouth had encased her nipple. He sucked hard as the crowd went wild.

When he pulled away, Brie whimpered in protest, wanting more.

"Would you like me to light the other one?" he asked, his voice hoarse with desire.

"Please, Master."

He repeated the performance, letting it burn on her left nipple a second longer. Brie's pussy contracted in pleasure when she felt the coolness of the towel, followed by the warmth of his lips as they landed on her nipple. Sir reached between her legs. "So wet," he murmured as he kissed her, stroking her clit gently with his finger.

This time when he pulled away, her pussy was pulsing with need. Instead of relieving the ache, Sir placed a large blanket over her. He kissed her forehead. "Allow yourself to enjoy the aftereffects of fire play, téa."

Sir began cleaning the area, but continually came back to touch and whisper his praise of her as he gave her sips of water. People began to disperse, but there were a few who remained. Brie was certain they were subs who wished that they could trade places with her.

Brie stared at the ceiling and smiled. *Luckiest sub in the world.*

# A Desperate Move

Once Sir was sure Brie was fine to move about, he informed her that he had one last meeting to attend. "I do not care for leaving you so soon, téa. You may continue to observe the other scenes or retire in the back to be alone for a few minutes." He tilted her chin up and graced her with his stunning smile. "I admire your trust in me, little sub. It was beautiful to witness."

"You have earned my trust, Master. I would do anything you ask."

"Then I ask that you trust your natural instinct, téa." He put his hand gently on her chest. "If you ever feel a checking in your spirit telling you to stop, I expect you to honor it."

She looked into his magnetic eyes. "I will, Master. I promise."

He nodded. "Good."

Sir turned her around and smacked her on the ass. "Now, go off and find something you want Master to try."

She glanced back at him and grinned. "If it pleases you, Sir."

Brie wandered through the crowds, searching for something unusual, something that called to her pussy—so to speak.

"Brie…"

She peered to her left and saw Faelan standing beside her. Her heart jumped into her throat. "Go away!"

"I won't touch you and I won't stop you if you walk away, but I need you to hear me out."

Brie backed away, looking around desperately for Sir, but he was nowhere in sight. "Mr. Wallace, I got in serious trouble the last time I talked to you."

"You weren't the only one, Brie, and I am sorry. I should have talked to Davis first as per protocol. However, I did get permission to talk with you tonight in this public area. There's no reason to be concerned."

Brie scanned the crowd again, unsure if it was really okay to talk to him, but then she remembered Master saying that he wanted her to meet with someone tonight. Faelan interrupted her thoughts, stating, "Brie, you need to listen. I *need* you to understand."

She frowned, not understanding what possible good it could do. However, Sir wanted her to speak with him, so it was her duty to listen. "Understand what, Mr. Wallace? Nothing you say can change what's transpired. I don't see how talking will help either of us." She stared at the floor, unsure where to look in a situation like this.

"Brie, I'm sorry for any pain I've caused you." Faelan's voice caught. "But you should know that you've changed my life. Given me direction and hope. I can't stand the thought of you not knowing the significance of what you have done or how I feel about you."

She looked up into his soulful blue eyes. "Okay, I forgive you."

He shook his head violently. "No, I will not be satisfied until you understand."

Brie crossed her arms, sighing irritably. "Fine! You said you didn't have relations with Mary. I believe you, but I will never understand why you didn't tell me that night. Why did you avoid the question and act like I was in the wrong for questioning you about it?"

"Because you were wrong to question me. It was the same as saying you didn't trust me. I don't know Mary. Why would I jeopardize *us*, what *we* had, for a stranger? It upset me that you understood me so little."

She frowned. "But it wasn't just that. During the interview, you were so flippant with your answers, as if you didn't care enough to take the interview seriously—or me, for that matter."

"I thought you were mine," he answered candidly. "I thought the interview was simply a formality for us." He moved to touch her, but stopped himself. "You and I…we are meant for each other. Two people cut from the same cloth. I knew it when I met you. Damn it, Brie! I thought you felt the same way."

She looked at him with renewed sympathy, but stuck to her guns. "You seemed so overconfident that night, like I was more of a conquest, not someone you actually cared for. And then the way you acted with Mary…"

"I fucked up that night, blossom. I admit that. But you need to know where I've been, why you mean so much to me."

Faelan's potential confession frightened her. Brie glanced around again, searching for Sir in the crowd.

He spoke in a low tone so that others could not hear. "I killed someone, blossom." She didn't believe what she'd just heard, so she inched closer to hear him more clearly. "At sixteen, I killed a boy my age while driving home at night. I was lighting a cigarette and the match fell. I ran a red light, but didn't know it until I looked up and saw the other car, just before I crashed into it. The poor kid never had a chance." He stopped, taking a ragged breath.

Brie said nothing, but in her head she imagined the other kid, eyes wide with horror as his death raced towards him—no way out.

"It should have been me. I should have been the one to die that night. No way should that kid have paid for my carelessness."

"That's so awful…" she said sorrowfully.

His blue eyes had a haunted look when he spoke. "I will never forget the terror on his face in the glare of the headlights, or the sound at impact." He shuddered and abruptly turned away from her.

Brie was tempted to touch his shoulder in order to comfort him, but she resisted the urge, knowing it could be misconstrued by others.

When Faelan faced her again, he'd regained his composure. "Brie, I have lived every day since then imprisoned inside walls of guilt and self-hatred. It ruined any chance at a normal life and I often wished I was dead. Until you happened."

She shook her head. "I didn't do anything."

He smiled at her. "The day you fell into my arms I felt a spark of life, a connection. Then when I saw you at the beach and realized what you were training to be, everything fell into place. I *knew* I was meant to be your Dom and I was single-minded in my quest to win you over. Even Davis agreed. Why else would he allow me to join the training, take me under his wing and give me additional lessons? Why?"

"I don't know. I can't answer that."

"Of course you can't," he said in a reasonable voice. "Because you and I are meant to be together."

"No! I did my best not to lead you on," she protested.

"But it made me want you all the more. You felt the chemistry between us, you can't deny it."

"Chemistry does not equal love—"

"We hardly had any time together, Brie. I am certain if we spent quality time together, you would feel differently."

Brie growled in frustration. "You're not thinking straight. I have already made my decision. There is no going back now. That's the problem. You're so sure about things that you never *listen*."

He held up his hands in agreement. "Okay. You're right. Go ahead; it's your turn to talk. I'm listening."

Brie knew her words would not be easy for Faelan to hear, but she needed to be completely honest with him. "Yes, it's true. I felt an attraction towards you, but my heart was already taken. Even I didn't realize how completely until the night of the ceremony."

"You said 'felt', as if it's in the past. Are you saying you don't feel attracted to me now? Can you honestly say that?" he insisted.

"There you go again… *Listen* to me, Mr. Wallace. I am in love with someone else. I have already chosen the man I will serve. I'm sorry about what happened to you in the past, truly I am. But it doesn't change anything. You have to move on."

He shook his head and smiled sadly. "Brie, you and I never had time to get to know each other on a personal level. I want that. I want you to know the real me. Reject me if you must, but do it with a full understanding of who I am. Do not base it on a few encounters during a couple of scenes."

The vulnerability he was displaying physically hurt Brie. She had never suspected the depth of his feelings. It made what she had to do so much harder.

Brie took a deep breath before beginning. "I believe that everything that happened on graduation night—"

Then she heard *his* voice behind her. "What are you doing, téa?" Sir's tone was controlled, but accusatory.

Brie felt her stomach drop, realizing she had made a terrible mistake. "Mr. Wallace…said you gave him permission to speak with me. I thought he was the one I was supposed to meet with tonight, Master."

Sir's reply was simple and direct. "Have I given you permission to speak to Mr. Wallace?"

Brie's lip trembled. "No, Master."

Sir faced Faelan and shot his next words at him. "Mr. Wallace, you have ignored my edict. I directed you not to speak with my submissive. The fact you had the audacity to lie to her on top of it illustrates your lack of maturity and decorum. Leave now. But let me be perfectly clear—you are not to communicate with Miss Bennett or come within fifty yards of her. Do you understand?"

The entire club had become silent as the scene played out between the three of them. The crowd respectfully watched the confrontation. Faelan glanced around, possibly looking for supporters among the group, but found none. He nodded curtly to Sir, but his eyes traveled back to Brie. "Don't reject me, blossom. Not without getting to know me first."

"That's it!" Sir roared. He gestured to the manager of the club and two staff members surrounded Faelan, taking hold of his arms and physically forcing him out of the club.

As he was being dragged out, Faelan yelled, "I love you, Brie! I love you more than he ever could. You have to give me a chance. We're meant for each other…"

Sir's neck pulsed with rage, but he did not respond. Instead, he turned his attention back to her. "You were told *not* to speak to Mr. Wallace."

It was humiliating to have the entire club witness her mistake, but Brie was far more crushed to have failed Sir a second time. Would he disown her now?

She wanted to fall at his feet and beg for forgiveness, but it would only anger him further. So she stated with conviction, "I was misled, Sir. I will not let that happen again."

He snarled, "It is obvious that the boy is in need of correction." Sir looked around and motioned the club owner over to him. "Until Mr. Wallace learns respect, he has no business being amongst others in the community."

"Understood, Sir Davis. You don't have to worry about seeing his face around here again."

Brie couldn't help hearing the discontented sighs of several of the submissives around her. Faelan was a favorite among the eligible subs.

"It's time I teach Mr. Wallace I mean business," Sir announced to the club owner before leaving Brie's side and heading out the door.

Several people tried to follow him, but the owner shooed them away. "Nothing to see here, folks. Go back to what you were doing."

A sub next to Brie muttered, "God, she is such a bitch! Just *had* to ruin it for the rest of us. Already has Sir and now she's taken away Faelan from us."

Brie glanced over, half-expecting to see Mary, but it was a short-haired blonde who stuck her tongue out at her.

What had started out as the perfect evening had quickly deteriorated into a humiliating spectacle. She wanted to escape, *needed* to escape from the resentful stares of the submissives surrounding her and the utter disgrace she felt. However, Brie remained where she was, staring blankly at the BDSM scene playing out before her, wondering what was going on between Sir and Faelan. The Domme was enthusiastically whacking the jiggling buttocks of her submissive with a wooden paddle. The crack of the paddle broke through Brie's anguish, helping her not to cry. *Just concentrate on them*, Brie commanded herself.

Until she overheard, "Do you think he will publicly disown her when he returns?"

Her greatest fear voiced out loud ruined her resolve. Tears streamed down her face as she ran through the crowds to the back of the club, seeking out a private room. Once found, she collapsed on a chair, wiping away her tears. *Sir is a good Master. He will not disown me. He won't…*

"Brie, are you okay?"

She looked up to see Tono standing in the doorway.

"What are you doing here?" She could just imagine Sir walking in on her talking with Tono. "Go away!" Then she remembered who she was talking to and corrected herself, begging him, "Please, Tono. Please go away."

He left without further question. A short time later, Sir strode into the room. Brie fell to her knees. "Sir, I did not mean to disobey. I'm sorry." She bowed her head to the floor, swallowing her tears.

"Stand up, Brie."

She slowly got on her feet, but kept her head lowered.

"Look at me."

Brie bravely looked up and was greeted with a grave expression, but she took heart at the tender look in his eye.

"I understand why this happened."

A single tear fell from her cheek.

"There is no need for tears. I did say you were to meet with someone tonight." He brushed the wetness from her cheek, chuckling lightly. "Tono said you ordered him away."

Brie nodded, unsure why that was funny, but she was relieved to see his smile.

"*He* was the one I wanted you to speak with tonight."

"I didn't know, Sir."

"No, you did not. It is fortunate that you chose not to speak with Tono due to that very fact. You are learning, téa." He leaned down and kissed her lightly on the lips.

He sat down on the couch and Brie naturally knelt down at his feet, laying her cheek against his strong thigh. Once Sir touched her, all worry evaporated.

"Brie, I know you have lingering feelings for Tono and I am not threatened by them. He is a mature Dom who respects your decision." The tone of Sir's voice softened as he stroked her hair. "I know you, téa. I understand that you suffer from guilt. I'd hoped tonight your heart would be eased by speaking with him directly."

His hand stopped mid-pet. "Naturally, I did not foresee Wallace's breach of protocol, but that will end." Sir lifted her chin to look her in the eye. "If he comes anywhere near you again, you are to ignore him and leave. If he dares to follow you, seek protection from the nearest person you trust. Although we reached an understanding tonight, I am not entirely convinced he will leave you alone. He admitted to me he has the misguided hope that he can still win you over, even though you are collared. Until he understands that reality no longer exists, he will remain a problem."

"Sir, I'm—"

"I do not blame you. Do not apologize again. But I want to know what he shared with you tonight."

"He told me about the accident."

"Yes. A terrible circumstance indeed, but do not let it color your feelings towards him. One must come to terms with one's past to be effective as a Dominant. It should never be used to garner sympathy from a sub."

Brie was hesitant to voice the one thing that Faelan had stated the first time he'd cornered her that still played in her mind. "Sir, he claimed I am his reason."

Sir shook his head in disbelief. "He is a fool to put that burden on another. I understand his desperation, having been there once, but it is still no excuse. Wallace will be good to no one until he works through his demons."

It was so easy to be open with Sir that she shared her biggest fear. "I am afraid Mr. Wallace will turn away from his natural talent. He has often said we were cut from the same cloth and in a way, I agree with him. He didn't realize who he was until he met me." She looked up at her Master. "Well, Sir, I didn't realize who I was until I met you."

"The difference, babygirl, is that you have not been solely dependent on me. I am certain that if I had truly turned you away at the collaring ceremony, you would have found another. I cannot imagine you stalking me out of desperation, hoping to win my affections. You are confident in who you are. Wallace isn't there yet."

Brie looked down at the floor, a twinge of fear stabbing her in the gut. "What if he doesn't recover from this, Sir?"

"You are not responsible for the world, Brie. Wallace is stronger than you think and the call of dominance will not let him rest. At this point he sees you as his, but he will come to realize you were only a stepping stone to his true mate."

Sir's words brought comfort to Brie's soul. "Thank you, Master."

"The challenge is getting him to see beyond his own desires so that he can embrace the future." He cupped her chin. "However, that is *not* your job. You will only hinder his growth if you intervene in any way."

"I understand, Sir."

They were silent for several minutes. Brie basked in her Master's soothing caress. It comforted her that he did not react to Faelan with irrational jealousy. In all things, Sir remained the teacher, seeking the best conclusion for all the individuals involved.

"Now, Tono is a different story," Sir stated.

Brie looked up at him questioningly.

"Tono is a good man. I have nothing but respect for him as a person and a Dom. I believe it would be in the best interests of both of you to sit down and discuss what happened the night of the ceremony."

"If it pleases you, Sir," she answered doubtfully.

"It is easy to underestimate the power of closure. I have found that loose ends tend to cause needless doubt and pain."

Despite his bravado, Brie wondered if it would hurt Sir on some level to see her with Tono.

He laughed under his breath. "If it is my jealousy you are worried about, téa, let me assure you that is not a concern. I have faith in your commitment. You asked to be collared of your own free will, despite the risk of rejection. I am confident of your love, just as you should be confident of mine. I am a condor, my dear."

Brie was unsure what the reference meant. Condors were not handsome birds and, as far as she knew, they were carrion eaters. Not romantic in the least, but she was reluctant to ask because of the look of tenderness he bestowed on her. She would definitely have to google it.

# Thane

"I think it would be best if we leave through the back," Sir advised. "Your discussion with Tono will have to wait."

"Yes, Sir." She was grateful to be leaving, feeling far too emotionally raw to deal with any more drama.

"Everything you feel is written on your face." He had said the same thing the night he'd put the protection collar around her neck, after the second evening of class.

"I am grateful you can read me so well, Sir. It eases my mind, even though it alarms me."

He chuckled softly. "It should. You can hide nothing from your Master." Sir stood up and held out his hand. She gracefully rose to her feet and took hold of his arm as he guided her through the back hallways.

The night was warm. Brie found it pleasant to stroll with Master in the dark, loving the sound of his confident stride on the pavement. As they rounded the front of the building, Sir stopped and commanded, "You will walk to the car and get in. Do not look anywhere but straight ahead."

He nudged her towards the car while he stayed back. "Why are you still here?"

"Brie!" Faelan called out.

Brie hurried her steps, her eyes fixed desperately on the car. *Do not look, do not look back…* she commanded herself.

"Blossom, I'll wait as long as it takes to prove the depth of my love for you."

Sir's voice was like ice. "You were told to leave, Mr. Wallace. I am dialing the police as we speak."

Brie made it to the car and slipped into the seat, then shut the door. She heard their heated exchange, but could not make out the words. Sir eventually got into the car, slamming the door.

He said nothing until they were close to his apartment. "He's a stubborn cuss, I'll give him that much."

Brie didn't say anything as they walked into the high-rise, although she nodded to the doorman when Sir didn't respond to the man's greeting.

Faelan's persistence astonished Brie, and it did not help to serve his cause. By not respecting Sir's position, he was only making a fool of himself and tarnishing his reputation, as well as that of the school. Brie did not want that for Faelan, especially after all he had suffered.

"Téa, make me a martini," Sir said when they entered the apartment.

She had watched him enough times to feel confident imitating the process. She doubted her martini would compare to his, but she smiled when she shook the drink vigorously. *Shaken, not stirred, Sir.*

He had been on the phone the entire time she was making the drinks. She walked up to him, holding the martini up, careful not to spill. Sir smiled as he took it from her, but did not stop his conversation on the phone. "Yes, I think it is for the best. I am glad you are in agreement."

Brie went back to the kitchen to retrieve her drink. It had to be Faelan he was discussing, but who was he talking to and what was he planning? She knew Sir would not put up with his latest actions, but she desperately hoped that Faelan would not be banished from the BDSM community.

She returned to stand next to her Master, sipping her first attempt at a martini. It was definitely not as good as Sir's.

"Hard to believe, I know."

Sir chuckled at whatever the caller had just said. He clinked glasses with Brie and took a sip. "No, I agree. However, you have my expectations set unrealistically high. Do not disappoint me." He took another drink, his face suddenly becoming solemn. "Affirmative. There are times when it takes an extreme catalyst to force change."

Brie was certain he was talking about Faelan now.

"I need to make arrangements. Expect a call in a couple of days." He paused, and then the smile returned to his face. He looked down at Brie. "That would be a definite yes."

Sir snapped the phone closed. "I am not a man who will be pushed. However, when an opportunity presents itself, I'm not foolish enough to ignore it." He said no more, but seemed much more relaxed after the phone call. She breathed a sigh of relief, taking another sip of her mediocre martini.

He nodded towards the Tantra chair. "Your Master is feeling amorous. Strip down, téa, but leave the boots on tonight."

Brie set her drink on a side table and took off her clothes sensually for her Master. She couldn't help noticing the outline of Sir's erection straining against his pants. She swayed her hips in a seductive manner to entice him further as she ran her hands down her thighs and over the smooth black leather of her boots.

Both had been aroused by the fire play they'd engaged in earlier, but neither she nor Sir had experienced release. It heightened Brie's sense of excitement now.

"Undress me," he commanded.

Brie smiled as she began unbuttoning his shirt, feeling the familiar stirring in her loins as she exposed his muscular chest. She wanted to run her hands over his dark chest hair, but followed his order and undid his leather belt next. It excited her that Sir was observing her as she undressed him.

She unzipped his pants and pulled them down, helping him out of each leg. Brie looked up at him from the floor, in awe of his commanding masculinity.

"Stay." Sir left her, walking back to his bedroom and returning with a blanket. He moved over to the Tantra chair and lay down, placing the blanket on the floor. He looked at her and ordered lustfully, "Come."

The butterflies started as she approached him, moving with catlike grace towards her Master. He offered his hand for balance as she lifted her leg and positioned herself over his shaft. Brie closed her eyes as she lowered herself onto his rigid member, letting out a moan of pleasure when he grabbed her hips and forced himself inside her depths. He then took the blanket and threw it over her shoulders, covering them both.

In that warm embrace he kissed Brie, moving her tight pussy up and down his shaft slowly, sensually. "I wanted to take you at The Haven, but I resisted, knowing it would be far more satisfying to wait." Sir did not kiss her wildly. Instead, he was tender and controlled. Not at all what she had been expecting. It caused her to slow down and enjoy the teasing way his tongue played across her lips.

"I want you to touch yourself."

Brie reached beneath the blanket and played with her wet clit. She became a little more adventurous and felt the rim of her opening as Sir pushed his cock in and out of her swollen lips. Apparently it turned him on as well, because Sir groaned.

His pleasure encouraged her to continue exploring with her fingers, playing with his shaft as she felt their physical connection. Eventually, he took her hand and lifted it to his lips, licking her fingers. It was such an intimate gesture, a soft whimper escaped Brie's lips.

He smiled, placing both of her hands on his chest as he continued to pump his shaft into her with unhurried movements. Brie tilted her hips and rolled with each thrust. They both cried out at the intensity of the new angle. He pressed farther into her then, each stroke rubbing her clit as he cradled her ass and maximized the effects of his slow lovemaking.

Brie was surprised when Sir stopped and caressed her face. He pulled her close and breathed into her ear, "I love you, Brie."

Those words had power over her. She closed her eyes, hardly able to breathe. "I love you, Sir," she whispered.

"Say that again, but call me by my name."

She stopped her movements and gazed deep into his eyes. "I love you, Thane."

He crushed her to him, kissing her passionately. They both sought to meld into one another. It was like a dream, their open emotion mixed into the physical act of making love. In that moment there was no Dom, only a man desperately in love with his woman.

When he came, Brie threw back her head and shouted, "Yes, Thane, yes!"

He stopped in the middle of his release so she could feel the pulsing of his orgasm. With his shaft still throbbing inside her, he reached between her legs and caressed her to a sweet climax. She collapsed on his torso afterwards, totally and utterly in love with the man.

He tucked the blanket around her gently. "I find myself in new territory, téa."

She smiled, her cheek pressed against his chest. "How so, Master?"

He paused. "Love is a challenge for me."

She lay there listening to his heartbeat. Finally, she braved the question she was dying to ask. "Am I your first, Sir?"

He said nothing, but squeezed her against his chest in response.

She didn't know why, but she suddenly blurted, "I promise to be gentle, Sir."

He pinched her ass playfully. "Be gentle? Who do you think you are? You deserve to be punished for that."

She propped herself on his chest, grinning at him. "I wish everyone could be this happy."

She saw a flicker of sadness in his eyes when he answered, "Yes. Wouldn't that be ideal?" She wondered if the pained look had something to do with his father. The last thing she wanted was to lose this feeling of closeness. She kissed his shoulder lovingly before laying her head against it. They stayed in that position for a long time, staring at the lights of the city under the warmth of his blanket.

"I'm so happy, Sir. I never want this moment to end."

His voice rumbled in his chest. "Never wish for stagnancy, Brie. It is important to grow—in our case, to grow together. You may be interested to know that I have just arranged an overseas trip for the two of us."

She lifted her head. "Overseas, Sir?"

"Yes. It will give Wallace time to regain his senses with you nowhere in reach."

She couldn't hide her excitement. "Wow, I've never traveled out of the country before, Sir!"

He looked at her questioningly. "Do you have a passport?"

Brie shook her head.

"No matter. We leave in a week, which will allow you time to finish up at the shop and get your passport in order."

"I can't believe it! Where are we going? I hope it is someplace exotic…"

His laughter was low and tantalizing. "I'm unsure if the destination matters. We won't be getting out much, my dear."

She bit her lip to stop from giggling. It sounded a lot like a honeymoon. The idea of traveling with Sir as his partner made her weak inside.

"Brie, there is something that concerns me."

Her bliss instantly disappeared. "What is that, Sir?"

"You have never spoken of your parents."

Brie let out a sigh of relief. "Well, there's really not much to say. They're in Nebraska and live quite ordinary lives, Sir."

"Tell me about them."

She smiled, glad his request was something so simple. "Well, my dad's name is Bill and he's forty-three. My mom's name is Marcy and she's a year younger." He looked at her expectantly, so she continued. "Dad works as an accountant these days and Mom has been a preschool teacher for years. Really, that's about it, Sir."

"Do they know about us?"

She hesitated. "No, Sir."

"Is there a reason?"

Brie looked at him earnestly. "They wouldn't understand, Sir."

"We don't have to detail our sex lives, Brie. However, they should know that you are in a committed relationship."

She gave him an uneasy smile. "Sir, I don't know how my parents will take the news that you are only ten years younger than my dad."

"Whether they like it or not, they should be told. It is irresponsible to keep them in the dark."

Brie lowered her eyes, knowing he was right but dreading the confrontation. She nodded her acquiescence.

"I will set up a layover so that I can meet with them in person before we leave the country. Hopefully it will help ease their minds about us."

She kissed him tenderly on the lips. "I love that you are so thoughtful, Sir."

"I expect you to call your parents tomorrow and explain that we have been seeing each other for the last six weeks. Do not lie, but keep the details simple." He looked down at her with a half-smile that made her heart flip-flop. "I am interested in meeting your parents, téa."

"They're good people, Sir, but old-fashioned and fairly ordinary."

"Your parents raised an exceptional daughter. That makes them interesting to me."

Brie blushed and kissed him again. She'd already decided not to mention his age when she talked to them on the phone. She wanted her mother and father to judge Sir on his own merits, not any preconceived ideas they might hold. Surely once they met him in person, they would see what an incredible man he was.

Sir stirred underneath her. "Let's finish our martinis in the bedroom." He got up and handed Brie her drink with a wicked little grin, clinking his glass against hers. "There are a few things I want to teach you before we head off to Russia."

Brie followed him into the bedroom, shaking her head in disbelief. *Sir and Rytsar together?* The mere thought of it made her lightheaded and weak.

# Brie's Russian Fantasy

# New Toy

Sir walked into the bedroom nonchalantly, while Brie stumbled over herself as she followed behind him. The knowledge that they were headed to Russia to see the Dom, Rytsar Durov, had her completely discombobulated.

Master commanded her to lie on the bed, her legs spread open for him. She did as he'd asked, watching while he retrieved something from his extensive rack of toys in the back of his closet. Although most Doms displayed their instruments, Sir seemed to enjoy the suspense of his sub not knowing what he would use until the scene was about to begin.

He came out holding up a white device that looked suspiciously like an oversized microphone. Were they going to sing karaoke together? A burst of laughter nearly escaped her lips, but she squelched it.

"I can tell by the amusement on your face that you have no idea what this is," Sir stated.

She nodded, trying to look properly serious.

He held up the device, which had a round head that tapered into a long handle and a short electrical cord that hung from it. There was nothing sexy or kinky about it. "This is a tool of choice for Durov. I feel you should be familiar with it before we go. There is no doubt in my mind that it will be used while we are there."

Whatever it was, the toy was clunky and unsexy. Brie couldn't imagine why the Russian Dom would prefer it.

Sir stripped before plugging in the toy and joining her on the bed. "It only has two speeds."

He flipped it on and a low rumbling emanated from the toy. *A vibrator…* Her whole body suddenly tensed. *Is that huge thing going inside?*

Sir's laughter filled the room as if she'd voiced her fear aloud. "No, téa. This is an external toy."

Brie relaxed back on the pillow, breathing a sigh of relief. However, she couldn't miss the mischievous glint in his eyes when he ordered, "Open your legs wider."

Now she was nervous.

He announced, "I think the lower one should prove enough for you."

Brie was surprised, considering she always used the highest setting on her little bullet vibrator. A low vibration was just an irritating tease. *Maybe that's part of Sir's evil plan…*

Sir placed it on her clit. It, and all of the surrounding area, rumbled with the low but intense vibration. She moaned softly. It was pleasant.

When he adjusted the angle slightly, her clit instantly became erect and began to quiver. Brie settled farther into the pillow, her back naturally arching in pleasure.

"You like the feel of the Hitachi, do you?"

Brie sighed with satisfaction. "It's very nice, Master."

His eyes got that mischievous look again, causing her concern. "I want you to give in to the orgasm. Don't force it, just let it come naturally."

Her breath quickened. This wasn't going to be a session of orgasm denial, so why was Sir wearing an impish grin?

She closed her eyes and concentrated on the intense, all-encompassing vibration. She mentally embraced the stimulation and Brie could feel the spark burst into flame as the orgasm started to build in her core. It wasn't coming in a rush; no, this was a slow burn that could not be denied because of the sheer size of the toy. Her clit could not escape the teasing vibrations.

Brie opened her eyes and her heart skipped a beat at the lust in her Master's stare. It was obvious he enjoyed bringing her to climax. However, the look held something more she could not define—it made her feel that this was both an act of love for her and dominance over her.

Without any struggle, she reached the edge. "I'm coming, Master," she purred as her hips lifted slightly of their own accord. Sir kept the vibrator directly on her clit throughout her climax, making it almost too intense.

When it ended she melted onto the bed, but only momentarily, for Master was not finished. His wicked grin widened when she started to whimper.

Brie's freshly-come pussy could not handle the intense stimulation of the vibrator now. "Please, Master. Too much."

"I command you to take it," he stated.

Brie squirmed under the vibrator, but there was no escaping the giant head. Her clit burned in protest and she instinctively moved away, but Sir's hand landed on her pelvis.

"Stop moving."

When Brie became still, he lifted his hand from her. However, the intensity of the vibration was driving her insane and she protested again, "Too much, too much!"

Sir leaned forward and said in a husky whisper, "Harness that feeling and come for me."

Brie's bottom lip quivered. How could she? It was so concentrated it was almost painful. Thankfully, the lesson of the beam came to her. During her session with the violet wand, Sir had instructed her to hold onto a pole. If the stimulation became too much, all she had to do was let go. Having that level of control had helped her tolerate more intense stimulation.

This situation was similar in that Sir was giving her a level of control again. He was not holding her down; Master had commanded she remain motionless of her own will.

With great effort, Brie stopped fighting the vibration. She willed her body to relax and give in to the stimulation, to embrace it. Slowly, her muscles obeyed and the vibration went from painful to wanted. She arched her back and pressed herself into the toy.

"Good girl," he murmured.

Brie let out a loud whimper as the second, far stronger orgasm took hold of her body and wrung her out with its powerful contractions. She was trembling afterwards, still writhing from the merciless vibration.

Her eyes began watering. "Please, Master! No more…"

"One more, téa."

She groaned in protest, but mentally accepted his command. Brie closed her eyes and calmed her feeling of panic. *One more… Sir is asking for only one more.* Brie slowed her breathing until it was deep and even. Once she was calm, she could better concentrate on the intense fire between her legs.

Having already come twice in rapid succession, it did not take her long to urge the third once she'd embraced it. The final orgasm felt like an exorcism when it struck. Her thighs began shaking violently. She screamed when Sir slipped his finger into her pussy and her muscles repeatedly clamped around him when she climaxed. This one went on forever, ebbing and then returning with a vengeance as the vibrator rumbled on.

Finally, the toy was lifted off her clit and she melted into the pillow, tears in her eyes. Brie never knew orgasms could be like that—extreme, but equally torturous.

Sir turned it off and put the device down. "God, you are beautiful when you come like that."

She slowly turned her head towards him, every movement an effort.

He swept away a strand of her sweat-drenched hair. "Impressive, téa."

Her body so wrung out that even talking was difficult, Brie whispered, "What is that thing called, Master?"

He smirked. "A Magic Wand."

She snorted and looked up at the ceiling. "More like a Merciless Wand."

"If it's merciless you want, it's merciless you shall have."

Before Brie could voice a protest, Sir moved between her legs and thrust his hard cock into her. She cried out as he began fucking her over-stimulated pussy.

"You are hot like fire, woman!"

Brie's clit was still buzzing from the vibrator, and his forceful thrusts just added to the dizzying effect.

"I'm going to come, and come hard," her Master proclaimed.

Her screams were more like whimpers as he revved up for the final act. The sound of their sex was enticingly juicy because of how wet and excited she was.

"Master, I…" she began, but lost all train of thought as he pounded his cock into her like a jackhammer. Only three words followed: "Oh…my…God!"

He grunted like a ravenous lion as he gave in to his desire, pumping his seed deep within her. Master pressed up against her sex with the last thrust and her pussy gave its final encore, a fluttering climax to milk his cock.

Sir kissed a tear that remained on her cheek. "And that, my dear, concludes your introduction to the Magic Wand."

# A Little Dish on Clark

Brie held up her philosophy textbook from college. "Why do I still have this? I'll never use it."

Lea giggled. "Give it to charity. I'm sure some poor college student would appreciate not spending a hundred bucks for the book."

Brie turned it over and looked at the price tag. "A hundred and eighteen bucks, girl." She flipped through the pages. "I think I cracked it open maybe…um…three times. The teacher didn't like teaching from books." She tossed it in the 'give away' pile and dug back into the box.

Lea had volunteered to help Brie move in to Sir's apartment. However, Sir had suggested the two first sort through the boxes, dividing them into three piles: 'keep', 'toss', and 'give away'. It was proving to be a daunting task.

Lea held up several DVDs. "What are these?"

Brie broke out into a grin. "That is my documentary, missy. I like to keep it on as many different formats as I can so there's no chance of losing it." She dug into her pocket. "Here it is on my USB drive."

"What? You keep it with you all the time?" Lea asked in amazement.

"Not normally." She laughed. "But Sir wants me to start working on it again." She looked around guiltily. "I know we should be working, but you wanna take a peek at what I have so far?"

Lea nodded vigorously.

Brie grabbed her computer and the two sat on boxes as she loaded it up. "I've been working on the first time you came to my apartment. Do you remember that night, after our first auction?"

"Oh, Master Harris! He was so damn sexy in his doctor getup and with all those naughty instruments…"

"Yeah, you pretty much were crushing on him that night."

Brie hit play and the two started giggling as they listened to their detailed summaries of the day-long auctions.

"We were such newbies then," Brie snickered. She pointed to her face in the video. "See, that's me, trying not to look totally freaked out when you talk about him inserting the instruments."

Lea leaned in to take a closer look, and burst out laughing. "I had no idea. I thought you shared my lust for the man."

"No, I thought you were nuts to want to play 'doctor' with anyone."

Lea sat back. "Well, that's funny, since you spent time with Master Harris yourself, and if I recall right, you loved it."

"*Doctor* Harris was nice, but he couldn't compare to Rytsar."

Lea shifted uneasily, causing Brie to wonder if her girlfriend still had a major crush on the doctor.

Lea lifted her hands up to her face and batted her eyes, imitating Brie's excitement from that night. "Just look at the way you're glowing as you talk about the Russian. I thought for sure you had fallen in love with the Dom, the way you were gushing."

Brie hit pause on the computer. "Well, I admit I definitely had a crush on Rytsar." She smiled self-consciously. "I actually cried when the night was over."

Lea burst into giggles. "That's my stinky cheese, falling for every man she scenes with."

"Like you're any better! Remember how sad you were when Master Harris sent me an apple?"

Lea rolled her eyes. "You already had the handsome Russian *and* Tono. As if you needed another man on your chastity belt."

Brie bumped her shoulder. "I still think you and Master Harris would make a fine pair, you know."

She looked at Brie coyly. "Oh, we have enjoyed a few scenes since…"

"No!"

Lea giggled again. "Don't try collaring me with the man, girlfriend. I'm enjoying myself too much right now. So many directions I could go—I can't decide."

Brie decided to ask the question that she'd been longing to ask for weeks. "What about Ms. Clark?"

Darn, if Lea hadn't turned bright pink all over.

"Spill the beans, girl!" Brie demanded.

Lea looked positively love-struck when she answered. "We haven't actually scened together since graduation, but she's taken me to a couple of clubs. Let's just say, I think there's a deeper connection brewing between us."

The thought of dating Ms. Clark made Brie shiver—and not in a good way. "So, have you learned anything more about her?"

Lea's voice dropped down to a whisper. "I think she has a thing for the Russian."

Brie was so shocked, she blurted, "What?!"

"Shh… I'm only telling you because you're my best friend."

Brie shook her head to clear it. "OMG, things are suddenly making sense. That's why she was so weird when he won me at the auction…and it explains her strange reaction when he rated me higher than she expected." She giggled into her hand. "Mistress Clark and Rytsar? I can't even picture it."

"Well, apparently neither can the Russian. Poor Mistress Clark is suffering from unrequited love."

"But…*Ms. Clark*? Is she even capable of submitting to someone else?"

Lea shrugged. "Guess it just takes the right individual."

The revelation put the Domme in a whole new light. Ms. Clark was looking for love—no different than the rest of humanity. She'd just managed to hide it under an exterior of impenetrable force.

"I always thought she was of the 'female' persuasion," Brie protested.

"Oh, no, I have seen her with male submissives. God, she is sexy when she subdues them."

"Really?"

"Yeah, that woman is multitalented. You don't know this, but she has many admirers. Unfortunately, the only one she really desires is the one who turned her down."

"What? Rytsar knows how she feels?"

"Yeah. From what I gather, Sir was somehow involved. Whatever happened, she ended up very hurt and resentful."

"It's a wonder she still works at the Center."

Lea gave her a sad smile. "I think Mistress Clark holds out hope the Russian will change his mind, and she wants to be here when he does. I can't tell you how unhappy she was when Sir quit, as he's her only link to Rytsar."

Brie shook her head slowly, unable to process this new side to the female trainer. "How is it that a dominant personality could think that way?"

"Love does strange things to people," Lea answered. "But I tell you this, if I could take Ms. Clark's pain away, I would."

Brie looked at her friend, understanding the deeper meaning behind the statement. "So are you telling me that you're in love with her?"

Lea tilted her head and looked at Brie with a solemn expression. "At this point I'm not sure if I can distinguish between love and lust. All I know is that the world is a much better place when I'm around her. She makes me feel alive like no one else, not even the doctor."

A random thought flashed through Brie's head. "Does that mean you're jealous of Rytsar?"

Lea became flustered, which was so uncharacteristic of her. "I… Hmm… Good question. I'll have to get back to you on that."

*Ms. Clark in love with Rytsar…what a tangled mess!*

"Brie."

She nearly jumped out of her skin when she saw Sir in the doorway. How long had he been standing there? Brie stood up and addressed him. "Yes, Sir?"

"There has been a change of plans. Marquis just called, claiming Celestia is in dire need of company. He said she's been lonely since returning home from the hospital. We'll be leaving in an hour." He looked at her laptop sitting on the box. "Finish what you can and reschedule for a later date."

Brie felt guilty, knowing she had wasted time gossiping with Lea when she should have been unpacking. "We will, Sir."

"Lea."

Her friend looked up at Sir with a guilty expression, as if she had failed him too.

"I am glad you came today. Brie never laughs as much as when she is with you."

He left them without any reprimand.

"That was so sweet of him to say," Lea cooed.

"My Master is a good man."

"The best!"

Brie put her computer away and the two made quick work of three more boxes before Lea had to leave. Sir escorted them both out, giving Brie the meal he had cooked for Celestia while the girls had finished their work. Whatever it was, it smelled delicious—far beyond anything Brie could have prepared.

"Thank you, Sir Davis. You really didn't have to make me a meal, but thanks," Lea joked, grabbing the meal from Brie.

Sir shook his head good-naturedly as he took it back. "Watch yourself, Lea."

Brie was amazed at Lea's boldness. Not too many people were brave enough to joke with Sir. It made her love Lea all the more. "Call you tomorrow?"

Lea gave her a big hug. "I'm counting on it, subbie."

On the drive there, Sir surprised Brie by stating, "Although I have made dinner, there is something I want you to cook especially for Marquis Gray once we get there."

She hid her disappointment with a smile. Having to cook for Marquis was humiliating, especially after the egg fiasco just before graduation. "Yes, Sir."

He winked at her. "I know he will appreciate it."

She wondered about this sudden trip to visit them and asked, "Is everything okay with Celestia, Sir? Is she having trouble recovering from her emergency appendectomy?"

He chuckled. "She is well enough. I think this is more for Marquis' sake. He has been at home taking care of his sub for more than a week, and I think it is driving him mad."

Brie was struck again by the paradigm shift—first with Ms. Clark and now with Marquis. She had always imagined him to be almost Zen-like in his approach to life. The idea that Marquis was going stir-crazy seemed so…human.

"I couldn't help over hearing part of your conversation with Lea," Sir stated. "During our stay in Russia, Ms. Clark's name is not to be mentioned."

Brie couldn't imagine what had happened to provoke such a command.

"I won't, Sir."

"I personally don't care for gossip, but in this case it was beneficial. You needed to be aware of that dynamic so you would not mistakenly mention it. Although the incident occurred years ago, there are still raw nerves on all sides."

"May I ask what happened, Sir?"

"You may ask, but I will not answer. It is a private matter."

Brie cringed, feeling bad for prying. Humbled, she assured him, "I will not ask again, Sir. Please forgive me."

"Lea is a natural gossip. I know that is not your nature."

She didn't want Sir to think badly of Lea. "I promise we will work hard next time to make up for today."

"See that you do," he replied as they pulled into the driveway of a sprawling, ranch-style home. He added, almost as an afterthought, "It would be nice to be settled, Brie. I've never been a fan of boxes."

Sir's comment warmed her heart. It was his way of saying that he wanted her there permanently. She blurted, "I love you, Sir!"

His devastating smile set her heart aflutter as she got out of the car, but those feelings of momentary bliss disappeared as soon as she stood on Marquis Gray's doorstep.

# I'm a Condor

Sir rang the doorbell and told Brie to stop fidgeting. "You will do fine," he promised, just as the door opened.

Brie tensed when she saw Marquis Gray. It had only been a couple of weeks, but she had forgotten what a commanding presence he had until those dark eyes greeted her. She quickly looked down, not wanting to be reprimanded.

"Well, isn't this a nice surprise?"

"I doubt you could call it a surprise when you demanded we come," Sir replied with a smirk.

"No need to speak of it to Celestia. I wouldn't want her to feel she was a burden to anyone."

"I suspect she is not the problem," Sir murmured as he held up the dish he'd prepared. "This is for later. My sub is going to make you an appetizer first."

Through hooded eyes, she watched Marquis for his reaction. She did not miss the look of revulsion that flitted across his face. "How kind of you."

She wasn't sure if he was speaking to Sir or to her, so she kept her head down. She was determined not to fail him—or Sir.

"But first, you two really must see Celestia. She has been cooped up here since I brought her home from the hospital after the surgery, and she is in dire need of company."

Brie followed Sir as Marquis led them through the house. It looked like the model homes one saw in magazines. Tall, vaulted ceilings, an expansive fireplace, tons of perfectly placed knick-knacks. Not what she had imagined for Marquis at all. It made her wonder if Celestia had been the decorator. If so, she was quite talented. The place maintained a homey and inviting feel, despite its perfection.

Marquis took them to the great room. It was equally impressive, with its wall of books, large screen TV, and huge bay window. The room had it all, including a smiling Celestia, who was lying on the couch.

"May I, Sir?" Brie asked.

"Of course."

She walked to Celestia's side and knelt beside her, grabbing her hand. "How are you? I was so scared when I heard what had happened!"

Celestia's angelic voice was as pure as Brie remembered. "I am doing well, Miss Bennett. Marquis is overly protective of his sub. He won't let me do anything while I recover."

"Doctor's orders," Marquis corrected.

Celestia smiled up at her Master. "You take good care of me." He offered his hand and she kissed it tenderly.

It was sweet. The two had a special bond Brie adored.

"It is good to hear you are well, Celestia," Sir said kindly. "You are greatly admired and your bad health was a distress to us all."

Celestia bowed her head. "That's very kind of you to say, Sir Davis."

"Miss Bennett," Marquis said, "I hear you have had issues with Mr. Wallace since the collaring ceremony."

She looked at him warily, only nodding when she glanced into his perilous eyes. They penetrated her to the core.

"I've spoken to him once and we will be meeting with him as a panel while you are in Russia. He is in significant need of direction. However, I can't help but wonder what you feel for the young Dom."

She looked to Sir before she spoke. He nodded, so she answered Marquis openly. "I care about Mr. Wallace, but only as a friend."

"That must stop."

She looked at him in shock. She was about to protest, but remembered his position and asked respectfully, "May I ask why, Marquis Gray?"

"He cannot distinguish the difference. He is convinced you feel the same and will not be able to move forward if he continues to receive mixed signals from you."

Sir put his hand on Brie's shoulder, stating, "I've already told her what to do if she encounters him again."

"I am not talking about that, Sir Davis. I am talking about her private thoughts. I personally believe those connections are equally potent. Even the simple act of dwelling on Mr. Wallace continues a link that needs to be severed. Until he is in control of his emotions, you should banish all thoughts of him."

Brie thought Marquis was being overdramatic, but then she thought back to the many times she had fantasized about Sir during her training. She'd felt a very real connection to him then, and look at them now…

She glanced at Sir, not wanting to commit to anything he did not agree with.

Sir addressed Marquis. "Although I doubt Brie will have any thoughts of the boy while we are in Russia, I believe it is a valid point."

Brie nodded to Marquis. "Then I will sever my thoughts, Marquis Gray. I don't want him to hurt anymore. Faelan deserves a fresh start."

"Fine." Marquis looked down at Celestia lovingly. "I believe my sub is due for some sustenance."

Sir inquired, "May we have free rein of your kitchen?"

"Certainly."

Sir guided Brie into the immaculate kitchen. He looked through the refrigerator before giving her directions. "It looks like you have all the necessary ingredients." He shut the refrigerator door and faced her. "I want you to create the best damn omelet he's ever eaten."

Brie felt her stomach sink to the ground. Her worst nightmare! *Cooking an omelet for Marquis?* "Only if it pleases you, Sir," she replied, stating her reluctance respectfully.

He chuckled. "It pleases me."

Her sigh was heavy when he left the kitchen. *An omelet for Marquis… Oh, the humanity!*

Brie gathered the needed ingredients, including his favorites: green onion, bacon, and Swiss. She counted out the eggs and noted there were only enough to make three omelets. She hoped it would be unnecessary to use them all.

While the others talked in the adjacent room, Brie set to work. There was a sense of excitement, despite the fear. She knew how to cook this omelet and if Sir wasn't willing to partake of her skills, at least Marquis could.

It only took two tries to make a perfect omelet. Sir had provided a covered plate so that she could properly display it. With pride, she placed the silver lid over it and walked into the room to join the group, the plate held proudly in both hands.

"Ah, you look as if you have created a masterpiece," Marquis complimented as he sat down on the couch next to Celestia.

"I could not have done it without your patience, Marquis Gray. I am grateful," she said with a bow as she placed it on the coffee table, along with a fork and napkin.

"I am anxious to try it."

Everyone watched as he lifted the lid—Celestia with her pleasant smile and Sir with a playful smirk. Brie bit her lip in anticipation.

The look on Marquis' face would have been comical if she hadn't been the one to make the dish. "Oh, no…" He quickly slammed the lid back down and closed his eyes.

The room was silent.

He said, in a voice of forced calm, "Miss Bennett, I appreciate the effort you put into the dish. However, after our last session in the kitchen I have sworn off omelets forever."

Sir put his hand over his mouth to hide his snicker. Celestia, on the other hand, took pity on Brie. "I would love to sample your work."

With much effort, Marquis took off the lid again and cut a small piece for her. He lifted the fork to her lips and turned away as she chewed.

"It's simply lovely, Miss Bennett. So light and fluffy. Thank you."

Brie bowed. "My pleasure, Celestia."

"Whose idea was it to cook the omelet tonight?" Marquis asked as he cut another piece for Celestia.

Brie said nothing.

"I see." Marquis turned to Sir. "Your idea of a joke, Sir Davis? It wasn't enough to put me in charge of the cooking unit last session, I take it."

Sir bit back his amusement. "I wanted you to enjoy the benefits of your labor, Gray. It was only fair. You know how I detest eggs. The whole Center smelled of them for a week."

Marquis actually smiled then. "You have an overly sensitive nose, Sir Davis." He raised his eyebrow and stated, "Surely you're not suggesting I chose that particular dish with you in mind?"

"That is exactly what I'm suggesting."

He chuckled. "Unfortunately, I ended up punishing us both." He gave Celestia another bite before addressing Brie. "Although the sight of this dish nauseates me, I must compliment you on the work. I can tell it has the right texture, and apparently you remembered what I prefer in an omelet. Kudos, Miss Bennett." His praise gave her an unexpected thrill. "And..." he lifted the fork to Celestia's lips again, "my sub seems to enjoy the flavor. A job well done. How many tries did it take?"

Brie said proudly, "Two."

"A vast improvement indeed. There is hope for you yet."

"Thank you, Marquis Gray."

Sir spoke up, "Unfortunately, we must cut this visit short. Brie and I both have work to do tonight, but I have your meal warming in the oven."

"It was lovely of you to come, Sir Davis. Miss Bennett," Celestia said, trying to get up.

Marquis gently pushed her back on the couch. "Stay still," he chided. "I'll see them out."

As they walked to the front of the house, Marquis told Sir, "To be honest, I questioned whether you would be a good match for Miss Bennett, despite her infatuation with you. Especially when I heard the reports of her interactions with Mr. Wallace afterwards. However, tonight those concerns have been silenced. I see a peace in her eyes I have not seen before."

Brie's heart nearly burst with joy when she heard his observation.

"It is good to hear you acknowledge that fact," Sir replied. "I did not make the decision lightly, nor did I do it solely for my own benefit."

"Understood," Marquis answered. "But one had to question your intentions, based on your previous actions."

"What one might label as a 'breach of protocol', another might see as a fated encounter," Sir responded.

Marquis shook his head as he opened the door. "Regardless of whether I agree with you or not, I wish you both safe travels. Miss Bennett, I hope you will visit again soon. I am sure my sub will enjoy your tales of Russia."

"Thank you, Marquis Gray. Please tell Celestia how happy I am to see her looking so well."

"I shall. The same can be said for us. It is good to see you thriving, Miss Bennett."

The drive home was agreeably quiet. Sir seemed as satisfied by the night's events as she was. It pleased Brie that he had openly acknowledged his feelings for her in front of Marquis. Although Sir hadn't used the L word, the meaning was the same. She assumed it was a big step for him.

The night still had one pleasant surprise left. After they returned to the apartment, Sir told her to work on editing her film while he polished a presentation he was to give the next day.

They sat on the couch beside each other with their computers. It was so pleasant and sweet that Brie decided to google something she'd been curious about. Sir had once told her that he was a condor, and said it with such tenderness that she knew it held significance to him. She typed in the word 'condor'.

Brie glanced over the stats of the bird, noting that she had been right. They were a type of vulture—not sexy in the least. However, the California condor was the largest bird in North America. It wasn't until she got to the behavior of the creature that she finally grasped Sir's meaning. She was surprised to learn the birds lived to be incredibly old—like fifty to sixty years—and the males waited until they were sexually mature before picking a female. Her heart skipped a beat when she read the words, 'condors mate for life'. That was what he'd meant!

'I'm a condor' had to be the most romantic thing she'd ever heard.

She glanced at Sir, hardly able to contain her joy.

He looked up from his screen and smiled. "What?"

"You're a condor, Sir."

He raised his eyebrow. "Yes, I am."

She smiled shyly. "I'm a condor, too."

# Her Parents

Brie was grateful to finish out her last day at the tobacco shop. Her boss had given the two new employees the day off so that it was just like old times—just the two of them. Although it was bittersweet to leave Mr. Reynolds behind, she couldn't wait to be free of the place. It was *so* mind-numbingly boring compared to the life she was leading now.

At the end of the day, Mr. Reynolds handed her a small gift.

"What's this?" she asked, both surprised and touched.

"A little remembrance. It has been a pleasure working with you, Brie. You will be sorely missed around here. My only consolation is that I will see you on an odd holiday or two."

"What? Don't you get together with your nephew more often than that?"

"No. He's a busy man. I understand."

She smiled brightly. "I'll see if I can change that."

"Open it," Mr. Reynolds encouraged.

Brie carefully unwrapped the pretty paper. She lifted the lid and smiled as she took the gift out of the box. It was a keychain with a tiny pack of Treasurer cigarettes hanging from it. The very cigarettes Sir had asked for the first night they'd met in the shop. "Mr. Reynolds, how did you know?"

"Thane was surprisingly open when he asked about the cute little cashier at my shop. He knew very well we don't carry those pricey cigarettes here."

Brie held it up to admire. "I will *treasure* this always," she said with a giggle, giving him a hug. "Truly, it means a lot to me. This little shop is where Sir and I met, where my life really began. Every time I look at it I will smile and think of you."

"I'm glad you like it, Brie." He discreetly wiped a tear from his eye, shaking his head. "This shop won't be the same without you."

She gave Mr. Reynolds another hug. It was hard saying goodbye to the man who'd been a father figure to her since she'd moved to California. She smiled at him sadly, knowing she wouldn't see him on a daily basis after this.

He shook the melancholy look from his face. "So, enjoy yourself in Russia. Be sure to take pics, but only show me the ones you can post publicly," he joked.

It was still weird having Mr. Reynolds aware of her alternative lifestyle, but it was comforting too. He was the only person outside the BDSM community who knew about it—well, besides his wife.

She pulled her keys from her purse and placed them on the new key-chain. "There—now you'll be with me wherever I go."

Brie gave him a final kiss on the cheek before heading out of the door. She turned around as she walked away from the small, brick building. "Bye, tobacco shop. It's been real and it's been fun, but I can't say it's been real fun." She snickered to herself as she jumped in her car.

Her new life had officially begun, and tomorrow she was heading off to Russia. But first, Sir had to meet her parents.

Brie was a jumble of nerves as they drove up to her parents' Nebraskan home. She had a bad feeling about the visit, but Sir would not be swayed. She stared out of the window of the rental car, looking at the old place. She'd spent her teenage years here in the small, two-story house on the corner lot, with her devoted but overprotective parents.

"I always hated bringing my boyfriends home to meet my parents," she mumbled, "especially my dad, Sir."

"Is there a point to telling me this?" Sir asked, a hint of humor in his voice.

"Dad would rather I set my sights on my career than waste my potential by getting involved with someone, Sir."

"Understandable…" He got out of the car and opened the door for her.

She took his hand hesitantly. "They're not exactly open-minded either."

"You have mentioned that before, Brie. We're only sharing our status as a couple," he reminded her gently as they walked up to the house.

Brie looked up at her Master as they stood on the front porch—strong, chiseled features, with a decidedly mature appearance. She was afraid his age would be an issue for them, but hoped her parents could see past it.

She closed her eyes, trying to quiet her nerves as Sir reached over and rang the doorbell. It seemed like forever before she heard the unlocking of the latch and the door finally swung open. Her mother, a short, rotund woman with bright green eyes, greeted them with a smile that quickly turned to a concerned frown as she looked Sir over.

"Hey, Mom!" Brie gave her a quick hug to ease the tension. "This is my boyfriend, Thane Davis. Thane, this is my mom, Marcy Bennett."

Sir held out his hand and smiled. "It is an honor to meet you, Mrs. Bennett."

Her mother took his hand and blushed as she shook it. Brie could see it in her mom's eyes—that glimmer of attraction towards the commanding Dom—but it disappeared as soon as her father entered the picture.

"What is your name, sir?" her father asked, in a voice already laced with judgment.

Despite the uncomfortable moment, Brie burst out in a nervous giggle. *Sir…*

Her dad glowered at her before addressing Sir again. "Well?"

"My name is Thane Davis, Mr. Bennett." He held out his hand. "It's a pleasure to meet you."

Her father looked at his offered hand with disdain before engaging him. "I am a frank man, Mr. Davis."

"I find frank talk refreshing," Sir replied.

"What the hell is a man my age doing with my little girl?"

Sir seemed untroubled and asked, "Wouldn't it be best to discuss this inside?"

Brie's mother scanned the neighborhood, as if suddenly afraid the whole world could hear them. She stammered, "Oh! Yes… Come in, come in," gesturing them into the house frantically.

Sir put his hand on the small of Brie's back as he guided her forward. It helped to calm her already frayed nerves. This was not starting off well…

They sat down in the front room, the unused room reserved only for company. Brie's first instinct was to kneel at Sir's feet, feeling in need of his comfort. Instead, she sat beside him.

Her parents sat opposite them with disparaging looks on their faces.

Sir responded to her dad's question. "Actually, there is only an eleven-year difference between us, Mr. Bennett."

"Only?" He turned to Brie. "You never mentioned you were dating an older man, daughter."

Brie bowed her head in shame, knowing now it had been a mistake. "Dad, I love Thane. I didn't mention his age because I wanted you and Mom to meet him in person. I was sure once you met him, you would see what an exceptional person he is."

Her mother frowned again. "We did not send you to California so some 'producer' could turn your head with promises of fame."

Brie shook her head, mortified at her accusation that he was a lecher. "Mom—"

Sir put his hand on Brie's knee and smiled. "I assure you that my intentions are honorable…and," he added drolly, "I am no producer."

"Don't tell me you want to marry her!" her father retorted.

Brie blushed a deep shade of red. Marriage had never been discussed and it was embarrassing that her father was bringing it up now.

She was grateful when Sir answered him with unrattled calm. "No. However, you should know that I care deeply for your daughter."

Her dad laughed. "Oh, I can just imagine how deep your feelings are for my little girl."

Brie squeaked, "Dad! It's not that way at all! We love each other."

His smile was patronizing. "Brie, I believe you have fallen in love with this shyster, but I don't believe for a second your feelings are returned. He wants only one thing from you."

Brie covered her face with her hands. It was dreadful to have Sir treated with such brazen disrespect by her parents. She wanted to curl up and die.

Sir's voice remained reasonable. "If it were as you say, would I be here meeting you in person?"

"I think you came hoping to throw the wool over our eyes, but we aren't twenty-two like Brianna."

Sir sat farther back on the mauve couch, a subtle show of confidence in an uncomfortable situation. "I'm sure you agree that this visit was necessary. I'm in a serious relationship with your daughter and came to meet you out of respect for your position as Brie's parents."

"Is that right?" Brie's father asked sarcastically. He turned to Brie and demanded, "Have you been over to meet *his* parents?"

Brie gasped and then looked down, shaking her head. Oh, how she didn't want to go there—not *now*!

"My father is dead and my mother left when I was fifteen. We have been estranged ever since."

Brie's mother's expression instantly changed. "Oh…I am so terribly sorry."

But leave it to her father to go right for the jugular. "How did he die, Mr. Davis?"

Sir did not hesitate. "Suicide."

His answer had Brie's mother wringing her hands and saying repeatedly, "I'm so, so sorry…"

However, Brie's father had the opposite reaction. "That alone makes you unsuitable for our only child. Your father was unstable. I do not want an emotionally weak man to have anything to do with my daughter."

Brie could not remain quiet any longer, horrified by her father's callous response. "Dad! Thane's father was a famous violinist who suffered a tragic death. What a terrible thing to say."

Her mother gasped. "Not Alonzo Davis, the musician who killed himself after—?"

Sir interrupted, his voice devoid of emotion. "Yes, Alonzo was my father."

For once, Brie's dad remained silent. It seemed her mother couldn't stand the suffocating hush, so she popped out of her seat. "Let me get us some tea. Everyone likes tea, right?" She disappeared into the kitchen before anyone could answer.

It broke Brie's heart that Sir had wanted to meet her parents, but all they had done was put him down from the moment they'd opened the door. "Should we go, Thane?" she asked, feeling desperate to run.

"No," he replied, squeezing her knee reassuringly.

The room stayed uncomfortably silent until her mother returned with the iced tea. She poured everyone a glass and sat down, asking in an overly pleasant tone, "So, how did you two meet?"

Sir was kind enough to humor her. "I met Brie at the tobacco shop where she worked."

Her father instantly picked up on that. "Worked?" He looked at Brie with concern. "Don't you work there anymore?"

"No, Dad. Yesterday was my last day. Thane wants me working on the documentary I mentioned. The one the well-known producer has shown interest in."

Her mom piped up, "Oh, you mean the documentary about your girlfriends learning the ropes in Hollywood?"

Brie struggled not to snicker. *Learning the ropes…*

Sir stated proudly, "Your daughter has real talent as a filmmaker. I asked her to quit so that she can devote her time solely to the project."

Brie's father's eyes narrowed. "What? Are you supporting my daughter now? Paying her rent?"

"We're living together," Brie corrected.

"Are you, now?" her father said, looking straight at Sir.

"We are in a committed relationship," Sir replied smoothly.

"What kind of child have I raised?" her mother lamented. "You barely know this man and you're already living with him?"

Sir's reply was quick and to the point. "What kind of daughter have you raised? You have raised an intelligent, talented woman, one who is respected and cherished by those who know her. Simply put, you have raised a beautiful person, both inside and out."

Brie blushed under the unreserved praise of her Master.

Her parents were left speechless. Finally, her father cleared his throat. "Yes, we agree that Brie is an exceptional woman, but she is still young. I don't like the idea of her being fettered in a relationship."

Brie wanted to giggle. *Fettered…* Her father's choice of words was perfect.

"I will say it again. I care deeply for your daughter."

"I don't trust you," her father shot back. "After what happened between your parents, I don't see how you could be anything but a philanderer or an utter control freak. Either way, neither is healthy for my daughter."

Sir didn't seem intimidated in the least. "Although I do admit to a need for a certain level of control, I too want what's best for Brie. If it turns out I am not what she needs, I'll willingly step aside."

Brie's father made a grunting sound as he sat back in his chair, digesting Sir's words.

Her mother pleaded with her, "Brie, honey, why the rush? I don't understand how you can go from just meeting each other to living together. Give it time; give yourself a little space before you commit yourself to something like that."

Her dad looked at Sir suspiciously. "Why did you really come today, Mr. Davis?"

"I plan to take your daughter out of the country. We are headed to Russia and I felt it was important for all of us to meet."

"What?!" Her dad turned to her mother, a look of sheer disgust on his face. He turned back to Sir. "Just because your father was rich and famous does not give you the right to do whatever you want or…" he looked directly at Brie, "take whatever you want."

Brie couldn't stay quiet any longer. "Dad, this isn't a case of me asking your permission to go to Russia. We came today so you could meet the man I love. That's it. I don't need your permission for anything. I'm twenty-two, remember?"

He stood up, fuming. "Do you know how stupid that sounds? Twenty-two. You're still just a kid!"

She closed her eyes, collecting herself before replying, "I'm an adult, whether you want to face that fact or not."

"You're not an adult!" her father answered emphatically.

Her mom moved over to her father, putting a hand on his shoulder. "Bill, we need to be reasonable here. Brie could have kept us in the dark and taken off to God knows where." Her eyes started to tear up. "She's all we have. I couldn't bear not knowing where she is."

"My point exactly," Sir stated.

Brie's father snarled at him, "You do not have permission to take her, Mr. Davis."

Sir nodded his understanding but answered calmly, "Then I leave the decision to your daughter."

It was time to change the traditional dynamics of child and parent. Her parents needed to see her as an adult, free to make her own decisions—

and her own mistakes. "I respect you both, but I am choosing to go with Thane to Russia. Either you can accept my decision…or not."

Her father wouldn't even look Sir in the eye when he spoke. "I do not approve of you, Mr. Davis. However, it is obvious I have no influence over my daughter so I will do as she says and accept it, but do not think for one second I am happy about this."

"I will take good care of her."

Her father snorted in disgust.

"Don't you dare let anything happen to our Brie, Mr. Davis," her mother added. Her mother grabbed her daughter in a death grip. "I've missed you so much, Brie darling! We never talk anymore…and now this."

Her father said gruffly, "If anything should happen—anything at all—little girl, you call me and I will be on the next flight out to get you."

"You don't have to worry, Dad," she said, reaching out to give her father a hug. He moved out of her reach, making his feelings painfully clear.

"It will be unnecessary to come for her, Mr. Bennett." Sir said, getting up and pulling a card from his breast pocket. He held it out to the man. "But if you wish to speak to her, this is the number to reach both of us. Keep in mind the time difference and the fact we will be out sightseeing much of the day and into the night."

Her father refused to take the card.

Her mom let go of Brie to take it from Sir. "Thank you." She added apologetically, "I am truly sorry about what happened to your family."

Brie saw it even if her mother did not—that brief flicker of pain before Sir replied. "It was an unfortunate situation but life moves on, as it should."

"Yes," her mom agreed, patting him hesitantly on the shoulder.

Sir smiled kindly. "It was nice to meet you, Mrs. Bennett." He looked over to her father. "To meet you both." Then he glanced at Brie. "Shall we?"

Her mother waved as they walked out to the car, but her father just stared at Brie with an expressionless face. It was terrible to feel this new and unwelcome barrier between them, but she knew Sir had been right to insist on meeting her parents. It was better to be upfront than to hide like a child.

When they were back in the car, Brie looked at Sir sadly. "My parents were awful to you."

"If they had reacted any different, I would have been concerned. They love you and want to protect you. That is a healthy response, in my estimation."

Brie leaned over and kissed him on the cheek. "You're a good man, Sir."

He chuckled lightly. "And now that we have that over, our trip can begin. I hope you're ready, little sub." His smirk made the butterflies start again.

*Oh, Master…*

# Sir's Past

When they boarded the overseas jet, Brie's mouth fell open. She had never been on a plane so humongous before. Sir escorted her to a first class seat. She giggled as she went to sit down. She had never thought she'd fly first class—ever.

On the seat she found a blanket, an eye mask, slippers and even premium bottled water. She gathered all of them in her arms and smiled at Sir. "I feel so special."

He chuckled. "You're easily satisfied."

Sir stuffed his items in the seat pocket in front of him. Brie followed suit. Then she started playing with the button on her chair. Instead of the seat only going back a fraction of an inch, this one kept going and going until she was practically lying down. She giggled at Sir. "It's like a bed!"

He had an amused look on his face. "You might want to put that up, Brie. People are still boarding the plane."

She immediately adjusted the seat back and looked out of the window at the workers below. They were busy loading the last of the luggage. "I can't believe I'm going to another country, Sir."

"I am sure this will be the first of many trips. I suspect you'll be traveling often when you're filming."

She turned to him, filled with gratitude. "You think I'll succeed, don't you?"

"I never had a doubt after watching your entrance video."

She blushed. "Well…that one doesn't really count. It was a stationary camera shot. Not my best work."

"I disagree. It was an award-worthy short."

She giggled again, burying her head in his shoulder. Brie lay against him until the plane was ready to take off. She looked out of the window when the engines started. "I love this part. The roar of the engine, the shaking of the plane, and then that sick little feeling you get when you first lose contact with the ground." Brie sighed happily. "I love flying!"

"We'll see how much you love it ten hours from now."

She looked at him and smiled. "Sir, anywhere with you is lovely."

He shook his head, but she saw the slight upturn to his lips.

Once the plane was in the air, Sir put his seat all the way back. She followed his lead, turning towards him so she could stare at his handsome face.

"Don't just stare at me, Brie."

She looked away, embarrassed. "I can't help it, Sir."

He chuckled softly. "Make conversation then."

With permission given, Brie gazed at him again but was silent for a moment. Her heart thumped in her chest as she built up courage to say the one thing that had been bothering her since their visit with her family.

"Sir, my parents seem to know more about your past than I do."

He looked at her with a somber expression. "Yes, it is unfair to you."

She didn't press further, but she waited expectantly.

He took a deep breath but then said nothing. Minutes passed in strained silence. Brie consoled herself that he still wasn't ready to talk about it. She was surprised when he finally spoke.

"You should know that my parents were envied when they were young. The two complemented each other like the sun complements the moon. He shone with brilliance; she equaled him in her loving reflection." He smiled, as if he was remembering something treasured.

But his smile faltered as he continued, "Unfortunately, my mother grew jealous of his fame, no longer content to act as his reflection. She found power in cheating on him behind his back. I became aware of her infidelity when I was thirteen, but I kept it hidden, thinking I was protecting him…" Sir paused. When he continued, his jaw was clenched as if it physically hurt him to speak the words.

"I remember the day as if it were yesterday. I can still smell the exhaust fumes from the school bus as it pulled up to my stop. I saw her car and *his*, and then my dad drove up in his Ferrari. He wasn't scheduled to arrive for another two days. I pushed my way through the line, trying to get off the bus, hoping I could prevent what was about to play out."

Sir closed his eyes, obviously reliving it in his mind. "I ran, but he had already disappeared into the house. I headed directly for the bedroom even though I knew it was too late. I entered the room to see my father pointing a gun at my mother. He vacillated between aiming it at her and the naked boy toy. For a second, I thought he would shoot her dead, but then he lowered it. The only thing he asked her was, 'Why?' My mother said nothing."

He opened his eyes and stared blankly ahead. "He turned to me and said, 'I'm sorry, son', put the gun to his head and pulled the trigger before I could move to stop him." Sir's voice caught, but he cleared his throat and continued. "I ran to him, begging him to hold on even though I knew…"

Sir turned to Brie, the rawness of his pain written clearly on his face. "I watch the life ebb from his eyes…heard his death rattle. It is a terrible thing to witness—the death of a loved one." Sir looked away. In the barest whisper he added, "It haunts me to this day."

Silent tears rolled down Brie's cheeks as she put her hand on Sir's and squeezed tightly, wanting to impart her strength.

His voice was devoid of emotion when he spoke again. "My mother was a convincing liar. She kept my father's estate and all his assets while she trashed his reputation to protect hers. She stripped everything from him… So I disowned her, legally distancing myself from the whore."

Brie braved a question. "How did you move on from it, Sir?"

"I am my father's son. I must strive for excellence in everything I do. I went to college, graduated with honors. Even though I had sworn myself away from women, my Italian blood would not be satisfied. I was wired to explore the female body. Thankfully, Rytsar introduced me to the BDSM lifestyle in college. Although he has preferences that I do not share, I found the lifestyle itself fascinating. Yet, it was the level of trust required in the D/s relationship that was the most appealing. It was the only sane choice for me."

"I'm glad you found a way to move past it, Sir."

"On the outside it may appear that way, but for most of my adult life I have been emotionally dead. My satisfaction has been in helping others explore their limits, because I have been unwilling to explore mine."

"And now, Sir?"

In answer, he covered her in a blanket and put the mask over her eyes. "Try to sleep, Brie. I have a feeling Durov is going to keep us entertained from the moment we land."

Brie woke to Sir's light touch. "We're here."

She popped up in her seat and pulled off the mask, then quickly gathered her things. "I can't believe it!" she whispered, conscious of the other travelers still snoozing. She was thrilled to be one of the first ones off the plane. Sir led her to the immigration area, where she was confronted with the long lines.

"And this is where we wait," Sir said with resignation.

Brie pulled out her passport in anticipation, but the lines weren't moving. She craned her neck to see what the holdup was just as a severe-looking security guard with mirrored sunglasses grabbed the passport from her hand.

"Hey!"

Sir tried to take it back, but two similar men showed up. The one with her passport took Brie by the arm, dragging her away. Sir attempted to follow her, but the other two men held him back. He fought against them, but was unable to break free.

"Brie, I will come for you! Don't do anything or say anything until I find you."

"Sir!" she cried, reaching out for him.

She was led to a small room filled with black and white monitors. Once they were inside, the door was locked and she was directed to sit down by a daunting woman built like a bulldozer. Brie sat down reluctantly, noticing another male guard behind her. She had no idea what was happening and was tempted to make a break for the door.

The large woman snapped a command Brie did not understand. The woman said it again and tried to spread her legs apart.

Brie fought against her, slapping the woman's hands away. *Are they going to do a body cavity search?* She began to panic.

"*Nyet!*" Brie cried, saying one of three words she knew in Russian.

The male guard behind her leaned in, inches from her face. All she could see was the reflection of her own terrified expression. He said in perfect English, "Open your legs."

*I know that voice!*

Brie timidly removed the sunglasses and looked into his piercing blue eyes. "Rytsar."

He stood up and rocked the room with his laughter. "*Radost moya,* you recognize your previous Master. I'm impressed."

Brie glanced at the screens and saw a camera shot of Sir. He was still fighting against the two guards. Rytsar followed her gaze. "Ah, yes. My friend is not happy, is he?"

He nodded to the woman, who immediately left. "I wanted to spare you both the long lines, but… Well, I could not help amusing myself. What do you expect from a sadist?"

*A sadist?*

She looked at the friendly Russian Dom again, believing he was just making a joke. Brie turned her attention back to the screen and watched as Sir was taken out of the line.

Rytsar's mirth greeted Sir as he entered the small room. "All is well, *moy droog.* Your sub has not been touched."

Sir held out his arms and Brie raced to them, grateful to be in his protective embrace.

"She seems to be satisfied with you. Would not even open her legs for me," Rytsar said, chuckling.

Sir kissed the top of Brie's head. "I'd forgotten your propensity for practical jokes. Should have seen this one coming."

"Yes, I was surprised you did not. However, it was far more amusing that you didn't." He smiled charmingly at them both. "Shall we be off, then? I am anxious to introduce you to my friends."

Brie was surprised to learn that Rytsar lived in an old mansion. She should have suspected it with all the aristocrat talk, but she'd never quite believed it until they pulled up to the large estate. The impressive red brick home even sported narrow turrets, giving it a regal appearance.

"This is really your home?" she asked in awe.

"It has been in the Durov line for centuries," he replied without arrogance.

Brie glanced at Sir. He seemed unaffected by the grandeur. She decided to take his lead and not react to the splendor of the place, even as they walked through the halls and she saw the gold accents, painted ceilings, and antique furniture begging to be admired.

"Please take a moment to refresh yourselves before you join us in the dungeon. My friends are dying to meet my American comrade and his new sub."

All Brie heard was the word 'dungeon'.

"I assume we just head downwards?" Sir inquired.

"Titov will direct you." Rytsar pointed to a servant, who nodded curtly.

"Fine." Sir took Brie's hand and guided her upstairs. Once inside the privacy of the room, Sir gathered her into his arms. "I know this seems a bit much, but I did warn you. Rytsar has eccentric tastes. It's not too surprising he has his own dungeon."

Brie thought back to Rytsar's statement that he was a sadist. It conjured all kinds of frightening scenarios. "Will I be asked to scene, Sir?" she squeaked.

"No. Tonight we are guests and will simply observe. It is no different than visiting one of our clubs back home. I suspect his friends want to show off their various talents. However, you should be aware that Rytsar's tastes run on the sadistic side. I am sure his friends are of equal bent."

Brie sighed nervously. Although she had witnessed a few scenes at The Haven, it was not something she had personally sought out. Not having expressed interest in masochism, she had been spared the more sadistic side of BDSM play during her training.

"Take this opportunity to explore new horizons, Brie. It is part of the reason I chose to come here. It is my belief you cannot know your desires or limits unless you expose yourself to them."

Brie understood Sir's reasoning and even agreed with it, and yet she still felt uneasy about exploring the darker side of pain.

# The Dungeon

The two followed Titov down a long flight of circular stairs. Before they reached the bottom, Brie heard screams echoing from the other side of the door. She swallowed hard and tried to keep a peaceful countenance.

Sir whispered in her ear, "Remember, the subs are masochists. This is their preference."

Brie nodded as they entered. The cries quickly died down as everyone turned to look at them.

Rytsar's voice rose over the crowd. "Welcome, *moy droog*!"

He walked over to greet them both. "We have been waiting impatiently for you." He turned to the crowd. "Please, continue the entertainment."

Immediately a whip cracked and a piercing scream filled the air.

Rytsar gestured proudly to the expansive underground room. "I have it all here. The ultimate playground of kink." Brie glanced around the dark and ominous dungeon. The floor was made of unforgiving stone, the walls of rough brick, and large wooden support beams dotted the room. Attached to the beams were chains and cuffs of various lengths and materials, some of which were already adorned with naked submissives.

In the farthest corner, Brie noticed several large metal cages. But the wall that held a plethora of whips, floggers, canes and other tools—the number of which was staggering—captivated her imagination and left her speechless.

The anguished cry of a submissive grabbed her attention. She glanced around at women bound to St. Andrew's crosses, benches, or leather swings, being whipped, fucked, or tortured with unknown instruments. Brie struggled to take it all in.

Sir felt her tension and suggested, "Why don't we visit the scenes individually, Durov? You can explain to my sub what is transpiring."

"Certainly," he said, nodding to Brie.

Rytsar guided them over to a woman spread out on a bench, bound by chains. She had a large metal collar around her neck, making it impossible for her to move. "Andreev enjoys subjecting his sub to clitoral torture." The Dom had already attached nipple clamps, but there was an extra chain that led down to her pussy. He was in the process of pulling back the hood of her clit and attaching the clamp to the loose skin. "Clit exposure allows for more intense play," Rytsar explained.

The Dom rubbed her naked clit, making the sub whimper pitifully. He then picked up a lit candle and leaned in, licking her erect clit before dripping the wax directly on the exposed sex. The girl screamed, but didn't call her safe word. Brie saw clearly that her pussy was red and swollen with excitement.

A more lustful cry caught Brie's attention. She turned to a lanky female chained to a pole being whipped with a cat o' nine tails. Rytsar grinned. "My personal favorite, the cat o' nines. Such exquisite torture."

She struggled to wrap her head around the fact Rytsar was a sadist. He had been demanding but playful the day she'd scened with him. Based on his actions that day, she never would have suspected his underlying need to deliver pain. Brie suddenly realized that what had been a mind-blowing experience for her must have been mere child's play for him.

As Rytsar continued to show off his dungeon, she kept glancing back at the girl on the pole. Despite her pained screams, the Dom had already made the girl come twice. Brie couldn't help wondering if she was missing out somehow. All of the women in this dungeon seemed to be thoroughly enjoying themselves despite—or because of—the pain.

Later that night, when she was lying in bed, safe in Sir's arms, she broached the subject. "Master, do you have sadistic tendencies?"

He did not answer her question; instead, he correctly read into her inquiry and turned it back on her. "Has tonight's exposure awakened a latent desire, téa?"

*Clever Master.*

"I was frightened by some of the things I saw tonight, but I wonder, Sir…is it a true fear or just fear of the unknown?"

"I noticed your interest in the cat o' nines," he commented, nibbling her neck. "Would you like to taste its sting?"

She hesitated, the idea of it unsettling—yet alluring. "Yes."

"Then I shall speak to Durov tomorrow."

"What? Aren't you going to scene with me?"

"No. I shall defer to Rytsar Durov's expertise."

"Then I would rather not," she answered quickly.

"I believe you should," he replied, sucking on her earlobe. "How else can you know your desires if you do not explore them?"

She tried to imagine herself tied to the pole receiving painful strokes, but as much as it enticed her, it frightened her equally as much. "Will you be there with me, Sir?"

"No, Brie. I would detract from the scene." She tensed in his arms. "Do not fret, little sub. I will request a simple whipping session, no audience and no intercourse involved."

She nestled deeper into his arms, suddenly excited and terrified by the prospect of scening with Rytsar. "What if I only last one stroke, Sir?"

"Then you will know where your limit lies. This is an exploration, not an endurance test."

She smiled and kissed him. "Yes, Sir."

She closed her eyes, reminding herself of that the next day, when she was naked and bound in chains before Rytsar.

The broad-chested Russian removed his shirt and smiled down at her. "I am thrilled to introduce you to my 'nines', *radost moya.*" He held up his multi-tailed whip reverently so she could admire it. The baldheaded Dom walked around her slowly. She remembered the ferociousness of the dragon tattooed on his muscle-bound shoulder. Like the dragon, Rytsar was beautiful—but dangerous.

Goosebumps rose on her skin as he caressed her with the tails, her body anticipating the violent sensations the knots were about to provoke. He pressed the handle to her lips. "Hold it, while I prepare you."

Brie opened her mouth. The leather tasted of the salt from his hands. He proceeded to twist her hair, pulling her head back. The chains clanked in reaction to the sudden movement. "We shall see how deep your dark fantasies lie, my willing sub." He deftly tied her long hair into a knot with a leather string.

Rytsar had already placed a Magic Wand between her legs and bound her to it so that the vibrator was firmly pressed against her clit. Once her arms were pulled taut above her head, he turned the wicked toy on. She squirmed, her pussy instantly responding to the vibration.

"I use this tool on submissives new to the dungeon. It helps acclimate them to the ecstasy of pain."

She moaned, a quiet panic setting in. The dark oppression of the dungeon, along with the lonely silence of the great room, made her anxious. However, it was the nagging sense of fear that had her entire body on alert.

Rytsar ran his hands over her naked skin. "I can feel your fear, *radost moya*. It…turns me on."

It was disconcerting to think her genuine fear was an aphrodisiac for the Russian Dom.

"Subjecting a submissive to intense pain is much like deflowering a virgin. I enjoy the journey of penetrating a sub's will with my desire."

Brie realized she was breathing erratically and forced herself to calm down, afraid of fainting before they even began. Rytsar walked away from her and towards the wall of instruments. With growing dread, she watched as he thoughtfully chose a malicious-looking flogger from the wall.

Rytsar did not explain himself. He simply walked back to her, cutting the air with the whip to warm up his muscles.

Brie closed her eyes, readying herself for the initial stroke, but *nothing* could prepare her for the fire he evoked. She salivated against the tangy leather of his cat o' nines, trying to keep her cries at bay as Rytsar lashed her back with solid, unyielding strokes. She whimpered loudly, the chains dancing around her as she rocked against the force of his blows. This was no gentle warm-up.

The sound of her lashing echoed throughout the dungeon, filling her ears. She did not drop the handle from her mouth to call out her safe word, but tears ran down her face as she forced herself to accept the onslaught.

When Rytsar finally stopped, the air seemed to still reverberate with the echoes of her surrender. He came up behind her, caressing her cheek. "The tenseness of your muscles, the whimpers against the leather, your sweet, sweet tears…they call to me." He caressed her fiery back and then patted her ass lightly before giving the Wand a small adjustment. Brie moaned as she focused on the intense vibration, which helped to cut through the wall of pain.

"Your body must grow used to my pleasure. Much like a child learning to walk, it requires guidance." His hot breath caressed her ear as he whispered, "You're quite desirable right now, *radost moya.* So vulnerable and scared. It takes strength not to ravish you."

He laid the flogger down and took the cat o' nines from her lips. He slowly wiped her saliva from his instrument, dragging out the anticipation. "This will hurt. I make no excuses. I want it to hurt. I want you to react to the pain." He abruptly threw the towel down and moved into position behind her.

This scene was unlike any experience she'd ever had. He wasn't trying to 'carry' her into subspace; he was taking her there kicking and screaming. *I want this*, she reminded herself as fresh tears ran down her cheeks. Brie was determined to face this fear, to embrace the experience despite the fact she was terrified.

"Focus on your clit as I strip your back," he commanded, just before the first lash of the tails came into contact with her skin. All illusions of bravery evaporated as she released an all-out scream. There was no controlling this pain. It was sharp, cruel, and more terrible than she'd ever imagined.

A second stroke immediately followed, not allowing her even a breath between. She shrieked, pulling against the chains, her back feeling as if it had been laid open and raw.

Then she felt his hot breath against her cheek. "Color?"

Brie gasped, "Red…ish yellow." There was a part of Brie that desired to know if she could defeat the pain, overcome its fierce power and enter subspace.

"Good," he replied. He reached between her legs and turned up the vibrator.

Brie threw her head back, her whole body shaking. Maybe the next hit would be enlightening or stimulating on a level she hadn't experienced before. *Fear will not control me!*

She heard each step magnified as he repositioned himself. She felt the swing of the cat o' nines before it came anywhere close to her. Her scream erupted when the evil knots impacted on her skin. Hot lava radiated from each point the cat o' nines made contact with her back. Rytsar followed it up with a second, equally forceful stroke.

Brie screamed and then sobbed uncontrollably. This was not pleasurable or enlightening. It simply hurt beyond anything she had ever experienced—and she couldn't handle it any longer. "No more," she begged between sobs, "no more…"

"So soon, *radost moya*?" Rytsar stroked the back of her neck lightly several times and then grasped it possessively, making her knees weak. She swayed back and forth in the chains, while the vibrator between her legs continued its relentless teasing.

"I have so much more I wish you to experience."

There was an urging in her spirit to acquiesce to his need, but her lessons at the Submissive Training Center had prepared her for moments such as this. She shook her head and called out clearly, "Red."

He chuckled. She felt his sharp teeth as he bit the back of her neck, wrapping his arm around her tightly. A deep and startling orgasm shook through her body. Brie twitched in her bonds until it had passed, completely stunned by it.

Rytsar kissed the bite marks he'd left before releasing her from the chains and removing the toy from between her legs. He had to support her as she stumbled to a padded table nearby. The Dom directed her to lie on her stomach.

She jumped when she first felt the icy salve. Rytsar smoothed it onto her wounds as he spoke in a low, calming voice. He shared his memories of their first encounter, recalling details that brought the scene back to life.

"My American captive…beautiful, passionate, frightened but willing. It is a good memory for me."

She smiled, nodding her agreement. Brie vividly recalled that day. She'd been inexperienced when he'd won her at the auction, yet he had managed to fulfill her fantasy in every sense of the word while making her feel worthy of his attentions.

As Rytsar continued to reminisce, his masculine hands gently tended to the wounds he had inflicted. His aftercare was so tender, so kind; it almost made up for the pain she'd endured under his hands.

When he had finished, Rytsar helped her off the table and gathered her into his arms, albeit carefully. "You did well, *radost moya.* Your Master will be pleased."

She shook her head against his chest, not buying it.

He murmured seductively, "I can help you learn to enjoy the pain."

She had no doubt he had the ability, but it was not what she desired. Brie worried Sir would be disappointed as she walked behind Rytsar back to her Master.

Sir immediately put down his work and stood up when they entered the room. "How was the experience?" he asked Brie.

Her bottom lip trembled in answer.

He turned to Rytsar with a look of concern. "How did she fare, Durov?"

"It was a decent beginning."

Sir looked her over again, his eyes unreadable.

Rytsar kissed the back of Brie's hand before returning her to Sir's care. She dropped to the floor and bowed stiffly before the Russian Dom. "Thank you, Rytsar Durov."

He nodded his acknowledgement and slapped Sir on the shoulder. "Trainable, but no masochist."

"I suspected as much," Sir replied evenly.

Rytsar bade them goodbye and left them to their own devices.

Sir helped Brie off the floor and smoothed her worried brow with his fingers. "That is fortunate news, téa, for I am no sadist."

# Performance

Rytsar spent the daylight hours while they were there taking the two all over Moscow, introducing them to the cuisine, the culture, and national treasures like St. Basil's Cathedral in Red Square, and the quiet grandeur of the Novodevichy Cemetery. Brie was amazed by the history represented all around her and the many riches to be found in the numerous museums. However, it was the smiles of the Russian people she treasured most. She had expected stoic faces greeting her on the crowded streets, but she was met by grins and snatches of English wherever she went.

Sir had specifically instructed her to act vanilla outside the confines of Rytsar's home. "I want you to interact with the culture. It will serve you well in your career. Experience the nuances of every culture you encounter."

That freedom allowed Brie to fully drink in the foreign environment. She smelled, touched and tasted everything she could, and interacted with anyone who gave her a sideways glance.

When they weren't sightseeing, they were enjoying the unique entertainment provided by their host. Rytsar spared no expense showing his good friends all that Russia had to offer, including a private performance of a well-known Russian opera. However, there was a condition to admission to this particular performance.

As Sir zipped up her sleek, crystal-studded gown, he casually mentioned to Brie, "Durov has asked you and me to entertain his guests this evening."

She waited until he'd finished to turn around and ask him, "I thought we were going to an opera, Sir?"

"We are. Our performance takes place after the show."

Her heart skipped a beat. "What kind of performance?"

He turned her back towards the mirror, looking at her in the reflection. "Durov has asked us to scene together. He wishes his comrades to observe a different type of power play. Durov was greatly influenced by what he observed visiting America as a college student."

Sir had insisted she wear her hair up for the evening, giving him free access to her neck. He kissed the nape of it tenderly. "It changed the flavor of Durov's sadism, so to speak."

"May I ask how, Sir?"

Sir looked at her thoughtfully. "Suffice to say, his partner's satisfaction is of consequence to him now. It was not always the case."

Brie lowered her gaze, a shudder going through her. She had watched Rytsar scene several times since her session with him. He was hard on his submissives, sometimes frighteningly so, but he knew how to please them and he was affectionate afterwards. What he had been like before, she could only imagine.

It made her think, though… All of Rytsar's friends were sadists. The submissives they played with were experienced masochists.

"Is something wrong?" Sir asked.

She forced herself to reply, even though she was reluctant to voice her inadequacy to him. "Sir, I am but a child compared to the submissives these men are used to."

"Do you put down my sub so easily, téa?"

Brie bowed her head, smiling to herself. How easy Sir made it to be his. "No, Master."

"Tonight we will play out a short scene of my choosing. Nothing elaborate. Just a Master playing with his sub for the pleasure of others."

She nodded, still looking at the floor.

"Téa."

She looked up, gazing into his warm, confident eyes as he turned her back around. "All that is required is that you please me. No one else in the room matters."

Brie breathed in his truth. *No one else matters…*

Sir escorted her down to the front row of the mini-theatre in Rytsar's mansion, so that all the men in attendance could admire her. Brie's nipples instantly became erect in response to their intense stares. Everyone knew they were the entertainment for the evening—after the opera.

Brie sat down with practiced poise in between Rytsar and Sir. The Russian nodded to her pleasantly, but said nothing. He lifted his finger and the lights dimmed just before the curtains opened.

Sir leaned towards her and whispered, "This is the Russian opera *Ruslan and Lyudmila.* It's one of the few Russian operas that are more…fanciful in nature." He kissed her cheek. "I think you will enjoy it, téa."

He was acting as if they were simply there to enjoy the performance, so she followed his example and focused solely on the opera. Brie was enthralled by the lavish costumes and extravagant sets that graced the stage. The actors must have been true performers because their voices were exceptional, ringing strong and true. The same could be said of the talented musicians. Rytsar had not provided a simple home performance; this was on par with any Broadway show.

Brie held her breath when the flying dragon appeared on the stage. The huge creature was made of billowing bolts of gold silk. It was enchanting and otherworldly. But she was horrified when the opera took a brutal turn, making her question Sir's assurance she would enjoy it. It wasn't until the final act that all was made right. The ending was wonderful and sweet, the way only fairytales can be.

Brie clapped her hands zealously when the curtains finally closed.

"I see that you enjoyed yourself," Rytsar commented with satisfaction.

"Very much, Rytsar Durov. It was…magnificent."

"I would have to agree," Sir interjected. "You surpassed my expectations."

"Not an easy thing to do, peasant," the Russian replied, laughing. "But I was determined."

"It's an experience I will never forget," Brie exclaimed. "Never!"

"I hope to say the same of your performance."

Brie suddenly felt lightheaded. She was about to scene in front of the prominent Doms of Moscow.

"Without the expensive costumes and sets, all eyes will be on you," Rytsar continued. "Not exactly fair, is it?"

"None of it is necessary," Sir replied matter-of-factly. "In fact, I would go as far as to say it is not the action itself, but the intention behind it, that truly carries a scene."

Sir tilted Brie's chin up with his finger, giving her a lingering look that said clearly, *I lead, you follow.* She nodded in understanding and then proceeded to melt when his firm lips met hers. She stood up with renewed confidence when Sir offered his hand.

Rytsar led them out of the theater and across the hall. Servants on either side of two massive wooden doors opened them as the group approached. Brie swallowed nervously as she passed through the doorway into the unusual room. The floor was made of dark wood a shade just shy of midnight and glossed to a perfect sheen. A long, red carpet made a path to a small, low-lying table made of gold in the center of the large room.

The table itself was encircled by unlit candles lining the floor. As she walked towards it, she noted the single line of chairs had been set six feet back, surrounding the table in a horseshoe pattern. The unusual seating allowed not only for the unobstructed view of the table, but also of a huge mirror on the opposite wall.

Brie began trembling as Sir guided her to the table. She had to step over the barrier of candles that separated them from the audience. Sir placed his hands on her shoulders, turning her towards the mirror. "Look at me, téa." She looked into the reflection as the men gathered and sat down. She understood now—the mirror was there to enhance the experience for both the participants and the observers.

He whispered in her ear, "Focus on your Master."

As she looked at Sir in the mirror, her confidence returned. When all of the gentlemen were seated, the doors closed and Brie heard the distinct sound of a large metal bar sliding into place. It added a thrill of fear, knowing they were locked in. For better or worse, she was to remain until the scene was complete. Thankfully, she was in Sir's trusted hands.

Rytsar spoke to the group in Russian. After his speech, he repeated it in English for their benefit. "We have come tonight to enjoy the unique performance of Sir Davis and his submissive, téa. They have witnessed our brand of dominance and have consented to share a scene of their own. Sit back and enjoy their unique dynamic."

Rytsar nodded to Sir before he sat down. The circle of Doms was so near that she could hear their subtle movements and even smell their various colognes. It was unsettling to have the audience so close. Brie looked into the mirror again. *Sir…*

She watched as he slowly unzipped her gown. Then he kissed her neck as he eased the material off her shoulders. The dress fell and pooled at her feet. Suddenly she was naked except for her garters, fishnet stockings and six-inch heels. Exactly the way Sir preferred her.

His hands roved over her breasts, and then he began pinching and squeezing her nipples as he lowered his lips onto her bare shoulder. His eyes did not leave her as he looked at her reflection. She was mesmerized by his hungry gaze.

Brie tilted her chin upwards and pressed the back of her head against his chest, giving in to the magic of his caress. She tapped into the sexual energy of those around her and ground her body against her Master.

He lifted her right arm above her head and ran his fingers down the side of her breast, the concave of her waist and the swell of her hips, tickling her skin with his light caress. Then he turned to a servant, who handed him a long red cord. Sir doubled up the rope and then began to tie it around her right forearm, starting at the wrist, creating an intricate, braided pattern as he went.

She watched, fascinated by the Kinbaku feel of it. He tied the cord off at her elbow, leaving the ends to hang like a fringe. He leaned in and said, for her ears only, "A warrior's cuff."

Her interest was piqued as he raised her arm again. The vibrant shade of red radiated power and his words infused her with a sense of courage and purpose. She smiled at Sir in the reflection, suddenly feeling worthy of this public display.

One of her Master's hands glided over her stomach, then moved between her thighs, while the other captured her breast. She gasped as his fingers slid into her moist depths. She glanced at the mirror again. It was a visual representation of their relationship. He the masterful, confident Dominant and she the powerful, yet wholly devoted sub.

"Lie facedown on the table, arms and legs outstretched," he commanded quietly.

Brie slid onto the table with catlike grace and laid herself out for him. Sir took his time as he removed her shoes, stockings and garters. His movements were sensual and confident, making her wet with anticipation.

She was startled to hear the sound of chains as Sir pulled up a cuff from underneath the table. It was attached to the leg. He secured her wrist, glancing at her briefly with a smirk. He continued until she was completely chained to the table.

So far he had done nothing more than undress her and bind her, but she was already quivering with need. It would not take much to set her body humming.

Sir nodded and a servant handed him a large swab and container. Brie glanced to the right and saw another servant standing with an extinguisher held elegantly in his hands. *So it's to be fire play tonight.* No wonder Sir had insisted she put her hair up.

The servant lit the swab and stepped back just before the lights lowered. The room was completely silent. There was no accompanying music for the scene. Brie found it made for a more intimate connection with the audience. Every movement of Sir's, every gasp from her lips was heard by their observers.

And Brie did gasp when she felt the cool alcohol coat her skin. Sir began with her back, making simple designs, lighting them on fire before he swept them out with his hand. He moved down her legs and even lit the soles of her feet, making her yelp when heat from the flames licked the sensitive areas.

As with the undressing, Sir took his time, building anticipation for both Brie and the audience. She noticed that Sir let the flames burn longer as he advanced in the scene. It required more of her concentration, as the heat was intense. Each time she was just about to cry out 'yellow', Sir would wipe the flames from her skin.

He began creating more detailed patterns on her back. Brie wondered if the designs had significance, because the men grunted in response when he lit them on fire.

Then he spoke the first words since he'd asked her to lie on the table. "You and I seek the path together." She felt him making a trail of a spiral circle with the cool liquid. Brie held her breath as he tapped it with the flame. The fire danced down the path he'd created.

He swiped it away and made a new design. She could identify the sideways eight easily, knowing exactly what the symbol meant. "No matter what the future brings, you and I are connected."

Sir lit the symbol for infinity on her back. She let it burn not only on her skin, but into her soul, almost regretful when he swept it away.

He then lit the ring of candles on the floor, one by one, before putting out the fire in his hand.

Brie looked into the mirror and felt a pleasant chill when she realized Sir was staring at her, his look cavernous in its depth and intensity. She could fall into those eyes, losing herself forever…

With the same slow precision he'd used to tie her up, Sir undid her bindings. He pulled her towards him on the smooth surface of the table and ordered her onto her hands and knees. He took off his clothes, his gaze never leaving hers in the reflection of the mirror. He caressed her bare mound gently and then smacked her on the ass. The satisfying sound of it echoed in the room and low chuckles emerged from the men.

He explored her pussy again, concentrating his efforts on her clit. "No coming," he instructed, rubbing at just the right tempo to start the chain reaction. Brie bit her lower lip when Sir slid his fingers into her pussy, going straight for her G-spot. She gasped when he caressed it, rolling his finger over the area slowly, pleasurably, until her body pulsed with electricity. He pulled his finger out and replaced it with his shaft.

Brie moaned when she felt his cock press against her. He smiled in the mirror, shaking his head in response to her unspoken request. Sir thrust forcefully, filling her with one solid stroke.

She arched her back to take the full length of him, holding back tears of joy as her Master claimed her. Brie watched as he grabbed her hips and began fucking her without restraint. It was an erotic scene, with the red warrior cuff he'd made contrasting against her white skin, the curves of her round ass in his hands, and the look of ecstasy on her Master's face.

Brie let out a primal scream that echoed throughout the room, desperate to express her passion and need for Sir. He met it with a roar of his own as he emptied his essence deep inside her.

He pulled her up to him, one arm across her chest, the other hand concentrated on her pussy. "Come for me, téa," he whispered through gritted teeth.

Brie threw her head back and allowed all the emotion and sexual electricity to release at once. She writhed in his arms as the powerful climax washed over her, blurring her senses. Afterwards, she lay against him like a ragdoll.

Sir murmured in her ear, "My beautiful goddess, see how you have captivated the audience."

Brie glanced discreetly at the men surrounding them. Their eyes were trained on her, holding varying looks of admiration and ravenous need. It was empowering to be admired by so many Doms, but she knew the truth.

"Master," she whispered.

"Yes, téa?"

"No one else in the room matters but you."

# The Taking

Katia, one of Rytsar's favorite submissives, insisted on taking Brie out for a day of shopping. With only a few more days left before her return to the States, the Russian beauty with grey-green eyes suggested taking Brie to bargain for souvenirs at the Izmaylovo Market, a place popular for its rows upon rows of folk art, jewelry, and Russian crafts.

Sir gave his blessing, but told Brie before she left, "I have arranged a special rendezvous for us today. Do not get so caught up in your shopping that you resist."

"Of course not, Sir."

"Do not resist," he repeated. She noticed the glint in his eye, hinting of something clandestine. She felt a tingling in her loins. *Is there a kidnapping in my future?*

Brie spent hours perusing the individual shops, constantly on the lookout for Sir, but he didn't show. Eventually she stopped anticipating his arrival and immersed herself in the joys of bargaining with the shopkeepers and joking around with Katia.

After an especially good bargaining session, Katia suggested they celebrate. "Shall we stop for a drink, Bennett-téa?"

Brie liked the cute nickname Katia had given her, combining her last name with Sir's pet name. With her hands already full of purchases, she readily agreed. "Sounds lovely!"

Brie tried to keep up with her long-legged friend as they navigated the backstreets of the city, but it was a struggle with her bulky packages. "Wait,

Katia!" she shouted when the girl rounded a corner ahead of her. Brie ran to catch up, but couldn't find her when she made it to the corner. She ran on to the next street, but couldn't find Katia anywhere. Brie doubled back, not knowing what else to do.

Chills went down her spine when she first heard the confident footsteps behind her. Even though she knew it must be Sir, her survival instincts kicked in. The feeling of being chased was frightening even though it was thrilling, causing a reaction she had no control over. Brie understood she wasn't supposed to show resistance, but she got ready to bolt.

A strong hand covered her mouth, pulling her roughly backwards. Brie's cries were muffled as she fought for her freedom. She was dragged, kicking and screaming, into a van and then everything went dark as the door slammed shut.

"Shhhh…shhhh…" her captor whispered as his powerful arms held her tight against him. Brie realized she was in the hands of Rytsar and whimpered, relieved but still suffering from the adrenaline rush of her abduction.

He forcibly bound her wrists and ankles together, securing them so that she was properly hogtied and unable to move. Before he placed the gag over her mouth he kissed her deeply, his tongue caressing the inside of her mouth.

Brie heard another man speak Russian. He was out of her line of sight, but she could have sworn it was her Master. The men's exchange was lively. If it was indeed Sir, she suspected he was giving Rytsar a hard time for kissing her. The van screeched to a halt and the two switched places, with Rytsar now at the wheel.

She was rolled onto her side and blindfolded. Hands roved over her body, rough and demanding, but she knew with certainty it was Sir. He ripped at her clothes, exposing both her breasts and pussy. Then he pressed his hand against her bare mound and spoke Russian in a low, ominous tone as he pushed his fingers inside her. Instantly, she became a willing but helpless captive.

Brie moaned into the gag when his lips landed on her skin and she felt his teeth on her neck. Sir knew exactly how to subdue her for play. She did not move or make a sound as he rolled her onto her stomach.

Brie wondered if this was a take on her warrior fantasy. She quivered at the thought of her pleasure being increased twofold. There seemed to be only one problem—it didn't appear Sir wanted to share her.

Brie giggled into her gag.

Sir fisted her hair, pulling her head back. He growled into her ear, sending shivers of fearful pleasure as he ripped away the remainder of her skirt and slapped her ass hard. He let go of her then and moved away. It was her punishment for getting out of character.

*That will not happen again, Master*, she promised him silently.

Brie wondered where they were taking her and what their plans were. She knew they weren't going back to the mansion, because the drive had been far too long already. She'd lain on her stomach for so long that she was desperate to catch a full breath. Brie wiggled slightly in an attempt to find a more comfortable position, but was unsuccessful and groaned in distress. Sir quickly turned her on her side, brushing his hand over her body before abandoning her again.

Rytsar said something and the two started arguing. Brie wondered if Rytsar had wanted her to suffer for longer, but he did not have the final say—which seemed to irk the Dom. It was certainly interesting having best friends scene together like this.

Brie was extremely grateful to Sir for rolling her over. Even though Rytsar's hogtie was exciting in its tightness and constraint, she found it far more provocative now that she could breathe again. It gave her the opportunity to fantasize about what was going to happen. Brie couldn't stop herself from imagining taking both Sir and Rytsar at the same time, but she immediately dismissed the idea. Sir had been much too quick to switch places with Rytsar after the Russian had kissed her. It appeared that her Master was a possessive lover… Brie thought back on her warrior fantasy. It revolved around a young maiden losing her virginity. She was curious what 'virginal' territories these two planned to plunder.

The van slowed to a stop and she heard Rytsar exit the vehicle. The door of the van slid open and the northern wind blasted in, taking her breath away. Brie was dragged to the cold edge of the van's floor and covered in a blanket before she was lifted up and carried between both men.

They spoke in hushed tones, possibly going over the sequence of events. The men stopped, and then she heard a key in a lock and the creak of a door being swung open. The instant they walked over the threshold, the warmth and crackling sounds of a fire greeted her. She was carried to another room and thrown unceremoniously on a hard bed.

The blanket was ripped away. She felt the hands of both men pulling off the remnants of her clothes—the squeezing of a breast, the rubbing of her wet clit—and then they were gone.

She listened to them moving about, the clinking of glasses and laughter. Were they celebrating her capture or what was about to commence? Her loins contracted in pleasure at the thought of two highly experienced Doms playing with her.

Brie heard someone enter the room. She whimpered, keeping to her character but also hoping to instigate a response. The low rumble that escaped from his lips let her know it was Rytsar. She stiffened as he approached, unsure of his intent, remembering their last session together quite clearly.

His hands were rough as he untied her from her bonds and removed the gag and blindfold. Then he massaged her limbs, loosening up the muscles that had been bound for so long. But the handsome Dom was not finished. He proceeded to bind her wrists together again. Then his hand trailed down her body until he grasped her ankle and secured it to a leg of the simple bed set in the center of the room. He did the same with the other.

"Please don't hurt me," she begged, keeping in character but secretly meaning it. He grunted in reply, his face remaining stoic—not a reassuring response. Rytsar grabbed her bound wrists and pulled her towards him so that her body was completely stretched and her head hung over the edge of the bed. He secured her wrists so that she was immobile.

Despite her real fear, Brie's pussy responded to his rough treatment, moistening itself for possible entry.

He chuckled to himself as he looked her over, obviously pleased with his work. He called out to Sir, who entered with a smile on his face. Sir's expression quickly changed to one of lustful avarice when he beheld his helpless sub.

He nodded to Rytsar and then gazed back at her. The intensity of his stare made her squirm. She was no longer his submissive—she was his powerless captive.

Sir descended on her, surprising her with the fierceness of his kiss. He grabbed her long curls in one hand and her chin in the other, forcing his tongue deep into her mouth. At the same time, she felt Rytsar's fingers on her inner thigh. He said something wicked-sounding in Russian as he explored the folds of her wet pussy. She groaned as the Dom expertly teased her clit.

Sir's kiss suddenly became more heated. He released her face and his hands moved down to her breasts. He flicked her nipples, making them taut before his lips left hers and he encased one with his eager mouth. He sucked hard on one while continuing to pull and tease the other.

Meanwhile, Rytsar rimmed the entrance of her pussy with his fingers without penetrating. Brie's body instinctively tried to arch in response, but could not because of the restrictive bindings. It caused a gush of moistness that Rytsar rubbed against her already sensitive clit, causing her pussy to contract in delicious pleasure. As soon as he felt her respond, Rytsar pulled away and left the bed.

Brie concentrated on Sir. He'd pressed her breasts together and was sucking each nipple alternately. She thrust her head back, giving in to the electrical current he was shooting directly to her groin.

Then she heard it…the distinctive sound of the Magic Wand. This time Brie's whimper was quite real. Rytsar chuckled under his breath, anticipating the orgasmic torture he was about to unleash. Brie's whole body tensed when she felt the vibration on her pussy.

Sir pinched her nipples as his lips returned to her mouth. She closed her eyes as her whole body began to tremble with the vibration. The Russian Dom was forcing a quick orgasm. However, Rytsar commanded, "*Nyet,*" just as she was about to crest.

Brie cried out as she fought against the desperate need to release. Sir pinched her nipples harder, giving her something to latch onto other than the fire within her loins. With a valiant effort, she avoided the orgasm.

Rytsar seemed pleased and eased up on the vibrating pressure against her clit. Sir got up and moved to the head of the bed. He unzipped his pants and presented her with a raging hard-on.

Brie looked up at him, but did not open her mouth, in keeping with her character. He pressed his cock against her lips. The warmth of it enticed her. She pretended reluctance as she opened her mouth and he forced the head of his shaft inside.

"*Sosat' moy chlen,*" he commanded gruffly.

There was no need to translate that order. Brie began sucking his cock with timid relish. While Sir enjoyed her services, Rytsar pressed the vibrator against her clit with renewed fervor.

Brie moaned on Sir's cock as Rytsar played with her pussy. She took it all in, loving the dual attention. Her mouth was delightfully occupied by her Master while her clit danced with the vibrator.

Master thrust deeper down her throat, demanding full access. She relaxed her muscles to allow his sexy invasion. However, Rytsar was not playing fair and she found herself about to come again without any warning.

"*Nyet,*" the Russian Dom said with amusement.

Brie's muffled cries met his command.

Sir stroked her throat with his hands, feeling the swell of his cock inside her. The pressure of his fingers distracted her enough to stave off the climax, but just barely.

Rytsar eased the vibration momentarily. Brie wasn't sure how much she could take, but all her concerns fell away when Sir held onto her face with both hands and began fucking her mouth. Suddenly, it was just the two of them as he derived pleasure from her throat and she reveled in giving her body over to him. Brie closed her eyes and drifted into an ethereal bliss.

Instead of coming in her throat, Sir pulled out and released on her chest. She moaned with satisfaction as he spread his semen over her skin. It was a psychological and visual claiming. "I am Sir's…" she murmured aloud.

Rytsar's blue eyes flashed with impish joy as he pressed the vibrator against her and turned it onto the higher setting. She had no hope and whimpered in protest.

Sir knelt down by her head and growled passionately into her ear. She felt a deep contraction in her pussy in response to his voice. Then she heard the welcome word, "*Da,*" come from her Master's lips. She followed his order and came fiercely in honor of both men. Her hips could not lift into the air, so she remained still as the muscles of her vagina pulsed powerfully and her feminine juices flowed in release.

The wand was removed and then Brie felt Rytsar's warm tongue as he gave her still reverberating sex a prolonged lick, while Sir seized her mouth and kissed her deeply. The double kiss was the perfect ending to the scene, and Brie sighed in satisfaction when they pulled away.

Rytsar began untying her ankles while Sir took care of her wrists. Her Master kissed her one more time before helping her to her feet. She wobbled a bit, weak from the session, so Master picked her up and slung her over his shoulder, carrying her through the spacious cabin to a bathroom in the back.

The place had a rustic feel, but everything was of the finest quality, including the tub. It was free-standing with golden claw-feet. He set her down and gently pushed her towards it. Obviously she was meant to clean up before the next scene. Brie immediately started the water as she watched Sir leave. She could barely hear their manly voices over the rushing water of the tap. It was deliciously provocative to contemplate what they might do next.

When she'd finished her bath, she was surprised to find Rytsar waiting for her just outside the doorway. He took hold of the back of her neck, sending a chill of possession through her. He guided her to the main room where Sir was waiting for them.

Her Master watched silently as Rytsar tied her to a chair. After binding her wrists behind her and her legs to the chair, he picked up a set of gold nipple clamps connected by a chain. He smiled as he manipulated each nipple, readying it for the clamp. Then he pulled on the sensitive skin, attaching the clamp to the areola so that when he released it, her nipple stood erect and begging for attention. Rytsar moved to the other, performing the same procedure before tightening the pressure on both.

The Russian Dom flicked her nipples playfully, sending an immediate burst of fire to her nether regions. She tilted her head back and closed her eyes, taking in the sensation. He made one quick swipe against her slit and grunted his approval before returning to Sir.

The two sat down at a small table and began a game of chess. With her nipples throbbing and her pussy wet, she watched the Doms battle it out in a contest of strategy and wit. They laughed and chatted in Russian the entire time, but there was an underlying intensity to their play. Despite being friends, the two were fierce competitors.

Watching the men play chess, she better understood their success as Doms. Each was able to see several moves ahead and anticipate what the other was planning. The two were closely matched, making it a long and passionate game.

Sir glanced at her several times during the match, apparently liking what he saw. Each time she felt his eyes on her, she melted inside. It would take only a simple touch and she would come for him. It was during one of his glances that Rytsar moved a piece without Sir's knowledge. When

Master looked back at the board, Rytsar moved another piece and knocked Sir's king over with a smug smile.

Sir shook his head and looked over the board as if he couldn't believe it. Rytsar glanced at Brie and winked. It was a wicked thing to do. She debated whether to tell Sir, but found there was no need as he quickly identified the false move. He shot Rytsar a humorous look before knocking his king over and declaring himself the winner.

The two broke out in laughter. Then Sir looked at Brie again, his luminous eyes sucking her in, hypnotizing her. He stood up and she held her breath. As he approached, she squirmed in the chair, knowing the power of his touch. She whimpered when his lips came dangerously close to hers, and then he moved to her ear and whispered, "Téa."

Her pussy erupted in a small orgasm. Sir reached between her legs and felt the last of its tremors. He smiled before walking away, leaving her alone in the room with the Russian. She glanced in Rytsar's direction. He stared at her as if he held some dark and delectable secret he was unwilling to share.

Sir returned, dressed in a thick coat, boots and a traditional Russian hat. Brie had to admit he looked charming as a Russian and smiled bashfully at him when he approached. He was carrying a fur for her.

He put it down to release Brie from the chair. Before he untied her, he freed one nipple from the metal clamp, sucking hard on her breast to reduce the pain. She held her breath as he freed the other and encased her nipple with his warm suction. Brie groaned in pleasure. Sir looked up at her before releasing her nipple from his mouth with a sensual pop.

He undid the bindings, picked up the fur, then helped his naked sub into it. Her Master placed a matching hat on her head last, pulling it down over her ears. He gazed at her tenderly. "*Krasivaya*."

She wasn't sure of the meaning, but knew by his tone that it was meant as a compliment. Brie wrapped her arms around his bulky frame and pressed against him. Sir helped her into her boots and then took her hand to lead her outside.

The scenery was unbelievably beautiful in its winter splendor. The cabin was next to a secluded lake covered in a thick sheet of ice. Large flakes drifted down lazily, changing direction only when a frigid breeze caught hold of them. She stuck out her tongue to catch one of the huge flakes and giggled when one landed on her nose and melted.

Instead of taking her to the lake, Sir headed into the forest. They walked until he stopped in front of an incredibly tall, ancient-looking tree. Sir pushed her back against it, and opened her coat without warning. The freezing air caressed her naked skin, making her nipples stand to attention, but soon Sir's warm hands were caressing them.

His fingers moved to her clit and he growled in English, "Your pussy has come twice, but it has not been satisfied. Let me remedy that." Sir unbuttoned his coat and fumbled with his pants. He pressed her against the tree as he thrust his cock inside her.

Brie cried out in satisfaction, overcome by the feeling of Master's shaft. So hard, so perfect, so needed… He grunted and lifted her up, giving her all of him. Her fur coat protected her from the roughness of the bark as he pushed into her with abandon.

"Oh, Sir! Oh, God, Sir, yes!" she cried.

He slowed down and looked into her eyes. "I love everything about you, Brie. Your passion, your mind, your body, your need…all of it." His lips landed on hers again as he made love to her in the forest. Brie watched the large flakes gather on his head and shoulders as he took her. It was magical, this unexpected coupling in the forest.

"I love you," she lifted her mouth to his ear, "Thane."

He went wild then, seeking deeper access. Her screams echoed in the forest as she gave herself over completely to his passion. His grunts soon turned into groans as he came close to climaxing.

She closed her eyes so she could feel the moment it happened—the thickening of his cock, the deeper thrusts as he released his essence. "Thank you, Sir. Thank you, Master," she murmured into his neck as he gave his final thrusts.

Sir pulled out and set her down, then buttoned up her coat and readjusted her hat. He whispered hoarsely, "I have one last surprise." He zipped his pants and buttoned his coat before taking her hand.

Master took her on a leisurely stroll back to the cabin, allowing her a chance to admire the winter scenery. He pointed out a herd of deer on the other side of the lake. Brie smiled, overcome by the natural beauty of the place. The mountains surrounding them were covered by clouds and the deep silence of the falling snow made it feel like they were the only people in the world.

Brie squeezed Sir's arm. "I love this place."

He patted her hand. "As do I, téa, as do I."

# A Gift

When they returned to the cabin, Sir helped her out of her winter clothing and told her to warm herself by the fire. She gladly complied, curling up on the hearth as close to the warmth as her naked skin would allow.

Sir asked Rytsar in a joking tone, "Did you miss us?"

"You, no. *Radost moya*, yes."

He chuckled good-naturedly. "Fair enough. I find her company far more agreeable than yours as well."

Rytsar slapped him hard on the back. "Time for some vodka!" He marched to the kitchen and brought back three glasses and a plate of small pickles. He smiled gleefully at Brie. "Tonight we make you a real woman!"

Brie had avoided joining the drinking games the men had enjoyed nearly every night. Today it didn't look like that was going to be allowed. Rytsar handed her the first glass and passed the other one to Sir.

"Brie, you are expected to drink it in one gulp," Sir reminded her.

She looked at the large amount Rytsar had poured into the glass and shook her head.

"Do not insult the host," Rytsar reprimanded, holding up his glass and a pickle.

Sir picked up one of the green appetizers and motioned to Brie. "You should take a bite after you down the drink. It helps, trust me."

Brie picked up a small pickle and looked at it dubiously.

"*Za zdarov'ye!*" Rytsar toasted with a mischievous grin.

Sir held up his glass in response to the toast.

They both looked at her expectantly, so she held up her glass and smiled.

Both men exhaled deeply to one side and then threw back their heads and gulped the drink down. Brie was horrified and amazed to see them drink so much at once. Before they were finished she exhaled quickly and threw her head back. She struggled to take a gulp and then another to down the burning liquid. She was about to take a breath when Rytsar tipped the glass back up.

"Drink," he commanded with a wink.

With determination, she downed the entire glass, tears pricking her eyes as her whole nasal passage burned from the strong alcohol. "Eat," he said kindly, taking the glass from her and holding the pickle to her lips. She struggled not to cough as she took a small bite.

Rytsar grinned and smacked her on the back. "Well done, *radost moya!*" He immediately poured another glass for all three. Brie looked at Sir nervously.

Sir's smiled was reassuring. "Russian tradition, little sub, but you can call your safe word."

"No!" Rytsar laughed. "*Radost moya* is no coward." He handed her back the glass with the same amount of liquid as the first time. The alcohol was already warming her entire body. It was an agreeable feeling, now she'd got past the initial unpleasantness.

She held up her glass to show her willing participation.

Sir nodded his approval and gave the next toast. "To all the pigheaded aristocrats in the world."

Rytsar looked properly insulted, but he and Brie clinked glasses.

It was just as much of a struggle as the first time, but she drank it all without any help. Afterwards, she took a big bite of the salty pickle and grinned at both men.

"You are now an honorary Russian," Rytsar proclaimed, giving her a spirited pat on the back that sent her tumbling into Sir's arms.

"Had enough?" her Master asked.

It took a few seconds to formulate the correct answer with all the warm yumminess coursing through her. "If it pleases you, Sir."

He put her glass down and answered, "It does, téa. I think you've had enough." He gave his own glass back to Rytsar. "I, however, would like another."

Rytsar gladly filled it up. "My turn for the toast."

Sir nodded with a grin. "You *are* the host."

Brie had expected to hear a witty insult. Instead Rytsar said, "To you, *moy droog*. You have seen me through great troubles."

Sir's face suddenly became solemn. "Same here, my friend." The men clinked glasses and downed their drinks, giving each other a heartfelt embrace afterwards. It was the most vulnerable Brie had seen Sir, other than with her. In that moment, she understood how close the two really were—like brothers.

Rytsar cleared his throat afterwards. "One more?" he asked, holding up the vodka bottle.

"No. I need to remain clear-headed," Sir replied.

Rather than giving Sir a hard time, Rytsar nodded and poured himself a drink, then downed it easily. He gave a satisfied sigh and smiled at Brie. "Nothing like vodka to open up the soul."

Brie giggled, flying on the warm cloud that was consuming her from the inside out.

"Come, Brie," Sir commanded. She looked over to see him sitting on the couch with his legs spread open.

As she approached Sir, she asked, "How would you like me, Master?"

He patted the area next to him. She giggled, finding it funny that he didn't want her between his legs. She gracefully sat down next to her Master. Sir told her to lay her head on his lap, and he began stroking her hair.

Rytsar joined them, sitting on the other side of Sir. He sighed loudly after he'd sat down. "I will miss you, peasant. It has been good to have you in my homeland."

Sir continued petting Brie's hair as he spoke. Tingles of electricity ran down her spine as his deep voice rumbled. "It is a shame it must end, Durov. This has reminded me of old times."

Rytsar chuckled. "*Da*."

Brie closed her eyes and fell into the pleasant warmth of the vodka and the soothing feel of Sir's touch.

Her Master continued, "I can't imagine why I waited so long to visit."

"It's all right, idiot."

Brie giggled on Sir's lap. They definitely sounded like brothers.

"Did your sub just disrespect me?" Rytsar asked.

"I'm not sure." Sir lifted her chin. "Did you just disrespect my long-time friend, téa?"

Brie looked at him and smiled. "No, Sir. I respect your friend very much."

He smiled and cradled her face. "I suspected as much."

Rytsar huffed. "If giggling is a sign of respect, I need another drink." He got up and poured himself an additional glass.

The warm feeling coursing through Brie must have been coursing through Sir, because he suddenly changed positions, pulling her up and kissing her forcibly on the lips. "Undo my pants and grind on me," he growled huskily.

Brie quickly obeyed and straddled him so she was face to face with him. She eased her pussy over his cock and coated it with her slick excitement as she moved up and down the length of his shaft without taking him inside her. He grabbed her hips and helped to guide her movements.

"Your pussy is so beautiful, téa."

She felt warm butterflies stirring. "Thank you, Master."

"Let me inside."

Sir lifted her off, removing his clothes before positioning her pussy over his rigid cock again. She slowly guided his shaft into her, purring as she settled down fully on his manhood.

He threw his head back and groaned. "I love the feel of you."

She ground hard against him, needing him deeper. She was oblivious to the world as she made love to her Master…until she felt manly hands on her ass.

Sir leaned forward and whispered into her ear, "My gift to you."

Brie whimpered as she felt Rytsar's fingers explore the valley between her legs. A tingling chill coursed through her body at the thought she was about to DP with both men.

Sir caressed her cheek. "Normally, I like to be the one teasing your ass, but not this time." He kissed her on the lips before adding, "I want to look into your eyes today."

She caught her breath, his words having a physical effect on her.

"Such a sexy ass," Rytsar complimented. He kneaded her buttocks several times before inserting a lubricated finger into her anus.

Brie whimpered again. The thought of what was about to happen threatened to undo her.

"It's okay, little sub. We will start off gentle," Sir said, teasing her.

She moaned as Rytsar pressed his finger in farther. "She is extremely tight."

Sir gazed directly into Brie's eyes and smiled. "Don't worry, she loosens up with play." To Brie he said, "I know your desires, téa. Even those you are afraid to voice aloud. The two of us want to give this to you. It will be our first time as well, as he and I have never scened together like this before."

"Oh, Sir…" Brie whispered.

Rytsar asked in a husky voice, "Are you ready, *radost moya*?"

Brie closed her eyes and nodded.

Sir reprimanded her softly. "Open those pretty eyes."

She looked at Sir as the round head of Rytsar's cock pressed against her. *Breathe*, she reminded herself as he separated her buttocks and pushed a little harder.

"Open for him, téa," Sir commanded, before they locked lips.

She became lost in his kiss, but cried out when the head of Rytsar's cock breached her entrance. It stretched her achingly, but she found it immensely satisfying. The Russian grabbed a fistful of hair and pulled her head back as he held onto her waist with his other hand.

Sir stared up at her lustfully, watching her varying expressions as she accepted Rytsar inside her. Soft mews escaped her lips as her body struggled to take both men at once.

The Russian Dom leaned forward and bit her on the shoulder blade. Growling against her skin, he left a trail of bite-marks on her back. She cried out in passion and felt him thrust his shaft even deeper.

Sir wrapped his hand around the back of her neck, drawing her to him. "Deny us nothing, téa," he said, kissing her bottom lip.

"Yes, Master," she murmured breathlessly. Rytsar started on her right shoulder blade, causing Brie to moan again.

"I want to feel my cock deep inside you, *radost moya.* I will pump my hot seed deep in this tight ass."

His dirty words had a positive effect as her body received another inch of his shaft. "More," she cried, but her body resisted farther advancement, despite her willingness.

Sir sneaked his hand down and smacked her on the butt. The sexy sound of it turned her on. "Again, Master," she begged.

"Make room," Sir told Rytsar as he wound up to spank her properly. The second stinging slap caused her to yelp in pleasure.

Rytsar's deep groan greeted their play as his cock sank all the way in. Brie felt chills as her body accepted the fullness of both men. She panted against Sir's chest, savoring the moment.

Sir gave her time to adjust before he seized her hips for leverage and pulled out so he could thrust back inside her. Rytsar waited to ascertain his rhythm before grabbing her waist and alternating his strokes. The men kept the rhythm slow but consistent, allowing her body to grow accustomed to the movement before they began fully thrusting inside her.

Brie screamed the first time they each gave a full stroke. It was almost too much. Sir kept his eyes on her. "Give in, téa."

She closed her eyes as a tingling sensation grew from her core and slowly spread outwards.

"Good girl."

Brie opened her eyes for Sir and basked in the glory of receiving both cocks deeply. Pleasing both Doms at the same time was deliciously decadent—the ultimate fantasy.

Rytsar changed things up when he stopped thrusting and grabbed her by the shoulders, forcing her up so that her back was against his chest. He wrapped one hand around her throat and nibbled on her neck as he clasped her right breast possessively with his other hand. "My cock missed you, *radost moya.*"

Brie moaned, her body remembering quite well the last time he'd taken her.

Sir used the opportunity to rub his fingers vigorously against her clit. Her pussy was already on fire, engorged with fierce desire. She twitched in Rytsar's arms as Sir stoked the flames. She thrashed her head against the Russian's chest, a captive to the orgasm they were about to unleash.

She started screaming, unable to form coherent words. "Ah... Ahh...!"

Brie turned her head and bit down on Rytsar's wrist in desperation. He roared his approval, forcing his cock deep into her ass as his hand tightened around her neck. "Yes," he growled hoarsely. "Come for my cock, *radost moya.*"

She looked down at Sir, her whole body melting when she saw the intensity of his gaze—as if he could swallow her whole. He mouthed the words, "Come now."

It was a confusion of sensations as her pussy tried to contract but could not, being stretched unnaturally tight. Instead, it became an intense burning that radiated from her pussy and blew through her. Her scream caught in her throat as her senses were blinded by the rush.

When she regained her awareness, she found herself staring down at Sir while Rytsar breathed low, haunting words into her ear, probably Russian—Brie was oblivious.

Rytsar let go of her and she returned her head to Sir's chest, reveling in the unique subspace they had evoked.

Brie purred, "Yes," when they started up again, thrusting deep into her body. She became a ravenous canvas for them, anxious to be transformed into something new by the two sexual artists.

Sir ordered her to cross her arms behind her. He then wrapped her in a tight embrace. "Fuck her," he commanded of Rytsar, while he remained still, buried in her quivering pussy.

Sir effectively became her bindings as he gave Rytsar free rein over her ass. Instead of pumping into her hard, he experimented with different angles. It took time until Rytsar found the one that made her shudder all over.

Being held captive by Sir was sexy on all kinds of levels. She listened to his heartbeat as Rytsar began stroking her at the perfect angle. Each thrust brought a symphony of pleasure. She reveled in the feeling, allowing it to carry her higher.

Rytsar grunted as she tensed. The sound of his lusty pleasure turned her on further. She felt her pussy start to pulse in time with her Master's heartbeat. She was sexually in sync with him, and the thought of it sent her to the edge.

"Master, I want to come for you."

"Yes, téa."

Tears of joy ran down Brie's cheeks as she lost herself. She heard the lustful releases of both men as they rocked her body with their orgasms, and then all became warm and silent. She floated higher, as if in a dream, the alcohol enhancing the natural high of her subspace.

When she felt Rytsar move, she protested. Sir chuckled beneath her. "All good things must come to an end, my little flyer."

It was with reluctance that she returned to earth as the lonely sound of a cell phone echoed in the other room.

Rytsar finally disengaged to answer it. He returned, holding the cell phone out to Sir.

Sir took it and answered in an official tone, not giving away the fact he was naked and buried inside his sub.

The person on the other end was speaking so fast, Brie could not make out what was said, but she grew concerned at Sir's serious expression. "We will be leaving in a few days. Surely, that will leave enough time." He paused again. "I'm afraid so."

Brie quietly detached herself from him, trying to conceal her worry.

When Sir finally snapped the phone shut, he surprised her by laughing.

"What's going on?" Rytsar demanded.

"Sorry, friend. I'm not allowed to speak of it. But I need to see if we can't get a flight out sooner."

He turned to Brie with a wistful look on his face. "Well, babygirl…it looks like your life is about to change."

# *Brie Faces her Master's Fears*

# His Pride

Rytsar was an influential man in Moscow, and was able to secure Brie and Sir a flight back to the States. On the drive to the airport, he complained, "I do not like this sudden leaving, *moy droog*. Nor the secrecy behind it."

Sir smirked. "Sorry, I was instructed not to divulge any information. You will know it as soon as Brie has permission to share."

Rytsar looked at her, defiance flashing in his eyes. "I had better be the first you inform, *radost moya*."

She opened her mouth, ready to assure him that he would be, but Sir interrupted. "Make no promises."

Brie suddenly became worried. *How serious is this secret?*

Rytsar frowned at Sir, sounding deeply offended. "I deserve to know."

Sir placed his hand on the Russian's shoulder. "There is no need to get your feathers ruffled, my friend. I simply think Brie will want to share it with others first. Rest assured, you will be told in a timely manner."

He growled in dissatisfaction. "I do not care to be left in the dark."

"It seems fitting you should suffer after your airport shenanigans. To abuse my sub in such a manner when she'd barely stepped onto Russian soil…"

"She handled herself fine, *moy droog*. You were the one who had me in stitches," said Rytsar, laughing.

Sir shrugged off the laughter at his expense. "Insulting me won't help your cause. Brie is capable of putting you farther down the list of people to call."

The Russian gave Brie a domineering look and barked, "Don't."

She struggled not to smile. It was humorous that the secret Sir was keeping was bothering Rytsar almost as much as it was bothering her.

Once they were safely on the plane, a private business jet with only a few prominent Russians on board, Sir shared the remarkable news with Brie. "Mr. Holloway has run into an unforeseen snag in his latest project. They are on a forced hiatus while it is being ironed out. His insistence on confidentiality is to prevent already gun-shy investors from backing out of his project before he has a chance to remedy the situation."

Brie stared at Sir, not really hearing anything after he mentioned the name 'Holloway'. Her heart began racing. *This is my big break!*

Sir continued, "He only has a few days, but said your documentary has been on his mind. He wants to see it in three days' time."

That was when reality hit. "Three days, Sir?"

"Yes. That's why I cut the trip short. You will basically have forty-eight hours, by the time we make it back to LA, to finish editing your documentary."

"It's not enough time," she protested.

"It *is* enough time," he corrected, "since it is all the time you've been given."

She bit back the feeling of panic and nodded. "Yes, Sir. I will make it work."

He covered her with a blanket. "Go to sleep, Brie," Sir commanded. "This will be the only chance you have for the next three days."

Obeying him was nearly impossible, but she forced herself to count sheep and then gave up on that, concentrating on Sir's breathing instead. It eased her into slumber—the reassuring force of his presence.

She had to fight back the thought that kept invading her head: *This is the beginning…*

Brie spent the next two days hunched over her computer, drinking coffee and eating apples at Sir's insistence—his idea of a more healthy energy booster. He took it upon himself to cook and care for her so that she could focus solely on editing the film.

Brie lived and breathed her documentary, from her first night at the Submissive Training Center to the last, when she, Lea and Mary had contemplated what the future held for them. She was obsessed with the last part of her footage, where both Lea and Mary had questioned her choice to be collared. At the time, she had only been considering Tono and Faelan, with no idea how the night would end up playing out.

However, it was difficult to listen to Mary. Brie had to fight back the bile rising in her throat when Mary mentioned wanting to take a spin with Faelan. Lea had jumped on her for it, but Brie had actually defended Mary. At the time she'd mistakenly thought the backstabber was her friend.

It shocked Brie just how many times Mary had called her an idiot for wanting to get collared. Her claim that Brie just needed to 'play the field' in order to find better Doms had been a lie. The truth was that Mary hadn't wanted Brie to be happy at all, and had been willing to do whatever it took to prevent it.

Mary was the lowest, most spiteful person she knew. Brie's only consolation was that despite her nemesis' best efforts, Brie had still got her happy ending. Although graduation night hadn't gone the way she'd envisioned, the end result had been far better than Brie could ever have hoped for. It turned out that Mary's hatred had been unable to stop what was meant to be.

Brie imagined seeing Blonde Nemesis in a club someday and walking up to her just to say, "Thanks for being such a backstabbing bitch. I couldn't be happier because of you."

It was difficult not to cut Mary out of the film altogether. Just seeing her beautiful but stone-cold face brought back a flood of emotions. Her nemesis might have become a capable submissive, but she was a wretched excuse for a human being.

There was only one problem: Brie knew Mary added to her documentary. Despite failing miserably as a friend, Blonde Nemesis was an 'interesting character'. That was how Brie had decided to think of her as she edited—just a two-dimensional character. To see Mary any other way only caused her pain.

Once Brie had selected the scenes she wanted, she spent the rest of the time finding and timing the music to match, as well as adding graphics and text. It wasn't going to be a polished piece of work by any means, but the meat of the story was well represented.

When she announced she was finished, Sir asked to watch it. "I want to see what you've been able to create." He sat down and pulled her to him, wrapping his arm around her waist. She'd missed his touch over the last two days in her mad rush to get the project completed, and was thrilled to feel that familiar electricity his touch evoked.

Brie was nervous when she hit play. She tried not to be obvious as she observed his reactions while he watched the film. Her heart soared whenever he smiled, but she saw the look of genuine concern when Brie spoke of the incident between Mary and Tono.

Because Brie hadn't become friends with her yet, it was simply Brie's impressions of the evening Blonde Nemesis had flipped out. The girl had been purchased by Tono at an auction, but had had a psychological breakdown in his care because of her failure to disclose her serious underlying issues.

Brie was surprised to see Sir's smile return when Lea questioned Brie about her Kinbaku experience with Tono. Brie had been flying high after such an incredible and unusual bondage session with the talented Dom. It was apparent she'd fallen for Tono that night by because of her actions and words, despite Brie's attempts to edit. She had wanted to avoid hurting Sir, but had remained true to the documentary.

Sir maintained that smile when, later in the film, she shared with the other two girls about her day with Faelan after he'd won her at the auction. The only times she saw Sir twitch uncomfortably were when she talked about her growing feelings for Sir himself.

When the credits rolled across the screen she turned it off, but was startled by his silence. Finally, Sir turned to her and said, "This is a telling piece."

She smiled uncertainly. "Do you feel it is worthy of distribution?"

"You have done a fine job depicting your journey as a submissive…the insecurities, triumphs and eventual growth. Your humor is a nice touch."

She blushed at the compliment, but she still wanted to know. "Thank you, Sir. But…do you like it?"

He touched her cheek lightly. "Your raw honesty in the film has given me new understanding of your personal journey. I hope you are prepared for the exposure, Brie. You are quite open in this film. There are many people who do not understand the lifestyle and will attack you for it."

"I've taken that under serious consideration, Sir. I fully accept what will come because of this film."

He tilted his head slightly. "Even with your own parents?"

She sighed, hating the thought of it. "Yes, Sir. I am willing to face anyone who does not understand."

He stood up and walked to the expansive window overlooking the city.

She stayed where she was, very aware that he had not answered her question—not directly—so she quietly asked it one more time. "Sir, did you like it?"

He held out his hand. She instantly got up and approached him, then knelt at his feet. He put his hand on the top of her head. "I admire this piece of work you have created. However, I cannot say 'like' is a word I would use. I can foresee that this will subject you and the other two girls to unnecessary strife." He helped her onto her feet. "That being said, considering how much time you've had to edit it, I find it an exceptional piece of work."

She wrapped her arms around him. "Thank you, Sir. It means so much to me to hear you say that."

He lifted her chin to look into her eyes. "No matter how this affects our lives, I am proud to stand with you in this moment."

*I love this man!*

Brie stood on her tiptoes to kiss him. "I'm truly honored, Sir."

He grasped the back of her neck and kissed her deeply. "I believe we both need to connect on a more intimate level."

Brie's heart leapt with joy. "I've missed your touch these last few days, Master."

"As have I. Undress and kneel by the Tantra chair while I select a new tool for you."

She felt weak inside as she removed her clothes and folded them neatly by her feet. Brie walked over to the lounger and knelt beside it, waiting for his return. In mere seconds, she'd gone from a tired filmmaker to a willing submissive. It was a glorious transition.

Sir was naked when he walked back into the room, his strides confident and lithe like those of a predator. He held only a spreader bar, but this was different from the previous one he had used on her. This bar had *four* cuffs on it.

"Today you learn a favorite Kama Sutra position of mine, téa."

"It is my pleasure to do so, Master."

"It is challenging in its depth."

Brie moaned softly, the thought of it making her loins ache with pleasure.

Sir placed the bar on the floor and asked her to stand before it. He buckled each ankle to an outer cuff, the bar forcing her legs apart. Then he commanded, "Give me your left wrist."

Brie bent down and Sir secured her wrist to the middle of the bar. He took her right wrist and did the same, leaving Brie standing with her legs straight, her head between her knees and her ass in the air.

He stood up and moved behind her to admire the view. "Your ass is a piece of art, woman."

Sir rubbed his hands over her buttocks and down her back. Brie glanced at the window to stare at her reflection. It was a defenseless pose, leaving her completely open to Master's whims.

"I see your pussy is swollen with desire, téa." He spanked her mound lightly, sending bursts of sensual electricity to her core. Her nipples hardened in response. He slapped it again with a little more enthusiasm, making her whimper with pleasure.

"Your pussy has missed its Master."

"Yes, Master. It's desperate for you."

He caressed her ass again, squeezing and releasing the flesh, randomly patting her mound when the urge struck. Brie struggled to keep her balance as he played with her.

Sir ran his finger over her wet slit and commented, "You appear ready." Instead of plowing into her, he walked into the kitchen. She heard him take down a glass and make himself a martini.

He knew exactly how to play her mind and body. Waiting for his attention in this suggestive pose was extremely effective. She glanced at the window again and smiled.

Sir walked back in several minutes later and stood beside her, sipping his martini. "The position is called the Second Posture, but I modify it slightly for the added benefit the chair provides. It requires flexibility and arousal to accomplish. Are you aroused, téa?"

"Yes, Master."

"Remember this position, as I plan to use it often." Sir put down his drink before he slipped his arm under her stomach. Brie squealed when he lifted her off the ground. She felt like a sexy sack of potatoes, completely at the mercy of the man who carried her.

He deftly laid her on her back, the Tantra chair cradling her body with its gentle curvature.

Brie relaxed in the chair, but Sir instructed, "Legs straight up."

Brie obeyed and watched in excitement as Sir straddled the chair and sat facing her, his cock resting on her bare mound. He grabbed the bar and pushed her legs towards her head, lifting her buttocks off the chair and her pussy at an inviting angle to receive his manhood.

Sir smiled as he slid his shaft into her and pressed his torso against her legs, still holding onto the bar with one hand. Brie let out a gasp as he thrust deeper, the angle of the chair and his position demanding that she relax in a major way.

He rolled his hips slowly, allowing her body to appreciate every inch of his shaft as he slid in and out. It was a challenge to take him this way, but with her legs straight the position was particularly stimulating to her G-spot. He gazed down at her and whispered huskily, "This is just the beginning."

Sir pressed harder against the bar, forcing her legs farther back, nearer to her head. She commanded her muscles to loosen and accept the awkward position as Sir gained deeper access.

"It becomes less about the thrusting and more about the depth as you relax, téa," he said huskily. Brie had been concentrating on relaxing her muscles and had failed to notice the look of ecstasy on her Master's face until now.

She smiled up at him, encouraging him to push the bar farther. With his patience and her willingness, he eventually pushed her legs all the way back until her feet and wrists were next to her head. Sir stopped thrusting and held onto the bar with both hands, looking down at her with a mixture of love and passion.

He pulled out and then slowly pressed his cock back in, letting her body embrace his fullness to the very base of his manhood. Then he began rocking back and forth—the head of his hard shaft in constant contact with her G-spot, rubbing it heatedly. "My cock cherishes you as much as I do, téa."

She nodded, unable to speak due to the demanding position.

"Let it love you to release."

Her eyes focused solely on his as she felt the tingles and chills caused by the deep stimulation. Her nipples almost hurt, they had constricted so tightly, while tiny goosebumps rose on her skin. She was a captive of his love in every sense of the word as the buildup reached its crescendo and she gave in to the feeling. Her pussy caressed his cock in rhythmic adulation.

Sir stared down at her. "I love you," he said as his cock joined in the dance, releasing his seed deep inside her.

*Hearts and bodies connected as one…*

Sir gently pulled away, easing her legs down and unbuckling her from the spreader bar. He let it drop to the floor and gathered her in his arms, pressing her head against his shoulder. The gesture was so tender, so moving that Brie began to cry. He seemed to understand and did not question her or ask her to stop.

"Forever," she whispered.

# Dreams Deferred

Brie stood before Mr. Holloway, confident that her documentary would wow him. The fact he had called her in to see it spoke of his vested interest in the project.

"Please, Miss Bennett, take a seat," he said in a firm, manly tone.

Brie looked him in the eye as she gracefully sat down. Sir had instructed her to treat the producer the way she would any business contact, despite the fact he was a known Dom.

She smiled amiably. "Thank you for offering to see my work, Mr. Holloway."

"Marquis Gray spoke highly of you and believed your work would reflect the same level of excellence he has come to expect from you in other areas."

Brie felt heat rise to her face, honored that he felt that way. "I hope I can do justice not only to his confidence in my abilities, but to the Training Center itself. It has changed my life, in ways I could never have imagined."

"Let's waste no more time then," he said affably.

Brie handed over the documentary—her baby—without hesitation. She watched him slip the DVD in and hit play. The large TV screen lit up with her introduction. The music started off light and soothing as the words 'Art of Submission' floated across the screen with images of submissives bowing, presenting, or kissing the hands or feet of the dominants. The music quickly became hard and pounding as more provocative images flashed onto the screen, depicting bondage, flogging and fire play.

Brie had ended the intro with pictures of the three girls with their silly nicknames: 'Lea the Lovely', 'Brie the Bodacious' and 'Mary the Magnificent'. She'd decided to keep the humor of their experiences at the forefront of her film. Becoming a submissive was a complex journey—one that not only involved facing fears and pushing limits, but also encouraged the pure joy of self-discovery.

She watched Mr. Holloway clandestinely as he took in her work. The man had his hand on his chin. His gaze never wavered; his lips never twitched. He was a master at masking his emotions. When the ending credits concluded, he turned off the TV and sat without saying a word.

With all her dreams on the line, such treatment should have put her in a tailspin of anxiety, but she knew it was good and stared back at him pleasantly, saying nothing. After several long, agonizing moments he spoke.

"It was not what I was expecting."

Brie swallowed hard, shocked by his reaction, but she kept her composure. "What was your expectation?"

"I had hoped for a more in-depth exposé of your training experience. That girl, Mary—you hardly touched on her issues and you left the end nebulous concerning her future. You also concentrated more on Lea's humor than her personal struggles. The only person I feel I know after watching your film is you, which is not bad…however, you have other personalities in the film who were not tapped into."

She took a deep breath before replying. "You are correct. I did not dig deeply into their personal lives. I didn't want to infringe on their privacy, especially with Mary, who has painful issues in her past."

"It is those issues that will make this film interesting. We need to know their pain and discomfort, just as you shared some of yours."

"I doubt they'd want to expose themselves like that, Mr. Holloway. Their willingness to publicly identify themselves as submissives was courageous enough. I am prepared to risk full exposure, but I do not expect the same from my friends."

"Well, you do not have a noteworthy film without it. You need more footage, individual interviews in which you delve into the darker aspects of their journeys. In fact, I would wager even you have held back some of your more difficult trials."

Brie nodded. "You are correct again. I consciously made the decision not to burden the viewer."

"Then it is not really a documentary, is it? It is a piece of well-packaged fluff. I expected a documentary, and *that* I did not get."

Brie took a deep breath and exhaled silently before speaking, grateful for Tono's breathing lessons at a time like this. "I thank you for your time, Mr. Holloway." She got up to leave, completely devastated but hiding it under a pleasant smile.

He motioned her back to the chair. "I want my documentary, Miss Bennett. Go back to Ms. Taylor and Miss Wilson and get their real stories. Go to the Training Center and video some of the scenes you allude to. I would also like to see interviews with the trainers. This film has potential, but not as it is now."

"I am fairly certain I will not get the consent of both submissives. I had a hard enough time getting what little I did get from the one."

"Miss Wilson?"

"Yes," she answered.

"It is her story that will sell the film. I don't care what you have to do, it is imperative you get her to agree."

"We did not end on good terms, Mr. Holloway."

He smiled wolfishly. "All the better."

"And if I cannot get her consent?"

He sat back slowly in his chair. "Then you don't have a film, in my opinion."

Brie's heart dropped. There was no way Mary would agree—not the Blonde Nemesis. "I will see what I can do. How soon do you want the completed film?"

"In a month."

She shook her head to clear it. A month was not a reasonable amount of time for all he wanted her to add to the documentary. However, this man was her best chance and she wasn't about to question him on it. "Shall we set up a meeting for in a month, then?"

He gave her a look of approval. "Had you made any excuses, I would have turned down the project. You may see my assistant on the way out to schedule our next meeting." The imposing man stood up and handed back the DVD. "I expect great things from you, Miss Bennett."

She took it with a feeling of disappointment, sad that her little film had failed to impress him. *What will Sir say?*

She nodded to the respected producer and headed for the door.

"I like your sense of humor, Miss Bennett. Do not lose that in the remake. You'll need the balance."

She turned around and smiled. "Thank you, Mr. Holloway. I find humor makes everything easier to digest."

Brie walked out of the building and got into her car, feeling shell-shocked. He had not rejected the film, but it felt like it—especially knowing that Mary was the key. She rested her head on the steering wheel and closed her eyes. That was not how she'd thought the meeting would go, and now she would have to go back to Sir and tell him her film wasn't good enough.

She jumped when someone knocked on her driver-side window. Brie looked up and saw Sir staring down at her. He made the motion for her to unroll the window. "I wanted to be the first to congratulate you."

Her bottom lip trembled.

Sir paused for a second and then smiled. "Let's go for a walk, babygirl."

Brie got out of the car and Sir placed his hand on the small of her back, guiding her through the crowds of people hustling down the sidewalk. His touch brought welcome peace to her soul.

"How did it go?" he asked gently. "I can tell by your body language and silence that you aren't happy, but I can't imagine he rejected it."

She struggled to talk without her emotions choking her voice. "Mr. Holloway rejected what I have now."

"But..."

"If I can get Mary's and Lea's consent to do more personal interviews, along with a host of other things within a month's time, he'll accept it. Well...he'll consider it, at least. But Mary will never agree to it, Sir. It's done." She held back a sob and turned away from him.

Sir directed her to a ledge so that she could sit down. He stood over her, allowing her time to collect herself. "I understand your disappointment, Brie. However, the door has not been closed. He is providing you with an excellent opportunity. It is not over—this is just beginning."

Brie looked up at Sir, unable to hide her misery. "The last thing I want is to talk to Mary again, much less ask a favor of her, Sir. To realize my dream I have to face my worst nightmare."

"I take it as a good sign. The unresolved issues between you two need to be addressed. It seems the universe agrees and is forcing the issue."

"Anything but that..." she whimpered.

He said quietly, "You are no longer a child."

It was humiliating to be put in this position. Mary had wronged her, Mary was the one at fault, but it was Brie who was expected to mend the rift the betrayer had created.

"Brie, let me give you a piece of advice, one I learned after my father's death. No matter how it may appear to the casual observer, you cannot know the truth unless you know all sides. I would refrain from making judgments until you speak with Miss Wilson directly."

Brie bowed her head. *Yes, Sir knows too well the cost of unjust judgments.* His words brought clarity in a sea of doubt and frustration. "I'll speak to her, Sir. But I already know it's going to end in disaster."

Sir chuckled. "I doubt that. I remember seeing the two of you together. There were times of honest camaraderie between you. Don't be so quick to dismiss that because of one incident you have yet to discuss."

"You have more faith in her than I do, Sir."

"My faith lies in you, Brie."

She stood up and wrapped her arms around his waist. "Thank you, Sir. I needed to hear that."

His strong arms embraced her and he lifted her off the ground. "You are meant to accomplish great things. To whom much is given, much is expected." He kissed her firmly on the lips.

Brie melted into his kiss, and laid her head against his chest when he set her back down. "As long as I have you, I know I can't fail."

He squeezed her tighter. "I have news of my own, little sub."

Brie looked up and smiled. "What is it, Sir?"

"One of the business contacts I made in Russia has plans for expansion into America. They've asked to meet in New York."

She was genuinely pleased. "Your dreams of expanding your business are coming true, Sir."

"Like yours, they are not happening the way I anticipated, and yet a unique opportunity has presented itself." He traced the collar fastened around her neck and added with a charming smile, "I believe you are my luck."

His words warmed her heart in ways he could not imagine. For a man who'd struggled in the past to communicate his feelings, Sir was becoming exceptionally expressive.

She squeezed him tighter. "I'm thrilled to hear it, Sir."

"There is a hitch, however. They are meeting later this week. I'll need to leave tomorrow to get my contacts set up and presentation ready."

A cold shiver of realization ran through her. "Will I be going with you, Sir?"

"No, Brie. You don't have time to spare on another trip. I regret that I cannot be here as support."

She sat back down on the ledge, trying to keep the tears of disappointment at bay. Brie thought what a funny creature she was—one moment flying high, and the next drowning in despair.

"Brie, do not let this deter you from your goal. Even when I am not near, my love and support are yours."

He'd said the L word in public without a second thought, his concern for her so great that he wasn't even aware of it. That one word changed everything in an instant.

She looked up at him, trying not to smile foolishly. "I won't, Sir. Although I wish you could be here if the meeting with Mary does not go well."

Always thinking ahead, Sir immediately suggested, "You should take Ms. Taylor with you and present the opportunity to the two at the same time. If Miss Wilson is not receptive, leave with Ms. Taylor. She can act as your moral support and a buffer if you require it."

Brie nodded, her confidence returning. With her best friend Lea by her side, she could face the Nemesis. Only Lea truly knew the trials she had suffered with Mary, anyway.

"I'd say we are both due a lavish night of celebration, Miss Bennett. Perhaps a quiet Italian dinner by the ocean and a ride along the coast."

She looked at him demurely. "Whatever is your pleasure, Sir."

"You are my pleasure, téa," he said, gathering her back into his arms.

Sir told Brie to pick out an outfit he would like, but added the stipulation there were to be no bra or panties involved. Brie walked into their closet, her eyes widening at the choices. Sir had purchased several outfits she had yet to wear and they were exquisite—and yet…

Brie walked out of the bedroom with a confident stride that spoke of her assurance as a cherished submissive. When Sir saw her, there was a slight moment of obvious surprise, and then his lips curled upwards in pleasure.

"My student."

Brie glided up to him dressed in her Submissive Training uniform: the leather corset, short skirt and her thigh-highs with six-inch heels. Tonight, per his request, she had forgone the red thong underneath.

"Are you pleased, Master?"

He kissed her in answer, reaching under her leather skirt. Brie ground against his hand. Sir licked his finger afterwards, smiling sensually before picking up a velvet box from the counter.

Inside were the pearls that he'd given Brie the night he'd scened with her as 'Khan'. Sir placed the strand around her neck, letting it hang between her breasts. "Perfection, téa."

Sir went to get dressed himself and left her with the instructions, "While you wait, I want you to come up with a use for those pearls tonight."

Brie played with the pearls around her neck, a sly smile forming on her lips. She knew *exactly* how she would use them.

It was her turn to look surprised when he came back out. He was dressed in the same tux he'd worn the night he'd collared her. Seeing him walk towards her in the black Italian suit made her knees weak. "You look beautiful, Sir."

He cocked his head. "Beautiful? That's not a word I hear often." He chuckled as he took her evening coat from the hook in the hallway and slipped it over her shoulders. Sir whispered in her ear, "Still my elegant property."

Brie purred. When she had played out the scene with Sir as her Khan, it had been exciting but full of emotional angst. This time the barriers were gone; she was simply a devoted sub in the hands of her Master.

"I love you, Master."

He cupped her chin. "I don't think you know the depth of my feelings for you."

Chills ran down her spine as she looked into his eyes. Unlike Marquis' gaze that bored into her soul, Sir's called to her like a perilous song, inviting her to lose herself completely.

He walked her out of the building to a waiting limousine. She smiled and pressed herself against him as they waited for the chauffeur to open the door. Brie remembered the last limousine ride, one that had been full of passion but had ended in utter frustration.

*Not tonight…*

Brie slid onto the long, leather bench seat, feeling lightheaded with expectation. Sir joined her, putting his hand on her thigh, but he remained silent. For the entire ride he did not speak. He simply stared at her with a look of longing and some unknown emotion—an almost raw vulnerability. It reminded her of their first time alone together.

Her heart started to race. What could it mean? She met his gaze, asking silently, *What are you trying to tell me, Sir?*

The limo stopped on the coast at a quiet area of beach. Sir helped her out of the car and escorted her towards the water on path of red tiles that had been laid out artfully for them. The footpath led to a lone table in the sand, surrounded by fiery tiki torches. A man dressed like a chef stood with a chair pulled out for her.

Brie smiled. "What's this, Master?"

"A quiet Italian meal by the ocean," he replied.

Brie sat down to the elegantly set table and stared across it as her Master sat down. This was too much—something extraordinary was happening tonight. She could feel it in her bones.

The chef removed covers from two plates, one with small grilled pieces of bread, and the other with colorful vegetables and a small bowl of oil. Sir pointed to the bread. "*Fettunta*, spread with olive oil, grilled with garlic rubbed on top. Best garlic bread you'll ever taste." He pointed to the other. "*Pinizimonio*, fresh vegetables to dip in the seasoned olive oil."

"It looks delicious, Master."

Sir picked up a slice of bread and consumed it with a look of rapture on his face. Brie was captivated by the vibrant vegetables and took a slice of bright yellow bell pepper, dipping it into the olive oil seasoned with black pepper. She brought it to her lips, trying to look alluring. A drip of oil fell before she could get it into her mouth. It landed on her chest, then rolled slowly under her corset and between her breasts. She looked up, hoping Sir hadn't noticed. The twinkle in his eyes said otherwise.

"Take off your top, téa."

Brie ignored the stranger standing beside her and undid the ties, letting her corset fall to the sandy beach. Sir stood up and with his finger, he caught the trail of oil. He lifted his index finger to his lips and licked it off. "I think you would taste good covered in olive oil."

He sat back down and took a mushroom, dipping it into the oil. Then, smiling at Brie, he devoured it. She blushed. Sir could eat her any way he wanted…

The chef poured them each a glass of wine, before moving back to a grill she hadn't noticed flaming in the distance until now. Sir was right—her favorite, hands down, was the garlic bread; hard, crunchy, infused with the taste of garlic and the tanginess of olive oil. She had to stop herself from eating the whole plateful. *Submissives are not greedy*, she reminded herself, *even if they secretly want to be.*

After several minutes, the chef returned with a covered plate. He placed it before Sir and lifted the cover with a flourish. A thick, juicy steak sat alone on the platter. It was not the pasta Brie had expected.

Sir took the knife the chef handed him and cut into it at an angle. Brie was shocked at how red it was, like rare—*really* rare.

He speared the piece of meat and held it up to admire. "*Bistecca alla Fiorentina.* A simple dish that impresses the most discerning palate."

Sir held it out for her to eat, but she did not open her lips to take it. With trepidation, she admitted, "I don't eat rare meat, Master."

He shook his head. "You have not tried this. Trust me, téa."

She opened her mouth, but only to please him, even though she was certain she would choke on it.

"It is seasoned simply and grilled only for a few minutes on each side, to let the true flavor of the beef shine through," he said as he put it in her mouth.

Brie let the bloody meat touch her lips and held back the urge to gag. Sir was watching her intently as she chewed, so she closed her eyes to concentrate on the flavors, divorcing herself from the fact it was basically raw animal tissue. The simple salt, pepper and garlic seasoning, along with the splash of olive oil, heightened the flavor of the steak. This meat *definitely* had flavor, but it was delicate and melted in her mouth.

She opened her eyes after she'd swallowed the enticing morsel. "Delicious."

Sir sat back with a satisfied grin. "Of course."

The chef took the knife from Sir and cut the rest of the meat into thin slices, then added a small bowl of white beans to the table.

"Is it to your liking, Sir Davis?" he asked.

"It is an excellent piece of meat. Thank you for the entire meal, Chef Sabello."

"My pleasure. I would do anything for the son of Alonzo."

Sir nodded gratefully.

Chef Sabello poured the last of the wine, made a small bow and walked into the darkness, leaving them alone on the secluded beach.

Sir scooped up a forkful of beans and said, "*Fagioli bianchi* are a bit like your mashed potatoes, a required accompaniment of the meal."

Brie took her own forkful of white beans to taste. Like everything else she had eaten that night, it was simple. A little bit of salt, oil and garlic, with a savory herb she couldn't identify. The simplicity of it made the ingredients stand out all the more.

"I love everything about this meal, Master. I've never had anything like it."

He chuckled. "Yes, I'm sure you were expecting pasta, possibly a meatball or two."

Brie giggled, instantly thinking of the animated movie *Lady and the Tramp*, when the two dogs shared the long noodle. She smiled bashfully at Sir as she imagined his lips coming closer to hers as they ate the single noodle from both ends.

Instead, she shared the same piece of mouthwatering meat and bowl of white beans with her Master. It was all the more wonderful because this meal had been a part of his childhood, something he desired to share with her.

Before they'd finished, Brie noticed a change come over Sir. He became quiet again. She could barely get her last mouthful down, wondering what was about to happen—not allowing herself to dream.

"I value sharing this with you, téa. This is a part of my past, the foods I grew up on. It pleases me that you enjoy them."

"I am honored you want to share them with me, Master."

"There are other things I long to share."

Brie's heartbeat increased. She got up from the table and walked over to him, to kneeling down at his feet. "I cherish your trust in me…"—she almost said 'Thane', but chickened out—"…Master." She kissed the back of his hand in reverence.

He petted her head with his other hand. Sir cleared his throat, but did not speak. She felt an aura of tension radiating from him that was delightfully disconcerting. Her body responded by trembling with expectancy.

"Master?" she asked, looking up at him.

He smiled briefly, but shook his head. "No. Not yet… I think it's time we took a drive." Sir got up from the table and commanded, "Gather your top, téa. No need to dress."

Brie felt wistful leaving the romantic meal behind, already treasuring the memories. She returned to the limo bare-chested. The chauffeur did not bat an eyelid as he opened the door for them.

# Pearls in the Sand

Once again Sir sat next to Brie, his masculine hand on her thigh. But this time his need filled the small space. His fingers traveled upwards, tantalizingly slow in their progress, centimeter by aching centimeter.

Brie quivered under his touch, her breaths becoming rapid and shallow. Ever closer to her sweet spot he came, as his warm breath caressed her neck. His hand moved under her skirt, so close… A small cry escaped her lips when his finger finally touched the soft folds of her pussy. He kissed her neck as he made quick work of her excited clit. Soon she was grinding against his hand. His lips moved down to her nipple and he began sucking as his fingers progressed to her opening. With the same drawn-out playfulness, he teased her, rimming the entrance but not providing penetration. She whimpered in need.

Sir's lips moved up to her ear. "What do you want, Brie?"

"I need you, Sir. I need you inside me."

With the cruelty of a good Master, he pulled away and sat back in the seat. "Not yet. You need to learn patience, sub."

She wanted to groan in frustration, but kept silent. *You want me, Sir. Take your willing sub.*

He shook his head, as if he could hear her thoughts. But he soon moved over to the window separating them from the driver and knocked on the glass. It slid down and he told the chauffeur, "This is the place coming up."

The driver turned the limo around and parked on the side of the road next to the coastline. Sir opened the car door and helped her out himself. Brie was still topless, but he wrapped his arm around her so that she was not exposed as he helped her down a path to a small beach surrounded by protruding rocks. She struggled to traverse the rocky path in her heels, so Sir picked her up and carried her. "I'm curious, téa. How will you use the pearls tonight?"

"It's a surprise, Master."

A lustful grin spread across his face. "I see."

When they'd reached the private alcove at the bottom, he set her down and played with the pearls around her neck. "Much like you, I struggle with surprises."

She looked up at him, smiling seductively. "Would you like me to show you then, Master?"

"Yes, your Master would like to see your use of pearls, téa."

She dropped to the hard-packed sand and began by taking off his shoes and socks. Then she relieved him of his slacks, pulling his briefs down along with them. She stood back up, undid his tie and unbuttoned his shirt. Sir sloughed off both his jacket and shirt, so that he stood completely naked before her.

Brie slowly gyrated to the rhythm of the ocean waves as she rid herself of her remaining clothes, so that she too was *au naturel.* He reached out for her and she moved into his embrace. Brie closed her eyes as she laid her head against his warm chest.

"My goddess," he murmured.

Brie looked up at him and smiled. "Would you please lie down on your back, Master, so that I may show you my pearls?"

Sir lay down on the ground, his eyes never leaving her. Brie knelt beside him and ran the pearls between her lips, looking at him suggestively before taking them off. With slow, sensuous movements, she lightly caressed his skin with the smooth pearls, causing goosebumps to appear. She concentrated on his chest first, but twirled the pearls lower and lower, towards his pelvic region. Just as they were about to touch his hardening cock, she reached down to his feet and started upward.

He groaned in lustful frustration as she teased him as cruelly as he had teased her. As she moved up to his thighs, she bent over and allowed her nipple to 'accidentally' graze his cock. It twitched in response to the brief contact.

She wanted his cock coated in her juices before she began, so she curled the pearls into a spiral circle over his bellybutton. "For safekeeping," she said with a smile, before standing up and turning so she was facing away from him. She straddled his hips and wiggled her ass seductively, before slowly lowering herself. She knew she was giving Sir a fine view of her ass in the moonlight.

He took hold of his cock so that it was waiting for her. Brie pressed against the tip of his hard shaft and then lowered herself all the way to its base before pulling up again. She looked behind her and asked, "Does Master like?"

He growled and grabbed both ass cheeks, forcing her back down in answer. Brie rode his shaft, enjoying the angle of the position and the control she had over his cock—when he allowed it. Once he was properly coated, she lifted herself off his shaft and settled down between his legs. She picked up the pearls and began slowly wrapping his cock in them.

Then she held onto them with both hands and began stroking him with the numerous round beads. Sir tilted his head back and closed his eyes—a good sign.

Brie rolled the pearls up and down his shaft, kissing and licking the head of his manhood as she did so.

"Harder," Sir groaned.

She pressed her hands together for more friction, adding a twisting motion to her movement. He stiffened underneath her, making Brie purr with excitement.

"Teeth."

She grazed the ridge of his shaft with her teeth, being careful not to bite down too hard. Sir shifted and she knew he was close. She moaned loudly, as excited as he.

Sir shuddered. He grunted as his hips thrust forward and his come filled her mouth. Brie pumped his cock in rhythm with his thrusts, eagerly swallowing her Master's essence. He grabbed her head as he guided her mouth for the last couple of surges, and then he held her still as his body shuddered one final time.

When he let Brie go, he pulled her onto his chest and wrapped his arms around her. She lay in his arms for several minutes. She listened to both his rapid heartbeat and the crashing of the ocean waves in the background. His hands ran down her back, caressing her skin with their electric touch, and then they suddenly stopped.

"Brie."

She lay still, holding her breath.

"You know that my feelings for you run deep."

"As do mine, Sir."

"How deep?" he asked. She lifted her head and saw that he was smiling.

"I love you more than life itself."

He instantly stiffened and his eyes clouded over with pain. Somehow, in declaring her love she had said something wrong. The look of torment on his face spoke of old wounds having been ripped wide open.

"Thane, I love you!" she said in desperation, not wanting to lose their intimacy.

He just stared at her as if he was seeing someone else.

She could feel Sir pulling away from her emotionally, almost as if it were a physical separation. "I don't understand," she cried. "Help me to understand, Sir."

When he spoke, his voice was calm but strained. "Get dressed."

She untangled herself from his embrace and put her clothes on, tears streaming down her face. Had her allusion to death hit a raw nerve? Could that simple error have been enough to upset him this profoundly? It didn't make sense, but he gave no reason for his hurtful behavior.

She went to pick up her strand of pearls lying in the sand, but he said, "Leave them."

They walked back to the limo in deathly silence.

"Put your corset on," he told her once inside the limousine, before turning his head and looking out of the window.

The ride home was every bit as uncomfortable as the end of their first limo ride had been. When they finally pulled up to the high rise, Sir instructed, "Go to bed. I don't expect to return until much later."

When her tears started up again, he closed his eyes and added, "I will explain…later."

The chauffeur opened the limousine door and Brie obediently left, although inside her heart was breaking.

A staff member opened the lobby door for her with a broad smile as the limousine pulled away. As she walked inside, Brie snarled under her breath. *I fucking hate limos!*

Sir did not return until dawn. Brie had been up all night waiting for him. It took everything in her not to run to confront him. Instead she lay curled up on the bed, her eyes swollen from crying.

He entered the bedroom and quietly undressed before joining her in bed. "I assume you got no sleep."

"No sleep, Sir."

He pulled her to him in a spoon position. "We both need to rest. Close your eyes, téa."

Sir offered no explanation, but just having him beside her, wanting her near, was enough to quell her questions for now. She did as he asked and closed her eyes, giving in to a troubled sleep.

It wasn't until hours later that Sir stirred. Brie turned towards him and simply said, "Sir?"

He brushed her cheek lightly. "You said something, Brie…something my mother used to say to my father. You couldn't have known. I do not blame you."

She wanted to speak, but he put his finger to her lips.

"I told you once that I am undecided about fate. I do not know if your words are meant as a warning or a challenge to me."

She shook her head in protest.

He leaned forward and kissed her on the forehead. "I am taking it as a challenge. I have never dealt with my past. You are forcing me to face it straight on."

When Sir took his finger from her lips, she told him, "I didn't mean to hurt you, Sir."

"I know. It was said in love, but what are the chances you would answer with her words?"

"I would *never* hurt you in that way, Sir," she declared passionately.

"And that is where the quandary lies, for I am certain my mother would have said the same thing in the beginning."

Brie was hurt that he was comparing her to his mother—hinting that she would end up betraying him. She tried to pull away, but Sir grasped her arm. "Brie, in my head I know you are not the same, but right now…" He let go then, and turned away from her.

With fear and trepidation, she asked, "Sir, what are you saying?"

Sir looked back at her, the expression on his face uncharacteristically open and unguarded. "Time. I need time, Brie."

She caressed his masculine jaw, rough with stubble. Smiling through her tears, Brie answered, "Sir, we are condors. We have a lifetime to find our way."

# Animal Sex

---

Sir made Brie stay at home when he left for the airport later that day. He claimed he didn't want her to waste a single minute away from her project. "Look through what you already have that you can use to enhance your film. Decide what questions you want to ask both girls. You will need to be prepared before you approach Miss Wilson. You will also need to get permission from the Training Center for those extra shots the producer wanted. There is far too much for you to do to be wasting time at the airport seeing me off."

She nodded her agreement, but deep down inside she felt he was running away from her.

The second the door shut, life seemed to leave the entire apartment. It felt as if a part of her soul had left with him.

"Pull yourself together, Brie. You're not a weak-minded little girl who can't exist without her man."

She spent the night going back over her documentary footage. She concentrated on Mary, wanting to see if there was anything she could pull from it. She came across the moment when Mary had broken down in front of the camera, demanding she turn it off. Brie had been in the middle of giving her a compliment. In an instant, Mary's countenance had changed and she'd become hostile. Brie replayed it several times, zooming in on the girl's face. She swore she could see a look of longing in Mary's eyes, just before the walls came crashing down and the girl flipped out.

Maybe Sir was right. It was possible Mary was not a back-stabbing bitch. Well…not *only* a back-stabbing bitch.

As she was readying herself for bed, she was surprised to see the velvet box on the dresser. Curious, she opened it and gasped, clutching the sandy pearls to her chest. Sir had gone back for them…

She slipped under the covers wearing only the pearls. Unfortunately, the large bed only reminded her that he was gone. She curled up on his side of the bed and breathed in Sir's smell on his pillow. It was comforting and helped her to fall asleep. Brie knew it would be a long week ahead without him, but she had been an independent person before. There was no reason she couldn't survive—no, *thrive*—on her own.

She was sure the time apart would only help to make their reunion that much more passionate, if that were even possible.

He held out his hand and helped her out of the Mustang, then slammed the car door in his haste. She could feel the animal lust radiating from her Master. He wanted her, he *needed* her…

Brie trembled as she waited for him to unlock the door. She had a feeling he would be rough with her tonight. His eyes shone with dangerous desire.

When he put his hand on the small of her back, she swallowed nervously, letting him lead her inside. This was it. There was no turning back from the ravenous meal he was about to make of her.

He shut the door and dropped his keys on the hallway table, then commanded as he guided her down the hallway, "Everything off except for the panties. I plan to rip those from your body myself."

He stopped, so she immediately followed his orders and stripped before him, trying to keep the grace of a trained submissive even though she was surprisingly nervous. His sheer maleness overwhelmed her, making it difficult to concentrate.

"Beautiful," he complimented as he pushed her down to her knees so that her mouth was inches from his cock. She knew what he wanted without being asked and unbuckled his belt before unzipping his pants. She eased his throbbing member out of his briefs and opened her mouth to take him.

He grabbed a handful of hair and guided her lips to his cock. "That's it. Suck hard," he snarled lustfully. Brie took the head of his shaft into her mouth and sucked with uninhibited passion, concentrating on the sensitive ridge while her hands worked the base. He groaned in satisfaction, throwing his head back. "Oh, God, those lips…"

She moaned as he forced his cock deeper down into her throat. She wanted to be used in this way, an object for his pleasure. He fucked her mouth without regard for her. Brie relaxed and let him have his way. She was turned on by this selfish need he could not control. She understood it, they both needed the connection and she was thrilled to have the ability to please him.

He finally pulled out, forcing her head back to look at her. "I need to eat you." He helped her to her feet and then pushed her against the wall, ripping her lace thong off her body. With strong arms he grabbed her waist and lifted her up, then putting his hands under her buttocks, he lifted her higher. She squeaked when he commanded that she position her legs over his shoulders. She balanced herself precariously, afraid of being so high—until his tongue found her pussy and she went still. Brie pressed her back against the wall and she found support holding onto his head, all fear gone as he consumed her.

Even his mouth was rough—biting, probing, sucking—but she loved the carnal feel of it. "Yes!" she cried. "Devour me, Master!"

His growl tickled her clit. He returned to his passionate cunnilingus, licking the entire length of her before rimming her ass. She instinctively bucked, taken by surprise by his aggressive tongue.

Brie screamed as she began to tumble forward. With superhuman strength, he caught her and eased her to the floor. "You bad girl… Now your Master must teach you a lesson." He pointed to the center of the living room. "Crawl over there to receive your punishment."

She got on all fours and crawled across the hard marble floor like a cat in heat. She was frightened of her punishment, but desirous of it nonetheless. Once she'd made it to the middle of the room, he commanded gruffly, "Spread your legs wide, and put your left cheek to the floor so you can watch me."

She laid her head against the cool stone, making soft mewing sounds as he approached. He spanked her hard on her right ass-cheek, the sound of it echoing in the room. He slapped her again on the left, and she whimpered. She was sure he had left a handprint that time. He rubbed his hands over both cheeks, bringing a warm caress to complement the tingling sensation he'd created.

He slapped her twice more with the same stinging force, and then he bent down and bit her fiery skin. Brie moaned in ecstasy, the erotic feel of it making her pussy ache.

"Shall we try this again?"

He spread her ass cheeks wide and licked her pussy, starting with her wet opening and traveling all the way up to her anus. Although she gasped when she felt his tongue touch the forbidden area, she did not move. With a hunger she hadn't experienced before, he licked her length the same way several times, like a tiger. The wickedness of it had her mewing in pleasure. He bit her fleshy ass before giving her one more satisfying slap.

He pressed his cock against her pussy without entering as he straddled her thighs, whispering into her ear, "What do you want?"

"I want you to fuck me."

"You want me to fuck you deep enough to hurt?" he growled hoarsely.

She closed her eyes and voiced her deepest desire. "I want my body to resonate with your thrusts, Master."

He turned her head towards him and kissed her hard, then he held her chin and looked deep into her eyes. It made her shudder, for his gaze reminded her of a ravenous creature's—one that meant her harm.

Part of her yearned for escape. Despite her fear, or because of it, she willingly opened herself to him. "Take me, Master."

He mounted her then, ramming in his cock while holding her waist painfully tight. "I'm going to fuck you like you have never been fucked."

The onslaught began. Brie screamed as he took her violently, just the way she'd asked. Every thrust hit so deep that it sent a wave of painful electricity through her, but it was addictive and she cried out for more.

He was ferocious in his taking of her, fisting her hair and pulling her head back as his powerful hands left bruising caresses. He continually changed angles, seeking to dominate her pussy in ways it had never been conquered.

With each strong thrust, Master was laying his claim. She could feel it approaching, an orgasm like she had never experienced before, born of possession and pain. "Yes, Master, yes!" she cried through grateful tears.

His roar filled the room. "Come for your Master, blossom!"

Brie instantly woke, drenched in sweat, her heart racing as her pussy convulsed in the aftershocks of a powerful orgasm. She reached around desperately in the dark. "Master…? Sir…?"

She found there was no one else in the bed. She lay back down, reality finally sinking in. This was the third night since Sir had left that she had dreamed of Faelan. The intensity of it lingered on her skin like an unwanted caress.

It had seemed so real that she could not free herself from feeling it was an act of betrayal against Sir. Brie hugged herself, tears falling freely down her cheeks. She lay in the bed, trying to rock herself back to sleep, whispering, "No more…"

# Trust

Another morning dragged into existence. Even though Brie understood it had only been a dream, the guilt of it weighed heavily on her heart and would not leave her. It cast a dark shadow over her spirit, so much so that she put off going to the Center in hopes of the dreams passing, but she knew could not waste any more time.

Still feeling out of sorts, Brie headed to the Training Center. She hoped that she might catch Lea while she was there, needing to spend time with her best friend.

When she arrived, Brie went to the front desk and asked for the new headmaster.

The girl smiled pleasantly and asked, "Would you like me to call up Headmaster Coen?"

Brie was surprised the panel had chosen Master Coen rather than Master Anderson to take Sir's place. Although Coen had years of experience working at the Center, from what Brie had observed during her training, Master Anderson had more extensive knowledge and was more affable, as well.

"That would be good, thank you," she answered. Brie stood at the desk waiting for him, her nerves increasing with each passing minute. She had hoped to meet with Master Anderson, who she knew would support the film project. Master Coen? He was an unknown.

The beefy trainer—now headmaster—stepped out of the elevator and walked towards her with his typical stoic face. "Good day, Miss Bennett. What brings you to the Center?"

"My film project, Headmaster Coen. Would it be possible to talk to you about it in private?"

"Certainly. Follow me."

Brie watched his large muscles bulge under his dress shirt. She'd experienced the power of those arms when he'd spanked her…and used a hairbrush. As they took the elevator down to the Training Center itself, she forced herself to break the silence.

"I appreciate you taking the time to talk with me, Headmaster."

"Although I am wading through a mass of paperwork, I have a few minutes I can spare."

She didn't know how to respond so she kept silent, grateful when the elevator doors opened.

As they walked down the hallway to Sir's old office, she was confronted with feelings of déjà vu. Brie closed her eyes for a moment and could almost hear the sounds of Lea and Mary laughing with her in the hallways. It was so strange to think that part of her life was over.

Headmaster Coen opened the door and gestured her inside. Even though the books and pictures on the shelves had changed, it still looked like Sir's office—including the hook attached to the ceiling. She hid her smile.

"What is it you need, Miss Bennett? I have no time for niceties."

"Yes, Headmaster Coen. I have been asked by Mr. Holloway to shoot footage of the school grounds and the equipment used during training."

"I do not have a problem as long as you do not shoot footage of any of our students."

She bowed her head. "Thank you, Headmaster Coen. He also asked that I get interviews with the trainers themselves, and possibly footage of some actual scenes."

When she saw him frown, her heart skipped a beat. So much was riding on his answer. "You may speak to the trainers. If any are willing, you are free to interview them. However, I do not want our training filmed."

She swallowed hard, unsure if simple interviews would be enough for Mr. Holloway.

Headmaster Coen sat back in his chair and sighed. "If—and it is a big if—you can find a trainer and a willing sub on our staff who will consent to being filmed, I give you permission to film one session."

Brie couldn't believe it. Master Coen was giving her exactly what she needed. She stood up and bowed. "Thank you, Headmaster! You don't know how much this will help."

"There is one stipulation, however."

Brie sat back down, afraid that he was about to rip it all away.

"I must approve of any footage you shoot on our school grounds. I will not interfere with footage you've filmed off the campus, but I insist on having the last word on anything shot here."

"Of course, Headmaster Coen."

"You are free to explore the school and film, provided you do not disturb anyone here."

"I won't, Headmaster Coen." Brie bowed low one last time before leaving. She looked around to make sure no one was watching, and then leapt into the air. She had cleared her first obstacle!

Brie spent the day getting shots of the various rooms that had been used for her practicums, including the first one with the spongy floor and mirrored walls. She remembered vividly that first night when she'd tied the blindfold over her own eyes and presented herself to a complete stranger. That room had been the setting for significant firsts, including her first scene with Faelan when he had been training as a Dom. Visions of her recent dream flashed before her eyes, so she quickly left the room without mentioning the latter experience on film.

Brie moved on to Mr. Gallant's classroom next. Her mind had been opened to the world of submission by the tiny but infinitely wise man. His presence seemed to linger in the classroom even when it was empty.

Brie walked to the bondage room next, the one with the table that she'd first noticed on the website. This room held her most cherished memory—it was where she and Master had begun their physical relationship. She had planned to take a panorama of the room, but decided against it. It was something too personal to share with the rest of the world.

Brie headed down to the auditorium. It was the most significant room in the whole Training Center. This was where she'd been challenged the most. From watching her fellow classmates perform to navigating her own demanding practicums, this was where she'd discovered her power and limits as a submissive. She sat down in one of the chairs and let the memories flood over her.

She was so lost in her private thoughts that she did not hear him behind her until Marquis Gray spoke. "Good afternoon, Miss Bennett."

Brie turned around to see the formidable trainer. His ghostly white skin contrasted against the dark tones of the auditorium. She immediately stood up and bowed out of habit.

"You no longer need to bow, Miss Bennett. I am not your Master."

Brie blushed and looked to the floor, afraid to gaze into his dark, penetrating eyes. "Old habits die hard," she answered.

"Headmaster Coen said you had something to ask me."

Brie felt nervous butterflies start. Being around Marquis was intimidating enough, but when she was trying to conceal something from him, his presence was almost painful. She looked at the camera in her hands, avoiding eye contact at all costs as he sat down beside her.

"I was wonderin—"

"Miss Bennett, look at me."

With apprehension she stared into his dark gaze, holding her breath. She had never been able to hide anything from the experienced trainer.

"You are not doing well," he stated.

She shook her head slightly, afraid she would start to cry if she spoke.

"Gather yourself and explain."

It took a few moments before she could begin. "I have been tormented by dreams, Marquis Gray."

"What kind of dreams, Miss Bennett?"

"Dreams of Faelan."

His expression darkened. "Have you spoken of it to Sir Davis?"

She felt a pit start to grow in her stomach. "No, Marquis Gray."

He shook his head in disappointment. "Describe these dreams to me."

"It has been the same dream the last three nights. It starts right after the collaring ceremony. He takes me to his house as my new Master, and…" She closed her eyes, forcing herself to finish. "We consummate the relationship."

"So in the dream you have chosen Faelan over Sir Davis?"

"Yes," she said meekly.

"How do you feel when you wake up?"

"I feel horrible. It seems so real that I…" she turned away in shame, "…physically respond to them. I feel like I've cheated on Sir."

He was brutally to the point with his question. "Is guilt the reason for your pain, or do you feel regret?"

She protested violently, "No, never regret!" She looked at him in desperation. "Marquis, these dreams are unwanted and yet I am haunted by them when I wake."

He penetrated her with his gaze. She met it bravely, needing him to understand her torment. Finally he spoke. "The dreams are not your responsibility, Miss Bennett. However, your thoughts when you're awake are. Be honest with me—have these dreams changed your feelings towards Mr. Wallace?"

"No! My heart belongs to my Master. Marquis, I cannot live with these feelings of guilt. It's killing me inside. Please help me," she begged.

"I would suggest two things, Miss Bennett. Meditation will help you clear your mind when you awaken, so that this does not affect your waking hours."

She nodded in understanding. "Yes, Marquis. I will do that."

"You must also tell Sir Davis. Be prepared for his displeasure. You should have gone to him first. If you were my sub, I would punish you for such a breach of trust."

Brie felt the pit in her stomach turn into a wave of nausea. What would Sir think of her now?

Marquis replied, "Face the consequences with humility, Miss Bennett, and learn from them. Now, what was it that you needed to ask me?"

Brie ignored the swirling emotions threatening to overtake her and answered the trainer's question about her project. "Marquis Gray, would you be willing to let me interview you about your work here at the Center?"

"Yes, I agree to do a short interview. Mr. Holloway spoke to me of it the other day." His smile was genuine. "I would like to assist you in this."

She was moved by his offer to help. "Thank you, Marquis Gray. Thank you for everything you have done. I know I would not have this opportunity if it weren't for you."

"You are incorrect, Miss Bennett. Your dedication and hard work brought this opportunity, not me."

She would have disagreed, but she knew better than to argue with Marquis Gray. "Then I will simply thank you for your willingness to interview with me."

He nodded curtly. "We will do the interview seven days from now. You may want to check with Mr. Gallant. I believe he's come in early tonight as well."

Brie perked up upon hearing Mr. Gallant's name. She hadn't seen her teacher since graduation. "I will do just that, Marquis Gray."

He raised his eyebrow. "Do not fail to tell Sir Davis about what we discussed."

She blushed with shame and murmured, "I won't. Thank you for your advice."

"You are alumni now, Miss Bennett, but you will forever remain one of my students."

Brie quickly gathered her things, anxious to see Mr. Gallant again and escape from the disgrace lingering in the room. Seeing her teacher would lighten her heavy heart.

She found the small but commanding Dom in his classroom, setting up for the night's class. She was touched when his face broke into a smile the instant he saw her.

"Miss Bennett, what a pleasant surprise."

She held out her hand and he shook it warmly. "How is the new class, Mr. Gallant?"

"Green and uncertain, but with promising potential."

"Do they remind you of us?"

"No, this group is much more competitive with one another. It will take a bit longer to tame their immaturity."

"May I ask how Candy is doing?"

He looked at her thoughtfully before answering. "That's the girl you recommended, am I correct?"

"Yes, I've been curious how she's faring in class, and if she got rid of the abuser posing as a Dom."

"I cannot speak of her personal life, Miss Bennett. But, as far as her studies are concerned, I am pleased to say she is excelling."

Brie grinned. "I can't tell you how happy that makes me, Mr. Gallant!" She gave him a knowing look. "I'm thrilled someone was willing to sponsor her."

Mr. Gallant didn't blink an eye. "Yes, it is fortunate."

Brie had been told that he was Candy's benefactor, but true to form, Mr. Gallant kept it to himself, not being one to boast.

"In some ways I'm jealous of Candy," she said wistfully, looking around the classroom. "I really enjoyed learning in this room with you."

Concern overshadowed his smile. "Are you satisfied with your new life, Miss Bennett?"

She realized he was picking up on her unease, so she smiled reassuringly. "Yes, Mr. Gallant. I'm overflowing with satisfaction at being collared to Sir."

He seemed appeased by her answer and replied, "That warms my heart to hear."

Brie wanted to hug him, but as a collared submissive she held back the urge. "I came by to ask if you would be willing to do an interview with me for the documentary. I've already gotten permission from Headmaster Coen."

"I am truly sorry, Miss Bennett, but I cannot," he said with regret. "There are family members on my wife's side who would not understand. I will not risk her exposure."

Although Brie was extremely disappointed, she hid it well. "I understand, Mr. Gallant. It sure has been good talking to you again. You made my day, really."

"I miss your enthusiasm, Miss Bennett," he replied. "My wife and I would enjoy having the two of you visit us. After the documentary is complete, of course. I know you have no time to spare these days."

"So true. With Sir off working in New York City and me finishing my project, things are a little crazy right now."

Mr. Gallant frowned. "Sir Davis is away?"

"Yes. But he will be back soon. It's just a week-long business trip."

"I am sorry to hear that, Miss Bennett. It seems regrettable to be separated so early after your collaring."

Brie shrugged her shoulders. "I'm fine, Mr. Gallant. With both of us busy, I can't complain. Please don't concern yourself."

"Very well," he answered, although he did not look convinced. "I need to continue preparing for class. I hope to see you around over the next couple of weeks."

Brie left Mr. Gallant so she could wander the halls of the school, trying to find extra shots, but she soon felt out of place as the Training Center began to fill with people. She looked for Lea but could not find her, so she headed for the elevators to return home.

To her surprise, Ms. Clark was standing before her when the doors opened.

"Miss Bennett."

Brie put her eyes to the floor and mumbled, "Ms. Clark."

The Domme stepped off the elevator and addressed her. "I was told you are doing interviews for your film. Is that right?"

Brie nodded, unsure if she was going to get a lecture about upholding the integrity of the school, a favorite topic of the trainer.

"I will interview with you."

Brie was so shocked, she looked up without thinking. "You will?" When she saw Ms. Clark's stern expression, she instantly looked back down.

"Of course. I believe the perspective of a Domme should be included."

Still recovering from the shock, Brie replied, "I agree."

"Fine. Marquis said you are doing his in exactly a week. I will be available the day after." She did not wait for Brie's response. She walked away, her heels clicking seductively down the hall.

Brie hit the elevator button, still reeling from the shock. The thought of interviewing Ms. Clark made her cringe inside. No doubt Mr. Holloway would approve of the added drama.

The minute she entered the lonely apartment, she dialed Sir's number. Brie dreaded the phone call, but did not hesitate.

Sir could immediately tell something was wrong just by the tone of her 'hello'. "Explain what has happened," he stated, his voice calm and sure. It helped to ease her nerves.

"Sir, I need to tell you that I have had the same dream three nights in a row. It's so real that I…" Her voice trailed off as she lost her courage to continue.

He chuckled, the relief easy to hear in his voice. "You're calling about a dream? Did I die in it? Well, don't worry. I'm fine, babygirl. No need to fret any longer."

"No, Sir… I had a dream about another man."

His tone suddenly became deadly serious. "What man?"

"Faelan, Sir."

He paused before insisting with forced calm, "Explain this dream in detail."

Brie recounted her dream, not leaving out any details, as much as she was desperate to. She would not make the mistake of holding back something he might consider significant, no matter how mortifying it was for her.

The phone went silent. Finally, she asked in a choking gasp. "Sir?"

"How did it make you feel?"

"Every night I wake up feeling I've betrayed you, Sir. Marquis Gray questioned if my feelings have changed for Faelan, but they have not. These dreams are coming out of nowhere and I just want them to go away."

He said coldly, "Marquis Gray?"

Brie backtracked, realizing she was just digging herself into a deeper hole. "I saw him today at the Center. I didn't want to tell him, Sir, but he insisted. He also was adamant I tell you as soon as I got home."

"Your Master should always be the first you tell," he said in an icy tone. "The fact you have had these dreams for three nights has me questioning your silence."

She blurted, "Sir, I thought they would go away. I thought you would think I was silly or worse, that I actually desired Faelan. Master…after what happened the night before you left, I've been afraid to do or say something wrong."

"So you said nothing."

"Yes," she admitted miserably. "I want to please you, but I also feel a need to protect you, Sir. But in the end, all I ever do is fail you." She stifled a sob, feeling unworthy of his collar.

"Your protection is not what I want from you, Brie. I want your honesty at all times."

She struggled to get the words past the lump in her throat. "Yes, Sir."

"I do not hold you accountable for dreams. You can let go of any feelings of guilt over that. However, I am disappointed."

"I know I deserve to be punished, Sir. Punish me, please."

She heard him sigh heavily. "I'm uncertain if your dreams are a result of our discussion before I left, but I believe your reluctance to tell me is directly related. It is a vicious cycle. Your fear causes you to be silent, and your secretiveness causes me to question your trustworthiness."

"Yes…" she agreed sadly.

"Brie, anything that causes you discomfort must be shared, no matter the reaction you fear will result from it. Without trust, you and I are nothing."

The truth of his words cut like a knife. "Please punish me."

"I am not without understanding, Brie. As my sub, you need to have faith I will react in a reasonable manner. Our last parting caused you to question that. I give you my word that, even if I need time to digest what you share, I will give you the benefit of the doubt. But only if I hear it from your mouth and *not* another's."

"I promise, Sir. But please, I feel the need to be punished."

"Then your punishment shall be that unfulfilled need."

She whimpered. Brie had never thought in a million years that not being punished could hurt so much.

"Remember this lesson so that we do not have to revisit it again."

After she'd hung up the phone, she let out a painful sigh. This precarious dance of trying to navigate his tragic past—and her foolish missteps—made their relationship difficult and hurtful. Brie could only hope that their love would be enough.

# Dangerous Liaisons

Brie knew she could not put off her meeting with Mary any longer. She'd asked Lea to feel out Blonde Nemesis' mental state before she made her first attempt at contact. Lea reported that Mary was willing to get together if it was at a club, not at the Training Center and *not* at Sir's apartment. Brie wondered at the strange request, but remembered Sir's advice to meet Mary on her terms. Before she committed, she called Sir to make sure he approved.

"No, you may not go to The Haven."

Brie was hurt at Sir's lack of trust. "Sir, I don't plan to scene. I will just talk with Mary and Lea and leave afterwards."

He laughed, a response that surprised her. "I am not concerned about you scening, Brie. However, you should know that Mr. Wallace has been given permission to return to the club. I've been informed he is there every night. It would not be appropriate for you to go, especially alone."

Brie wanted to avoid Faelan and all the chaos he would cause if they were to meet. "Understood, Sir."

"There are several clubs that will do, but they are on the outskirts of the city. See if Mary is open to meeting at one of them instead."

Sir could not know how much his trust in her meant. "Thank you, Sir! I will happily make that suggestion."

"Good luck, Brie. Call me after your meeting."

It turned out that Mary was open to visiting another club, and suggested one that had just reopened. She'd heard it was more edgy than The Haven and wanted to check it out. Neither Lea nor Brie had heard of it, but it was in a central location for them all. Brie picked up Lea in Sir's Lotus. The look on Lea's face when Brie pulled up was priceless.

"Oh my, Brie! Does Sir know you're driving this?"

"Of course. He told me to take his car whenever I want. I'm hoping to impress Mary. Maybe if I let her take a spin she will sign my consent form."

"Do I get to drive it if I sign?" Lea asked.

"Umm…I'll have to ask Sir."

"What?! You trust Mary to drive this hot little sports car more than me?"

"You forget I've seen your poor vehicle. I know the kind of driver you are. How many dents does it have? Fifty?"

"Brie, you're a cruel friend. I'm going to seriously reconsider this whole documentary thing."

"What? And miss out on telling the world your lame jokes as you shake your big boobs? It's an idle threat, girlfriend."

Lea's eyes lit up. "That reminds me, I have a new one."

Brie groaned as she punched the gas pedal and sent both of them slamming into the seats. *Oh, the power of Sir's car!*

"How do you know you have a cheap Dom?"

Brie rolled her eyes. "Just hit me with it."

"He asks you to take off your collar to walk the dog."

Brie actually laughed out loud. "Okay, that was good. You can use that in the interview."

Lea clapped her hands. "I have a good feeling, Brie. I think tonight is going to exceed your wildest dreams."

She sighed nervously. "I hope so. I've never wanted anything as much as this. Well, let me amend that. I have never wanted anything except Sir more than this."

Lea bumped her shoulder and giggled. "Get thee to The Kinky Goat, woman!"

When they arrived a half-hour later and parked, the girls looked at each other and laughed. "This can't be it," Brie stated.

"It says Kinky Goat," Lea replied, pointing to an old, neon sign.

The club was in a rundown section of town and had the vibe of a biker bar. "Is it safe?" Brie asked, reluctant to leave Sir's car unattended.

Lea jumped out of the car. "Where's your sense of adventure, Brie? You've become an old married woman since getting collared. Live a little!"

Brie locked the car and set the alarm. She sincerely hoped she wouldn't regret this…

When they entered the establishment, several of the patrons turned to stare at them. Brie suddenly felt like fresh meat on display and wanted to turn around, but Mary was waving at them from the bar.

"Come on, stick-in-the mud," Lea joked, dragging her over to Mary.

Brie sat down unenthusiastically. She stared at Mary, and Mary stared at her—neither willing to make the first move.

"I have a great joke," Lea started.

Mary broke the silence to avoid it. "How have you been, Stinky Cheese?"

Brie answered half-heartedly, "Good, and you?"

"Could be better. Could be a hell of a lot better."

Brie didn't want to pussyfoot around the elephant in the room. "Why did you do it? Why did you let me think you fucked Faelan at the graduation ceremony? Why on earth would you do that to a friend?"

"It's always about you, isn't it, Brie? Did it ever occur to you that I had feelings for Faelan?"

"What? Like you did for every guy I showed an interest in?"

"See! There you go again. You think I liked those men because you did? Hell, no! You and I have the same tastes, but for some damn reason they always go for you," Mary spat out angrily, then took a drink of her rum and Coke.

"Are you seriously telling me that you love Faelan?"

"Love is too strong a word, and something you throw around like candy. I want him on a level I have never wanted another man. You'd probably call that love, but that would be stupid."

Brie snorted. "Oh, yeah. Call me stupid, but at least I'm honest about my feelings. You just push everyone away."

Mary waved her hand and ordered a round of drinks for the three of them. "You are such a bitch, Brie. You think you're all goodness and light, but you are a bitch underneath. Guys are idiots and fall for bitches like you all the time."

Lea spoke up. "Look, Mary, don't take out your frustrations on Brie. She cares for people and that's something you wish had, even if you hate her for it."

Mary stood up and looked like she was going to throw her drink in Lea's face, but Brie put her hand firmly on Mary's wrist.

"Maybe I *am* a bitch, because you're right—you and I are a lot alike, and you are the biggest bitch I know."

Mary looked at her in shock and then started laughing. Brie joined in and soon all three girls filled the bar with their laughter.

A sleazy wannabe Dom eased up to them. "You do realize laughing is not allowed. Sit down and shut your mouths and I may treat you to my whip."

His uncouth approach was comical. Brie looked at Lea and then Mary. The three burst out in giggles, embarrassing the 'Dom' enough that he left.

"Oh, my God, I've missed this!" Lea stated.

Mary sat down and sipped her drink before admitting, "Me too."

Brie grinned at the two girls. "I've felt lost without my other Musketeers." She gave Mary a humorous snarl. "I just couldn't get past you betraying me like that."

"I was honest for the first time in my life and look what happened. The guy tossed me away like garbage and my friends turned on me."

Brie suddenly felt the weight of her rejection and grabbed Mary's hand, squeezing it tightly. "You're right. I sucked as a friend because I never considered you were telling the truth. Well…that's not quite true. When I went to present my collar I saw the look on your face. It helped me to have the courage to present it to Sir instead."

"You should be bowing at my feet, thanking me," Mary answered.

Brie took a sip of her drink as a peace offering, even though she didn't care for rum and Coke. "Yeah, that'll happen…"

Lea held up her drink. "Here's to the Three Musketeers reuniting!" The three clinked glasses. Brie noticed the sleazy wannabe Dom raised his glass too. It was pathetic, so she turned her back on him.

"Lea said something about the documentary," Mary started. "Don't you dare tell me you need me to spill my guts on film."

Brie took a gulp of the drink for liquid courage and smiled, throwing all caution to the wind. "That's exactly what I need. I showed the piece to a big-time producer and you know what he had the nerve to tell me? And I quote: 'You don't have a film unless you get Mary's story'."

Mary smiled. "Hah!"

"I'm completely serious."

Mary got a superior look on her face. "So the great Brie Bennett came here tonight with her tail tucked between her legs to beg for my story."

Brie replied dryly, "There will be no begging, bitch."

Mary bristled at her tone and was about to let Brie have it when Lea stepped in. "Hey, Virginal Mary, I thought this was a club but all I see is the lame-o bar."

Mary turned to her. "You're an idiot, Lea. The action takes place in the back." She pointed to the double doors across the room. "I'm told all kinds of fun happens behind those doors."

"Yeah, like it could even compare to The Haven," Brie retorted.

Lea rubbed her hands together gleefully. "Why don't we check it out and see for ourselves?"

Brie knew Lea was attempting to defuse Mary's anger, so she went along with it. "Why not?"

Mary looked at her scornfully. "I'm shocked the collared Brie would consent to having fun. Won't your Master get mad and punish you?"

"I'm not going to scene, you ignoramus. I'm just curious."

"Well, hell, so am I!" Lea answered, getting up. "Let's go…"

Brie followed the other two into the Play Arena. She was shocked at how rundown and grimy the place was. She looked around, not impressed by the old equipment. Everything about it felt icky and slimy.

She glanced over at a girl bent over a table. The blindfolded sub had a ball gag in her mouth and was dripping saliva profusely. Her hands were tied behind her back, and her legs were spread and bound so that her pussy was splayed out for all to see. Written on her ass were the words, 'Fuck Doll'.

Brie looked away when a random guy dropped his pants and warned the girl that he played rough and was going to make it hurt.

She quickly moved on to another scene with a Domme and two subs. The male sub was dressed in a black leather hood and matching collar. His cock was restrained by a painful-looking metal gadget that fastened around both his balls and the head of his cock, making the shaft bend in an unnatural manner. He was standing over the female sub, who was lying on a rickety bench. She was licking his balls enthusiastically while the Domme fucked her with a lengthy black dildo strapped on at the hips. The Domme's strokes were long and ruthless.

"Now, thumperboy, you better not get any harder or it's going to hurt." She slapped the female. "Suckle those balls, slut. Make it hard for him." She laughed wickedly as she spread the girl's outer lips and thrust even deeper.

Somewhere in the back, Brie could hear a girl whimpering as a whip cracked repeatedly. "Shut your piehole, cunt, or I'll make it really hurt."

Overall, the place lacked the cleanliness and allure of The Haven, so Brie opted out. "I'll meet you back at the bar. Don't take too long, you two," she warned.

Brie sat at the bar, feeling on edge. She took a sip of her drink and snarled. Leave it to Mary to order her a crappy drink. After several minutes, Brie started drinking it out of sheer boredom. Even though she didn't enjoy the taste, at least it gave her something to do.

She waited impatiently, getting more agitated by the minute. That was when the sleazy wannabe Dom came over to make his move. "I see your girlfriends have decided to have a little fun. Why don't you and I join them?"

Brie shook her head, and was surprised to feel a little lightheaded. "Look, I'm collared." She touched the beloved collar around her neck for emphasis. "I don't scene with anyone except my Master. It's rude of you to even ask."

The guy didn't seem to care and sat down beside her. "We're both grown adults here. What we do doesn't have to leave this place. It's just you and me enjoying a little time together." He reached over and stroked her arm.

Brie pulled away, but her reflexes were unusually sluggish. "Don't…"

He smiled. "Don't what? Don't flirt with the sexiest girl at the bar?"

Her limbs began to feel heavy and weak. She looked at her hands, wondering what was wrong. But then she remembered the sleaze sitting next to her and barked, "Go."

He ignored her demand, opening his mouth to show off the stud in his tongue. "I'm going to make you come."

Brie giggled at the ludicrous thought.

He grinned at her lustfully, taking her response as consent. "I'm going to ram your ass with a dildo while I eat your cunt."

She let out a snorting giggle, as if she were drunk. Brie looked at her drink, but it was still half full. She couldn't explain why she thought he was so funny.

"After you come, I'll tie you up and make you pay for laughing at me earlier."

She broke out in a peal of laughter as she watched the room begin to move of its own accord.

"I think you would make the perfect fuck doll, princess. Don't you?" he said as he grabbed her arm.

Despite her confusion, Brie's internal alarms sounded loudly and she struggled against his firm grasp. "No…"

"No means yes and yes means no," he replied with a sly grin.

She had to think for a few seconds to answer him. "Yes."

He grunted in triumph. "I knew you wanted it. Come with me." He pulled her off the chair.

She struggled against him, but she could barely stand and fell into his arms. "That's it, come with Daddy," he encouraged, guiding her towards the double doors. "Daddy's going to have all kinds of fun with you tonight."

Brie no longer resisted, desperate for his support when the floor began to wobble beneath her feet.

"Let her go," a deep voice demanded from behind her.

"Stay out of this," the sleaze answered.

"I'm serious. I will count to three. Let her go or you will leave with a mouthful of broken teeth."

The sleaze held onto Brie tighter. "This one's mine."

"One…two…"

Brie suddenly felt herself falling. Solid arms caught her and lifted her up.

"You're safe, kitten."

Brie focused on his hazel eyes just before everything began to spin.

She woke up feeling groggy and was surprised to find herself lying on a couch. *This isn't Sir's apartment!* The place had the feel of a bachelor pad, with its minimal décor and large entertainment system.

Brie began to hyperventilate, remembering the sleaze who had been holding her just before she'd passed out. A number of scenarios went through her head, each one more terrible than the last. A sob escaped her lips.

"You're awake."

Brie knew that voice and turned towards it in relief. "Baron…"

He got up from his chair and walked over to her. "What the hell were you thinking, kitten?"

"How?" she asked, so woozy she was unable to form sentences.

"How did you get here? I found you being dragged off to have sex with a lowlife. What were you thinking going to a place like that?"

All she could manage was, "Lea? Mary?"

"They're fine. I sent them home and brought you here to recover. There must have been something in your drink. Probably that bastard, but no one saw him do it and I couldn't get him to admit to it, despite my powers of persuasion. So I decided to give him a personal warning just in case. He won't be fucking a girl anytime soon."

Brie shuddered, realizing how close she'd come to being raped.

"Why…you?"

"Why was I there? I heard it'd reopened and went to look after newbies who might wander into the place. That club is bad news. I never thought I would find one of our graduates there, much less three of them."

Brie buried her head into the couch. "Sir?"

"Yes, I called him to let him know what's happened. He's on a plane flying back as we speak."

Brie began to cry. Baron lifted her up off the couch and embraced her.

"You're safe. Nothing happened."

She sobbed, soaking Baron's large shoulder with her tears. Finally, she choked out a weak, "Thank you."

He held her tightly. "You're okay, kitten. Nobody hurt you."

She gulped through her tears, "You…are…a good…man."

His warm chuckle rumbled in his chest. "No. I simply cannot abide women being abused."

"Baron…" she gasped, still struggling to think straight.

He crushed her in his safe embrace. "Don't speak, kitten. Sit here while I make you something to eat." Baron put her down and repositioned the pillow so she could sit up. He returned a short time later with a bowl of oatmeal and some hot tea.

"Drink," he commanded, bringing the cup up to her lips.

Brie opened her mouth and the warm liquid brought its soothing relief, caressing her throat. He put the cup down and lifted a spoonful of the hot cereal to her lips.

"You'll feel better soon."

"Thank you," she said. A tear fell down her cheek.

He wiped it away. "No need to cry."

Baron gave her another spoonful. She looked around his apartment, noting several photos of a beautiful woman with dark skin, an inviting smile and a collar around her neck.

"Your submissive, Baron?" she asked, pointing to a photo.

He looked at the photo and nodded slowly. In a quiet voice he added, "We're parted."

Brie frowned, sad to learn that Baron was alone.

"Eat," he insisted, letting her know it was not a topic up for discussion.

After the bowl was empty and the last sip of tea had been drunk, he tucked the blanket around her and ordered her to sleep. She settled down, not thinking sleep was possible.

"Brie…"

She felt a gentle nudge and heard her name again. *Master's voice.*

Her eyes flew open and she saw Sir's beloved face. He sat beside her and pulled her onto his lap, rocking her as if she were a child. She buried her face in his chest and cried with relief.

"Shhh, babygirl. I'm here now…"

# Lovers to Friends

The fallout from the incident affected Brie in ways she could not have imagined. Sir was angry with himself. "Here I was so concerned about Wallace that you ended up going to a *den* of wolves. Well, that won't happen again, Brie," he stated forcibly.

Brie worried about what it would mean for her—for them both. Sir seethed with a quiet anger she could not reach past. She was grateful when he finally decided to speak with his friend Master Anderson. After several visits with him, Sir set up a long meeting with Marquis Gray.

She had no idea what had been discussed, but when Sir returned from Marquis Gray he seemed more like himself. "Sit with me, Brie."

She moved over to him and sat on the couch. "Yes, Sir?"

"I realize I have not been easy to live with lately, and you have suffered for it."

"It has been difficult, Sir," she admitted, bowing her head.

"Brie, unfortunately you are collared to a man haunted by ghosts of the past. I have been shaped by those events and cannot react the way most people do."

"I accept that, Sir."

He swept her hair back gently. "You are a challenge for me in so many ways, téa." She looked at him questioningly. In response, Sir pressed her head against his chest and held her tightly against him. "I couldn't save my father, but I damn well am going to protect you."

She smiled, content in her Master's caring embrace.

They spent the afternoon unpacking the rest of her boxes, making her stay more permanent for them both. During their work, Sir came across the wax casting Tono had made of her. He held it up and stared at it for a while before announcing, "I believe I will call Tono and ask if he can come over tonight. The meeting has been put off for far too long."

"If it pleases you, Sir," she answered. Brie wondered how she would feel when she saw Tono. So much had happened since graduation—it seemed like a lifetime ago.

When the doorbell rang later that evening, Brie felt only peace as she opened the door to her former training Dom. Tono's eyes were as gentle and kind as she remembered, despite the reality of their past. He handed her a bottle of sake.

"It is good to see you, Miss Bennett."

It was strange hearing him call her 'Miss Bennett' and not 'Toriko'. She took the bottle graciously. "Thank you, Tono Nosaka." She gestured him inside, then closed the door slowly behind him, struck by how surreal it was to invite Tono into Sir's apartment.

"Thank you for coming, Ren," Sir said, getting up from the couch. He shook Tono's hand and then instructed Brie, "Set the sake in the kitchen and start a pot of water boiling."

Brie bowed and followed his orders, assuming the boiling water must be the way to warm sake. When she returned to Sir, she was surprised to see his hand on Tono's shoulder and a serious look on his face. Tono nodded once and turned to Brie.

"You are completing your documentary. It pleases me to hear it."

She avoided his gaze, suddenly feeling uncomfortable. The last time they'd talked, he'd told her how proud he was of her work and that he would support Brie's career as her Dom. Guilt clouded her heart, making it painfully clear that she was *not* ready for this meeting.

Sir answered for her. "Yes, Brie is working diligently on it. Mr. Holloway has some suggestions she is currently filming. Why don't we move to the kitchen and Brie can tell you about it?"

Tono and Brie sat at the table while Sir took out a small flask. Brie couldn't bring herself to speak, so she watched as Sir poured the sake into the flask before placing it in the boiling water.

"What were you asked to add?" Tono inquired.

Brie blushed and turned to him, smiling hesitantly. "Shots of the Training Center, interviews with trainers, and…more in-depth interviews with Lea and Mary."

Sir interjected, "That is how the three inadvertently ended up at the club."

Tono nodded in understanding.

Brie felt heat rise to her cheeks, knowing that Tono had been informed of the incident at The Kinky Goat. She looked away, feeling the shame of the experience wash over her.

She felt Sir's hand on her shoulder. "But that is not why I asked you to come tonight." Sir set three sake cups on the table and poured the warmed sake into them before sitting down. "How is your family, Ren?"

"My father returned to Japan last week. My family in general is in good health."

"To your family's continued good health," Sir stated, holding up a small sake cup.

He handed Brie her sake, and she held it up before sipping the warm rice wine. It had a plum flavor that was slightly sweet and incredibly tasty.

She stared at the cup, trying to build up the courage to ask, "Was your father relieved when I did not choose you?"

Tono waited until she looked up and met his unwavering gaze. "He feels you made the appropriate choice, Miss Bennett."

Brie looked back down at her cup, unsure how to respond.

"Ren, it is fine to call her Brie. 'Miss Bennett' is too formal given your history together."

Tono picked up his cup and nodded. "To both of you."

"I'll drink to that," Sir answered.

Brie lifted her cup and swallowed the last of the sake in it. Sir immediately filled up Tono's and Brie's cups and announced, "I'm heading off to the spare room to unpack Brie's remaining boxes. I want to give you two a chance to speak freely."

An uncomfortable silence filled the room when Sir left. It was broken when Tono said, "Brie, I understand your choice."

She looked at him sadly.

He shook his head. "No, I do not need or want your sympathy. You made your choice. I accept it."

When Brie did not answer, Tono leaned forward. "Your guilt does not honor me or what we shared." He sat back in his chair slowly. "Seeing you happy is my only consolation at this point."

"I…I never meant to hurt you."

"Someone was going to get hurt. I knew what was at stake going in. I do not regret our time together, Brie. Do you?"

"No, Tono Nosaka, I do not."

"Then we both move on, better for the time we shared together."

"Yes," she agreed.

They both drank their sake and he poured another round before stating, "I am looking into working with couples new to Kinbaku. There are many who would like to learn the art."

"I'm sure there are, and you would be the perfect man to teach them. You have a patient soul and a true talent."

"I'm currently looking for a sub to join me for the beginner courses. Most only want to be involved if there are advanced rope techniques or suspension involved."

"That's a shame. Even your simplest work is inspiring."

He laughed good-naturedly. "Yes, I remember how easily you gave in to the rope."

She joined in his laughter. "I think a lot of that had to do with your 'breathe with me' technique."

"I will not deny there is method to my madness."

She dared to look the handsome Japanese Dom in the eye. "I think you are an exceptional person, Tono Nosaka."

His expression softened. "I feel the same, Brie. So this is where we go from lovers to friends."

She picked up her cup. "To you, my friend."

"To us."

Tono shared some of his recent foibles in scening, including one with a new sub. The girl had had a panic attack while he had been hoisting her up, but her reaction had been to giggle hysterically. Everyone watching had thought she was having a wonderful experience, but he'd noticed her rapid breathing. He had asked her if she had reached red, but she'd shaken her head and giggled louder.

After several minutes, he had decided something wasn't right and had cut her down. She'd grabbed onto him, laughing all the way to a private room. The entire club had laughed along with her even as they'd abandoned the scene.

"When I asked her why she'd answered no to being red, she told me she'd heard, 'Do you eat sweetbread?'"

Tono had Brie laughing so hard that Sir came out to investigate.

"What is going on here?"

Brie was pointing at Tono, snickering. "Sweetbread!"

Tono shrugged. "She's easily amused."

Sir nodded in agreement. "Yes, it doesn't take much." He looked at her and smiled—the first relaxed smile since his return.

With the pleasant buzz of the sake flowing through her veins, she momentarily forgot Tono was there and purred, "I love you, Sir."

He walked over and kissed the top of her head. "I try to convince myself that being easily amused is not the reason you chose me."

She broke out in another peal of laughter that both Doms joined in on. The night ended on that light note.

Sir asked Brie to see Tono out while he stayed in the kitchen to wash up. She walked Tono to the door and smiled when he held out his hand to her.

"Good night, Brie. It's been a pleasure."

She took it, grateful they no longer had that awkward barrier between them. "Likewise, Tono Nosaka."

After shutting the door, she returned to Sir to thank him, but the amorous look in his eyes told her he had other things on his mind.

"Come to me, téa."

She glided over to her Master's wet hands, and squealed when Sir swept her off her feet. He started towards the bedroom, pronouncing, "I'm going to fuck your sweetbreads."

Brie giggled all the way down the hall.

# The Solution

Sir insisted that Brie meet with Mary and Lea again, but this time in the safe confines of the Training Center. "I will spend time with Master Coen while you three speak. There are several issues he and I need to go over, now that he has taken over as headmaster."

Brie was curious, knowing that Sir had recommended Master Anderson take over the position when he'd resigned, so she asked, "Sir, how do you feel about the panel's choice?"

"I made my recommendation. However, I am confident Coen will make a fine headmaster."

"What will Master Anderson do now?" Brie hated the thought of future subs missing out on the experienced Dom's unique skills.

"He is taking over Coen's training position, but has not committed to staying longer until he sees how this new session plays out."

"I hope he stays, Sir."

He looked down at her with a smirk. "Want to feel the bite of his bullwhip again, téa?"

Brie shook her head. "Not for that reason, Master. I want him to stay because he's your friend."

Sir surprised her by giving her a peck on the cheek. "You are a sweet little thing."

Sir treated Brie to a spirited drive to the Training Center in his Lotus. The sports car was like an extension of his body and he knew precisely how to use and abuse it for his enjoyment. He kept Brie's heart pounding the entire way, helping to temporarily relieve her of the anxiety she felt about meeting Mary again.

She walked into the college, laughing as she hung onto Sir's arm. Business students standing at the entrance turned to see what the commotion was about. Brie buried her face in Sir's arm. "Sorry, Sir." She knew as a submissive she was not supposed to bring attention to herself.

He chuckled, patting her hand. "It's all right, Brie. The students here are far too serious. They could do with a little laughter."

Sir took her to the lower level and walked her to the meeting room where Lea and Mary were waiting. He handed Brie her briefcase and nodded to the two women. "Good afternoon, Ms. Taylor, Miss Wilson."

They both greeted Sir, but Brie was surprised to hear a hint of repentance in Mary's voice.

Sir nodded to them both and turned back to Brie. "I will be meeting with Headmaster Coen in his office. Go there when you are finished."

"Yes, Sir," Brie said, bowing gratefully. Whatever happened today, Sir would be there to support and encourage her. She watched him walk down the hall before she entered the room.

Lea ran to her, then hugged her tightly. "Oh, Brie, I'm so sorry about what happened. Are you okay?"

"I'm fine. Baron stopped the creep before anything happened."

"But it must have been frightening, knowing what almost… And we were right there," Lea said with tears in her eyes.

Mary snarled, "As soon as he brought you into the Play Arena, I would have been all over his ass. No way would I have let him touch you! What, did he think we wouldn't notice or wouldn't care?" Brie could tell Mary was boiling with pent-up rage.

Brie walked over to her and put her arm around Mary's shoulders. "I know you would have protected me."

Mary's voice was rough with emotion. "I never meant for that to happen, Brie. I know you blame me—everyone does."

Brie squeezed her shoulder in reassurance. "No. I don't, and I know Sir doesn't. I should have trusted my gut when I saw how rundown it was, but like you, I was curious."

Mary pulled away, but slowly, as if she wanted the contact but felt uncomfortable with it.

Brie turned to Lea. "So let's sit down and talk about the documentary. It's the whole reason we got into that mess in the first place."

"I'm in—whatever you want, however you want it," Lea said, sitting down beside her.

"No," Brie said. "Hear me out before you agree to anything."

Lea propped her chin up with both hands. "Okay, shoot!"

"Mr. Holloway wants your honest stories. He won't settle for superficial crap. But if you do this, you will become an easy target for the haters out there. It could get really ugly." She looked sympathetically at Lea. "And you'd have to tell your mom everything. Is that something you're willing to face?"

"Obviously you are," Lea stated. "If you're willing to jump into the lions' den, I'll jump with you."

Both Brie and Lea stared at Mary.

"What the hell? I don't even know why you're asking. I told you from the beginning I wasn't going to get all personal. Did you really think I would change my mind?"

Brie suddenly had an idea, realizing exactly how to sway her. "I remember a story you once told me. One about a little girl who watched *It's a Wonderful Life* and decided to become a pharmacist so she could save lives. Well, I think you could save lives with this film. From the abuse you suffered and *survived*, to learning the importance of full disclosure in a scene, the mistakes you and I made could prevent others from suffering the same consequences—or worse. I plan to include what happened to me at The Kinky Goat," she added with seething rage, "because I don't want any girl to fall victim to a creep like that." She wiped away the angry tears that fell from her eyes. "Mary, everything we've learned—all of it—will be lost if you don't agree to do this."

Mary just glared at her, saying nothing.

Brie leaned forward and said with confidence, "I know you aren't a coward."

Mary responded by growling and pushing away from the table. Brie simply sat there and stared at her, letting it sink in.

"No means no!" Mary hollered, getting up from the table. She paced around the room furiously, muttering to herself.

Lea gave Brie a cautious thumbs-up.

Finally, Mary sat back down. "I know I will regret this and hate you for the rest of my life."

Brie opened her briefcase and pulled out the consent forms. "Now, there's no need to sign this today. Read it over; make sure you understand everything before you sign, anyway."

Mary grabbed it from her and signed it immediately.

"What are you doing?" Brie cried.

"I know myself. If I take this home I'll tear it into a million pieces." She glared at the form and then shoved it in Brie's face. "Better take it from me now."

Brie quickly placed it back in the briefcase and shut the lid. "I don't think you're going to regr—"

"Shut up, Brie. Just shut up," Mary snarled.

Brie knew better than to push her any further. A nervous happiness started to build inside. It was really happening… Mary, her Nemesis, her frienemy, had agreed.

"So do you guys want to see what I already have?"

Mary shrugged, but Lea clapped her hands. "Damn tootin', I wanna see how I look in this film." She asked with a grin, "Does it make my boobs look bigger?" Lea adjusted her breasts with her hands for dramatic emphasis.

"Naturally," Brie answered, pulling out her laptop as the other two gathered around. "Now, feel free to tell me what doesn't work for you. I'll be filming a lot of new shots, so I have plenty of room to play."

They spent the next hour and a half laughing their way through six weeks of training. Brie kept sneaking glances at the other two, overflowing with happiness. This journey they were on had not ended at the Center like she'd thought—it was truly just beginning.

Brie walked to Sir's old office, listening to the sexy echo of her heels in the hallway. Surprisingly, one of the most useful things she'd learned was how to walk in six-inch heels. It had given her a seductive power she'd never had before, and she basked in the glory of it as she swayed her hips.

She knocked on the office door. Even though she knew Master Coen was headmaster now, it surprised her to hear his voice order from within, "Enter."

Brie opened the door and had to catch her breath. Sir was holding a thin iron rod in his hands. She took a step back and then dropped her gaze to the floor. *The brand!*

"Well, it appears it's time for you to go," Headmaster Coen told Sir. "Thank you for your time."

She sneaked a peek and saw Sir put the brand in a thin wooden box, before shaking Coen's hand. "My pleasure, and thank you for this," he added, holding up the box.

Brie shuddered.

Sir winked at Brie as he walked her out. "How did it go, Brie?"

She immediately forgot about the brand and grabbed onto his arm. "Sir, Mary said yes!"

"Excellent."

"You were right. My assumptions about Mary were way off."

He looked at her compassionately. "I have found that is normally the case, Brie. What we think to be true has nothing to do with reality."

She pressed closer to him. "You're so wise, Master."

"You have called me 'wise' once before. Did I not tell you that I prefer intelligent, quick-witted or experienced?"

She giggled, remembering their conversation at the club after Master Anderson's bullwhip session. "Yes, Sir. I do recall you saying that a *long* time ago. Can you forgive your wayward sub for forgetting?"

He slapped her on the ass. "I should take you home for a thorough spanking, so that it will remain fresh in your mind."

She wiggled her butt suggestively. "If it pleases you, Sir."

When they arrived home, he handed her the dark wooden box to carry up to the apartment. He was not letting her forget that it existed. She stood in the mirrored elevator, staring ahead, her body tingling with fear. She noticed that Sir looked completely relaxed and unconcerned, as if this was an everyday happening. Would he try to brand her tonight?

*Will I let him?*

Brie looked down at the box with tears pricking her eyes. The fear evoked by Master Coen's 'mock branding' still resonated in her mind. Sir was asking too much…

As devoted as she was to Sir, Brie did not want to endure the pain of the brand—even if it would please him.

When they entered the apartment, Sir sat down on the couch and asked her to kneel at his feet. "Give me the box, téa."

Brie held it up with shaking hands.

He opened the wooden box reverently and smiled. He picked up the simple iron rod with a handle on one end and a 'T' on the other, and twirled it between his fingers. "There are two things I am quite aware of, téa. You are not a masochist, and you are afraid of this brand."

He looked down at her. Brie nodded in agreement, not trusting herself to speak.

"You will not wear my brand until you beg for it. Until that time, it will remain in this box, unused." He gave her a benevolent look, adding, "I promise—even if it means you never ask." He placed it back in the box and closed the lid, latching it. "Put it on the top shelf of our closet."

She rocked back to her feet and walked down the hallway without speaking, grateful he was not forcing it on her. She pushed the wooden box far into the back of the closet, with no desire to feel its skin-melting touch. However, knowing that Sir wanted her to wear his brand was powerful. Even more potent was the knowledge that he was leaving it up to her.

She walked back to him and settled at Sir's feet once more, purring silently as he ran his fingers through her hair.

"I know this will not come as welcome news, téa, but my clients are returning to Russia and have requested I join them. The purpose of my visit is to observe their factory practices, so that their managers can be properly trained for the relocation."

Brie looked up at him, unable to hide her disappointment.

"This will be at least a three-week trip."

She opened her mouth to protest, but thought better of it.

"But I am not leaving you alone again. Completing your film is paramount and you need support for that. Normally, I would suggest you stay with a friend, but given recent events, I am not comfortable with that option. After much thought and soul-searching, I have come up with a solution I think will serve both our needs."

"I don't understand, Master." Brie shook her head, an icy chill running down her spine. "I have a feeling I don't want to understand."

He lifted her chin, forcing Brie to focus on him and not on her growing concern. "Your safety and well-being are the only things that matter to me. Since you cannot come with me, I will leave you here in the hands of another."

Her heart skipped a beat. "Master?"

"I will give him full rights as your Master, bar one."

"Rights?" she cried out in alarm.

"In every way you will serve as his submissive. However, he will not have the right of penetration. I expect you to obey every command without question or suffer his punishment when you fail. I have instructed him not to be lenient with you."

"No..." The weight of Sir's abandonment crushed Brie's heart like a heavy stone.

"Téa, this is my command. I cannot stay and I will not leave you alone. You must obey me in this."

"Please, Master, don't ask this of me."

"I am not asking," he replied.

She bowed her head, struggling between shock and grief.

"Look at me, téa." Brie forced herself to look into her Master's eyes, unable to hide her feelings of resentment. He said with gruff emotion, "I have promised to protect you. I can do no less."

"But...giving me to another? Don't you love me?" she whimpered.

"It is the force that drives me. You need to be supported, not only as a submissive, but in your film endeavors." He caressed her cheek tenderly, his gaze certain and kind. "My love for you is without question, Brie."

She jumped when the doorbell rang.

He nodded. "Answer it."

Brie fought with her conflicting emotions. She did not have to answer the door. Sir could not force her to give herself to another Master. If push came to shove, she had the option to leave...

"Obey me," he commanded with gentle firmness.

Looking into his eyes again, she saw only love for her. Sir was not asking her to do this for himself. This was a sacrifice of love on his part.

She got up and walked to the door, her heart pounding as she reached for the doorknob. Which trainer would it be? Marquis? He was a disciplinarian and had an interest in helping her with the film. Or would it be Master Anderson, the bullwhip master who was also Sir's good friend? Either would be a challenge she wasn't sure she was ready for.

Brie took a deep breath and opened the door.

His soothing gaze washed over her like a wave in the ocean.

"Toriko…"

# Brie Learns Restraint

# The Contract

Brie stood holding the door open, staring at Tono in shock.

"Invite him in, téa."

She shook her head slightly to regain her bearings before bowing to the Dom. "Please come in, Tono Nosaka." She stepped aside to allow him to pass, not daring to look in his direction.

In a daze, Brie closed the door and walked back to Sir, then knelt at his feet—her place of comfort. Tono sat at the other end of the couch, beside Sir.

Sir began petting her hair lightly. "She just became aware of the arrangement."

"Her thoughts?" Tono asked.

"I do not know." Sir lifted Brie's chin. "What do you think, téa?"

Her lips trembled when she spoke. "If I am to serve another, then Tono is a fine choice, Sir."

Sir glanced over at Tono. "She is still struggling with my decision."

Tono addressed Brie. "Do you wish to serve me, toriko? I will not allow you to serve under me unless it is your desire."

Brie dropped her eyes to stare at the floor. "I do not understand what this arrangement entails, Tono Nosaka. I cannot answer you."

"Spoken like an intelligent woman," Sir commented, kissing the top of her head. "I will keep you in suspense no longer. Ren and I still have to iron out the details. Come join us at the table. I want you to be fully aware of what I am asking of both of you."

Sir stood up and went to his desk to retrieve a file. "I had this drawn up. Naturally, it is subject to change, depending on our discussion tonight."

Tono followed him to the kitchen table, with Brie several feet behind both men. Her head was buzzing like a hornet's nest with thoughts…and fears.

Sir indicated that Tono should sit opposite him, but he pulled the other chair close to himself and commanded gently, "Sit."

Brie sat down robotically, and kept her eyes glued to her lap. *This isn't really happening…*

Her Master pushed the folder across the table towards Tono. "Read over the contract. Anything you do not agree with or need clarification on, I want to address now. This is as much for téa's benefit as for yours."

Brie heard Tono turn the pages slowly as he read over the contract. When he was done, he asked, "Do you have a pen?"

"Of course," Sir answered. "Téa?"

Brie obediently stood up and retrieved a pen from the desk. She returned to Sir, but he nodded towards Tono. She held it out with an open hand, her insides quivering when he made physical contact. "Thank you, toriko."

Such simple words, yet everything had changed with Sir's decision. This man would soon be her Master—if she allowed it.

"It states the duration of this contract begins tomorrow and ends exactly three weeks from that date?"

"Actually, that should be amended to 'or upon my return'. Should I arrive earlier, I would expect to regain my rights as her Master and should I need to stay longer, I would want téa to remain in your care and under your protection."

"Understood." Tono scribbled something in the margin and continued, "I see that I am not allowed to 'lend' her to another, but I want to clarify that you have no objection to her being part of a demonstration. Although she will be working on the documentary, I plan to have her assist me in a weekly class. Will that be a problem?"

"As long as completing the film is your top priority, I do not have an issue with her participating in a class. However, you must be the one in charge of téa. No one else touches her," Sir stated emphatically.

"Even to recreate a knot?"

Sir sighed and closed his eyes, rubbing his temples. "Simple guided instruction is fine. However, I do not want her to scene with one of your inexperienced Doms."

"I would never put Brie in that situation," Tono assured him. Brie noted that he wrote the words '*guided instruction only*' in the margin.

"I see I am not allowed to take her from the city limits."

"No."

"Because my classes take place at The Haven, I see no conflict."

"Ah, but The Haven may be an issue. I do not want Brie running into Wallace there."

Tono nodded in agreement. "We shall enter from the back and proceed to the training room. We will in no way provoke an encounter. However, if he seeks us out, it will be dealt with."

"I do not trust the boy—yet. Although Marquis is working with Wallace, I still consider him a threat to himself and Brie."

Brie was surprised to hear that Faelan was being personally instructed by Marquis. She wondered if it had anything to do with her talk with the trainer.

"Acceptable," Tono replied, looking farther down the contract. "I will need further explanation of the 'no penetration' clause."

"It is simple enough. There is to be no penetration of her anally, vaginally, or orally with any tool or body part."

"Does that include kissing?"

Sir stared at Brie's lips for several moments before answering. His voice was gruff and low as he replied grudgingly, "I will allow kissing."

Tono took the pen and clearly wrote, '*kissing excluded*'.

Brie blushed. It was strange to have these two men discussing such things. She looked to the floor, her heart beating erratically.

"It states I am in charge of her care, protection and well-being. Are there any specific needs you require me to meet?"

"Naturally, her documentary comes above everything else. I expect you to give her the time and environment necessary for her to succeed in meeting her deadline. I am not opposed to having her performing necessary tasks for you, as long as it does not jeopardize the project."

"You and I are agreed on that."

Sir snorted. "Just as important to me, I expect you to keep her safe, Ren. No run-ins with Mr. Wallace, no unescorted clubbing while I am gone… Keep her safe."

"I assure you, she will be looked after."

"After what occurred during my last trip..." Sir shook his head angrily. "I cannot be reasonable on that score."

Brie glanced at Sir, noticing his clenched jaw and the throbbing vein in his neck. As much as this action seemed extreme, she understood the motive behind it. It was his need to protect her that had inspired the unusual arrangement. She understood and would receive it as such.

"I would suggest you text me while you are away. I will give you an update whenever asked." Tono scribbled more notes onto the contract. "Toriko, you should be aware that you are expected to contact Sir Davis every Sunday morning to speak for one hour."

Although she knew she should be thrilled contact was allowed, the idea of only speaking to Sir once a week crushed her heart. She felt tears coming, but fought them back.

"There is another stipulation, Brie," Sir added. "I expect you to exercise at exactly six every morning at a local gym minutes from Ren's home. I will be exercising at the same time, only it will be four in the afternoon my time."

Brie felt a sense of relief. Although they would not be talking every day, there would be a daily connection nonetheless. She looked at him and whispered, "Thank you, Sir."

"I assume you have no issues with that?" he asked Tono.

"It seems like a healthy solution," Tono replied with a smirk, "on many levels."

Sir smiled in reaction to Tono's jesting, but it disappeared when he added, "It is important that Brie submits to you fully. I do not believe it is possible to serve two Masters, but I do not want the connection between us to be lost."

Tono put the pen down. "I understand my place, Thane. Temporary Dom. I will treat the role as such." He looked at Brie compassionately.

Sir stood up and held out his hand. "You are an honorable man, Ren."

Tono took his hand and shook it. "Toriko's well-being is equally important to me."

Sir slapped him on the back the way Brie had seen him do with his good friends. "I am counting on it." He picked up the pen and handed it to Tono. "If téa agrees, sign the contract and initial the addendums."

Tono turned to Brie. "Are you willing to become my sub based on these parameters?"

She stood up and bowed to him formally. "Yes, Tono Nosaka."

"Fine, we are all in agreement," Sir announced, sounding as if a big weight had been lifted from his shoulders.

After Tono had signed it, Sir took the contract and added his name and initials before sliding it across the table to Brie.

Brie looked at the pages for the first time. It looked official, like a legal document. Sir handed her the pen, but cautioned, "Read it thoroughly, Brie, before you sign."

She sat back down and read each line meticulously, trying to grasp the concept that she was being transferred to another as she read her Master's wishes in black and white. She hesitated for a moment before finally adding her name to the document, a feeling of apprehension tugging at her heart. She looked up at Sir's confident face and those fears abated.

Brie held out the contract to him. He took the paper and gave her a tender kiss.

Then he turned back to Tono. "I will drop téa off at eight tomorrow morning. She will be packed for the three-week duration. Is there anything you would like her to bring?"

Tono responded immediately with one request. "I would like toriko to bring her favorite vibrator."

She blushed again. Oh, God, what did the next three weeks hold for her?

That night, things were different with Sir. He asked her to lie on the bed, then slowly removed her clothing himself. He caressed her skin as if he were a blind man wanting to 'see' her through touch alone.

She closed her eyes and took in his cherishing contact, wanting to hold onto the feeling so that it would comfort her when he had gone. Brie held back tears, not allowing herself to think about tomorrow.

There was a shift of the bed as Sir settled lower. She gasped and opened her eyes when she felt his tongue between her toes. Brie struggled to stay still as he sensually took a toe in his mouth and sucked lightly.

"Sir…" she whimpered.

"Stay still, little girl."

He moved to the next one, his wet tongue licking in between her toes—the most sensitive area—before taking it into his mouth. She threw her head back and breathed out slowly. It was extremely sexual while being incredibly ticklish—an addictive combination. She moaned when he took her big toe into his mouth. How was it possible that Sir could cause her pussy to contract in pleasure by sucking on her toes?

He moved to the other foot, slowly licking her instep. It made her squirm and struggle.

"Be still."

She instantly stopped her movements and closed her eyes again, her pussy moistening in response to the attention of his mouth.

"Play with yourself," Sir commanded huskily.

Brie slipped her fingers between her legs and started rubbing her slippery clit, craving the extra pleasure. It aroused her to no end knowing that Sir was watching.

His tongue caressed the crease in her smallest toe and she squeaked. He chuckled and nibbled on it lightly as he watched her press her fingers into her pussy.

"Deeper."

She pushed two fingers deep into her vagina and ground against her own hand.

"That's beautiful, téa. You are going to play with yourself until you come." Sir returned to nibbling her toes.

Brie revisited her clit and began flicking it with her fingers enthusiastically. She moaned as his teeth grazed her skin. The first pulse announced her upcoming orgasm. "Sir…"

"Are you close, téa?"

"Yes," she whispered.

"Wait until I bite down."

She nodded, keeping her pussy at the high level of arousal without tipping over. She'd suspected he would make her wait, and he did. But it was glorious to be so deliciously close, to have his attention centered on her.

She opened her eyes and looked up at the ceiling, smiling as she wondered when…

He cradled her foot and turned the sole upward. Brie lifted her head to watch. He met her gaze as he lowered his mouth onto her instep and bit her sensitive skin.

She let out a small gasp as her body exploded in an energetic orgasm. She pressed her fingers against her clit to increase the sensation as her pussy pulsed against her hand.

As soon as it had passed, he released her foot and grinned lustfully. He looked so damn masculine as he crawled between her legs, pushing her thighs apart with his body.

His cock rested at her entrance, but he did not thrust. He gazed down at her instead. "Do you remember the first time I took you as your Master?"

"Of course, Master…" she whispered.

"I plan to take you just as slowly. Feel the depth and width of my love, téa," Sir said as he breached her opening.

Brie held her breath, every fiber of her being concentrated on his shaft. He slid inside a fraction at a time—achingly slow, deliciously arousing—but above all else, the feeling of his love enveloped her.

"I love—" she whispered, unable to finish, the intensity of the feeling choking her.

He looked down as he began to thrust. "I love you, too."

To have not only his dominance expressed, but his love fully communicated in words and actions sent her over the edge. Her spirit floated upward from sheer happiness, and then he took her even further…

"I will always love you, Brie."

He'd used her given name. Brie could not trust herself to speak, but met his every movement, the two becoming one in their emotional dance of souls. When Thane eventually came inside her, she wrapped her legs around his hips and drew him in deeper.

This was her Master. Whoever had control over her, this wonderfully perfect but flawed man owned her heart.

She fell asleep in his arms, no longer dreading what the future held.

# Transfer of Power

Brie packed quickly, her hands trembling as she placed the last of her clothing in the suitcase and zipped it closed. Sir grabbed it and nodded to her.

*I will miss you…* she cried in her head.

Sir had been unusually quiet and curt with her this morning. Neither of them wanted this parting, but Brie dutifully followed him out of the apartment.

The drive to Tono's was silent, but full of unspoken conversations. Would their relationship survive such a test this early on? Brie was suddenly scared again. It was not Tono she feared, but her natural attraction to him. *Will I grow to love Tono too much…?* Brie shook her head, hating her doubts.

"What is it, Brie?" he asked, noting her headshake.

She blanched, ashamed of the reason for her misgivings. "It's nothing, Sir."

He let it drop and stared forward, concentrating on the road.

When they pulled up to Tono's home, Sir turned off the engine and stared at the simple rock garden in the front yard. "We will say our goodbyes now. Once we enter Nosaka's house, I will present you to him, along with the key to your collar."

Brie grasped her collar, shaking her head.

Sir smiled gently, pulling out the key from under his shirt. "The original key remains with me, téa. You are my sub; this arrangement does not change that."

She nodded and wiped away the tear that had formed in the corner of her eye. "I don't want you to go," she whispered, and then looked at her lap, trying hard to keep her emotions in check.

"No tears. Consider this a lesson. Embrace it and learn from it. It is a characteristic of yours that I greatly admire."

"Sir… I am unsure if I am allowed to ask, but I have a personal question about your trip."

"All questions are allowed, even those I may choose not to answer."

Brie voiced a concern that had been burning in her heart ever since he'd announced he was heading back to Russia. Before she lost her nerve, she blurted, "Will you be entertaining Rytsar's subs while you're there?"

His laughter filled the small sports car. "No, téa. This is a business trip. I will have no time for such play." He added in a more serious tone, "I would not damage the newly forged trust between us. This separation will be hard enough without adding that element to the mix."

Brie smiled, letting out a sigh of relief. Of course he would be thoughtful of their growing relationship.

"It is time, téa. Look up and tell your Master goodbye."

She met his confident gaze, but could not stop her bottom lip from trembling. "Goodbye, Master."

He grazed her lip with his finger. "Be my good girl. Follow Nosaka's orders dutifully and with a servant's heart."

"Yes, Master." She could not stop an errant tear from escaping.

Sir wiped away the wetness with his thumb without mentioning it. "I look forward to seeing your completed documentary and hearing about the lessons you learned from Nosaka on my return."

Brie spoke the words that had been pounding in her head, in time with her heartbeat, since she'd woken up that morning. "I will miss you…"

He smiled, but she noticed it did not reach his eyes. "For the first time since my father's death, I am experiencing that emotion as well. I do not care for it, but I assume it is a positive sign."

Brie took his hand and kissed it, choking down her emotions.

His countenance changed to that of a trainer, his voice unemotional and firm. "So now you begin your three-week adventure in the hands of another. Do not burden him with tears. Look at it as the unique opportunity it is."

She accepted that his defensive barrier had reared its ugly head again. "I will, Master."

"The transfer is a formal, but simple ritual. I will present you to Tono Nosaka. You must bow at his feet. When he places his hand on your head, it signifies his acceptance of you as his temporary submissive."

Sir exited the car and walked around to open her door. He pulled her small suitcase from behind the seat and then held out his arm for her to clasp. "Head held high, but at a respectful angle. Chest out."

Those were the same words he'd used the night he'd collared her. She forced herself to smile, even though each step towards the house was killing her inside.

Tono opened the door moments after Sir rang the doorbell. The Asian Dom was dressed in a traditional brown kimono that matched his chocolate-brown eyes. "Welcome, Sir Davis. Won't you both come inside?"

Sir guided Brie ahead of him. "Thank you, Nosaka. I plan to keep this short."

"As you wish," he replied, closing the door behind them.

Tono escorted them into the open living room. Brie vividly remembered the lack of interior walls and the modest décor that spoke of his Japanese background. His home radiated tranquility, helping to calm her nerves.

Brie was disheartened that Sir hadn't been exaggerating about not wasting time. "I present to you my sub, téa." He nodded to her.

Brie instantly knelt at Tono's feet, in an open kneeling position. She closed her eyes when she felt his light touch on her head and had to struggle to hold back a sob in response to the physical transfer of power.

"I accept your sub, téa, for the duration we have agreed upon," Tono answered.

"Here is a key to her collar."

Tono took the small key and closed his hand tightly around it, bowing to Sir respectfully.

"I leave her in your capable hands, Tono Nosaka." With that, Sir turned around abruptly and left, without addressing Brie again. She couldn't believe he was really gone until she heard the roar of the engine as the Lotus sped away. The lonely echoes of it could be heard long afterwards.

"Toriko."

Brie looked up, biting her lip, trying not to cry. He held out his arms to her.

Brie stood up and accepted his embrace. She closed her eyes, fighting the feeling of abandonment enveloping her. To combat it, she concentrated on matching her breath with Tono's. *This is your life for now…*

His calming voice rumbled from deep inside his chest. "He needed to leave for his own peace of mind."

She pressed her head against him and nodded meekly in agreement.

"Are you ready to serve your Master, toriko?"

She broke away and bowed at his feet again, reconfirming her commitment to him. "It would be my honor, Tono."

"Remove your shoes and place them at the front door. Then fill the kettle with water and bring it to me after it boils."

While she followed his instructions, Tono exited out of the back door. Brie stood by the stove, not allowing herself to think. She listened intently to the water warming in the kettle instead. There was something soothing about the sounds of the water as it slowly reached a soft, rolling boil. Waiting gave her time to adjust to this reality.

Tono was a wise Master.

*Master…* Brie shook her head in protest, but stopped herself short. Tono had chosen to serve as her Master during Sir's absence. He deserved a willing sub. Sir expected it, and Tono merited no less.

When the water came to a raging boil, she took the teakettle off the stove and joined Tono outside. The sounds of trickling water and birdsong greeted her.

"Good," he replied when he saw Brie. "Place it on the table and sit beside me."

She did as he had asked, kneeling on the small pillow beside him. Brie broke out in a smile when she saw the tea set, the one he had painted with his signature orchid. "I remember this."

He poured the water over the tea leaves to let them steep. "If I recall correctly, you consumed a lot of tea that day."

Brie giggled to herself. "I certainly did. I've never forgotten that lesson, Tono." She paused, then added, "Thank you."

They sat in respectful silence waiting for the tea to steep, the sounds of nature filling in for the lack of conversation. It was…heavenly.

When Tono deemed it ready, he poured the tea and offered her a cup. He said solemnly, "It is an interesting place we find ourselves, isn't it?"

"Yes," she agreed, waiting until he took his first sip before taking hers. She purred when she tasted it. "I forgot how good your tea was, Tono Nosaka."

He smirked. "You and I have similar tastes, little slave."

It would be so easy to fall into this role with him… She looked deep into his brown eyes and whispered, "To be honest, I'm scared."

He nodded, not seeming surprised by the admission. "This is a precarious role we have been given. To act as partners, but to remain detached."

*Is it possible?* she wondered to herself. Brie took another sip of the warm liquid, grateful for its soothing effect.

He took a piece of jute from his pocket. "Hold out your left wrist."

She did so, watching with curiosity as he wrapped it several times around her wrist and tied a beautifully intricate knot. "I have the right to remove your collar, but I do not think that would be wise. Instead, I am giving you this." He lifted her wrist to his lips and kissed the knot. "A visual reminder of my mastery over you, but one that does not replace your original commitment."

She lightly touched the jute and smiled. "It is an honor to wear this, Tono Nosaka. Thank you."

He surprised her by grasping her jaw and giving her a kiss. It was a simple, closed-mouthed kiss, but immediately focused her attention on his masculinity.

"I have agreed to refrain from intercourse. However, you should be aware that if I were free to do so, I would ravage you right now on this table." He picked up his cup and sipped his tea slowly. "Understand my feelings. It is with great restraint that I will walk these next three weeks with you."

"Why have you agreed to do this?"

"I find it a worthy challenge. There is no other man who cares for your well-being as much as I do…other than Sir Davis. I could not allow you to flounder alone, or in the hands of a man not suited for you."

"But at what cost?" she asked quietly.

"I love you, toriko. That is my reality. What is imperative to me is that you are safe and able to complete your project. On that score, Sir Davis and I are in complete agreement."

He read the concern on her face and added, "It may be because of my Eastern upbringing, but I accept this role. You and I are connected.

Choosing another Master did not alter that fact, although it changed the dynamics between you and me."

Brie took another sip of tea, overcome by the wisdom and compassion of the man beside her. She put her hand over his. 'I am glad to be here…Master."

He grunted and moved his hand away, pouring more tea for them both. "From now on, you will call me simply 'Tono', as you did in the past."

She drained the cup slowly in congenial silence, until a plane flew overhead. She couldn't help but think of Sir and felt a painful ache in her chest.

Tono interrupted her thoughts with instructions. "I want you to go to my bedroom. There you will find the clothes I have set out for you. Wear nothing underneath. You will remain barefoot at all times while in my home. Return to me after you're dressed and present yourself."

Brie rocked off her heels and stood up, bowing to Tono before walking back into his home. She found a red kimono waiting for her on his bed. It was similar in style to the one she had worn for him during the photo shoot, but this one was more modest in length.

She undressed and slipped the silken kimono onto her shoulders. It caressed her skin like a lover's touch, making her smile. On the bed lay a sash. She did her best to wrap it around her waist in an artful manner.

Tono laughed when he saw her. "That's all wrong." He stood up and moved over to Brie, untying the sash. The kimono fell open, exposing her naked flesh. He stared at her appreciatively for several moments before repositioning the kimono and instructing her on how to tie the sash properly. Tono moved behind her and cinched it tight.

She ignored the sexual electricity that sparked from the contact. "Thank you, Tono."

"You will practice tying the sash ten times before bed tonight."

"Yes, Tono."

He went back to the table and sat down, patted the pillow beside him. She joined him as he refreshed their tea and told her to partake. They both put their lips to the cups at the same time. So simple, and yet an intimate act to share with him.

Being here with Tono, caressed by beautiful silk, leisurely drinking tea within the confines of his exquisite garden seemed as natural as breathing.

# Revealing Dreams

After tea, Tono instructed Brie to work on her documentary. He followed her into the bedroom, where he had set up a desk for her work station. It looked incongruous with his simple Oriental décor, but it had everything she required to complete the project.

"I wanted you to have the best tools to work with, toriko. I am proud to be a part of your dream, even if it is simply providing you with the environment in which you can produce it."

Brie wrapped her arms around her new Master's waist. "My words cannot express—"

"There is no need. It is my pleasure as your Master. Sit here while I watch your genius."

She smiled bashfully. "The tea has made its presence known, Tono. Let me excuse myself first." When he nodded, she entered the bathroom.

She was about to close the door when Tono ordered, "Leave it open," while he sat down at the desk.

Brie took a deep breath as she mentally accepted the review lesson.

She sat down on the toilet, upright and with all the grace she could muster as her pee trickled into the water. Despite the flush on her skin, Brie appreciated the stripping away of her pride that exposing such a private act to inspection evoked.

He nodded his approval when she came out of the bathroom. "I saw the moment of hesitation, but much more natural the second time, toriko."

"I am still learning, Tono," she responded, suitably humbled.

"As each of us are, little slave. That should never stop."

Brie returned to the desk and uploaded her documentary onto the fancy new computer. "It still needs a lot of work, Tono. This is really a rough draft of sorts…"

Tono chastised her. "Hush. I want to see it without explanations. This is what you presented to the producer, correct?"

"Yes."

"Then that is all I need to know."

Brie knelt down on the ground beside him and the two watched her original movie. Unlike Sir and Mr. Holloway, Tono was full of expression as he watched. He laughed out loud, but looked visibly upset when Brie spoke of Mary's breakdown while in his care.

After the ending credits, he clapped. "I don't care what your producer said—that is a masterpiece." He picked her up and twirled her in the air. "We must go out and celebrate!"

Tono would not let her change, bur allowed her to wear traditional Japanese sandals to dinner. The two went to a local pizza joint, where they stood out like sore thumbs in their Japanese attire. She slid into the seat, quite mindful of the fact she was naked under the kimono. It enhanced the awareness of her own femininity.

She looked across the table at Tono. With or without physical contact, there was an arousing connection between them. It amazed her how Dominants could easily change a normal, everyday experience into something sensual and alluring, even something as innocuous as eating pizza. She bowed slightly when his gaze fell on her.

The hustle and bustle of the place was momentarily forgotten as she stared into his chocolate-brown gaze and received his silent praise.

The waitress scooted over. "Mr. Nosaka, great to see you again! What can I get started for you?"

"I would like you to bring my three favorites, Miss Mallory."

"Three whole pies?" she asked, looking surprised.

"Yes," he answered, with a playful smirk in Brie's direction.

The waitress dutifully wrote down his order, obviously knowing Tono's favorites without asking. "My pleasure, Mr. Nosaka. I'll get Tony started right on those." Her blush and subconscious hair-flip as she walked away from the table let Brie know the girl had a crush on her new Master.

"I came across this place by accident. Best pizza in the world," Tono announced proudly. His enthusiastic claim was that much cuter considering he was wearing a traditional kimono.

Miss Mallory was quick to deliver his requested favorites, but became flustered when she spilled his glass of water while trying to make room for the three pizzas. He gently clasped her wrist, his touch immediately calming the girl. "It's fine. Don't worry about it." He soaked up the water with several napkins and handed them to her with a nod.

The girl smiled appreciatively. "Thank you, Mr. Nosaka." She turned to Brie, acknowledging her for the first time. "He's a good man."

Brie reached over the food and put her hand on Tono's, squeezing lightly. "I know."

The look he gave her was unreadable, but he broke the contact, demanding that she partake.

Brie gladly succumbed to the temptation set before her. Tono hadn't been kidding; it *was* the best pizza she'd ever tasted, with the unusual toppings and brick-fired crust. Her favorite by far was the simple white pizza with spinach, smoked mozzarella and garlic, but she very much enjoyed the sesame chicken with spicy sweet and sour sauce, and the unexpected surprise of the pizza pie with turkey sausage, red onion and pecan.

With Tono's encouragement, she spent the entire meal discussing her film and sharing her plans for additional scenes. She'd never had such a captivated audience before. Tono listened intently, his enthusiasm for her work deliciously contagious. His sincere excitement tickled Brie and gave her hope that she would be a success.

When they had finished their meal, Tono stood up and offered his hand to her. Brie took it, and felt the eyes of the other diners on her. She moved with grace, deliciously aware of her nakedness beneath the thin material. Tono put his arm around her waist and escorted her away from the table, to the envious stares of several women. She felt a thrill of pride as she walked out of the door beside him.

While they strolled back to his place, she laid her head on his shoulder. "I've never had so much fun discussing my work. Thanks, Tono."

He wrapped his arm around her shoulder. "I knew you were good, but I never understood how truly talented you are. This will be a huge hit."

She grinned gleefully. "It helps to hear it. It's easy to doubt yourself, especially when you've put so many hours into it. It all becomes a blur and then you start wondering if you're fooling yourself by thinking any of it is good."

He stopped and physically turned her to face him. "You are no fool. This is a true gem. Do not lose sight of that, toriko, no matter what obstacles are thrown your way."

Tono's confidence had a significant effect on her. He'd infused her with renewed conviction. Even if Mr. Holloway did not bite, she felt certain her documentary would be produced.

"Toriko, I was excited before about your documentary, but now that I have seen it…I am inspired," he said, pressing her body against his in a heartfelt hug. Her body reacted to the contact, wanting to melt into the embrace shamelessly.

Tono pulled away and they continued walking in silence. It was a delicate balance, this act of giving herself to a new Master. Her submissive heart wanted to please him, but she could not dishonor her true Master by giving in to her need.

Part of her wished that she could live two alternate lives—one with Sir and one with the extraordinary man beside her.

That night, Brie made sure to practice tying her sash ten times before undressing for bed. Tono nodded his approval, and then pulled a straw mat from the corner of the room. He rolled it out, then placed a pillow from the bed on the mat and handed her a folded blanket.

"When I was a child I slept on the ground. It is where you will sleep now."

Brie was surprised, but bowed in thanks. "It is my honor, Tono." She dutifully lay on the mat next to his bed, feeling a bit like a pet. But to her surprise, it was not a negative feeling. She curled up in the blanket and closed her eyes in contentment when the lights went out.

She surveyed the room, impressed by the group of people attending. So many beautiful women dressed in colorful gowns, hiding behind decorated masks. She lightly touched the one covering her own eyes, elated to be wearing the color crimson. It marked her as *his*; everyone knew the one to whom she belonged.

Brie was asked to dance by a dashing young man wearing a mask of gold. She accepted his request and they began moving to the old-fashioned waltz. "You are divine," he whispered in her ear.

"Why, thank you," she replied unashamedly as he twirled her.

He handed her a note, and then left her on the dance floor alone. She opened the red envelope and read the words: *Meet your Master in the library.*

Brie kissed it, then fairly skipped off the dance floor, thrilled by his summons. She sauntered down the large hallway and took a deep breath before opening the large wooden door of the library.

The room was dark except for the crackling fire burning brightly on the opposite side of the room. The light of the flames glimmered off the covers of thousands of books lining the walls, and silhouetted the high-backed chairs and the table positioned near the fireplace.

Brie did not see anyone in the room, but shut the door quietly and headed towards the fire, intoxicated by the unknown.

"Stop."

She held herself still, melting at the sound of his voice. Two figures appeared from the shadows—a man wearing a crimson mask, and another with a black mask that complemented his silver hair.

"We are going to play a game, pet."

Brie's heart skipped a beat. His games always proved challenging. "Yes, Master."

The gentleman in the dark mask sat down while her Master moved up behind Brie. His warm breath tickled her neck. "But first, I must undress you."

She felt his hands at the back of her neck as he unzipped her dress and let it pool at her feet. She had been instructed not to wear a bra or panties, so she stood naked except for her high heels before the two men.

"She has lovely breasts," she heard the stranger say.

"That's not all that is lovely about her," her Master answered, slipping his hand between her legs. She felt his middle finger press into her pussy and she moaned softly.

He growled in her ear. "The rules of the game are simple. He watches and directs. You do what he says."

Brie nodded in understanding, goosebumps covering her skin despite the warmth of the fireplace. *What will be asked of me?*

"I want her bound to the table."

Brie looked at the table and noticed for the first time the glint of metal.

"On your back. Put your wrists in the iron restraints," her Master ordered.

Brie had never been bound by hard metal before. She lay down on the table and placed her wrists in the metal cuffs. It positioned her so that her ass lay at the edge of the table. She had to lay her neck on a leather strap screwed into the wood.

Her stomach jumped when her Master locked her first wrist into place. The restraint was unforgiving and hard. The helpless feeling the cold iron evoked was arousing. He locked the other—both were tight enough that she could only wiggle slightly. He moved to her legs next, locking them into place so that her thighs were spread wide and her high heels pressed against her ass. The clank of the metal sealed her fate, making her weak inside.

Then her Master returned to her head and wrapped the leather restraint around her neck. She'd never had a neck restraint before, and it frightened her. He tightened it so that she felt the constant pressure of the leather on her throat and could not move without causing herself discomfort.

Never in her life had she felt more exposed or vulnerable. She whimpered softly, her fears setting in—but not enough for her to call her safe word.

"Is she wet?" the stranger asked.

Her Master leaned forward and felt her pussy with his fingers. He chuckled. "Yes."

"I expected as much."

She watched as her Master undressed and stood beside her, waiting for instructions.

"She would look good in gold."

Brie's eyes followed her Master as he moved to the other end of the table, picked up a golden butt plug and held it up for examination. Brie squirmed as he coated the large tool in lubricant.

He moved out of her line of sight as he bent over to insert it. "Be a good sub and take the entirety of it."

Brie gasped as the tip penetrated her tight hole. It was just like the restraints— solid and challenging.

She was forced to look at the ceiling as he eased it deeper into her ass. The butt plug opened her up and stretched her. She gasped softly, struggling to relax.

Brie's heart was thumping rapidly by the time her sphincter clamped around the stopper. It was as if a rod had been placed inside, restraining her in yet another way.

She swallowed hard, feeling the leather press uncomfortably against her throat when she did so. It took great will to remain calm.

The older gentleman replied, "Now that she is prepped, I think she needs to be fucked."

Her Master laid his hand on her thigh and trailed his fingers across her skin. "Would you like me to gag her first?"

"No."

Brie felt her pussy gush with wetness as her Master moved into position to take her. She was an object to be enjoyed. Unable to move without discomfort, she was completely at his mercy.

She whimpered when the head of his cock rubbed against her slick outer lips. Despite her fear, despite her distress, she wanted him to use her in front of the stranger. She was desperate for it.

"How easily a goddess becomes a slut," the gentleman observed.

Brie closed her eyes and accepted his words. She was a slut—a slut who needed her Master to dominate her with his cock.

She groaned as he pushed inside her, filling Brie completely. She cried out, needing to pull away, but unable to because of the metal restraints. She was his to do with as he wanted… Only one thing stood in his way—a safe word that she refused to call out.

"Who am I?" he growled, grabbing her thighs and thrusting with greater force.

"Master!" she screamed.

Her Master took her cry as an invitation and began to fuck her hard. He fucked her like a man possessed. Everything blurred as she fell into his unleashed passion.

"Brie!"

She felt like she was falling into the darkness and flailed about, trying to save herself.

"Brie, wake up!"

She opened her eyes and stopped her struggling when she realized she was in Tono's bedroom. She forced herself to let go of the dream, but echoes of Faelan's domination still lingered over her.

"It's Faelan…" she sobbed, burying her head in the pillow.

Tono lifted his blanket and ordered, "Come to me, toriko."

Brie lifted herself off the floor and slipped under his covers. Tono wrapped his strong arms around her and held her protectively. "It was just a dream."

She shuddered from the intensity of the images and the lustful energy coursing through her. She nestled closer to Tono. "Make it go away," she begged.

"He will no longer haunt you, toriko," he said with finality, and ordered her to go back to sleep.

She lay in his arms and was amazed that the memories of the dream began to slip away as she listened to Tono's even breathing. It wasn't long before she followed him into a deep, restful sleep.

# Disclosure

"Brie," Sir called out.

His clear voice demanded attention. She opened her eyes expecting to see him, but quickly realized she was in Tono's bed. She looked at the clock and saw it was five forty-five. She couldn't afford to be late on her first day.

She slid out of the bed, trying not to disturb Tono as she quickly gathered her workout clothes and got dressed. Luckily, the workout center was only a five-minute drive. Sir had arranged her membership, so all she had to do was flash her card to the staff member at the door.

This was her first time working out with the complicated exercise machines. All she'd ever done was lift five-pound weights and jump rope. She found a vacant elliptical machine and attempted to get it to start. After she had pressed many buttons without success, an elderly man took pity on her and instructed her how to use it.

Brie looked at the clock. It was already five after six; she'd missed five minutes with Sir. She started running in place, vowing that she would not be late again. She closed her eyes and called out to him in her mind. *Sir…*

It thrilled her to know that he was on the other side of the world, possibly even using the same equipment while thinking about her. Despite the great distance, she swore she could feel his warm presence surrounding her.

It seemed only natural to tell him about the dream about Faelan as if he were there. She closed her eyes and had a silent, one-sided conversation with Sir. She went on to describe her first day with Tono, and how much fun she'd had discussing the film the night before. *Thank you, Sir. Thank you for asking me to serve under a kind Master while you are gone. I have a better understanding of why you have chosen this for me.*

Brie was sad when the hour was over and she had to say goodbye. She looked up at the ceiling and subtly threw a kiss upwards. "Goodbye, Sir. Until tomorrow."

Upon returning to Tono's home, she was instructed to dress in her kimono and meet him at the dining table. Like the table in the backyard, it was low-lying piece of furniture with pillows surrounding it. She sat down opposite Tono and smiled. He'd already prepared breakfast for them. It consisted of a mixture of rice, egg and vegetables—not the kind of breakfast food she was used to.

He handed a bowl to her and smiled when he noticed her surprise. "I believe in a hearty Eastern breakfast to start the day. It will give you the energy for all you need to accomplish. Pour the tea, toriko."

She felt self-conscious as she filled his cup, blushing when a drop fell from the spout onto the table. She poured hers next, with no better results.

He said kindly, "I will teach you later."

Brie was grateful, wanting to please Tono as well as learn the proper tea etiquette.

"Today you interview with Marquis. Is that correct?"

"Yes, Tono. I'm nervous about it."

"Have confidence in your purpose and you can overcome any uncertainties."

She reached over and touched his arm. "You are a very wise man."

"Wise, toriko?" He shook his head. "That is reserved for men like my father. I prefer sage-like."

She giggled, his response reminding her of Sir. Brie said in an overly dramatic voice, "Yes, oh sage-like Tono."

He grabbed her wrist and pulled her onto his lap, then pulled up her kimono to smack her naked ass. She squealed when he delivered a firm, stinging slap. He grabbed a handful of her hair and pulled her head back so he could look her in the eye. His eyes sparkled mischievously. "Say it with respect, toriko."

She hadn't expected such treatment from the gentle Dom. Brie responded solemnly, "Yes, my sage-like Tono."

"Better," he replied. He pulled the kimono down and helped her off his lap.

She picked up her bowl of rice and began to eat, attempting to hide the smile on her lips. He certainly was not what she'd expected.

Brie arrived at the Training Center early to make sure she was ready for Marquis' interview. It would not do to keep the trainer waiting, especially when he'd already done so much to help her with this documentary.

She went to the receptionist at the front desk. "Hi. Can you tell me if Marquis Gray has arrived?"

The young woman smiled. "Actually, he has not, Miss Bennett."

"Would it be all right if I—"

"Fancy meeting you here."

Brie's heart nearly stopped at the sound of Faelan's voice. She whispered to the receptionist, "Call Headmaster Coen up immediately."

Faelan sounded genuinely hurt. "Why, Brie? Are you really so cold to me now?"

She turned around slowly, but did not speak.

His blue eyes locked onto hers, so she instantly looked to the floor.

"You have haunted me, blossom. Every waking moment since that damn collaring ceremony."

Brie edged towards the elevator. Unfortunately, Faelan did not take the hint and followed her.

"You haunt my dreams as well."

She gasped, made a beeline for the elevator and mashed the down button several times. The mention of dreams had Brie envisioning the lustful dream encounters she'd had with the Dom.

"I know you still think about me, Brie. I can feel it…especially at night."

She shook her head violently, staring at the elevator doors, willing Master Coen to show.

"What are you doing, Mr. Wallace?"

Brie breathed a sigh of relief at the welcomed sound of Marquis Gray's voice.

"I came to reschedule our next session and came across Miss Bennett at the front desk."

"Why would you attempt to engage her?"

"I needed to speak with Brie."

"You have been instructed not to, and everything about her posture shouts her discomfort. Take heed."

At that moment, the elevator doors opened to Master Coen's impressive presence. Marquis guided Brie inside. "Take her down, Headmaster. I will join Miss Bennett in a few minutes."

Brie glanced up as the doors closed. Faelan was staring her down, his eyes dark with lust.

"Unfortunate timing," Headmaster Coen stated.

Brie nodded and the two stood in silence until the doors opened to the lower floor.

"I was in a meeting. Go ahead and set up your camera in the room I designated for this interview while you wait for Marquis Gray."

"Thank you, Headmaster," Brie said as she bowed respectfully.

He huffed and headed back down the hallway, mumbling to himself, "This is getting absolutely preposterous."

Brie went directly to the small classroom she'd been given to interview Marquis. She set the camera on the tripod first and then erected her light reflectors, adjusting them several times until she was satisfied. Next, she got out her list of questions and read over them a multitude of times, gradually getting more nervous as time passed.

She waited a full half-hour before Marquis joined her. His stern countenance let her know not to question him about Faelan. "Would you please sit here, Marquis Gray?" she asked, pointing to the seat.

He did so, stating stiffly, "I apologize for the lateness."

Brie smiled, trying to lighten his dark mood. "I truly appreciate you taking the time to meet with me today."

"Let's begin," he instructed, not allowing time for any small talk.

Brie turned on her camera and made a few last-minute adjustments before sitting down next to it, so that it would appear as if Marquis was speaking to the camera when he answered her questions.

"First, I want to thank you for meeting with me today, Marquis Gray."

"My pleasure, Miss Bennett," he replied, without a smile.

She jumped into interviewer mode, not wanting to waste a second of his time. "I am sure many are curious about how one becomes a trainer for the Center."

"It is not something you strive for. The Submissive Training Center looks for individuals who show extensive skill in a particular area. However, they must also have the patience needed to work with students."

"May I ask how you came to work at the Center, then?"

"Headmaster Coen, who was simply a trainer at the time, noted my flogging skills and felt I would be a good match to be on the panel of trainers. I was not interested, until there was an incident with an inexperienced submissive at a club I frequented. I did not witness the abuse myself, but I saw the aftereffects. I regret I was not able to help the young woman, but I determined then that I would make it my mission to empower submissives so that such maltreatment would cease."

"Can you elaborate on the incident, Marquis Gray?"

He raised his eyebrow. "Suffice to say the girl was permanently hurt. That is all I will say about it."

Brie knew better than to push the trainer, and went to her next question. "May I ask how you became a Dominant in the first place?"

"I come from a large family with eleven siblings. I noticed early on that the religious beliefs my parents subscribed to valued appearances more than reality. I could not accept such duality." A slight smile haunted his lips. "Instead, I sought inner enlightenment through pain, similar to the monks of old. Once I'd achieved a sense of self, I desired to help others attain it."

"How old were you?"

His eyes pierced her when he answered. "I was ten."

Brie's jaw dropped, but she quickly recovered. "When did you have your first scene with another person?"

"I was thirteen. The girl was seventeen. She was lost. I aided her in regaining her inner purpose."

Brie had not expected such an answer, and had to think fast on her feet. "How do you feel pain helped her to achieve that?"

"A person's tolerance for pain varies with the individual, but there is a point common to all where pain forces you to focus on the present. Too much pain and that focus is lost. However, if you can maintain the correct level, you can keep a person at a point of awareness that is enlightening. Initially, that was my goal when I started flogging. However, I quickly realized the sexual allure of pain for many. I enjoy delivering both."

Brie's loins trembled—she knew very well the pleasure he was capable of delivering. She cleared her throat self-consciously. "Going back to what you said earlier, you mentioned that your family is religious. Does that mean you believe in God, Marquis Gray?"

He stared straight into her soul. "Yes, I believe in a higher being."

Again, she was stunned by his answer. She'd never considered that practitioners of BDSM would also believe in God. "What religion are you…if I may ask?"

"I do not follow any conventional religion, Miss Bennett. Religions are far too concerned with judgment for me to have any interest."

"I see." Brie was floundering. This was not the direction she'd thought the interview would go. She looked at her sheet and asked the next question on it, realizing how horribly unqualified she was to give such an interview. All she could think was, *Poor Marquis…*

With feigned confidence, she asked, "Marquis Gray, having worked with you personally, I was struck by your ability to…for lack of a better word, read my mind. Is that a skill you have learned due to your exposure with so many subs, or does it come naturally?"

"I do not read minds, Miss Bennett. I discern intent and motivation."

"Have you always been able to do that?"

"Yes."

Brie felt a nervous flutter in her stomach at the thought of Marquis reading people even as a young boy. "That is fascinating. You must have been an interesting child growing up."

Although his expression did not change, she could tell by the way he shifted in his chair that it was not something he wanted to discuss. Mr. Holloway had asked for more intimate details from the subs, but he hadn't said anything about the trainers. It didn't feel appropriate to force the issue.

Moving to something light and generic, she asked, "What is your favorite aspect of being a trainer at the Center?"

"That moment a submissive embraces the totality of what and who they are. Once they reach that level of understanding, they are empowered to live out their lives without compromise."

She was struck by the empathy Marquis had for the students. It was more than simple training; he was truly passionate about improving the lives of the submissives he worked with. She couldn't help wondering if that was the case for all of the trainers. If so, what would she learn about Ms. Clark when she interviewed her the next day?

"So the training that the school provides goes beyond training submissives to master particular tasks?"

"The sole purpose of the Center is to train and educate dedicated submissives so they can realize their full potential. That cannot be achieved by merely learning 'tricks', Miss Bennett. It is a lifetime objective that requires a complete understanding of one's strengths, weaknesses, and personal needs."

She was grateful he had so clearly and eloquently expressed her own experience at the Training Center. "Marquis Gray, I am sure many people are interested to learn what fulfillment you get from flogging a female submissive."

His smile was disarming. She knew women were going to eat it up. "I enjoy the exchange of power, Miss Bennett. Knowing that she trusts me enough to lay down her needs and desires for mine is exhilarating. I also derive pleasure from helping her transform the stimulus I give into something sensuous and beautiful. The connection with her during the scene is unique and cannot be duplicated in any other setting."

The sensations she'd experienced during their many sessions together flooded her mind, and she found herself blushing. Brie fiddled with the equipment to distract herself, hoping he wouldn't notice.

"Turn off the camera, Miss Bennett."

Brie did so immediately, groaning inside. Why was he able to read her thoughts—*no, correct that*—her intent and motivations so easily?

Marquis was not smiling. "This conversation is not meant for public consumption." He moved his chair closer to her before he spoke. "Mr. Wallace is woefully misguided in his conduct, but I understand his motivation. I believe today's encounter necessitates a formal meeting between you two in order to end the unnecessary drama his infatuation is causing. I will speak to both Sir Davis and Tono Nosaka after we finish here."

The idea of meeting with Faelan had Brie spiraling out of control. Marquis gazed into her tortured eyes. "There is no need for concern, Miss Bennett. I am personally mentoring Wallace and have suggested counseling to help him move beyond his past. It is the root of his unhealthy obsession with you. I thought he was further along—however, his behavior today refutes that. It must be confronted."

"Will Sir be at the meeting, Marquis?"

"My opinion is that it should happen sooner rather than later. I believe the connection he has with you can be severed cleanly if done in a timely manner."

"I will only meet with Mr. Wallace if Sir agrees, Marquis Gray. Even if you and Tono punish me for it, I will not without my Master's approval."

Marquis chuckled. "You are feisty but devoted. It pleases me to see it, Miss Bennett. Unfortunately, time is short. This interview is over. However, I was told by Headmaster Coen that you are looking to film a scene with a trainer. I am willing. Did you have a particular submissive in mind?"

Brie's mouth curved into a smile. "If I had my choice, I would choose Lea Taylor."

"I will inform Ms. Taylor after class tonight then. I assume you want to film a session with the flogger?" He gave her an amused look. "Unless you'd prefer her to receive a good caning."

*Lucky Lea…* Brie wasn't sure she could handle watching a sexy scene between Marquis and Lea without imploding, but she knew that it would serve her documentary well. "A flogging session would be perfect, Marquis Gray. Thank you."

Marquis stood up and shook her hand formally. As he was leaving, he threw out an offhand comment without bothering to look back. "Be sure to bring a towel, Miss Bennett."

When she returned home, the concern on Tono's face alerted her to the fact he had already spoken to Marquis. "I'm questioning if it is necessary to hold your hand wherever you go, toriko."

Brie sighed. "What were the chances *he* would be there?"

"Fate seems determined to bring you two together."

"Why?! It was so uncomfortable, Tono. Faelan wouldn't leave me alone, and when he mentioned the dreams I almost fainted."

"Faelan specifically mentioned them?"

"He accused me of haunting his dreams and said that he knew I was thinking of him because he could feel me at night."

"Did you tell Marquis this?"

Brie looked at him warily, wondering if she had screwed up again. "No. Sir said to always speak to my Master first."

"Fine advice, but Marquis should know, since he is working with the boy. I will mention it to Sir Davis first, before I call Marquis Gray." When he saw her worried expression, he added reassuringly, "You have done nothing wrong, toriko. In fact, based on what I've heard, you handled the entire situation exactly as you should have."

She nodded, grateful to hear his words of praise.

"After I'm finished speaking to them, you will join me and share your impressions of the interview today. In the meantime, boil the pot of water. I will teach you the proper way to pour tea." He pulled away from her and went out of the back door, closing it behind him.

Brie listened to the water boil as Tono spoke on the phone outside. It was difficult to know she could not speak to Sir, but there was comfort in the way Tono was handling the situation. He was respectful of her true Master, but Tono remained in command of her.

With a few words and simple orders, he had her calm and awaiting her first lesson in tea etiquette. He seemed to have the uncanny ability to bring serenity to her soul, no matter the circumstance.

# Interviewing the Domme

Brie had gone over her questions for Ms. Clark over and over again. She'd changed them multiple times, only to go back to the original set. Marquis Gray's interview had been so unpredictable that she could not begin to imagine how her interview with Ms. Clark would play out.

It was with trepidation and excitement that she returned to the Submissive Training Center the next day. Thankfully, there were no unexpected confrontations with Faelan to throw her off her game this time.

Brie set up the interview room, then sat pensively waiting for the female trainer—the Domme who had caused her such grief during her six weeks of training. Although Brie had come to respect Ms. Clark, she had never grown to like the woman.

How could she? Ms. Clark hated her guts for no apparent reason.

Which made Brie all the more curious as to why the woman had offered to do this interview. Whatever the motivation, she was going to take full advantage of her time with Ms. Clark. Although Brie was a submissive, she was playing the role of filmmaker now. It allowed her all kinds of latitudes she'd never had with her former trainer.

Like most Dominants, Ms. Clark was punctual. Brie took a deep breath before standing up to shake her hand. "Thank you for coming, Ms. Clark."

"You may call me Mistress tonight."

"Okay…" Already, Ms. Clark was pushing her Dominant role on Brie.

Brie pointed to the chair and adjusted the focus of the camera once the trainer had sat down. Ms. Clark was staring straight at the lens, giving Brie the willies and rattling her confidence.

*No, I'm the interviewer! I control this scene…*

Brie went straight for the jugular by asking her age. "How old are you, Mistress, and at what age did you realize you were a Dominatrix?"

Ms. Clark looked momentarily shaken but she answered, looking Brie straight in the eye. "I am thirty-two, Miss Bennett. To answer your second question, I understood my role when I was in my freshman year of college."

Brie jumped on her answer. "Was there some incident that caused you to realize that, or had you felt it all your life and simply realized it at this point?"

"I was given the opportunity to top and I found it unusually satisfying. I haven't looked back since."

Brie could sense Ms. Clark was hiding something—there was vulnerability in her eyes that Brie hadn't seen before.

Despite their unpleasant past, Brie had no interest in exploiting that. She switched to a simple question. "How did you become a trainer at the Center?"

"Sir Davis asked me to join the panel. We had known each other in the past and he felt I had the skills and female perspective the Training Center was in need of. You may be interested to know that I was the first female hired to serve on the panel."

That was certainly news to Brie. Sir had personally invited Ms. Clark, a woman he'd known since college, to serve with him at the Training Center? Just how well *did* her Master know Ms. Clark?

"You must be proud of that distinguished accomplishment."

"After my appointment, they made it a policy that a female must be represented on each panel."

As impressive as that sounded, Brie had seen the trainer lose her composure. She did not have the same high regard others seemed to hold for the Domme.

Hoping to uncover the trainer's underlying motivation, she asked the same question she'd asked Marquis Gray. "I'm curious as to why you chose to be part of the Submissive Training Center, Mistress?"

The woman looked at her shrewdly. "The simple fact is I enjoy training new subs. Their untarnished state makes it easier to strip away their egos. It is an entertaining process to see what lies underneath."

Had Ms. Clark's unkind treatment of Brie simply been for training purposes—to strip her bare? No—as much as Brie wanted to believe it, she couldn't. There was more to her harsh treatment than the trainer was letting on. Brie hoped the next question would provoke the Domme to open up.

"Have you ever played the role of a submissive?"

A brief flicker of emotion quickly turned into a hard stare. "I have allowed a Dominant to top me for educational reasons, but I have never been a submissive."

Brie couldn't help thinking, *But I bet you wanted to be, didn't you?* "So Mistress, is it something you would ever consider?"

Ms. Clark tilted her head slightly, narrowing her eyes. "Why do you ask, Miss Bennett?"

Brie felt her skin crawl; her paddling session with the trainer instantly sprang to mind. "I know some Dommes who enjoy reversing roles, Mistress."

"Do not confuse me for a switch, Miss Bennett."

Brie could feel the trainer's defensive walls going up, so she changed the line of questioning accordingly. "What is your tool of choice?"

The Domme answered with an evil curve to her lips. "I favor the cane, Miss Bennett. A good caning can subdue the most errant submissive."

It sounded like a promise…

Brie felt a sudden chill travel down her spine and had to remind herself that Ms. Clark had no power over her anymore. She laughed nervously.

There was no missing the glint in the Domme's eye. What was this interview—a power play?

Brie became outraged at the thought. "Why did you agree to this interview, Mistress?" she asked, point blank, tired of playing games.

The startled look on the trainer's face gave Brie a feeling of control, boosting her confidence. But Ms. Clark was not about to reveal her true motive, and took several seconds to formulate an acceptable answer. "I believe it is important people understand that Dommes play an important role in the BDSM community. Being a Dominant is not a male-exclusive role, just as being a submissive is not gender-related. It has more to do with a person's character type and his or her sexual desires."

Getting the upper hand gave Brie the courage to voice the one question she had been dying to ask. "Mistress, why do you hate me?"

Ms. Clark gritted her teeth as she pointed to the camera.

Brie turned it off and waited in silence. *Oh, this is going to be good...*

"That is not a professional question. I expected better from you, Miss Bennett. I do not see you lasting long in the film industry."

Brie did not respond, waiting for the question to be answered.

Ms. Clark's voice was cold. "I do not hate you. That would require too much energy and you are certainly not worth that."

Brie ignored the insult, knowing it was a bait and switch tactic. She was not biting.

As the silence dragged on, the trainer snarled. "Your arrogance is not befitting a submissive. I find you immature, selfish and rude."

"So is that why you hate me?"

Ms. Clark snapped, "I said I do not hate you. Let me add obtuse to your list of faults."

"What is the real reason you agreed to this interview, Ms. Clark?"

The Domme growled under her breath. "You are like an itch I must scratch. Everything about you rubs me wrong, and yet..."

The woman did not finish.

"And yet what?"

Ms. Clark stood up, taking off the microphone. "We are done here." She exited the room, leaving Brie alone, completely stunned.

*What the hell was that?*

Brie packed up her equipment and went to find Lea. She knew the sub was waiting for her, and she *needed* to talk. On her way, Marquis Gray stopped her in the hallway.

"Have you spoken to Ms. Taylor yet?"

"No. I was just on my way to see her now."

"Then it is fortunate I caught you. Tonight looks like the only time our schedules coincide. Can you be set up in an hour in room six?"

"Yes, I can certainly do that. Thank you very much, Marquis Gray."

He nodded. "I look forward to it."

Brie hurried off to find Lea. She found her friend in the sub lounge, sitting on the couch, looking quite pleased with herself. But the instant Lea saw her, she jumped up and gave Brie a huge hug. "Thank you! OMG, when Marquis said he wanted to scene with me, I about died! Thank you, girlfriend!"

Brie hugged her back. "Yeah, I won't lie. When he asked who I wanted him to flog I was tempted to say, 'Me!' But since it can't be me, then I want it to be you."

Lea squealed, "I love having you for a best friend!"

Brie gave her a long, hard squeeze. It was good to see Lea again. "Girl, I had the weirdest interview with Ms. Clark."

Lea grabbed her hand and forced her to sit on the couch. "Tell me about it. I was wondering how it went."

"Well, she was intimidating and rude like she always is with me, but it all changed when I asked her why she hated me."

"You asked her that on camera?"

"Yeah. I've never understood it and I finally just cracked. I *had* to know."

"What did she tell you?"

"She made me turn off the camera before she would answer, but then she gave me the whole 'you're rude and not submissive enough' routine. I pressed her further and she claimed I'm an itch she needs to scratch."

Lea's jaw dropped in disbelief. "She was coming onto you?"

Brie burst out laughing. "No! I have no idea what she was trying to say. I even asked her, but she just up and left the interview."

"Go back… What exactly did she say?"

"Something like, 'I'm like an itch she must scratch. Everything about me rubs her wrong and yet…'"

"And yet what?"

"I don't know! That's what I asked her and she ended the interview."

Lea shook her head sadly. "Mistress has been extremely aloof since you and Sir returned from Russia. I have no idea what's going on with her."

"It must be something to do with Rytsar; it has to be. Ugh…I hate mysteries! Sir won't let me talk about it, but it's killing me not to know what happened between those three, and why I am somehow caught in the middle of it." She slumped on the couch and whined, "It's not fair…"

Brie understood that Sir did not care for gossip, but was it really gossip when she only wanted to find out about Ms. Clark's past because it was affecting her personally? "Did you hear anything more about Rytsar from Ms. Clark?"

Lea leaned forward, exposing her overflowing bosom to Brie. "Funny you should ask. Right before you left on your trip, she opened up a little about Sir. Whatever mistake she made with Rytsar caused the Russian to go ballistic. His reaction was swift and terrible. Sir stepped in, which is why Mistress holds your Master in such high regard. I have never heard her say anything bad about Sir," she laughed, "other than that he was an idiot to collar you."

Brie hit her friend's shoulder. "I didn't need to hear the last bit, Lea."

"Well, I need to keep you humble. It's my job."

Brie looked up at the clock. "Nuts, I better get things set up for your flogging."

Lea squealed again. "I'm so excited!"

"Well, if you want it to happen, you'd better help."

"I'd do anything for you, Stinky Cheese."

Brie gave her another hug. "Thanks. I really freaked out after Ms. Clark's interview, but now I think I have a better understanding. Unfortunately for me, I am just an innocent bystander who happens to remind Ms. Clark of her past—a past she wishes she could change. Maybe that's what she meant by me being an itch she needs to scratch."

Lea looked at her sadly. "I wish she would just let Rytsar go. There are others who want to love her, but she won't let anyone near her."

Brie shuddered. "I still don't get you, Lea. You can do much better than Ms. Clark, trust me."

"Oh, like you can do better than Sir?"

Brie's laughter filled the room. "Oh, no. I got the best of the best."

Lea pressed her breasts together and tilted her head comically. "And that's why Tono is your Master now?"

Her attempt at a joke stabbed Brie in the heart. She closed her eyes, trying not to cry. "Lea…"

Her best friend instantly apologized, wrapping her arms around Brie. "I'm sorry. That was uncalled for. Please…" She put her forehead against Brie's. "Please forgive me."

She knew Lea hadn't meant to be cruel, but glared at her anyway. "You don't know how close you were to losing that flogging session. I was considering making you a cameraman while *I* enjoyed the pleasure of Marquis."

"Can I make it up to you with a real joke?"

"Absolutely not!"

# Sexual Release

Brie focused the lens on Marquis and felt a small thrill when he looked directly at the camera. "Are you ready, Miss Bennett?"

Her loins tingled, even though she was not part of the scene. "I am, Marquis Gray. Act as if I'm not here. I want people to see the intimacy between a Dominant and a submissive. But Lea, whenever you can, verbalize what it feels like for the audience. Oh, and one more thing, Marquis. If it would be okay with you, when you turn on the music, could you keep it low enough that I can hear the thud of the flogger and any exchanges between you two?"

"Very well, Miss Bennett," he answered solemnly. The sound of Mozart filled the room until he turned it down significantly. "Will this do?"

Brie gave him a thumbs up.

Marquis beckoned Lea to him, while still speaking to Brie. "My only requirement is that you do not interrupt the scene once I begin."

"Of course, Marquis."

He turned away from her and ran his hand through Lea's hair. Brie took it as her cue to begin filming. Her body responded as if she were the one receiving his attention.

Marquis ran his hands over Lea's body, lingering at her impressive breasts. "Undress and kneel, facing the far wall. Hands at the back of your neck."

Lea quickly peeled off her clothes and knelt down gracefully. While she was undressing, Marquis took off his shirt and went to the table Brie had set up to pick out a flogger. He grabbed a large black one. "First, we warm the skin."

Lea nodded to signify her understanding.

Marquis swung the flogger slowly in a sideways figure eight pattern, lightly slapping her back with the soothing flogger. Brie knew the feel of it. It looked scary because of its size and many tendrils, but it was made of supple leather that was actually soft to the touch.

The sounds of light thudding and Lea's satisfied sighs filled the small room. Brie's own skin tingled in wistful anticipation. The thuds became louder as he increased the force of impact.

"Color, Lea."

"Green, Marquis. It feels like a warm massage."

The Dom put down the large flogger after several minutes, then picked up one that had fewer tendrils that were also thinner in width. "Now that the skin is warm, I'll increase the sensation."

Brie noticed that Lea's skin was lightly blushed. She did a quick close-up so it would be apparent to the viewer.

When she pulled back, she caught Marquis in graceful motion. He used fluid, solid strokes with the thinner, more challenging flogger. He concentrated on the left side of Lea's back and then moved over to the right, always precise, aiming for the fleshier areas of her skin.

"So beautiful," he murmured under his breath.

Brie saw Lea's muscles stiffen and then eventually relax as her body become accustomed to the more demanding strokes. Her friend's satisfied moans caused Brie to roll her eyes as a trickle of wetness escaped her soaked panties. *I really should have brought a towel…*

When Marquis put down the flogger and turned on the Mozart, Brie's entire body trembled. He returned to Lea with a silk ribbon in his hand. He rubbed it over her bright pink skin, whispering things to Lea that Brie wished she could hear. Her girlfriend turned her head towards him and they kissed. It was long, deep and passionate.

Eventually Brie closed her eyes, still keeping the camera focused on them. Their impassioned kiss was too hot, causing Brie's loins to ache. *Oh, Sir…*

Brie opened her eyes again when she heard Lea cry out. Marquis was using a red flogger this time, the flogger with thin leather tendrils. Brie had not personally experienced their sting, but knew Marquis' natural talent brought a person to the edge without taking them over to the unbearable.

Unlike Rytsar, Marquis did not enjoy delivering pain; he enjoyed producing clarity before he sent his submissive into subspace.

Brie melted and the camera slipped for a second. She righted it and held her breath as Lea was taken into glorious subspace.

"Marquis…oh, Marquis," her friend gasped.

The music carried the three of them as he stroked Lea's back with the flogger in time with the music. It was beautiful, sensual, erotic…

Marquis Gray's masculine grace was accentuated by Lea's response to each stroke. Truly, they were poetry in motion. A tear ran down Brie's cheek as she watched. She understood the connection the two were experiencing.

Brie was tempted to slip a finger between her legs, desperate to relieve herself of the sensual ache watching them caused, but she was a professional now. The camera shot was more important than her throbbing need, so she silently suffered for her art.

She watched Lea's back arch. "Give in to it," Marquis encouraged lustfully.

Lea let out a passionate cry as her whole body shook in ecstasy. Brie let out a whimper of her own, swept away by Lea's climax.

Marquis must have heard her, for he glanced in Brie's direction before setting down the flogger and kneeling next to Lea. He wrapped his arms around her and spoke softly, complimenting her body, her sensuality and her spirit.

After several minutes, he helped Lea into his lap and caressed her face as she slowly drifted back to reality. Lea smiled up at Marquis and giggled like a giddy girl. The trainer leaned over, kissing her on the lips. "Charming…"

Brie turned off the camera and closed her eyes, trying to force her racing heart to slow. How she longed to trade places…but no, that was not true. What she longed for was Sir. She sent out a mental message: *I need you, Sir.*

When Marquis helped Lea off the ground, Brie immediately began putting her equipment away. She needed to get out of there—needed fresh air, and quick.

She jumped when she heard Marquis behind her. "Did you get what you were hoping for, Miss Bennett?"

She didn't dare look at him when she answered. "I got the shots I needed, yes. Thank you, Marquis."

He chuckled under his breath. "I wager you could do with some aftercare."

A shiver ran through her. She said nothing, but her hands refused to cooperate and she dropped her tripod. When he offered to pick it up, she assured him that he'd done enough.

She gave Lea a quick hug. "Sorry, gotta run. Great stuff, Lea. Both of you!"

Brie couldn't get out of the Training Center quickly enough. She found it difficult to concentrate on the roads as she headed home. It wasn't until she saw the valet that she realized she'd headed straight to Sir's apartment. With a groan, she waved the valet away and turned the car around, heading for Tono's.

She burst through the door, dutifully taking her shoes off before collapsing on the floor.

"What's wrong, toriko? Bad day?"

She looked up at Tono in tortured desire. "Help me…"

His countenance changed as he lifted her up and held her close. Brie was certain he could smell her desire. It literally coated her panties.

"I can taste your need," he said, but his voice was not full of lust; it was cool and controlled. "What happened to cause this?"

She sighed. "I had to film Marquis and Lea today. It was…a stimulating scene."

He pulled away and stared into her eyes for several moments before giving directions. "Take a shower and meet me on the mat, unclothed."

Brie felt a twinge of apprehension. What would he ask of her? Would she be able to resist if he crossed the line? In her excited state, she wasn't so sure.

It was with a flood of relief that she stood under the hot, pelting water of the showerhead. It momentarily took away the sexual angst. She reluctantly turned off the shower and dried off in front of the large bathroom mirror. Her honey-colored eyes stared back at her, luminous with need and a touch of fear.

"Toriko…" Tono called from the other room.

The sound of a lone flute floated in the air, letting her know what was about to take place. She took a deep breath before rejoining him. Brie bit her lip when she saw Tono sitting on the mat in his black kimono, with jute in his hand.

She joined him on the mat, kneeling before him. Her stomach jumped when his fingers made contact with her skin. Without asking, he took her wrist and wrapped the jute around it.

"Observe what I do, toriko. I want you to understand the intricacies of the bindings. These are basic, but can still be used for more complicated designs."

Her heart rate sped up as she watched him bind one wrist to the other. He then began a pattern, weaving the rope between each of her fingers, caressing her skin sensually with the jute. She longed to close her eyes and give in to the feeling as she listened to the lone flute call her, but it was not what he had asked of her.

When Tono was done, he held up her hands so she could see the intricate work before he untied it and bound her again so that she could observe it a second time. He left her wrists bound when he was finished, starting on her legs next.

He told her to sit with her ankles together and, using a new rope, proceeded to bind them together. She watched in fascination as he tugged and pulled at the rope, creating tight yet beautiful bonds with simple knots. He untied it, and repeated the procedure for her benefit.

Tono then got up and retrieved something from the bedroom before kneeling behind her. "Breathe with me, toriko."

His words brought a smile to her lips. Brie closed her eyes, embracing the sensual feeling of the bindings as she matched the rhythm of his breaths. He explored her skin with his hands while lightly kissing the back of her neck. "I will bring the release you need," he murmured.

His hands left her momentarily. Brie opened her eyes when she heard the distinctive sound of her little bullet.

She whimpered as he wrapped his arm around her and his fingers made their way between her legs. The instant the little vibrator made contact with her clit, she let out a long and frustrated moan.

"Don't resist," he commanded, pressing it against her.

Brie leaned her head back on his chest. Her nipples became hard with need as the fire began to build inside.

"I desire your orgasm."

She gasped as she allowed the vibration to take her over the edge. Her whole body froze just before the fiery pulsations began. She pushed against Tono as her body released the pent-up sexual energy she'd been suffering from.

"Little slave..." he whispered.

He lifted the bullet from her wet clit, ran it over her stomach and up to her breasts. He tickled her hard nipples with the toy and then returned to the source. Brie stiffened as her clit began dancing with the vibrator a second time.

"I demand another."

She whimpered as her body greedily accepted the challenge. The build-up was slow, but she could tell it was going to be powerful—possibly even painful in its intensity. "Tono..."

"Trust me, toriko."

He helped to build the strength of the orgasm by moving the bullet over her clit, letting the fire burn and then switching the angle so the flow was interrupted momentarily, until he built it up again.

With her hands and legs tied, she was at his mercy—his wonderful, thrilling mercy. Her legs began shaking first, announcing the impending orgasm. She tried to keep in rhythm with Tono's breathing, but began panting uncontrollably.

"Tono..." she cried.

"Let it consume you, little slave."

That was actually her fear. It felt like the orgasm was about to consume her completely—mind, body and soul. He tightened his grip, pressing Brie hard against him. "Come for me."

The simple bindings, the tightness of Tono's embrace, the relentless vibration of the bullet and her own images of Sir caused a fiery explosion within her core. As it burst forth, she screamed in pleasure and fear. Brie struggled against Tono as it swept through her. The power of the orgasm obliterated everything, almost claiming her consciousness before it ended.

She groaned in satisfaction, her body tingling long after her release. Brie opened her eyes, her body and mind finally free from the desperate need that had eaten at her. She took a deep breath and turned her head to smile at Tono. "Thank you, Master of the Rope."

"It was not just for you, toriko. I was confronted by your need the minute you entered the house. Without immediate intervention, I would have fulfilled it in a manner outside the bounds of the agreement."

"I shouldn't have agreed to film Marquis. I was just asking for it…" she said, rolling her eyes at her own foolishness.

"Knowing your attraction for flogging, I would have to agree," Tono answered with a smirk as he began slowly untying the knots.

When he was finished, she asked, "Would you allow me to practice on you?"

He hesitated for a moment, but handed over the rope. "Let me see what you've learned."

# Ties that Bind

Brie took the cord and folded it in two. She wrapped it around his wrists, pulling the rope through the loop in the middle. She looked up at Tono and smiled as she pulled it tight. She wound it around his wrist several times and looped it under before starting between his fingers.

Brie laughed when she was done. The knots were different sizes, his fingers spread far apart and the ends dangled unattractively. Still…he was bound and she found it surprisingly sexy.

She lifted his hands up and gently, but forcibly, pressed her body against him so that he lay down on the mat with her on top. Brie felt his rigid cock against her stomach. Obviously he found it as erotic as she did.

It seemed a shame that she had enjoyed an earthshattering release, but he had been denied his. Brie opened his kimono so that his shaft rubbed against her naked skin. Still holding his arms, she whispered, "Don't move."

Brie rubbed her abdomen against his hard cock, rocking her hips sensuously. Tono shook his head, but did not resist. She moved against him, increasing the pressure between them. She felt the wetness of his pre-come and moaned, knowing that she was bringing him close. She was drawn to his lips…

Tono gave a deep-throated groan when she kissed him, his manhood spasming between them, but he refused to come. He suddenly brought his bound wrists down around her, capturing her in his embrace. "Do not do that again."

Although he said it without malice, she wondered at his words. Was he displeased with her?

"Untie me," Tono insisted after releasing her from his embrace. She fumbled with the poorly formed knots. It took extra time to set him free because of her amateur attempt.

Once free, he stood up. "Stay." He left her and retreated to the bedroom. He returned with an armful of rope and the silver ring he used for suspension. She shivered in anticipation.

"This will be demanding on you, toriko. The bindings and pose will challenge your body."

Her heart sped up, but there was no way she would turn down such an opportunity. "I long to be challenged, Tono."

He sat down on the mat and laid out the long lengths of jute beside him. He motioned her to him. "Kneel, facing away from me."

She did as she was asked, her whole body buzzing with excitement. Tono started with her chest, binding it tightly, framing her breasts with the rope. The subtle touches as he pulled and adjusted the rope were hypnotically sensual. This time there was no music, just the slap of the ends of the rope as they smacked the floor with each pass.

He bound her arms one at a time, covering them in a decorative three-inch diamond pattern. He moved down to her abdomen, attaching a rope from her chest as he bound it in the same ornamental pattern.

She gasped softly when he reached between her legs and pulled the rope taut against her clit and up the valley of her ass. He fastened it in the back, pulling it even tighter before tying the final knot. The pressure was arousing, causing her body to react.

"Tono, I've wet the jute."

He chuckled under his breath. "To be expected, little slave."

He continued down her legs with the diamond pattern. The bindings were tighter than normal, but not challenging. When he had tied off the rope at her left ankle, he told her to lie on her stomach. While she followed his orders, he began fastening the silver ring to the ceiling. He tested it out with his full weight before returning to her.

He pulled her arms back and secured them so that she felt like a swan in mid-flight. Tono lightly caressed her back and thighs before taking her right ankle. He pulled it backward towards her wrist. She lifted her chest off the ground to accommodate the position as he secured her ankle to her wrist. Brie imagined she looked like a dancer with her arms thrown back and a leg gracefully kicking backwards.

He made it even more challenging when he finished the pose by binding her left ankle to her other wrist. Tono was right. It was a demanding pose, and she hadn't even been lifted off the ground yet. It was unpleasant to have her body weight centered on her torso and chest.

He ran his hands over her skin again, soothing her with his touch. "Breathe with me, toriko," he gently reminded. Brie concentrated on matching his breath, staving off the discomfort. He quickly bound the rope at several points and slipped it through the ring. "And now you fly."

He began slowly lifting Brie off the ground. Instantly, the jute began to tighten and dig into her skin. The tightness around her chest was more acute than before, but there was also a sexual pressure added with the rope resting on her clit.

"Breathe with me," he reminded her again.

She closed her eyes and forced her body to accept the challenge of the jute. Once Tono had her lifted and secured, his hands returned to her, caressing her skin as he made minor adjustments to the rope.

"As Dom, I am the one in control, little slave."

"Yes, Tono," she said as she slowly twisted in the air. She wondered if he was talking about her grinding against his cock.

"What you did provoked me, toriko."

She looked up at him, unable to tell if he was joking or not. "Tono, I wasn't trying—"

"I do not care to be topped." He reached over and slapped her ass with a biting smack. She squeaked, surprised by his move and slightly turned on by it as she swung back and forth from the force of the swat.

Brie squirmed and whimpered as he continued to slap her ass cheeks, making them warm with his punishment. She'd never known the sexual allure of being spanked for misbehavior. It felt like a guilty pleasure, one she knew she should not enjoy, but her wetness exposed her true sentiments.

Tono paused and she thought he was done, but then his hand landed on her warm buttocks again. The tingling feeling on her skin moved straight to her pussy. The next swat really hurt. Brie cried out in alarm. It hurt—oh, God, it hurt—but it was so damn sexy coming from her gentle Master.

"No more topping."

"No, Tono, no more topping."

"Now that you have been punished, I will take my pleasure."

Tono left her side to rummage through an ottoman that also acted as extra storage. He pulled out a plastic mat and laid it under her before picking up a long, red candle and lighting it in front of her.

Brie whimpered in pleasure as he dripped some of the hot wax on her tingling buttocks. He slowly moved up her back. She groaned as the wax made thin trails on her skin. He moved to her front and slipped the candle into a tight loop he had created previously with the rope.

Tono grabbed Brie's chin roughly and kissed her as melted wax dripped onto her shoulders. Her pussy pulsed against the jute and she moaned loudly.

He untied his kimono and moved behind her. Brie's loins contracted in anticipation. Tono ran his hands over her body, caressing the skin, sliding them over the rope until his fingers rested on the slick jute binding her pussy.

He put one hand on her ass. Although she could not see his actions, she knew what he was doing because of his jerking movements and low grunts. Knowing Tono was masturbating on her was an incredible turn-on.

Another drip of burning wax hit her shoulders just as he groaned and hot liquid covered her ass and pussy.

"Yes, Tono, yes…" she moaned.

After he was done he pushed on her thigh, causing her to twist around slowly on the rope. Brie closed her eyes and took in the extreme sensations of constricting jute, the pull of gravity, hot wax, warm semen and flying…

She heard the clicking of a shutter and opened her eyes to see Tono taking photos of her. She managed a slight smile before she closed her eyes, moving towards the promise of spiritual flight, but Tono pulled her back.

"No, toriko." He stopped her spinning, blew out the candle, and lowered her to the floor. She wondered if this was another aspect of her punishment, but as he untied her he explained, "It is not safe to stay suspended in that pose for long."

The deep indentations the rope had left began to burn as the blood rushed back into her skin. Tono eased it by rubbing her down, forcing the blood to return quickly. He laid her across his lap afterwards and meticulously removed the wax from her skin, allowing Brie to bask in the afterglow of the experience.

When he was done, he asked Brie to join him in the shower.

She followed Tono into the bedroom and watched as he shed his kimono, his toned body causing an instant reaction. As he walked into the bathroom, she couldn't help appreciating his firm ass. Why did he have to be so beautiful?

Brie reminded herself that the Training Center had specifically chosen this Dom for her because he was the embodiment of her top attributes in a man. It was no wonder she was physically attracted to him.

Tono handed her the bar of soap. It slipped out of her hand and she was forced to pick it up from between his legs. Her gaze took in his handsome stature as she slowly stood back up. To calm her unwanted attraction, she turned away and concentrated on replaying the procedure for binding in her mind while she soaped up.

He exited the shower first, as she was rinsing off. She stepped out a few seconds later to find Tono drying his wet hair with a towel. It seemed so natural and cute, as if they'd been a couple for years.

"Join me in bed when you are dry, toriko," he said as he tossed the towel on the counter, then left the bathroom.

Brie wondered what he had in mind. She quickly dried off, then slipped into bed with him. Tono pulled her close, causing nervous butterflies in her stomach. When she felt his warm breath against her neck, Brie was certain she knew where the night was heading, and wondered if she would be forced to use her safe word.

She couldn't have been further from the truth.

Tono's voice was grave as he spoke. "I told you once that my father does not share the same connection with my mother that you and I have experienced."

Brie shivered as if cold water had been splashed on her at the change in his tone, and only nodded in response.

"My mother is overbearing, incapable of submitting her will."

Brie stared at the wall and admitted her confusion. "I don't understand, Tono."

"Although my father is a Master in the community, he is not Master in his own home."

She closed her eyes, worried about the answer to her next question. "What does it have to do with us?"

"What you did, although enjoyable, still angered me."

She turned and gazed into his chocolate eyes. "Tono, I didn't mean to top you."

"I understand your heart, toriko, but anything that even hints to it rubs me the wrong way."

"But you didn't stop me," she protested quietly.

"I was controlled by desire," he replied, stroking her cheek lightly. "Which is something else I do not care for."

It upset her to have displeased her Master. "I am genuinely sorry, Tono. I never—"

He silenced Brie by kissing her on the lips. "We each have our own triggers, toriko. Now you know mine…"

# Master's Voice

Brie anxiously awaited her first conversation with Sir. Tono suggested that she take the call in the backyard garden, where she would have not only privacy, but peaceful surroundings. On the outdoor table were two items—her cell phone and a small gift box. Her curiosity was piqued.

She stared at the phone, knowing that Sir would call exactly on time but hoping against hope he would break protocol, just once. Precisely at eight, the phone rang.

She answered it without allowing another ring. "Sir?"

"Brie."

A flood of warmth moved through her at the sound of his voice. "I've missed you, I've missed you so much, Sir!" She had to hold back the tears that threatened to break her.

"Are you well?" he asked.

"I'm so much better now. I love hearing your voice." The sound of his laughter tickled her beyond measure, and she pressed the phone against her ear, not wanting to miss a word.

"I am equally pleased to hear your voice, my little sub. Are you serving your new Master well?"

After last night's misstep, she was unsure how to respond. "I'm doing my best, Sir."

"It is all I ask. I'm sure Nosaka will fill me in if there are any issues that need my attention. Have you had any more dreams or encounters with Mr. Wallace since I last talked with Tono?"

"No, Sir."

"Any other issues that are concerning you?"

There was only one she wanted to express. "I miss you."

Brie longed to hear how much he missed her, that he was coming home because of it. Instead, Sir responded, "But you are well, and you are getting your filming complete?"

"Yes, Sir," she answered obediently. Brie was desperate to hear his voice rather than her own, so she asked, "Is work going well? Are you making good progress?"

"There is adequate progress being made." He switched the line of questioning back to her. "Do you feel you will be able to make the deadline for the documentary?"

"Yes, Sir. Tomorrow, I'll be editing the interviews I did the last couple of days. I am making adequate progress, too."

"Good. Your success is as important to me as my own."

"As is yours to me, Sir."

"Have you been my good girl and exercised every day?"

"Of course, Sir! It's my favorite way to start the day."

His warm laughter thrilled her. "I look forward to it as well. However, I desire a deeper connection. I want to bring structure to our daily encounter."

Brie was intrigued. "I would like that very much as well, Sir."

"There should be a package near you."

She smiled. "There is, Sir."

"Put the phone down and lift the lid. Read the note to me."

She slowly untied the bow and lifted the lid of the pretty box. Inside was a small envelope on top of a piece of jewelry. She opened the envelope and pulled out the note, then picked up the phone to read his words. "*Wear this each morning while you exercise.*"

"Good girl. Now describe the jewelry to me."

Brie put down the note and picked up the unusual blue and gold piece with one hand, while she held the phone to her ear with the other. "It's beautiful, but it's nothing like I have ever seen. The three-inch glass is cobalt in color and curved like a finger, but it's thicker on one end. It's rounded and smooth with a gold decoration attached to one side of the glass. The gold has a pretty filigree design etched in it. Instead of being attached to a chain, the thin elastic material looks suspiciously like a thong, Sir."

"If that is true, Brie, where would the jewelry go?" he asked.

As she examined the piece, it dawned on her that the glass was meant to be inserted into her vagina so that the gold decoration covered her clit. "Is this pussy jewelry, Sir?"

"You could call it that," he said with amusement.

Brie's loins moistened at the thought of inserting the rounded glass into her vagina. What would it feel like? What would it look like? She couldn't wait to try it on and find out.

"Tomorrow morning, wear the jewelry and think of your Master."

"Sir, I won't be able to think of anything else!"

"I will be thinking of you wearing it as we exercise together," he said lustfully.

Brie shivered at the thought. "I can't wait for tomorrow, Sir." With his gift and simple command, he had completely changed the experience of her morning routine.

"There is one more thing in the box, Brie, but I don't want you to open it until our conversation is over."

She tingled with excitement at knowing there was another surprise. "May I *please* open it now?"

His answer was emphatic. "No."

She didn't waste time begging. "Thank you in advance, Sir. I can't express how touched I am by your gifts." She played with the bow on the box. His thoughtfulness was proof he was missing her. He might not have said it in words, but this was more than enough.

Their time on the phone ended far too quickly. Before she knew it, she was listening to Sir saying goodbye. Then the buzz of a dead line took over. She struggled to hold the tears at bay as she picked up the box and looked for his final gift, but she didn't see anything. Brie lifted up the satin lining and found another note, written in Sir's elegant handwriting.

She took it from the box with trembling fingers, knowing it must be important.

*In the cold Russian snow, a flower catches my eye.*
*Breaking through the icy shards*
*In the sea of white, its radiance springs hope.*
*Its tenacity stirs a hardened heart,*
*Adding to its allure.*

*It is a strength to be admired*

*A miracle to behold.*

*Delicate, with the heart of a warrior*

*Rare in its beauty*

*Priceless in its worth.*

*Everywhere I look, I see this tiny flower blooming in the snow and am reminded of you.*

*~Love, Thane*

Warm tears threatened to fall on his poem. She wiped them away, crushing the note to her chest. The romance of a poem and the love expressed in his words filled her heart with a level of peace she'd never known. She sat there, completely entranced by it.

Everything she'd experienced took on a different meaning. The realization that time and distance had no effect on the strength of their love was powerful, life changing. Nothing could prevent it from growing deeper—nothing.

Brie experienced a significant paradigm shift in that moment. With renewed conviction, she stood up and entered Tono's home. She walked over to Tono, greeting him with a bow.

"A good conversation?" he asked.

"Very good, Tono."

Looking at the box in her hand, he explained, "Your gift arrived yesterday, but I was instructed to wait until the phone call to give it to you."

A deep, overflowing love for Tono filled Brie's heart. Not the romantic love she had felt for him prior to now, but the deep-seated love of a kindred spirit. "Tono, I want you to know how honored I am to be your submissive." She bowed low at his feet.

"I accept your gratitude, toriko, but must ask what has brought this sudden need to express it."

She looked up at him with tears in her eyes. "I finally understand… I cannot love you as a mate, but the intensity of my love for you has not changed."

He nodded and indicated they sit down. "Love can be redirected, toriko. Given time, the sexual attraction will dissipate as we move forward with our lives. But to deny the feelings we have would be foolish and unnecessary."

She smiled and held out her hand to him. He took it and squeezed gently. "I ask again, what brought you to this conclusion?"

"Something Sir did today brought me deep inner peace. No time, distance, or personal struggles can separate us. I believe that to my very core. With that realization, I can now accept my love for you. Ever since my decision at the ceremony, I have seen that love as a threat to my relationship with Sir, but now I understand it is not."

"No, it is not, toriko. As a man of principles, I would never allow myself to come between you. But I will admit that being with you in this capacity has been enlightening."

She looked at him warily, afraid Tono would say that she had failed him.

He laughed. "You believe you have disappointed me?"

Brie looked to the floor. "I *know* I have, Tono. Have you forgotten last night?"

He waved it off. "That was minor, toriko. No, I am speaking of the routine and comfort of a mate that I have experienced with you. I am no longer satisfied with the solitary life I lead." Brie felt a twinge of guilt. This would have been his life, had she chosen differently. He continued, "I am now consciously listening for the soul call of my partner."

Brie was thrilled to hear it. "Whoever she is, Tono, she will be worthy of your love. You deserve only the best."

He looked away from her. Instead of responding, Tono changed the subject. "Tomorrow we have our first class together. How do you feel?"

She answered, accepting the change of topic without question. "If I only have to accept your bindings, I will have no troubles."

"Even with an audience of amateurs?"

"I won't even notice," she said with a small grin. "You have that effect on me."

"True," he agreed with amusement.

"How may I serve you today, Tono?"

"Due to tomorrow night's class, I want you to spend the entire day working on your film. As you can't cook and I can't spare the time, I will order in our meals. While you work on the documentary, I'll prepare my notes for the class and go over them with you tomorrow before the session."

"It sounds like the perfect plan."

He banged his fist on the table for dramatic effect. "Make it so, little slave."

Brie got up from the table but paused, looking back at him shyly. "May I hug you, Tono?"

A warm smile spread across his face. "Yes, toriko."

She moved into his open arms and closed her eyes as he enfolded her in his manly embrace. "Can I tell you that I love you, Tono?"

"Yes."

"I love you, Tono Nosaka."

He rested his chin on the top of her head. "I love you too, toriko. That will never change."

# Unforeseen

Brie entered the gym wearing her special jewelry underneath her sweats. She'd modeled it in the bathroom earlier that morning. It was beautiful, making her look as if she had a clit of gold. None of the blue glass showed—just the shiny jewelry and the thin, black thong with a stylish gold clasp in back. She had twirled several times to admire it from every angle before slipping on her sweatpants.

With each step, her outer lips rubbed against the glass, causing a subtle pressure on her clit and making Brie acutely aware of the jewelry's presence. *I feel you, Sir…* she thought with a smile on her lips as she made her way to the car.

The gym was busy, as was usual that early in the morning. Brie found an unoccupied elliptical and started running.

*Oh, the rubbing…*

Brie closed her eyes and fantasized about her Sir.

She was bound with her arms high above her.

"Open," he commanded, placing a cloth gag in her mouth and tying it tightly behind her head. "There will be no kissing or speaking, although you are allowed to moan."

He disappeared from her line of sight. She could hear him rifling through his assortment of instruments and tools, but Sir returned with nothing in his hands.

When he saw her look of surprise, he gave her a sexy smirk. "Don't you remember, Brie? I told you I believe in the power of touch…"

His hands caressed her skin, sending electric flutterings throughout her body. "You've missed your Master's touch, haven't you?"

She nodded, then moaned into her gag when he cupped her breasts and lightly pinched her nipples. He bent down and took one into his mouth. The contact created a deep ache—a desperation to connect, to be filled with him, body and soul.

Brie groaned, pressing herself into him as he began to suck. Sir broke the suction and stood back, smiling mischievously. "I can sense your need. Shall I tease you some more?"

She shook her head, knowing he would not listen to her.

Sir came back to her and slipped his hand between her legs, rolling his finger over her swollen clit. Brie threw her head back and moaned loudly. It wouldn't take much…and then her Master knelt down.

Brie squirmed in her bindings when she felt Sir kiss her clit reverently.

*Oh, God, sweet torture!*

"So good…" he murmured gruffly. Sir rapidly flicked his tongue over her clit, setting it on fire with his expertise.

She looked down at his face, buried in her hairless pussy, and felt the stirrings of an orgasm.

Brie started running faster, teasing her clit with the jewelry as she exercised and fantasized for all she was worth.

*Make me come, Sir!* she cried in her head.

Heart racing, pussy throbbing, she let her fantasy take it up a notch. Sir moved behind her and fingered her anus. "I'm going to fuck your ass, my dear. No foreplay, just good old-fashioned thrusting from a hard cock. Do you think you can handle it?"

Brie nodded, whimpering when he placed his rigid member against her tight hole.

Sir grabbed her waist and, with one solid thrust, forced the length of his cock deep inside her.

Brie let out a small cry when she came.

"Are you all right?"

Brie looked over at the elliptical beside her. It was the stately older woman she had become good acquaintances with. On the second day, Elizabeth had struck up a conversation after they were done exercising. The lady seemed nice and not overly intrusive, so that Brie had come to look forward to their short conversations every morning. It made it that much more embarrassing to be caught orgasming in front of her now.

"I think I might have tweaked a muscle. It's nothing, really," Brie said, trying to control her blush.

"You need to be sure to listen to your body, young lady. Don't overdo it."

"Yes, ma'am." Brie agreed. She increased the resistance on the machine and closed her eyes to shut out the rest of the world. *Sir, I'm so naughty! Do you want me to be naughty again?*

Brie had a satisfied grin on her face by the time she finished up her hour at the gym. She hadn't thought it was possible to maintain a physical relationship while being far apart, but Sir had managed it with this simple trick.

Her imagination had no problem convincing her body the hardness between her legs was Sir's princely cock. Knowing he was fantasizing about her at the same time had been enough to send her over the edge. How incredibly wrong to orgasm in a crowded gym while she was exercising, but she adored the wickedness of it!

Brie got off the machine a sweaty but happy mess. She headed towards the lockers, but stopped cold when she saw Faelan just outside the gym, waiting for her. She looked around, unsure how to avoid a confrontation with the Dom.

"What's wrong? You look like you've seen a ghost," Elizabeth said, joining her at the lockers.

Brie pointed Faelan out to the older woman. "See that man? His name is Todd Wallace and he's stalking me. I can't leave this place until he's gone."

Elizabeth looked him over through the glass door and tsked. "Tell you what. I'll go out there and talk to him. When his back is turned, you scoot over to the coffee shop next door. I'll meet you there when the coast is clear."

It seemed like a reasonable solution. "Okay. But please, whatever you do, don't let him see me."

Elizabeth put her hand on Brie's shoulder to reassure her. "It'll be a piece of cake. By the way, I'd like a double latte."

Brie nodded dully, trying to keep her fear in check. She had a feeling Faelan would smell it on her.

She watched the elegant woman exit the building and engage Faelan. Brie didn't know what Elizabeth said, but he willingly followed her into the parking lot, away from the entrance. Brie held her breath, walked out of the door and straight into the café.

She didn't allow herself to breathe until she was seated at a table in the back. Both lattes were sitting on the table, getting cold, by the time Elizabeth finally joined her.

The woman sat down gracefully, placing her purse on the empty chair next to her. "You have nothing to worry about, Brianna. That boy was simply waiting for a friend. His name is Tommy. Such a nice lad."

Brie wasn't convinced. "How do you know his name is Tommy? Fae…Todd could have been lying to you."

Elizabeth laughed as she picked up her cup and took a tiny sip. She made a face before setting it back down. "I asked for his driver's license, dear. You're not dealing with an amateur."

Brie was stunned. "How could you possibly get him to show you that?"

The older woman smiled craftily. "I have my ways…"

Brie held up her cup to make a toast. "Thank goodness for friends in unexpected places." She swallowed the lukewarm brew, not minding the temperature.

Elizabeth smiled and clinked mugs with her, but put hers back down without drinking any. "It was my pleasure, Brianna."

In the short time they spent in the café, Brie learned that Elizabeth was the proud owner of a new spa in LA. "I recently moved from New York, where I previously ran a spa called Serenity. All the Broadway stars frequented it; it was truly divine…" she said wistfully. "However, the cold winters finally got to me and I thought LA sounded like a nice place to retire. But I miss my clients, so I started up a sister spa."

It turned out that Elizabeth was single, but seemed quite content as a free agent. "I find I am still too young to settle down. Too many delectable men to enjoy, including that handsome boytoy I just met."

Brie's jaw fell open. "You made a pass at Tommy?"

Her laughter was pleasant, but controlled. "Hell no, honey. *He* made the pass at me."

Brie had to admit the woman oozed confidence and sex appeal, despite the gray in her jet-black hair.

"So what do you do for a living, Brianna?"

Brie sighed in frustration. At this point, her documentary was still under wraps, so she replied, "I'm an unemployed film director. Still trying to make connections so I can get my work noticed."

Elizabeth smiled with perfect crimson lips. "Maybe I can help with that. I see all kinds of high-end clients at my spa. I could put in a good word for you. Do you have any business cards I can pass out?"

Brie was only half listening, wondering, *Really, who wears makeup to work out?* She dug in her purse, looking for a card. Although she had business cards, they were outdated because of her old address. She handed one over, apologizing as she did so. "The cellphone number and email are correct, but unfortunately the address is not."

Elizabeth's long red nails caught Brie's attention as she took the card. Everything about the woman was meticulously perfect.

*Is she a Domme…?*

The older woman looked the card over critically. "I have a friend who owns a printing shop. I am sure he could print up a few hundred of these free of charge. Do you have your new address?"

"Actually, I was planning to leave my address off the next set of business cards. It's unnecessary in this day and age. If someone needs to mail me something, they can just message me."

Elizabeth pursed her lips and nodded. "True enough. So would you like me to have new ones printed up? A business card should reflect the professionalism of the person it represents. This screams 'amateur' to me. Ricky would do a far better job."

Even though her critique was unsolicited, Brie had to agree with Elizabeth's assessment. "If it's no trouble, I guess that would work. But I have to ask, why would he do it for free?"

The older woman raised her eyebrow. "Why, indeed?"

Brie noticed that her new friend had glanced at her collar several times throughout their conversation. She was fairly certain the woman was a Dominatrix. However, Elizabeth made no mention of it. The lady kept the conversation light and short. "Until tomorrow, Brianna. Hopefully you'd be open to doing this again sometime soon, stalker or no stalker."

Brie giggled. "This was nice. Consider it a future date."

"Good," Elizabeth said, as she got up to leave. The lady had a sexy sway to her hips, one that grabbed the attention of a male customer. He got up and opened the door for her, staring at her ass for several seconds before going back to his coffee.

Elizabeth knew how to win over the male population, even in workout clothes.

Brie was surprised that she felt anxious with Tono in the room. She'd been on stage countless times during her training, and she'd been part of several club scenes, but this felt different. These were complete newbies and she could sense their collective nervousness.

She surveyed the class of twenty-four. Most were couples ranging from their twenties into their thirties, but there were several who looked to be in their forties and beyond. It was an interesting range of ages.

Tono had requested Brie only wear a thong underneath her clothing. Once the class was quiet, he introduced the two of them and asked Brie to remove her clothes.

Brie gracefully removed her skirt and blouse, to the quiet gasps of two women in the front row. It reminded her of an art class with a nude model.

She accepted their surprised stares willingly, focusing her attention on Tono to distract herself. He held up his tools for the evening: several bundles of jute and a pair of medical scissors. He then handed out a pair of scissors to each of the students. "This is my gift to you. Keep it within reach whenever you practice the art of Kinbaku."

He went on to share the history of Kinbaku as he unwound a section of jute. He explained how it had morphed from being a form of torture to an erotic exchange between two people.

"Americans often use the term Shibari. It is my personal belief that the two are similar, but different. Shibari focuses on the art—the beautiful image created by the bondage itself. Kinbaku, on the other hand, is about the process—the connection between the couple. It makes no difference to me if you call it Shibari or Kinbaku. However, in my class I will only use the term Kinbaku, with the understanding that your success has less to do with how the bondage looks, and more about how you interact with your partner during the exchange."

Tono turned the flute music on and adjusted it to a soothing background noise. "It is important to create a peaceful setting. One in which your partner can lose herself in the act of binding." He ran his hands over

Brie's naked skin as he continued talking. "Contact is essential during the scene. You seduce as you restrain."

He stood behind her and wrapped one arm around her chest, just under her breasts, pressing her against him. "Breathing in sync is an effective tool for connecting." He leaned down and whispered loud enough for them to hear, "Breathe with me, toriko."

Brie smiled as she laid her head back against his shoulder and closed her eyes. Even though it was second nature to sync with him, it immediately calmed her. After a minute or two, Tono pulled away and began to wrap the rope underneath her breasts, where his arm had been moments before. He explained each step as he went, unwinding and redoing as he made the simple chest harness.

His hands lightly brushed her nipples as he worked, keeping them hard and receptive. When he was done, he tightened the harness just a little more, causing her pussy to tingle with need. It didn't matter that he was using basic techniques; Tono knew exactly how to seduce her—and the audience.

He tied her wrists next. "This is visually and emotionally powerful. After you bind your partner in this way, lift her arms above her head. You now have freedom to explore her body with your fingers and the extra length of rope." Tono used the dangling jute from her wrist bindings to lightly slap her skin.

She was intrigued that he was demonstrating techniques he had never used on her before. Brie assumed that it was for the benefit of those who might never proceed further than these simple skills. She loved Tono all the more for it. Although he was a highly experienced Master, he had taken into account the level and comfort of his students.

Tono tied a new section of jute to her chest harness and brought it between her legs. "Be aware of the amount of pressure you place on her clit. You can take what is meant to be pleasurable and make it unbearably painful if you are not careful. It is necessary to ask your submissive how it feels as you experiment with the tautness of the rope. You can always loosen or tighten based on her response. It is not a sign of weakness; it is an indication of your commitment to her well-being."

Brie moaned softly as he applied just the right amount of pressure with the jute. He turned her around to show the class how to attach the rope in the back, and then positioned her to face the crowd again.

Tono lightly touched her pussy with two of his fingertips as he adjusted the rope. It seemed unintentional, until he explained to the class, "A simple touch in erogenous zones while you work has the power to drive your partner wild."

Brie bit her lip and nodded. She heard giggles coming from some of the ladies in the group. Oh, yes—she knew they wanted him to touch *their* erogenous zones.

Tono handed out a length of jute to each individual in the class. "It is important to know how the jute feels on your own skin, whether you plan to do the binding or have the binding done to you. My first assignment requires you to take off your shoes and socks so that you can bind your own ankles together." There were many nervous chuckles as people followed his instructions.

To demonstrate the procedure, he had Brie sit on a chair. She watched in amusement as the class made humorous attempts to bind themselves according to Tono's directions. Brie noticed there was one female who seemed especially quick to catch on, but the majority had about as much talent as Brie herself did. It was entertaining to watch.

She observed Tono correct and encourage each person individually. His patience was extraordinary. It was truly an honor for Brie to be a part of this introduction to Kinbaku. She wondered if the students understood they had a gifted Master in their midst.

Tono ended the class by untying Brie from the jute with lingering caresses and plenty of kissing. She could feel the sexual tension rise in the room, and suspected many of the couples would be experiencing passionate encounters of their own after class.

He commanded Brie to dress, and then had the class thank her for the demonstration. She blushed at their applause and bowed to Tono.

The applause increased, with a few enthusiastic hollers to round out his accolades. It took a full half-hour before the classroom emptied. His students felt the need to personally thank him before they left. It was gratifying to hear their enthusiasm and impressions of the first night of class.

Brie was surprised when several of the women came over to thank her, as well.

"It was lovely to watch your connection together."

"Miss Toriko, I hope my husband and I can create that kind of harmony."

Brie smiled. "I am sure you will," she encouraged. "The breathing is crucial and very sexy."

"Yes, it was sexy to watch! How long have you two been together?"

Brie wasn't sure how to answer, and chose to willfully misdirect instead. "Actually, this is our first class…"

Once the classroom had cleared out, Tono held out his hand to her. She walked into his embrace and the two simply drank in the joy of the experience.

"This is a good thing, Tono."

"Yes, it is, toriko."

"Thank you for letting me be a part of it."

"The pleasure is mine, little slave."

He picked up the rope and smiled as he bundled each strand. "I am surprised to find that teaching the correct method to those new to the art is as satisfying as teaching advanced skills to the experienced."

"They are lucky to have this opportunity," Brie said, looking forward to next week's class. "Truth is, I feel lucky too."

He kissed her on the lips before handing her the last bundle of jute. "We make a good team, you and I."

She fell into a comfortable routine with Tono that second week. Brie did not live each day in quiet desperation for Sir's return, choosing instead to embrace the unique life experience Tono offered.

However, Brie was still overjoyed when Sunday rolled around, knowing she would get to hear Sir's voice. The day held special excitement because not only was she going to get to speak with Sir in the morning, but she had an interview set up with the girls that afternoon. She had decided they should gather at Mary's apartment, believing the tight-lipped woman would be more open if she was in her own environment. It would also serve to feed Brie's curiosity about what kind of place Mary had.

Just before she left for the gym that morning, Brie inserted the pussy jewelry and rubbed the gold appreciatively. The beautiful piece fit as if it had been made for her, and had the added benefit of teasing her clit with its slight pressure. She decided to wear a half shirt and flattering shorts to match her sexy attire.

Brie left the house quietly, being careful not to wake Tono. She remained silent until she slipped into her car, where she spotted a small pot of purple and yellow flowers sitting on the passenger seat. Brie picked the small pot up and cradled it in her arms. They were crocuses, the flower Sir had mentioned in his poem. She knew their name, having googled it after reading his romantic words.

Brie looked at Tono's home and smiled. She had no idea when he had placed Sir's gift in her car, but she would be sure to thank him on her return.

It thrilled her to have received so many thoughtful gifts from her Master. Not only the sexy jewelry and the romantic poem, but now she could add flowers to the list. She lifted the colorful flowers to her nose and kissed the delicate petals. "I love you, Sir!"

It was with a joyous heart that she pulled up to the workout center with a single crocus tucked behind her ear. But once she entered the building, she stopped dead in her tracks. "It can't be…"

He tilted his head slightly and asked, "It can't be what?"

Brie didn't waste a second, jumping into his arms with utter abandon. "Sir!"

He held her tight, rocking her back and forth in his embrace. "So you're glad to see me?"

"Best present ever!" she exclaimed. "I got your flowers this morning, but I never dreamed I would see you today."

Still holding her with one hand, he lifted her chin and kissed her in front of everyone in the gym. Her whole body tingled with electricity and for a moment, time stood still as she reveled in their soul connection.

Brie wanted to protest when Sir finally put her back on the ground. He looked down at her tenderly, touching the flower in her hair. She tiptoed to kiss Sir again, but stopped when she noticed the color completely drain from his face.

Sir growled under his breath. "What is *she* doing here?"

# Brie Discerns Master's Heart

# The Beast

In a fluid motion, Sir moved Brie behind him as he stepped forward to face the threat alone. "You have no business being here."

Elizabeth smiled easily, as if she had expected such a negative response. "It's a free country, Thane."

"Who is she?" Brie asked, stunned at Sir's odd behavior towards the woman, suddenly afraid she knew exactly who it was but not able to believe it.

"No one," he answered angrily, taking Brie's hand and turning to leave.

"Are you really such a coward, Thane? I had expected you to grow into a man by now."

The entire gym was now focused on the scene being played out before them.

"Come, Brie," Sir said with forced calm, guiding her towards the door.

Brie was shocked to feel him literally shaking with rage, the air around him rife with hostility. She kept up with his long strides. They were both desperate to get away from the situation as swiftly as possible.

From behind her, she heard, "Don't walk away from your mother, boy."

Sir didn't break his stride as he pushed through the door and shouted, "I have no mother!"

Brie stole a glance back at Elizabeth. The woman lifted her chin and smiled at Brie condescendingly. A cold chill coursed through Brie's veins as she realized how easily she had played into Elizabeth's hands. But she could not fathom how the woman could be Thane's mother. She looked far too young.

"Keys," Sir snapped.

Brie dug the keys out of her pocket and handed them to him. "Sir, I didn't kn—"

"Not now, Brie."

He slid into the driver's seat and she automatically slipped into the passenger side, grabbing onto her flowerpot and clutching it to her chest.

"Seat belt," he barked.

Brie belted herself in as Sir revved the engine loudly and took off with a squeal of tires and black smoke.

He drove like a man possessed, going above the speed limit for the foggy conditions, which were normal that early in the morning. At all times he remained in control, but he drove with a dangerous focus that unnerved her.

Sir did not proceed to their apartment. Instead, he headed for the California hills that overlooked the city. The atmosphere inside the vehicle was alarming. She had never seen Sir so upset. He stared at the road, his jaw set, his eyes narrow—a seething mass of tension. Brie was afraid that if she dared to touch him, he would explode.

She buried her face in the flowers and said a silent prayer.

Sir suddenly pulled off to the side of the road and jumped out of the car. She scrambled out too, unwilling to leave him alone.

He stormed to the edge of a steep embankment and held his arms out wide in the swirling fog, screaming with his fists clenched towards the sky. The sound of his cry broke Brie's heart. It was full of pain on a level she had never experienced. His screams of agony were swallowed up by the surrounding mist.

Sir roared again, but it was full of a rage that frightened her. He looked around wildly and then focused on the hard trunk of a large tree. He began punching the rough surface in blind anger, not caring about the damage he was doing to his fists.

Brie cried out, wanting to stop him but understanding, on a deeper level, his need to unleash the furious wrath within him. After countless sickening thuds, he fell to his knees and slumped against the base of the tree.

She ran to him then, wrapping her arms around Sir, trying to impart every ounce of her strength to him.

Sir wept—a deep, raw release of emotion that had been buried for years. She didn't say anything as she held onto him, needing him to know he was not alone in his grief. Finally the sobs ceased and he became silent. Time stood still in the white mist, silent and cold, while he struggled with his grief and pain.

"I love you," she whispered.

Sir responded by pulling her to him and tucking her into his arms. She lay on the ground, her head buried in his chest. He held her in silence, words unnecessary as he took comfort in her presence. But it wasn't enough to fill the emotional abyss. Sir pulled at her clothes, removing them hurriedly until his fingers met the resistance of her jewelry. He grunted and looked down for a second, ripping it from her and replacing it with his cock.

Sir climbed onto Brie, like a drowning man climbing into a boat. She became his means of survival as he filled the cavernous void in his soul with her feminine offering. Brie opened herself to him, willingly accepting her role. Sir's groans were subdued as he took her deep and hard. Brie looked up at the swirling mist, tears streaming down her face as she cried for Thane the young adolescent and Thane the man.

All that pain, held inside for years, was now exacting an excruciating toll as it erupted with violent force. The desperate coupling seemed to go on forever, his anguish too great for him to find release. Eventually he stiffened inside her and cried out in painful relief.

Sir pushed off her and lay beside Brie on the ground, watching the swirling mist as his breath slowly returned to normal.

When he finally turned to Brie, his anguished gaze penetrated the depths of her soul, causing her to shiver from the chill of it, but she did not flinch.

"Seeing that woman," he said hoarsely, "it's as if it happened yesterday. I see him on the floor, struggling for breath, blood everywhere." Brie felt him shudder beside her. "She just stood there and did nothing, cold as ice." Sir growled as he looked back up at the sky. "It should have been her on the ground. To this day, I wish it had been her."

Brie put her arms around him, but remained silent.

"She wants something from me…"

She pressed against him, wanting to bring comfort and assurance. "Maybe she needs to make amends."

He frowned. "She never showed remorse, never asked for forgiveness. There would be no reason for her to seek it now. I can only think of one thing that would motivate her."

Brie was afraid to voice the obvious question.

Sir continued, speaking his thoughts. "She knew I wouldn't have given her permission to see me…so she went through you." He snorted in anger. "As devious and selfish as I remember."

The mist had slowly given way to the warmth of the sunshine. Sir stared up at the sky as the sun broke through the haze. "It's time we head over to Ren's."

He gently dressed her, as if she were breakable, like china, and then picked up the jewelry and placed it in his pocket. Sir helped Brie to her feet, holding her close for several minutes.

She understood that this had been a significant victory. Sir had survived the unexpected encounter with his mother.

The drive to Tono's was silent but reverent.

Brie wondered if her Asian Master had been told of Sir's early return. Tono's calm expression when he opened the door hinted that Sir had already forewarned him.

"Welcome to my home, Sir Davis," he said.

Brie was technically still Tono's sub and was unsure how to behave with both Masters. She looked at Sir, who nodded towards him.

Brie bowed. "Tono, how may I serve you?"

"Go change into your normal clothes and pack, toriko, while I speak with Sir Davis."

She bowed again before leaving the men. She was excited to be packing to rejoin Sir back at home, but there was a sense of sadness as well. The thought that Tono would face a lonely house after they left hurt her heart.

Brie returned to find them engaged in lively conversation.

"I asked Marquis about Wallace when you told me what happened at the gym. The boy claimed he was nowhere near the workout center the morning Brie saw him."

"Do you believe him?" Tono asked.

"I didn't until this morning."

Brie knelt down at the end of the table between both men.

Sir turned to Brie. "How close were you? Are you certain it was Wallace?"

Brie thought back to that morning and shook her head. "No, Sir. The man looked like Faelan, but I cannot say with one hundred percent certainty it was him."

Sir's face contorted in anger. "Knowing her, I'd be willing to bet it wasn't."

The idea that it hadn't been Faelan blew Brie's mind. "I'm sorry, Sir. I *never* suspected Elizabeth was anything but a kind acquaintance."

"One who now has your business card."

She lowered her eyes. "Yes, Sir."

He lifted her chin. "I do not blame you, Brie. She is a cobra, beautiful to look at but deadly to handle."

Tono sounded appalled. "I was not aware of a business card exchange."

Sir growled angrily. "In a normal world, it would mean nothing. Had I known she was on the prowl again, Ren, I would have insisted you keep Brie with you twenty-four seven."

To Brie he said, "You will have to change your cell phone number and email account immediately. I can assure you, the woman will not leave you alone after this. I may have thwarted her plans, but she will not deviate from her primary goal. She is a tenacious beast."

Brie was disheartened she would not only have to change a phone number she'd had for years, but she would also have to inform everyone of the changes to both accounts. She felt like an idiot.

"What does she want?" Tono asked Sir.

"It's simple—money."

Tono was silent. When he spoke next, his voice was full of compassion. "It is unfortunate that you must deal with such a creature."

Sir's nostrils flared. "Yes, but I will *not* allow her to ruin my life a second time. I would prefer it if you would not mention her to anyone. The fewer people involved, the better."

"It shall remain between us." Tono glanced up at the clock on the wall and informed him, "I do not know if you are aware that toriko has a meeting in four hours, with Ms. Taylor and Miss Wilson."

Brie quickly assured him, "I will reschedule it, Sir."

"No! I do not want my early return to interfere with your plans. You will do the interview as scheduled."

Brie couldn't stand the thought of Sir being alone, today of all days. "Sir, it is no—"

"Brie, you will do the interviews as planned," he stated firmly.

She bowed her head, realizing she had offended him. "Of course, Sir."

Tono addressed Brie. "Toriko, I will need a model for this week's class, since you will not be available to attend. Is there someone you would recommend as your replacement?"

Brie was disappointed she would not be joining Tono's Kinbaku class, but she knew who would make a fine stand-in. "I think Lea would do well."

"Naturally you would suggest Lea," Tono said with amusement. "However, I agree and can see her being a good choice. I'll see if she has any interest."

*Dang, that Lea!* Brie thought with a grin. *She's so going to owe me…*

Tono stood up and moved to the center of the room, calling Brie to join him.

She looked into his chocolaty brown eyes with a sense of sorrow. As much as she was anxious to be with Sir, her time with Tono had been emotionally profound.

"Give me your wrist, toriko."

Brie held up her wrist to him and watched as Tono untied the jute that signified his ownership. He turned her palm upward and kissed her wrist tenderly. "I release you."

Brie knelt down and bowed her head. "Thank you, Tono. It was an honor to serve you."

He put his hand on her head. "I return you to your Master's service."

Brie felt a physical lifting as he took his hand from her. She stood up and bowed one last time as a sign of her utmost respect for the Dom.

"Brie," Sir called to her.

She returned to him and knelt at Sir's feet. When his hand touched the crown of her head, a jolt of electricity coursed through her. "Stand before your Master."

When she stood up, Brie looked into his eyes. She could see the inner struggle he was attempting to hide. "What is your pleasure, Master?"

"Gather your things. We are leaving."

Tono handed her the small suitcase and her wrist tie. She smiled as she closed her fingers around it. She would keep it as a memento, a reminder of the lessons she had learned under his care.

"Serve your Master well," he said with finality.

The dynamic had officially changed. "I will, Tono Nosaka. I will not forget the lessons you have taught me."

"Good." To Sir, he added, "If assistance is needed in any capacity, do not hesitate to call."

Sir took his hand and shook it warmly. "I will keep that in mind, Ren. Thank you. Your help and support will not be forgotten."

Opening the door to their apartment was the best feeling in the world! Despite having been abandoned for two weeks, his place still held the faint aroma of Sir. Brie took in the smell with relish. *Home…*

"Brie, it was a long flight and I am exhausted," he said gruffly, guiding her towards the bedroom. "Take off your clothes and lie in bed."

She did so dutifully, wondering what he would ask of her. Sir pulled Brie into his embrace once he joined her on the bed. There was no animalistic coupling, no emotional exchange—nothing. He simply fell asleep with her cradled in his arms.

It gave her great joy to be his safe haven. "I will always be that for you, Sir. Always…" she whispered passionately.

# Girl Chat

Lea gave Brie a huge hug later that afternoon, when they met outside Mary's apartment.

"Guess who I got a call from!" Lea gushed.

Brie smiled as she started gathering her camera equipment from the car. "A Kinbaku Master?"

Lea eagerly grabbed one of the light reflectors to help her. "Yes! Oh-em-gee, Brie! I cannot believe it. Tono Nosaka called me an hour ago and asked if I would work with him. Can I just say that knowing you is the best thing that has ever happened to me?"

Brie giggled. "I'm glad you're happy, Lea."

"Tell me how I can repay you. I'll do anything—just name it," Lea exclaimed, beaming with happiness.

Since Brie's arms were full, she asked, "How 'bout you ring the door-bell?"

"You got it!" Lea did a graceful pirouette before ringing the bell.

Despite only having a small apartment, Mary took her sweet time to answer the door, asking before she opened it, "Who is it?" as if she wasn't expecting them.

Lea immediately answered, "It's the plumber. I've come to fix the sink."

Mary swung the door open and looked at Lea oddly.

Brie knew the cartoon skit Lea was quoting was a favorite of hers, so she explained to Mary, "You're supposed to say 'who is it?' again."

Mary frowned, but gave in to Lea's puppy dog look. "Fine. Who is it?"

Lea said in a louder voice, "It's the plumber. I've come to fix the sink."

Mary ignored Lea and turned back to Brie, stating in an uninterested voice, "I don't get it."

"You have to ask again."

Mary didn't even crack a smile as she repeated the question one last time.

Lea gasped out the words, "It's the plumber… I've come to fix…the sink." She grabbed her chest, twirled around several times before falling to the ground, 'dead'.

Mary stared at her momentarily, and then said to Brie, "Come in."

Brie giggled as she stepped over Lea's prostrate body and entered Mary's apartment.

Mary shut the door and locked it, leaving Lea lying outside on her doorstep. "Glad I have one less idiot to entertain."

"Hey!" Lea yelled from outside.

Mary walked over to her sofa and sat down with a self-satisfied smile.

Lea began pounding on the door. "Let me in, guys!"

Although Brie thought it was humorous, she took pity on her friend and unlocked the door.

"Party pooper," Mary complained.

"Look, I need both of you for this interview."

Lea pouted. "Didn't you think it was the least bit funny?"

"No!" Mary answered emphatically.

Lea looked at Brie for support.

"Well, it was funny the first time you did it to me. Not so much today."

Lea grabbed her chest, twirled several times and collapsed on the floor.

"Nope, not any funnier," Brie replied.

Lea got up in a huff. "You two have no sense of humor."

"Trust me, Lea. It's you, not us," Mary stated. "There is nothing funny about that."

"That's because you don't know the cartoon," Lea said earnestly. "You see, there's this parrot in the house. The plumber knocks on the door and the parrot asks, 'Who is it?' The plumber keeps answering until he finally gets so frustrated, he has a heart attack. It's an old rerun of Electric Company I used to watch with my dad."

"That explains it," Mary said.

Lea looked at her questioningly. "Explains what?"

"You dad is as much of an idiot as you are."

Lea's face contorted into an ugly scowl as she got ready to let loose on Mary. It was the last thing Brie needed, so she piped up, "Hey, Mary, you got anything to drink?"

Mary shrugged. "Only rum and Coke."

Brie groaned, remembering the last time she had had that particular drink was at the Kinky Goat. It brought a wave of bad memories, but it was the quickest way she could think of to relax the tension in the room. "Make it a double."

Mary turned to Lea. "And you?"

"Make mine a triple. It's the only way I'll be able to stand you."

Brie laughed, thinking back on their first outing together. Despite the passage of time, not much had really changed between the girls.

Mary took care of the drinks, which gave Brie a chance to examine Mary's apartment. She was shocked to see a wide variety of Disney mementos, from little music boxes and posters to pillows and snow globes, all scattered throughout the room. It reminded her of a little girl's bedroom rather than an adult's apartment.

Brie picked up one of the snow globes and watched the glitter swirl around the little redheaded mermaid. When Mary came back with their drinks, Brie asked, "So you're into Disney, huh?"

Mary gave her a nasty look. "Yeah. You got a problem with that?"

"No. It just isn't something I would have expected from such a tough bitch like you."

Mary's expression softened as she handed Brie the drink and took the globe from her. "I love everything Disney. I'm a serious collector."

Lea glanced around the room. "No doubt! I'd say you're like a crazy obsessive collector."

Before Mary could take offense, Brie held up her glass. "Here's to the Three Musketeers—Mary the Mediocre, Lea the Lame and Brie the Beloved."

"Brie the Bitch is more like it," Mary snapped.

Lea rolled her eyes. "Mary, you show no spark of creativity. Clearly, it's Brie the Butt."

All three laughed as they clinked glasses, and Brie forced down Mary's favorite drink. She hid her shudder as she swallowed it, and then got to work setting up the camera and light reflectors while the other two chatted.

She focused on the moment instead of on Sir, whom she had left at the apartment all alone. It had nearly killed her to leave him.

"Okay, my plan is to keep things the same as we've always done. We're simply going to sit and talk like we used to after every session. No need to notice the camera. This is just about subbies getting together to dish."

Mary nodded her approval. "Good. I would have punched you in the throat if you'd tried to get a close-up of a tear or something."

Lea laughed. "Are you even capable of crying, Mary?"

"No, that ability died long ago," she quipped, taking a sip of her drink.

It was an honest answer given lightly, but with deep significance. Brie instantly thought of the little girl Mary had once been, and her heart ached for her. This was going to be a difficult interview. She hoped Mary would be resilient enough to survive it.

The girls started off talking about silly things to break the ice, but soon the conversation turned to a serious topic when Mary brought up Brie's time with Tono. "So…how is it living with the Master of the freakish rope tricks?"

Brie smiled. "Tono has been a wonderful Master to me."

"Did he tie you up nice and tight and fuck you silly?" Lea asked.

"He tied me up all right, but I only got a spanking."

Lea giggled. "A spanking? I never thought Tono had it in him."

Mary interjected, "Of course he does. He was doing an excellent job with my spy fantasy just before I had my little 'episode'."

Brie suddenly felt the urge to share. "Mary, you should know that Tono became visibly upset when your breakdown was mentioned while he was watching the documentary."

Mary closed her eyes. "Yeah, whatever."

"Why would it surprise you that he cares about you?"

Mary pursed her lips. "The guy never knew me. Must have been a kneejerk reaction."

Brie was offended by her brush-off of Tono. "He is a genuine person, damn it. Don't you dare belittle his heart."

Mary held up her hands. "Don't get all weird on me Brie. I didn't mean to put down Rope Freak."

"Why do you have to make everything a joke?" Brie complained.

Mary stared at her without speaking, but then sighed deeply and answered, "I…I'm not used to it, don't trust it."

Lea said what Brie was thinking. "Do *not* base your opinion of the male population on your father. He was a fucked-up piece of shit."

Mary held up her glass. "Yes, he was."

"Do you still have contact with him?" Brie asked.

Mary threw her head back and laughed. "Fuck, no! Do you think I'm crazy?"

Brie forged onward with a more difficult question. "What do you think his reaction will be when this film comes out?"

"He won't care. The guy never cared about me, good or bad. I was just his punching bag after my mom left. There isn't a shred of human kindness in that man. He's a worthless excuse of manmeat, take my word for it."

Brie clinked glasses with her. "Okay, he's worthless manmeat. But surely someone had to have been looking out for you as a kid."

The color drained from Mary's face. She looked like she was about to clam up, but then she gulped down her drink and spoke. "In second grade, I told my teacher. She treated me like I was lying to get attention. You know what she said?" Her voice changed as she imitated the woman's voice. "'Your father is under a lot of pressure, young lady.'"

Lea put her hand to her mouth in shock. "No way…"

"I didn't say anything after that, but damn if my third grade teacher noticed the day I cringed after she touched my arm. I told her everything and two weeks later Social Services came to our home. My dad played everything off as if I was a klutzy kid, and they bought it. The fucking social worker bought it hook, line, and sinker."

Brie looked at her with compassion. "I can't imagine how that must have felt, Mary. Finally being heard and then having it all fall apart."

Mary snarled. "It hurt like fucking hell, bitch! He beat the crap out of me and told me if anyone noticed this time, he would find new ways to hurt me." Mary downed the rest of her drink in one gulp. "I never told another living soul after that, until I was forced to explain what happened with Tono."

Brie asked a harder question, concerned that Mary might not respond but feeling it was important to ask. "How do you feel your childhood experience shaped you as an adult?"

Mary's resistance dissolved as she let out a faint, anguished cry, turning away from them both. "Truth? I'm damaged goods."

The vulnerability Mary exhibited tore at Brie's heart. She put her arm around her and whispered so the camera wouldn't catch it. "You are the strongest woman I know. He did not break you. You not only survived, you overcame his brutality."

Mary shrugged off her hug, but said under her breath, "Thanks." She got up and headed to the kitchen to make another drink before returning. "What else do you want to know? Have at it, bitches. This is your only chance."

Lea piped up, "So did you become a masochist because of your dad?"

"No!" Mary growled angrily. "I hate that you would assume that."

Brie had also presumed that was the case. "Can you explain?"

"I am not a masochist. I don't *like* pain, but I endure it. It's like I have a driving need to defeat it. Like…" She let out a long, ragged breath. "If I was able to bear it without fear, I would finally be the victor over him."

Brie felt tears burn her eyes but Mary glared at her, letting her know that such an emotional response was not acceptable. Brie switched her mindset to that of a director and asked, "So what attracted you to the D/s lifestyle, then?"

Mary held her chin up. "In submission, I find control. It's the only time I have power over my past."

"Wow, that is really profound," Lea said in awe. Mary just rolled her eyes.

Brie was equally impressed, but kept it to herself. Nothing but an indifferent reaction would satisfy Mary. She turned to Lea. "What about you, Lea? What made you want to become a submissive?"

"Well…I am adventurous by nature. I want to try it *all*, nothing held back. In D/s, I find equally adventuresome souls. It's exciting! Anything and everything is allowed as long as we both agree. I don't care how weird it is—I want to try everything at least once!"

"You're a twit, Lea," Mary stated. "Everyone has their limits. You can't convince me otherwise."

Lea grinned at her enthusiastically. "Well, I haven't found mine yet. Sure, there have been a few things I won't try again, but all of it has been interesting. Wouldn't change a thing."

Brie had to ask, "So how will your parents react when you tell them about this film, Lea?"

Her bosom suddenly blossomed a nice, deep shade of pink that crept all the way to her cheeks. "Well…I'm not sure. My parents have always been my biggest supporters. They're the ones who've encouraged me to explore the world." She looked at the camera guiltily. "I think… I believe they'll be surprised that this is the direction I have chosen, but I don't expect they will love me any less."

Mary stepped in. "What about you, Brie? How will *your* parents handle their perfect little girl going all kinky on them?"

Brie choked on the horrid rum and Coke she was drinking. She hadn't counted on being on the other end of the interview. "My parents? Um… They won't handle it very well. It'll be embarrassing for them, living in a small community with small town values and all. But I trust, as much as it will be a struggle for both my mom and dad, that in the end they will support my decision. Like most parents, their greatest desire is my happiness. Well…" Brie shrugged and grinned. "I've never been happier in all my life."

"Of course," Mary said condescendingly. "'Oh, Brie, our little baby who can do no wrong.'"

Brie snapped at her, "It's not like that at all! I know the news is going to hurt them, but I have to believe they will eventually come around because they love me, and I hold to the belief that love conquers all."

Mary grabbed a pillow in the shape of Pumbaa, the warthog, and hugged it to her chest. "I have a theory. People who are given lots of love as kids attract lots of love. Those who never received it will never know its power."

"What a depressing way to go through life," Lea complained.

But Brie felt only sympathy for Mary. "Haven't you ever loved someone?"

Mary hugged the pillow even harder. "Possibly…" Her vinegar tone returned as she announced, "But it was unceremoniously rejected, which totally proves my point."

Brie wondered if she was speaking about Faelan. The fact Mary would bring it up a second time was significant. Rather than risking embarrassing her on camera by exposing her crush, Brie asked, "So have either of you considered settling down with one Dom now that you've had time to check out what's out there?"

Brie was pretty sure she knew the answer, but felt the viewers would be interested in their responses.

Lea giggled. "Are you kidding, Brie? I love being a submissive for the Center's Dominant training. It is so sweet seeing the new Doms come in, a little unsure of themselves, but leave full of confidence about their calling. It's so damn sexy!"

"But there's no one you would like to settle down with, Lea?" Brie pressed.

She made a pretty little pout. "Maybe, but I'm not sharing who with the rest of the world." She stuck her tongue out at Brie.

Brie laughed and then turned to Mary. "What about you?"

For the first time, Mary did not have a smart comeback. She just shook her head and looked away, sipping at her drink.

Brie took the attention away from her, grateful for Mary's candidness. "I'm still ecstatic with my choice of Dom." She sighed happily and hugged herself.

"So Brie, how does it differ having a twenty-four seven relationship?" Lea asked.

Brie appreciated the chance to share her experience on film. "During training it was more about succeeding in the scene, wanting to get the most out of it. But having this one-on-one interaction with my Master on a daily basis has brought a level of depth to our relationship I never thought possible."

"You're one lucky bitch," Mary grumbled into her glass.

Brie smiled at her with encouragement. "I've said it before, but I believe you and I are a lot alike. Your day will come, Mary, you just have to own it."

"Thank you, Pollyanna," Mary huffed, getting up to mix another drink. "Always sweetness and light, sweetness and light…"

It hurt to have Mary throw her heartfelt words back in her face, so Brie responded with spite. "It is not all sweetness and light, bitch. It is hard to integrate two lives on such an intimate level. Both Sir and I have struggled, but it's because of those struggles that we have grown stronger."

"Can I just say how sick I am of hearing about your perfect life? Fucking sick of it!" Mary spat back.

Lea stepped in to defend Brie, as she had in the past. "Mary, being jealous of Brie is pathetic. In the end, you create the life you have. Despite your father, your crappy childhood, and some idiot who didn't love you back, this is *your* life! You decide today how the rest of your days will play out."

Brie was left speechless. Instead of making a stupid joke, Lea had laid out a sobering truth.

"That's it!" Mary threw the pillow across the room. "I don't have to listen to any more of this shit. Get the fuck out of my apartment, both of you. Now!"

Brie put her drink down slowly, unsure if Mary was serious—but the woman was deadly serious. Mary manhandled Brie off the couch. "I said get out!"

Lea helped Brie gather her camera equipment while Mary went on a cussing spree, the likes of which Brie had never known.

It was with great relief that they made it out, just as Mary slammed the door behind them. "Never again!" Mary screamed from behind the door. "I am never trusting you two bitches again!" Brie heard the lock slide into place.

Lea shook her head at Brie. "What the fuck?"

Brie shrugged her shoulders. "I think we must have touched on some of her greatest fears. I feel terrible, Lea. She opened up so much today, and now she's in there hurting and feeling more alone than ever."

"It's her own fault, damn it," Lea retorted.

"Yes, but she was trying to reach out today. I hate that it ended this way."

"Ain't nobody gonna be able to help that bitch."

Brie frowned. "I refuse to believe that, Lea. Everyone deserves happiness, especially someone as wounded as Mary."

Lea put her arm around Brie. "You can't save the world, girlfriend. You're just going to get hurt if you try. Rabid dogs bite the hand that tries to comfort them, and Mary is as rabid as they come."

Brie laid her head on Lea's inviting bosom and accepted her hug. "Why don't you tell me a joke?"

"Yay!" Lea squeezed her tighter. "So, you know you've got a serious kink if, while driving up a mountain pass, you read a sign that says 'Chains required' and the first thing that pops into your head is, 'Are whips are optional?'"

"I love you and your stupid jokes, Lea," Brie chuckled as she looked at Mary's window. *And I love you too, Mary the Mediocre. Don't you dare give up—bitch!*

# Tender Revelation

Brie let the unpleasant ending of the interview fall away from her as she raced back home to Sir. She hadn't told her friends that he was even home, wanting that secret to remain hers a while longer.

She entered their apartment and was startled to see that it was dark. Had he escaped the solitude of the place and gone somewhere else? She was about to call out Sir's name when she heard his voice. "Put your camera equipment down on the floor and strip where you stand."

Brie's heart fluttered as she hurried to do his bidding. She closed her eyes, holding back the tears, realizing how much she'd missed his authoritative sensuality.

"Kneel on the ground, put your shoulders on the floor and spread your arms on either side of you."

A chill went through her as her breasts made contact with the cold marble. She hid her smile in her long hair as she lay there waiting, listening…

She heard the soft clink of glass and imagined him sitting at the kitchen table, enjoying his martini while he made her await his next command. The anticipation rendered her wet and ready.

He prolonged the moment. Brie assumed he enjoyed the temporary postponement of their desires as much as she did.

When she heard him stand and start walking towards her, Brie let out a soft whimper of excitement. His stride was confident and strong, making her loins ache for him.

Sir stood before her, not saying a word.

Brie held her breath, waiting for his next order.

"Don't move," was his only command.

Her body trembled as he stepped behind Brie. "Such a fine ass."

"Thank you, Sir," she whispered.

He lightly ran his fingers over her round curves and said, "I shall partake of it tonight."

She shivered in delight.

"Stand."

Brie stood up and he pressed himself against her. "Put this on."

Brie bit her lip when she saw that it was the pussy jewelry he had given her while he was in Russia. She took it from him, stepped into the thong-like ornament and eased the blue glass into her opening until the outer piece was snug against her clit. He leaned over her shoulder and stroked her golden femininity.

She laid her head back and moaned in response.

He kissed her shoulder. "Hold your hair up, téa."

Brie held up her brown curls and gasped when he undid the collar around her neck. She wanted to protest, but held her tongue. Sir replaced it with a heavy leather collar with a steel ring at the front. The smell of the leather and the weight of the collar were intoxicating.

He attached a leash to the ring, the snap of the metal causing her loins to contract in sexual anticipation. He eased her hands down, biting her earlobe sensually before lightly yanking on the chain, escorting her out of the hallway and into the living room. "Come, téa."

She followed him to the Tantra chair, feeling lightheaded. To be with her Master in his apartment again was a dream come true.

Sir knelt down and secured the chain to the leg of the chaise longue, then instructed her to lay her stomach against the lower curve of the chair so that her ass was in the air.

Brie glided over the smooth leather with catlike grace, the chain jingling pleasantly as she did so. She turned her head to watch their reflection in the glass of the expansive window.

She observed Sir slowly undress. Each piece of clothing he stripped off revealed more of his handsome physique, from his toned chest to his firm thighs. She held her breath as he removed his briefs and she glimpsed the extent of his arousal.

Sir glanced up and caught her staring. She immediately lowered her eyes, but he told her, "I want you to watch, téa. Watch your Master dominate this body he has longed to play with for two weeks."

She raised her gaze again and visually worshipped the body of her Master. She adored the hair that covered his chest and the dark patch of pubic hair that framed his manhood. In every way, he was masculine and erotic.

He ran his hands over her smooth skin, lighting her senses on fire. Two weeks apart had made her body desperate for him. Goosebumps covered her skin—her need was so great.

Sir picked up something from the side table and she watched him massage his cock with lubricant. She let out a little gasp, her body anticipating the delicious plundering about to take place.

He caressed her ass with his slippery hands, moving the tiny string that held the jewelry in place out of the way before coating her in preparation for his taking. "Are you ready for me, téa?"

She whispered, "So ready, Master."

Sir wiped his hands on a towel before he laid his body on top of hers, resting his shaft in the valley of her ass. "My cock is going to find its way," he growled in her ear.

Brie watched their reflection as Sir rolled his hips, rubbing his shaft against her sensitive sphincter. He teased her as he hovered over the area and then slipped on by, again and again.

She whimpered softly but did not move, loving the frustration of his roguish teasing. He played with her until her body ached to be filled. She moaned when he changed angles and his rigid cock pressed hard against her taut hole.

Because of the addition of the jewelry filling her pussy, the round head of his manhood seemed much too big for the access he demanded, but they both knew how eagerly she would grant it. The tight outer muscle eventually gave way to his insistent pressure, and Sir pushed himself in. Brie watched his progress in the mirror as he controlled the speed and depth of his cock.

His satisfied sigh made her quiver inside. Nothing was as thrilling as pleasing Master, especially in this intimate way.

"Oh, téa…"

The way she was lying on the Tantra chair gave her no leverage to push against his gentle thrusts. She was completely at his mercy and whim—the collar and chain emphasizing that fact in a primal way. She was suddenly reminded of the brand in the closet and asked hesitantly, "If you were to brand me, Master, where would you put it?"

He grunted, placing his fingers just above her tailbone and caressing the area lightly. Her pussy contracted in fear and longing. The idea of being permanently marked as his was exciting, but the pain…the agony of burning flesh still frightened her.

Sir leaned down and bit her shoulder, deep enough to leave teeth marks without breaking the skin. Brie moaned as her pussy pulsated in an impending orgasm. She shifted slightly, to stave off the pleasure.

"Good girl," he whispered, as he thrust even deeper.

Brie closed her eyes, concentrating every fiber of her being on the friction of his cock rubbing against the tight constriction of her ass, as the jewelry inside moved with each thrust and teased her clit in the process. In this position, with the added pressure of Sir's jewelry, she felt the first flutterings of subspace.

Sir's demanding, yet sensual contact, his confident domination of her, and the delicate, clinking chain at her neck started a tingling sensation she associated with flight. "I love my Master," she purred.

"Your Master loves you," he replied, giving more emphasis to every thrust.

Brie started moaning softly, hardly aware she was making noises as she let their connection carry her away. She was floating on a cloud of pleasure, content in the love that surrounded her.

He wrapped his hand around her throat, just under her chin, and lifted her head back, kissing her forehead. "This man loves you."

Sir released the warmth of his come inside her, causing Brie to cry out in pure ecstasy, taking her even higher. She let out a long sigh of total bliss, unable to respond to his declaration of love. Her body answered for her, coming around his shaft in loving adulation.

Soon after, he pulled out and repositioned the little string. He unbuckled the leather collar and replaced it with the original silver one. Brie's soul lifted when she heard the gratifying click of the lock, signifying their commitment to each other. Sir picked her up and carried her to the bedroom. Neither spoke, both riding the emotional wave of their connection.

Sir placed her gently on the bed and lay beside her, lightly playing with a strand of her hair. "I have not felt this whole in a long, long time."

She smiled, thrilled that her love had the power to heal.

Although he had been staring at her, his focus moved past her as he spoke. "Seeing her again, although painful, has brought back a flood of memories for me."

"I can only imagine, Sir."

"Would you like to see a picture of him?"

"Please."

He jumped off the bed and rifled through his closet, coming out a minute later with a framed picture. He handed it to her as he lay back down on the bed, putting his arm around her.

It looked like a professional shot taken for a magazine. Alonzo Davis had had long, dark hair and bronze skin. His face had been striking, but it was his eyes that riveted Brie. It was as if she was looking into Sir's eyes. She let out a gasp of surprise.

"Not what you were expecting?" he asked.

"I didn't expect to see so much of you in him."

"Actually, it would be the other way around," he said, chuckling as he took the photo from her and stared at it intently.

"He must have been very popular with his female fans," Brie complimented, touching the picture reverently. "He was an extremely handsome man."

He agreed, "My father had a legion of concert groupies. Women who went to every event—some who even sent him their panties in the mail. But he only had eyes for my mother. His fans respected him for that."

Sir put the photograph on the bedside table, facedown, and lay back on the pillow. "But my mother managed to tarnish his reputation in the months immediately following his death. Most people who still remember my father believe he was a shameless womanizer. I hate that she did that to him."

Brie put her hand over his and squeezed gently. "Maybe we can change their perception."

Sir discounted her suggestion. "People would rather believe scandalous lies than the truth."

"I don't believe that, Sir. I think people long to know the good around them. They've just been blindsided so many times that they assume the worst."

He snorted. "Well, it's too late to repair it now. Most people don't know who my father was, and those who do couldn't care less." He stared at the ceiling and sighed heavily. "Life goes on."

Brie laid her head on his chest. "Thank you for showing me his picture, Sir. It makes me feel closer to you."

He put his arm around her. "It was time."

She lifted her head. "Sir, would it be all right if we put his picture in the living room? It doesn't seem right to have him hidden in the closet when he was such an exceptional man."

Sir closed his eyes and didn't speak for several moments. "Brie, I still see visions of him dying when I look at this photo."

Brie kissed his chest and murmured, "When you are ready, then…"

# Master Anderson's Influence

Brie woke up alone. That *never* happened with Sir. She scrambled out of bed and threw open the bedroom door. She was immediately assaulted by a savory aroma of onions, bacon, and garlic. Brie hurried to the kitchen, but stopped as soon as she saw him.

Sir was dressed in only his black sweatpants while he stirred a large pot with a wooden spoon. He looked so damn sexy standing there in the kitchen alone. She hesitated to disturb him, and slinked back to hide around the corner so she could still take in the charming sight.

He must have sensed her presence. Without looking in her direction, he instructed, "Come and sit down, téa."

She was naked and hoped she would not dampen her seat while she watched her handsome Master cook. "Good morning, Master."

Still stirring the pot, he explained, "I woke up this morning with the sudden urge to create my father's favorite meal. I know this does not qualify as a breakfast."

Brie smiled, more touched than she could express that he had cooked such a personal dish for her. "I've had plenty of savory meals at Tono's, Sir, and actually have grown to appreciate more hearty meals in the morning."

He glanced back and smiled at her. "As fetching as you look sitting at my table naked, I need you to get a pair of bowls and two soup spoons."

She immediately popped out of her chair and gathered the needed items, along with napkins and glasses. She set the table and then placed the crocuses in the middle for an added touch.

Sir nodded his approval. "The dish is called *ribollita* and includes a host of vegetables, including carrots, cabbage, celery, and kale. But what makes it delicious is the pancetta." When she tilted her head, he handed her a small piece of round, bacon-like meat. "Taste."

She took a small bite. It was more delicate in flavor than bacon because instead of the smoked flavor, it tasted of Italian herbs. "Very nice, Sir."

"It's not just the meat, but the cannellini beans and sourdough bread that elevate it to favorite food status." Sir explained with a smirk, "I even added a small amount of tomato paste for color, but not enough to taint the dish." He went back to stirring the pot. "I thought you might like that."

Brie finished the last bite of pancetta and licked her fingers before answering. "I like it very much, Sir. Thank you."

He took the bowls from the table and ladled the thick stew into them. He brought them back to the table and added a generous sprinkling of parmesan cheese and a drizzle of olive oil, before sliding a bowl over to her with a look of satisfaction.

She took a deep sniff of the steamy mixture and smiled. "It smells heavenly, Sir."

He sat down and lifted his spoon, waiting for her to do the same. Together they spooned up healthy portions, and he cautioned her to blow on hers. She couldn't help smiling as they both took a bite.

The stew had the consistency of oatmeal, the bread having soaked up all the stock. The combination of the savory meat with onion and garlic gave the whole dish an Italian profile, but the soaked bread reminded her of a French dip, a favorite comfort food of hers.

She purred after she had finished her first bite. "Sir, I understand why this was your father's favorite meal. It's the best stew I've ever tasted. I could eat it morning, noon, and night."

"I'm pleased you approve," Sir replied, his eyes sparkling.

The two of them ate the meal in pleasant silence, savoring every morsel. She could almost imagine Alonzo standing beside them, smiling in satisfaction. Brie wondered if Sir could feel it too.

After breakfast was over, he beckoned her into his lap. She gratefully climbed into it and laid her head against his shoulder.

His masculine hands lightly stroked her soft skin. "Brie."

She smiled and looked up at him. "Yes, Sir?"

He gazed into her eyes and said nothing. Then Sir pressed her head against his chest again. "This was good," he finally stated.

Brie felt certain he had wanted to say something more, but she readily agreed with him. "Yes, it was the second best way I can imagine waking up." She glanced at him and blushed when she asked, "Do you think you could teach me how to cook it?"

He chuckled. "You? Hmm…"

She bit his bottom lip playfully.

Sir grabbed her face with both hands and kissed her soundly. "Yes, girl who can't cook. I will teach you." He lifted her off his lap and slapped her ass. "But not now. Clean up the kitchen and then ready yourself to visit Master Anderson."

Brie made quick work of the kitchen. She was thrilled at the prospect of seeing her old trainer again, mainly because she knew that Master Anderson was a good friend of Sir's. It would be beneficial for Sir to discuss his mother with someone who knew him well. However, she also liked the trainer on a personal level. Master Anderson had always been kind and respectful to Brie, even when he had held a bullwhip in his hand.

They arrived at his home before ten that morning. The trainer was out in the front yard, picking weeds. It was the last thing Brie would have imagined a Dom doing. Of course, he did it with his shirt off so that his thick arm muscles were properly displayed. She scanned the houses nearby and noticed several ladies 'watering their lawns'. Evidently, Master Anderson was doing his part to beautify the neighborhood.

The impressive trainer stood up and swept the dirt from his hands with an inviting smile on his face. "Well, if it isn't my old buddy, ex-Headmaster Davis, and his sidekick, Brie."

He grabbed Sir in a manly hug and slapped his back several times. Sir returned the gesture with more resounding thuds.

"Good to see you, Brad."

"Likewise."

Brie blushed when Master Anderson turned to grace her with his intense green stare. "May I?" he asked Sir.

"If you must."

Brie squealed as Master Anderson picked her up and twirled her around in the air several time. He set her back down, grinning. "Young Brie, it's always a pleasure to see you."

Sir shrugged. "It's something he used to do in college, but I thought he had outgrown that juvenile habit."

Master Anderson smiled charmingly, nodding at the neighbors. "It gives all the married women watching something to daydream about. I don't have the liberty to touch them, but that doesn't mean I can't tease them a little."

Sir grunted. "Looking to cause trouble, are you?"

"No, I just enjoy bringing a little spark to their lives. You should see how they gather when I practice my bullwhip out back."

Brie giggled. She could just imagine the stir he caused among the lady-folk.

"You're going to get yourself hogtied and feathered if you aren't careful, Brad."

Master Anderson laughed. "It might surprise you to learn that a few husbands have asked for tips. Seems the woman here have developed a taste for the bite of a whip. Naturally, I steer them towards crops. Safer for everyone that way."

Brie piped up, "Maybe you should teach a class on the bullwhip. I know Tono's session on Kinbaku was very well received."

He smiled down at her. "Maybe I should, young Brie. Point well taken."

"How did you enjoy being an official trainer at the Center this time around?" Sir asked.

Master Anderson directed both of them towards the house. "It was an experience, Thane. The overall atmosphere has shifted under new leadership. There is no question that the rules are being adhered to, but…it lacks something vital since you left."

Sir slapped him on the back. "I think you just miss the ribbing we used to give each other after each session." He chuckled to himself. "I must say, it was agreeable working with you again."

Master Anderson opened the door for them and ushered them in. "So, Thane, what brings you here so soon after your return to the States?"

Sir did not answer him until they had all taken a seat in Master Anderson's study. Upon seeing it, Brie was reminded of her last visit here, the night she'd hosted the trainer's party—a night of many memorable encounters.

She settled down at Sir's feet, resting her head lightly on his thigh.

"I had an altercation with *her*."

He held such disdain in his voice that Master Anderson did not need to question to whom he was referring.

"When?"

"The beast befriended Brie while I was gone. I was met with her unpleasant presence upon our reunion."

"The nerve of the bitch!"

"You would not believe the lengths she went to. It's not only pathetic, but desperate. So desperate, it's given me insight into her motives."

"What could she possibly want? She took everything."

"I have to assume she is alone and destitute," he said coolly.

"But why come to you? I thought the woman was skilled at parting men from their money."

"I'm not certain what brought her to this point, nor do I care." Sir glanced at Brie with a look of regret. "But now Brie has to deal with the consequences of the unwanted reunion."

Master Anderson spoke with the candor of a good friend. "To be blunt, I am glad you have her with you. This is not something you should face alone." He stood up, walked to the expansive bookshelf lined with liquor bottles and poured both of them glasses of Scotch. "Have you spoken to your uncle about it?"

Sir shook his head as he answered, "No, not yet. Besides you and Nosaka, no one knows of her return. I think it's best to keep it that way, but I agree that he should be warned."

Brie had forgotten that Mr. Reynolds was related to Sir's mother. How would he react to the news? She couldn't imagine the kind old man being brother to such a spiteful woman.

"Yes—in fact, the sooner the better, Thane. He should not be surprised by her the way you were. You remember how it ended between them."

"Yes…" Sir said distractedly, as if he was remembering the event. "Unc felt as if he was to blame for what happened. Foolish on his part."

Master Anderson held up his glass. "No more foolish than you."

Sir snarled ominously as he took a drink. "Shut up."

"You know you came today because you needed someone to be honest."

"Don't be so sure."

Master Anderson finished his drink and grabbed Sir's glass without asking, filling it up with more Scotch.

When he handed it back, Sir stated, "You should know I don't care to drink before noon." Then he looked at Brie. "Would you like some, téa?"

His question did two things. It acknowledged that he cared about her well-being, but by calling her by her sub name, he was also informing her that she was there to observe and not participate in the conversation unless commanded.

Brie did not want the liquor to dull her response to him. "No, thank you, Master."

Master Anderson sat back down. "I thought a little Scotch was in order. It's not every day that Ruth Davis comes to call."

Sir shot up off the sofa and roared, "Do *not* use my father's surname with that woman!"

Brie was confused for a moment, until she realized that Sir's mother had even lied about her name. The woman had lied about everything…

Master Anderson got up and placed his hand on Sir's shoulder. "A mistake, my friend."

Sir exhaled angrily, but sat back down.

Master Anderson returned to his chair with a calm air about him. "How are you planning to handle it, Thane?"

"I am siccing my lawyer on her. He'll find out soon enough what's really going on." Sir directed Brie, "Don't let her get anywhere near you. The woman is toxic in every sense of the word." He looked back to Master Anderson. "The beast was able to finagle Brie's business card from her."

"I'm sorry, Master," Brie whispered.

"Téa, I do not fault you, but it illustrates the lengths to which she will go."

Master Anderson assured him, "I will keep an eye out for the beast. But after so many years, I'm not even sure I'll recognize her."

Sir laughed unkindly. "She probably went bankrupt because of her face. The whore looks the same—it's unnatural, like looking at the picture of Dorian Gray. She's made herself into a freak of nature in her frantic attempt to keep the only thing of value she has left—her looks."

"I honestly can't imagine her looking the same after all these years," Master Anderson mused.

"The only thing that gives her away is the gray in her hair. Gives her a cougar look, which must be advantageous to her somehow."

"I can see the value in keeping some of the gray. Imagine jumping into bed with what you thought was a young chick, but unwrapping an old woman."

Both men laughed, but Sir's expression quickly soured. "I've struggled all these years, knowing she was alive but my father was not. The only thing that kept me sane was the assurance I would never see her again."

Master Anderson put his glass down and said solemnly, "Thane, you never dealt with it. No matter what the future holds, I believe you will navigate your way through this and be a better man for it, when all is said and done."

Sir picked Brie up and pulled her close to him. "My sub seems determined to challenge me in this area, whether it's intentional or not."

Master Anderson picked up his glass again and raised it to them. "Then it's the perfect match, is it not?"

Sir kissed the top of Brie's head and then let her go, commanding, "Téa, go to the kitchen and whip up something for lunch. I would like to spend time with Master Anderson alone."

Brie bowed, thinking, *Oh, God. Whipping up 'something' for Master Anderson, the gourmet chef?* "My pleasure, Master."

The men exited through the back door, leaving Brie all alone in Master Anderson's house. She wished she could sneak over to the door to hear what they were discussing. Listening to these two Doms converse was fascinating, because with every exchange she learned a little more about Sir.

She glanced around the impressive kitchen. It was the kind of setup that belonged on a cooking show. Although Sir's also had marble countertops and stainless steel appliances, Master Anderson had a ton of extra cooking tools that would make a chef's heart palpitate. However, they just confused Brie.

She decided to stick to the basics. There was no point in trying to impress either man, for Brie knew she would only end up embarrassing herself. Instead, she concentrated on what Sir liked, and what she could cook semi-decently. Brie checked through Master Anderson's refrigerator to make sure he had the needed items before she began.

Brie cooked the bacon in a pan first. It was one thing she was good at, having been given the task by her mother from an early age. Her mother didn't trust her with much in the kitchen, but bacon was one of Brie's specialties. She prided herself on getting it to that 'just crisp but not overcooked' stage.

Soon Master Anderson's house was filled with the delicious smell of bacon. While she let it rest on a paper towel, she set to work on the cheese. Normally she just used American, but Master Anderson did not have 'fake' cheese in his kitchen. Instead, she went with Gruyère, fontina, and for a personal touch a little Brie de Meaux. It would be a white grilled cheese, but that made it seem more gourmet to her.

The kitchen had the kind of grill you would find in a diner. It looked intimidating to operate, but Brie messed with the temperature until it seemed hot enough. She spread butter on the bread and placed the sandwiches on the heated grill. They sizzled pleasantly upon contact. Brie grabbed a spatula and watched the cheese intently as it slowly began to melt.

In her best cooking show voice, she announced, "You will find that the combination of cheeses will meld together to create the ooziest, most gooey grilled cheese you have ever eaten. Adding the bacon gives it a more savory flair, for those men of yours who need a little meat on their plates."

She lifted a corner of one sandwich and smiled. "You want to wait until you get a golden brown color. Too soon, and your grilled cheese will be unpleasantly mushy." She looked at the pretend camera. "Totally *not* delish!" She flipped the sandwich over. "If you wait too long, then you get the dreaded barbecued grilled cheese, and we ain't talking Memphis-style, people."

Brie set out three plates and grabbed a sprig of fresh parsley. Then she lovingly placed the sandwiches on the plates and stood back with a proud smile. "And that, my friends, is how you cook a killer grilled cheese!" She bowed gracefully, then turned to the pretend camera and ran her fingers across her throat. "Cut!"

She hurried to open the back door to let Sir know that lunch was ready, but stopped short when she saw the two men. Master Anderson was instructing Sir how to handle the bullwhip. Her knees almost gave out as she watched Sir swing the whip back and forth before hitting the bottom of the post with a loud snap.

Master Anderson shook his head and repositioned Sir's arm. This time, Sir stared at the post with intense concentration before swinging again. He lashed the post directly in the middle. It was as if Brie could feel the sting of it on her back, and she almost dropped from the impact.

Both men looked in her direction. Brie realized she must have made a noise and blushed. To cover it, she announced with a respectful bow, "Lunch is ready, Master." She hoped it wasn't obvious how much she was trembling.

"We'll join you in a minute, téa."

Brie bowed again and shut the door. She made her way back to the kitchen to finish setting the table, but her mind was not on her task. *Sir is practicing the bullwhip.*

He knew her feelings about the bullwhip. He had asked her the night she'd scened with Master Anderson at The Haven. It frightened her, the thought of being whipped again…

Maybe it was simply a way to relieve his stress. Men often bonded over physical activity. Typically it was over a game of basketball, but considering their kinky inclinations, chatting over a bullwhip seemed perfectly natural, right?

The men walked in, both sweaty from their workout. Brie looked at Sir through hooded eyes as he sat down. He winked at her before looking down at his plate. "I see you went with an American classic, téa."

Master Anderson pulled the bread apart to examine it more closely. "But with a uniquely Brie twist to it," he added with a smirk. He reassembled the sandwich and took a bite, announcing afterwards, "You went with a blend of three creamy cheeses. Good choice. The outside is nice and toasted, the cheese properly melted, but I can't say I care for the selection of meat. I think a slice of tomato would suffice."

Sir took his own bite. His face showed little expression as he chewed. After he had finished, he glanced at Master Anderson as he informed Brie, "Naturally, I disagree with the addition of tomato. I believe by replacing the bacon with pancetta you would have a fine sandwich, téa."

Brie wanted to burst with pride. Her first culinary success with Sir! He had eaten what she'd served him ever since she'd become his submissive, but this was her first real triumph. She wanted to squeal with happiness and struggled to keep quiet. It was only a grilled cheese sandwich, after all.

It seemed that Sir was more relaxed after his practice session with Master Anderson. He was more like himself during the meal, but insisted on leaving shortly after.

"I thank you for your time, Brad. As always, talking with you gives me a healthy perspective."

"Think nothing of it."

"Now you can go back to teasing the neighborhood."

Master Anderson grinned. "Think of the thrill you would cause if both of you joined me in weeding the front garden. Two bare-chested men and a little sex kitten in a miniskirt. I'm sure we could get the entire neighborhood out for the show."

Sir shook his head. "You need to get a permanent sub."

"Gardening has a calming effect, Thane. Maybe you should look into it."

Sir scoffed and walked out through the front door. "Come, téa."

Master Anderson said to Sir as he left, "Don't forget what I said about Wallace."

Sir stopped and turned to address him. "I'll set up a meeting tomorrow. It will be a relief to Marquis, who has been pushing for it since Brie's encounter with him at the Training Center. Personally, after yesterday's trouble I need to tie up those loose ends. The beast alone is enough for me to deal with."

"Good luck. Give me a call afterwards. In fact, why don't you drop by, and you can practice some more?"

Brie's eyes widened when Sir agreed. He was serious about learning the bullwhip! That could only mean one thing—he meant to use it on her. A cold chill ran through Brie, but an enticing shudder accompanied it. The knowledge that she was *his* and that this was an area he was going to push her in was…exhilarating.

# The Wolf Howls

---

The meeting with Todd Wallace took place at The Haven. Faelan had refused to have it at the Training Center, stating that it should be on neutral ground.

Sir had been puzzled by his assertion that it was not neutral ground, but Brie understood. Both she and Faelan had been students at the Center. No matter how much experience they accumulated, they would always be pupils of the school.

The owner of the club had set aside a quiet room in the back for the meeting, away from the playful chaos. When they arrived, Sir turned to Brie. "At all times, be open and honest with him. If he sees the slightest hesitation, he will read it as you hiding your affections for him. Although Wallace is unusually talented, he remains emotionally stunted."

'The death of the young man in the car crash…" Brie said softly.

"Yes, it is the reason for his immaturity, but not an excuse to behave dishonorably."

"I will remember that, Sir."

"Look him in the eye."

"Yes, Sir."

Tension filled the air, but it immediately dissipated the moment Sir touched her, just before he guided her into the room. "You are an exceptional person, Brie. Beyond being a submissive, beyond your film talent, you are a kind soul," he said, brushing her cheek with his hand. "A true rarity."

Brie pressed her cheek against his hand, closing her eyes in contentment. "You make me a better woman." She opened her eyes and gazed into his. "I love you, Thane."

He returned her smile. "I love you." Sir kissed her then, their connection born of love and admiration.

When Brie entered the room, she knew with certainty that not only could she do this, but she could do it with the purity of love Tono had shown her. She noticed that there was only a single table with four chairs in the room. Faelan was seated directly in front of her, with Marquis Gray sitting on the right.

Faelan stared at her from across the room. Despite the situation and the people involved, she was irresistibly drawn to those deep blue eyes.

"Welcome," Marquis Gray said, directing Brie to the chair across from Faelan, and Sir to the one directly opposite him.

They all sat down in uncomfortable silence. But Brie followed Sir's orders and looked Faelan directly in the eye, despite her natural inclination to stare at her lap.

"Well, isn't this quaint? It's like I'm in jail. Here we have my lawyer, sitting next to me," Faelan said, pointing to Marquis Gray, "and there, you have the warden."

Brie smiled to herself at the comparison.

Marquis spoke up. "He has a few things to go over with you, Miss Bennett. Both Sir Davis and I will remain silent unless we can add clarification to the discussion."

Faelan looked down at a piece of paper in front of him and snarled. "No!" He swept the paper aside. "I am not going down a list." He stared at Brie. "You and I are going to have a genuine conversation, with no pretenses."

Brie noticed that Marquis discreetly slid the paper back over to him.

"That's acceptable to me, Mr. Wallace," she replied.

"To begin with, you will *not* call me Mr. Wallace. That just sounds wrong."

Brie looked in Sir's direction for guidance. He did not speak, but nodded slightly.

"Okay… Todd."

Faelan sat back in his chair and snorted. "That's only a slight improvement."

She wasn't willing to argue the point, so she forged ahead. "The reason we are here is to—"

"No, that's not how this is going to play out," he stated firmly as he took over. "As you know, I have lived in darkness most of my adult life. The guilt of killing someone has eaten at me like a cancer."

Brie replied compassionately, "But it was just an acciden—"

He held up his hand. "There's no point in continuing that line of thought, Brie. I've talked to a counselor and I'm not about to rehash it with you."

She looked down at her lap but immediately looked back up, realizing she was subconsciously falling into the submissive role with him.

"That day… The day you fell into my arms I finally saw a spark of hope. You were a light in the suffocating darkness consuming me." Faelan grinned at her. "I can't explain why, but there was an instant connection made I've never felt before." He leaned forward and asked her, "What did you feel that day?"

Brie took a deep breath before she began. Sir had instructed her to be honest, so she kept that her primary goal. "I was grateful that you saved me from a bad fall and I thought you had nice eyes. Honestly, I felt nothing more than that."

Faelan sat back and nodded. "When I saw you tied up later, while I was jogging on the beach, I almost lost it. I thought you were being kidnapped and raped."

Brie blushed. "That was an awkward moment for both of us." She looked upon Faelan with empathy. "But I appreciate that you were trying to help."

"I will never forget the sight of you, Brie. Knowing that you were naked under that robe when you came to the door. Seeing you caress the collar around your neck… The possessive way the Russian lorded over you." Faelan paused. "That was the beginning of a new life for me."

Brie interjected, "I didn't feel that way, Todd. In fact, I didn't realize who you were until the cops were about to leave."

"You felt no connection, not even then?"

She shook her head. "Not even when you formally introduced yourself the next day. All I could think was that you were the last thing I needed."

He looked at her intently. "You needed a Dom, that's why I fell under the radar. As soon as I realized what you were, I understood what you required. Since that day, I have endeavored to become the man you needed."

Brie felt a twinge of guilt. "I never asked you to."

"You say that, but I know the first time we scened together you felt the connection, Brie. Don't deny it. Don't you dare deny it in front of these two men."

She gazed into his blue eyes, not shying away from her answer. "Yes, I admit it. You surprised me that day. I was impressed by you, despite my reservations."

"That's because I understand who you are, Brie. Yet, it's more than that. You and I are cut from the same cloth. We're both young and adventurous. We both hide an animal that no one else sees."

This time Brie looked away. It was true; there was a side of herself that only Faelan seemed to bring out. It was a side that was wild and dangerous.

He continued, "After our scene, with every interaction you were playful and inviting. Especially when I had to punish you and your two girlfriends."

It was embarrassing to have him bring that up in front of Sir. Brie shifted in her seat, remembering quite well the night he'd commanded she use her vibrator for a half hour without orgasming. It had been a long and frustrating night, which had only served to make her desire the young wolf more. "It was an unfair punishment," she responded.

His eyes sparkled mischievously. "I thought of you that night, Brie. Thought of your glistening, wet pussy struggling not to come because *I* commanded it."

Brie shivered under the power of his domineering confidence and broke their gaze again.

"Such descriptions are not necessary," Marquis Gray warned quietly.

"Brie," Sir said.

She forced herself to look into her Master's eyes, embarrassed by the feelings Faelan evoked in her—feelings she knew were obvious to both Sir and Marquis Gray.

"Remember what we talked about," he reminded her.

Brie bowed her head in response and turned back to face Faelan. "It was an order I completed because I was in training and it was my duty, Todd."

He smiled at her knowingly. "It drew you closer to me so that you were ready when I won you at the auction. There, you gave yourself over with no reservations. Do you remember that night? You opened up and released the animal that lay buried deep inside. That's when you finally understood, as I did, that we were meant for each other."

Brie's heart constricted. She knew her next words would wound him. "As much as I enjoyed our time together, I never loved you."

Faelan dismissed the unwanted truth. "You've said that before, but I still maintain you can't know that for certain. You and I were never given the chance to explore our feelings for each other because of the Headmaster." He gave a slight nod towards Sir without looking at him.

Brie smiled sadly. "I suppose you're right. You never had a chance because I love Sir. I have loved him from the very beginning."

Faelan growled. "Which is completely against school policy, I should point out. I'm sick and tired of being lectured by the trainers of this school about protocol when the very man who ran the Training Center desecrated it." He leaned forward and said in a low voice, "I know for a fact you chose him at the collaring ceremony because he manipulated you."

She closed her eyes, dreading sharing the hurtful truth with him. A truth even Sir did not know.

With renewed determination, she opened her eyes to face Faelan. "At the collaring ceremony, I planned to ask Tono to be my Master. If his father hadn't scorned the match, I would have become his submissive that night, not yours."

Faelan shook his head in disbelief.

Brie didn't even dare to glance at Sir when she continued, "It's true, Todd. Although I have lusted after you, I realized at the ceremony I could never partner with a man I did not love."

The room went deadly silent. "I don't believe you," he finally stated.

"I was always upfront with you about how I felt."

It was as if Faelan hadn't heard her. "How could you love that one-trick pony? It was painfully obvious to everyone but you that you wouldn't have been happy with Nosaka."

Brie's hackles went up. How dare he ridicule Tono by calling him that? She took a deep breath, refusing to start an argument with Faelan. "You have no idea what you're talking about. At the collaring ceremony, I realized it could not work between us with his father being against the match. Which was a good thing, because it pushed me to do what my heart truly wanted." She glanced at Sir and smiled. "Sir is the only man whose collar I ever want to wear."

Faelan snarled and then turned on Sir. "Why the hell did you train me if you were planning to steal her away?"

Sir met his anger with an equal level of calm. "When you approached me about training as a Dom, I recognized your potential. Despite my better judgment, I took you under my wing because I understood your pain and knew this was a healthy direction for you to pursue. Unfortunately, I did not appreciate how immature you were, and am glad to hear you are getting professional help now."

"Is that supposed to be meant as an insult?" Faelan demanded.

"No. It's a simple fact that you cannot guide a submissive well if you are unable to control your own emotions."

Faelan threw back his head and laughed. "Oh, like you? What right do you have to tell me what to do? Answer me that, 'Headmaster'!" Faelan looked earnestly at Brie, reaching out for her across the table. "Did you catch what he just said? Your 'Master' admitted that he can't guide you properly. At least I'm doing something about it. It's not too late, Brie. Get out while you still can, in front of both of these men, so there's no question it came from you."

Brie took his outstretched hand and squeezed it. "Todd, I am content with my choice of Dom. I love Sir. Loving him makes me happy—far happier than I've ever been."

Faelan snarled. "It's not right! He's too old for you, *and* too arrogant."

She answered quietly, "'Arrogant' is a word I would use to describe you."

"Confidence, Brie. Not arrogance. I am confident we are good together and confident that we were meant for each other."

Brie smiled sadly. "You claim to love me. If that's true, then you should *want* me to be happy. I am happy, truly happy with Sir."

She saw him swallow hard, even though his confident expression never changed. "You've been brainwashed."

That flippant statement pissed Brie off. "Don't belittle my feelings like that. I love Thane Davis. You have to accept that."

"Brie, 'Headmaster' can have any girl he wants, but I *need* you."

She felt his desperation, but refused to give in to it. "As much as I care about you, Todd, I would never wear your collar."

His eyes narrowed. "So you will turn away my love without any thought or consideration."

"I know my own heart," Brie answered.

"And you're condemning me to a life without love?"

"No." An image of Mary instantly came to mind. "I know of at least one person who cares about you, but you are oblivious to it."

His blue eyes flashed with vehement anger. "There is something you should know about me, Brie. I run either hot or cold. I am a passionate man and cannot be lukewarm like Nosaka. I will *not* be your 'friend' after this. If you tell me it's over, I will not acknowledge you when our paths cross again. For me, you will cease to exist."

His declaration hurt. The idea that Faelan would cut her out of his life completely had never occurred to Brie. "Does it have to end that way?" she asked, shocked.

"If I'm to keep my sanity, yes."

Brie looked at Marquis Gray, hoping he would impart some wisdom to Faelan, but he remained silent. She closed her eyes then, trying to keep back the tears that threatened to fall.

Faelan pleaded with her one last time. "Brie, I know you have feelings for me. Don't let this be the end of us. Don't."

There was no question what her answer must be. She opened her eyes and gazed into those beautiful ocean blues of his. "If that's how you want it to be, then I guess this is goodbye."

He stared at her as if he hadn't heard.

Marquis Gray spoke up. "Before we conclude this meeting, there are several things we need to go over."

Faelan's voice was hollow when he answered Marquis. "It is unnecessary. Everything listed there has just been taken care of."

He stood up slowly, as if in a daze, and left the room without another word. The sound of the door closing made Brie's heart sink. Her bottom lip trembled, even though she willed herself to remain composed.

"I don't think the meeting could have gone any better," Marquis stated.

Brie nodded, even though she hated how it had ended. The pain in Faelan's eyes would haunt her forever.

"So what was on that list?" Sir asked Marquis Gray.

"We were going to set boundaries, but he's right. It is unnecessary now."

"Come here, Brie," Sir said with compassion. She melted into his embrace, needing his love to combat the ache in her heart. "You did what was required to set the boy free."

She nodded against his chest without looking up.

"Go ahead and cry, téa," he added softly.

The tears began to fall as she let out a deep sob. Sir held her tightly as she released the pain and guilt. When Brie was finally quiet again, she lifted her head and noticed that Marquis Gray had gone.

She felt bad and automatically apologized. "I'm sorry, Sir."

He smiled as he dried her tears. "For what? I know you are an emotional creature. It is something I value and choose to nurture."

As they prepared to leave the room, Brie stopped him and asked, "Sir, do you need me to clarify anything I said during the meeting?"

"Nothing you shared came as a surprise to me. Have you forgotten that you wear your heart on your sleeve, téa? It is something I find reassuring." He swept her hair back and kissed her tearstained cheek.

She laid her head against his broad chest and sighed. "That was hard, Sir. Harder than I imagined."

"Wallace's response was unusual, but in the end it may be the healthiest way for him to deal with it. I cannot fault him."

Brie nestled into Sir's embrace, feeling heartbroken for Faelan, but hoping that he was finally and truly free.

# Release

Things became more settled after the meeting. Brie had met Faelan once already in public and, true to his word, he had not looked at or spoken to her. Although it was disconcerting for Brie, the new arrangement had freed Sir as well. Their relationship no longer carried the weight of Wallace's obsession, and he became more lighthearted as a consequence.

Brie knew something was afoot when she walked into the apartment and found a note beside a package. She picked it up and read:

*Buy the items on the list and make a rainbow roll for your Master.*
*Leave it on the kitchen counter.*
*Retire to the bedroom.*

She smiled as she opened the package. Inside was a sushi-making kit with a cookbook. During her stay with Tono, he had instructed her in the basic skills of making sushi rolls, but she had no idea what a rainbow roll consisted of. Flipping through the colorful illustrations, she quickly found it and grinned. It looked like beautiful art. Thin slices of uncooked tuna, salmon and avocado were laid over a California roll. She quickly wrote down the ingredients and headed to the store.

Brie loved it when Sir gave her tasks like this—simple assignments that were completely vanilla in nature, but the outcome would be anything but. She shopped with a secretive smile on her lips, her sexy mission giving a sense of intrigue to the whole shopping experience.

When she returned home, she was surprised to find that the apartment was still silent. Brie speculated that Sir might be off with Master Anderson again. It inspired a vision of Sir cracking the bullwhip against the pole. Goosebumps covered her skin as she began working on the sushi roll.

She was determined to impress Sir with what she had learned under Tono's tutelage. Although her roll ended up being somewhat lopsided, the slices of raw fish and avocado covered up that fact. She stepped back to admire her handiwork.

Brie added a note of her own next to the plate: *I love you, Master.*

She skipped down the hallway to their bedroom, wondering what he had planned next for her.

The bed itself had been prepared for her with a new bedcover, golden handcuffs at the headboard and leg restraints at the bottom. On the pillow, she saw another note.

She felt butterflies in her stomach as she reached over to pick it up. In his precise handwriting, she read:

*Take the hood on the nightstand and put it next to the pillow.*

Brie glanced at the nightstand and saw an unusual hood of silk. It was black with golden thread woven in a striking floral pattern. As beautiful as it was, a shiver ran down her spine as she put it beside the pillow and handcuffs.

*Undress, leaving only your panties on.*

Brie quickly stripped down, folding her clothes and laying them on the nightstand before climbing onto the bed to read her next order.

*Lie on your back and restrain your legs so they are open wide for me.*

Brie's heart beat fast as she bound her own legs for Master. It felt deliciously wicked. She lay back on the bed to read the final instruction.

*Secure the hood around your head and cuff yourself to the bed.*
*Wait.*

Brie was not a fan of hoods, but she dutifully put the silken material over her head and secured it loosely around her neck. Then she lifted her hands to the cuffs and tightened one around her left wrist. It was a bit of a struggle to secure the second, but she felt a sense of satisfaction when she heard the metal clink as it locked into place.

Now she was bound and ready for Master.

She lay there in a state of sexual arousal, waiting for him to claim her. The thin material of the hood allowed Brie to hear clearly. She caught the faint sound of movement in the kitchen and felt a thrill of excitement, knowing Sir had been in the apartment the whole time, silently observing her actions without her knowledge.

Brie waited with bated breath, the anticipation of his taking driving her wild with desire. When he finally entered the bedroom, she could *feel* his presence. Sir stood there for several moments in silence. She imagined him at the door, admiring her body, enjoying the scene he had created.

She found it alluring that he had chosen a different cologne to wear for the evening. A simple alteration of scent gave a whole new feel to their encounter.

She felt the bed shift when he sat down next to her. Brie gasped when he placed a piece of the cold sushi roll on her stomach. With thoughtful precision, he decorated her body with the meal she had prepared for him.

He stood back up, and a few seconds later she heard the click of a camera. Brie smiled under the hood, grateful she would be able to see his artwork later.

Sir returned to her and blew on her stomach before retrieving a piece of sushi with his mouth. Her heart fluttered at the contact.

How she loved being Sir's vessel…

Brie heard his low grunt of pleasure and wanted to burst with pride. Another culinary success! Sir ate the piece he had placed on her nipple. The slow, sensuous way that he picked it up with his lips could make a girl come.

After he had swallowed the bite, his lips came back down and he sucked on her sensitive nipple. Brie wanted to press herself against his mouth, but stayed completely still so as to not disturb his feast. Sir continued his leisurely tasting, teasing her mercilessly as he went.

To Brie's mortification, partway through his meal her stomach gave a long, thunderous growl. Sir chuckled.

Her cheeks burned with embarrassment under the silk. *Why now?*

Sir undid the tie of the hood and uncovered her mouth. He kissed her on the lips before placing a piece of sushi into her mouth. Brie chewed it gratefully, hoping it would quiet her stomach's noisy protests.

She started to say, "Thank y—" but Sir put his finger to her lips, signifying that speaking was not allowed.

He kissed her again and gave her two more pieces before tying the hood back in place and finishing his meal. Her entire body was tingling by the time he was done.

Sir left the bed and she soon heard soft violin music fill the air. Brie wondered if it was a recording of his father's playing. The music was hauntingly beautiful and infused with raw emotion.

He returned to her side, running his hands over her body and leaving trails of fire wherever his fingers touched. They finally rested on her panties. He felt her mound beneath the wet lace and groaned.

Brie's pussy answered by pulsing against his hand. Sir gave a low growl as he literally ripped the panties from her body. Now she was completely exposed to her Master—tied, hooded, and cuffed for his pleasure.

Instead of moving between her legs and taking her like she'd expected, Sir lay beside Brie and played with her pussy. He began by teasing her clit first, getting her wet and desperate. Then he pushed two fingers inside and began caressing her G-spot.

Brie threw back her head and moaned as he made her loins contract in pleasure from the direct stimulation. He had played with her that way many times before, and her body responded by slowly building up to an intense orgasm.

That was when Sir changed tactics.

He repositioned himself and slipped his fingers back inside her velvety depths, this time pumping his hand at a vigorous rate. Brie was taken by surprise by the ferocity of it.

She moaned and began squirming as the slow buildup suddenly became an inferno of intensity. So intense, in fact, that she began to subconsciously fight against it.

Sir did not let up. His fingers rubbed against her G-spot at that alarming speed. Brie fought against her bonds harder, trying to get away. But without a means of escape, there was only one viable choice for her.

She commanded herself to let go. Brie consciously stilled her body and mind to accept his passionate invasion.

As soon as she did, a chill went through her as her pussy contracted in violent pleasure, and a literal gush of wetness burst from her. Brie cried out in surprise at her watery release.

Sir's fingers left her and she heard him suck them as he tasted her wet climax. "Good girl. Let's try that again."

Brie was a slippery mess when he inserted his fingers back inside her still-quivering pussy and began pumping again. She arched her back to better allow the aggressive stimulation.

For a second time, she felt the intense buildup. "Oh, Master!" she screamed as a second powerful orgasm claimed her. Liquid flowed from her, splashing droplets everywhere.

"What is that?" she whispered from beneath the hood.

"It's your female ejaculation, my dear," he answered, kissing her through the silk. "And I must say, it tastes as sweet as rain."

He moved down to her pussy and started to eat her.

Brie was unsure if she could take further stimulation. "Please, Master. No."

"No is not an option, babygirl."

Sir swirled his tongue over her clit and growled when she tried to struggle. Brie instantly became still.

He licked her clit in a long, hard, rhythmic manner. Brie could imagine Sir's cock thrusting into her as it brushed against her clit, instead of his tongue. It didn't take long before her pussy began twitching with a need for sexual release.

This kind of climax was familiar and comforting to her. She began mewing as his expert tongue brought her to the edge. She willingly gave in to the waves of pleasure, easily coming for her Master.

After the last wave had dissipated, he climbed on top of her and thrust his cock into her wet, overly sensitive pussy. The head of his shaft rubbed against her extremely swollen G-spot with concentrated abandon. This time she did not resist the stimulation, wanting to come around his cock.

Brie let out a loud, passionate scream when she washed his rigid shaft in yet another watery orgasm. Sir answered her by coming deep inside her pussy, the mixing of their essences complete.

"Sir… Sir…" Brie whimpered afterwards, overwhelmed by the experience and finding the darkness of the hood unsettling.

He immediately removed it and smiled down at her. "I'm right here, Brie."

She looked into his eyes in wonder. "I've never experienced anything like that."

"I was curious how you would respond to it. It requires a loss of control on a level that many women, even devoted subs, find difficult." He lifted himself off her and slid his hand down between her legs. "I love how slippery sweet you are. I have acquired a taste for you and will be demanding a sample whenever the urge strikes, téa."

Brie trembled at the thought.

Sir was releasing her from the restraints when the violin in the background began to play an achingly poignant melody. He stripped off the bedcover before lying down beside her and closing his eyes.

With pride in his voice, Sir confided, "My father used to play this song for me. He laid out all his emotions whenever he played, holding nothing back…"

It was so beautiful that a tear fell down Brie's cheek as she listened. "I can feel it, Sir. It's as if he is speaking to me through his violin."

Sir opened his eyes and gazed at her, finally nodding in response when tears welled up in his eyes.

Brie cuddled up next to him and they lay there, listening to his father speak through the song. The life and vitality Brie found in the touching piece belied the fact that his father was no longer living.

The ache in her heart grew when the song became lighthearted in nature. She could just imagine his father playing with Sir as a little boy. The love and passion in the music hinted at the beautiful relationship they must have had. Brie wasn't sure how Sir was able to listen to it without falling apart.

Once it returned to the hauntingly sad melody, she felt Sir's chest rise and fall in jerky movements and knew he was silently crying. She cried along with him, choking back the sobs as she soaked his shirt with her tears.

Brie instinctively knew there was healing to be gained from his painful release…

# Wicked Game

Brie spent every waking hour working on her film the week before she was to present her documentary to Mr. Holloway. This was her last chance with the producer—either he would be satisfied with her changes, or he would withdraw his interest and she would have to start from square one, trying to find someone to take on her project.

There was no way Brie was going to let that happen.

Sir supported Brie in her work, demanding little from her as she poured her soul into the documentary. Not only did he take care of all the meals, but he handled her laundry. It made Brie extremely uncomfortable to see him take over tasks that were hers alone, but when she attempted to help, he reprimanded her harshly.

"Brie, you are disobeying a direct order. I do not want to see you do anything else until that documentary is complete. Do you understand me?"

Brie answered with a miserable, "Yes," frustrated that she was not only failing to care for her Master, but she had managed to disobey him in the process.

While she worked tirelessly on her project, Sir concentrated on coordinating his business in Russia while still meeting the needs of his American clientele. It kept him busy, but he still made time to visit Master Anderson on a daily basis.

It gave Brie nervous butterflies every time he left. The daily visits meant that Sir was taking his lessons seriously, and soon she would be feeling the sting of his newfound expertise.

Just before he was about to leave for another lesson, the doorbell rang. No one ever visited Sir without prior arrangement. Brie ran to the bedroom to throw something on as Sir went to answer the door.

She was worried it was bad news, but breathed a sigh of relief when she saw that it was Mr. Reynolds, Sir's uncle.

"Good to see you, Unc," Sir said, giving him a more heartfelt hug than normal before inviting him in. Mr. Reynolds smiled when he saw Brie, but his reserved manner let her know something was up. She immediately joined Sir on the couch.

"To what do I owe this unexpected surprise?" Sir asked pensively, picking up on Mr. Reynolds' unusual demeanor.

"I have been visited by…" He paused, as if unwilling to even say her name out loud in front of Sir.

"The beast?" Sir answered for him.

Mr. Reynolds let out a long, anguished sigh and simply nodded.

"What did she want?"

Mr. Reynolds sounded as if he was in pain when he replied, "I'm sorry, Thane."

Sir's voice became tense. "Sorry for what?"

"She's determined to see you."

Sir snarled. "You know I don't care what she wants. I refuse to speak to a woman who is dead to me."

Mr. Reynolds looked at him with an expression Brie could not read. "I would do anything to protect you, but she's crazy."

"Did she threaten you?" Sir asked with an eerie calmness, as if it had happened before.

"I'm not worried about us. Thane, I came to warn you. Ruth is determined to see you, no matter the cost."

"Did she say what she wants?"

"No. I tried to get it out of her to spare you, but she was closed-mouthed about it. Claimed it's a matter of life and death."

Sir growled angrily. "There is nothing she can say that I want to hear." He stood up and started pacing in front of the window that overlooked the city. "I want her out of my life, once and for all!"

Mr. Reynolds closed his eyes and groaned. "I know, Thane… I'm sorry for this. For all of it."

Sir snapped, "It is not your fault!" He recovered his inner calm before continuing, "This has no reflection on you. What is imperative is that we eliminate the problem before she can cause any further damage."

"How can I help?"

"All I ask is that you do not engage her again. Call the cops if you have to, but do not give her an audience. As long as we present a united front, all her conniving will be for naught."

Mr. Reynolds looked ill when he told Sir, "The reason I came straight over is that she threatened to head to the school next."

"The security staff has been apprised of the situation. They will be on the lookout for her. Do not concern yourself."

Mr. Reynolds said with confidence, "Thane, she will not go quietly."

"Fuck!" Sir began pacing again. Brie could feel the tension in the room rising to dangerous levels. "She will not ruin my life again. I will *not* allow it!"

"Sir, what are we going to do?" Brie asked, suddenly afraid for him.

"What am I going to do? I'll wait until I hear from the Center. It's possible she's bluffing and I refuse to react to idle threats."

No sooner had he spoken than his cell phone rang. Sir looked at the caller ID and frowned. "What is it?" he demanded when he answered the call. "Good God, Rachael. Call the police. I'll be there as soon as possible. Hopefully, she'll leave of her own accord."

Sir snapped the phone closed and asked his uncle, "Will you come with me?"

"Of course. No need to ask."

Sir turned to Brie. "You'll stay here. I do not want you getting involved with her again."

She insisted, "But Sir, my place is by your side."

"No, Brie. Work on your documentary while I am gone." Before she could protest, he added, "Obey me."

Brie held in her objection and watched both men leave the apartment in a rush. What could his mother have done to cause Sir to go against his better judgment?

She sat down with her computer and tried to edit her work, but she couldn't concentrate. She kept contemplating what was happening at the

Center. What kind of mother would threaten her son? What was the woman capable of?

Although Brie appreciated Sir's protective nature, she wanted to be with him—*needed* to be with him.

She began pacing the apartment, contemplating driving down to the Center without his permission, until she heard a polite knock on the door.

Brie walked up to it hesitantly. She took a look through the peephole and saw a courier holding a manila envelope.

Brie asked him through the door, "Could you just leave it on the doorstep?"

"No, ma'am—I need a signature from the person it's addressed to. A Brianna Bennett."

She immediately thought of Mr. Holloway. "Could you slide it under the door?"

"That's highly unusual, ma'am."

"But could you do it anyway?"

The man grumbled as he bent down and forced the envelope under the gap at the bottom of the door. "The pen won't fit," he complained.

"Not a problem; I have a pen. Just a sec."

Brie picked up the manila envelope and looked it over. It was big enough for legal documents and was addressed to her, although she noticed it did not have a return address on it. She went to the desk, signed her name on the slip for the courier and stuffed it back under the door.

He huffed as he bent down to pick it up. Brie peeked through the hole to watch him leave. Despite the man's obvious irritation, he tipped his hat before he left. "Thank you, ma'am."

Brie was pleased with the cautious way she had handled the exchange and eagerly tore open the manila envelope. Inside was another envelope, but it was addressed to Thane Davis. His name looked as if it had been written by a woman.

A feeling of nausea came over Brie and she had to sit down. The letter must have come from his mother…

Whatever was written in that letter might reveal the reason she was back. Brie was desperate to find out what it said, wanting to understand what kind of threat this woman posed to Sir.

Brie stared at the envelope for a long time, part of her wanting to destroy it and part of her wanting to secretly read it. There was no part of her that wanted to present the note unopened to Sir, but that was exactly what she decided to do.

When Sir returned home an hour later, he came alone. Although he looked cross, he was no longer irate.

Sir seemed relieved when he saw her sitting on the couch. "Whatever game she was playing, she ran off before I got there. Guess the threat of involving the police was enough."

Brie looked up at him, unable to hide her guilt.

"What is it, Brie?"

"A letter came while you were gone."

He looked at her apprehensively. "A letter?"

"I knew better than to open the door, Sir, but I let the courier slip it under. It was addressed to me. I thought it was from Mr. Holloway."

"But…"

"But when I opened it, there was a letter inside addressed to you." She glanced at the envelope on the table.

Sir looked at it in disgust and went to the kitchen. He came back and said, striking a match, "Whatever this is, it's gone now."

Just before the flame touched the paper, Brie blurted, "But Sir, maybe this will tell you her motive. You said yourself that you can't prepare to fight her until you know what it is."

Sir stopped and stared at the envelope, letting the match burn until it singed his fingers. He blew the match out and then set the letter back on the table.

He sat down next to Brie. "The fact it's here tells me two things. One, she knows where I live and two, she knows that you live here with me."

"I shouldn't have signed for the letter, Sir. I'm sorry." Brie bowed her head, feeling as if she had betrayed his trust.

"It doesn't matter. The only thing she learned from this little stunt is that you are an extremely trusting individual." Sir sighed, glancing at the letter again. "Either this will tell me the real reason she wants contact and it will infuriate me, or this is a clever lie she's concocted, which will infuriate me even more." Sir rubbed his chin, trying to decide if he wanted to open Pandora's box.

Finally, he picked it up and ripped the envelope open. He unfolded the letter and glanced at it before throwing it down. "Bullshit!"

Sir stormed out of the room. Brie hesitantly picked up the note to read it, and was shocked to see there were only five words.

*I am dying of cancer.*

Brie couldn't believe it. She ran to the bedroom to comfort Sir, but he was still in an uncontrollable rage. When she entered the room, he shouted at her, "That bitch does not have cancer any more than I do!" His laughter was low and angry. "Oh, but isn't she clever?"

"But what if it is true, Sir?"

He replied coldly, "I wouldn't care. She should know that. This is her clever way of garnering other people's sympathies. Look at the poor beast, dying of cancer while her son stands back and does nothing to help. Well, that's exactly what I plan to do. She can rot in hell. In fact, I would prefer it."

Brie was taken aback by his wrath.

Sir looked at her and snarled. "This is how she does it. She pits us against each other. She expects me to begin resenting you for giving me the letter, and you to be horrified that I would react to such news with indifference."

Brie crossed the room and stood beside him, stating her support in words as well as with her proximity. "There is nothing she can do to tear me away from you, Sir. I understand your righteous anger towards her and I believe you when you say that she's lying. I stand behind you and support you, Sir."

"No, Brie." He pulled her into his embrace. "You stand *beside* me."

She wrapped her arms around him. "Nothing can separate a condor from its mate, Sir."

He lifted her chin and smiled for the first time that night. "Brie, that is the only truth I need. You are a wise little sub."

She cocked her head. "*Wise*, Sir? Aren't I far too young to be described as wise?"

His spontaneous laughter was music to her ears. It delighted her heart to hear it.

# Believe

Brie couldn't stop the buzzing in her ears. After weeks of shooting and retooling her documentary, her time had finally come. She bit her lip and closed her eyes, trying to rein her nerves in.

"Brie, what's wrong?" Sir asked.

He'd insisted on being with her as she waited to be called in, although he would not be present during the meeting itself. Sir felt it was important this was her success, and hers alone.

"Sir, I've never felt like this before. I think I'm going to faint, I'm so nervous."

He put his hand on her knee and gazed into her eyes, imparting his confidence. "You will not let your fears get the best of you."

She nodded, needing to hear his reassuring words.

"You have reworked the film to his specifications while remaining true to your vision. The work is better for it. However, if Mr. Holloway chooses to turn it down it will be his loss, for you *will* find someone to produce it."

Brie took a deep breath and smiled. "Yes, you're right, Sir. Someone will pick up my film if Mr. Holloway does not. This film is a winner—I can feel it in my bones."

"Hold onto that truth and do not let your nerves control you. Be self-assured without being arrogant and you will do well."

That extra shot of confidence was all she needed. "Thank you, S—"

The receptionist interrupted their conversation. "Mr. Holloway will see you now."

Sir stood up with Brie and gave her a quick kiss before letting her go. "Knock him dead, Brie."

She let out a nervous sigh and then shook her head. *No! My nerves are not going to control the moment.* Brie consciously released the tension and stood up straight, her chest out, her head at a respectful angle.

"That's my girl," Sir commented as she walked away.

Everything was perfect until she greeted Mr. Holloway and he barked an order to sit down. The inflection in his voice let her know the man was on edge and irritable. Not at all what she needed for her big moment.

Brie held out her hand and shook his. "Thank you for seeing me again, Mr. Holloway." To ease the tension in the room, she started off the conversation with a compliment. "As you know, sir, I admire your expertise and took your suggestions to heart as I reworked this film. I trust you will be as impressed with the changes as I am."

"I'll be the judge of that," the producer grumbled, grabbing the disk from her hand. He slid it into the player, then sat back in his chair, closing his eyes as if he couldn't be bothered to watch it.

Brie swallowed hard. It was one thing to be turned down because her work legitimately sucked, but it was quite another to lose out on her chance because the producer was upset about something she had no control over.

The lively music of the introduction started up. Brie had chosen something that would instantly grab the viewer's attention. She smiled, knowing the hard bass and driving beat were impossible to ignore.

Mr. Holloway opened his eyes a crack and watched as the opening credits showcased the three girls and the two trainers she'd interviewed. He sat up and took notice when a short teaser clip of the flogging scene flashed onto the screen.

Brie silently cheered, even though it still remained to be seen if she could keep his attention throughout the entire film, especially since it was twenty minutes longer with the additional scenes.

*Believe…*

Images of Sir, Tono and Marquis Gray came to mind. Brie turned her attention back to the screen and smiled as she watched her beloved film unfold.

Sure, Mr. Holloway might have a few questions or suggestions, but damn, the film was not only hot, but informative and riveting. Mary's part especially had taken on a life of its own. It was easy to see the vulnerability in her mannerisms and hear it in her voice as she talked about the effects of her abuse. However, Brie had assured Mary that she would not come off as a victim in the film. It had been Brie's mission to show how strong and courageous she was, despite her abusive past. Mary was not a person to be pitied. No, she was an inspiration.

Although Mr. Holloway watched the film with no emotion evident on his face, Brie did notice his keen interest when Marquis' scene with Lea came up. Even now, having seen it at least fifty times while editing, Brie felt the sexual stirrings that watching Marquis' masterful skill evoked.

When the scene was over, Mr. Holloway glanced over at her and stated, "That was powerful."

Brie hid her pride with a humble nod.

He did not speak for the rest of the film, but he did watch it in its entirety, then shut off the machine as soon as the ending credits began.

Mr. Holloway folded his arms and settled back in his chair. "What do you think of the film, Miss Bennett?"

Brie decided to be completely honest. "It is my masterpiece. The film explores the forbidden world of BDSM, but in a way that is not intimidating to the average viewer or irreverent to the lifestyle. I was pleased with the additions you requested because it gives the film a more emotional hook, without being simpering or demeaning."

He chuckled. "I especially enjoyed the added flogging scene. How did you manage to get permission from Coen to do that?"

Brie smiled. "Mr. Holloway, the staff at the Center stand behind what they do. I believe they are committed to giving an accurate picture of what submission can look like."

She was surprised that he frowned. Everything had appeared to be going well, but he definitely did not look happy and she felt the air leave her lungs.

"This has been a shitty week. No, the reality is that the last two months have been shitty. The last thing I wanted today was to like your work. I don't need the hassle. In truth, all I want to do is take a long vacation and forget the last few months ever happened. But it doesn't look like that's going to happen now."

Brie was finally able to breathe again. "I'm pleased to hear that, Mr. Holloway."

"I bet you are," he snarled, as if she had wronged him by creating quality work. "I'll show this around to a couple of my friends and get back to you next week. Looks like I'll be scrapping my last project in lieu of this one."

Brie stood up and gave him a firm handshake. "That is excellent news. I look forward to hearing from you."

She started towards the door, hardly feeling the floor beneath her feet.

"Oh, Miss Bennett. I highly suggest you take a vacation within the next couple of days. You won't have any downtime once the ball starts rolling."

"I'll keep that in mind, Mr. Holloway. Thank you."

"I'm serious—tell Davis he'd better set it up now, because I won't tolerate complaints later on that he never has time with his sub."

"I'll be sure to inform him, sir."

"Good." He waved her off as he picked up the phone and growled at his receptionist, "Get in here, damn it. We've got to revamp the whole fucking schedule…"

Brie shut the door behind her and walked towards Sir with a grin she could not hide. His confident smile greeted her. "I take it that it went well?"

"Yes, Sir."

"How well?"

"He said you should set up a vacation this week because there won't be any breaks in the foreseeable future."

His eyes lit up. "You did it!"

"I did it, Sir."

His warm laughter filled the office. "My babygirl, a famous filmmaker."

"Not yet, Sir, but soon."

He kissed her, still smiling when their lips met. "I think I will take the good producer at his word and arrange a quick trip. There is one place in particular we need to go," he informed her, as he rested his hand on the small of her back and guided her down the hallway.

"Where's that, Sir?" Brie had expected he would say Russia, but what came out of his mouth completely surprised her.

"We need to revisit Nebraska."

Brie nearly tripped over her feet. "Nebraska, Sir?"

"Something this important must be done in person."

In one fell swoop, he had sucked away all the joy she had previously felt. Speaking with her parents was going to be an exceedingly difficult conversation. "Very well, Sir."

"Take heart, little sub. I have someplace else in mind afterwards. A place I haven't been to in years."

Now her interest was piqued. "Where's that, Sir?"

"That, téa, shall remain my secret. I know how you cherish surprises."

Brie groaned. She couldn't stand not knowing and decided to probe with little questions. "Does it require a passport, Sir?"

"I will not answer any questions on the subject," he replied. But once they had left the building, Sir lifted her up and slung her over his shoulder, slapping her hard on the butt.

Brie squealed, trying to wiggle out of his arms. "What was that for, Sir?"

"That was your congratulations spanking."

Her attitude immediately changed. "Oh, well then, I'd like another, Sir."

"Too bad, my dear. You must wait." He set her down with a smirk.

"You are a cruel Master." She pouted as a group of businesswomen hurried by, staring at them reproachfully.

He leaned down and winked at one of them when he answered her. "Sometimes you must be cruel to be kind."

Brie took his hand and wove her fingers between his. "To be honest, Sir, I enjoy your cruel ways."

His eyes took on a mischievous glint as he squeezed her hand and walked her into an alley. "I suddenly have a craving for you, babygirl."

Brie's loins tingled as she followed him. She glanced back, noting the people walking on the sidewalk less than fifteen yards away.

"Panties off."

Her heart beat wildly as she stepped out of her panties and handed them to him. He slipped the thong into his jacket before pushing her against the brick wall. "I want to taste you," he growled huskily as he slipped his hand up her skirt.

Brie leaned her head back against the wall and let out a quiet moan as his fingers began caressing her pussy.

"That's it, téa. Relax as I finger-fuck you in broad daylight."

She peeked at the crowds walking by, aroused by the wickedness of what the two of them were doing.

Brie had to hold back her cry when his fingers slipped in and he began caressing her G-spot. "Let go," he whispered hoarsely as he forced her orgasm with his powerful hand.

She held nothing back, embracing the strange sensation as her body tensed and eventually released in a burst of intense pleasure. "Good girl," he praised as he knelt down and tasted her dripping wet pussy. His groan was a total turn-on.

She looked up at the patch of sky between buildings as Master continued to tease her clit with his tongue. Suddenly, she got an uneasy feeling and turned her head to see that an older gentleman had stopped in the alleyway to watch.

"Sir…"

Her Master gave her one last swirl of his tongue and then stood up, adjusting her skirt before wiping his mouth with relish. He leaned in and said lustfully, "Delicious," before taking her hand and escorting Brie past the voyeur. Sir didn't even glance in his direction, as if what they had done was a common occurrence that required no explanation.

The two of them continued down the bustling street hand in hand, like any vanilla couple in love.

Brie looked up at Sir, unsure if the happiness she felt could ever be topped. Her film was going to be seen all over the world and her Master loved her.

Could life get any better than this?

# *Brie Visits Master's Italy*

# Challenge at The Haven

To celebrate her documentary, Sir took Brie to The Haven that night. It was hard not to tell everyone why she was so happy, but she'd promised Sir she would keep her recent success under wraps until she'd had a chance to talk to her parents. Sir insisted that they do it in person. Brie knew the discussion would not go well, so she buried it in the back of her mind and embraced the festivities and kinkiness of The Haven.

She saw that Tono was in the middle of a sensuous scene in one of the largest alcoves. There were a considerable group of Kinbaku enthusiasts watching his precision and skill. Brie stopped to admire his artful work.

The Asian Dom's hands glided over the sub as he finished adjusting his knots before lifting the girl into the air. Brie heard a woman beside her gasp and knew she was imagining herself in Tono's ropes, flying under his power. It was a common fantasy many of the subs shared.

Brie looked again and realized that she recognized the submissive being suspended. It was Candy, the girl she had met on the bus months ago—the one to whom she had given Sir's Submissive Training card. The look of ecstasy on the girl's face contrasted starkly with what Brie remembered from the light rail. At the time, Candy had been in the service of an abusive wannabe Dom. She'd had the look of the worn and beaten, but to see her now one would never know it was even the same person.

Brie smiled to herself, glad she had made the sacrifice of the card when she'd felt the urging. As much as she had wanted to keep it as a memento, it was worth the joy she was experiencing right now at seeing Candy so happy and fulfilled.

Tono turned to secure a last tie and noticed Brie in the audience. He gave her a slight nod and then continued with his scene, whispering to Candy. The girl moaned in pleasure when his hand rested near her mound. He was the master of incidental touches—simple contact that could drive a girl wild.

Brie turned to say something to Sir, but he was no longer by her side. She moved through the crowd, anxious to find him. She tripped on a crop left carelessly on the floor and collided face first with a muscular chest. Brie looked up and was shocked to see Faelan staring at her. He was equally thrown off by the unexpected impact.

His blue eyes held her mesmerized for a brief moment before he pushed away from her and grabbed the woman beside him. He fisted the blonde's hair and pulled her head back to kiss her deeply.

Mary's surprised whimper shocked Brie even more than running into Faelan had. The two kissed long and passionately before Faelan broke the embrace. "Do you want to scene with me?"

Blonde Nemesis' eyes sparkled with expectation. "What kind of scene?"

"A little knife play," he suggested lustfully.

"I'm in."

"Good. I plan to play rough tonight." He escorted Mary through the crowd, leaving Brie behind without any acknowledgement. It was strange to be treated in such a bizarre manner, but Faelan had warned her that she would no longer exist in his world after she'd chosen Sir over him.

Brie could tell Mary was happy to play his impromptu sub in a scene, but it worried her. Brie was afraid Faelan was only using her. The fact was, Mary genuinely loved the guy and deserved much better than that.

Scanning the crowds, Brie was even more anxious to find Sir after her unexpected encounter. She finally spotted him on the other side of the large common area, engaged in conversation with Master Anderson. She started towards the two, but was stopped by her former trainer, Ms. Clark.

"What are you doing in the club alone?" Ms. Clark demanded.

Brie glanced down to avoid looking her in the eyes as she tried to respectfully move past her. "I'm not alone, Mistress. I'm trying to rejoin my Master."

Ms. Clark put her hand on Brie's shoulder and squeezed her sharp fingernails into her flesh. "Don't be flippant with me, sub," she snapped.

This time Brie looked her straight in the eye. "I am not being flippant, Ms. Clark." She tried to twist out of her grasp, but the Domme's hold was too tight.

Ms. Clark's eyes narrowed. "I have half a mind to take you in the back and teach you respect, Miss Bennett."

"Get your hand off my sub."

Ms. Clark instantly obeyed and addressed Sir. "I didn't realize you were here, Sir Davis. I was simply trying to protect your property."

"Touching my sub is never an option, Samantha. I believe *you* are the one who needs the lesson in respect."

"I'm certain you missed the exchange between Wallace and your sub just a minute ago."

"No, I did not."

"Then you understand my concern."

"No." Sir glanced at Brie. "Join Master Anderson."

"Yes, Master." Brie hurried to Master Anderson's side, wishing she had eyes in the back of her head. What had Ms. Clark been thinking? Nobody touched another Dom's sub without permission, not even trainers.

When Brie reached Master Anderson, she turned around to see Sir had one hand wrapped around Ms. Clark's wrist to prevent her from leaving as he spoke to her. The look on the Domme's face announced her discomfort. Obviously, whatever he was saying was upsetting to her.

The Domme tried to speak several times, but Sir interrupted and continued his lecture. It pleased Brie to see it. Someone needed to put that arrogant woman in her place.

The trainer shook her head violently, but it wasn't until she nodded that Sir let her go.

Sir came to Brie and announced, "Ms. Clark has something to share with you. Follow me."

Brie looked up at Master Anderson, who looked visibly troubled. His discomfort alarmed her.

She followed Sir and Ms. Clark. The Domme marched ahead of her angrily, clicking the studded heels of her thigh-high boots. Brie couldn't help focusing on the pointed heels, noting that they looked potentially lethal.

Ms. Clark headed to a private room with comfortable seating. She refused to sit, but gestured Brie towards a chair. Brie looked to Sir, who nodded his approval. She sat down hesitantly, curious about what was about to transpire.

"Go ahead, Samantha. Explain your past with Rytsar and how that has caused your odd fascination with my sub."

"I am not fascinated by your sub," Ms. Clark protested indignantly.

"In all the years I have known you, I have never seen you behave this erratically with a submissive before."

"I'll be damned if I am going to open up about my past in front of a student, Sir Davis."

"Ah, but she is no longer a student. Miss Bennett is now a respected and collared sub. You seem to forget that whenever she's around."

The Domme looked at Sir and pleaded, "Don't make me do this."

"You brought it upon yourself." He addressed Brie before leaving the room. "See me afterwards. I'll be practicing with Master Anderson in the whipping area."

Brie let out a barely audible gasp as her pussy contracted in fear. She found her voice and replied dutifully, "My pleasure, Master."

When he shut the door, Brie had to control the urge to run to it and fling it back open. The resentment radiating from Ms. Clark could kill a girl.

The Mistress sat down and crossed her legs, showing off the pointy, metal-studded tips of her lethal heels. It felt like an unspoken threat to Brie. She took heed and looked to the floor, not wanting to piss the Domme off.

"If this must happen, then we will make it short. Despite what your Master said, I am not fascinated by you in the least. But you already know that." She paused, then added menacingly, "Don't you?"

Brie nodded with her head down. There was no way she would be foolish enough to disagree with the woman.

Ms. Clark grumbled at the ceiling, "God, I can't believe he's making me do this!"

It was arousing to know that Sir had that kind of power over the Domme.

"I knew Sir Davis in college. I met Rytsar Durov through him. There was chemistry. Only barrier—he is a Dominant and so am I. It makes for a difficult partnering."

Ms. Clark seemed to be waiting for Brie to respond, so she said quietly, "I can only imagine, Mistress."

The trainer snorted angrily. "I was confident in my role as a Dominatrix and I was young…" Her voice trailed off for a moment. "I made a critical mistake one night." The room filled with the woman's rising anxiety.

Was Ms. Clark going to cry?

But Brie's former trainer cleared her throat and finished with a simple statement. "Needless to say, it ended my chances with him." She sighed as if she was relieved her short speech was over.

Brie dared to look up and ask, "But what does that have to do with me?"

Ms. Clark's face contorted in revulsion. "When Sir Davis announced that he was inviting Rytsar to the first auction, I couldn't wait to see what he would do with someone so inexperienced and disobedient. But something happened that night." She gave Brie a death glare. "What did he see in *you*? You're nothing special! You're a failure as a submissive and yet you had him wrapped around your finger—the renowned Rytsar. You had them all eating out of your hand. It was unfathomable to me!"

Ms. Clark got up and stood over Brie, her animosity hitting Brie like palpable waves. Brie trembled under the weight of it. "If you ever tell anyone what I've shared here, I will permanently hurt you. I don't care about the consequences. Do you understand?"

Brie had to swallow down her fear to answer. "Yes, Mistress."

"So run along to your Master, you worthless cunt."

Brie got up and made a beeline towards the door.

Ms. Clark laughed behind her. "Maybe this was cathartic for me after all. I will have to thank Sir Davis."

Brie's heart was racing as she made her way back to Sir. She tried to act calm, although her interaction with Ms. Clark had been both terrifying and enlightening.

"Did she explain it to your satisfaction, Brie?"

She nodded, wanting desperately to enclose herself in his protective embrace. "I understand now, Sir. Thank you."

Ms. Clark sauntered up behind Brie. "Miss Bennett proved to be an apt listener. It actually feels good to get that off my chest." Her red lips curled up into a dangerous smile.

"You will not mistreat my sub again, Samantha." Sir lowered his voice so passersby would not overhear. "I tell you this as a friend. We all assumed once Miss Bennett finished training, you would return to your professional demeanor. That has not been the case. Should you continue to struggle in this area, I will be obligated to advise Headmaster Coen to rethink your tenure."

Ms. Clark raised her head proudly. "I assure you that is unnecessary."

"I'm aware that Miss Bennett challenges you. Frankly, she seems to have that effect on people. But that in no way excuses your appalling behavior. Now apologize to my sub. It is apparent you upset her during your *talk*."

Ms. Clark rolled her head from side to side, cracking her neck before replying. "As you wish, Sir Davis."

Again Brie felt a surge of excitement at knowing that her Master held that kind of power over the Domme.

Ms. Clark turned to Brie. "I apologize for being blunt."

Sir immediately corrected her. "Being blunt is acceptable, and something that would not have upset her." Brie loved that Sir knew her so well.

Ms. Clark insisted, "I needed to be clear that speaking about what I shared is not acceptable."

Sir's eyes narrowed. "It was unnecessary to threaten my sub, Samantha. A simple, 'You are not allowed to share this' would have sufficed. Brie is obedient."

Ms. Clark opened her mouth to protest, but Sir stopped her. "The fact she looks you in the eye on occasion does not reflect on her character as a person. She would honor your request without question."

The Domme clamped her mouth shut and glared at Brie. She took a deep breath and forced out the words. "I apologize for not respecting you as a sub, Miss Bennett."

"Thank you, Ms. Clark," Brie answered, lowering her eyes and bowing slightly. She understood the will it took for the Domme to humble herself like that. The level of respect Ms. Clark had for her Master was clear.

The Domme's smile returned as she spoke to Sir. "After this little episode, I plan to speak with your friend when he comes to visit again. I believe a conversation between us is long overdue."

"That would not be wise, Samantha. Let sleeping dogs lie," Sir warned.

"Your wisdom only goes so far, Sir Davis. There are times when a person must take a risk and become master of her own fate."

"I will not protect you again if it comes to that. You are too old to play the fool."

Ms. Clark crinkled her nose. "Too old? I'm just hitting my prime."

The Mistress strode off as if she were queen of the world. Brie observed two submissives fall in line after her. What Lea had said was true. Ms. Clark could have anyone she desired—all except the one man she wanted.

"Are you ready?" Master Anderson asked behind her.

Brie turned and her knees gave way when she saw the large bullwhip in his hand. Sir supported her and said with a chuckle, "No need to worry, little sub. There will be no blood tonight."

"Unless your Master screws up," Master Anderson joked.

"If I do not do well tonight, it reflects solely on you, *Master* Anderson."

"A teacher can only do so much," he replied, letting his bullwhip unwind, accentuating its dangerous length.

She watched with morbid fascination as Sir pulled a black bullwhip with a blood-red tip out of his bag. It made a slapping sound as it unfurled to the floor. She looked up at him nervously.

"Are you scared, téa?"

She nodded.

"Does it turn you on?"

She blushed when she confessed, "Only because it's you, Sir."

"I may not be a sadist, but I do enjoy challenging you, little sub. This will be a test for me as well." He ran his fingers between her trembling legs. "Yes, that is exactly the wetness I was striving for. Shall we begin?"

Sir escorted her to the chains and commanded her to undress fully and stand on the red 'X'. It felt a little like déjà vu as Sir put her small wrist above her head, strapping the cuff into place.

Brie's nipples hardened in fearful expectancy when he took her other wrist and secured it. She could hear the crowd gathering. Everyone enjoyed watching Master Anderson's expertise with the bullwhip.

As both men removed their shirts, Master Anderson informed the audience, "Tonight is simply a practice session. Sir Davis has been working with a fence pole for several weeks. Now it is time to practice on human flesh."

Brie could hear the excited chatter amongst the crowd. She suspected some of them *hoped* to see blood tonight.

Sir's hands ran over her body as he readied her for the experience. Whereas Rytsar had enjoyed her fear, Sir dispelled it. He tied up her hair and then kissed the nape of her neck. This was not a session meant to frighten; this was an extension of his sensual skills using the bite of a whip.

She held her breath when he pulled away from her, the fear sinking in. Brie's heart began racing as he positioned himself behind her. The smell of the ocean that was unique to this particular alcove in the Haven helped to calm her nerves. She'd never fully appreciated how different scents could prove valuable to a sub during a scene until now. Brie focused on the smell and immediate sensations, forcing back her fears of what was yet to come.

Master Anderson instructed Sir. "Keep your stance in mind. We'll start off light. Watch me first."

She imagined him winding up and then felt the light lick of Master Anderson's whip on her back. She smiled. It was pleasurable. Brie had forgotten how gentle the bullwhip could be, and she purred with pleasure.

Sir warmed up before giving Brie her first taste of his whip. The waiting made it that much more arousing and frightening.

"Are you ready, téa?"

"Yes, Master."

The light caress of her Master's whip took the experience to a whole new level. Brie moaned in satisfaction.

He continued to warm her skin with gentle strokes from his bullwhip, making the encounter delicious, not distressing. The control Sir showed was a testament to the amount of time he'd practiced.

"Now that her skin is prepared, it's time to increase the sensation," Master Anderson stated.

Brie forced herself to stay relaxed as she waited for Master Anderson to take his stance. He described his actions to Sir as he caressed her back with a more demanding stroke. It was strong enough to take her breath away.

She took a quick glance behind her and noticed that a larger crowd had gathered as Sir stepped into position behind her. Brie closed her eyes. There was no fear, only anticipation as she waited for her Master's stroke.

But Brie cried out in surprise and pain when the end of his whip made contact. It was much harder than Master Anderson's. She heard Sir mutter under his breath, "Fuck!"

"To be expected, all part of the learning process. You flicked your wrist at the end," Master Anderson explained. "Try again, but be conscious of that."

Brie did not realize she had tensed until Master Anderson commanded, "Relax, Brie."

She took a deep breath and let it out slowly. The chains clinked above her as she twisted in place. The movement helped release some of the tension, so she stilled herself for the next stroke.

"That's my good girl," Sir praised.

Brie trusted Sir completely, honored to be his first. Despite his extensive experience and the numerous subs he had trained, this was something exclusive—shared only between them. It pleased her to serve him in this way, the two of them a team as he learned to control the bullwhip.

Sir took his time before taking his next swing. Brie gasped at the challenge it provided, but it was not overwhelming as the first had been.

"Color, téa?"

"Green, Master."

He grunted in satisfaction and began to take her into flight as he stimulated her back with well-placed strokes. Brie moaned in her chains as she began to lose herself to the sensation. Brie could sense the crowd, and it enhanced her experience. Their excitement played into hers. It was a glorious feeling…

Eventually, the rhythmic contact stopped. Brie swayed dreamily in the chains, ready to be released by her Master, hoping he would take her.

"I suggest you give her one more with bite before we end the session," Master Anderson advised Sir. Brie's heart skipped a beat as he explained, "It will do two things. For you, it will let you navigate the force required for a harder stroke that does not cause damage. For your sub, there is an erotic allure to experiencing the fierceness of the bite you can deliver. Every time you caress her with the whip, no matter how lightly, her pussy will drip because she knows it's your choice not to strike her harder."

Brie shivered in her chains. Although she agreed with Master Anderson, she did *not* want to feel the harsh bite again. Still flying on her sub high, she was unable to hold back the tears rolling down her cheeks.

Master Anderson demonstrated the motion it took to deliver a welt-worthy strike in the air first. Brie jumped each time she heard the crack of the whip beside her.

"Are you ready, sub?" Master Anderson finally asked, preparing her for his more forceful strike.

Brie understood that this was necessary to help hone Sir's skills. Despite her fears, she forced herself to answer with confidence through her tears, "Yes, Master Anderson."

He did not wait. With a quick and sure stroke, the tail of the whip cut across her back. Even though she had faced the biting power of his whip before, Brie was surprised by the shooting pain and screamed. She bit her lip afterwards, stilling her thoughts. She had experienced this once before. She knew how to transfer the pain into something sensual if she centered herself.

Brie could hear the concern in Sir's voice when he got into position behind her, and asked, "Color, téa?"

Although her skin was on fire, she knew she could handle another stroke and she *needed* to take it from Sir. "Yellowish-green, Master."

Master Anderson cautioned Sir, "Concentrate and deliver. Do not hesitate or you will either damage the skin or deliver an inadequate stroke and be forced to do it again."

Brie closed her eyes and smiled to herself. Her Master and she were one in this moment. This would be a challenging test for them both.

Her pussy tingled at the sound of the whip just before it came in contact and transformed into burning fire across her back. Brie did not hold back and screamed in both passion and pain.

Then she felt Sir beside her, his hand running lightly over the mark he had just left on her back. "It looks good on you, téa." He growled into her ear as his fingers traveled up her arm and began releasing her from the cuffs, "You did well, little goddess."

He picked her up and carried her to a chair in the corner. While she rested there, he removed his pants and underwear, revealing his hard cock. Sir lifted her up and sat down, turning her to face the crowd before impaling her on his waiting cock.

Brie moaned loudly, her body grateful to have the burning sensations on her back transferred to fire in her nether regions. Sir pressed her head down and picked up salve from a small table nearby. He rubbed the cool lotion over the marks on her back.

The sensuality of his loving aftercare made her aroused on an almost spiritual level. Sir grabbed her hips after soothing her back and moved her up and down on his shaft.

She threw her head back as she braced her hands on his thighs to help deepen his thrusts.

Sir's satisfied grunt increased her pleasure. The two moved as one as he powered his manhood into her repeatedly. Time no longer had significance as Brie closed her eyes and gave in to the erotic thrill of Sir's possession.

"Are you going to come for your Master?"

She nodded, readying herself for his command.

"Three… Two…" Brie whimpered in response to his slow countdown. On cue, her pussy began pulsating with her impending orgasm.

"One…"

He forced his cock deep within her and held her still.

Brie's vaginal muscles squeezed and released his cock with their vice-like grip. He answered by grabbing her bound hair and tilting her head back farther as he shuddered deep inside her. Then Sir wrapped his arm around her torso and pulled her to his heaving chest, growling softly, "I love you, téa."

She smiled, lost in the ecstasy of the moment. *I love you, Master—heart and soul.*

Brie stayed in his arms, oblivious to the crowd dispersing until Master Anderson broke into her reverie. "There is another couple waiting for the area, Thane. Would you like me to begin cleaning it?"

Sir released Brie and helped her disengage from him. "No, we will take care of it ourselves."

Brie cleaned the chair and then moved to the 'X' on the floor while Sir dressed and cleaned the cuffs, saving his bullwhip last. After he finished, Sir commanded Brie to dress, all except her top. Just like her first time with the bullwhip, she was given the privilege of showing off her well-earned marks.

As they moved through the club, Brie found it difficult not to gloat. In one day she had secured the future of her documentary and faced the bullwhip a second time. Her happiness only increased when she saw Mr. Gallant and his wife.

Sir stopped before them and formally greeted the pair. Brie noticed Mr. Gallant had his arm protectively wrapped around his statuesque Amazonian wife, just as he had at the collaring ceremony. Despite his small stature, the man exuded a self-assured confidence that garnered natural respect.

"You both appear to be doing well, Sir Davis."

"We are, Gallant. Fate seems to be smiling down on the two of us today."

"Glad to hear it." He added somberly, "That was quite some unpleasant business with your mother at the Center."

"I do apologize for the unseemly disturbance." Brie noticed that Sir abruptly changed the subject. "Téa, say hello to your former teacher."

Brie's smile was genuine as she addressed him. "It is wonderful to see you again, Mr. Gallant." She loved the man who acted as a father-figure and wise mentor all rolled into one glorious person.

She was pleased when he nodded his approval. "You're positively radiant, Miss Bennett."

Brie was fairly bursting, desperate to share about her film, but she dutifully kept the news to herself. "Life only seems to get better and better, Mr. Gallant. One of the best things that ever happened to me was stepping into your classroom that first night."

Brie glanced at his exquisite wife and found herself captivated by the brand the dark beauty wore on her upper arm. The lighter color of the raised scar made it very noticeable. The brand itself was a simple pattern of two curvy Ms, one above the other.

She was struck by the woman's serene face and could tell she was devoted to her Master. Yet it surprised Brie that such an elegant woman would allow herself to be branded like that. Brie wanted to ask her about the pain involved, but was afraid Sir would take it as a sign that she was considering it for herself. Instead, she said, "I am curious what your brand symbolizes."

The woman lovingly caressed the raised marks. "Two birds in flight." She smiled at Brie, her foreign accent making her statement that much more enchanting when she answered, "My Master guides me to higher levels of awareness."

Mr. Gallant kissed her shoulder and replied, "In the process, she continues to take me to new heights as well."

Brie put her hand over her heart and cooed, "Aww… that's so sweet!"

Mr. Gallant seemed surprised by her reaction and said succinctly, "Simply the truth, Miss Bennett."

Sir wrapped his arm around Brie's waist. "The natural progression of a healthy D/s relationship."

Brie looked up at Sir in admiration and wonder.

*Pinch me now…*

# Their Disappointment

Sir pressed his lips against her forehead. It was reassuring in nature, but reminded her too much of a benediction—a benediction given just before she willingly walked to her own death.

"How can this go well, Sir?" she whimpered.

"It depends on your definition of 'well', Brie. If you are upfront about the film and answer all of their questions truthfully, then I will consider it to have gone 'well' enough."

His wisdom infused her with confidence. "Yes, Sir. Upfront and honest, that's all I have to keep in mind. The rest of it will fall into place as long as I do not shy away from the truth."

Sir encouraged her further. "Brie, my advice is not to take a negative response as their true response. You cannot know how your parents truly feel until they have had time to adjust to the news. Shock tends to evoke erratic behavior."

"I will try to remember that, Sir."

"In the end, what they desire is the truth, even if it is difficult to hear."

She took another calming breath and announced with more bravery than she felt, "I'm ready."

He gave her a wink as he exited the car. "As am I…"

Sir opened the door for Brie and together they walked up to the house, a unit—partners in crime.

When Brie's mother opened the door, she greeted them pleasantly enough. "How nice you could make it back so soon after your last visit."

From the living room, her father exclaimed, "There is nothing *nice* about this visit, Marcy. They come bearing bad news, I guarantee it."

Brie shook her head. Why did her father always have to make things harder than they had to be?

Her mom shut the door behind them and gestured the two towards the couch.

Sir stopped and informed Brie, "Before we sit, I was hoping to speak to your father in private."

Brie's eyes widened. *Could it be?* Her heart beat wildly at the thought of Sir asking her father for her hand in marriage.

"Although I do not like this sound of this, I will meet you in the study, Mr. Davis. The ladies shouldn't hear what I have to say. Follow me," her father snarled, rising from his chair.

That left Brie and her mom alone, looking awkwardly at each other.

"Is he asking what I think he is?" her mother asked, sounding stunned.

Brie shrugged, but she couldn't hide her glee. "I don't know, Mom. To be honest, he and I never talked about it."

She sputtered, "Let's hope not… It's too soon… There is no way your father would consent."

As if in agreement, Brie's father yelled loud enough for the neighborhood to hear, "Over my dead body!"

Brie groaned as a heated discussion began. One that was too muffled to understand, although the hostility was easy to hear.

"Why don't we go out on the back porch?" her mother suggested.

"Sure," Brie replied, looking down the hallway in misery. *Poor Sir…*

Once they had settled on the porch swing, her mom blurted, "It sure is hot this summer. We've gotten so little rain—"

Brie couldn't care less about the weather and interrupted her. "Mom, why does Dad have to be so unreasonable?"

Marcy frowned. "I don't think your father is being unreasonable at all, young lady. It has only been a few months since you announced you two were dating."

"But Thane loves me, and he is the most amazing man I've ever met. It is an honor to know him, much less be his girlfriend." *'Girlfriend' sounds so weird…*

"If he loves you, then he won't mind waiting a year or two before making a lifelong commitment. You are only twenty-two. Far too young to consider such things."

"But Mom, weren't you barely twenty when you got married to Dad? You always told me when it's right, it's right, because that's how it happened with you."

Her mother said with an air of superiority, "But we had known each other for years, darling. We weren't strangers like you two."

"Mom, I would be willing to bet that I know Thane far better than you knew Dad when you two married."

Her mother huffed at her remark. "*We* went to high school together!"

Brie giggled. "Well, Mom, Thane and I went to school together, too."

"What do you mean?"

Brie was too scared to explain it more than once, so she answered, "When Dad and Thane come back out, I'll tell you everything. Just trust me when I say that I am confident in my choice of Thane as my partner, and there are legitimate reasons I feel that way."

They sat in uncomfortable silence as the two men continued to have it out with each other in the study.

Her mother asked, "Brie, do you understand why your father is so protective of you?"

"No, Mom. I'm a grown adult now, yet he still he treats me like a baby."

"Sweetheart, do you remember that incident when you were a child? When you were beaten and stabbed with a needle?"

Brie looked to the floor—for a brief second she felt the stab of the needle, the humiliation and terror of the moment. "Of course I do, Mom. I was scarred by that experience." But then Baron came to mind and Brie physically relaxed. She gazed into her mother's eyes. "Until recently." Brie smiled as she assured her mom, "I'm okay now."

Her mother took Brie's hand in hers and squeezed it. "I'm grateful you feel that way, but your father has never forgiven himself. It has eaten him inside knowing that he wasn't there to protect his little girl. Since then, your father has done everything in his power to keep you safe."

Brie suddenly made the connection as her entire childhood flashed before her eyes. "Is that why we moved to Nebraska?" she asked in disbelief.

"Of course. He wanted to raise you in a small town, away from gangs and violence. It about killed him to let you move to California after college."

That revelation softened her heart towards her father. All these years he had carried the burden of that terrible day, but she had never known it. Brie tried to ease her mother's mind by explaining, "Mom, I'm an adult now. I don't need Dad's protection anymore."

Her mother squeezed her hand harder. "We love you, Brie. You can't expect us to stop caring just because you're getting older. It doesn't work that way. It's a parent's right to worry."

It hit Brie then just how deeply her news was going to upset her parents. It was so much more than just the embarrassment of the film they were going to struggle with. BDSM seemed like abuse to an outsider. It was imperative she help them understand the truth.

"Mom, you need to trust that I am happy and confident in the life I have chosen. You can see how happy I am, can't you?"

"I'll admit you are glowing today. But just because you are in love now doesn't mean it will last."

Brie smiled, silently asking for patience. "Answer me this. When you told Grandma and Grandpa you were getting married, how did they take it?"

Her mother rolled her eyes, chuckling when she answered. "They wanted us to wait a few years."

Brie nodded in agreement. "See… I think it is a completely normal reaction for a parent. But it's like you've always said, Mom. When it's right, it's right. I love Thane. We were meant for each other."

"But his age is disconcerting, Brie."

She protested. "It's only eleven years, Mom. When I'm thirty, no one will even bat an eyelid."

"You are twenty-two *now,*" her mother stated firmly.

Brie was about to argue the point when both men burst out of the study.

"Marcy! You will not believe what this bastard has been doing to our daughter!"

Brie rushed into the house and over to Sir's side. He sat down on the couch with an air of calm, but she did not miss the flush on his skin. It was nothing compared to her father, who was a deep lobster red.

"Stay away from that bastard, Brianna!"

Brie sat down next to Sir and raised her chin in defiance. "Don't be disrespectful to my boyfriend, Dad."

"Don't you mean 'Master'?"

"Wha—?" her mother gasped.

*So Sir did not ask for my hand…* Brie realized he'd simply informed her father about his role in her life. It made sense, and she suddenly felt embarrassed for entertaining such a silly idea. She appreciated that Sir was man enough to face her father's wrath head-on, but now it was time to bring her mother into the discussion. With trepidation, Brie began, "Mom, Thane and I have chosen to live a Dominant/submissive lifestyle."

Her mother stared at them in confusion. "What does that mean, Brianna?"

Her father growled, "He acts as her 'Master', Marcy. He chains our little girl up and beats her."

"That's not it at all, Dad!" Brie cried in frustration. She reined in her emotions and turned to her mom, stating more calmly, "Dad is exaggerating. You need to *listen* before you make any judgments about us."

Her father's reply was cold and harsh. "Why would we listen to the girl who is being abused?"

Brie popped off the couch and put her hands on her hips. "Dad, do I look like I am being abused? I love the way Thane makes me feel."

"Brianna," her father snapped, "you know nothing else. You have only had this poor excuse of a man to compare against."

"That's not quite true…" Brie sat back down and took a deep breath before she broke the news. "I have been in the service of several exceptional men."

Her mother's jaw dropped. "Are you a…lady of the evening?"

Brie closed her eyes, biting back the torrent that threatened to escape from her lips. She felt Sir's reassuring hand on her knee and used it to maintain her control.

Sir told Brie, "I have explained to your father the dynamic of our relationship and the fact I was headmaster of the school you were trained at."

"School?" Brie's mother stared at her and then turned on Sir in disgust. "How dare you take advantage of our daughter? You…you *pervert*!" She stood up and demanded shrilly, "Get over here, Brie, right this instant or I'm calling the police."

Brie's nostrils flared as she struggled not to lose it. "We are doing nothing wrong, Mom! It would be stupid to call the police, but go ahead. Be my guest. Make a fool of yourself, see if I care!" Brie faced her father. "I came here to tell you something exciting about my film career. I think you would be proud if you knew, but you refuse to listen so I am not going to tell you. I'll just leave so you can find out about it along with the rest of the world. I don't need to deal with your intolerance."

Her father held out his hand to her. "Brianna, I will listen if you step away from him and tell us your news. I want to know the words you speak come from you and not your puppet master."

Brie was about to refuse when Sir spoke up. "Do as your father asks."

She was surprised by his response, but dutifully got up from the couch and walked over to her parents. Both of them gathered around her in a protective manner. Brie glanced back at Sir. He simply nodded, encouraging her to speak.

She looked at the concerned faces of her mother and father, understanding the time had come to be upfront with them. No matter how this played out, she had Sir's arms to fall into when it was over.

*I can endure this…*

Brie began by telling them about her documentary and the fact it had been accepted by a popular producer. Her mother sat down partway through her description of the film, looking bereft.

"Brie, you are going to let the world know about your lack of morals?"

"No, Mom. I am going to share the incredible experience I've had and explain in an entertaining way this lifestyle I have chosen."

"So you expect us to be proud of you?" her father said with contempt.

"Can't you at least support me? You can ask me anything. I *want* you to understand why I have chosen submission as my path."

Her mother put her hand to her mouth in horror. "I just realized that everyone in town is going to know what you do. How can I hold my head up ever again?"

Brie was hurt, but needed her mother to be on her side. "Look, Mom, you don't have to agree with what I do, but I would still like you to see the film." She said hopefully, "I brought an extra copy with me."

"I refuse to watch a porno, especially one starring my daughter!" her father fumed. "Brianna, I have never been so disappointed in you in all my life."

"It is not a porno, Dad! You don't know me at all if you think that."

"You're right. I do *not* know you at all. You have become a stranger to me." Her father looked past Brie and added, "Do you understand how much I loathe your 'boyfriend'?"

Brie tried to appeal to his fatherly nature. "Dad, I understand that you want to protect me and I can even appreciate that you think Thane is the wrong person for me, but I'm telling you that I love Sir and trust him completely. I've never been happier or felt more cared for."

She saw a look of pain flit across her dad's face and realized she'd hit a nerve she hadn't meant to. "That man is a bad influence," he stated icily.

She looked back at Sir and smiled. "No. He's the best thing to ever happen to me."

Brie's mom forced a thin smile and said in a curt, parental tone, "I respect you have a will of your own, Brie. You believe this is what you want, but you are too young to know what's good for you. You're easily influenced because of your tender age."

"So basically, in your eyes I am still just a child?" Brie asked incredulously.

"Yes, Brianna," her father affirmed.

"Well then, it all comes back to the fact that I'm legally an adult. I have the right to make this choice. It's my life. I would rather have you hate me than pretend to be someone I am not."

"I could never hate you, Brie," her mother protested, giving her a hug. "But this is not the life I want for you." She tucked a lock of hair behind Brie's ear. "It's morally wrong, sweetheart."

"How? I'm in a committed relationship. What is morally wrong about that?"

Her mother shook her head, not accepting Brie's answer but not having a quick comeback to dispute it.

Her father warned Brie, "Nothing you say will ever convince me that what you are doing is acceptable."

"I understand, Dad. But this is my calling. I can't change who I am, even if it disappoints you."

"Then leave. If my opinion doesn't matter, I don't see any point in discussing this further. You're willfully planning to embarrass us in front of the nation. The truth is, you care more about yourself than your own parents. As disappointed as I am, I *accept* that. But I do not respect your choice of 'partner' or the lifestyle you have chosen."

Brie looked to her mother and whimpered, "Mom?"

She stared at Brie with a look of misgiving. She looked to her husband before stating, "I agree with your father."

Brie was stunned and stood there frozen, as if in a trance. Were these really her parents? The people who had loved and raised her since birth?

Sir's warm voice filled the room. "Brie, I think you have accomplished what you set out to do here."

His gentle reminder helped her to refocus. If this was all her parents were capable of giving at this point, then she would have to accept it. Hopefully, there would come a time when they would welcome her back with open arms—once the shock dissipated. *But if that day never comes…* She looked at them both sadly, bereft at the thought.

Brie couldn't keep the tears back when she told them, "Okay, I will leave because you asked. But consider this: you always taught me to follow my heart, no matter the cost. That's what I am doing now. I hope someday you will understand and be proud."

She took Sir's arm and started towards the door.

He father declared behind her, "I will *never* be proud of you for this. Never!"

# Lesson: His Belts

Sir opened the car door and helped Brie into the rental. She remained silent, still in shock over her parents' rejection. Just before they pulled away, her mother ran out of the house. "Brie, can I have the film? I want to see it before the rest of the world."

Brie gratefully pulled the disc out of her purse. "Of course. Mom, I *want* you to see it. I'm really proud of this film."

"I can't guarantee that your father will ever watch it, but I will. I need to stay connected, even if I disagree with what you are doing."

Tears of gratitude ran down her cheeks. "That means a lot to me, Mom."

Her mother gave Brie a quick hug through the car window before running back into the house.

Brie turned to Sir. "Thank you for getting me out of there before I cracked."

His smile was forced. "I struggled myself, Brie."

She leaned over and pressed her head against his shoulder. "Are you okay, Sir?"

"Your father is a provocative man. His heart is in the right place, but his methods are…off-putting."

Brie snorted with anger. "Off-putting? That's far too kind. He was horrible."

Sir turned towards her. "All I have to do is put myself in his shoes, and it makes it easier to accept his reaction."

"So you told him about us, Sir?"

"I felt it was important to do it man-to-man."

"I'm sorry it didn't go better with my parents."

He started the car and muttered under his breath, "It went...well enough."

Brie sat back in her seat and stared at her parents' home through the rearview mirror as they drove away. Would she ever be welcomed back into her childhood home after this? Even if she was allowed to visit, would she ever *feel* welcomed again?

"We have to give them time," Sir stated with confidence.

Brie sighed miserably. "Yes, they just need time..."

Although Brie was glad to be traveling with Sir again, the pain of her parents' rejection tempered her excitement when he informed her that he was taking her to Italy. She sat down dutifully beside him at the airport gate with a forced smile, trying to hide her feelings of despondency.

Sir handed Brie his phone. "Call Rytsar. Let him know the secret you've been keeping from him. He's been insufferable ever since we left Moscow."

Brie gave a weak smile as she pressed the speed-dial button for Rytsar and waited. It took several rings before he answered. The Dom shocked her by spitting out a string of irate Russian words before she had a chance to speak. Brie looked at Sir in surprise, shrugging her shoulders.

He smirked as he pointed to his watch.

Brie groaned inside, realizing she'd caught Rytsar while he was sleeping. Sir was evil, on so many levels. She said in her brightest voice, "Hi, Rytsar, it's Brie Bennett. How are you?"

He grumbled more Russian profanities.

"I'm sorry to have called you at such a bad hour, but Sir just gave me permission to tell you my secret."

He growled, "Inform your Master that he's a *mudak*." He paused, and then barked, "Go on."

She blushed when she realized Rytsar was serious. She put her hand over the phone and repeated his exact words to Sir.

"Hang up on him," Sir ordered with a grin.

Although she hated doing it, Brie pressed the off button.

The phone immediately rang back. Sir grabbed the phone from Brie, taking his time in answering it. "What was that, Durov?"

Brie could hear a litany of angry utterances coming from the phone. Sir took his rant with a bemused smile. "For your information, Brie just finished talking with her parents and I was under the impression you wanted to be the next in line to know. Sorry I was mistaken. Talk to you later… Oh… What was that? Ah, you do want to speak to Brie after all? I thought you might." He chuckled evilly. "Who's the *Master* now?"

He handed the phone to Brie while Rytsar was still cussing him out.

"Hi, Rytsar, it's Brie again."

Rytsar immediately stopped his tirade and took a deep breath. "Good morning, *radost moya*."

"I have some exciting news to share!"

He laughed. "I've already deduced it."

She was intrigued. "Please tell me."

"You're pregnant. Why else would you wait weeks and tell your parents first?"

"Oh-em-gee! I'm *not* pregnant, Rytsar. I am too young to have a baby! Are you kidding me?"

She heard Sir chuckling softly. She looked at him, pointing to the phone and shaking her head in amusement.

Rytsar sputtered. "I'm sorry… I meant no offense."

Brie stifled her laughter, not wanting to offend the Dom. "It's fine, Rytsar. I forgive you." She was too excited to hold back the news any longer. "If you can believe it, my documentary now has a popular producer behind it!"

"That's impressive, but why all the secrecy, *radost moya*?"

"We were told to keep it quiet until it was official."

"So, no baby Brie in eight months?"

She laughed at the absurdity of it. "No. Sorry to disappoint you."

"And here I was looking forward to being a *dyadya*. Ah, such is life… Congratulations on your documentary nonetheless. I am honored to have bound and fucked such a talented woman."

Brie was instantly reminded of her warrior fantasy that the Russian Dom had so artfully played out for her. She looked at Sir and blushed. "Um…thanks for the congrats."

"I assume I'm mentioned in your film."

"Of course!"

He said in jest, "Then it is guaranteed to be a hit."

She giggled. "Naturally…"

The blaring sound of their flight being announced over the intercom drowned out his reply. Sir gestured for Brie to give him the phone. She handed it back to him, grateful Sir had given her a chance to share the news with a friend who would be glad to hear it.

After Sir hung up, she thanked him and added, "I needed that, Sir."

"It is important for you to experience the positive along with the negative." He picked up their carry-ons and directed her to the gate. "I trust you will find the next ten hours very positive."

She was already excited to be taking another international flight with Sir, but she was speechless when she saw their first-class setting for the trip. Sir's seating area next to the window looked like a small suite. Not only did he have a large-screen TV, but the length of his private area covered four airplane windows. It was like a hotel room in the sky.

"I never knew there were such things…" she said in awe.

He sat down in the large leather seat and beckoned her to him. "Have you ever heard of the Mile-High Club?"

She giggled as she sat on his lap. "Isn't that where people have sex in airplane bathrooms?"

He shook his head with an amused smile. "Only if the person is desperate and enjoys unsanitary conditions."

"To be honest, Sir, I never thought having sex over a toilet was very sexy."

"Nor I, although I must say you did a fine job of making it look tantalizing during Master Coen's challenge."

Brie grinned as she recalled her bathroom stall antics involving a camera, clothespins and a naughty hairbrush.

Sir whispered in her ear. "We are about to have sex in the air, little sub. I assure you it will not be on a toilet or in the way you are expecting."

He had her full attention now.

"I don't suppose you will let me in on your wicked secret, Sir?"

He surprised Brie by giving her an answer. "It shall be a lesson on belts."

Being spanked was something Brie found sexually arousing. The idea of being hit with a belt terrified her on a level she could not explain. "Sir?"

He smiled with an ease that reduced her building apprehension. "Tonight you will learn the power and allure of your Master's belts." He produced six leather belts, of varying widths and shades of brown, from his carry-on bag. She suddenly understood why the airport staff had kept Sir behind to question him about his luggage. What man need six belts on a flight?

"Hold out your hands."

He laid the belts in her open palms so she could feel and smell his tools of choice for their upcoming scene. Brie stared at them with a sense of pleasurable dread. Surely he would not beat her with the six different belts…

She glanced at Sir. His playful smirk, along with his raised eyebrow, begged the question—did she trust him?

A perky stewardess appeared, asking Sir what he wanted to drink. He ordered for them both. "We would like your finest merlot."

"Yes, sir!" the young woman answered cheerily.

Brie pouted as she walked away. "I hate when other women call you sir."

Her Master chuckled under his breath. "I can appreciate that. It's something I do not experience, as téa is not a common word."

"In some ways, Masters have it easier…" Brie teased.

He looked at her with feigned sympathy. "A Dominant is expected to be in charge. That takes much forethought and planning, little sub. Both sides of the coin have their benefits and disadvantages. Thankfully for us, it is a pleasant balance."

Brie wrapped her arms around his neck and purred, "Yes, it is, Sir. Very pleasant, although I am hesitant about your plans on this flight."

He snuck a hand down between her legs discreetly, caressing her femininity. "As I suspected, your hesitancy is also marked by juicy anticipation."

Brie closed her eyes in frustration. Why did her body have to betray her like that? She was genuinely scared, but there her pussy was announcing she wanted what she feared. Being true to her heart, she opened her eyes and faced him. "Sir, belts scare me."

He caressed her cheek with the back of his hand. "But you trust your Master."

She nestled herself against his chest and murmured, "Always."

"Good, because I have been looking forward to this lesson for a long, long time."

Brie muffled her whimper in his shirt. *Will it hurt too terribly much?*

"Here you go, sir, our very best!" The stewardess handed the wine to him with a winning smile—the kind of smile that could set a sub's nerves on edge.

The girl looked at Brie, who was still holding the bouquet of belts, and informed her in an overly friendly voice, "You will need to sit in your own seat, ma'am. The plane is readying for takeoff."

'Ma'am' was not a sexy or respectful title compared to 'sir'. Brie resented that it made her sound like an old lady.

Sir took the belts from her and gave Brie a peck on the cheek before releasing her from his lap. She made her way to her own private seating area across the aisle from his. The middle seats did not have the same level of privacy, but they had all the other luxuries.

Brie started pressing buttons and opening compartments to discover all the amenities the plane offered.

The stewardess cleared her throat. Brie looked up and blushed with embarrassment. How unsophisticated could she get? She was handed the glass of wine and told to buckle her seatbelt.

Sir gave her a weary look after the woman left. "You act like such a child sometimes."

She sighed, disappointed in her lack of decorum. Brie stared at her lap and offered her apology. "I'm sorry, Sir."

"Curiosity killed the cat, Brie. Or in your case, it got her ass whipped."

Brie looked up at him in concern. "Please, Sir. I won't play with any more gadgets, I promise."

He shook his head in disbelief. "I was joking, Brie. Do you honestly think I would punish you for your adventurous spirit?"

"It's just that…you are so worldly and refined, Sir, and I am…"

"Bewitchingly curious," he finished for her.

The engines started up, announcing the beginning of their long flight. Brie smiled at him as she sat back in her seat. She buckled herself in, tightening the seatbelt around her waist, and sighed contentedly. Although he challenged her in daunting ways, Sir was good for her—building her up, helping her to be confident and fearless despite her lack of experience. Someday, she would be the sophisticated woman he deserved to have by his side.

As soon as the airplane rose to cruising altitude, Sir stood up and motioned Brie to him. She looked at the six belts lying beside Sir's seat and began shaking in fear. He noticed when he took her wrist to guide her to his chair.

"Brie, this is going to be a positive experience. There is no need to fear me."

She swallowed hard, whispering, "The belts frighten me, Sir. I'm not sure why."

He slid the privacy partition closed, stating, "Then this is a necessary lesson, Brie."

Brie's heart began to race as he ordered, "Take off everything, including your panties, but leave the skirt on."

She undressed and felt her nipples grow hard. Out of fear or exhilaration? She couldn't tell.

Sir adjusted the seat so that it leaned back at a forty-five degree angle. "Kneel on the chair, ankles at the edge, wrists resting against each armrest."

There was a mirror on the back wall. It faced a similar mirror above the TV screen on the opposite side. Not only did it give the small area a sense of more openness, it also allowed her to look at herself and gave her a limited view of Sir.

He picked up the first belt. Brie expected that he would fold it in half to spank her with it. Instead, he knelt down and secured her right ankle to the chair.

Brie looked into the mirror and smiled. *Belts as restraints!*

She glanced down to watch as he belted her ankle into place. These belts were specially modified, with holes created just for this purpose. It made her wet to think of Sir altering the belts as he contemplated how he would use them on her.

He was quick to belt her other ankle and both wrists. The fifth belt went around her waist. Brie was unsure of its purpose, but the possessive feel of having his belt cinched around her made her loins hot.

He then took off the chain around his neck and undid her collar. It surprised her, because he'd insisted she wear it on the plane, even though they'd had to remove it while going through security. She was curious why he'd been so adamant about it when he was taking it off now.

Sir placed her beloved collar inside a small drawer, along with his key, and picked up the sixth belt. It was wider than the others. Brie bit her lip as he placed the belt around her neck and tightened it. It was loose enough to feel comfortable, but restrictive enough to keep her aware of its presence.

She looked in the mirror and saw Sir's reflection staring back at her. She was covered in Master's belts. It was an erotic feeling, being bound by Sir like this.

"Who are you?"

"Téa."

"Who owns you?"

"You do, Master."

Sir undid his tie and rolled up his sleeves. Keeping eye contact with her, he unbuckled the belt around his waist and slowly pulled it out of the belt loops. Brie let out a tiny gasp, her helplessness and fear somehow accumulating into something deliciously thrilling.

"Not a sound," he commanded as he lifted her skirt.

Brie was surprised he had not given her a gag. In a public place like this, she would have appreciated it. Instead, he was expecting her to remain in complete control. Then it dawned on her that this was similar to the lesson on the balance beam. She'd had to concentrate on remaining still while he teased her with the electricity of the violet wand.

The man was remarkably wise in planning out his scenes.

Sir grabbed the end of the belt around her neck and applied just enough pressure to focus her attention solely on him. With his other hand, he began lightly slapping her ass with his belt. The sound of the hard leather striking her skin was sultry. The feel was similar to a light flogging.

"Do you like, téa?"

She remembered his command to be silent and only nodded slightly. The belt around her throat did not allow for freedom of movement.

Sir continued to warm her buttocks with the belt, hitting with more power, but not bringing the biting pain she had feared. He concentrated on his work, keeping the tension around her throat while carefully placing the strikes of the belt so that they covered every inch of her skin.

Every once in a while he would stop to stare at her in the mirror. The lust radiating from his eyes made Brie weak.

"We're almost done here," he announced. She watched as he pulled back for a more forceful strike. Brie closed her eyes and squelched the cry that erupted in her throat when the belt made contact with her skin. It was challenging, but not overwhelming. Just enough force to bring biting pleasure.

He let the belt fall, the buckle clanking as it hit the floor. Then he caressed her skin with his free hand, the hint of a smile playing on his lips. "I shall never tire of this ass."

Sir moved into position behind her. She watched him unbutton his pants and ease his cock out of his briefs. He stroked his shaft several times before pressing it against her wet pussy. Sir pulled a little harder on the belt around her neck, forcing her to arch her back as he slipped inside.

"Good girl," he said quietly.

Not crying out during the session with the belt was nothing compared to keeping silent as her Master fucked her. The unique position he had restrained her in gave him a stimulating angle, one that allowed his cock to rub hard against her G-spot with every thrust.

He upped the sensation by grabbing the belt around her waist and using it as extra leverage to pound her deeper. Brie panted hard, wanting to scream—to fill the airplane with the sound of her pleasure.

She kept her eyes on Sir, in total love and lust with the man who possessed her.

As he reached his climax, Sir threw his head back and grunted quietly. Brie closed her eyes and concentrated on the feel of his cock releasing the warmth of his seed deep within her, while the pressure of the belt at her neck reminded Brie of her place—she was totally and completely *his*.

# Isabella

Sir's family lived on an island, an hour's journey by ferry from the main coast. Brie found that fact completely enchanting, but the city itself turned out to be captivating in its own right.

Brie couldn't hide her grin as Sir guided her through the narrow streets of his father's island hometown of Portoferraio. The old apartments were charming, with their brightly painted doors and colorful shutters.

Sir explained as they walked, "People mainly take the bus or walk here. As you can see, cars are impractical."

Brie looked at the narrow streets and nodded in understanding. She squeezed his hand and announced, "I prefer walking, Sir."

He placed his hand on her back and guided her through a group of chatty women. One of them looked at Sir and then took a second glance. He didn't seem to notice, but the woman whispered to the others and they all turned to stare at him. Brie wondered if it was possible the group recognized him.

Sir took her up a steep hill where the street had tiny steps the entire way up. He led her to an attractive apartment with a vivid red door.

He took a deep breath before he knocked. From deep inside the building, Brie heard a woman complaining. After what seemed an exceptionally long time, the door finally opened and a middle-aged woman complained at them in Italian. However, she stopped midsentence when she saw Sir. He smiled at her and put his finger to his lips.

The woman's eyes widened and then she threw her arms around him. Brie stepped back so they could greet each other properly. The woman grabbed his hand and started dragging him inside, shouting up the stairs.

Sir glanced back at Brie. "I told my aunt to keep it a secret. My grandmother does not know it's me." He winked at her. "This should be amusing."

Brie followed closely behind him, anxious to see the look on his grandmother's face after so many years of separation. She saw a little old lady hunched over in a chair facing the balcony. Sir's aunt touched her shoulder and pointed towards him.

The elderly woman turned and time stood still in the small room.

Her face lit up when she recognized her grandson. The tiny woman struggled to stand as she reached out for him. He was by her side in an instant.

His grandmother grabbed Sir's cheeks, pulling his face close to hers.

"*Nonna*," he said with tenderness, wrapping his arms around her small frame and picking her up off the ground.

Tears of joy ran down the woman's wrinkled cheeks. "*Nipotino…*"

Brie felt tears prick her own eyes as she watched the touching reunion of grandmother and grandson. She reflected on the pain the old woman must have felt at losing her talented son eighteen years ago to suicide, but that was not all she had lost. She'd lost her grandson as well, due to the traumatic circumstances surrounding her son's death. How tragic for them both…

An elderly gentleman slowly made his way down the stairs from the floor above. He looked at Brie in confusion and then turned to stare at Sir.

"Thane!" he shouted, a toothless grin spreading across his sunken face.

Sir held out one hand to him while still holding onto his grandmother. "*Nonno*!"

The old man was all skin and bones, but had a vitality that filled the room. He took Sir's hand and shook it vigorously, laughing with gusto.

Sir's aunt couldn't contain her excitement and impulsively hugged Brie. She understood the woman's joy and returned the hug, glad to be included in the moment.

Sir gestured Brie to him and said something to his grandparents. The old woman let go of Sir briefly and pinched Brie's cheeks with her thin fingers. "*Grazie mille.*" Brie was shocked when his grandmother kissed her right on the lips before letting her go.

The little old woman grabbed back onto Sir, looking as if she would never release her hold again.

The love flooding the room was overwhelming and the joyous look in Sir's eyes was a sight to behold. Brie had never seen him so open and vulnerable, except on a few occasions when he was alone with her. It made her heart sing to see him truly happy.

Although Brie could not understand a word spoken, she quietly found a seat in the corner and enjoyed the role of silent observer to the jubilant reunion of Sir with his grandparents. It was obvious there was a lot of catching up to do, since words rushed out of the mouths of all involved.

But the chatter stopped the moment the door opened from below and a woman's sweet voice laced with an Italian accent called from downstairs. "Is that you, Thane Davis? Is it really you returning from America?" Sir looked in the direction of the voice and had to act quickly as a beautiful brunette threw herself into his arms.

The entire atmosphere in the room changed. The aunt glanced at Brie nervously and then looked to his grandparents, who now only had eyes for the woman in Sir's arms.

Brie noticed the subtle way Sir held the beauty at bay, but there was no mistaking the look of attraction in his eyes. They knew each other—they knew each other well…

"Isabella, what are you doing here?" Sir asked.

"What do you mean? Why wouldn't I be here, Thane? I ran as fast as I could as soon as I got word you were back!" She tiptoed and gave him a peck on the lips before he could stop her.

Sir held her at arm's length. "Bell…"

The brunette smiled at him playfully, not heeding his subtle warning. "I have waited all these years because I *knew* this day would come."

Sir directed the girl towards Brie. "Isabella, this is Brianna Bennett."

Brie stood up, ready to shake hands with a woman who looked to be the same age as Sir. However, the color drained from the beauty's face as she stared at Brie. Isabella said nothing to her, focusing her attention back on Sir.

"A friend?" she asked hopefully.

"We're a couple, Bell."

The woman shook her head in disbelief and pushed away from him, then ran down the stairs, crying hysterically.

Sir looked at Brie. "I have to go after Isabella. Stay here." He headed down the stairs, jumping down two at a time to catch up.

The room was suddenly silent and uncomfortable. To escape it, Brie headed out to the balcony. There, she inadvertently witnessed the encounter between Isabella and Sir on the streets below.

Sir held her firmly with both hands, even as the woman tried to pull away. He was talking to her, although Brie could not make out what he was saying.

Isabella began hitting his chest in anger but then collapsed into his arms, sobbing violently. Sir held her like a lover as he comforted the brunette.

It hurt Brie to see it and she collapsed, staring at them through the iron bars. Who was that woman?

Sir's grandfather came out to join her and held out his hand to Brie. She was hesitant to take it, but allowed him to help her back to her feet. He pointed to the sea and began talking to her. Even though she didn't understand his words she pretended to, grateful for the distraction. She listened to the strong timbre of his voice, admiring his commanding gaze, and silently wondered if all the men of Sir's lineage were natural Dominants.

When Sir finally returned, he came straight to Brie and put his arm around her. He said something to his grandfather, who frowned but nodded curtly.

Sir spoke to Brie next. "We are leaving so you and I can talk." He led her from the balcony to the stairs, but stopped to give his grandmother a kiss goodbye. The old woman started arguing with him, holding onto his hand in a death grip.

It was heartbreaking to see Sir attempt to gently pry himself from her tight grasp. The terror on his grandmother's face spoke of her fear that she would never see him again, but Sir's grandfather barked a command and she let go.

Sir guided Brie down the stairs to the sound of the old woman's pleading.

As soon Sir shut the door behind them, he leaned against the building, taking a few moments to gather himself before commanding Brie to walk beside him. While they strolled down the street, he explained, "Isabella was my childhood sweetheart. Our families are extremely close, and it was assumed by all that we would marry when we were older."

"I can tell you have a connection," Brie replied lightly, even though it pained her to say it.

"We were very close...once."

Brie wasn't sure she wanted to know, but she forced herself to ask, "What happened, Sir?"

He took his time to answer her, looking troubled when he finally spoke. "After my father died, I wanted nothing to do with love, marriage, or women." He paused and then stated candidly, "I sent Isabella a letter explaining that I never planned to marry."

Those last words cut Brie to the quick. Even though they had never talked of marriage, she had secretly hoped someday he would marry her.

Sir continued, "I explained in the letter that I would not be returning to Italy and broke off all contact with her. It has been that way for eighteen years. I never considered that Isabella might await my return; that she held onto the belief I would come back for her one day. Unfortunately, that unspoken hope compromised her subsequent relationships."

Brie heard the regret in his voice and her heart constricted.

Sir took her hand and held it tightly. "Both families expected the marriage. I do not doubt that even now they hold out hope." He stopped in the middle of the street and turned her to face him, stating solemnly, "I'm sorry, Brie. I do not know if my extended family will be any more receptive to our union than your parents."

"I can handle it, Sir," Brie assured him, grateful that he was stating his intention to fight his family's wishes.

Sir brushed her cheek with his thumb and smiled before they continued down the street. After several minutes, he let out a deep sigh. "Oh, Isabella… What a waste."

There was nothing she could say in response. It was romantic and heartbreaking that his childhood sweetheart had waited for him all these years. There was a part of Brie that wanted to hate her, but in all honesty, she only had empathy for the woman.

# Condor Love

After a day of exploring the island of Isola d'Elba with its luscious greenery, rocky cliffs and mixture of sandy and pebbly beaches, the two were invited to dinner at Isabella's family home. Although Brie wanted to avoid her like the plague, Sir insisted they attend.

"This is my family, Brie. To turn down this invitation would be the same as turning down your parents. We will use this as an opportunity for everyone to meet you. To see the extraordinary woman I see."

Despite the doubts that assailed her, she knew showing a lack of confidence would only cause others to question Sir's choice. It was with a courageous heart she faced the evening with Isabella, determined to act secure in her role as Sir's partner.

Isabella's parents lived in an expensive home on the beach. This was no traditional Italian apartment. This was a modern home with a breathtaking view of the sea. It appeared that Isabella had very wealthy relatives.

Brie was surprised that everyone welcomed her with smiles and hugs. If she hadn't suspected their true feelings, she would have missed the slight reservation in their welcoming embraces.

Isabella came out of the kitchen with a beautiful smile framed by rosy cheeks. Brie was struck by how stunning she was with her sparkling eyes, those perfectly shaped lips and that womanly sway to her hips. "Welcome to our home! I have spent the entire day cooking your favorites, Thane. I had a suspicion you have not had traditional food in a *very* long time." She turned to Brie. "It is my hope that you will enjoy it as well, Miss Bennett. We believe food is an expression of the soul."

Brie understood her meaning. In her own experience, she'd felt closer to Sir whenever he'd shared one of his favorite dishes with her. Because of that, it seemed almost sinful to have Isabella cook for him now. Her jealousy got the best of her and Brie secretly prayed the dinner would be a disaster. Unfortunately, the smells floating from the kitchen belied that hope.

Isabella disappeared again to finish the meal, while the huge family gathered around a massive table and the wine began to flow. Brie watched Sir covertly, noticing how comfortable he was, how frequently he smiled and how easily he laughed. It was heartwarming to see.

When Isabella finally returned, a troupe of women got up to help her, filling the table with a bounty of authentic Tuscan cuisine. Brie quickly glanced over the table, hoping to see tomatoes somewhere in one of the many dishes. Naturally, Isabella knew him too well for that.

Isabella loaded a plate and placed it in front of Sir with a proud smile and a hint of a blush. She then made a similar plate for Brie.

Sir explained to Brie, "You are expected to eat every bite. If you do not, the family will consider it an insult."

Brie stared at the plate piled high with food. There was no way she could finish it all. It felt as if she was being set up for failure with a capital F.

She heard Sir's quiet chuckle. He bit the bullet for her, asking Isabella for a '*piastra*'. Isabella looked at him oddly, but handed him a fresh plate. Sir took a little of everything from the bountiful meal. He slid his plate over to his grandfather, slid Brie's plate in front of him and placed the new one beside Brie.

A hush fell over the table. Sir grinned and rubbed his stomach. "*Non Italiano.*"

The group laughed and began partaking of Isabella's incredible feast. Sir winked at Brie and held up his fork, inviting her to eat.

Although what was sitting on her plate was far more than Brie would eat normally, it was manageable. "Thank you…Thane," she said quietly as she picked up her fork and chose the same item he did.

When Brie tasted Isabella's gnocchi, she closed her eyes and stifled her moan of pleasure. It was soft and light, almost melting in her mouth as she chewed. Her heart sank. There was no doubt about that Isabella was a damn fine cook. Why did the woman have to be beautiful, loyal *and* talented in the kitchen?

It was with joy and sadness Brie finished the entire plate. Everything on it, even the seafood items—which she normally didn't like—was simply prepared and delicious. To Brie, each bite had been an added nail in the coffin of her own inadequacy.

After much laughter and lively discussions in their enchanting native tongue, the group retired to a large room with plenty of seating and an expansive window overlooking the coast.

Sir directed Brie to a seat while Isabella separated herself from the family. When Isabella picked up a guitar, Brie's heart sank.

*Not this too…*

Isabella took a few minutes tuning the guitar and then took a seat on a stool directly facing Sir. She smiled shyly and announced, "I haven't played for years now, but *Papà* insisted. I apologize in advance."

Sir nodded, a silent encouragement Brie recognized. Her seeds of jealousy began to sprout into life. Sitting there next to Sir, Brie felt like she'd already lost him.

Isabella's fingers danced over the strings, filling the room with a soulful melody. Although there were a few little mistakes, they did not detract from the beauty of her song.

Then Isabella sang.

Her voice was disarming, reminding Brie of the tale about sirens who lured seamen to their deaths with their beautiful voices. Although Brie could not understand the words, the emotion behind them was clear. Isabella was singing a love song to Sir.

First with the food, and now with the music, Isabella was making love to Sir through untraditional means. She was reminding him, as well as showing Brie, why Sir had fallen in love with her all those years ago.

It wasn't just Sir Isabella was ensnaring with her many talents. Brie was equally captivated by the beautiful and talented woman. She knew if she were a man, she would want this woman for her own. A lone tear ran down Brie's cheek at the revelation.

"Are you okay?" Sir whispered.

She wiped the tear away. "The song… It's just so beautiful, Sir."

He looked at Isabella and smiled. "Yes. Yes, it is."

In that moment, Brie's fate was sealed.

She knew what she needed to do, but lost her courage that night. Instead, she lay beside Sir, savoring the warmth of his love for just a little longer.

It wasn't until the next morning that she found the strength, sitting in the little espresso café Sir had taken her to. Brie took a deep breath, praying she would not cry until it was over.

"What's wrong, Brie?"

"Sir… Thane…"

He looked at her with concern. "This must be serious."

She nodded.

"You have my attention."

She looked away from him, unable to keep her composure while looking into his eyes. She stared out of the window at a couple walking hand in hand. That wasn't helping, so she averted her eyes and focused on a bird pecking at crumbs. "You seem happy here, Sir."

"I am," he answered cautiously.

"I have never seen you this way before. It's…wonderful."

"If that is true, why can't you look at me?"

Brie's bottom lip trembled when she spoke. "You belong here, Sir. This is your home. These are your people. You deserve the love and support you've found here."

He shook his head in irritation. "You are not making yourself clear, Brie. Spit it out."

She braved a look into his magnetic eyes and the tears began to fall. "You told me that condors mate for life. I believe that. However, I think there is one instance that can split a pair apart, besides death." She let out a sob and had to stop for a second, swallowing hard to get rid of the lump that had formed in her throat. "I think a condor's love is so strong she will let her mate go if she knows he will be happier with another."

Sir stared at her and said nothing.

Brie closed her eyes and commanded herself to stop crying. She was sacrificing her heart, but she didn't want to do it with tears. His silence let her know she had read the situation correctly.

"Brie."

She opened her eyes, prepared to have her heart shattered for him.

He pushed his chair back and commanded, "Come here."

She did so unwillingly, terrified he was going to have her bow before him to release her from her collar. To her relief, he directed her to his lap instead. She climbed onto it and laid her head against his chest, listening to his heartbeat. It was for that heart she was sacrificing herself.

"I did not understand until this moment how much I needed you to say that."

Her heart broke into a million pieces. Brie held him closer, not wanting to let him go despite her decision to set him free.

Sir nestled his face in her long hair. "I would never have expected such a gift from you."

She answered sadly, "I love you, Thane."

His laughter was low and warm. "Yes, you do."

"Your happiness is everything to me."

"As you are a submissive, I am not surprised you feel that way." He cupped her chin and gazed into her eyes. "But I will never let you go."

"Sir?" Her heart hadn't dared to hope.

"You are mine. There is no other."

"Isabella?"

"Is a part of my past."

"But, Sir, the woman is beautiful, talented and can even cook."

"You are beautiful, talented, and you…are learning to cook," he added with a kiss on her forehead.

Brie whispered, "But Sir, Isabella is an extraordinary woman."

"I concur. However, she and I together do not equal *us*. I am not the boy she once knew. She cannot meet the needs I have now." Sir cradled her cheek in his hand. "You are my soul's complement. I love *you*."

Brie started crying without any chance of controlling it.

"Would you give up on us so easily, Brie?"

She struggled to answer him through her tears. "No, Sir. I love you too much."

Sir kissed her salty tears. "I believe this is the greatest gift I've ever been given—my happiness in exchange for your heart." He lifted her chin and kissed her gently on the lips. "Silly girl, my happiness is you."

Brie melted into his embrace, the relief of not losing him announcing itself as a painful sob. She buried her face in his chest.

"I am honored by the depth of your love, babygirl." He put both arms around her and held her tightly.

Brie felt an incredible rush, as if she had been reborn and given new life.

# Captive

"There is a special place I want to take you, Brie," Sir informed her as they walked down to the docks. He helped her onto a simple sailboat and introduced her to a man she'd met at Isabella's dinner party a few nights before.

Sir explained, "Pietro was a friend of my father's. We used to go sailing together when I was a child."

The older gentleman took her hand and put it to his lips. "*Sei bellissima.*"

Brie blushed, knowing he'd said something about her being beautiful. "*Grazie,*" she replied shyly.

Pietro gave Sir a long and emotional hug. When he pulled away, there were tears in the older man's eyes. It was obvious to Brie that seeing each other brought back treasured memories for both men.

Sir directed Brie to the front of the boat while they set about getting it ready to sail. She basked in the warmth of the sunshine, feeling like the Queen of Sheba when the boat began to pull away from the dock.

Brie secretly pretended this was her boat and they were her two manly servants. It was a naughty fantasy, considering her place, but she threw her head back and drank in the power and delight the image brought.

Eventually, Sir joined her. He looked incredibly sexy with the wind whipping through his dark hair, like he was meant to be on the ocean as a captain—or a pirate.

He took in a deep breath of the sea air. "I love getting out on the water."

"I do too, Sir. I love the smell and the feeling of freedom it inspires." She looked out over the expanse of blue. "It spurs the adventurer in me."

He pulled her up to stand beside him, holding her close. "It appeals to a part of my soul that lies dormant until I'm on the water again."

She enjoyed the wind playing with her hair. It was a moment she wished she could capture and bottle, to be savored often in the years ahead.

"You see that little island?" he asked, pointing over her shoulder at a speck on the horizon. "That is our destination. My father used to take me there as a boy."

She snuck her hand around his waist and snuggled against Sir, grateful that he was including her in retracing a part of his past.

"It's been more than eighteen years since I've been," he said pensively, as if he was shocked by the passage of time.

Sir told Brie to undress down to her bathing suit while he helped Pietro lower the sails as they approached the tiny island. Brie heard a satisfying splash when the sailor dropped the anchor over the edge of the boat.

The two men talked for several minutes before Sir rejoined her. "He'll come back in four hours. That should leave us plenty of time to play."

*Play?* Maybe this was more than a walk down memory lane.

Without any warning, Sir picked her up and threw her into the water. Brie yelped as she fell and the cold sea enveloped her. She popped her head back up and took in a deep breath, only to hear Sir say, "You better start swimming towards the shore, princess. I am about to capture you."

He started peeling off his shirt, looking at her lustfully.

The thrill of the chase infused her with giddy determination. Brie started swimming for all she was worth, heading towards a small alcove on the island. Even though she was smaller than Sir, she was a good swimmer and thought she could make it before he caught up.

She heard a splash. Sir was coming for her…

Brie kept her eye on her destination. He would not apprehend her easily if she could help it. Brie tried not to think about his long, powerful strokes as she swam until she felt hands grabbing at her legs. She screamed and was rewarded with a mouthful of salt water.

Survival mode kicked in as she made her way to the shore, crawling onto the sandy beach gasping desperately for breath. She glanced behind her and saw that he was rising out of the water.

This time Brie let out a terrified scream and jumped to her feet, sprinting across the tiny beach towards a wall of rock ten feet high. She looked behind her and felt butterflies. Sir had the look of a hungry predator about to devour his lunch.

Brie found she was trapped and darted to the right, but he cut off her escape. She switched to the left, but immediately changed direction, trying to trick him. Sir was not fooled, and he lunged.

She sprinted, but he grabbed her around the waist and brought her crashing to the ground. Brie struggled under his weight, fully caught up in the terror and excitement of being captured.

Sir grasped her wrists and pushed them into the sand as he lay on top of her. His low laughter helped to calm her wild struggles.

He ignored her protests as he pulled the strings on her bikini, leaving her naked and exposed. Brie thought he would take her then, but he stood up and threw her over his shoulder, leaving her little suit discarded on the beach.

As he walked towards the rocks, he slapped her ass hard. "Did you really think you could escape me, princess? I could have captured you at any point."

It appeared he was giving her the opportunity to play out a version of her Queen of Sheba fantasy. She tested it out by replying snottily, "Do not touch me, you filthy swine. My father will have your head for this!"

He laughed loudly. "I don't care who your daddy is, princess. Your cunt is mine."

She smiled to herself, thrilled by his choice of scene.

Brie was about to protest when he put her down next to the cliff. "Climb," he ordered, pointing to the rock.

Brie looked closely and noticed someone had carved handholds into the cliff face. She stepped back and folded her arms across her bare chest. "I will not!"

Quick as lightning, Sir had her bent over and was slapping her ass with enough force to bring tears. She totally deserved it and loved playing the bratty princess. Being a naughty submissive did have its benefits.

When he let her up, she wiped away the tears defiantly, refusing to speak.

"Climb," he commanded.

With her head held high, she faced the rocks and started her ascent, knowing that he was admiring her pinkened ass from below.

When she reached the top, the ground leveled off to a grassy area surrounded by trees and vegetation. It was so beautiful that Brie stopped for a moment to admire it.

She heard Sir moving below her and got her mind back in the game, trying to scramble away as soon as she crested the top, but Sir wrapped his hand around her ankle and pulled her back down to the ground.

He was on top of her in a second, squeezing the breath out of her with his weight. "You must have mistaken me for one of your imperial fools…but I am no fool, princess." He bit her shoulder, causing her to cry out in passion. "You like that, don't you? I bet I know what else you like," he said hungrily, feeling the wetness between her legs. He added, "But I don't care what you want."

Sir pulled her onto her feet and slung her back over his shoulder, carrying her to a dead tree in the middle of the field. He put her down and pressed his large hand against her chest, pushing her against the bark. "Don't move."

"No one tells me what to do," she protested.

He stared into her eyes with such a look of possession it stole her breath away. "I do."

She lost herself in his gaze and nodded automatically.

He smirked. "That's right, princess. I control you." He whipped out a piece of rope from his swim trunks and tied her wrists together before lifting her arms above her head and slipping her bound wrists over the end of a broken branch.

Sir stood back and admired her stretched form.

"Don't look at me," Brie snapped.

"Not only will I look at you," he stated. "I will touch you." He brushed her nipples and slipped his hand between her legs, forcing a finger into her pussy. She gasped, pressing against the tree as she tried not to give into her lust for him.

"I feel your excitement. Your cunt tells no lies." He pulled his finger out and ran her wetness across Brie's lips. "Taste."

She licked her lips and sampled her salty sweetness before turning her head away as if in disgust.

He grabbed her chin and licked her lips. "Luscious…"

Sir thrust his tongue deep into her mouth, plundering her like the pirate he was pretending to be. Brie's body betrayed her, eagerly responding to his aggressive nature. It knew him too well to deny her Master pleasure.

"You are a wanton creature," he teased, leaving her desperate and needy as he looked around as if searching for something. Once he spotted what he was looking for, he left her, stating, "Your captor has better things to do."

Sir walked off leaving Brie bound to the tree. She sighed in contented frustration. She *loved* the way Sir played with her.

Brie watched curiously as he walked up to a crooked olive tree that split into two rickety fingers. He picked up something in the crook of the base and studied it. Then he counted out his steps as he walked farther away from her.

When Sir finally stopped, he rolled a large rock over in a sandy gullet. He knelt on the sand and began digging with his hands.

Brie shook her head, wondering what the heck he was up to. After many minutes of laborious work, she heard him cry out in triumph. She was dying to know what he'd found.

Thankfully, Sir satisfied her curiosity by walking back to her, hoisting a small chest over his shoulder and wearing a charming grin. It gave him a delightfully boyish appearance.

He put down the old chest and unlatched the rusty closure. Before opening the lid, he looked up at Brie and explained, "My father and I came out here to fish and play pirates every summer when I was a boy. He always hid something in the chest for me to find. I didn't think there would be anything this time, but old habits die hard. I had to check, but I can't imagine what he put in here."

Brie watched in fascination as he lifted the lid.

"Ah." Sir pulled out a bottle covered in sand. He wiped off the label and then sat down on the grass, shaking his head. "*Papà*…"

Brie watched silently from the tree, wishing she was free to go to him.

Sir held the bottle and stared at it as if he was being bombarded with memories. Finally, he spoke. "It is tradition in my family to share a bottle of Brunello di Montalcino as a rite of passage when a boy became a man. My father must have buried it when he visited my grandparents after his last European tour…" He added quietly, "How could he know he would never return?"

"Oh, Sir…" she said sorrowfully.

"No, Brie. I will not mourn him on this island." He looked into the trunk and took out a corkscrew. "I can think of an appropriate use for this wine." He stared at her as he licked his lips. "And I think he would approve."

Sir uncorked the old bottle with a satisfying pop and took a long sniff, closing his eyes to take in the bouquet. "Amazingly, it is still sweet." He lifted the bottle up and nodded at the sky before taking a swig. "Ahh…that's fine wine, *Papà*."

Sir walked over to Brie and shared the drink with her by taking another long draught from the bottle before kissing her. Red wine flooded her mouth with hints of musky berries and vanilla. She smiled when he pulled away. "That's delicious, Sir."

He cupped her breast and raised his eyebrow. "This is how I plan to enjoy his gift." Sir poured the red liquid onto her breast and leaned in, sucking on her nipple seductively. He lifted her wrists from the branch and untied her before forcing her down on her knees. Sir slipped out of his trunks and poured the wine over his rigid cock. "Suck me," he ordered.

Brie smiled, grateful for the chance to please her Master. As much as she'd enjoyed playing the spoiled princess, her joy was in pleasuring him. She ran her tongue over the length of his cock before concentrating on the smooth head of his shaft. When she pulled away, he poured more wine over it. She opened her mouth and took in the stream of the fermented grape. It was so wickedly hot to drink from his cock.

The wine ran down her chin and dripped onto her breast. He knelt down and put the bottle on the ground, ordering, "Lie on your back, but lift your ass off the ground."

She lay in the grass and lifted her butt up, spreading her legs for him. Sir ran his hands over her thighs, looking at her greedily. He took a swipe of her swollen clit with his tongue before picking up the bottle and pouring the wine over her pussy. He lapped it up with obvious pleasure.

"The best way to drink wine, babygirl." Sir did it again, drenching her sex with the red wine, but this time he settled in for a long session of cunnilingus. Brie moaned as he took her clit between his teeth and sucked hard before fluttering his tongue over it. She bucked against him, surprised by the intensity. He held her still, his fingers digging into her skin helping to state his authority over her.

She cried out when her pussy began pulsing in pleasure. He did not let up, demanding her climax with his tongue. "May I?" she asked between gasps.

He said nothing, but increased the pressure and tempo of his tongue as he inserted two fingers into her and began pumping vigorously. There was no stopping such aggressive stimulation and Brie's pussy burst with love for Sir.

He lapped up the mixture of wine and her watery juices, groaning in satisfaction as Brie's thighs trembled with aftershocks. He looked up from her mound and growled, "I'm coming for you, princess." He crawled up between her legs to position himself.

Sir took her face in his hands, looking her in the eyes as he plunged his cock into her fiery depths. "There is no escaping me…"

Brie focused on his mesmerizing gaze as he took her as his submissive, his goddess, his lover.

It was difficult to leave Isola d'Elba the following day. The hardest part by far was Sir's goodbye to his grandmother. The tiny woman started crying before Sir even announced they were leaving. She refused to let Sir go, whimpering, "*Non andare via*," over and over again.

Even his grandfather's stern command could not get her to release her desperate gasp on Sir. Brie could not bear to watch him pulling away from the sweet old woman again, and looked away.

It must have broken Sir's heart as well, for he called out Brie's name. When she met his gaze, he asked, "Would you be willing to return in six months?"

Brie nodded vigorously, thrilled at Sir's suggestion.

He turned back to his grandmother. "*Sei mesi, Nonna.*" She shook her head as if she didn't believe him. Sir touched his forehead to hers and said firmly, "*Sei mesi.*"

"*Promettere*?" the tiny woman whispered.

Sir smiled. "*Sì, Nonna.*"

Her tight grip slowly loosened, but the tears did not stop. She looked at Brie and commanded, "*Promettere.*"

Sir told Brie, "She is asking you to promise that I'll be back."

Brie took the old woman's arthritic hands in hers and said with confidence, "*Promettere.*" Whatever it took, Brie would make certain her grandson returned to her in six months' time.

With a gentle smile on her lips, his grandmother patted Brie's cheek and said in broken English, "Good girl."

Sir took Brie's hand and escorted her down the stairs before the old woman's tears began again. He guided her through the narrow streets, just as he had the first day they'd come to the island, but everything felt different now.

Brie had faced a lover from his past and their relationship had grown from the challenge of it—they were more united as a couple.

She felt the refreshing tonic of the island, the love of his *famiglia,* and the healing power of his father's gift would give them the strength they'd need for whatever lay ahead…

# Birthday Girl

Brie woke up wondering if Sir knew.

"Good morning, babygirl."

He grinned as he pulled the sheet away and presented her with a morning gift. Brie took his hardening shaft in her small hand and began caressing it with self-indulgence. Waking up this way was always a treat—making that connection with Sir before the day had a chance to break in.

She swirled her tongue around the ridge of his cock and sighed contentedly as she took the warm head of it into her mouth.

Sir tilted his head back and groaned, making Brie wet with his pleasure. She tasted his pre-come, which signaled that her mouth was exactly what his manhood desired.

"I want you to swallow, téa," he commanded.

She smiled with his cock still in her mouth. Her lips made a popping sound when she opened them to answer. "My pleasure, Master."

She tickled the frenulum with light flutterings of her tongue before taking the length of him deep in her throat. He grabbed the back of her head and began guiding her up and down his shaft, but it seemed this morning he wanted to take it slow—real slow.

That pleased Brie. When she concentrated on him like this, it invited a spiritual connection with him. As odd as it seemed, it stopped being about getting Sir to climax and became more about pleasing him. Sessions like this could last an hour, and in that time she would read his changing needs and fulfill them, all without bringing him over the edge.

It was during those long morning sessions that Sir would speak to her openly about her triumphs and failures. Always in a positive way that empowered her to succeed in the future.

"I noticed you were more relaxed last night, little sub. I do not think I have ever taken you so deeply in that position before."

Brie looked up at him and smiled without losing her rhythm or suction.

"Your body seems to be much more capable of yielding than it did the first time I taught you that position."

She nodded in agreement, still pleasuring his cock as she listened to his critique.

"Yet I know, téa, as deep as I can force myself into your pussy, there are areas here," he touched her temple lightly, "that you still have locked away."

She opened her mouth to protest, but he pushed her back down on his cock.

"Yes, little sub. I see it in your eyes, that hope I will not ask this or that of you. However, it is my intent to continue to push. Do not mistake my inaction at this point as future protocol."

Brie's heart rate sped up, wondering what he had planned for her. That welcomed excitement of being his and knowing whatever he asked would open a whole new world of sensations made her tremble inside.

"I, too, have areas I have been hesitant to tread. Just as I challenge you, I test my own boundaries."

He lifted his hand from the back of her head, allowing her to disengage from his cock.

"I love being yours," she purred.

He smiled as he brought her lips back down on his shaft and pushed for deeper penetration down the tight muscles of her throat. She willingly opened and took his entirety.

"That's my good girl. Now play with yourself as I come."

She drank his masculine release as she flicked her clit with enthusiasm. His praise and pleasure were gifts enough on this, her special day.

Sir reached down between her legs and joined in her fingering. Soon her pussy was surging with its own pleasure. He leaned over and whispered, "Happy birthday, babygirl."

That night, Sir presented Brie with a golden corset, a matching thong, black hose and a beautiful pair of stilettos. He told her to put them on and model the outfit for him.

When she came out of the bedroom, he had her turn before him so he could admire her pretty new ensemble from various angles. He whistled in appreciation as he picked up a delicate tiara from the table.

"Come to me, birthday girl."

Brie glided to him and smiled as he placed the delicate piece on her head.

"Perfect," he proclaimed with pride.

His praise was more precious than any gift.

Sir hadn't told her what his plans were for the evening, but the fact she was not wearing anything to cover her shapely bottom let her know it would be an in-house affair.

When the doorbell rang, he said with a mischievous glint in his eye, "Let the festivities begin…"

Sir placed Brie in the hallway and handed her a silver tray. He pulled out a silk blindfold from his suit pocket and told her as he tied it, "Stand still and follow my instructions, birthday girl."

Her body tingled with excitement as she wondered what surprises Sir had in store.

Sir opened the door and stated matter-of-factly, "Set the food in the kitchen, we will serve drinks in the living room."

A stranger's voice answered. "Thank you, Sir Davis. It is our honor to serve you tonight. We will make your night memorable."

"Actually, not garnering my notice would be considered a success by my standards."

"Of course."

Brie heard several people move past her without acknowledging her existence. She quickly surmised they were the caterers by the drifting aroma of exotic foods. After several minutes of listening to them setting up, the doorbell rang again.

Sir answered it and greeted the visitor. "Glad you could make it."

Brie was curious who it was and stood there anxiously, wishing she could take a quick peek.

That was when Sir revealed the game he had planned for the evening.

"As the invitation stated, you are not to speak until you leave your gift on the tray. *But* only give it to téa if she can guess who you are after your kiss."

Brie felt the heat rise to her cheeks as the mysterious visitor walked towards her. However, she noticed there were two sets of footsteps. One was definitely female. It was easy to tell by the sexy click of the woman's heels.

She had to commend Sir. *What a naughty and exciting way for a birthday girl to greet her guests!*

Brie held her breath as the first person leaned over and pressed his lips against hers. The chemistry of the kiss immediately alerted her as to whom it was, but it was the feeling of peace that sealed the deal. Brie smiled while his lips were still on hers.

When he pulled away, she announced confidently, "Tono Nosaka."

"Well done, toriko." She felt him drop something onto her tray. It was so light she surmised it must be a card.

The second person positioned herself for the kiss. Brie was all kinds of nervous, not really wanting to kiss a female. The image of Ms. Clark came to mind and she involuntarily shuddered.

However, her fear was dispelled the instant the soft lips met hers. An unexpected thrill went through her at the intimate contact, despite the gender of her guest. Brie had no idea who it was and silence filled the air as she contemplated who Tono might bring as a date. Thankfully, Brie heard a stifled giggle.

"Lea!"

"Damn, girl, I almost had you stumped and I could have kept my darn present." Lea dutifully placed her card on the tray.

"Do you have a joke for me?" Brie asked half-kiddingly.

"That's your present, girlfriend."

Brie pouted. "Then you can take it back, Lea. Really, I insist."

Lea patted her cheek in a motherly way. "No, sweetie. I'm not rude like you. While you stand there looking all pretty, I believe Tono and I will enjoy the delicious yumminess coming out of the kitchen."

*Are Tono and Lea a couple now?* Brie wondered.

"Yes, please enjoy," Sir told the two. "Since you are our first guests, they are still setting up the bar, but y—"

The doorbell rang, announcing new mystery guests.

Sir excused himself to answer the door.

Brie quivered. Who would be the next to kiss her? The pressure of guessing was exhilarating, but failure would be humiliating—there would be embarrassment for both parties if she guessed wrong.

Sir gave the same directions and a single male walked over to her. He lifted her chin and kissed her possessively, teasing her with his skilled tongue. Brie knew that kiss, but could not believe it.

"Rytsar?"

He placed his gift on her tray. "*Radost moya*, we meet again…"

Brie heard Sir slap his back with excessive force. "It was supposed to be a simple kiss, not an invasion."

Rytsar chuckled and answered with his seductive Russian accent, "I could not resist."

The two moved off to join Tono and Lea, leaving Brie alone. It was interesting to be the center of the party, but to play the role of blind observer.

She heard the clinking of glasses and Rytsar's guttural laughter just before the doorbell rang again. Brie bit her lip as she felt Sir walk past by her to answer the door.

This time it was a large group of people, all laughing and chatting. She distinctly heard Headmaster Coen's voice and felt sure he would be an easy one to pick out.

Most of the group moved past her and went directly to the kitchen. Only a few stayed behind to deliver gifts.

Brie couldn't help smiling when the first leaned over to kiss her. The scent of perfume let her know this was *not* Headmaster Coen. The woman's lips were supple and she surprised Brie by slipping a little tongue across her closed mouth.

Brie pulled back in astonishment. Which woman would dare to kiss her so brazenly? Brie shook her head, knowing the female was the wrong height to be Ms. Clark. That left only one person in her mind.

"Mary?"

"Seriously? There is no way you could know it was me." Mary pressed her fingers on the edges of Brie's blindfold. "You must be able to see. I thought for sure the tongue would throw you off."

"Ha! It was the fact you were so bold that gave you away, but I'm surprised you came. Last I heard, you'd disowned me."

"I had a little talk with Sir Davis and he persuaded me that you still need me. Who am I to deny such a convincing man, especially when I know he's right?" Mary grabbed Brie's chin and shook her head back and forth forcibly. "And aren't you just the cutest little gift table? Hope you like standing there while the rest of us enjoy your party."

Brie grinned. "I hope your present is worth the lackluster kiss you just gave me."

Mary grabbed her face in both hands and gave her a long and overly passionate kiss that left Brie breathless. Blonde Nemesis leaned in close and said affectionately, "Bitch."

Brie heard shifting of feet and knew that Mary's little performance had been appreciated by the male population watching.

"I'm off to get a rum and cock. Oh wait, I meant Coke…" Mary's laughter trailed behind her.

The next person took the tray from her before pressing his lips lightly on the back of her hand. The sweet but nonsexual gesture gave his identity away.

Brie bowed her head, pleased that he had come. "Mr. Gallant."

"Very good, Miss Bennett. Happy birthday. Another year down, a lifetime yet to enjoy." He handed back her tray and placed his gift upon it.

The person who followed wore aftershave, which hinted at his gender, but the kiss was sweet and gentle. When he pulled away, Brie furrowed her brow. Although it seemed remotely familiar, she was stumped. It was comparable to seeing a face she knew but could not place.

Brie tilted her head. "Could you kiss me again?"

Sir answered for him. "No, téa. Only one kiss allowed."

Brie sighed nervously. No one was coming to mind—she had no answer to give. "I'm not sure, Master."

"Still, you must provide a name," he insisted.

The possibility of being wrong in front of all these people was daunting. She stood silently, going over every Dom she'd been with.

Her guest took pity on her and leaned in, rubbing his cheek against hers. When she felt the hard scar tissue, Brie broke out in a smile, thrilled to be in the presence of the Dom.

"Captain."

"Yes, pet. Happy birthday. I must say, you look lovely collared."

She blushed with pleasure, grateful to be reconnected with the military hero. "Thank you, Captain. My birthday has been made better because you are here."

He chuckled lightly. "That is kind of you to say, pet." He placed his envelope on the tray and moved on.

A large hand with beefy fingers grasped her shoulder and firm lips met hers. There was no doubt who it was.

"Headmaster Coen," Brie said with a coy smile and bow. "I am honored you came."

"Tonight I'm simply Master Coen. No pomp and circumstance allowed."

"Yes, Master Coen."

Brie became curious when the next man stood before her and patted the top of her head as if she were a little girl. She was surprised, realizing that the man did not want to kiss her. Who would Sir invite who would react in such a way besides Mr. Gallant? Well, the answer was simple enough.

Brie grinned as she greeted him. "Mr. Reynolds!"

"Happy birthday, Brie." He placed his card on the tray, adding, "I miss you at the shop, but I hear big things are ahead for you. I couldn't be prouder. Congratulations. It couldn't happen to a nicer person."

"Thank you, Mr. Reynolds. Do you realize if you hadn't given me the job at the tobacco shop, none of this would be happening now?"

He said firmly, "Nonsense, Brie. I guarantee you were destined for success no matter how it found you. It is my pleasure to know such a fine young lady." She blushed at his kind words.

Mr. Reynolds moved to the side to make room for the final guest. She could smell his unique, spicy scent as he leaned forward, which alerted her to his identity even before he kissed her. Baron's thick lips pressed against hers, causing a pleasant warmth in her nether regions.

"I know you..." she murmured during his kiss. When he pulled away, she added, "Thank you for coming, Baron."

He dropped his envelope on the tray. "It's good to see you glowing like a birthday candle on your birthday, kitten."

"I'll never forget what you did for me, Baron. You literally saved me that night at the Kinky Goat."

"And I will forever be in your debt," Sir stated beside her.

"No, Sir Davis," Baron said with conviction. "You introduced me to Adriana. Even though we are parted, I am a better man for having known her. The debt of gratitude is mine."

Brie could hear the thudding sound of Sir patting Baron's muscular shoulder. "We all miss her. She was a remarkable woman."

It wasn't until then Brie understood that Baron had not broken up with his submissive, as she had first assumed. Her heart broke for the kindhearted Dom. "I didn't know she died, Baron," she whispered.

"Do not let it trouble you, kitten. This is your special day. Keep glowing; it makes me happy to see it."

She forced a bright smile, even though her heart hurt for him.

"That's better," Baron complimented.

She heard Sir walk away with him.

The party was in full swing. Brie caught snippets of conversations, much laughter, and the tinkling of glasses and utensils on plates. It was surreal but strangely exciting to be on the outside listening in. Brie cherished Sir's ability to think outside the box. He had given her an experience she could never have imagined and would never forget.

# The Uninvited

This time when the doorbell rang, Sir ran his fingertips over the swell of her breasts as he passed. Brie purred, aroused by her Master's touch.

"Good evening," Sir said when he opened the door. "I was concerned you wouldn't make it tonight. Please come in and kiss the birthday girl."

Brie was glad to hear manly steps, afraid that Ms. Clark might join the party. The new guest stopped before her and waited.

After several moments, Brie licked her lips and giggled nervously. Did he expect her to do something first?

The wave of masculinity that washed over her when their lips finally touched rendered her speechless.

"Well, téa?" Sir asked.

She answered quietly, "Marquis."

"Yes, pearl. Celestia wanted to come tonight, but family obligations took precedence. She hopes you understand."

"Of course, Marquis Gray. Please let her know that she was missed."

He placed their gift on the tray. "I will tell her that." Marquis added as a side-note to Sir, "You should consider strapping her down with her ass bare next year. I am curious if she would be as adept at knowing who canes her."

Brie trembled at the suggestion.

"Sorry, Gray. That privilege is mine and mine alone."

"A pity."

Sir responded sarcastically, "But let me show you to the kitchen. I believe there is an egg dish with your name on it."

"Oh, I wouldn't leave your station just yet, Sir Davis. I saw two guests parking as I entered the building. They should be arriving shortly."

A few seconds later the doorbell rang. Master Anderson's laughter filled Sir's apartment.

*This will be easy…*

His laughter suddenly stopped as if he had just remembered the rules to the game. Heels clicked up to her first. Brie held her breath as the smell of Cashmere, a perfume she found particularly alluring, enveloped her.

The woman's lips were firm, but inviting and her kiss compellingly feminine. Brie had never thought kissing a woman could be this much of a turn-on, but she found herself aroused by the gentle yet commanding kiss.

When she pulled away, it left Brie confused. Who would Master Anderson bring along with him who could kiss like that?

She would have considered Candy, the sub she had met on the subway, but she immediately dismissed her as a possibility. It had to be someone she knew well. Sir had been consistent in that part of the game.

"I honestly don't know, Master."

"No guesses, téa?"

Brie strained her eyes underneath the blindfold, wishing the material was thinner. She shook her head. "That kiss has left me confused, Master."

Brie could hear chuckles throughout Sir's apartment.

So it was a trick. Was it a man dressed and perfumed as a woman? *No…those lips were definitely feminine.*

"No gift for you," Ms. Clark replied frostily.

A cold chill ran down Brie's spine. *No!*

The mere thought of enjoying her kiss made Brie nauseous. She suddenly understood *exactly* how Ms. Clark had felt when Brie had given the Domme cunnilingus. It was not a pleasant feeling to be aroused by someone you disliked. If she could, Brie would have wiped her mouth to rid herself of the lingering sweetness of that damn kiss.

Master Anderson took pity on Brie and kissed her soundly, erasing the taint of that unwelcomed encounter.

"Thank you, Master Anderson," Brie said with sincere gratefulness.

He placed his gift on the tray. "I forgot we were playing this little game or I would have kept silent at the door."

"Admit it, you're just a loudmouth," Rytsar replied, coming up to join the conversation.

Brie giggled, enjoying the camaraderie of the three Doms who'd attended college together.

Sir moved beside Brie and was in the midst of taking off her blindfold when the doorbell rang again.

"Odd…" Sir muttered as Master Anderson answered the door for him.

The air seemed to leave the room when the door opened. No one spoke a word. The silence was deafening and made Brie exceedingly uncomfortable.

Finally, Brie heard Faelan growl, "What kind of game are you playing, Davis?"

Sir left Brie's side, stating angrily, "Rest assured, you were *not* invited to tonight's celebration."

"I was told to come to this apartment and deliver a note to a man named Alonzo."

"By whom?" Sir asked, his voice deathly calm.

"A woman by the name of Elizabeth. So tell me, *Sir* Davis, who the fuck is she? And who the hell is Alonzo?" Brie could hear the building ire in Faelan's voice.

Neither Dom was someone to trifle with. Brie knew things were about to get ugly between the two as she felt the negative energy crackling in the air. Brie ripped off her blindfold just as Mary moved past on her way to Faelan.

Sir answered Faelan tersely, "Neither are any of your business, Wallace. As far as I'm concerned, you can take that letter and shove it up her ass."

Mary smiled at Faelan as she approached the seething Dom. "It appears this 'Elizabeth' person was playing some kind of joke. Why not have a little fun at her expense? I can think of several things we can do with this letter. Shall we discuss it over dinner? Say, at my place?"

Faelan glared at Sir as if he was still convinced this had been Sir's doing, but he left without incident. Mary followed closely behind, obviously pleased with herself.

Sir shut the door, but Brie could feel the rage radiating from him. Rytsar grasped his shoulder. "Don't let her win the day."

Sir nodded. He glanced at Brie. It pleased her to see the ire slowly melt away from his countenance as he gazed at her. Finally he said, "I think I must turn you over my knee and spank you, téa. I did not give you permission to take off the blindfold."

Relief flooded her soul as Brie looked to the floor, hiding her smile. "Yes, Master. I need to be punished."

He strode over and took the tray from Brie's hands, handing it to Master Anderson, and informed her, "You will open these another day."

Sir picked her up and slung her over his shoulder, carrying her into the living room. Seeing that the couch was already occupied, Sir laid her over the taller curvature of the Tantra chair so that her ass was in perfect alignment for spanking.

"I think twenty-three swats are in order, don't you?"

The group voiced their approval.

Sir ran his hand over her bare ass cheeks before delivering his first smack. The sound of it echoed through the room and was forceful enough to make her skin tingle pleasantly.

"One…" Sir called out,

Brie looked up to see Lea grinning at her.

*Oh, this is fun…* she thought.

She let out a squeak at the second, more commanding swat.

"Harder," she heard Rytsar assert.

Sir was not one to follow another man's order. "Two…" He delivered a feather light smack and then followed it up by teasing her clit through the thong.

"Did all that kissing turn you on, téa?" he inquired, before slapping Brie's ass solidly twenty-one more times. Brie loved every minute of it as her friends watched her receive her full set of birthday spanks.

Sir ended it by saying, "Happy…"

Brie whimpered as he called out each word and spanked her with enthusiasm. "…birthday…my…tasty…little…sub."

Her buttocks smarted after his birthday wish. Sir rolled his finger over her pussy, the gold material soaked with her desire. Then he bent down and delivered a tender kiss to her red ass, whispering into her ear, "I plan to play with you tonight, princess. After your little party is over."

That simple comment had her dripping with anticipation.

He helped Brie off the chaise and gestured to the servers. One hurried over and presented two identical martinis to him on a golden tray.

Sir took them both and handed one to Brie. He looked to the friends gathered and said, "I raise my glass to this remarkable young woman beside me, in honor of the day she graced the world with her divine presence."

Brie was both pleased and embarrassed by his words. She gazed at the smiling faces of her friends and trainers, feeling a tremendous sense of joy.

Sir continued. "Here's wishing her much success in her blossoming film career."

"To Brie's future," Rytsar echoed.

Everyone raised their glasses in unison and drank to the toast.

Brie was overwhelmed and found it difficult to speak. "Thank you for coming tonight...and thank you for helping me grow as a person." She felt she might cry, so Brie finished quickly with, "I have never known such happiness."

The night played out like a beautiful fairytale, except for one uncomfortable moment.

Brie couldn't help noticing Ms. Clark staring at Rytsar the entire evening. There came a point when it became obvious to Brie that the Domme had finally determined she would engage the Russian Dom.

Ms. Clark presented herself before Rytsar and then sank to her knees in supplication. The whole room fell silent.

Sir quickly moved over to her, hissing, "Don't. This is not the time or the place."

Rytsar's icy stare made it apparent that Ms. Clark's dramatic gesture had not been appreciated. *What can Ms. Clark have done to the man to evoke such a callous response?*

The Domme raised her chin haughtily as she stood back up. "Another time, perhaps." She left the party soon after.

For the first time, Brie's heart ached for the woman. Ms. Clark had just humiliated herself in front of her peers in the hopes of reconciling some past mistake with Rytsar, and been unequivocally shot down.

The Russian Dom, although a sadist, had always seemed a thoughtful and generous man. Brie had to assume whatever Ms. Clark had done to him must have been something truly unforgiveable.

To witness such a scene was uncomfortable for all, but especially hard for Lea. She glanced at Brie. It was obvious how upset Lea was to see Ms. Clark hurting, but she did not leave Tono's side to run and comfort the Domme. That really surprised Brie and made her realize that she needed to arrange private 'girl talk' time with Lea. She was determined to find out what was going on with her best friend.

The tension in the room eased soon after Ms. Clark's departure, once Master Anderson decided to play a humorous round of 'pin the tail on the *pony*' with a willing sub. Brie had never laughed so hard in her life.

But the night turned into something intensely memorable when the server came out carrying her birthday cake. He set it down on the coffee table so everyone could admire it.

Brie walked up and put her hand to her lips when she saw the design. In the middle of the sheet cake were two condors flying around a yin-yang symbol. But it wasn't the traditional black and white design. The light side was represented by the sun and the dark side by the moon. Meaningful to Brie on so many levels…

Sir said tenderly, "Make a wish, Brie."

Her lips trembled as she attempted to blow out the candles, but it took several tries because she was so touched. She shrugged afterwards, explaining to her friends, "Oh, well, I didn't need a wish anyway. I already have everything I want." She smiled up at Sir.

"That's so cheesy, Brie," Lea teased.

Everyone laughed at Lea's perfect pun.

Brie grinned unashamedly. "Sorry, girlfriend. It's the truth."

She glanced around the room packed with people she held in high esteem, appreciating how incredibly lucky she was. As the festivities began to wind down, Brie found herself staring at Sir from across the room. He was laughing with Rytsar and Marquis. Sir looked genuinely happy—as happy as he had been in Italy.

She realized that he had made a family here that was every bit as dear to him as his blood relatives. This was the life he had purposely chosen.

Sir must have felt her gaze, because he glanced in Brie's direction. Her heart fluttered when he winked at her. How was it possible that one man could captivate her heart and soul?

As she continued to stare at him in loving admiration, a calm resolve flowed over Brie. She knew with clarity what she desired—what she *needed* to make her happiness complete.

# *Brie Surrenders her Heart*

# Birthday Presents

The moment the door had shut behind the last guest, Sir swept Brie off her feet. He did not speak as he carried her to the bedroom.

Her heart fluttered when she looked into her Master's eyes. There was no doubt he had special plans for his birthday girl. Brie buried her face in his chest and grinned. There was no better gift than to be Sir's plaything.

"Gold suits you, téa, but I prefer nude," he stated as he set her down next to the bed. He turned her around and unhooked the corset, then let it fall to the floor. Sir traced the lines left on her skin made by the corset laces, sending pleasurable sensations to settle between her legs. His fingers deftly relieved Brie of her panties as well.

"Yes, much better," Sir complimented. He pushed her gently onto the bed, grinding his hardening cock against the flesh of her ass.

"What should I try tonight that I haven't tried before?" Sir mused. He disappeared into the closet and returned with golden anal beads, a hairbrush and a delicate ball gag. He held up the metal gag and smiled charmingly as it swung back and forth in his hand. "Only the most beautiful ball gag for my birthday girl."

Although Brie was charmed by the elegance of the gag, the anal beads concerned her. "It's my first time with the beads, Master."

"I'm aware of this, téa. I enjoy introducing you to firsts and this one's been long overdue."

He seemed to be waiting for a response. Brie smiled to reassure him, opening her mouth to accept the gag. Normally, she did not care for ball gags but this one was unusually cute.

The metal ball was smooth and cold against her tongue. Sir secured it in place and turned her back to face him.

"Ah, my beautiful girl…" His hands ran down her curves to rest on her fleshy rump. He leaned over and growled into her ear, "I'm going to fill you with golden beads and slowly draw them out at the peak of your orgasm." Brie gasped as his thumb caressed her anus and he lightly applied pressure. Her pussy pulsated in response to his touch, despite her misgivings.

Sir left her side to turn on the stereo. Brie smiled when she heard the passionate melody of a lone violin. She was sure it was Alonzo's; the intensity of his playing added to the atmosphere in the room.

Sir took the lubricant off the bedside table and began liberally coating the metal beads. Each one was larger than the last, strung together with black cord.

Brie watched him work with curious fascination. It was humorous to think she had enjoyed butt plugs, the insertion of a long, flowing tail and even the challenge of double penetration, but never a common strand of anal beads. She was actually nervous.

Though she was an experienced sub, there were still a few items she found wicked and forbidden, and anal beads happened to be one of them. She assumed it stemmed from a childhood incident when she'd played a game of Truth or Dare with some neighborhood boys…

~~~~

*The twins were same tender young age as Brie, so it didn't seem weird to her when Marcus and Tommy suggested playing Truth or Dare in the backseat of their daddy's car. Cloaked in the darkness of twilight, she didn't feel any shame when they dared her to get naked in front of them. It seemed natural at the age of six. Besides, she'd been equally curious what boys looked like close up.*

*Everything was innocent enough until one of the boys produced a toy with pretty beads. Marcus said he'd found it in his mommy's dresser, and dared her to stuff the plastic beads up her butt. When she baulked, he assured her that if she did, he would try too. The over-eagerness of the boys frightened her a little, but she wasn't a quitter or a cheater—which was what they were calling her.*
~~~~

*Brie took the beads from him, but wasn't really sure what to do. When Marcus offered to help, she agreed and turned around, laying her chin against the top of the seat while she gazed out of the car's rear window with her naked butt in the air.*

*Just as he pressed the first bead against her tiny hole, headlights flooded the car. The boys' mother was coming home from work. The woman jumped out of her car and raced to them, screaming hysterically. The boys whined as they desperately tried to dress, begging Brie to get her clothes back on.*

~~~~

It had been a bad experience for all three; the lectures, the punishment, the shame…

"Lie down on the bed, téa, legs tucked under so your ass is presented."

Brie climbed onto Sir's bed, closing her eyes and sighing anxiously. Even though she was twenty-three now, and it was Master who wanted to play, there was a part of her that was leery of that simple sex toy.

Sir put the beads down and began rubbing and kneading her buttocks. Brie purred, letting the past melt away.

"That's it, babygirl. No reason to tense."

Brie automatically whimpered when he pressed his finger against her sphincter.

"You will find this enjoyable, téa. Relax…"

She trusted Sir and willed her body to allow his play. Sir swirled the smooth bead around her sensitive anus, teasing her with it before slowly inserting the bead inside. Her muscles stretched and then eagerly clamped around the golden bead, giving her a sense of fullness.

Sir began teasing her with the second one, which was slightly bigger than the first. "One by one, you will take all my beads," he stated, gently forcing them inside.

Brie moaned softly, liking the feel and challenge of the beads as well as the mystery of how they would feel when he pulled them back out. Each insertion felt like a delicious invasion; each tiny surrender made her wet.

"Good girl," he complimented when he was done. Sir stood back to admire his work. "You have the look of a toy, babygirl. All I have to do is pull on the string to bring you to life."

Brie looked behind her and smiled as she swayed her heart-shaped ass seductively as if to say, *Please play with me…*
~~~~

Sir picked up the brush and Brie readied herself for a swat. Instead, he took a handful of her hair and brushed it. Her scalp tingled from the contact of each individual bristle and she purred. He brushed through her long mane again, tugging lightly on it before running the brush through it.

She lifted her head back, her eyes half-closed in pleasure.

Sir said nothing as he continued to run the brush through her locks, continuing the movement down her back, past the ends of her hair. The bristles grazed her skin, caressing her with tiny points of ecstasy.

"Ooomm…" she moaned with the ball in her mouth. What he was doing felt so sensuous and loving.

Sir brushed her hair slowly and meticulously, stimulating her back with the instrument. Then he stopped and grabbed her waist, thrusting his shaft into her pussy several times before resuming the brushing.

It was delicious, the tantalizing myriad of sensations: the tingling, the light scratches, the fullness of the beads and Sir's commanding cock. She wished it could go on forever; however, Sir had much more in mind for Brie that night.

"On your back, téa, legs wide open."

She lay on the bed, moaning as she watched Sir kneel down and bury his face between her thighs. She arched her back as his tongue lapped her wet pussy just before unleashing its divine torture on her clit.

Panting and moaning soon filled the bedroom when his middle finger found its way inside her, and Sir began caressing her already swollen G-spot. He played her pussy in tune with the song, increasing the sensations to a concentrated level, only to ease away when the tempo changed. He knew his craft well, building her impending orgasm to startling heights.

Brie thrashed her head back and forth, craving blessed release.

Sir looked up from between her legs and chuckled. "Shall I take pity on my birthday girl?"

She nodded vigorously, the metal ball preventing her from screaming, *Please, I beg you!*

"Lay your head back, téa. Close your eyes and concentrate on the sensations I am about to create."

Sir began swirling his finger around her G-spot as he pulled the string attached to the beads taut. Brie's heart skipped a beat in anticipation, but suddenly he stopped. Sir reached up and undid her ball gag. "Eyes closed, my little sub, but I want your mouth open and vocal."

She smiled, remembering her first critique on the very first day of her training. "Yes, Master."

Sir resumed his ministrations, making her loins blaze with desire as he aggressively caressed her pussy. He pulled on the string, causing Brie to momentarily stiffen in fear. *Will it hurt?*

"Relax, babygirl. Let your Master have his way."

She concentrated on the raging orgasm, teetering on the precipice. "Have your way, Master," she pleaded.

A powerful contraction gripped her when his lips met her clit. She had no control now…

When the next contraction hit, Sir began slowly pulling out the first bead. Her body was a hotbed of electrical bursts, but the sensations instantly became focused on the erotic pressure of the bead, causing her anal muscles to spasm with orgasmic energy.

A new sound escaped her lips. It was the cry of her inner animal voicing its satisfaction.

Brie's body took over—her hips thrust upward; her thighs trembled uncontrollably from the intensity and longevity of the orgasm as Sir continued to tease her to climax by slowly and calculatedly pulling out bead after golden bead.

There was nothing left of her when he was done. She was floating on a cloud of sensations, sexually content on a level previously unknown to her.

Brie heard her Master's voice calling to her through the erotic mist in her mind. She had to focus on it to understand what he was saying. "Birthday girl."

Her eyes fluttered open and a slow smile spread across her lips. "Oh, Sir…"

He leaned over and kissed her forehead before collapsing beside her on the bed. "I take it you liked your gift?"

"Best present ever…"

He wrapped his muscular arm around her and let her continue to ride the ecstasy of the experience. Cuddling with Sir was just as prized as the mind-blowing sex.

Eventually he nuzzled her neck. "I was somewhat concerned tonight."

She turned her head and gave him a questioning look. "About what, Sir?"

"What your response would be to the beads."

"Why? I love everything you do to me."

"Your father informed me of your past experience with them."

Her jaw dropped. *Sir knew?*

"I fully expected you to tell me your history with the beads, but you never said a word."

Brie's mind was still reeling at the fact her father had told Sir about that humiliating experience. "But why would my father tell you, Sir?"

"He felt certain that childhood experience damaged you to the point you were susceptible to participating in similarly base activities. I assured him that you had shown no interest in anal beads, which seemed to pacify him somewhat." Sir raised his eyebrow. "Little did he know that he had given me your next lesson."

"I can't believe my father told you," Brie cried, covering her face.

Sir took her hands away and gently laid them on her chest. "I am grateful he was forthright since you failed to be as open."

Brie met his gaze, needing him to understand. "Sir, it's just that I trust you completely. I knew you wouldn't hurt me."

He ran his fingers through his hair. "Communication and trust are the foundations of our relationship, téa. I should never walk into a scene unaware that it holds a possible trigger for you."

"You're right. I'm sorry for putting you in that position." She lowered her eyes, but soon snuck a peek at him, curiosity driving her to ask the obvious question. "What else did my father share with you?"

He smiled, raising his eyebrow mischievously.

Brie stuck out her bottom lip when he did not answer, pleading with her eyes.

Sir chuckled and rolled off the bed to grab her tray of gifts. "Ready to open your presents?" He must have known he had her, because there was no way Brie could pass up a chance to find out what was inside all those envelopes.

He laid the tray on the bed and rejoined her. Brie searched through the gifts, wanting to open Lea's first. She grinned at Sir. "I can't wait to find out what she got me!"

His smirk belied the fact that he already knew.

Brie ripped open the envelope and read her message:

*I have created the perfect gift for you, Brie! I can hardly stand having to wait. Turn the card over to reveal your special surprise.*

She grinned at Sir as she turned it over, but then her smile disappeared. There was nothing written on the back. It was completely blank.

"Is this a joke?" she asked, waving the card at Sir.

He chuckled. "She's *your* friend."

Brie tossed it on the bed, formulating a plan to get even with the girl. She picked up Tono's envelope next.

"Interesting that you would choose that one," Sir commented off-handedly.

She tilted her head, now curious. "Why?"

"Their gifts are interconnected."

Brie giggled. "So Lea *did* get me a present after all!"

She was much more careful when she opened Tono's. He'd used special rice paper and painted his signature orchid on the front. She pulled out the thin parchment and read a simple haiku, each line written in traditional Japanese script, with the words written in English for her underneath:

*Together as one*
*In desire and spirit*
*An erotic gift*

Brie read it several times, but was unsure of its meaning. "Sir?"

He smiled, but shook his head. "Your surprise is not for me to reveal."

"But you know what it is?" she queried.

"Yes, little sub. There will be no more questions on the subject."

"Are all the gifts going to be equally mysterious?" she pouted.

He held up the tray and winked. "There's only one way to find out."

Brie took Rytsar's from the pile because it was extra thick and promising. What she pulled out looked like an official government document, but it was written in Russian. She held it up for Sir to see. "I don't know what this is."

He took the document and looked it over. A slow grin spread across his face. "It appears that Durov has given you the cabin by the lake."

Brie took the paper back and crushed it to her chest. "I can't believe he did that! When can we visit Russia again?"

Sir took the deed from her and folded it up carefully, stating, "Not for a quite a while, téa. Somebody has a documentary to introduce to the world."

"Then this must be the first place we visit—after your grandmother's, of course."

"I concur," he said agreeably.

Brie picked up a black envelope with her name neatly printed in silver. She found a photograph inside of a beautiful two-toned flogger of royal purple and black. On the back it read:

*A gift crafted especially for you. Enjoy its character, pearl.*
*Sincerest regards, Marquis*

"I wonder where it is," she mused, realizing that he had been limited by what could be placed on her tray.

"I believe Marquis left a package behind when he left."

"Oh, I can't wait to feel it! Well, maybe I can. I love opening gifts too much," Brie picked up another envelope. She found a wondrous variety of treasures within the cards, from a certificate for a designer leash from Captain to a weekend getaway compliments of Baron. Mr. Gallant had given her a formal dinner invitation, while Headmaster Coen had arranged a private play session for two at the newest club soon to open in Los Angeles. But Brie's personal favorite was a small framed picture of Sir standing beside Mr. Reynolds and his wife. It had been taken the night of the collaring.

Master Anderson's gift, however, tickled her because it had a humorous element:

*Inside your Master's car—on his seat, in fact—sits an indoor herb garden. This gift will benefit you in two ways, young Brie. Your Master can experience the tranquility of gardening, albeit on a smaller scale, and you can use the fruits of his labors to flavor your ever-improving culinary attempts.*
*Yours truly, Master Anderson*

Brie snickered as she handed over the card for Sir to read.

The last one on the tray was from Mary. Brie was extremely curious as to what Mary would consider an appropriate gift.

*This is my home phone number. I give you permission to call me, night or day. I don't normally give it out, and never to women. Consider yourself privileged, bitch.*
*~Mary*

Brie giggled, but understood how huge the gift was. Although she already had her cell phone number, giving Brie access to her home phone was the closest Mary had ever come to treating her like a real friend. She looked at Sir and smiled. "Mary gave me her number."

"Good. I think it's important you two keep in close contact, especially with the documentary coming out. You may need each other's support."

Brie put down the card and stared at him. "Do you really believe my work will be received badly, Sir?"

He played with a lock of her hair. "I believe that you will create polar reactions with it. Some will celebrate you for introducing them to the world of BDSM, while others will revile you for the debauchery you have unleashed on the world. Both reactions will be a challenge, and I want you surrounded by people who will keep you grounded. Miss Wilson is one such person."

Brie realized the gift might not be as personal as she first thought. "Did you suggest that she give me her number, Sir?"

"No, Brie. The only influence I had was in reminding her of your unique journey together. It was her decision to come to the party, as well as the type of gift to bring."

Brie kissed the phone number on the card. "It means a lot that I am the first girlfriend she's ever given her number to. But I must admit I'm tempted to call her at all hours of the night, just to test her resolve."

Sir frowned.

She kissed his downturned lips. "I'm just kidding, Sir. I would never be so immature." She made a mental note not to joke about Mary around him, but she knew Lea would have totally thought that was funny.

Picking up the photo of Sir, Brie stared at his serious, but gorgeous face. "You look so handsome, Master. I love this picture because it captures that moment before you collared me. You had no idea what was headed your way that night."

He took the photo from her and examined it critically.

Brie traced the outline of his face in the picture. "This is the look of a handsome condor, Sir. One about to claim his mate."

He tickled her ribs, causing her to squeal and squirm. "Such a disobedient little thing she was, too. What the hell was I thinking?"

# Condor Devotion

Brie smiled as she listened to the sound of his steady heartbeat. With his arms wrapped around her, she was safe to revel in the afterglow of his lovemaking. These moments were a little taste of heaven on earth.

Sir stirred beneath her. "Let me get up to turn out the lights. Stay here."

Brie's heart started racing when he got up and left the room. This was the opportunity she had been waiting for. She headed directly for the closet and got on her tiptoes to reach for the thin wooden box.

She carried it out and laid it on the bedside table. Taking a deep breath, she undid the latch and opened the lid, then took out the branding iron. In a fluid motion, she turned and knelt facing the door, her head bowed and the iron rod held up in petition.

She bit her lip as she waited for Sir's return, her heart beating like a hummingbird's wings. There was no fear in the offer, simply the deep-seated need to be marked as Sir's.

He entered the room and stopped in his tracks. "Téa."

She looked up at him from her kneeling position and begged earnestly, "Please…"

He stepped forward and took the brand from her hands. "The pain will be significant, téa. This is not a simple tattoo and cannot be covered up later should you dislike the results."

"I understand, Master."

He knelt down beside her and placed the rod back in her hands. "I cannot guarantee how the brand will heal, or what it will look like afterwards. It may not be pretty."

"Before I made any decisions, I googled it, Sir. I understand the risks." She touched his cheek, which was rough with five o'clock shadow. "I *need* to feel your mark on my skin. I want it to hurt."

"Why?"

She lowered her eyes, unsure if she could clearly explain the desire in her heart. "So that it counts. This brand will mark a profound point in my life…on my body and in my mind. A rite of passage. It will require both strength and courage to receive this brand of yours, but I've never wanted something as much."

Brie felt so strongly that she couldn't bear the thought of him denying her request, so she braved calling Sir by his given name. "Thane, my skin tingles with need of it; my soul cries out for it."

His eyes flashed with an emotion she could not identify. He cleared his throat and said huskily, "You should know I will not be the one to do it. Master Coen is the only one I trust to brand you."

She looked down to hide her smile, pleased her request had been granted.

Sir helped Brie to her feet. "This is as significant as a collaring, téa. I leave it up to you whether you want witnesses."

Brie wrapped her arms around his waist, pressing her cheek against his chest. "Sir, I would like it to be just us, under the stars."

He crushed her against him, but said nothing for several moments. Sir's voice was gruff with emotion when he spoke again. "I will give you a week to reconsider, téa. The passion you feel now may lose its luster as the date approaches."

"With all due respect, Sir, I don't think that will happen."

His fingers lightly caressed the small of her back—the area to be branded. His touch left her lightheaded and tingly all over. Brie sighed in contentment. "I love you, Master."

The night of the branding, Brie felt nothing but peace. There was no question in her mind that this was what she wanted. She'd been curious as to whether the fear of the hot iron would deter her from going through with it, but the reality was that the pain was what attracted her to the act. It wasn't a case of needing the pain for pain's sake; it was the challenge it presented. She wanted to make a great sacrifice to Sir. Even though she was not a masochist, if the act wasn't painful, it would cheapen the gift.

Brie felt akin to a Native American warrior as they drove out to meet Master Coen. She was out to prove her worth by way of a trial she had willingly accepted. It was both thrilling and terrifying.

Sir took her to a secluded beach under the stars where the muscle-bound Headmaster Coen stood waiting for them beside a fire ring with red-hot coals.

Brie briefly glanced at the flames and saw the iron rod nestled in the coals. For the first time she felt a quiver of fear and found it strangely exhilarating.

"Good evening, Davis." He nodded to Brie. "Miss Bennett."

Sir held out his hand. "Thank you for coming tonight."

"I am honored to be part of such a sacred event."

"Yes, thank you, Headmaster Coen," Brie echoed. "It eases my mind, as you and I have been through this once before."

He chuckled lightly. "Unlike last time, Miss Bennett, there will be no mind-fuck. If you get cold feet, you have only to say the word up until the moment the hot iron touches your skin. After that point, I will be committed to giving you a proper brand."

Brie took a nervous breath, the weight of what she was about to do hitting her full force. "I will do everything in my power not to move when that time comes, Master Coen."

"The branding itself is a quick process, but you'll find the challenge comes in the healing afterwards. It will take months for the burns to settle down and up to a year for the brand to heal. You also run the risk of infection. Do you understand what you are committing to?"

"I do, Master Coen. I understand and accept the risks."

"Fine." Master Coen turned to Sir. "I'm satisfied."

"Good." Sir then asked Brie, "Would you like to have a drink in honor of your courage before or after your branding?"

Hearing the word 'branding' spoken so casually caused her loins to contract in fearful pleasure.

*I'm really going to do this…*

"Afterwards, Sir. I want to be fully aware. I need to embrace this experience, body and soul."

Sir pulled a gag from his pocket. Brie had requested it, feeling it would give her a sense of control to be able to bite down on the cloth and muffle any screams she might make.

Brie turned and opened her mouth, allowing him to tie it securely in place. Afterwards, Sir turned her back to face him, cupping her cheeks in his warm palms. He stared deep into her eyes, caressing her soul with his intense gaze. When he seemed satisfied with her resolve, he commanded, "Undress for me, téa."

Numbness took over as she slowly undressed before the two men. The moment became surreal when she folded her clothes. Master Coen directed her to press her torso against the smooth trunk of a huge tree that had washed ashore. Even lying on its side, the log came up to Brie's waist.

"It will give you the support you need during the branding," he stated. "If you concentrate on leaning into the trunk, you will avoid flinching and possibly ruining the brand."

Brie pressed her waist against the smooth trunk, surprised that she would not be bound as she had been at the Training Center. Instead, Sir moved around to the other side of the trunk and took hold of both of her hands, his confident smile giving her courage.

She took a moment to glance around her, soaking in the beauty of their surroundings: the small crescent moon, the ghostly white foam of the waves constantly hitting the beach, and the night sky sprinkled with stars. All of it added to this unique moment in time. Brie felt connected to the universe; humans throughout history had performed rituals such as this to mark moments of deep spiritual significance.

"Look into my eyes, téa."

Brie focused her gaze solely on Sir.

He stroked her cheek with one hand while still holding tightly onto her wrists with the other, not breaking their bond. "I brand you tonight not only to mark you as mine, téa, but to celebrate your devotion and courage as my submissive. To others it may symbolize my ownership over you, but to me it announces my undying commitment. There will be no other in my life. Even death will not stand in the way of my commitment to you."

Brie sighed contentedly. She looked into his eyes again, noting the burning flames from the fire reflected in them. *I desire no other man to be Master over me.*

"Are you ready?" Master Coen asked from behind her.

Brie closed her eyes for a moment. Up until now, it had been a mental surrender. Now it would become a physical one. Still…the peace she felt gave her the courage to nod her head.

The headmaster meticulously cleaned off the area to limit the risk of infection before leaving her side to get the hot iron from the fire.

Sir squeezed her hands tightly and commanded, "Look at me, téa. Do not look away."

Brie opened her eyes, her gag preventing a verbal answer. She hoped to take her brand in brave silence, but was unsure if she would have the strength.

She felt Master Coen approach and held her breath. She stared at Sir, repeating in her head, *This is my outward expression of the love beating inside my heart.*

"It is good you have an expert doing this, Miss Bennett," Headmaster Coen informed her, his voice calm and reassuring. "I know what's needed to provide the desired result without causing excess damage." Coen placed his beefy hand on her small waist and barked, "Do not move."

Brie trembled involuntarily just before he pressed the red-hot metal firmly against the area just above her tailbone. She shrieked into the gag as a white-hot current of pain exploded from her back into her entire body. Despite the extreme pain, Brie kept her eyes open, not wanting to lose contact with Sir—even when the sickening sound of burning skin filled her ears.

Sir's grip kept her grounded and his eyes conveyed pride and courage. It gave her the ability to remain still. When Master Coen removed the brand, Brie was surprised to feel instant relief. As he carefully put the iron down, the Headmaster informed her, "Your body is in shock. However, it won't take long for the pain to return. Before it does, I'm going to dress the area to keep it free from infection."

He placed a cool cloth on her back and Brie groaned in appreciation, but he soon took it away, explaining as he worked, "I'm placing a special bandage on your skin. It has been soaked in a silver solution to provide an extra layer of protection against infection. As per your Master's request, I will also add compression to the burn. It will help minimize the scarring." While he wrapped a stocking-like garment around her waist, Sir untied her gag.

The lack of pain and the special care being taken had her worried, and she naïvely asked, "I will still have a scar, won't I?"

Master Coen's laughter filled the night air. "You cannot avoid it, Miss Bennett."

Sir gathered her gingerly in his arms, explaining, "Although I want to admire your mark, téa, I would like it to heal as cleanly as possible."

Brie rested her head on his chest, suddenly overtaken by a case of uncontrollable shivering. Shortly after, the pain came back with a vengeance. She began to pant, fighting back the urge to cry at the intensity of it.

Master Coen came to her with ibuprofen and a canteen of water. "It will help with the inflammation, as well as the pain." Brie looked at it warily, unsure whether she should suffer a little longer to prove her devotion.

"Take it, téa," Sir ordered.

That immediately ended any questions she had on the subject. Brie closed her eyes as Sir lifted the canteen and she swallowed the cold water, letting it ease her parched throat.

"It is important you keep hydrated, Miss Bennett," Master Coen instructed. "It will aid the healing process."

Brie bit her lip and nodded, a whimper almost escaping. With each passing minute, she was finding the pain increasingly unbearable.

"Are you ready?" Master Coen asked Sir.

Brie was shocked to see Sir begin unbuttoning his shirt, exposing his handsome chest to the cold night air. "Sir?"

He positioned her to his right as he braced himself against the thickest part of the log.

Brie gasped when she saw Master Coen clean off the area above Sir's heart before picking up a second brand from the fire.

Sir smiled down at Brie. "Why are you surprised? I would never ask you to do something that I was unwilling to do myself."

All the pain she'd been suffering melted away momentarily as she watched Headmaster Coen approach Sir with the new brand. Instead of a capital 'T', it was lowercase to represent Sir's name for her.

"Can I hold your hand, Master?" Brie whispered, suddenly overcome with emotion.

"Yes, téa."

She took his right hand and cradled it in both of hers. He gazed down at Brie with an aura of calm. "I wear this brand as a reminder to you of your place."

"Brace yourself," Master Coen ordered, just before he positioned the brand over Sir's chest muscle and pressed the metal onto the skin above his heart. Sir squeezed Brie's hand hard, but his gaze did not waver and no sound escaped his lips.

The smell of burning hair and skin greeted Brie's nostrils, making her feel woozy. When Master Coen pulled away, Sir let out an energetic grunt and roared, "Fuuuuck!"

He grabbed the back of Brie's neck with his right hand and sought out her lips. He kissed her deeply, stealing the breath from her lungs with his passion.

"Davis, I need to dress the area," Master Coen stated, interrupting their impassioned embrace.

Sir reluctantly pulled away and grinned down at her, his eyes flashing with lustful excitement. "Always the caretaker, isn't he?"

As he cooled the area before placing on the bandage, Master Coen said dryly, "It's what makes me the perfect headmaster. I don't let my emotions get in the way of my duty."

Sir snorted. "Although you may be right in some instances, it does make you a stick-in-the-mud. You might want to loosen up a bit, *Headmaster* Coen."

Master Coen shook his head as he handed Sir the ibuprofen and water. "Says the man who was forced to quit the position because he let his emotions get the better of him."

Sir stated emphatically, "Smartest thing I ever did, Coen."

His lips met Brie's again. She closed her eyes and let herself fly through the swirling emotions of love and agony, proud of the fact she now carried the mark of her Master.

# Exchanging Places

The weeks following the branding had a sweetness to them. Even though her brand was excruciatingly painful, each day involved a ritual Brie cherished. She would clean and dress Sir's burn and he, in turn, would care for hers.

It involved lathering the branded area, then carefully removing any discharge before rinsing off and patting the skin dry. Sir did it with such tenderness that it reminded Brie of an aftercare session, and she found that time they spent together pleasurable, which offset the pain.

The day Headmaster Coen gave them both a clean bill of health and declared the first stage of healing complete, Sir surprised Brie with a unique challenge when they returned home.

He placed cuffs, rope, and a Wartenberg wheel on the table next to the Tantra chair and held out the blindfold. "Tonight, we switch roles."

Brie felt butterflies as she took the blindfold from him. "I get to be in control, Sir?"

"Yes, téa."

She looked up at her Master and asked, "Why?"

"As a Dominant, it is crucial to experience submission to understand the psychology behind the dynamic. I believe that for a submissive, it is equally important to understand the role of the Dominant."

She glanced at the blindfold in her hand, her loins stirring at the thought.

Sir continued, "I am curious what you have learned and how you will use that knowledge tonight."

Brie said confidently, "I have had only the best teachers, Sir. I am positive you will enjoy the experience."

He leaned over and stroked her mound as he growled into her ear, "Dominate me."

She groaned, her pussy moistening his fingers with her excitement. Brie pulled away and smiled wickedly as she gave her first instructions. "Remove your shirt and belt, as well as your socks and shoes. Lay them beside the chair neatly and kneel before me."

He kept his eyes on her as he slowly followed her commands. She felt her stomach flutter when he lowered himself to the floor. Brie bit her lip as she put the silk blindfold over his eyes and tied it securely behind his head. She stepped back to admire this new view of her Master. He looked so manly and vulnerable, kneeling down before her with his naked chest and black blindfold.

"Ah, the allure of the unknown. Where will I touch you?" she purred.

A smile played across his lips. It pleased her greatly that he remembered that he'd used those words on her right after the collaring ceremony.

"I want you to lie on the Tantra chair, Sir, hands above your head."

"On my back or stomach, téa?"

She'd forgotten to be specific in her instructions. "On your back, Sir."

He stood up and felt for the lounger, lying down on it with masculine grace.

Brie bit her lip. *Where to begin?*

She picked up the gold cuffs Rytsar had given her. Would he have ever expected they would be used in this way?

*Probably not…*

Brie grinned as she moved to the head of the Tantra chair, feeling incredibly wicked as she got ready to bind her Master. Brie's heart raced as she tightened each cuff around one of his wrists. She watched him open and close his fists, getting used to the restriction. It was an unexpected turn-on for her.

Moving back to stand beside him, she carefully straddled the chair so that her pussy hovered just above his cock. "Don't move, Sir…" she commanded before her lips landed on his hairy chest. She left a trail of kisses across his muscled torso, ending with a lick of his right nipple.

But his lips were irresistible, so she kissed her way up to them and claimed them for her own. She started off with light butterfly kisses and then nibbled on his bottom lip. His deep, passionate kisses called to her…but in true Dominant form, she denied her own pleasure to intensify his and pulled away.

"I know what I want," she announced. Brie left the chair and went to the kitchen to get a large strawberry from the pantry. The thought of feeding it to Sir made her quiver inside.

Brie returned and straddled him again, this time pressing herself against his hardening cock. "Open your mouth, Sir."

He did so immediately.

*Such a good Master…* she thought, warming up to her new role.

Brie put the ripe strawberry to his lips. "Take a bite."

She watched his teeth break the skin of the soft fruit and juice burst forth, covering his lips. She took the strawberry away and leaned over to lick the sweet nectar. "That's very nice, Sir," she complimented, before returning it to his lips. She enjoyed the sensual vision as he took another bite.

But the urge to consume his lips became too much for her. She discarded the rest and kissed him deeply, exploring Sir's mouth, running her tongue over his teeth, and sparring playfully with his tongue. She ground against him as she made love to his mouth.

His hands came down and he encased her in his cuffed embrace, pressing her against his shaft as he moved his pelvis in time with hers.

She tsked. "You are being very bad, Sir." Brie lifted his hands back up above his head and left the lounger to grab the rope. With a loop of the rope and a few quick knots she had picked up from Tono, she had Sir's cuffs secured to the chair so that he could not disobey her again.

"I apologize for my over-enthusiasm, téa."

She was not buying it. "I believe it was willful disobedience. Therefore you must be punished."

She could read amusement in his expression. "As you wish, téa."

Brie picked up the Wartenberg wheel before straddling him again. She ran the spiky wheel over the inside of her own arm to get an idea of what kind of pressure to use. "Ooh…" she gasped, having pressed too hard, leaving tiny but deep indentations on her skin. She would have to use lighter pressure on Sir.

Before she began, she warned, "Feel free to call a safe word at any point, for I will not be asking." It was another one of his best lines.

Sir grinned. "Thank you for the reminder, téa. You have me more than a little curious now."

She answered his curiosity by rolling the sharp wheel over his stomach without warning. He jumped at the wheel's first contact, but forced his muscles to relax even as goosebumps rose on his skin. She felt his erection harden even more underneath her as she continued to mark trails across his stomach with the wicked tool. It was clear that he liked the stimulation of it too much.

"Punishment should not be pleasurable," she observed aloud. She leaned over and put the wheel back on the table, saving it for later.

"I have something more effective in mind." Brie undid his pants and eased Sir's shaft from the confines of his briefs. She pushed the material away so that his handsome cock was exposed.

Using a strategy Tono was famous for, Brie teased Sir's cock. It became her plaything as she stroked it with the lightest of brushes, tickled it with the ends of her hair, and on rare occasion, gave it a chaste kiss on the tip.

Sir's groans and stiff cock let her know that she was having the desired effect.

"Naughty Sirs get teased, not pleased," she warned him.

Brie left the chair again and quietly acquired a piece of ice from the freezer. She didn't want him to have any clue what was coming.

Brie slipped off her panties before climbing onto him again. She wanted Sir to feel her warmth and dragged her wet pussy over the length of his cock, teasing the head of it with her opening before abruptly leaving him.

"Prove yourself worthy, Sir. Do not move," she commanded as she placed the ice on the base of his shaft. His balls immediately responded, retracting from the cold. She watched Sir grit his teeth as he held himself still. Brie slowly dragged the ice up the length of his cock and back down, then she leaned over and licked the cold water that clung to it.

Sir grunted in pleasure, making her stomach flutter again.

Brie retraced his cock with the cube of ice, knowing the thrill that opposite temperatures brought to one's senses. She licked his cock, this time taking the head of his shaft into her warm mouth and sucking hard before letting go.

"You are cruel," he complained lustfully.

Brie grinned, taking it as a compliment. She continued to play with the ice until it had entirely melted. As a parting punishment, Brie took hold of his manhood and slowly descended on it, deep-throating him for only a few seconds before pulling back up.

He groaned again, thrusting his pelvis upwards, silently asking for more.

Brie smiled when she saw the bead of pre-come form on the tip of his cock. It was going to taste delicious.

"Will you be good now, Sir?"

He smiled when he answered, "Yes, téa."

"Lose the smirk when you say that, Sir," she admonished.

She could see him struggle not to smile. It took a few moments before he could say with a straight face, "I will obey, téa."

"Good Master."

Brie wasn't quite ready for their session to be over. "I would like to get another toy, Sir."

Sir corrected her gently, "Reword the statement as a Dominant, téa."

Brie blushed as she rephrased it. "Remain still until I return, Sir."

Knowing that leaving him unattended while bound was unsafe, Brie ran down the hall and quickly gathered the candle and matches. She returned, giggling like a little girl and out of breath.

Brie realized that she wasn't coming off as very dominant. Not wanting to fail her assignment, she set the items down and took a couple of moments to gather herself by closing her eyes. She put herself in Sir's shoes—cuffed and tied down, his eyes blinded and his sex exposed, defenseless… It was her job to heighten the sense of anticipation.

She walked around the lounger slowly, liking the way her heels clicked on the marble floor. "We must remove these clothes," she announced. Brie pulled down his pants and briefs in a rough, swift motion.

*Oh, that was sexy*, she thought, feeling a sensual rush.

Sir's rock-hard cock affirmed that he felt the same. She denied her need no longer and took a long lick of his cock, savoring the tang of his pre-come. *Soon, Brie, soon…* she assured herself as her pussy pulsated with mounting desire.

She settled down on his cock again, her wet lips encasing him without providing the relief of penetration. She struck a match and lit the candle, letting it burn for several moments to allow the scent of jasmine to fill the air.

Just as she was about to pour it on his chest, Sir remarked, "Téa, you may want to cover the area in massaging oil first, unless your intent is to wax my body hair."

He said it nonchalantly, as if he didn't care one way or the other, but Brie could have died. She could just imagine Sir's body with a crisscross of missing hair after she was finished.

In a calm, Dominant voice, Brie answered, "That was the plan, Sir, but I do not fault you for voicing concern."

She placed the candle on the table and went back into the bedroom closet to procure the needed oil. She came back, taking long, confident strides so that her walk would echo throughout the apartment.

Before returning to his side, she removed all of her clothing, leaving only the stilettos on. Brie rubbed a glistening layer of oil over his chest, stomach, and pelvic area. Then she cleaned off her hands, picked up the burning candle and straddled him again.

Brie leaned down and whispered, "Embrace the hot caress, Sir..." as she slowly poured a small line of wax down his right chest muscle, covering his nipple.

He let out a long breath, but remained still and quiet.

Brie poured a second line, imitating the 't' brand on the left side of his chest. She poured a thicker line down the middle of his torso, starting at his sternum and going all the way down to his lower stomach. When she noticed the hot wax pooling in his belly button, she quickly spread it outward so the heat would not concentrate in that one area and burn him.

Brie shook her head, realizing that being the Dominant was serious business. Even a simple candle could cause harm if she wasn't careful. Although she had said she wouldn't ask, she needed to know. "Color?"

"Green, téa."

She breathed a sigh of relief and poured a second line to cross the giant lowercase 't'.

"I'm marking my territory," she explained.

Brie pushed herself down onto Sir's ankles so she had free access to his entire pelvic region. "I love your cock, Sir."

His passionate groan alerted her that he knew exactly what she meant by that statement. Brie carefully poured a thin line of candle wax down the length of his shaft. Droplets fell on either side, giving him extra sensation.

She poured the corresponding line of the 't' to mark his groin as hers.

"Now that's sexy," she remarked, blowing out her candle and picking up the Wartenberg wheel.

She rolled the instrument, starting at his knee and slowly trailing it up to his pelvis. This time, Sir moaned loudly. Brie felt a gush of wetness in response to his cry. Instead of asking him to state his color, she observed the thick hardness of his cock.

Just like last time, playing with the Wartenberg wheel seemed to have an erotic effect on him. She trailed it up the opposite thigh, stopping just before she reached his scrotum. His cock twitched of its own accord.

She turned around and lightly rolled it over the sole of his left foot. He gasped, trying hard to keep his foot still. It was entertaining, so she used the instrument on his right sole and received the same response. She used it on various parts of his body, keeping him guessing where stimulation would come next.

Brie was thrilled to see his cock pulsing with each beat of his heart, hard and ready for *her* pleasure. She had denied herself long enough. It was time to fulfill a fantasy she'd held for quite some time…

She rubbed the wax off his cock and cleaned off the oil with a warm cloth. Both actions only added to his sensual torture. Brie kissed his princely shaft, tracing her tongue across the ridge of his cock and tickling his frenulum for added fun.

"Téa…" he groaned.

"Yes, Master. Your time has come," she purred, as she eased her wet pussy onto his cock and slowly took the fullness of Sir into her body.

He threw his head back. "Oh, God."

"The third day of my training, I had a fantasy about you, Sir."

"You…did?" he panted as she moved up and down on his shaft.

"I did. And now you are going to make that fantasy come true."

He let out a low, tortured groan.

"In my fantasy, I told you not to hold back. To come quickly, thinking only of yourself. I want you to do that now."

He shook his head.

"Yes, Master. I am going to fuck you hard and you are going to come inside me with no hesitation." She added with mirth, "Do you understand?"

He licked his lips before replying with a strained, "I do."

"Good. My greatest pleasure is feeling your hot come inside me, Sir." Brie braced her hands carefully on his chest to avoid the brand. "Give me my pleasure."

Brie began fucking him with abandon, taking him deep and riding him hard.

Sir's back arched and his jaw went slack just before his pelvis began to thrust. Brie cried out as he released his pleasure in savage bursts. She screamed, "Yes! Yes!", forcing him deeper as he delivered his seed.

Chills went through her body, the power of his orgasm overwhelming and erotic. She stopped and laid her head on his chest. Her pussy began pulsing violently as she joined him, her inner muscles contracting around his cock in blessed release.

"That…was…amazing!" she gasped between breaths.

He gave her one final thrust. "I liked your fantasy, téa."

She listened to his rapidly beating heart, trying not to grin like a fool. *What an experience!* Topping Sir had been more exciting than she'd thought, although she was certain she hadn't made a good Domme.

"Undo the cuffs, téa. My hands are losing circulation."

Brie quickly disengaged herself to get the key. She noticed his hands were turning blue, a sign of tight restriction. "I'm sorry, Sir." She rubbed his wrists, trying to aid his circulation.

He chuckled. "No need to worry, little sub. No harm done."

"I never truly understood how hard it is to Dom a scene. It's a lot of responsibility, Sir, even though it has its perks."

He ordered her to straddle him, grabbing her waist and grinding against her. "You did an adequate job for your first time."

"I know I made several mistakes, Sir."

"Knowing your tools and how to use them is essential before you start a scene. But I will say that I was impressed with your use of the Wartenberg wheel."

She rubbed his chest with a pleased smile, gently taking off bits of wax. She admitted, "I thought because I had experienced candles that I knew enough to use them."

"I would have stopped you if I was concerned, babygirl."

She leaned over and kissed him on the lips. "At least you advised me before I gave you a full body waxing."

"Rookie mistake, and one I was not willing to suffer." Brie's head bounced up and down on his chest with the force of his laughter.

"I'm grateful, Sir. I love your hairy chest."

He pulled the blindfold off. "You have made me ravenous with all your teasing. Now I will require *you* to come, slave." Sir dug his hands into the flesh of her ass and thrust himself deep inside her pussy without warning.

She moaned at the forceful entry but quickly adapted herself to his rhythm.

"I will fuck you hard and fast until that pussy is quivering from over-use."

"Yes, Master. Use me, please…"

# Dinner with Gallant

Brie had been working long hours with Mr. Holloway's best film editor, Fehér, as well as his graphics team. The progress they were making was encouraging—so much so that Mr. Holloway had started contacting select theaters, offering them exclusive rights to the initial release. He explained to Brie, "Because it's a documentary, we pick a few key theaters and let word of mouth, as well as carefully placed press releases, draw interest. If I've done my job well, the bigger chains will start asking to show the film in their own theaters once it begins to build steam. Although documentaries are not an easy sell, they're not impossible," he said with a cunning smile. "And I like a good challenge." He exuded the confidence of a Dom, giving Brie pleasant shivers.

The prospect of the upcoming release was exciting, but equally overwhelming. The relentless schedule was starting to wear on Brie. She counted herself lucky when Fehér came down with food poisoning and they all went home early one afternoon. She phoned Sir, who instructed her to take advantage of the break and set up the belated birthday dinner with Mr. Gallant.

She was thrilled to finally be dining with her former teacher and his elegant wife. Brie had never had the chance to get to know the statuesque woman because Mr. Gallant was a private man, mixing his personal life with work as little as possible.

But tonight, as a special gift to her, she would be allowed into their personal lives. It meant the world to Brie. She greatly admired the man who'd been her teacher throughout her six-week training.

Brie undressed except for her beloved collar and waited for Sir at the door, following the ritual greeting he had assigned her at the Training Center. She smiled as she knelt, remembering his command: "Legs closed, arms behind your back so that your breasts are presented for my pleasure."

She bowed her head when she heard him. Sir entered and slowly shut the door behind him. He placed his keys on the counter before putting his hand on her head. Brie felt the familiar jolt of electricity her Master's touch inspired.

His low, commanding voice warmed her spirit. "Stand and serve your Master."

Brie stood up gracefully and looked into his luminous eyes. It was clear he had missed this simple ritual as much as she had due to her long hours working on the film.

"Go to the couch and lean over the arm."

Her heart sped up as she walked to the sofa and pressed her torso against it in an inviting pose for her Master. She purred when she felt his fingers petting her sex.

"I will take my pleasure now," he stated as he unzipped his pants and rubbed his cock up and down her outer lips. Before she was fully ready, he forced himself inside. Brie gasped. The friction and tightness were tantalizing.

He grabbed her hips and thrust with more power. Brie cried out, challenged by his strokes.

It seemed to turn Sir on, and he began fucking her with more gusto.

Brie closed her eyes and threw her head back. This was the exact connection she'd needed, the release her body and soul had longed for over the hectic weeks she'd suffered. Brie wanted to feel the thick release of her Master's come.

She pressed against him and moaned loudly to let him know her pleasure. Sir did not disappoint. Her buttocks rippled with his ardent pounding.

*Bliss…*

"Good evening, Sir Davis," the diminutive but commanding Dom said when he opened the door.

"Mr. Gallant," Sir replied, shaking his hand firmly.

Mr. Gallant turned to Brie and smiled. "And welcome, Miss Bennett. It's a pleasure to have you join us tonight. The other guests have already arrived and my wife is currently seeing to their needs, otherwise she would have met you at the door as well."

Mr. Gallant led them to a formal dining room. Brie was thrilled to see who was seated at the table. "Captain!"

The older gentleman with the misshapen face and sexy eye-patch stood up. "Miss Bennett, it's good to see you again."

The submissive sitting next to him was even more of a surprise. "Candy, I didn't expect to see you here!" Brie asked Sir, "May I go and hug her, Sir?"

Mr. Gallant corrected Brie. "In my home, we do not adhere to strict formalities. Consider it a vanilla setting and behave accordingly."

Brie was surprised by his request, but honored it. She looked at Sir, who gave her a slight nod.

She scooted around the table to give Candy a big hug. There was no missing the fancy pet collar gracing the girl's neck. Brie grinned. "Seeing you again is like getting an extra birthday present, Candy. I've often wondered what happened to you after you finished training."

Candy's cheeks colored an adorable shade of pink when she looked at Captain. "The night of my graduation ceremony, I was introduced to this gentleman. I have been captivated by him ever since."

Captain patted her chair, giving a silent command for her to sit back down. After Candy and Brie had taken their seats, he explained, "If you remember our night together, Miss Bennett, you may recall how I believed your blonde classmate was better suited for me."

"I remember the night well, sir, but not for that reason."

He chuckled politely. "Kind of you to say, Miss Bennett, but I was rather blunt. It turns out that you were correct. The outer shell of a woman does not matter. It is the heart that defines her." He looked at Candy thoughtfully. "I have never encountered such a loyal or tender-hearted creature." He petted her hair lightly. "She just happens to be a comely little thing as well."

Candy closed her eyes and leaned into his caress. It was easy to see she was equally enamored with him.

"To be honest, Candy," Brie explained, "when I saw you scening with Tono at The Haven a while back, I wondered if the two of you were a couple. I never suspected the Captain would be the one to capture your heart." She suddenly realized that sounded rude and added, "But he is a most wonderful choice."

Candy's eyes sparkled when she told Brie, "Captain wanted me to be certain, and allowed me the pleasure of many Doms before he consented to collar me as his pet."

"Youth should not be wasted on one as old as me," Captain stated.

Candy shook her head, smiling at him. It was a tender way to disagree with his statement. "Fortunately, Captain eventually came to the same conclusion I did." She touched his deformed face and said with confidence, "I was born to be his pet."

"Did I miss the formal collaring ceremony?" Brie asked, concerned her hectic life had prevented her from being at such a momentous event.

Captain answered for Candy. "No, Miss Bennett. I have no need for such pomp and circumstance. A commitment between us in private is as binding as any communal ceremony."

"I quite agree," Sir interjected.

Brie looked at Candy again, marveling at her youthful, glowing appearance. "You know, you don't even look like the same girl I met on the bus."

"I'm *not*. My whole life has changed since my training." She glanced at Captain again. "I never dreamed a Dom could love or care for me so well."

Captain lifted her chin up, gazing into her eyes. He stated proudly, "I enjoy spoiling my pet." It was sweet to see their blossoming connection.

Mr. Gallant guided his wife over to Brie and said, "Miss Bennett, I feel remiss. I have not introduced you formally to my beautiful wife."

Brie faced the exotic Amazon, whose dark brown skin contrasted beautifully against Mr. Gallant's pale skin. Their difference in height contrasted with equal and complementing severity.

"Miss Bennett, this is Ena. My wife and companion of fifteen years."

The submissives bowed to each other. Brie almost felt she was in the presence of royalty because of how elegantly Ena held herself, and how respectfully Mr. Gallant treated her.

Ena's voice was warm and dignified. "It is an honor to have you grace our home tonight, Miss Bennett. My husband has spoken fondly of you on numerous occasions."

"Truly, the honor is mine," Brie replied. "Your strong marriage is an inspiration to me."

Brie noticed Sir looked at her strangely. Had she spoken out of turn?

Ena's smile was enchanting. "That is kind of you to say, but it is my husband I must thank. He cares for me well."

"Nonsense, Ena," Mr. Gallant corrected. "Your intelligence and grace cover any inadequacies I bring to the table."

The beauty blushed and looked at Mr. Gallant coyly.

"And she remains modest to this day. Is it any wonder I cherish her?" He took his wife's hand and kissed it.

Her eyes held a look of such intense love that it touched Brie deeply. To still have that much respect and passion for one another after fifteen years together… She sat down beside Sir, feeling warm from their happiness.

"Should I get the girls now, Husband?" Ena asked Mr. Gallant.

Brie blurted out, "You have children?"

Ena smiled. "Yes, two young girls, aged eight and twelve."

Brie returned the smile, surprised and pleased by the revelation.

"Miss Bennett, it is the reason we keep to an informal protocol in our home. What looks informal to the outsider is actually formal between the two of us. We have transformed everyday phrases, titles and actions to have personal significance to us."

"That's ingenious," Brie complimented. "You can go anywhere and still remain as formal as you desire, even in public."

Mr. Gallant nodded. "It was born out of necessity. Raising two girls, it was important to us to keep our D/s life separate from them."

"But why?" Brie asked, intrigued.

"We both believe that someone who chooses this lifestyle should do it because it is an inner calling, not simply because they were exposed to it as children. I will be fine if my girls grow up and do not venture into this lifestyle. As long as they find mates who treat them with respect and love, I will be satisfied."

Sir inquired, "And if they decide to seek D/s?"

Ena replied with a pleased smile, "Then they couldn't have a better teacher than their father, could they?"

Brie was curious. "Is it difficult living this lifestyle with a young family, Mr. Gallant?"

"It takes careful planning and constant communication. Just like any marriage, children are a huge commitment. At times, their needs must supersede your own. However, that cannot be allowed to consume the marriage itself. For a D/s relationship—for any relationship, really—the partners must cut out time to care for and support one another. It's essential."

Captain put his arm around his pet. "Luckily, that is not something the two of us must worry about."

"Yes, Captain. We have many years to play," Candy agreed, fingering her new collar.

Brie lightly touched her own, and smiled to herself. She remembered when it used to rub against her neck, reminding her of its presence. Over the months, it had become a part of her. The only time she noticed it now was when Sir took it off for certain scenes. Those times that he did made her realize how safe she felt when the collar was securely around her neck, and how vulnerable she felt without it.

"So should I get them, Husband?" Ena politely asked again, with a slight bow of her head.

"Please do, my wife. I am certain they will enjoy meeting our guests."

When the two young ladies entered the dining room, they instantly ran to Mr. Gallant. "Daddy!"

The honest affection was endearing. Brie noted that the girls had an exotic beauty common with the mixing of races. Incredibly, the two girls were even more striking than their mother.

After formal introductions, the girls sat down on either side of Mr. Gallant. As Ena was placing the first of the dishes on the table, Candy suddenly said, "Oh, wait!"

Everyone stared at her.

"Um… You see, I have something for Miss Bennett." She quickly slid a business card over to Brie.

Brie picked it up with trembling fingers. It was worn at the edges, but still intact.

Candy apologized, "It isn't in the same shape as when you gave it to me. You see, I held it many times those weeks before training."

Brie looked down and smiled when she read:

*The Submissive Training Center*

*25 Years of Excellence*

Sir looked at its ragged condition and offered, "I have several in my wallet if you would like a new one, Brie."

Brie held it to her heart and closed her eyes in contented bliss. The card had made it back home…

"I meant to give it to you sooner," Candy explained, "but I kept forgetting. I knew how special it was to me and assumed by the wear when I got it that you might want it back."

Brie opened her eyes, suddenly feeling a little foolish. "No problem. It was yours to keep, but I'll admit I'm thrilled to have it in my hands again."

Sir chuckled. "All this sentimentality over a business card?"

"This is the one you gave me, Sir."

"Is it now?" he said, taking it from her. "Well, if that's the case, maybe we should frame it."

She had been thinking the same thing. "That would be lovely, Sir."

He laughed, kissing the top of her head. "I was only joking, but if it means that much to you, I'll frame it myself." He tucked the card in his wallet, which he then placed back in his suit jacket. When he glanced back at her, he gave a private wink.

Her heart did a flip-flop. Could she love the man more?

# Best Intentions

It had been a month since her birthday party, but what had happened between Ms. Clark and Rytsar still bothered Brie. Sir had always maintained that no questions were off limits, so one morning while she was straightening the kitchen, she inquired casually, "Sir, may I ask what happened between Rytsar and Ms. Clark? It was shocking to see her bow in front of him."

Sir gave an irritated sigh. "Durov knew you would eventually ask. He's given me permission to speak about it, because he was upset that your special night had been tainted by her unseemly display."

"But it wasn't his fault, Sir. I don't blame Rytsar. If you feel it's best I remain in the dark, I trust your judgment and will not ask again."

"It was for his sake that I have kept silent. I can only give you minimal details, but not one word can be repeated."

"I give my word not to tell anyone, Sir."

His eyes narrowed with anger when he started speaking. "I'm furious that she put him in that position in front of so many. It was inappropriate and manipulative. All these years I have supported her, but she pulled that even after I warned her not to."

"It seems she still has deep feelings for Rytsar."

"You may be surprised to know it was mutual in the beginning. The sexual attraction between the two was tangible. I remember how surprised I was, as they are both uncompromising personalities, but Dominants have been known to partner up. It's not unheard of, simply unusual."

Brie was more than a little startled to hear that Rytsar had once been attracted to the stern Dominatrix. "Hard to imagine either of them being willing to submit to the other."

He nodded. "Rytsar was an uncompromising Dominant even then, having been raised since adolescence to indulge in his sadistic ways."

"What do you know of Ms. Clark's background, Sir?"

Sir was curt with his reply. "It's irrelevant to the conversation, Brie. Suffice to say she took pride in her skills as a Dominatrix. Durov had failed to pursue her in the manner she was accustomed to and she felt slighted. It was her misplaced pride that caused that night."

Brie was almost afraid to find out—afraid that knowing might break her heart.

Uninterrupted, Sir continued, "I wasn't there when it happened, so I can only speak to what I witnessed. I knew Durov had gone off to celebrate the end of semester finals, so I was unconcerned I hadn't seen him the entire night.

"But around two in the morning I passed by his dorm room and heard muffled screaming. It was low and masculine—men were not something Durov was known to indulge in. When no one answered the door, I was forced to break the lock. I found him bound to his bed, gagged and tortured. His angry screams indicated it had not been consensual."

Sir looked away. "What had happened had scarred him as a man. It came as a shock when I discovered who'd done it."

When he turned back to Brie, his mouth was a hard line. She could tell it was difficult for Sir to speak about it, but he continued anyway. "After taking care of his physical wounds, I went seeking justice."

"I found Samantha crying in a corner of her room. Two things quickly became evident: she was drunk, and she was horrified by what she had done.

"In no way did it excuse her abuse, but she explained how she'd found Durov passed out outside his dorm when she was stumbling home after her own overindulgence. She'd helped him to his bed, where he'd passed out again. Seeing him helpless like that had done something to her. She'd suddenly got a wild hair up her ass to prove she was Domme enough to take him, convincing herself that if he experienced one session with her she'd win over his affections once and for all.

"After tying him up and gagging him so he couldn't resist, she'd woken him. According to her, Durov had remained unyielding the entire time, unwilling to give in to her dominance. In her drunken state, she'd become fixated on breaking his resolve. They'd fought a battle of wills where neither had come out the victor. She had left, furious she hadn't been able to break his ironclad will. What she'd failed to realize was that she had broken him in the worst way possible."

Brie stopped her work in the kitchen and sat down, horrified, imagining a myriad of reprehensible scenarios.

"Although he had every reason to press charges, he refused. He fell into a deep depression and almost quit college. Thankfully, that fierce Russian spirit kicked in and he eventually crawled out of his darkness and continued on with his schooling."

"What happened to Ms. Clark?" Brie asked, hoping for some kind of retribution.

"Samantha begged Durov to forgive her. She spent time in extensive counseling, gave up drinking and, per my suggestion, submitted to a well-known Domme for several months to experience submission for herself. She wanted to prove that she was repentant. Although it came as no consolation to my friend, it molded Samantha into an exceptional Domme."

"I take it he never did forgive her."

"None of her actions fazed Durov. As far as he was concerned, she was dead to him. He continued on as if it had never happened. When the two met in public settings, he simply ignored her. We all assumed he had moved on, but one night he flipped out for no apparent reason and pushed Samantha to the ground. He wrapped his hands around her neck and tried to squeeze the life out of her. I was barely able to break the stranglehold he had." Sir closed his eyes. "I came close to losing them both that night."

The pain Sir still carried was apparent to Brie, but she couldn't understand why he felt responsible.

Sir finished his account by stating, "Durov went back to Russia the next day. He claimed that time and distance were the only things that would prevent him from killing her."

Brie looked at Sir and dared to ask, "I don't understand, Sir. Why did you remain friends with Ms. Clark after she hurt Rytsar so seriously?"

He gave a long sigh of deep regret. "I was her mentor, Brie. I introduced Samantha to BDSM."

It would be difficult to keep such a shocking revelation to herself when she met with Lea and Mary the next day, but Brie refused to betray Sir's or Rytsar's trust. Instead, she planned to concentrate on discovering what was going on between Lea and Tono. She also wanted to find out what had happened to the note Sir's mother had tried to deliver through Faelan during Brie's birthday party. Mary should be able to satisfy her curiosity on that count.

Brie decided to meet the girls at the bar they had frequented when they had been training. It brought back a flood of enjoyable memories.

John, the head bartender, sidled up to them, looking Mary over with a flirtatious grin. "Long time no see, gorgeous." He turned to Brie and asked, "What happened to the long trenchcoats, Brie? I kind of miss the Goth look on you fine ladies."

Mary, who loved to torment members of the opposite sex, out-and-out lied. "I insisted we come here today. I missed…" she gave him a breathtaking come-hither look, "…the place."

"Well, I'm honored. Just for that, your drink's on the house."

Brie rolled her eyes. Mary was a ruthless user and abuser of her looks, but for some reason men just ate it up.

Once the drinks had been delivered, Brie asked, "So Lea, out with it. What the heck is going on with Tono?"

"Before I spill the beans, I have a joke for you."

Mary groaned. "No, not another one of your lame-ass jokes."

Lea smiled eagerly at Brie. "You know you're kinky when you keep Christmas lights up in your house to hide the real reason you have all those hooks in your home."

"That wasn't bad," Brie said, giggling as she noticed the small white lights over the bar. She poked Lea in the ribs as she asked, "Hey, John, why do you still have Christmas lights up?"

He gave her a goofy grin. "Eh, too lazy to take them down."

"I bet," Lea replied with an exaggerated wink.

"I don't know these two," Mary exclaimed as she moved to a seat farther away.

Lea turned her back on Mary in silent protest and smiled mischievously at Brie as she took a sip of her drink. "So Brie, you're the one who set Tono and me up. Why are you surprised we're together now?"

Mary scooted back over, shaking her head. "Something's not right here. You can't go from lusting over Ms. Clark to cozying up with Jute Freak."

Lea gave her a superior look. "I'll have you know we're living together, Miss Smarty Bitch."

Brie choked on her merlot and started coughing. "Wait. What?"

Lea just grinned and took another drink. It was obvious she was enjoying herself and had no plans to hurry her explanation.

Mary set her rum and Coke down. "Let me get this straight. Not only are you working with Tono, doing Kinbaku demonstrations, but you have partnered up and are living with him?"

"Why is that so shocking?" Lea asked, sounding offended.

Brie's coughing had ceased and she was finally able to speak. "This is the same girl who wants to explore everything while she's young and unattached? Seriously, Lea, how can you go from *that* to settling down with one Dom?"

Mary laughed unkindly. "I think I hear a little jealousy. You know you can't keep them all, Brie."

"It's not jealousy you hear, Mary. It's utter disbelief." Brie turned back to Lea. "What's the real story, girlfriend?"

Lea pouted. "You guys are no fun. I should have been able to run with this for weeks." When neither girl responded, she sighed. "Fine. Tono thought our sessions would go smoother and be more indicative of a genuine Kinbaku partnering if we got to know each other. He insists that Kinbaku is best showcased when the couple is in sync."

Brie lifted her glass. "I'd drink to that."

"So…kind of going along the lines of what you did with Tono, I suggested a temporary contract. I've been kind of curious what full-time subbing is like." She shrugged and smiled. "Besides, who wouldn't want to be trained by the sexy jute Master?"

"Me!" Mary stated emphatically. "I hate that weird rope crap."

"I take it Tono was agreeable?" Brie asked, still adjusting to the fact Lea and Tono were living together.

"He was hesitant at first. But after a couple of days he came up with a contract for me to sign."

"How long is it for?" Brie pressed, wondering if Lea was pulling her leg.

"Until the end of our classes together."

Mary snickered. "Just look at Brie trying to act all calm, but inside she's boiling over with jealousy. Admit it!"

Brie said coolly, "I'll admit no such thing. I'm surprised, yes, but jealous? No. I want Tono to be happy." She slid her hand over and squeezed her best friend's. "And, of course, I want Lea happy as well. It's just that I don't see you two as a match. I would hate either of you to get hurt by this temporary partnering."

Lea giggled. "Not everyone falls in love with the Doms they work with, Brie. You're just a hopeless romantic. I see it more as a business transaction. He gets a devoted sub— who can cook, by the way— and I get to be trained by a true master of the art. It's quite exciting, actually. This twenty-four seven stuff is really demanding, though. It's like you said, Brie—I'm learning new things about myself on a daily basis."

Brie nodded. "Isn't that the truth…?"

Lea clicked her tongue at Mary. "You should give it a try. Might mellow you out some."

Blonde Nemesis snarled. "Me, tied down? Not going to happen even for a month. This is the time to fly free, girls. To experience the world while you can. No one controls me unless I want them to. I wouldn't have it any other way. You're both idiots, but Brie's the worst."

Brie huffed. "Just because you can't commit doesn't make commitment wrong. Stop belittling my choice."

Mary's nostrils flared as she built up to an ugly outburst. John stopped by to check on them and noticed. "Looks like you could use another drink there, gorgeous."

Mary flashed him a fiery glare.

"Yep," he said nonchalantly, unfazed by her venomous stare. He hit the counter twice with his fist. "Looks like you could use a double."

As he walked away, Brie called, "You're the best, John."

Mary's ugly stare landed on her. It seemed like the perfect time to ask, "So Mary Quite Contrary, whatever happened to that note?"

Surprisingly, Mary's countenance completely changed and she smiled. "Faelan and I decided to have a little fun and froze it in a block of ice. We sent it back to that Elizabeth woman with a message. 'Will deliver when hell freezes over.'"

Lea laughed. "Funny, but harmless. Good one, Mary."

"Know what the cow did?"

Brie suddenly got a sick feeling in the pit of her stomach. "What?"

"She sent it back nestled in an ice chest, still encased in the cube of ice."

Brie frowned, sensing there was more. "Was that all?"

"No. She included her own little note. 'Hell may come sooner than you think.'"

"Whoa…" Lea exclaimed. "That's an ominous threat if I ever heard one."

Brie's heart started racing as the hairs rose on the back of her neck. She imagined Ruth's cruel but beautiful face, and felt a protective surge shoot through her veins. She would do *anything* to protect her friends.

"Mary, I'm sorry she involved you and Faelan in her scheming. It's not right, but nothing about that woman is right." Despite her anger, Brie also felt a pang of sympathy for Sir's mother. What if the crazy woman was truly dying and felt she had to resort to threats out of sheer desperation?

"I would like the letter. If it is in my hands, she won't have any reason to threaten you again."

"I'm big enough to care for myself, Brie," Mary answered irritably.

"I won't be able to rest until I've destroyed the damn thing myself. Please, Mary. Do this for me."

Mary shrugged. "You're a fool, Brie, but I'll let you nail your own coffin shut if you insist."

Lea growled, "Why are you always so negative, Mary?"

"Why are you such a ditz, Lea?"

Brie could sense that they were all on edge. There was no point in prolonging their suffering. Besides, the sooner she got rid of the offending note, the better.

"Do you mind if we go now?"

"And end this lovely girl-chat?" Mary snarked.

Lea stood up. "A minute less of you would be a gift." She gave Brie a big hug. "If you need me for any reason, call. You hear me?"

Brie laid her head against Lea's large bosom for a moment, liking the feeling of being nurtured that flooded over her. "I will, girlfriend."

"Come on, Brie-a-licious. Let's get this over with."

The two drove to Mary's apartment, where Mary retrieved the icebox. She opened it and whistled. "Must be a high quality cooler—the ice has hardly melted."

Brie took it and set it on the passenger seat of her car, slamming the door shut. "The sooner it's gone, the better for everyone."

Just before she drove off, Mary stopped her. "I think you're making a mistake getting involved in this."

Brie shook her head. "You don't understand, Mary. I would do anything for Sir. *Anything.*"

"I know Bouncy Boobs already said this, but I'll say it anyway. If you need me, call."

Brie waved off Mary's concern and jumped in the car. As she made her way back home, she kept glancing at the cooler. It reminded her a little of Pandora's box. Inside were words Sir's mother wanted him to see. Were they words full of hate or healing?

She knew Sir was off meeting with clients for the day, which was part of the reason she'd asked to see her friends. Thankfully, that left her plenty of time to get rid of the note. She hurried up the stairs and turned on the faucet full blast as soon as she entered the kitchen. Brie slid the heavy block of ice under the heated water and waited, pacing around the kitchen. She became nervous when it seemed to be taking too long. Even though Sir wasn't due back for hours she wanted the note, and any evidence of it, long gone by the time he came home.

*Brie, why did you bring it here?* she chided herself as she watched the ice block slowly melt. But she knew why…

She needed to know if the note held hope. Was it possible for Sir to make some semblance of peace with his mother before she died? It was Brie's greatest wish to help make that happen if she could. *No one is completely evil,* she thought. *Every person has goodness in them.* She was convinced that the threat of death could bring clarity to the darkest of hearts.

After what felt like forever, Brie got out a kitchen towel and laid what remained of the cube on the table. She searched through the pantry until she found the toolbox Sir kept there. She grabbed the hammer and started hacking at the ice.

At first it seemed unbreakable, but once the cracks started the ice fell away in shards. As Brie got closer to the center, she noticed that Mary hadn't covered the letter in any protective material. More likely than not, the letter inside would be unreadable.

*Maybe it's for the best…*

But Brie's curiosity was too great. She continued to hack away until the envelope was free. She stared at it for several seconds before grabbing the scissors and carefully cutting off the top. She felt like a criminal, but there was no stopping now. She *had* to know.

Holding her breath, Brie drew out the folded note and opened it. It was smeared, but still legible.

*Thane,*

*If my impending death means nothing to you, perhaps your father's violin will. If you do not consent to meet, I will destroy the violin. Yes, that damn instrument that has been in the family for centuries. It will cease to exist, just like your father.*

*So you see, son, Mommy has you by the balls.*

*Time to play by my rules.*

"What are you doing?"

Brie jumped, her heart threatening to burst at being caught. She put the letter down by her side and turned to face Sir. "I thought you were out…"

"I had a severe headache and decided to come home today to sleep it off. Little did I suspect my own sub would bang a worse headache into my brain. Now answer the question."

"I… I—" The tears started to fall.

"Is that from her?" he stated in a deceptively calm voice.

She nodded, her throat closed too tightly to allow speech.

"I won't even ask how it ended up in such a state." Sir's eyes bored into her with a coldness that stabbed her very soul. "You have betrayed me on a level I'd never thought possible." Sir strode over and took the note from her, crumpling it into a wad before turning on the gas stove.

Brie managed to blurt out, "She'll destroy the violin!"

He hesitated for a second before throwing the paper onto the flame. It took a while to catch fire, but soon the whole kitchen was filled with the faint smell of the burning paper.

He growled darkly under his breath after the note had burned itself out, and then turned on Brie. His gaze was clouded with anger. "I commanded you not to have any contact with her and yet I find you here, seeking out her correspondence behind my back. I have purposely disregarded every attempt at contact and then you do this…"

Brie was desperate to explain. "Sir, I wanted to destroy the note myself."

"The fact you disobeyed my orders on something so vital speaks volumes, Miss Bennett."

Brie whimpered, knowing the use of her surname was a bad omen. "Sir, she threatened Mary and Faelan for not delivering her message. I wanted to protect them and you from its contents. But before I destroyed it, I was overcome with hope that she wanted to make things right by you."

"Things will *never* be right between us!" he shouted.

Brie fell to the floor, bowing in supplication. "I'm sorry, Sir."

He asked, his voice as cold as ice, "Do you realize what you have done?"

She shook her head with her forehead still pressed to the floor.

"You have forced me to react. Had you simply destroyed it, I would be ignorant of her plan and unable to stop it. I thought she had gotten rid of the instrument years ago. Now I am obligated to liberate my father's violin from the beast."

She said in the barest of whispers, "You could pretend you don't know."

"No, Miss Bennett. That is something I *cannot* do." She heard the flip of his phone. "Yes, it's me. Simply state where and when. No, I will not." He paused for a moment, then snarled, "If it is a requirement then I must acquiesce." He slammed the phone closed and threw it onto the table.

"Get off the floor and clean up the mess you've made."

The apartment was full of a black rage that hung in every corner; there was no escaping it, even when Sir retired to the bedroom.

After Brie had finished restoring the kitchen to order, she took the ice chest and went to the basement garage to throw it in the dumpster. It didn't ease her misgivings, but she couldn't bear to have anything of that woman's near her.

She clearly understood Sir's intense rage, now that she had read his mother's hateful words, but it gutted her to know his anger was also directed towards her now.

As the rays of the sun disappeared behind the horizon, Sir emerged from their room. His haggard expression alerted her to the fact he was still suffering from a debilitating headache.

"Miss Bennett, I think it best that you find a place to stay tonight. Call me at noon so I can pick you up. You presence has been requested at the meeting tomorrow."

"Sir, I never meant—"

He turned from her to return to the bedroom. "I will need to meditate if I am to survive tomorrow. Goodnight." She heard him quietly shut the door.

With a trembling hand, she dialed and then sobbed into the phone, "Mary… I fucked up bad…"

# Confronting the Beast

Although she had been tempted to stay with Lea, it had been Mary's no-nonsense advice she'd needed. She'd warned Brie not to take the letter, but naturally, Brie had refused to listen. Well, she was listening now.

Mary gave Brie no sympathy, even remarking that it would be good if Sir uncollared her. When Brie broke down in hysterical tears at the suggestion, Mary quickly changed the subject.

"All you can do now is prove to Sir you understand you were wrong, and do whatever it takes to earn his trust back. If he wants to be done, then be a woman about it and leave with dignity. After all, you're the one who screwed up."

Brie struggled to breathe, unable to bear the thought of losing Sir.

Mary took pity on her. "But if he knows you at all, he'll understand that you were only trying to help."

"I was, Mary! That was my only motivation," Brie cried.

"Yeah, yeah… Good intentions or not, the simple fact is you disobeyed him on something deeply personal. He has every right to be angry. You have to accept what comes, Brie, and deal with it. Don't be a whiny baby about it."

But the idea of life without Sir killed Brie inside. "I can't lose him! Don't you understand that he's everything to me?"

Mary stared at her without a lick of sympathy. "If he would be happier without you, would you really deny him that?"

Brie crumpled into a heap on the couch. "No…"

"Then rest tonight. Be strong for your Master tomorrow. He'll need your positive energy, even if he dismisses you after the meeting."

Brie looked up at Mary, a sureness of spirit slowly taking over as she sat up straight. "Yes, you're right. I created this mess; it is my duty to see him through it."

Mary nudged her shoulder with her hip. "So go to bed and make me proud tomorrow."

Brie woke up, steeling herself for the difficult meeting. Ruth was a dangerous person—indifferent of others on a level that was terrifying.

She called Sir at exactly noon, afraid to hear the displeasure in his voice. It only rang once before he answered. His tone was formal and distant. "Where are you?"

"At Mary's, Sir."

"Expect me in twenty minutes." He hung up before she could respond.

She looked at Mary. "He's still pissed."

"To be honest, Brie, he probably isn't thinking of you. All of his focus is centered on navigating this meeting with the bitch. I only have to imagine how I would be if I was meeting my father to know how Sir feels."

Brie found solace in that. "My job is to serve as his strength."

"There's no need to wish you luck, then. You will succeed in that, I'm sure of it."

Brie felt only gratitude. "Thanks, Mary. You've given me exactly what I needed to survive this nightmare."

"A nightmare you created," Mary pointed out, in typical Blonde Nemesis fashion.

Brie waited for Sir outside. She had planned to jump into the Lotus when it pulled up, but Sir insisted on getting out and opening the door for her. It gave her some hope that he could find it in his heart to forgive her.

The ride was silent except for a few simple instructions. "Do not speak directly to her."

"Yes, Sir."

"Do not accept anything she says as truth. She is a master of manipulation."

"Understood, Sir."

"Keep out of my way."

"I will say and do nothing, Sir, unless you ask."

He turned to stare at her briefly. "I do not want you there. It is another power play I must endure, but it will not go unanswered." He hit the steering wheel with a vengeance, but said no more for the rest of the drive.

Sir pulled up to a high-end hotel and threw the keys to the valet without a word. He helped Brie out of the car and led her through the doors robotically. The vacant look in his eyes alerted her to the fact that his mind was elsewhere.

Naturally, Ruth was staying at the penthouse suite. Sir grunted his displeasure when the bellman pressed the button. The ride up was tense—even the young man sensed the gravity of their mood and coughed several times to hide his discomfort.

The elevator doors opened onto a small hallway and a two-door entry. Sir put his hand on Brie's back and guided her out of the elevator, then rang the doorbell without hesitation.

"Let yourself in," Ruth called from inside.

Sir waited until the elevator closed before opening the door. "Stay beside me," he commanded softly. They entered the spacious loft and he shut the massive doors behind them.

Ruth was lying on a red velvet couch in a flowing gown, looking every bit the part of a diva. "Right on time, like a good boy."

"Where's the violin?"

"No, son, not so fast. We need to talk first."

"Produce the violin or I will leave."

Ruth narrowed her eyes, studying him for a second before pulling herself off the couch and disappearing into the bedroom. She came back a few moments later, holding the violin away from her as if it were a piece of unwanted trash.

She laid it on the end of the sofa, placed a pillow over it and lay back down, her body a shield protecting the instrument. "Now we will talk. Take a seat," she said, gesturing to a small couch opposite hers. "Both of you."

Sir led Brie over and they sat down, facing Ruth, but Brie turned her head and stared at Sir's chest. She concentrated all her energies upon his heart.

"She's a mousey little thing, isn't she?" Ruth complained.

"I'm not here to discuss Miss Bennett. Why don't you just state your request and be done with the games?"

Ruth's laughter filled the room. "Request? It's a demand, son. Make no mistake about it. Desperate times call for desperate measures."

Brie saw Sir's lips twitch, but he said calmly, "Proceed."

"It's simple. I have plenty of cash overseas, but am temporarily unable to access it and I need it now. The only way I can survive this cancer is through non-traditional means. That takes money and lots of it, son."

"Are we still imagining we have cancer?"

Her voice became low and harsh. "You are a heartless bastard. Yes, I'm dying! But I see that has no effect on you."

When she got no response from Sir, she addressed Brie. "What kind of son treats his dying mother this way?"

Brie continued to stare at Sir's chest, but she felt a slow, angry blush creep over her face.

"Now you can see what a ruthless man he truly is. But at least you believe me, Brie. You've been on my side from the beginning and even helped me meet with him today. You're really precious to me, dear. You know that, don't you?"

When Brie did not answer, she laughed. "Thane, she reminds me of your father. That look of pure devotion…it will be the death of her."

"Enough!" he snapped.

"Mark my words, you will destroy her. You are, after all, your mother's son."

Sir stood up. "We're done here."

Ruth lay back on the couch. "No, we're not. There's still the issue of the money for my cancer treatment."

"How much?"

"It isn't cheap. It could run as high as a million."

"I don't have that amount of money lying around," he stated angrily.

"Well, then give it to me in installments. Half a million now, half a million before Brie's film comes out."

"Why then?"

"Insurance."

Sir pulled out his checkbook, calmly wrote out a check for five hundred thousand dollars from his personal account and held it out to her.

Brie felt sick to her stomach watching him give in so easily to the witch.

"Have Brie bring it to me, boy."

Sir gave the check to Brie and nodded, his eyes revealing neither anger nor defeat. She stood up and walked over to Ruth. The woman lay there, studying her like a piece of meat. With a dissatisfied grunt, she took the check. "Before I give her the violin, let me make sure this money is good."

She called the number on the check and verified the funds were available.

"Good boy." She sat up and pulled the violin from under the pillow. She held it out to Brie and, without warning, dropped it from her grasp.

With lightning-quick reflexes, Brie caught the instrument before it hit the floor.

"Pity," the woman exclaimed, folding the check and stuffing it into her brassiere.

Brie carried the violin with reverence back to Sir. He took it, looking it over briefly before commenting. "Do you have the case?"

"It's in the bedroom. Have your pet get it," Ruth answered in a disinterested voice.

With Sir's permission, Brie went to retrieve it. The case, lined with red velvet, was open on the bed. She closed it slowly, feeling power radiating from that simple violin case—a connection to the past.

Brie held it to her chest as she walked back to Sir. With the same reverence she had shown, Sir placed the violin inside and latched it shut.

Sir spoke to Ruth in a businesslike manner. "Where should I send the next check? I do not want to meet with you again."

"Agreed. Totally unnecessary to meet in person. I've gotten what I need from my heartless son." She lifted a card from the table and handed it to him. "Send it here two weeks before the premiere. Failure to do so will have dire consequences."

Sir took the card and tucked it into his jacket.

"There are three things you might find of interest, Ruth." He nodded towards the check. "One: that is a bogus account. You will not be receiving any funds from me. Two: I know that you had your medical records altered. I could only wish to get rid of you that easily. Three: my lawyer informed me that you are bankrupt—not a cent to your name. You are living on borrowed time and that time has finally run out."

She rose from the couch in a furious rage. "Foolish boy! I will *bury* you!"

Sir tucked the violin under his arm and said, "We're finished here."

"Finished is right!" Ruth screeched. "My threats are not idle, Thane. I will trash your reputation as thoroughly as I did your father's. You will lose everything. Money, honor…" she looked directly at Brie, "…love."

"Unlike my father, I am not dead and can defend myself."

Her laughter was hard and cruel. "You underestimate me, son. There will be nothing left when I'm through."

"I repeat, I am capable of defending myself. And yes, your threats *are* idle. I do not fear you." He put his hand on Brie's back and directed her towards the door.

Ruth hissed from behind them, "I'm coming after you too, precious. If I don't ruin you, Thane will."

Brie took a deep breath once the elevator doors had closed. It felt as if she had survived a physical battle. She was exhausted, both emotionally and physically. She glanced at Sir and was heartened to see a slight smirk on his face.

Yes, he'd won the hour.

Although Sir remained aloof when they returned home, he called her to him that evening and asked her to bow at his feet. "I actually contemplated uncollaring you, Brie, but something the beast said today caused me to reconsider. She is correct in likening your devotion to that of my father. It is also true that a part of my mother lives in me. I am capable of being heartless and cruel, but my father's unfailing passion beats in this heart. It is his legacy that I choose to live out."

Brie looked up hesitantly, afraid to hope.

"Are you repentant of reading the letter?"

"More than you know, Sir."

"Will you ever contact her again, in any way?"

"Never knowingly, Sir."

He snorted in understanding and amended his statement. "Will you immediately tell me if you encounter her unexpectedly?"

"Immediately, Sir. No hesitation."

He ordered her to stand. "As punishment, I could have you endure another session with rice or even a thorough beating."

Brie bowed her head, ready to accept his punishment, although she feared it would be much harsher than the first.

His breath was long and drawn out, as if he was completely exhausted. "However, I fear whatever the beast has planned will far surpass any punishment I could deliver. She will attempt to break you emotionally. It will get ugly, I guarantee it. Are you strong enough? If not, then I should set you free now."

She took offense at the offer and stated proudly, "I would die for you, Sir."

He growled, "Dying is not an option, téa."

Hearing her pet name uttered from his lips made her whole body sing with relief. "What I meant, Sir, is that I would suffer any hardship to remain by your side."

"You must be sure, téa."

Brie kissed his hand lovingly. "In good times and in bad, there is no place I would rather be than by your side."

"Then we stand together."

"As one, Sir."

His smirk from earlier returned. "I did enjoy the look on her face the moment she realized she'd been beaten at her own game."

"It was brilliantly delivered, Sir."

"After being forced into a corner, I spent the night devising my plan and setting the wheels in motion. As my mother said, 'Desperate times call for desperate measures.' The beast didn't stand a chance."

"Your father would have been proud."

"No," Sir said solemnly, "he would have been saddened that we were still fighting against each other, but I trust he'd have understood my actions." His gaze suddenly became sentimental. "Although I was against you being there today, your presence was…appreciated."

Brie smiled at him lovingly.

Sir took her hand and placed it over the healing brand on his chest. "This is where you remain. Always."

Burying herself in his embrace, she whispered, "Thank you, Sir."

When she walked into the bedroom that night, she found the violin lying in the middle of the bed. The two lay down on either side of it. She could tell he had something he wanted to share.

Sir touched the strings, making a light strumming sound. "This instrument has been in our family for over two hundred years. It was passed down from generation to generation to the most promising talent."

"I had no idea it was that old."

"My great-grandfather was an American who fought in World War I. He fell in love with the Italian language and culture after making friends among the troops and decided to relocate there after the war ended. He married the sister of one of his Italian comrades and set about propagating the world with eight children, the youngest being my grandfather. Although *Nonno* never stepped onto American soil, he carried the Davis name and was granted the family heirloom when it was discovered his son had exceptional talent."

Brie stroked the smooth wood, amazed so much family history was represented in one instrument.

"My American relatives invested in his education, flying my father out here when he was only twelve. For all intents and purposes, he grew up an American but never lost his love for his homeland. At least four times a year we would visit, even when his concert schedule became hectic. Family meant everything to him."

"What a rich childhood you had, Sir."

"True, I did." His eyes held a haunted look, but Sir smiled as he looked down at the violin. "After he passed, the only thing I wanted of my father's was this violin. Naturally, my mother refused to give it to me. I had assumed she'd sold it because of its considerable worth, but now I realize she kept it all these years for one reason."

Brie looked at him sadly. "Blackmail."

His eyes narrowed and his voice became dark. "Yes, but she failed to take into account that I *am* my mother's son. I am not so easily manipulated."

Brie ran her fingers over the strings tenderly. "Now it's back where it belongs." She smiled. "Is this the violin he always played, Sir?"

His expression softened. "Yes. My father would touch no other."

"So when I hear his music, I am hearing this instrument."

"Yes."

"Wow…" she said in admiration. Brie looked at it again, realizing it was a piece of Alonzo's soul in physical form.

Sir picked it up and placed it back in the case. "And now it can wait for the next in the Davis line to bring it back to life."

"A beautiful gift…"

His eyes shone with triumph when he replied, "A valuable legacy. One worth fighting for."

# Excitement at The Haven

Brie's Master was asked to join an impromptu meeting at The Haven with several of the other Submissive Training Center staff members. The discussion was to center on issues anticipated following the publicizing of the documentary. Sir had given Brie permission to roam the club until he had finished.

Sir was no longer worried about Faelan. After the formal meeting with the Dom, Brie had had no further trouble with him. It seemed Faelan had found his niche in the community with a little guidance from Marquis, and he was highly popular at the club these days.

From what Brie could gather from information Lea had shared, he had created an unusual routine at The Haven, inspired by the auctions at the Center. At the start of each evening, submissives were invited to fill out a form detailing a simple fantasy they wanted to play out that particular night. An hour before he was scheduled to scene, Faelan would announce the scenario that had captured his interest. The lucky sub would then spread the word, guaranteeing a large audience to watch it.

It was not only popular with the subs, but with fellow Dominants as well. They took the opportunity to observe the wide variety of scenes presented and select those that aroused them to recreate at home. Despite Faelan's young age, he was a master of role play and displayed advanced skills, having been trained by both Sir and Marquis. It made him a hot commodity in the community.

Although Sir no longer considered Faelan a threat, he reminded her, "If at any point you feel uncomfortable, seek Tono out. He has been made aware that I will be in a meeting tonight."

As Brie watched Sir walk off to join Headmaster Coen and Master Anderson, she felt a thrill. She hadn't been allowed this kind of freedom in forever, and she found it invigorating.

She stepped over to the first alcove and was surprised to find Marquis finishing a scene. Celestia, his collared sub, was bound to a wooden St. Andrew's cross, her back a crisscross of red marks, indicating that she'd received an intense flogging from him.

Marquis zipped up the bag that held his infamous tools. He approached his sub with predatory grace, turning her head and kissing her forcefully while she was still bound.

Celestia's moan resonated in Brie's core. It was the sound of a woman who had been flying high in subspace, brought back to earth by the overwhelming connection of her Master's kiss.

She heard him say faintly, "My beautiful star…"

Her eyes fluttered open and she smiled. "My heart."

Brie was moved by their simple exchange. She admired how each D/s couple had their own erotic dance. No two couples followed the exact same steps, but the deep level of trust and respect was consistent throughout the community.

Marquis released Celestia from the cross and cradled her in his arms, kissing her lightly. It was the romantic side of Marquis that Brie had been surprised by the first time she'd scened with him during training.

She smiled to herself, remembering the first day she'd met him at the Training Center. Oh, how Marquis Gray had frightened her with his dark, penetrating eyes and ghostlike figure. She understood now that looks did not define a person. It was one of many lessons she'd learned at the Center.

Brie quietly moved on to the next scene, wanting to give them privacy to bask in their aftercare.

At the next alcove she came across a Master punishing his slave. Brie had no idea what her offense had been, but he commanded his naked slave to mold herself to the 'Pole of Penance'. The girl walked over to the sleek metal pole and turned around to face the crowd, her face the picture of repentance.

Attached to the pole was a thick, black dildo. The slave bent over and pressed her ass against the toy. The multitudes watched as the girl began rocking against the large, latex cock. Her Master stood over her, obviously enjoying the sight of the dark phallus penetrating his sub. He grunted, stroking his cock as he watched.

The slave whimpered occasionally as she willingly ground against the toy, forcing it deeper into her ass.

"Hands above your head, slave," he ordered when the penetration was complete. He then tied her hands to a ring and pulled the rope taut. Brie could imagine how the girl must feel, with her body stretched by the binding and her ass stretched by the large toy inside her. Then her Master added a new element—the Magic Wand.

Brie whimpered along with her.

He held it in front of his slave, stating, "Disobedient slaves do not get the pleasure of orgasm."

The girl watched with a look of fear, knowing she was in trouble as he knelt down and bound the wand between her legs, securing it tightly against her clit.

"Please—no, Master," she begged.

Her Master's smile was playfully ruthless. "Do not orgasm or you will meet a much worse fate, slave."

The girl cried out when he switched it on. Brie knew the wand would be creating a delicious vibration between her thighs, and wondered how the girl could possibly hold out. When he turned the wand up to the higher setting, Brie decided to leave. Watching orgasm denial was almost as bad as experiencing it herself.

She moved on, looking for Lea, but stopped short when she saw Boa beginning a scene with his Mistress. He was dressed in black leather chaps and nothing else. His Mistress was wearing embroidered, royal purple silks wrapped tightly around her sleek body, her lips a matching deep plum.

Brie was surprised to see there were four men, including Boa, involved in the scene. It was quite unusual. Boa's Asian Mistress was in charge, so Brie assumed all four males and the one lone female must be submissives. She forgot all about Lea as she watched the tantalizing scene play out before her.

The girl was ordered to lie on a thin wooden bench. She was bound to it with violet ropes, one just under her breasts and a second binding across her hip bones. Brie noted that her head and pussy were positioned at the edges on either side of the bench. The furniture seemed to be specifically designed for fucking a sub at both ends.

*Ingenious.*

Brie was a little curious, though, because the girl's hands had been left untied. She looked at the other male submissives and noted that they were wearing similar leather chaps to Boa's. All four men had full erections; however, it was Boa's that drew Brie's attention. She'd never forgotten the challenge of taking his massive cock into her small frame. Just thinking about it now caused a deep ache in her loins.

The Domme grabbed a leather crop and walked over to the girl. "You are about to be banged by my four men. I expect you to please each one equally. I will correct you if necessary." She snapped the crop onto the girl's mound. The sub cried out in pain at the unexpected warning. "That's right. Mistress will be very strict tonight. I want my boys pleased."

"I understand, Mistress Luo," the female answered.

The Asian Domme walked up to each male individually and grabbed his scrotum, squeezing her long nails into his flesh. She leaned in close to his ear, to whisper something the crowd was not privileged to hear.

When she was done, the four men took their places: Boa between the girl's legs, the twins on either side of her and the remaining one at her head. The idea of pleasing all four men at the same time was both frightening and exciting to Brie. Boa was enough of a challenge on his own, and Brie wondered how the sub felt about her task.

She glanced between the girl's legs and noticed her outer lips were already red and swollen, indicating a very turned-on subbie. Brie had long since realized that a woman's vocalizations were never as reliable as the state of her sex.

A female could fake a scream of pleasure, but not an amorous pussy.

The Domme ordered, "Please the twins."

The sub immediately took a cock in each hand and expertly stroked the lengths of their shafts with an added rotation of her wrists at the end. Both men groaned in appreciation of her evident skill.

"Keep them satisfied, sub. Do not slow down, not even for an instant."

"Yes, Mistress Luo. It will be my pleasure."

The Mistress turned to Boa with a hungry look. "Boa, fuck the girl."

Brie bit her bottom lip as she watched the male sub position his colossal shaft against the sub's opening and then grab onto her thighs. The girl panted and groaned as he forced the impossibly large head of his shaft inside her.

Brie felt a trickle down the inside of her own leg. Oh, yes, her pussy knew well the sexy demand of Boa's shaft. She squeezed her legs together, feeling her clit faintly pulse with desire.

While he was still forcing himself inside, the Domme trailed the crop slowly up the girl's body, all the way to her throat and up to her chin. She smiled down at the female and said, "Lex, fuck her pretty mouth."

Brie shivered. She remembered the time she'd been on the doctor's table and Master Harris had deep-throated her while stimulating her clit with a vibrator. That was nothing compared to this. Brie stood glued in place, completely entranced by Mistress Luo's scene.

Lex began by massaging the girl's neck as he slowly eased his shaft past the back of her throat, but there was a moment of instinctual resistance and the girl momentarily paused the motions of her hands.

As promised, Boa's Mistress snapped the crop across her right breast.

The girl twitched on the bench, but she resumed the rapid hand movements even as she whimpered around Lex's cock.

It took time for the girl's muscles to relax enough to take the entire length of Boa's manhood, but Brie found it extremely sexy to watch the process—to see that huge cock force its way in.

Boa's Mistress walked around the scene, complimenting her male subs as she used the leather tab of the crop to caress the female. When the base of Boa's cock was pressed firmly against the girl's mound, the Domme asked, "Are you ready to come, boys?"

All four men answered in unison, "Yes, Mistress."

She leaned down and spoke directly to the girl. "You have done well, sub. This Mistress is pleased. Now it's time to enjoy the fruits of your labor."

The Domme stood up, slapping the crop against her hand as she announced, "I will count down from ten."

Brie was familiar with that technique—waiting to orgasm until the counting was complete. However, she had never seen it done with multiple partners before. Were they all so well trained that they would come as a unit?

She watched in fascination, holding her breath as the last few numbers were called out. "Four… Three… Two… One."

Boa shuddered deep inside the girl at the same time as Lex, while the twins covered her breasts with large amounts of come. Brie could hear the girl's muffled screams as the two men finished off deep inside her. Suddenly, the female stiffened and her whole body began to shake violently in a powerful orgasm of her own.

All four men stepped away at the same time and allowed their Mistress to approach the girl. "Delicious to watch," she commended. She looked up at the audience, which responded with appreciative applause.

The girl looked up at the Domme with half-hooded eyes, her chest still rising and falling rapidly as she recovered.

"Was it all you had hoped for?" the Domme asked, tracing the end of the crop around the young woman's breasts.

In a hoarse whisper, the girl replied, "Better…Mistress Luo."

"Good," she said soothingly.

Having watched the scene to completion, Brie decided to make her way to the bar, hoping to find Lea there—after a quick trip to the bathroom to rid herself of her soaked panties.

# The Wolf Bares His Heart

She found not only Lea at the bar, but Mary as well. They were sitting together in an intense conversation. As Brie approached, she was startled to spot Faelan standing nearby, casually drinking a beer. Brie passed by him, wondering if he would cause a commotion. But, true to form, the Wolf completely ignored her.

Lea lifted her purse off the empty stool between the two as soon as she saw Brie. "Dang, girl, you finally made it!"

"Sorry, I was watching a scene with Boa and couldn't pull myself away."

Lea grinned. "Oh, that Boa is one fine sub. I've had the pleasure of his cock on several occasions. It's like the first time every session because he's so freaking huge."

Mary interrupted, "Boa Shmoa. Let's get back to talking about Master O."

"Who?" Brie asked.

Lea looked at her in disbelief. "Haven't you heard? Master O is in town tonight."

Brie shrugged her shoulders, the name meaning nothing to her.

Mary explained, "He's a world-renowned master of blood play..." When she saw that Brie was still clueless, she seemed irritated. "Seriously, you didn't know he's coming to tour the club tonight?"

Brie looked around and noticed the unusually high number of eligible subs parading about. "Is that the reason this place is so packed?"

"Ah…yeah!" Lea teased. "Subs from all over California have come tonight, hoping he'll choose one of them to play out a scene."

They quickly brought Brie up to speed. Apparently, Master O was from Eastern Africa and had traveled the world in order to refine his unique skills. Mary claimed his work with needles was unsurpassed. "You would not believe the artful displays he can create using human skin as his canvas."

Even Lea, who wasn't a fan of blood play, was excited. "I really want to see his work up close. What I've seen in photos is amazing, and don't you just *love* his name?"

"What? Is it in reference to orgasms or something?" Brie asked.

"No, idiot," Mary snapped. "The 'O' stands for type O blood."

Brie laughed. "Aw… Well, that does make him sound a little more dangerous and less conceited."

Lea handed her a drink before asking, "Would you let him scene with you if Sir allowed it?"

"No way. I hate needles. But I wouldn't mind watching…I think." She shuddered involuntarily.

Lea turned to Mary. "What about you?"

Mary rolled her eyes. "Do you even have to ask?"

Brie noticed that Faelan shifted uncomfortably behind Mary. Was it possible he was jealous of Mary's stated interest in the visiting Dom?

"With so many subs to choose from, I wonder which one he'll select. This is going to be fun!" Lea squealed.

Brie grinned at her best friend. "What? Are you hoping he'll pick you?"

"Hey, I wouldn't turn the man down if he asked, but I can't say blood really turns me on, unlike some freaks I know," Lea replied, looking straight at Mary.

Blonde Nemesis snorted. "I wear the 'freak' title gladly. I'm the only truly adventurous one in our little group, Lea the Lackluster." She slapped Brie's back. "Hey, I've got to pee. Watch my stuff." She disappeared into the sea of people without looking back.

Faelan came up from behind and nonchalantly picked up Mary's purse, setting it on the counter in front of him before taking her seat and ordering another beer. The bartender slid it across the counter, where it landed perfectly in Faelan's open hand. He picked up the mug and took a long, hard stare at Brie before giving her a slight nod and tipping the mug to drink.

"So you're acknowledging Brie all of a sudden," Lea commented.

Faelan looked as if he were contemplating ignoring the question, but finally answered, "I'm moving forward."

Brie held up her glass to Faelan. "I'm glad to hear it, Mr. Wallace."

He glanced in the direction Mary had gone and stated, "People don't give that woman the respect she deserves, but that's about to change."

*Is Faelan actually being protective of Mary?* Brie couldn't believe it. "I agree; she deserves to be treated better."

He corrected, "What she deserves is for people to recognize the extraordinary woman she is and treat her accordingly."

Lea smiled into her glass as she sipped her drink. "Okay…"

Faelan took a long draught of beer and slammed the mug on the counter. "Do you realize that she's the only person since that car crash, all those fucking years ago, who actually cares about me as a man?"

Lea slammed her drink down, imitating him, and stated, "You have *tons* of girls at your beck and call, Faelan."

"I'm not talking about simple fucking, Lea," he growled.

He turned to Brie and stared at her with those intense blue eyes. "After the accident, the boy's family condemned me, and my family and friends have treated me with kid gloves ever since. I don't need sympathy, damn it! What I needed was a taste of reality. Well, Mary is all about shooting you between the eyes with reality."

Brie had to force herself not to smile. "That's one way to put it."

For some odd reason, Faelan seemed to be feeling unusually talkative. Brie gave Lea a little wink when he continued of his own accord, "She and I have struggled with demons from our pasts, believing if we could defeat them we would be free. But that isn't how it works."

Faelan suddenly had Brie's attention. He wasn't spewing some frivolous bullshit just to be heard—he was speaking from the heart. She met his gaze, transfixed. "How does it work?"

"You have to accept it and then let it go. You can't keep going back to revisit the pain." He took a long drink to let that simple truth sink in.

Brie was moved by his words. "Yes, you're right…"

Faelan put his beer down and looked at them both. "I killed a boy. It was my fault. I can't change it. Mary helped me see that I had imprisoned myself in that guilt and grown used to the pain." He closed his eyes and groaned. "That was where my true weakness was, in allowing myself to accept the pain to the point where I refused to let go."

He opened those hypnotic blue eyes and stared into Brie's with a soulful gaze that took her breath away. "I will never be that weak again."

She ran a finger along the rim of her glass, at a loss for words. "That is profound, Mr. Wallace."

Faelan addressed Lea. "Who could have guessed that seeing Brie tied up while jogging on the beach would mark the beginning of my re-entry into humanity?"

Lea shrugged. "It's crazy, the turns life takes…"

"Now I am determined to help Mary face that same truth. She has to let go of the pain she clings to. She thinks of it as her shield against the world, but in reality it's killing her."

Brie suddenly understood how perfect Faelan was for Mary. Only someone who had suffered deeply would have the authority to bring her through it. "I'm grateful she found you, Mr. Wallace."

He ignored her compliment. "I need you to support Mary. Do not let her down."

"Of course," Brie answered easily.

But Faelan was quick to add, "Even when she bites back…and she will."

Both girls had suffered Mary's backlashes in the past, but Brie appreciated the reminder. She assured him, "Through thick and thin, Mr. Wallace."

He lifted his glass and clinked it against both of theirs. "Do not fail her."

Tono came to collect Lea for the scene they would be performing together. He glanced at Faelan and asked Brie, "Is everything fine here?"

Brie smiled to reassure him. "Couldn't be better."

Faelan stood up and handed Mary's purse to Brie. "No problems here, old man." He left them and moved over to a group of fawning submissives.

Lea grabbed Tono's arm and squeezed it. "Can't wait for tonight's scene!"

Tono put his hand lightly on Brie's shoulder. "You know where to find me, should you need anything."

"Yes, Tono. Thank you. I think I'll hang with Mary for a bit longer."

Lea turned to Brie as they were leaving and whispered, "He promised to spank me this scene!"

Brie had to admit she was jealous, especially when all she could do was observe other people all night. Several subs descended on Lea's seat and fought over it, filling the space instantly. Brie guarded Mary's stool fiercely until she finally showed up.

"What took so long, Blondie?"

"Hey, I can't help it if Doms keep stopping to talk to me. I'm not allowed to be rude to them, now, am I?" she said with a self-satisfied smirk.

"Whatever..."

"I'm telling you, Brie. You're missing out."

Brie didn't want another lecture about being collared, so she changed the subject. "So what are your plans tonight?"

Blonde Nemesis answered with a cocky tilt of her chin, "Wouldn't you like to know?"

"Why do you have to be such a pain?"

"Haven't you always touted that we should be true to our hearts? Well, I *truly* don't want to tell you, so suck on that."

Brie groaned. *Why do I even try?* She suddenly heard frantic whispering all around her.

Mary stood up and announced, "He's here." She moved forward, trying to get a better look at the man. Brie got up to follow her, but couldn't stay close because of the crush of females. She satisfied her curiosity by watching the tall, midnight-skinned African from afar.

He studied each sub as he made his way through the crowd, stopping at every alcove to take in the scene but moving on abruptly, obviously on the prowl.

Even Brie felt a sexual attraction as he approached. He caught her eye, glanced briefly at the collar around her neck and moved on without pausing.

She let her breath out once he'd passed by. To scene with a man as imposing as Master O would challenge any sub, but the fact his expertise involved blood took it to an entirely different level.

The Haven did not allow blood play on its premises. Whichever sub was chosen tonight would be required to leave with Master O. Although that was normally frowned upon by the club, the Dom's experience and reputation allowed him to circumvent standard protocol as long as he procured a willing sub—and there were *plenty* who were willing.

It did not come as a surprise to Brie when Master O eventually approached Mary. Brie could feel the collective tension of the subs around her. They deeply resented his choice.

"Your name?" he asked in a dark, velvety voice.

Mary looked up and smiled, obviously pleased she had been the one chosen. She answered demurely, "It's Mary, Master O."

"I would like to scene privately with you…Mary." His voice dropped to a low growl when he spoke her name. The timbre of his voice had even Brie quivering.

Mary batted her eyelashes at the Dom, before bowing low in respect. Brie knew what a cherished dream this was—to experience blood play performed by a famed master of the sport. That was why it came as a complete shock when Mary answered, "I am honored, Master O, but I fear I must decline tonight." She gave him a coy smile, one that invited the chase.

Brie heard a gasp from one of the other subs.

The Dom appeared equally stunned. He looked Mary up and down reproachfully. "Ah, my mistake. You are unworthy of such an invitation." He turned his back on her, and began studying a group of girls nearby. Eventually, he picked a curvaceous sub with platinum hair to accompany him out of the club.

After Master O had left, a band of spiteful subs encircled Mary.

Brie heard one hiss, "You don't belong here. You pretend to be a submissive, reeling them in with your looks, but you're really just a fucked-up piece of white trash. He figured it out quickly enough though, didn't he? They all do…"

Another echoed the sentiment, "Worthless piece of trash."

Mary held her head up higher, but said nothing. It distressed Brie that Blonde Nemesis wasn't lashing out.

The girl's lack of response sent a chill down Brie's spine because she knew what it meant. Their words were hitting close to home—tapping into Mary's greatest fear. Brie tried to push through the circle, desperate to grab onto Mary before she bolted from the club, but there was no need.

Faelan appeared beside Mary and barked, "Enough!" He placed his hand on the back of her neck and squeezed hard. Brie could see her visibly relax under his vise-like grip.

The Wolf's icy stare bored into the two girls who had dared to insult Mary. "This submissive is worth ten of you."

The wayward subs' haughty gazes instantly fell to the floor.

Faelan spoke loudly enough for everyone within earshot to hear his command. "From now on, you are not allowed to speak to Miss Wilson. You are unworthy of such an honor." He glanced at the other girls and added, "That will be true for the rest of you if you dare to speak disrespectfully to her. Do you understand?"

Brie knew that each girl in the group longed to partner with him. His displeasure was a true hardship for them. "Yes, Faelan," they answered.

He nodded curtly.

"It's time to serve," Faelan ordered, guiding Mary out of the circle of women and leading her to the empty alcove he had reserved. It was then that Brie understood why Mary had declined Master O. She was to be Falean's sub for the evening and had sacrificed her desires in order to honor her commitment.

Like a moth to a flame, Brie drifted to the scene, curious what Mary had requested. Tonight, as per his protocol, Faelan addressed the gathering crowd, informing them of his choice. "Miss Wilson has asked to play the reluctant spy." He smiled ominously. "Enjoy."

Brie struggled to breathe. This would be the same scene Mary had flipped out on during her first Auction Day with Tono. Brie understood that it was the embodiment of her father's abuse, which Mary was still fighting to overcome. After what had just happened with Master O, it seemed like such a scene was a train wreck waiting to happen—with an audience who might enjoy the carnage.

Mary's eyes watered as Faelan covered her head in a black hood and secured it. He guided her to a wooden chair and began to bind her to it.

Tears fell down Brie's cheeks as she imagined Mary as a child, being bound by her father, apprehensive of the beating that was about to begin. Why did Blonde Nemesis insist on reliving her childhood over again?

Mary's words echoed in Brie's mind. "*I don't like pain, but I endure it. It's like I have a driving need to defeat it. Like…if I was able to bear it without fear, I would finally be the victor over him.*"

There Mary was, once again, attempting to defeat her father even if it cost her sanity.

*Please, Faelan, save Mary…* Brie begged silently.

The Wolf became rough as he finished the last of the ties. Brie heard Mary whimper underneath the hood.

"Are you afraid?" he asked lustfully.

"No."

His chuckle was low and menacing. "Oh, but you will be…" Faelan circled around her slowly. He knew how to play the crowd as he simultaneously played with his subs. Everyone in attendance was in tune with the scene he was orchestrating.

Unexpectedly, he grabbed her blouse with both hands and ripped it open. Buttons flew haphazardly onto the floor. He left her chest exposed as he turned and rifled through his duffle bag.

Faelan approached Mary, carrying a large knife and wearing a dangerous grin. "I will tell you a little secret, spy. Even if you do everything I ask, I am still going to hurt you."

One of the subs near Brie sucked in her breath.

Even Brie felt the aggressive eroticism flowing from Faelan and her body responded, remembering her time alone with him—the chocolate, the dancing, the bruises…

He slid the edge of the blade under her bra and cut it with a quick motion, releasing her breasts from their restraint. "How does it feel knowing you are powerless to stop me?"

Mary growled with real anger, "You will not break me."

"I *will* break you." He pinched her nipple and rolled his fingers against it, causing her to cry out in pleasurable pain. "I guarantee it."

Faelan knelt beside her, grabbing her breast roughly. He took her nipple into his mouth and bit down, then he pull back cruelly with the sensitive flesh still clamped between his teeth. Brie gasped when he did it again to the other one. It looked incredibly painful, but Mary didn't make a sound.

He grazed the edge of the knife against her skin, starting at her stomach and dragging it slowly between her breasts, up to the hollow of her throat. Faelan pressed it against her pulsing skin, leaving an indentation without drawing blood.

"I know this is what you seek." He tossed the knife, and its clatter as it hit the floor filled the air. "Which is why I will not give it to you."

Mary growled in frustration and turned her head away from him. "Coward."

Faelan grasped her chin violently, pulling the hood off and hissing, "Worthless trash."

Brie whimpered. *No…* Mary could not handle Faelan turning on her too. It would be the end of her.

Mary's stubborn spirit could not be silenced. She glared at the young Dom and challenged him, "Go on… Give me your worst."

He slapped her face, leaving a pink handprint on her cheek. "You will get exactly what you deserve."

Faelan put his hand under her skirt and forced his fingers between her closed legs. Mary gasped and then clamped her mouth shut, refusing to give him the satisfaction of her surrender.

"Are you ready to be broken?"

"Never."

"You *will* break," he taunted.

Mary stared him down, but flinched involuntarily when he raised his arm to backhand her. It was easy to tell that reality was blurring into her past. Brie could sense it, could feel the dangerous precipice Mary was teetering on.

Faelan swung, stopping an inch from her face. "No."

Mary's eyes popped open in surprise.

"Never again," he decreed. "You are not allowed to play out this scene. The past no longer has power over you." He bent down to whisper something into Mary's ear.

Her lips trembled slightly as she listened to Faelan. She stared ahead without speaking, his words seeming to have no effect until the tears began to flow. A heart-wrenching cry escaped Mary's lips.

Faelan pulled a small penknife from his pocket and swiftly cut her from her bonds, gathering Mary into his arms and holding her tightly as a flood of emotion tore at her. It was a terrible and powerful release that Mary couldn't control. Sheltering her, he picked her up and spirited her to one of the private rooms in the back of the club.

People stood gawking as they passed, wondering what had just happened. Brie pushed through them and began gathering Faelan's things. Her heart was racing as she picked up the large knife and the pieces of rope and stuffed them into the black bag.

Whatever Faelan had said must have affected Mary on a soul level. Brie had never seen the woman cry real tears—ever. She looked in the direction in which the two had disappeared. Tonight, the young Dom had broken the barrier no one else had. For the first time, Brie felt hope…for both of them.

Lea came running up just as Brie was sanitizing the area. "Oh-em-gee, Brie, what just happened? Everyone is talking!"

Brie smiled as she meticulously wiped down the chair. "Lea, I think Blonde Nemesis has found her Prince Charming. Faelan held the key to unlock her."

Lea shook her head in disbelief. "Someone actually got through to that woman? And it was the young pup, no less?"

"Mary caused quite a ruckus by rejecting Master O, but I'm so proud of her. She stayed true to her heart, despite the temptation the Master must have presented."

"Dang, girl—sounds like I missed *all* the action!"

Brie gave her an unsympathetic look. "Like I'm going to feel sorry for you, all tied up with Tono. But yes, it was amazing," she said wistfully. "So romantic, the way he stopped midway through backhanding her and said 'No'. But even more astonishing was seeing Mary really cry."

"Blonde Nemesis sobbing? I don't believe it."

Brie had seen the spark between them, and said with confidence, "Mark my words, Lea. I see a collaring in their future."

# Lea's Erotic Surprise

The last day of production, Sir sent Brie an unusual text as they were wrapping up: *Go to the boutique next to the studio.*

With a little googling, Brie found the closest shop and headed there when she was done for the day. Even though it had been an exhausting week, she couldn't wait to discover what Sir had planned for the evening.

A little bell rang above the doorway, announcing her entrance into the boutique, but there wasn't a soul in the shop. She looked around and saw a gamut of sexy clothing, from catsuits and lingerie to full-length gowns.

"Hello?"

Brie moved up to the counter and saw a large box with a small envelope attached. Her name was on it. She took it off and read:

*Go to the flower shop by our apartment.*
*Bring the box but do not open it.*

Brie picked up the giant box, grinning as she clutched it. What lay inside could be an evening gown, which meant a night out, or naughty lingerie for indoor play.

*Clever Sir.*

She texted him as soon as she was in the car. He responded with an extra assignment for her.

*Put your feet on the dashboard on either side of the steering wheel.*

*Play with yourself until you're on the brink of orgasm.*

*Proceed to the flower shop.*

Brie looked around at the busy sidewalk. She was nervous about masturbating in public, but did not want to fail Sir. She gingerly placed her high heels on either side of the wheel and scooted down a little so she wouldn't be as obvious.

Brie only received a few blank stares, so she reached between her legs and under her panties.

She suddenly understood the exhilaration of her assignment. Doing something wicked in broad daylight with the very real threat of detection was arousing in the extreme, which was also cruel, given the fact she wasn't supposed to orgasm.

Brie slipped her finger inside her pussy and coated it with her juices before pulling out and playing with her clit. It was already erect and sensitive. She swirled her finger over the responsive nub before giving it a good flicking.

Brie whimpered and had to stop. She was too turned on to tease herself that way. Using two fingers, she slid in and out of her pussy, gliding her slick fingers over the folds of her outer lips, only brushing her clit lightly on occasion. Oh, yes, that felt good—like a relaxing back-rub for the loins.

But she knew that was not what Sir had asked of her. Brie returned to the quick flicking, seeing how long she could take it. Her pussy began to burn with need, demanding a quick release to end the torment. She was inclined to spoil it, but resisted the urge.

*Just a little longer.*

She made the mistake of looking up and meeting the gaze of a man walking past. The unexpected connection sent her over the edge. She squeaked, removing her fingers and scrambling to sit up, her pussy beginning to climax.

*No, no, no…*

Brie did the only thing she could think of to stop the tidal wave. She slapped her face hard. The pain brought her off the precipice and back down to earth. *Success!*

The man was still staring at her. Brie slipped her two fingers into her mouth, sucking off the remaining juices. "Yum," she mouthed before buckling up and starting the car.

She headed to the flower shop with a mischievous grin on her face. Sometimes it was wickedly fun to be bad.

*Thank you, Sir.*

Brie kept glancing at the box as she drove. Wrapped packages presented a terrible temptation. Sir knew the added torture he was putting Brie through by preventing her from taking a peek. He was probably at home, sipping a martini, amused by the thought of it.

Brie entered the tiny flower shop and went up to the girl at the counter, but was unsure what to say to her.

"Are you Miss Bennett?" the woman finally asked, after looking Brie over.

Brie smiled in relief. "I am, but how did you know?"

"I was told to look for a particular necklace."

Brie fingered her collar and smiled. "I *love* this necklace."

"It is quite lovely. I haven't seen one like it before," the shopkeeper replied. She handed Brie a single stem covered in a series of delicate orchids.

Brie took it and examined the blossoms, admiring the perfection of each individual flower. "This is stunning."

"Yes, it is. I was instructed to pick only the best for you."

Brie didn't see a card with further instructions, so she asked, "Is there anything else?"

"No, this is all."

Brie was slightly confused. Orchids reminded her of Tono, but that couldn't be right, so she texted Sir after leaving the shop. Unfortunately, she got no response. Was he up in the apartment, waiting for her?

She stared at the orchid again, remembering the haiku Tono had written. It had mentioned an erotic gift… But OMG—what if she was wrong and showed up at Tono's place uninvited? It would be all kinds of embarrassing.

Playing it safe, Brie made a quick stop by the apartment. She wasn't surprised to see it dark and silent. She checked every room just to be sure before getting into her car and heading to the Kinbaku master's place.

Now her imagination was running amok. Why would Sir have Brie spend time at Tono Nosaka's? She remembered he had mentioned that Lea's birthday gift was linked to Tono's.

*Damn! Whatever they have planned is going to be freakin' amazing!*

Brie pulled up to Tono's house and stared at it, feeling disappointed. His house was dark too. She got out of the car, assuming that Sir had left a card for her on the doorstep. However, as she approached she noticed a slight flickering through the window, as well as the hypnotic sound of a lone flute.

She knocked lightly, trembling all over as she waited for Tono to open the door. Instead, Lea graced the doorway dressed in a vibrant red kimono, her lips stylized in black to look like those of a geisha.

"Miss Bennett," she said in a formal voice, "please come in."

Brie stepped through the entrance with her large present, which Lea took from her before shutting the door.

The room was a fairyland of red candles.

"Lea, this is beautiful!"

"Kind of you to say, Miss Bennett," Lea said, trying to hide her grin. "I am here to clean and prepare you for the evening."

That sounded deliciously promising.

"Please follow me," Lea directed, leading Brie to Tono's bedroom.

Brie whispered, "What's going on?"

"I have waited months for this, Miss Bennett. I'm not about to spoil the surprise now," Lea informed her. "So be quiet and enjoy my preparations."

Brie giggled under her breath. The sexual tension flowing from Lea told her that this was going to be better than anything she had imagined. Brie just hoped the evening wouldn't end in a bad joke.

Lea undressed her slowly, laying her clothes on the bed. She then spent an hour cleaning her body, shaving her intimate parts and fixing her hair. All the months of stress slowly evaporated under Lea's gentle hands.

"I like the look of your brand," Lea purred, lightly tracing the mark. It ached at her touch, but Brie found it strangely erotic.

"Does it still hurt?" Lea asked.

"Not as bad as it did. To be honest, the branding itself didn't hurt nearly as much as the weeks after." Brie looked behind her, wishing she could see it. "Still, I love wearing his mark and I love looking at his."

"Sir has one too?"

Brie suddenly felt guilty, as if she had given away a privileged secret. "Forget I said anything. Please…"

Lea could tell she was upset and assured her, "Don't worry, Brie. I'm going to see it tonight anyway."

Brie gasped and turned to face her. "What?"

Lea cursed herself as she turned Brie back around. "Forget I said anything. Enough talk."

Lea giggled to herself as she continued her sensual preparations. When her friend had finished, she gave Brie a hug and a kiss on the cheek. "Now to unwrap your gift, birthday girl."

Brie tore into the package. Had it been anyone but Lea, she would have shown more decorum, but her best friend knew how wrapped gifts intrigued Brie. She lifted the lid and found a kimono that matched Lea's, but in black. It was covered in intricate embroidery. Brie realized on closer inspection that there were tiny orchids covering the silk. "This is unreal," she exclaimed, picking it up to put it on. She twirled around, feeling the cool silk flap lightly against her warm skin. She felt so wonderfully spoiled that she hugged herself.

"Miss Bennett, although it is beautiful on you, I need to complete your dress," Lea said, returning to her formal persona. She slid the garment off Brie's shoulders and laid it back on the bed.

Lea took a pair of stockings, garters and lacy crotchless panties from the box. She helped Brie into them and then finished with the kimono, tying the sash tight around Brie's waist. Lea stood back and looked at her with the pride of a mother.

"Simply gorgeous, just as I envisioned." She dragged Brie to the mirror and they stood side by side. Lea had a red kimono and black lips, and Brie was her complement, wearing a black kimono and red geisha lips.

"We make a beautiful pair," Brie said, laying her head on Lea's large chest.

"We always have," she replied, smiling at Brie in the mirror. "And now for your big surprise. I'm getting goosebumps just thinking about it."

Brie saw actual bumps on Lea's arm. "What are you planning to do to me?" she questioned, suddenly worried.

"Just you wait, Brie. I've watched you from the beginning of training. I know what you like. I think tonight will top everything. *Everything*!"

"Please—give me a hint, at least."

Lea led Brie out of the room. "You're just going to have to trust me."

*Trust Lea?*

Sir and Tono stood waiting for her. Both men were naked from the waist up, which was heavenly to behold. Sir was dressed only in black silk pants, and Tono in red.

Brie noticed two rings hanging from the ceiling above them. They were new, and gave Brie an inkling of what was in store.

"You look breathtaking, téa," Sir said, holding out his hand. Brie glided over to her Master on a cloud of wondrous expectation.

"Lea," Tono called. Lea walked over to stand beside the Asian Dom, her smile wide and beaming.

"So it's téa and Lea tonight, is it?" Brie commented.

"Yes," Tono replied smoothly. "It is not unusual for two girls to share an experience of Kinbaku."

Brie looked at Lea, barely able to contain her excitement. "Kinbaku *together*?"

Lea grinned. "Not exactly…"

Sir turned Brie's head and kissed her, sending little ripples of electricity through her already humming body. His low whisper sent chills through her. "Stand below the ring, hands behind your back, and wait."

She walked under it, looking up to make sure she was in the exact spot. Brie put her hands behind her back and smiled as Lea did the same, facing her, not more than two feet away.

Tono picked up a length of jute and unwound it. Just hearing it hit the floor made Brie's pussy wet. He came up behind Lea and secured the rope just under her breasts. Lea looked at Brie without speaking. The glint of lust in her eyes said it all.

Brie shivered when she felt Sir's lips next to her ear. "I want you to watch."

He kissed her neck, scratching her skin with his five o'clock shadow, as though he knew he was driving her crazy with the contact. Brie watched as Tono expertly wrapped Lea in jute, taking away her freedom to move, to breathe deeply. Her own body ached to feel the rope and she swayed slightly in need of it.

"Completely still, téa," Sir commanded as he knelt down. Brie cried out passionately when he bit her on the ass.

Lea gasped. "Oh, Brie. That little cry of yours turns me on."

Tono swiped his finger between Lea's legs and commented casually, "Yes, it does."

Brie bit her lip, liking this dynamic already.

Tono looped a length of the jute down between Lea's legs on one side of her outer lip and cinched it tight, and then he brought down another, leaving her pussy unobstructed for his pleasure. Brie did not miss the light touches he placed on Lea's mound as he worked, or the glazed look in Lea's eyes as she began to give in to the seduction of the rope.

He pulled at her kimono, uncovering Lea's impressive breasts in an artful manner. The way he exposed her was so sensual that Brie felt a gush of wetness. Watching her best friend enjoying Tono's expertise was intensely arousing.

Sir rubbed his middle finger against Brie's clit. It pulsed with desire. "No coming yet, téa. Not until your Master gives permission." He caressed her with more enthusiasm, making Brie whimper. She closed her eyes and laid her head back against his shoulder, trying to be good.

When she opened them again, she saw that Lea's hands were bound above her head, the rope anchored to the ring in the ceiling. Lea looked like a Japanese doll decorated in jute. "You're beautiful, Lea," Brie told her.

Lea smiled slowly, the rope already having its euphoric effect on her.

Brie's heart skipped a beat when she saw Tono approach *her* with a new length of jute. Sir left Brie's side, moving over to Lea. He opened a case and began laying out a series of attachments.

*A violet wand…*

Tono slipped the kimono off her shoulders, letting it drape over the sash. He then lifted her arms. Brie trembled, waiting for the first caress of the rope. As with Lea, he placed the first under her breasts. When he cinched it tight, she gasped involuntarily. It had been a while since her body had embraced the call of the jute.

"I feel your need," Tono stated quietly, as he slowly crisscrossed the rope to lift and separate her breasts. She sighed, loving the tight and pleasing constriction.

Tono bound Brie in a different pattern than Lea's, leaving her back free of rope. As he worked, his hands teased but did not touch her mound. The spell of his seductive binding began to lift her soul. She let out a soft, contented moan. The slapping of the jute, the tugging, and the tight caress were sending her ever higher.

"Delicious, isn't it?" Lea whispered.

Brie nodded, not wanting to disturb the rush.

The buzz of the violet wand began, and Lea whimpered. Both girls were familiar with the distinctive sound. Brie opened her eyes and smiled at Lea. She was going to love Sir's electric touch.

Sir turned the device to medium, knowing Lea's affinity for it, and slowly moved the device up the inside of her leg. Lea started shaking as he got closer to her pussy. She stiffened and Brie could have sworn she orgasmed.

Brie cried out as she struggled to deny herself her own climax, and was surprised when no one reprimanded Lea for her lack of control. How was that fair?

Sir started up Lea's other leg, forcing Brie to take a deep breath. It was proving to be a challenging night. Again, Lea started shaking as Sir made his way up her inner thigh.

Fortunately, Tono distracted Brie, taking her wrists and quickly binding them together before looping the rope over the ring. As he pulled the jute taut, Brie was struck by a feeling of elegant femininity mixed with total helplessness.

"Ooh…" she moaned. She felt long and lean, with no ability to resist her Master's desires—the perfect combination.

Sir finished off his play with Lea by turning up the power and brushing her nipples. Lea screamed in surprise and then started giggling. It was so infectious that Brie couldn't help but giggle with her.

"Oh, Brie, that was good, so good…" she sighed when he was done.

Sir looked across at Brie and said, "And now it's your turn."

He carefully cleaned off the equipment and put it back in the case. Instead of bringing it with him, Sir walked over empty-handed, letting Brie know he had something else in mind for her.

Brie swayed in her bindings. There was no escaping whatever he planned to do. It was thrilling. Tono had done an excellent job of restraining her. She looked at Lea and mouthed the words, "Help me!"

Lea purred at her. "Never."

As Tono passed to return to Lea, he grazed his fingers lightly against Brie's nipple, sending tendrils of fire down to her groin.

Brie heard Sir unzip his bag, and then the distinctive thud as the end of the bullwhip hit the floor. Her body tingled all over. *Will he be gentle or rough?*

Lea's eyes lit up. Being so close to each other made it almost as if they were experiencing each action as one.

Tono's home was unique, with high ceilings. They were perfect for Kinbaku as well as accommodating a bullwhip. Brie heard Sir warming up as the end of the bullwhip snapped near her.

Brie found the whip challenging, like no other tool Sir used. It forced her to a level of submission she struggled to maintain. Her fear was real, but her trust absolute.

She was hyperventilating, but did not become aware of it until Tono spoke softly. "Breathe with me…"

His simple command was a welcomed reminder. She closed her eyes and listened for Tono's breath, which brought instant calm to her soul. She quickly became in sync with him and, with a stroke of genius, she told Lea, "Breathe with us."

The three became one as they took deep, soul-refreshing breaths.

Sir approached Brie and gently pushed her hair forward, exposing her back to him. "Are you ready, téa?"

"Yes, Master," she breathed out in a calm voice.

He stepped back and waited a few seconds, building the suspense.

She was actually relieved when she heard the rush of air as the whip came hurling towards her. Because of her heightened arousal, the light stroke sent a burst of sexual energy straight to her loins.

"Does it feel good?" Lea whispered.

Brie nodded.

"Yum…" her friend said, as if she could feel it.

The lick of the whip was stimulating and alluring. Just as Master Anderson had predicted, her pussy quivered with the knowledge Sir could deliver a fiery stroke…but he did not.

After several minutes of the sensual stimulation, he paused. "Now," he said ominously.

Brie felt the lash of the whip across her buttocks as she watched Tono smack Lea's ass. Both Brie and Lea cried out in unison. It was extremely erotic.

"Color, téa."

"Green, a brilliant green, Master," she answered, hoping he would do it again.

To Brie's delight, he cracked the whip across her ass repeatedly. The sharp burst of fire across her skin multiplied the burning in her groin. She enjoyed watching Lea receive her spanking, knowing her friend was feeling the sting of the whip vicariously.

It was incredibly sexy, but that darn Lea came again, right there in front of her. Brie had to close her eyes when Tono began playing with

Lea's clit. Why were they being so cruel? Wasn't this supposed to be *her* birthday present, not Lea's?

Sir finished the session with several light licks, like tender kisses. It was a sweet ending with the bullwhip, something she hadn't experienced before. He came up behind her and whispered in her ear as he caressed her smarting ass.

"Watching you receive my strokes, the way your beautiful ass rolls with each contact of the whip, the way your muscles tense and release…it is arousing, babygirl."

She turned her head towards him. "Thank you, Master."

His tongue caressed the outside of her lips as his fingers reached between her legs and teased her wet opening.

Brie moaned, feeling her pussy tensing for an orgasm. She cried, "Red… Red!"

Sir chuckled. "Your orgasm will be grand, téa. When I allow it."

He pressed his finger inside and teased her G-spot, making her thighs shudder involuntarily. "Yes, an orgasm of epic proportions, but not yet."

Sir nodded to Tono and both men began loosening the bindings. Brie watched as Tono made quick work of the knots and the jute fell from Lea. He then untied the sash and lifted the kimono from her shoulders, laying all three items on the mat.

The knots proved more challenging for Sir, but soon she felt the jute's release. The feeling of lightness it gave her was almost like a spiritual liberation. Looking at Lea's body covered in beautiful rope marks brought a smile to Brie's lips. She knew she carried the same lovely marks—a charming gift left by the jute for their Doms to admire.

Her skin tingled where the jute had been, extending the delicious experience.

Sir loosened the sash and slid the kimono off her shoulders. She stood before him, naked except for the hose, garters, and panties—his favorite look for her.

He ran his fingers over the indentations of the rope, sending chills through her. "Exquisite."

To Brie's surprise, Sir bent down and picked up one of the lengths of jute, then began binding her wrists again. Tono did the same, looping the end through the ring and forcing Lea's arms back up.

Brie bit her lip as Sir tightened the rope again, binding her arms tightly. What were they going to do now?

"Bend forward at the waist, both of you," Sir ordered.

The girls did, facing each other, now only a foot apart. With careful precision, the Doms released the tautness of the ropes until Brie's and Lea's noses were only inches from each other. Lea smiled at her and leaned forward, giving her a quick kiss on the lips. Both girls giggled.

"A little tighter," Tono suggested.

The two were pulled back just a fraction, so no contact could be made. When the adjustments were complete, they were tightly secured to the rings again.

Curiosity was killing Brie. "What are you doing, Master?"

Sir glanced at her and winked before addressing Tono. "I think they need to be silenced." He pulled a gag from his pocket and commanded, "Open." When Brie parted her lips, smooth silk instantly filled the gap. Sir tied it firmly and then stood back.

Instead of silk, Tono wrapped several strands of jute around Lea's mouth to act as her gag. Lea looked at her and wiggled her eyebrows, as if to say, *Aren't we naughty girls?*

"The time has come, téa."

She held her breath, hoping her ecstasy would be close at hand.

Sir instructed, "I want you to keep your eyes locked on Lea—do not let them stray. I am going to fuck you hard. I will be rough."

She whimpered, very much liking the sound of that.

"You are free to orgasm as many times as you want, as long as you continue to look into your friend's eyes. I want her to be able to count the number of your pleasures."

Naked and bound, Brie met Lea's gaze and thought, *Oh, this is going to be hot on a whole new level…*

Sir undressed behind her as Tono removed his clothing in front of her. She admired the Asian Dom's toned body, a perfect male specimen according to her own specifications. And now she was going to watch him in action—with her best friend, no less. It was all kinds of erotic!

Tono looked up with those chocolate-brown eyes and she suddenly felt like a deer in headlights, caught by their connection. Her heartbeat increased as both men took their positions. It was almost like watching a mirror as she felt Sir's hands on her waist and saw Tono grab onto Lea's hips.

Brie lowered her gaze and stared at Lea. This was it—they were going to be pounded at the same time, by two gorgeous Doms, while facing each other.

*It's good to be me…*

Sir forced Brie to arch her back more, and then penetrated her slowly until he found an angle he liked. He traced her brand with his finger, causing her pussy to contract around his cock. "No mercy for my goddess."

Sir grunted as he rammed his cock deep inside, the head of his shaft rubbing hard against her swollen G-spot. Brie screamed into her gag while her body invited the ferocity of it—*needed* it, in fact.

Lea's eyes widened as Tono began his own thrusting. Lea's breasts bounced crazily as he pounded with fervor. Neither Dom was taking it easy tonight.

Brie screamed into the gag again as the crest she had been teetering on for hours completely overwhelmed her and she experienced what she could only describe as a full-body orgasm. Every part of her seemed to tense almost to breaking point, and then explode in orgasmic release—from the tips of her toes up the entire length of her spine, to the individual hairs on her head.

Tears fell freely as she rode the intense tidal wave of pleasure.

Lea's face had screwed up in her own orgasm, but Brie's lasted far longer—far, far longer.

Sir finally pulled out and instructed her to breathe in deeply. She heard him coating his shaft in lubricant. It could only mean one thing…

Brie almost shut her eyes in pleasure when she felt him press against her sphincter, but Sir had given her specific instructions. She opened them and concentrated on Lea's pupils as he eased his hard shaft into her ass. Sir gave sexy, stinging slaps on her ass cheeks as he forced himself in deeper.

Just as he had before, Sir thrust leisurely until he found the perfect spot. He chuckled when he finally found it.

Brie tensed, but he murmured, "Relax, babygirl, relax…" He turned her head to kiss her. Once she had surrendered to him, his lips were fierce and demanding.

Sir grabbed a fistful of her hair, pulling her head back as he began thrusting into her with powerful strokes, over and over again. Reality blurred as primal sensations took hold. His cock was hitting her G-spot, but from a different angle, causing a different reaction. As soon as he stopped, her pussy caught up, gushing with liquid as it clamped down in a rhythmic dance.

Brie stared at Lea, but struggled to focus. As soon as the last contraction had ended, Sir started up again. It didn't take long for her body to respond with another, equally powerful orgasm.

Brie shook her head in disbelief. She knew her body well. Normally, with each consecutive orgasm the intensity and pleasure decreased, but not this time. She looked at Lea in wonder as Sir began again. There was no question he was going to make her gush for him a third time.

He started pounding again, and had no problem bringing her to that point almost immediately. She whimpered as another orgasm rocked her body and her pussy released a smaller ejaculation than before.

"We're getting close," he growled.

*Close to what?*

Sir began playing with her clit as he slowly caressed her ass with his shaft. It was too much, and she stiffened in a long, drawn-out orgasm.

*Help me…* Brie pleaded silently to her friend.

Sir commanded, "Come for me, téa."

At only the lightest pressure on her clit, with his cock filling her ass, Brie came for him again.

"Again."

Brie shook her head in astonishment as her pussy orgasmed on command, stealing her conscious thought with its intensity. Subspace called and she entered willingly, letting the tingly feeling take over while her body continued to listen and respond to Sir. Pure bliss and a level of heightened serenity carried Brie deeper within as Sir pounded into her again.

Everything fell away as she *became* sensation and found a whole new world to explore…

"Téa…"

A light tapping on her cheek caught her attention, and she listened more carefully.

"Téa… Open your eyes."

They fluttered open of their own accord, and she gazed into the loving eyes of her Master. She tried to smile, but her muscles were too relaxed to respond.

Sir leaned over and kissed her. "I sometimes wonder just how far you fly from me, babygirl."

She struggled to turn her head and saw they were lying on Tono's floor mat. The candles had been blown out, and the room was dark except for a single tealight.

"Sir," she croaked.

He put his finger against her lips. "No need to talk. Now that I have you back, we can go home."

*Home.*

When Sir picked her up, she realized she had been wrapped back into the smooth silk of her black kimono. She laid her head against his chest and smiled.

"Did you enjoy yourself?"

She nodded.

"How were your climaxes?"

She was silent for a few moments, trying to find the word she wanted to share. "Legendary."

# ...On the Way to the Theater

The night she had been waiting for all her life had finally come—the premiere of her first film, her *baby*. A film she hoped would change the world in some small, but positive way.

People were going to see more than just a simple documentary. The film revealed Brie's personal transformation from the shell of a girl she had been into the fully actualized woman she was now. Would people recognize the significant, soul-level change or only see the kink? As Sir zipped up the back of her blood red gown, Brie suddenly felt a twinge of fear.

"What's wrong, téa?"

She turned around with tears in her eyes. "What if they don't understand? What if they don't get it, Sir?"

"It's the risk you take. You cannot force people to see what you see. All you can do is present your truth to them."

She swallowed hard. "For the first time, Sir…" Brie gazed into his confident eyes, "I'm scared."

He smiled as he put his hand under her chin and tilted her head higher. "Why did you make this film?"

"To share a new world of desires and a level of satisfaction people might not know exists."

"Do you feel your documentary accomplishes that?"

She gave a half-smile, understanding where he was heading with the question. "Yes, Sir, I do."

"Then whatever happens tonight, it will have gone well enough, agreed?"

Brie pressed her forehead into his chest. "Well enough…" she echoed. "But if it were up to me, I would prefer 'well enough' to mean a huge success, with lots of positive press and millions of enthusiastic fans."

Lifting her chin again, he asked in a serious tone, "Is that why you did it?" His intense gaze pierced her soul and the arrow of truth flew straight into her heart.

"No, Sir."

"Do not waste your energies on the unimportant."

She tiptoed to kiss Sir's firm lips. "As always, you give me the perspective I need. Thank you, Sir."

"This journey we embark on tonight will be a challenge, I'm certain of it. But I said it once and I will say it again, so that we are clear. No matter how this affects our lives, I'm proud to stand with you in this moment."

A lone tear escaped Brie's eye and rolled down her perfectly made-up face. Sir brushed it away with his thumb. "Exude elegance and poise, confident in the knowledge you are mine, Brie."

She smiled, remembering he had said those words the night of her collaring.

He returned her smile and announced, "I have a surprise for you."

She was grateful for any distraction, thinking he'd gotten her flowers or jewelry. "What is it, Sir?"

"Your parents are joining us tonight. They're on their way here as we speak."

She swallowed hard, trying to keep the shock from her face. "My parents?"

"I asked them to come and support you tonight."

"And my dad agreed?" Brie asked, unable to believe it.

He nodded as he turned her back around and placed a delicate chain around her neck. "They may not care for the path you have chosen, but their love for you remains constant."

She touched the necklace, noticing that it fit right under the collar she wore as if it were a part of it. "What's this?"

"A little reminder," he said, kissing the nape of her neck.

Brie walked over to the wall mirror to look at it. The intricate piece rested on her collarbone. She leaned closer to see the silhouette of two condors in flight, their wings outstretched and touching, connected to one another.

She was in awe. "Where did you find this?"

"I had it made for you."

"It matches the collar so perfectly, Sir. I…" She turned to face him. "There will never be a more perfect gift." Brie glanced in the mirror again, smiling as she touched the condors. She believed the necklace held the same significance as a wedding band.

She put her hands on Sir's chest and gazed up at him. "I love you, Thane Davis." Her insides fluttered as she said his given name.

He leaned down and kissed her. "I love you too, Brie Bennett, with all the fierceness of a condor."

She could feel the light pressure of the birds on her neck when she kissed him back. Whatever happened, nothing could touch her. She was protected by Sir's love.

The ride in the limo was miserably silent. Despite the fact that her parents had come to support Brie, it was obvious they hadn't changed their minds about Sir or the BDSM lifestyle. She could feel the judgment rolling off her father in waves. He refused to acknowledge Sir and it mortified Brie.

She looked around the spacious limousine and shuddered. Nothing good ever came out of a limo ride.

Sir had insisted they act vanilla in front of her parents. It made for a strained and difficult trip. Brie was nervous about the premiere, so she placed her hand on Sir's thigh for comfort, although she would have preferred to be at his feet.

Brie tried to kill the deafening silence by forcing a conversation. "So Mom, did you watch my film?"

Her mother gave her father an uneasy glance before answering. "I did…"

"And what did you think?"

"Frankly, I found it shocking."

"Is that all?" Brie asked, leaning forward, hoping to hear something positive from her lips.

"I like your friend Lea."

Brie sat back, disappointed that was all her mother had to say. She looked out of the window and said, "Yes, Lea is a funny girl."

"Will all the men who used you be there?" her father asked coldly.

She turned towards him, looking her father directly in the eye. "The men who helped train and support me will be there. If you have nothing nice to say to them, say nothing at all. They do *not* deserve your contempt."

"That is my intention, daughter. I will remain silent," he replied, glancing at Sir briefly to emphasize his meaning.

Brie groaned inside. "Why did you come tonight, Dad? If all you're going to do is make me feel bad and insult the man I love by ignoring him, what's the point? You might as well have stayed home."

"I came, daughter, because the man beside you insisted I was needed tonight. It seems obvious to us both that he was mistaken."

"That's not true! I'm glad Mr. Davis invited us," Brie's mother exclaimed, clutching her husband's hand. She smiled at her daughter. "Sweetie, even though this is not the kind of premiere I ever dreamed I would be attending, I *want* to be here. You are everything to me."

"Will you both stay to watch the film?" Brie pressed.

Her father growled. "Do you realize the sacrifice this is going to be for me as your father?" He stared at Brie harshly. "Do you?"

"No, Father. I can't imagine," she answered simply, biting back an ugly retort.

"I am going to be exposed to things a father should never have to witness. On top of that, I get to live with the knowledge that the rest of the world has seen it too. You are *my* daughter, *my* little girl."

"I am the girl you raised to be an independent adult. If my happiness is important to you, then you no longer need to worry. I am not only happy, but content and successful. I am living my dream."

"And my nightmare," he mumbled under his breath.

"You know, Dad, I'm glad you're going to watch my documentary. At least you won't be able to make ignorant statements anymore."

"We're about to pull up," the limo driver interrupted.

Brie looked out at the crazy amount of people crowding around the theater. "I never expected such a turnout for a documentary film," she said in wonder. She was thrilled until she saw the protest signs.

*Oh, no…*

Sir saw them too. "Head up at all times, Brie. You are focused on me. No one else matters."

She remembered a similar lesson in Russia. She closed her eyes and repeated to herself, *No one else matters.* When she opened her eyes, Brie felt a new sense of calm.

She told her parents, "Follow us, but *please* don't speak to anyone. These people don't need extra cannon fodder to use against me or my film."

"Our lips are sealed," her father replied, his expression hard and unwavering.

Her mother looked at the angry multitudes milling outside the car and panicked. "Brie, I don't want them to hurt you!"

Sir assured her, "She'll be fine, Mrs. Bennett."

Sir then cradled Brie's face in his hands and smiled. "Your moment has finally come, Brie. Embrace it with pride and confidence." He kissed her deeply, right there in front of her father. The boldness of the gesture infused her with a rebellious self-confidence.

When the driver opened the door for them, angry shouts filled the vehicle. Sir made her parents go first. "Wait beside the car, and then follow behind us."

Sir exited next. He stood up outside the limo and held his hand out to her. Brie took it and squeezed it hard, needing his courage.

"Slut!" was the first word to greet Brie as she emerged from the limo. She looked at Sir and smiled. If that was the best they could do, this was going to be easy.

She was enamored by the red carpet at her feet and the velvet ropes sectioning off each side. Hundreds of flashes went off as Sir held out his arm to escort her down the carpet.

Brie looked into the barrage of flashing lights and saw news cameras as well. Brie assumed the coverage would be a good thing, whether it was for the documentary or the protesters.

She was surprised to see Master Anderson standing just inside the ropes, and farther down, Master Coen as well. She wondered if they'd been asked to walk the red carpet as well, since both were mentioned in the film.

"Miss Bennett!" one of the reporters called out.

Sir led Brie over to the woman. She smiled at the reporter as she nervously played with the condors around her neck.

"Can you tell us why you created this documentary?"

"Certainly. I wanted people like me to have a better understanding of the D/s lifestyle." She giggled. "To be honest, when I first learned about it

I was pretty shocked. But through my training, I've come to understand the beauty and power that can come from it."

"Beauty—I'll say! Just look at these hunky men you worked with," the reporter said, giving Sir a flirtatious wink.

Brie ignored her remark, and leaned towards the microphone. "I hope my documentary can open people's minds and bring couples closer together."

The reporter continued to flirt with him. "Closer is exactly where I'd like to be."

Sir frowned and moved Brie on to the next reporter in line. He leaned down and whispered, "Well done. Keep it about the film."

The male reporter she approached looked to be as old as her parents. Brie was already dreading his questions.

"Miss Bennett, this documentary is based on your own training. Is that correct?"

"Yes, it documents the six-week training I experienced at the Center."

"Did you go into training with the intention of documenting it, or was submission something you wanted to become skilled at?"

"Great question!" she complimented, realizing she had a true reporter on her hands. "I joined the Center because I was curious about the lifestyle after receiving an invitation from the headmaster of the school."

"When you say 'headmaster', you are speaking about the man standing beside you, Sir Thane Davis, and not the current headmaster of the school?"

It appeared that the man had done his homework. "That's correct. Because I studied film, it only seemed natural for me to document my days as I lived them. After I got to know the other students, I asked them to add their experiences as well."

"Would you say you are close to your fellow classmates?"

Brie looked farther down the red carpet and saw that both Mary and Lea were ahead of her, answering questions under the protection of Faelan and Tono.

She glanced back at the reporter. "Yes, I'm most definitely close to both. Although Mary and I have our differences, as you will see in the film, both ladies are exceptional friends."

He surprised her with his next question. "Miss Bennett, do you feel this documentary may end up hurting the BDSM community in any way?" he asked.

It was a sobering thought. Brie frowned when she answered, "I certainly hope not. It's my belief that knowledge is power. How can learning about something new and dispelling preconceived ideas be a bad thing?"

"We need to move on, Brie," Sir informed her, guiding her forward.

The next young woman in line looked so eager to interview Brie that she wondered if the girl might secretly desire to become a submissive herself.

With a wide, virtuous smile, the reporter asked, "Miss Bennett, are you concerned at all about the negative message this film will give to millions of women?"

Brie was taken aback. "What do you mean?"

"Violence against women. The utter contempt of social standards. Girls whoring themselves out to the highest bidder. Women allowing themselves to be treated like sex objects, or worse—animals. Is that really the message you want to send out to impressionable young ladies?"

"What you are talking about are the preconceived notions I hope to dispel with this documentar—" Brie stopped midsentence. She found herself staring into the eyes of Sir's mother, who was standing directly behind the reporter. Ruth wore a malicious grin on her perfect face.

From within the crowd a woman emerged, shouting, "Fucking whore!" The stranger threw something at Brie's face.

It crashed into Brie's skull when she tried to duck, the impact hard and painful. Sir immediately moved between her and the attacker, using his body to protect her as several people rushed up, pelting them with what she thought were rocks and shouting hateful words.

Time slowed down to a crawl for Brie. All the shouting and commotion became silent in the chaos. She glanced over and saw her father shouting angrily, but her mother stood frozen in place with a look of sheer panic.

Then Brie felt the ooze of blood from her forehead and down her cheek. She felt for the wound and was confused when she looked at her hand and saw yellow instead of red. A piece of eggshell that had been stuck to her hair fell to the crimson carpet at her feet.

Brie felt the sting of humiliation. Rocks would have been preferable.

Sir tightened his grip on her. "It's going to be all right. Marquis Gray is taking care of it."

She looked up and saw that a small army of staff members from the Training Center had descended upon the attackers and were 'escorting' them to police waiting nearby.

Now that the initial shock had passed, Brie was crushed by a wave of shame. She had just been egged in public and her beautiful dress was ruined. To make her humiliation complete, she heard the sound of hundreds of camera clicks. Brie pulled against Sir in the direction of the limousine, wanting to escape.

"No, babygirl," he said firmly.

She looked up at her Master—her hair matted with yolk, the tears ready to fall.

Sir pulled the decorative handkerchief from his pocket and smiled charmingly as he cleaned the egg from her face. He did it with such tenderness that Brie momentarily forgot the world.

After he was satisfied, he stuffed the dirty handkerchief back in his pocket and lifted her chin to kiss her. The kiss infused her with courage, reminding her that nothing else mattered.

Brie whispered when he let go, "Only you, Sir."

He nodded and held out his arm for her. She took a deep breath before holding up her head and smiling at the cameras.

Brie's mother came up and blurted out, "Wait just a second." She licked her fingers before rubbing them against Brie's temple. It was an action that Brie had hated as a child—mother-spit used to clean her face—but tonight it took on emotional significance.

Her mother stood back and looked her over. "Yes, all better."

"Thank you, Mom," Brie whispered.

She gave Brie a tight squeeze before stepping back to stand with her father.

Brie looked back and saw her dad nonchalantly brushing eggshell off Sir's shoulder. It was a simple gesture, but one that meant the world to Brie. It was the first sign of acceptance.

She mouthed the words, "Thanks, Dad."

He gave her a brief smile and then wrapped his arm around her mother's waist. "Shall we?"

They avoided the rest of the reporters, making their way directly into the theater. Brie could only imagine what the headlines would read in the morning.

"Why don't we both freshen up, Brie?" Sir said. "Your father can wait here for you, should you have need."

Brie liked the protective sound of that. She kissed her dad on the cheek before following her mom into the restroom. Although she had a dress polka-dotted with wet spots, Brie looked and felt tons better when her mother had finished cleaning her off.

Sir was standing beside her father, already waiting for her when the two emerged from the restroom.

"Beautiful," he complimented, kissing the back of Brie's hand tenderly.

"Well done, Marcy," her father praised after looking Brie over. "It appears we were needed tonight, after all."

Their small party was led to the reserved area, where she was greeted by Mr. Holloway, Lea and Mary. Lea rushed up to Brie, wanting to dish about what had happened outside, but Sir shook his head. "Tonight is about celebrating Brie's achievement, Ms. Taylor."

Lea reluctantly sat back down. "Can I at least tell a joke?"

Sir and Brie both answered, "No!"

Lea huffed and slouched in her seat. Tono gave her a gentle nudge.

She immediately sat up, her blooming blush coloring her ample chest a bright shade of red. "I'm sorry," she whispered to Tono, loud enough for others to hear as the lights began to dim.

It made Brie giggle. Even without her jokes, Lea was good for a laugh.

Brie eagerly watched the audience and listened for their collective responses once the film started. She loved every giggle and chortle, but cherished even more the lustful gasps when Marquis and Lea filled the screen. She noticed several audience members swiping at their eyes when Mary confessed her feelings of brokenness. To Brie's delight, as the credits rolled, the entire theater broke out in applause.

When the lights came back up, both Brie and Mr. Holloway were asked to stand and take a bow together. The theater roared with a second round of applause as people gave them a standing ovation.

Brie felt embarrassed by the focused attention and tried to sit back down, but Sir would not allow it. "This applause is for you. Accept it gracefully, Brie."

She faced the audience again and smiled, but she knew the applause was for everyone involved in the film, not just her. Brie gestured for Lea and Mary to stand with her. Mr. Holloway did the same with the film crew. It felt right, all of them standing together as one.

Finally, she convinced Sir to stand up beside her. Brie laid her head against his shoulder with a smile so wide it hurt and a heart that was completely and utterly content.

# The Aftershock

Brie's parents left later that evening. Her father said it was imperative they control the damage the film would cause in their close-knit community. Brie didn't mind. Her father had watched the film and had not spoken of it since. She figured he needed time to process it. So she spent a restless night in Sir's arms, worrying what the newspapers would say in the morning.

What she woke up to both astonished and pleased her. The front page of the *LA Times* read 'The Strength of a Dominant' and had a picture of Sir thoughtfully cleaning Brie's face after the attack. The same picture was plastered on the national news that morning. Instead of focusing on the film or even the protestors, all the news centered on was the unusual relationship between Sir and Brie.

Brie found out from the morning show that Sir now had a following of female fans, from young girls to grandmothers. Twitter was going crazy speculating about him and Facebook pages had been set up in his honor. Everyone wanted to know more about the man who'd defended Brie so gallantly.

Overnight, D/s went from being an obscure term used by kinky deviants to being something sweet and romantic. The morning news had 'experts' answering questions and a psychologist explaining in clinical terms the reasons why they thought people practiced BDSM. It was quite amusing, if not a little insulting.

Sir turned off the TV and folded the paper before putting it in the trash. "The firestorm has begun." Brie looked at the trash can, deciding to ask Lea later to save her a copy as a memento.

Brie smiled as she crawled onto the lap Sir offered. "Well, at least people are talking about it, Sir."

"I, for one, do not care to see my face everywhere."

Brie brushed her fingers over his jawline, which was rough with morning stubble. "But it's such a handsome face, Sir. I don't mind one bit."

He huffed in irritation. "It has serious repercussions, Brie. I doubt I will be taken seriously in the business world now."

Brie frowned, suddenly feeling nauseous. "I never considered that, Sir."

Sir chuckled at her statement. "Why am I not surprised?" He pulled her head back and gently kissed her throat before biting it. His lips moved up to her ear. "I understood the consequences, but never considered they would belittle my lifestyle in this way." He shook his head in disgust. "Facebook pages?"

"It's kind of sweet, Sir," Brie told him, kissing his chin.

"What it does is diminish my authority, Brie. We are not a sideshow to be gawked at and thereby dismissed."

She finally understood the gravity of the situation. "What do you suggest I do, Sir?"

"Only respond to serious inquiries and ignore frivolous issues meant to distract. Your duty is more than simply garnering press for the documentary—it is also about being respectful to the community we are a part of. Whether or not Mr. Holloway agrees, I believe that takes precedence over the film."

She understood his point and acquiesced. "I will do as you suggest, Sir."

The positive attention they had enjoyed quickly turned dark when rumors spread that Sir had abandoned his dying mother. As quickly as people had embraced him, they turned and crucified him.

'Woman-hater' became Sir's new title in the press. Clients he had worked with for years ended their association within hours of the accusations being released. The financial impact was terrible and swift.

Ruth had done her job well. She'd accomplished exactly what she'd promised. It broke Brie's heart to see his reputation decimated, but Sir seemed unruffled. In fact, he smiled when she asked why he was so calm.

"This is a litmus test, Brie. Any client who would react to such a rumor is not worth my time."

The next morning, everything changed yet again. Brie was watching the news with Lea and Mary. It amazed the girls how fickle the public could be and Lea was about to make a joke when Brie heard, "Next up, how you can help support Ruth Davis in her fight against cancer."

Brie called Sir immediately.

His answer surprised her. "Good. It's time the beast was flayed."

The girls continued to watch the television and were soon rewarded with a newsflash. Under Sir's orders, his lawyer had sent evidence of her falsified medical history to the major media outlets. It didn't take long before the news that Ruth Davis was cancer-free spread like wildfire and all donations were halted.

Reporters then set out to discover the *real* story behind Ruth Davis and left no stone unturned in their pursuit. Within days, the murky state of her financial affairs came to light, as well as issues in her past—including her infidelity and the death of her husband, Alonzo Davis.

The negative press quickly transferred from Sir to Ruth, and in the aftermath droves of women naïvely flocked to the documentary to find out more about the tragic hero they knew as Sir Thane Davis.

What they found instead was the power of submission.

# Farewell and Good Riddance

Brie was on her knees, back straight, breasts out, her hands behind her back. The clock was ticking in the kitchen, marking each second until Master's return.

She was startled by heavy pounding at the door. Brie cautiously approached it and peeked through the peephole, terrified it might be Sir's mother.

She was shocked to find it was Ms. Clark.

"Open up! Open up now—I demand to have answers!"

Brie ran down the hallway and threw on a summer dress before returning to the door. "Sir's not here, Ms. Clark, but I expect him in a few minutes."

Ms. Clark answered in a condescending tone, "Then let me in to wait for him."

"I have to get permission first," Brie called through the door. She texted Sir and was told to let the fuming Domme in.

Brie unlocked the door, quelling her unease as she allowed Ms. Clark to enter. Her ex-trainer brushed past her as if she didn't exist and headed straight for the couch. When Brie asked if there was anything she needed, Ms. Clark held up her hand and barked, "Do *not* speak to me."

Brie backed away slowly and returned to the door to kneel in the proper position until Sir's return.

The clock ticked loudly in the kitchen as the two waited. It was an unbearable silence, at least for Brie. Ms. Clark's anger was palpable and her contempt for Brie equally apparent. So she closed her eyes and entertained happy thoughts of being tied down by Sir, and of being tortured by his cock.

"Get that smirk off your face," Ms. Clark snapped.

Brie instantly frowned for the Domme's benefit, but in her head she begged, *Hurry home, Sir!*

Relief came when she heard his keys in the door. Sir dropped them on the counter and patted her head as he passed, letting her know she could stand up and join him.

"What are you doing here, Samantha?"

"Why? Why, Thane? Why do you hate me?"

"Calm down and explain," he ordered. "I have no clue what you're talking about."

"Tell your sub to leave," Ms. Clark demanded.

"No."

Ms. Clark looked first shocked and then dismayed. In a subtle act of defiance, she turned her back on Brie before explaining, "You told them to let me go and now I'm no longer working for the Center."

"Ah…" Sir took off his jacket and hung it up before joining her on the couch. "That had nothing to do with me, Samantha. That was your own fault."

"What the hell do you mean?" Ms. Clark demanded.

"Did you really think your stunt at Brie's party would have no consequences? All of the trainers were there, including the headmaster. With that one action, you demonstrated your utter lack of control. We'd seen it before with Brie, but unfortunately you never recovered, even after she'd left. The trainers must have decided it was time to give you the freedom you need to overcome that weakness."

"But you *know* I am a damn good trainer. How could you let them do this to me?!"

"I was not involved. But truthfully, I am in agreement with their decision. You need to move forward. It is time you break from the past that has held you down."

"What are you saying?" she said, her voice trembling as if she was about to cry.

"You have stuck by my side all these years with the mistaken hope that one day Durov would change his mind. I am telling you now—that will never happen."

"But… I don't believe it. Rytsar didn't press charges that night. I know he did that for me. He cared enough to protect me, despite everything. It was a horrible mistake and I've done my penance with unfailing determination. I've been waiting patiently all these years for his forgiveness. I've learned my lesson and am ready for him to grant it."

Sir shook his head. "Samantha, you are gravely mistaken. The reason he didn't press charges had nothing to do with protecting you. What you did to him was so degrading he could not stomach bringing it before a judge. To this day, you've never owned up to the damage you caused him."

"That's not true! I went to counseling; I quit drinking. Hell, I even became a submissive to another woman for him. Everything I did, *everything*, has been for him."

Sir's voice was harsh when he replied, "Everything you did has been for you, and you alone. You wanted him back, so you did those things in the hope that he would return to you. It's never been about him."

Ms. Clark glared at Sir, as if she hated his version of the truth.

He continued, indifferent to her wrath, "Samantha, it's possible to make a mistake so great you can never know closure with the person you have wronged. You can't undo the damage and you can't change the past. It's time to move on."

"But…" Her voice dropped down to a whisper. "Oh, God… "A tear fell down her cheek when she confessed, "I still love him."

Sir's response was stern but clear. "If you love him, you will move on."

Ms. Clark slumped on the couch, sounding hollow and weak when she asked, "How can I face a future without him?"

"Durov was never a part of your future."

It seemed surreal to Brie when Ms. Clark moved over and laid her head on Sir's shoulder. It was weird to see the woman underneath that hard exterior—like seeing a turtle without its shell.

Sir was gentle with her. He put his arm around Ms. Clark, saying, "You are an exceptional trainer and a skilled Mistress. There is no reason not to move forward with confidence. Claim the life you have put on hold."

She mumbled into his shoulder, "But the Center *was* my life."

"I understand, but trust me when I say you'll get used to it. It's a hard adjustment in the beginning. However, other things will take its place. My advice? If it gets to be too much, you can always visit. I know it's helped me."

Ms. Clark sat still in his arms for a few moments longer before sitting up and moving away from him, her hard persona back in place. "So that's it then. My time at the Training Center is officially over." She stood up and walked over to the window. "I have never felt so out of control of my own life before," she said as she gazed at the city below.

"That is only an illusion, Samantha. You were never in control, not until this very moment."

The Domme gasped. She closed her eyes and let it sink in. When she finally turned to face Sir, she stated, "I will miss your wisdom, Sir Davis." She glanced at Brie and her eyes narrowed briefly.

She focused her attention back on Sir. "Master Anderson is planning to move back to Colorado to start up a Training Center there. He's invited me to join him, along with Baron."

Sir put his hands behind his head and sat back on the couch, looking a bit stunned. "I'd actually forgotten that was Brad's original plan."

Brie wondered what Sir was thinking. Was he sad to lose his friend?

The stunned look was replaced with cool assurance. He stood up, telling her, "This will be a good opportunity for the three of you. I'm confident you will work well as a team."

Ms. Clark shook Sir's hand, stating in a businesslike manner, "It's been a good run, Sir Davis." She paused. Her voice was thick with emotion when she spoke again. "I will never forget your support these many years." She bowed her head. "Thank you."

He placed his hand on the top of her head in a silent exchange. When he removed it, the Domme looked up and smiled sadly. Then she turned and stared hard at Brie.

"I have always found you irritating and disrespectful. Why do you think that is, Miss Bennett? I have yet to put my finger on it."

Brie blanched at her blunt words and sputtered, "Maybe…maybe I'm too much like you?"

The Domme scoffed, "No. You couldn't be more my opposite." Ms. Clark walked up to her, invading her personal space to stare at Brie's mouth. The ex-trainer's proximity was unsettling, and Brie licked her lips nervously as she stepped back.

Ms. Clark leaned in even closer. "Maybe it has something to do with the fact such talented lips are wasted on you."

Brie had no quick comeback and had to watch silently as Sir said goodbye while he escorted Ms. Clark to the door.

The moment it closed, Sir turned around and said with a devilish smirk, "On your knees, now."

Brie sank down to the floor, automatically putting her hands behind her back.

Sir began unbuckling his belt as he approached. "Those talented lips are definitely *not* wasted on you."

The next goodbye was much more expected and enjoyable. Sir and Brie met with his mother in his lawyer's downtown office. Ruth had complained that it was far too stuffy and impersonal, which was exactly the reason Sir had chosen it.

When they entered the room, Sir asked Mr. Thompson straight away, "Are the papers ready?"

"Of course," he said, handing Sir the stack of documents.

"Excellent. Let's get started."

Ruth did not seem to care for his abruptness. "Wait one second, son. I think we need to have a little discussion first."

"This is the discussion. The terms are simple. I will provide you with transportation and supplies if you agree to go to China for three years as a medical volunteer."

"That is not having a discussion; that is telling me what to do. I'm your mother, damn it. I don't deserve to be treated like a common business transaction."

"I see no mother before me. What I see is a manipulative, self-centered beast with a total lack of a conscience. I hope the work you do over the next three years opens your eyes to the truth."

"Fuck you, Thane. And I'm not going to some third world country!"

Sir shrugged his shoulders, pushing the papers towards her. "You don't have to. However, people are out for blood, Ruth. I'm giving you a fresh start because I need to believe there is a human heart beating somewhere in that chest." He pushed a pen towards her. "You can worry where your next meal or lawsuit is coming from, or you can sign this and be gone within the hour. Your choice."

"I won't do it. At least not until we speak. Alone."

He pushed back his sleeve to glance at his watch. "You have two minutes to make a decision. After that, the offer is rescinded."

"You are a hateful bastard." She glared at Brie. "This will be you one day, girl. One day you'll be sitting in a lawyer's office, being told that you are no longer loved."

Sir cleared his throat. "One minute and forty seconds."

Ruth looked startled and grabbed the papers, looking them over. "Will I get an allowance afterwards?"

"No, you are only being supported for the three years you volunteer. After that, you are on your own. No contact with either of us will be tolerated on your return," he said, glancing in Brie's direction.

"Why would I ever sign this?"

"Because you have burned all your bridges. Show the public you're genuinely sorry for manipulating their good hearts by taking this time to give to others. Possibly in three years they will have forgiven you, or forgotten that you exist. It's a win-win, either way."

She looked at the document again and whined like a spoiled child, "But I don't want to go to China."

"Thirty seconds," Sir answered.

Ruth quickly scribbled her name on every page, then threw them at Sir. "Bastard!"

Sir gathered the papers and handed them to Mr. Thompson. He stood up without acknowledging her again, calmly walking Brie to the door.

Ruth came unglued. "Don't walk away from me, Thane. Don't you dare walk away from me, you fucking coward. You're a failure as a man. Everyone knows it. Beating up little girls and abandoning your mother like this. It's disgusting!" When she got no response, Ruth screamed, "You should have died with your father! You hear me?"

Sir opened the door without pausing, putting his hand on the small of Brie's back.

Ruth redirected her wrath. "That money's mine, bitch. Don't you think for one second you're getting any of my son's money. I'm his mother; it's *mine*!"

Sir guided Brie out of the door and turned to face the beast. "But I have no mother."

He shut the door on a torrent of profanities.

Sir winked at Brie. "Satisfying on so many levels."

Brie tightened her grip on him, extremely proud of the way he had handled the wretched woman. Sir had been compassionate without giving an inch of his soul.

He let out a long, ragged sigh as they waited for the elevator. "The beast is no longer my problem." Sir gave Brie a cheerless smile. "From now on, when I remember Ruth Davis, I will think of the woman my father once loved. The reality is that I lost both of my parents when I was a boy."

When they returned home, Sir quietly put the framed picture of his father in the living room. It marked his emancipation.

# Pearls

Sir's involvement with the documentary had caused his business to take a severe financial hit—a hit that would take years to recover from. Brie was shocked when he listed the number of clients he'd lost during a discussion with Master Anderson.

"Impressive," Master Anderson commented, showing only amusement at the amount.

But Brie was devastated. "I feel horrible, Sir. I never thought my film would impact your business so negatively."

He looked at her with compassion. "I always knew there'd be a significant cost, Brie. It's an investment I was prepared to make. I realized it would obligate me to pursue clients outside the States to offset the losses." When he saw her continued distress, he gestured for her to kneel beside him. "Unlike you—a girl who tends to make impulsive decisions based on her heart—I weigh the risks and act accordingly."

She rested her head on his thigh. "I do admire how you calculate the costs, Sir. It's as if you play a game of chess with life."

Master Anderson laughed at the statement. "Yes, that's exactly what you do, Thane."

Sir sounded amused. "I'm not sure I care for the analogy, Brie. However, it *is* true that while you are constantly surprised by the aftermath of your decisions, I rarely am."

"You're very wise, Sir."

"Tsk, tsk," Sir said as warning before lifting Brie over his knee, raising her skirt. "What did I say about that word?"

Brie struggled not to smile when she apologized. "I'm sorry, Sir. Not wise, definitely not wise. I meant knowledgeable."

He smacked her hard on the ass. "Try again."

"Sage-like."

"No." He spanked her even harder.

"Intelligent! Intelligent!" she squeaked.

He rubbed his hand over her red ass. "Acceptable." He pulled her skirt back down and returned her to her kneeling position.

Sir spoke to Master Anderson as if nothing had happened. "When will you be leaving?"

"By the end of the month. I already have a warehouse in mind. I plan to be there before renovations start."

Sir chuckled. "I'm certain your neighbors are going to miss you."

"It has been impossible. I tell you, ever since the documentary, the women won't leave me alone. What started out as harmless flirtation has quickly turned into cougar wars. Best to leave before someone gets hurt."

"Or shot."

Master Anderson grinned smugly, but his smile fell when he saw the herb garden on the counter. "Thane, I gave you this garden to take care of." He walked over and caressed the yellowing leaves. "They're screaming for light. You can't expect them to produce a pleasant flavor if you don't give them the food they require." Without asking, he moved an end table near the window and placed the small herb garden on it. "There. Now the plants will be happy, but you'll have to water them more."

Sir growled with irritation. "I never asked for a garden."

"But you *will* care for it. Think of it as a part of me when I'm gone."

"Great. Then I'll be sure to flick the leaves and poke the roots every time I water," Sir said sarcastically.

"As long as you water me, I'm okay with being flicked and poked."

Brie giggled on Sir's thigh.

Master Anderson glanced at his watch. "Unfortunately, as much fun as I'm having entertaining young Brie here, I can't stay longer."

Sir stroked Brie's hair one last time before he got up to see his friend out. "I trust you're still coming tonight."

"Of course. Wouldn't miss it."

Brie was pleased to hear that Master Anderson would be there. She'd been looking forward to the huge party at the Training Center all week. It was going to be the biggest gathering to date. Sir had said the film had been great for the Center, but the increased enrollment necessitated an expansion. A whole new wing was being built at the college to accommodate future classes. Everyone associated with the Center would be there to celebrate.

In honor of the event, Sir had purchased a special gown for her. "It only makes sense that the woman responsible for the expansion looks stunning for the party."

The gown was a black, sequined seduction with a high, modest neckline in the front and a low back that exposed the barest peek of her brand. Sir seemed to find it highly erotic, and kept grazing his hand over her mark.

Before they left, he surprised her by removing the condor necklace. Brie protested, "But I love that, Sir."

"Tonight you only wear your collar and this around your neck," he replied, holding up her strand of pearls. He looped it once and let the length drape gracefully down her back.

"My goddess, my slut," Sir murmured as he lightly bit her shoulder.

Oh, this was going to be a grand celebration indeed!

When they pulled up to the Training Center, Sir parked his Lotus in his old spot— reserved exclusively for the headmaster. Sir chuckled as he got out, stating, "Coen needs a little aggravation."

They'd come early to help with the set-up, but the commons area was already decorated with layers of black and iridescent pearl, giving an air of sophistication to the festivities.

Brie touched the hanging silks and cooed. "Wow, I love how elegant this looks, Sir. Very classy."

"Class is a given for anything associated with the Center," he responded with a smirk.

It took a second before she got his joke and started laughing, but Headmaster Coen cut her merriment short when he entered.

"Very funny, Davis. Repark your car *now*."

"You can't be serious."

The headmaster responded angrily, "I assure you, I'm quite serious."

Sir grinned like a mischievous schoolboy as he fished his car keys out of his pocket. He gave Brie free rein to explore the Center while he went to change parking spots.

As she walked down the silent halls, Brie was bombarded with memories: Baron's initial challenge and those damn six-inch heels. The experience of her first auction with Rytsar, followed by lessons on deep-throating. She'd learned to overcome her fear of the cane with Marquis, and discovered the joy of flying under Tono's skilled hands.

She made her way back to the commons, running her fingers against the wall and smiling to herself as she passed the bondage room. She remembered her second night at the Center, waiting in the hallway for Sir to unlock the door after class…

*Good memories.*

She was determined to drag Mary and Lea back here while the party was going on. It would be fun to reminisce together. Now that the film was complete and all the excitement of the release was over, she needed to set aside girl-time on a regular basis.

Brie was startled to see the silhouette of a man standing in the hallway ahead of her. It was definitely not Sir. She stopped in her tracks until she heard a hearty, "*Radost moya!*"

"Rytsar!" she cried, running to his open arms. "I had no idea you would be here tonight."

The Russian picked her up, laughing. "I am part of the Training Center experience, am I not?"

"Well…you are for me," she answered, struggling to breathe inside his powerful embrace.

*Such a sadist.*

When he had nearly squeezed the breath out of her, he set her down, chuckling to himself. "Why don't you run off with me? I will teach you the power of pain and you can teach me the power of *lyubov'*."

"Hands in the air. Step away from the sub," Sir ordered from behind him.

Rytsar put his hands up. "We've been caught before we could make our grand escape." He turned around and walked to Sir, grinning like a Cheshire cat. "*Moy droog,* I am still convinced I could make her into a masochist. I just need a few weeks alone with her."

Sir held out his hand to Brie as he replied, "Not going to happen, my friend."

Walking down the hallway with a Dominant on either side brought back memories of the cabin, and a pleasant warmth grew between her legs. She looked up at the handsome Russian and thanked him for her extravagant birthday gift, adding, "Rytsar, the cabin is really too much."

He threw back his head and laughed. "Truth, *radost moya*? It has to be the most selfish gift I've given."

Sir snorted, slapping him hard on the back. "I suspected as much…"

Brie asked Sir, "Would it be okay if I tell him?"

"Why not?" he answered with amusement.

"Rytsar, you are the very first person to hear," Brie said excitedly. "We're leaving in two weeks for Italy and you'll never guess—" She saw the glimmer of hope in Rytsar's eyes and knew what he was thinking. "No, you're still not an uncle."

He frowned, shaking his head at Sir in mock disappointment.

"I don't have time for babies, Rytsar. I'm going to begin filming my new documentary."

Rytsar raised an eyebrow. "Another film?"

"Yes! This one will be about Alonzo Davis, the man behind the talent." Brie grinned at Sir. "Recently, there has been a surge of interest in his music."

Rytsar slapped his hand on Sir's shoulder. "I'm glad to hear it, *moy droog*."

Sir answered somberly, "Yes, it's time people know the truth about my father, and there is only one person I trust to tell it." He kissed the top of Brie's head.

As they walked into the commons, Brie was thrilled to see that it was already filling up with people. She spotted Mary and Faelan across the room and asked, "May I, Sir?"

"You may speak to whomever you wish tonight."

She bowed and thanked Sir before bounding off to talk to Mary.

Unfortunately, Mary burst her bubble about girl-time with the first words out of her mouth. "Guess our big news!"

Brie noticed the possessive way Faelan had his arm around Mary and felt certain she knew the answer. She said playfully, "Is there a certain piece of neck jewelry in your future?"

Mary looked mortified. "No, you idiot! You know I'm not ready for that shit. We're going to join a commune."

Brie laughed at her reaction. She could tell Mary wanted a collar, and the tight hold Faelan had on her let the world know his feelings. It wouldn't be long…

"So a hippie commune? That's cool, Mary, but I can't see you as a flower child."

Blonde Nemesis rolled her eyes. "It's a BDSM commune, bitch. Everyone works for the community, but the beauty is that you can live your D/s life out in the open. It's kind of like The Haven, but twenty-four seven. Just think, Faelan could come up to me while I'm peeling potatoes with the group, order me to bend over and fuck me, just like that. Nobody would bat an eyelid because it's totally accepted. The vanilla world left behind."

Brie was amazed. "I never knew there was such a place."

"Oh, yeah, it's up north. There are even a few couples who have been with that commune for years. God knows the things we can learn while we're there. Imagine living with a bunch of like-minded people—what could be better?"

Brie didn't like the idea of losing Mary. "What about your job?"

"I'm taking a six-month sabbatical, so it's no big deal." Mary groaned dramatically. "God, I'm so fucking tired of being hounded by idiots who saw the film. I can't tell you the number of vanillas hitting on me. Hell, both Faelan and I could use a break from that crap."

Faelan spoke up. "We're young and free to leave our jobs temporarily. Seems like the perfect time to explore the lifestyle in more depth, don't you think?"

Although Brie was not excited about them leaving, she hung onto the fact that it was a temporary loss. "Yes, Mr. Wallace, I can certainly understand the allure."

Mary's eyes sparkled with excitement. "Brie, you'll never guess what happens the first night."

Brie couldn't hide her smile when she answered, imagining Mary with a ring of pretty flowers in her hair, dancing around a maypole. "I have no clue."

"The day we arrive, they throw a huge party for us." Mary looked up at Faelan with a lustful grin. "At sunset, Faelan will bind me to the center table and present me to the community. Then they'll spend the whole evening sampling the newest submissive. Doesn't that sound wickedly hot?"

The idea of being taken by a group of Doms was both hot and frightening, but Brie was certain Mary could handle it. Ever since that night at The Haven with Faelan, she'd been different. She seemed complete, as if she had found a part of herself that had been lost. Mary could still be a bitch, of course, but she seemed like a much happier bitch.

Unfortunately, Lea hit Brie with even harder news. Brie could sense something was up when Lea hugged Brie so hard and for so long that her friend's boobs nearly smothered her.

"Isn't tonight exciting, girlfriend?"

Brie shrugged. "It's just a party for the new wing. Nothing to asphyxiate me over."

"Well, maybe not." Lea giggled. "But look around you. All this is because of you. *You* made this happen, Brie."

She waved away Lea's comment. "Nah, it was all of us. I just happened to have a camera."

Lea pinched her cheeks and wiggled them painfully. "Aren't you just so cute? Can't accept a compliment to save your life."

God, Brie had missed this—the silliness of being a girl. "Hey, Lea, I was thinking of starting up our girl-time again."

Lea frowned. "Oh, I'm sorry, sweetie. I'm going to be busy packing."

Brie's smile froze on her face. She couldn't believe what she'd just heard. "What do you mean?"

"I'm headed to Colorado, baby!"

Brie's stomach sank. *It's Ms. Clark all over again.*

"Don't do it, Lea. Please don't go chasing after Ms. Clark. Don't make the same mistake she did by running after someone who will never love you."

Lea laughed and gave Brie another hug. "I'm not, silly! Master Anderson asked me yesterday if I wanted to be a part of his new Training Center. I'm going to be the lead submissive for the trainee Doms. Isn't that awesome?"

Brie kept the smile plastered on her face, even though her heart was breaking. She couldn't bear the thought of losing Lea as well. "That's an incredible opportunity."

"I know! I'm so giddy about it I can't even think straight. And Colorado is gorgeous with all those huge mountains. Who knows? I just might become a sub-bunny on the ski slopes."

Brie could just imagine males crashing into trees as Lea skied down the slope in latex, exposing her ample cleavage to the mountain men. "You might be dangerous in the snow, girl."

"Hey, I hear Colorado isn't too far from California. I'm sure we can get together between my sessions."

"Yeah, that'll be great," Brie answered, but that sinking feeling grew stronger. She was afraid it wouldn't happen, so she said, "Let's set it up right now, before we get too busy and forget. I don't want *anything* to get in the way of our girl-time."

Lea bumped Brie's hip with hers. "You got it, girlfriend." She got out her phone and they looked over the calendar, picking the first date available. "Master Anderson has everything planned out to the day. I think the weekend after the school's first six-week session should work. You know I'll need to dish all about it with you!"

"Perfect, because I'll need to hear every detail."

Lea set a reminder on her phone. "All set. I've got you in there."

"I'm holding you to it, Lea. Come hell or high water, the two of us are getting together that weekend."

"Nothing comes between us, woman!" Lea assured her.

Brie hugged Lea again, doing her best to hold back tears.

*No Mary and no Lea… Can it get any worse?*

She sought out Mr. Reynolds and his wife, needing some stability to cling to.

When Sir's uncle saw Brie, his face lit up. "We couldn't be prouder. To think I had such talent sitting in my tobacco shop. I'm embarrassed I had you stocking cigarettes."

"No need to feel that way, Mr. Reynolds. I was happy to do it. Well…I was willing, at least."

He chuckled, remembering those days. "That damn Jeff. He was a thorn in both our sides."

Brie couldn't help herself and gave him a hug. She grabbed his wife's hand and gushed, "It's just great to see you both again." She was struck by a brilliant idea and prayed Sir wouldn't mind. "I was wondering…"

"What, dear?" Judy asked, squeezing her hand in encouragement.

"Would you join us for Thanksgiving dinner? I would love to cook the meal for you."

"I'd advise you to decline and save yourselves," Marquis commented behind her.

Brie turned to face him. "I've gotten much better at cooking, Marquis Gray. Truly, I have."

He patted her head as he told Mr. Reynolds, "Offer to bring the turkey, stuffing, potatoes, as well as the gravy and you should be good to go."

She crinkled her nose at Marquis and assured Mr. Reynolds, "I can cook all those things…"

*If I google it,* she added in her head.

Brie eagerly continued, "It will be lovely, I promise. Please say you'll come. Thanksgiving should be about family."

"And not about edible food," Marquis interjected.

She stamped her foot, biting back a witty retort. Marquis was a respected Dom and she knew her place, but he was being wicked with his teasing.

"Of course we'll come, dear," Judy replied.

Mr. Reynolds readily agreed. "It's an invitation we would never turn down."

"Great!" Brie felt some of her joy return.

Brie focused her attention back on Marquis Gray, noticing for the first time that Celestia was standing beside him. "It's so great to see you again!" Brie cried, sighing gratefully as she hugged the gentle woman. It was a friendship that held possibilities.

She was about to extend an invitation for Thanksgiving dinner, but Marquis Gray changed the subject. "I never did hear if you enjoyed the new flogger, Miss Bennett."

Brie shivered just thinking about it. "The flogger is incredible, Marquis. I've never known one to give two different sensations at the same time."

Marquis' eyes shone with pride as he explained, "I had that one especially made for you with a combination of suede and oiled leather. The flogger is also balanced so that the wielder can use it for longer sessions."

Sir came up behind Brie and put his hand on her shoulder. "It's the finest flogger I've used, Gray. None finer."

Marquis seemed particularly pleased. "I have a similar one at home." He ran his fingers down Celestia's spine and Brie watched her quiver in response. "It's a favorite tool of ours." Marquis looked at Brie again and said, with a glint in his eye, "Wait until your present next year."

Tono came up and shook hands with the men before addressing Brie. "Amazing, the impact a simple film concept can have in the hands of a true artist."

She blushed at his compliment. "Thank you, Tono. It does amaze me that the Center is expanding and a new one is starting up because of the demand for training. I never guessed my documentary could effect that kind of change."

"That reminds me, Ren," Sir said, "I've heard rumors that you are going to start a national tour soon. Is that true?"

Tono glanced at Brie before he replied. "Yes. I've been contacted by a group of Kinbaku artists. Due to the increased interest, they are holding performances nationwide to promote understanding of the ancient art. I've been asked to lead it."

Brie's heart sank. *Not Tono too…*

She hid her disappointment, but felt compelled to ask, "Tono, you told me once that you preferred remaining in one place. What's changed?"

His smile was gentle when he answered, "I've become stagnant."

The meaning behind his answer was clear. He would be traveling the country to find the woman meant to be his complement.

"I wish you much success with the tour, Tono Nosaka," Brie said, bowing to him not as a submissive, but as a friend. She turned away, fighting to control her swirling emotions.

It was too much. Too many losses to swallow in one day.

Sir cupped his hand lightly over the brand on her back. "It's time, Brie." He led her to the stage.

As she mounted the steps, Brie forced herself to focus on the school's success so that her smile was genuine when she faced the large group. She scanned the crowd, and did a double-take when she saw two familiar faces she hadn't expected.

*What are my parents doing here?*

Sir put his arm around her waist and began, "I know many of you are familiar with the courage that burns inside the young woman who stands beside me." He looked down at Brie and stated proudly, "If you know her, then you know she has the heart of a lioness."

She burned with a heated blush, embarrassed to be praised so highly for her simple documentary.

Sir took his eyes off her to address the group again. "You may recall that a certain graduate of this school broke all protocol to offer her collar at my feet. You may also remember that it was *not* met with enthusiasm."

Several people chuckled in the crowd.

"I believe courage should be met with courage," Sir stated firmly. He reached into his pocket and pulled out a small box.

Brie watched in shock as he got down on one knee and held out the opened box. "Brianna Bennett, in front of everyone here, I am asking for your hand in marriage."

She glanced at the diamond ring nestled within. It sparkled with an eternity of promise.

When she looked back at Sir, time stopped. She took in the sight of her Master. It didn't seem right, seeing Sir on his knee before her in front of the people she knew and loved, but at the same time it was heartbreakingly beautiful.

For one fraction of a second—just one—she toyed with the idea of turning him down as payback.

But Brie's answer was loud and clear, so that there would be no doubt. "Yes, Thane Davis. I accept your proposal with all my heart."

He stood up and took her hand. Brie lost herself in the moment, aware of only one thing—her Master's touch as he slipped the engagement ring on her finger.

Brie stared at him in stunned silence.

Sir smiled as he explained in a lowered voice, "I asked permission to marry you the day your father and I spoke in the study. Needless to say, it did not go the way I'd planned." He cradled her cheek and stroked her soft lips with his thumb. "But I am a determined man, Brie Bennett."

She pressed her cheek into his hand and returned his smile. "I cherish your determination, Sir."

"I know your father isn't going to like this, but I will not be denied," Sir murmured as he fisted her hair and pulled her head back, giving Brie a possessive kiss that sealed his rights as her fiancé.

Brie stumbled slightly when he let go of her, overwhelmed by the kiss.

Sir announced to the group, "Please sit down and enjoy the meal my friend, Chef Sabello, has prepared for you. We are grateful you could join us tonight to celebrate our engagement."

*So tonight was never about the expansion of the school or my film. Clever Sir...*

The applause started up again as Sir led her off the stage to speak to her parents.

"Congratulations!" her mother cried, giving her a hug.

Her father's response was to turn to Sir and demand, "Was that really necessary? You were doing well up until...that *thing* at the end."

Sir wrapped his arm around Brie and said unapologetically, "Yes."

Brie ignored her father's criticism. "Thank you for giving us your blessing and for being here tonight. I—" Tears welled up, making it difficult to speak. "This means so much to me, Dad."

Her father held his arms out to her and Brie gratefully settled in his embrace. "I may not care for your choice of husband, Brie, but I am certain he loves you. In the end, that's what I care about most."

She stood on her tiptoes to kiss his cheek. "Dad, right now I am the happiest woman in the world."

Her father squeezed her tighter. "I guess that will have to sustain me when I suffer from doubts later tonight."

Brie spent the evening flitting from table to table, catching up with people who had been part of her training, including Jennifer, the redhead who'd been Sir's date the day they first met, and Greg, the Dom from her first encounter. *Everyone* who had been a part of her training was there—even Mistress Clark.

Although the Domme stayed behind the scenes for most of the evening, she came to Brie before leaving. "It seems congratulations are in order, Miss Bennett. Sir Davis is an exceptional man." Her gaze burned into Brie when she added, "He deserves an exceptional sub."

Brie chose to ignore the last comment, knowing the woman's history with Sir. She replied respectfully, "Thank you, Ms. Clark. I wish you success in Colorado."

"Yes... Well, thank you," she answered uncomfortably. It seemed that having Brie know so much about her personal life made the Domme jumpy.

*Who has the power now?* Brie thought, pleased with the subtle shift of control.

Before she could explore this interesting new dynamic, her parents came to say goodbye. She watched Ms. Clark walk away and suddenly felt an ache of sadness. She would miss the harsh woman. It was a disconcerting realization.

Brie was surprised her dad seemed cheerful. When questioned about it, he explained, "You know, Brianna, we had a chance to talk to Mr. Gray during dinner. He is a remarkable person. A man of deep faith and philosophical insight. We had a fascinating conversation tonight."

If there was anyone who could convince her father that the D/s dynamic was healthy and viable, it was Marquis. Brie glanced at her ex-trainer from across the room and smiled in gratitude. He nodded slightly, accepting her thanks.

"Shall we?" Sir stated, letting Brie know it was time to go.

Brie looked over the commons one last time, taking in the moment so she could remember every detail. Then she looked down at her ring and smiled. "We shall, Sir."

Sir took Brie on a little detour on their way home. She was surprised when he parked his sports car on the side of the coastal highway and set the brake.

"Take off your shoes."

Brie did as she was told, wondering what he had planned when he took a blanket from behind the seat and slipped matches into his pocket. He went to her side of the car and opened the door.

"Come with me, Brie."

Her heart fluttered as she took his hand. He lifted her over his shoulder and spanked her playfully on the ass before starting down the trail.

Even in the dark, Brie recognized the beach. She'd been here before, and had mixed feelings about it. Brie fingered the pearls around her neck, remembering how badly the night had ended last time.

Sir made it down the trail quickly and, to Brie's relief, passed by the spot where they'd had their tryst. He took her closer to the water and set her down next to a fire ring that had been prepared beforehand.

He laid the blanket on the sand and commanded, "Lie down, Brie."

It startled her that he hadn't used her submissive name.

She lay down on the soft blanket and watched as Sir lit the fire. When it was pleasantly blazing, Brie held her hand out to him. "I'm so happy, Sir."

He took her hand and lay beside her on the blanket. "Tonight I prefer we call each other by our given names."

Brie leaned forward and breathed his name in his ear like a forbidden secret. "Thane."

He smiled, turning his head to kiss her. "I like the way it sounds coming from your beautiful lips."

Sir began slowly removing Brie's clothes, beginning with her stockings. He rolled them down one at a time, lifting her foot once it was free to examine it as if it were fine art. He kissed each toe tenderly before he started on the gown. Sir undressed her with such controlled passion that he made the experience another form of foreplay.

He took the pearls from her neck, rolling the beads over her body—first her right nipple and then her left, causing them to contract into tight buds for him. He trailed the beads down her torso, making Brie giggle with his feather-light touches.

Sir smiled as the pearls traveled southward and brushed against her femininity. Brie gasped, her clit already erect and hungry for his pleasure.

"Do you remember the night I was Khan?"

She nodded, smiling as she bit her lip in anticipation.

"Open your legs," he commanded.

She could barely breathe as she spread her legs open and exposed her sex to him. Sir stared at her, admiring her mound without touching it. She loved it when he examined her with his heated gaze. It made her feel beautiful.

Sir fingered her pussy, separating her outer lips, which were already moist with arousal. He placed the pearls on either side of her clit and pulled them taut. "You know what comes next…"

Brie moaned softly as he pulled the beads along, each pearl caressing her clit as it rolled by. She lifted her pelvis, wanting more when he had finished.

Sir spoiled her and repositioned the pearls to begin again. "Do you want to know what I see?"

"Yes."

"Your clit dances as I pull the strand down, and I am aware that each tiny movement brings a jolt of pleasure to you. It's erotic to watch."

She turned her head to the side and bit down on the blanket, lifting her pelvis again in silent petition. He granted her wish and pulled the pearls against her swollen clit one last time. Then he put them to his lips as he gazed down at her and ran them across his tongue, tasting her.

"I have another use for pearls. Present your wrists to me." Sir began binding her with the strand of pearls as if it were rope. It was not simply decoration. He bound her tightly so she could not break free.

"Put your hands above your head, Brie."

She stared at him, feeling vulnerable naked and bound in the open like this. It was intoxicating.

Sir leaned over her and stated, "I told you that I would never marry."

"I remember," Brie replied, curious what had changed his mind.

"But I realized a simple truth after I collared you." Sir traced his finger over the collar on her neck and asked, "Do you know the difference in commitment between having a collared submissive and a wife?"

She shook her head.

He smiled down at her. "There is none. Even though I meant it when I told people years ago I would never marry, I hadn't met you yet."

A warm tear rolled down her cheek when she admitted, "Being your wife…it means everything to me."

He kissed her salty tear away. "It challenged me to grant your unspoken desire, but I am not a man to shy away from a worthy conquest. I had resisted the legal commitment because of my parents' past, but the simple truth is I was already fully committed to you." He leaned over her, his masculinity heightening all her senses. "The moment I locked that collar in place, our fates were sealed."

She looked up at Sir, admiring his handsome face framed by the stars in the sky. "I love you, Thane."

"I love you," he answered, as he began unbuttoning his shirt. He stared down at her lustfully as he undressed, revealing his toned chest first. She loved that it was covered in dark hair. He unfastened his pants next, pulling them down slowly to show off his muscular thighs. The last piece of clothing to go was his briefs. Brie smiled when she saw his erect manhood. The man looked magnificent naked.

Sir spread her legs and settled in between them. The head of his rigid cock pressed hard against her opening, demanding entrance.

Brie closed her eyes, savoring the feeling of her fiancé taking her slowly, a centimeter at a time. The peaceful sound of the ocean waves rolling in, along with the warmth of the crackling fire, added to the sensual moment.

"You are mine, Brie Bennett, spiritually and soon legally."

"Body, heart and soul," she murmured, sighing in pleasure as his cock slid in up to the hilt.

Sir cradled her face in his hands and demanded she open her eyes as he began rolling his hips. The depth of his penetration asserted his claim, but he was slow, gentle and loving in his taking of her.

He was her Master, but tonight he treated her as his goddess. Sir spent hours under the canvas of stars making love to her, exploring her body with his fingers, cock and tongue.

When she came, Sir whispered, "A lifetime to explore every facet of our love."

Brie gazed up at the stars shining in the night sky and smiled.

*And this is just the beginning, Sir…*

Thank you for following Brie on her unique journey. Your enthusiasm and support have truly blessed this author's heart.

~ *Lady Red*

## You can find Red on:

**Twitter:** @redphoenix69
**Website:** RedPhoenix69.com
**Facebook:** facebook.com/red.phoenix.904

### Red Phoenix is the author of:

*Brie Learns the Art of Submission*
* Available in eBook and paperback

(Submissive Exploration—A young woman enters a world of new experiences when she enrolls in the Submissive Training Center)

---

*Brie Embraces the Heart of Submission*
* Available in eBook and Paperback

(Submission of the Heart—After being collared, Brie learns that submission is sexier and more challenging than she'd ever imagined)

---

*Blissfully Undone*
* Available in eBook and paperback

(Snowy Fun—Two people find themselves snowbound in a cabin where hidden love can flourish, taking one couple on a sensual journey into ménage à trois)

---

*Sensual Erotica: The Erotic Love Story of Amy and Troy*
* Available in eBook and paperback

(Sexual Adventures—True love reigns, but fate continually throws Troy and Amy into the arms of others)

(Novellas and Novelettes available as eBooks)

## Novellas

*His Scottish Pet: Dom of the Ages*

(Scottish Dom—A sexy Dom escapes to Scotland in the late 1400s. He encounters a waif who has the potential to free him from his tragic curse)

---

*Varick: The Reckoning*

(Savory Vampire—A dark, sexy vampire story. The hero navigates the dangerous world he has been thrust into with lusty passion and a pure heart)

---

## Novelettes

*Keeper of the Wolf Clan*

(Sexual Secrets—A virginal werewolf must act as the clan's mysterious Keeper)

---

*In 9 Days*

(Sweet Romance—A young girl falls in love with the new student, nicknamed 'the Freak')

---

*9 Days and Counting*

(Sacrificial Love—The sequel to In 9 Days delves into the emotional reunion of two longtime lovers)

---

*And Then He Saved Me*

(Saving Tenderness—When a young girl tries to kill herself, a man of great character intervenes with a love that heals)

---

*Play With Me at Noon*

(Seeking Fulfillment—A desperate wife lives out her fantasies by taking five different men in five days)

# Connect with Red on Substance B

**Substance B** is a new platform for independent authors to directly connect with their readers. Please visit Red's Substance B page (substance-b.com/RedPhoenix.html) where you can:

- Sign up for Red's newsletter
- Send a message to Red
- See all platforms where Red's books are sold

Visit Substance B today to learn more about your favorite independent authors.

www.ingramcontent.com/pod-product-compliance
Lightning Source LLC
Chambersburg PA
CBHW030743030726
47497CB00001B/112

* 9 7 8 0 6 1 5 9 1 1 2 5 0 *